THE
YEAR
OF THE
LOCUST

TERRY HAYES

PENGUIN BOOKS

TRANSWORLD PUBLISHERS
Penguin Random House, One Embassy Gardens,
8 Viaduct Gardens, London SW11 7BW
www.penguin.co.uk

Transworld is part of the Penguin Random House group of companies
whose addresses can be found at global.penguinrandomhouse.com

First published in Great Britain in 2023 by Bantam
an imprint of Transworld Publishers
Penguin paperback edition published 2024

A CIP catalogue record for this book
is available from the British Library.

ISBN
9781804992159

Typeset in 9.90/12.60pt Sabon LT Std by Jouve (UK), Milton Keynes.
Printed and bound in Great Britain by Clays Ltd, Elcograf S.p.A.

The authorized representative in the EEA is Penguin Random House Ireland,
Morrison Chambers, 32 Nassau Street, Dublin D02 YH68.

Penguin Random House is committed to a sustainable future
for our business, our readers and our planet. This book is
made from Forest Stewardship Council® certified paper.

'AN **ABSOLUTELY TERRIFIC ESPIONAGE THRILLER,**
JAMES BOND MEETS **JOHN LE CARRÉ**'
JOHN SANDFORD

'Emerging dazed and somewhat
brutalized after two intense days
reading this utterly gripping,
elegantly written 650-page
plus thriller, I can say that it was
most definitely worth the wait ...
Kane is a fantastic character:
preternaturally brilliant and brave
humble and insightful' *OBSERVER*

'SURE TO KEEP YOU ON THE EDGE OF YOUR SEAT' *SCOTSMAN*

'With vivid descriptions,
some terrific action
sequences and
lashings of suspense,
the book ticks all the
boxes necessary for a
superior geopolitical
thriller' *GUARDIAN*

'The must read of the year for
the true connoisseur of the
classic espionage thriller ...
The Year of the Locust reaches
new heights in storytelling.
Wonderfully literate,
beautifully written, and
tightly plotted. This one will
stay with you a long time'
NELSON DEMILLE

'If Daniel Silva and Michael Crichton had written a
near-apocalyptic epic thriller, it might look something
like this. The spycraft is unflinching and authentic.
The stakes both global and intimate. The action
throat-clutching ... Read this now!' JAMES ROLLINS

For Alexandra, Stéphanie-Marie, Connor and Dylan.

More than I could have ever hoped for,
much more than I ever deserved.

'We have met the enemy and he is us.'

– Walt Kelly, *Earth Day* poster, 1970

The day after tomorrow...

PART
ONE

PART
ONE

1

I ONCE WENT TO KILL A MAN. AT OTHER TIMES, IN YOUNGER DAYS, I had followed my work through the neon-lit alleys of Tokyo, watched the sun rise over the Mosque of the Nine Cupolas and waited on the waterfront in Old Istanbul as a woman's tears fell like rain.

This time, it was way out east where the Aegean Sea runs into the Mediterranean and the Turkish sun beats down on a chain of tiny islands. The smallest of them was also the most remote – waves broke over the wreck of a freighter lying on a reef, dangerous currents swirled through hidden coves, and a fishing village, its wooden boats long gone, was nothing but ruins now.

I landed in late spring, put ashore by the Egyptian skipper of a tramp steamer who was wise enough not to ask many questions. I can still recall the breeze on my face and the heady scent of pine needles as I moved through a silent forest; as I have done for most of my working life, I stuck close to the shadows.

My target that day was a brave man, no doubt of it, supposedly a German out of Nuremberg – that beautiful old city steeped in so much dark history – and when I surprised him in the kitchen of his lonely villa, we both knew I had travelled a long distance, both in miles and in years, to arrive at such a deadly rendezvous.

I was a member of the agency back then and for many years had gone under the codename Kane. Five years earlier, the German had been a trusted asset of US intelligence in Tehran. What nobody knew, but found out soon enough, was that he was secretly working as a contractor for the Russians. It seems like everything is being outsourced these days, even espionage.

On a quiet Monday night he had gone for a late meal in the bistro at Tehran's gilded Espinas Palace Hotel and in the men's room had delivered the names of ten of our most valuable Iranian sources to a representative of Moscow Central. It is well known in the secret world that the spy agencies of Russia and Iran have worked hand in glove for years, so it was inevitable that the list of names would end up with PAVA, the brutal Iranian secret police. As a result, our network – built over many years at a huge cost in lives and treasure and, more importantly, a vital back door into the Iranian nuclear programme – was destroyed within hours. Even for the CIA, an organization that had known its fair share of failure, it ranked as an unqualified disaster.

The consequences for the eight men and two women who were unmasked as a result of our asset's betrayal were far more catastrophic. They appeared before a judge in a late-night trial and the next day workmen started to assemble ten towering construction cranes in one of Tehran's largest squares. While members of the public didn't pay much attention at first, their purpose soon became clear: it was to ensure that as many people as possible could witness the court's sentence being carried out. In many countries in the Middle East it is not enough that people are punished; everybody else must be warned.

Once the towers had been erected, the horizontal arms were attached. Coils of rope were fixed to the end of the jibs and late on a spring day four black prison vans brought the captives to the square. One by one, as the minutes crawled by, each of them was conveyed in a cage to the top of their own personal crane.

There, under the gaze of the crowd gathered below, Revolutionary Guards forced the terrified men and women on to a small platform at the end of each jib. They hung a sign on each prisoner's chest identifying them as a spy for the 'Great Satan', and a noose, popularly known in the country as the 'Iranian necktie', was then dropped over their head.

Thanks to the careful planning, people packed in the square were all afforded an unimpeded view of the ten figures above them. Against a clear blue sky, they seemed to be suspended between heaven and earth. Given the circumstances, I suppose that was exactly where they were.

A small huddle of men and women closest to the cranes – most likely relatives and friends – were on their knees, wailing and praying. They looked up as a uniformed man, a lieutenant colonel, climbed on top of one of the vans and spoke in Farsi through a loudhailer, his voice echoing across the square. He read out the name of each prisoner, the charge and then the sentence.

Finally, he lowered the pieces of paper and, more loudly, said a word which translated as: 'Ready.' One of the condemned prisoners – a man – heard the word and his courage failed: he screamed, calling on God to save him.

As usual, at least in my experience, such a plea had no apparent effect. In a well-practised routine, the Revolutionary Guards stepped forward and each placed their right hand on the small of a prisoner's back.

At this gesture, a heavy silence fell across the crowd, and a child, a boy aged about six, stood up from among the group of friends and relatives and stared up at one of the prisoners – possibly a mother or father – and started calling out a name. A woman beside him pulled him back down, the boy started to cry, and after what seemed like an eternity the man with the loudhailer gave the next order: 'Now.'

The Guards, in unison, pushed the prisoners forward. Ten pairs of feet left the wooden platforms and an involuntary gasp went up from the crowd. The relatives and friends watched shoes and sandals rain down as the victims fell through the air.

Plunging feet first towards the square far below, the coils of rope reeled out fast behind them. When the coils ran out, the ropes snapped hard against their anchors, the nooses tightened around ten throats, the prisoners jerked upwards, and their necks snapped in an instant.

Nobody in the crowd said a word; the only sound was the wailing of the families as the ten bodies swung gently in the warm Middle Eastern breeze.

I wasn't surprised that the crowd had reacted with silence. It has been my misfortune to witness a number of executions – several by firing squad, two by hanging and one when an elderly man had been strapped into an electric chair and forced to 'ride the lightning', as the guards on death row call it – and I can promise you: the terror on the face of a man or woman as everything they had hoped to be vanishes into eternity never leaves you. The memory of it will surface at 3 a.m. when everything you fear most in the world is on its way, coming up the stairs to find you.

Several days earlier – in the Espinas men's room – the German, in payment for the list of names, had received an attaché case containing a fortune in anonymous Swiss bearer bonds. I'm not a believer – nobody could ever say that about me – but two thousand years ago St Paul wrote something that, once heard, is not easily forgotten: the love of money is the root of all evil. It certainly was that night in Tehran.

From the moment the traitor had left his coffee cup, an old raincoat, two cigarette butts and a crumpled credit card receipt on the table in the bistro, entered the bathroom, made the exchange, exited via an adjoining cigar bar, swung on to the back of a waiting motorcycle taxi and vanished into the city, the agency's analysts estimated that ninety-two seconds had elapsed. Ninety-two seconds to turn yourself into a multimillionaire, destroy an entire intelligence network and sign the death warrants of ten colleagues. By any measure, he was a very good spy. As a self-taught freelancer, he was out of the box.

As you would expect, the CIA – the deeply flawed but occasionally brilliant organization where I had worked for the previous twelve years – made numerous attempts to find him, but none of them came close to success and, with more evidence of his double-dealing surfacing daily, his status grew until he became something of a dark legend to US intelligence. Worse still, the agency's analysts drilled down and found that over the years he had assumed so many fake identities that the Company was finally forced to admit one final chilling fact: they had no idea who he really was. Maybe he wasn't even German.

With his real identity a mystery – and, I suspect, out of respect for his impressive vanishing act – one of the agency's resident intellectuals gave him a name that soon took flight. She codenamed him 'the Magus', a sorcerer, a *magician*, a word with roots deep in antiquity. The Bible tells us the three wise men who brought gold, frankincense and myrrh to mark the birth of Jesus were all magi. So, the CIA – the company that throughout its history had pioneered so many of the dark arts of espionage – had finally met a wizard and a solo operator almost as good as itself.

Needless to say, that realization fuelled the frustration of the expensively tailored man in our corner office and encouraged him to redouble the agency's efforts to find him. Believe me, there has never been a shortage of testosterone at the highest levels of the intelligence world.

When even the much better-resourced search, led by a hand-picked team of data-miners and elite field agents, could find no trace of the Magus, the problem landed on my desk. It was a Friday and I was heading out for an early lunch – the Starbucks at CIA headquarters at Langley is, by many accounts, the busiest in the world – and I was aiming to beat the midday crush. My computer and floor safe were already locked when I heard the unique tone informing me that a high-priority message had just hit my inbox.

I decrypted it and saw that it contained the secret files relating to the betrayal in Tehran, horrifying footage of the public execution hacked from PAVA's cameras, and accounts of the string of failed manhunts that had followed. Accompanying it was a note from the director asking me to familiarize myself with the material and meet him in his office just before dawn on Monday. Being called to a meeting at such an ungodly hour by him wasn't unusual and there were some in the agency who claimed the early appointments were a ploy – he wasn't a workaholic, they would say, he just liked to create that impression.

As it happened, they were wrong: he was a driven, ambitious man who – though very few knew about it – had grown up in strange and difficult circumstances. Work, I had always thought, filled an emotional void for him and – to be honest – it wasn't unusual in an agency renowned for its eccentrics and misfits.

The director – silver-haired and still retaining much of the tall, athletic build that had made him a track star in college – had grown up as Richard Rourke, but nobody had used his given name in years. He was universally known as Falcon – ever since, as a young agent, he had entered Iran as part of a joint US–Israeli team tasked with crippling an array of nuclear centrifuges hidden in the rugged mountains near a town called Natanz.

The mission ended in disaster, but even though Rourke was the least experienced member of the team, he showed not only extraordinary courage but a remarkable coolness in extreme circumstances: at least five Iranians working for the agency ended up owing their lives to him. As word spread through the secret world of his midnight escape, under fire and stopping for nothing, driving across the border into Iraq with half a network of local collaborators in the back of his pick-up, the name Falcon stayed with him.

With arresting eyes and a firm line to his jaw, he was probably more imposing than handsome, but one thing was certain: he was the best-dressed man I had ever met. No matter the hour, no matter how fraught the situation, you would find him early in the morning in his office, or late at night in the operations centre, wearing a handmade Brioni suit, a silk tie and a Charvet shirt. Even his collection of cufflinks was a wonder to behold.

Once he had left front-line operations, he spent several decades climbing the greasy pole in Washington, and the clothes and the image were all part of that. In the corridors of power and the elite social salons of Georgetown he was seen as both accomplished and very sophisticated; a safe pair of elegant hands.

He was in his mid sixties by the time I received the summons to his office and, to be honest, I wasn't surprised to receive it. I had heard rumours that the latest search for the Magus was proving to be no more successful than its predecessors and I figured that sooner or later an elite member of US intelligence would realize I probably had the necessary skills to bring a new approach to the pursuit.

By a strange set of circumstances, I was one of a small cadre of spies who specialized in entering what are called Denied Access Areas – places under total hostile control such as Russia and Syria, North Korea, Iran and the tribal zones of Pakistan – so I had more knowledge than most about how someone who was being hunted to the death might evade discovery.

In short, the Magus obviously knew how to hide. And so did I.

2

MY EXPERIENCE AND UNUSUAL SKILLS MEANT THAT ON AN OTHERWISE unremarkable Friday – hurrying to get to lunch – I found myself once again about to take a cursory glance through a group of highly classified files.

As I opened the first of them, a strange thing happened – a silence deeper than anything I had ever known fell across my office, making me pause. I looked out the window: the wind which had been building towards a winter gale had dropped to nothing and the few leaves left on the trees were no longer rattling out a wild tattoo. Superstitious or religious folk might have said the strange silence meant the universe was commanding my attention, that the heavens were marking the moment when a covert spy opened a highly secret file and the planets began to align.

Fortunately, I didn't labour under any such illusions. From a life that is long past now, I have a science degree from a highly regarded college and I have always believed in a rational world. I had watched winter hit Virginia hard that year; most mornings there was a thick frost on the ground, and several times I had seen trees draped in exoskeletons of ice, and I knew what the silence outside really meant: heavy snow had started to fall nearby, deadening the noise of the world, as it so often does.

Worried about driving home in the coming blizzard, I closed the shades, heard the wind gather strength again and began to look through the files. Six hours later, having absorbed them, I sat in the deepening night, and thought about the difficulty of finding the Magus.

To complicate matters, I was certain that long before he had walked into the bathroom in Tehran he had prepared a series of new identities and bolt-holes, dozens of places and names he would have used and discarded until he was certain the trail was cold and he had been swallowed by the vastness of the world. According to the agency database, there were at least 200 million middle-aged white men on the planet; to an intelligence agent trying to locate one of them, that was a vast world indeed.

While his file at Langley held a full suite of his photos and biometrics, I had no doubt that immediately after leaving Tehran he would have stopped in the Swiss mountains at either Gstaad or Villars-sur-Ollon, exclusive villages that not only host the two most expensive boarding schools on earth but are also home to institutions of a far different stripe. Deep in their valleys, you can find unmarked clinics that specialize in secrecy and high-end surgery. Vladimir Putin's mistress had once given birth in one of them, and if the Russians have paid you a fortune, you can emerge from them with a different face, a new hairline, surgically altered fingerprints and magnetic shin implants that add inches to your height.

Alone in my office, I realized I was being asked to find a white male of indeterminate height and nationality, with a name we didn't know, in a place we couldn't identify, wearing a face we had never seen and leaving fingerprints that weren't his own. Maybe something in his distant past would help, except we had never found out who he really was. In Turkey they have an expression for such a task: they say it's like digging a well with a needle.

I stood up, walked to the window and opened the shade into the night, expecting to see that the blizzard had hit and heavy snow was gathering on the ground, but there was only the wind blowing in the trees. It was strange, I thought – that a silence should fall and then the winter storm never arrive. Thinking no more of it, I told myself that finding the Magus was an interesting conundrum, but if you took the vengeance and testosterone out of it, the mission didn't amount to much: he was long gone, living off the grid, no longer a threat to anyone.

Looking at the skeletal trees, I thought of something my father, dead these ten years past, had once told me: 'If it's revenge you're after, dig two graves'; and I toyed with the idea of suggesting to Falcon that the agency might do better to work on finding today's traitors and not worry so much about yesterday's. Thankfully, something stopped me.

Instead, I followed the Magus's trail and one of the insignificant items that he had left on the table at the Espinas Hotel led me to the island in the Aegean. I knew that he lived alone and, with the noon sun warming my back, red bougainvillea tumbling over the villa's walls and a black Sig Sauer 9mm in hand, I entered via a locked basement door, made my way through the silent house, and found him in the kitchen cooking pasta over a gas hob, quietly singing an Italian love song to himself. Not German at all, as it turned out.

He faltered mid-note, sensing my presence, and turned towards the dining room. We faced each other across thirty feet of balmy Mediterranean air and then, without hesitating, he took half a step, momentarily shielding his left hand from view. In one movement I slid the safety off and tightened my finger against the trigger—

I got no further; in the split second between my eye seeing and my hand reacting, he pulled off an extraordinary piece of tradecraft which hurled me – ears ringing, half deafened – backwards across the room and gave him twenty seconds to open fire with a pistol he had produced and escape into the garden. Once again, he was on the run, doing what he was best at: disappearing.

But, in the fullness of time, the real significance of those hours on the island had nothing to do with whether I had found him, or if the agency had managed to take its revenge. No, its importance was entirely different: quite by accident, the Magus had taught me a brilliant trick, a remarkable piece of tradecraft, that ended up saving my life.

Some time later, on a mission far more significant and vastly more harrowing than anything I had ever undertaken, I travelled across oceans of time, through a landscape ruled by fear, to the ruins of a once-great industrial complex. It was a Russian facility located in the former Soviet republic of Kazakhstan – and though few people would probably recall it now, it was the site of one of humankind's greatest achievements. It was there that I ended up in brutal hand-to-hand combat against terrible odds and – face to face with eternity – I reached into memory and recalled what the Magus had done. I can never forgive the man for his betrayal in Tehran, but there is no doubt I owe him an enormous debt of gratitude and, given the importance of my mission, maybe the world does too. Yet another example – as if any were needed – that life is full of irony.

While the mission reached its deadly conclusion at Kazakhstan's historic and decaying Baikonur Cosmodrome, it had started thousands of miles away, in the wild and lawless country where the borders of Iran, Afghanistan and Pakistan all meet. It is a lethal triangle, an area where peregrine falcons, the fastest creatures on earth, hunt at dawn and the life of a Denied Access Area spy is often measured in days.

I went there to rendezvous with an informer, a man who knew a world of secrets about the world's most dangerous terrorist group. I couldn't tell you that he was a brave man – he wanted money and passports to give his wife and children a better life – but I did know this: were he to be unmasked, his life expectancy would be even shorter than mine.

3

FOR A JOURNEY INTO THE HEART OF DARKNESS, IT WASN'T AN auspicious start. I flew into Karachi, Pakistan's largest city, on the hottest day in the metropolis's recorded history and it was only late April. When I stepped out of the air-conditioned arrivals hall the heat was so intense it literally stole my breath away.

The fifth biggest city in the world – and quite possibly the most chaotic – Karachi is home to twenty million people, nearly all poor, crammed into an area between a river delta on one side and the polluted waters of the Arabian Sea on the other. Five times a day the muezzin call the residents to prayer from three thousand mosques, the air is toxic with diesel, and the drinking water's not much better. Nothing prepares you for the assault on your senses. On the way across the car park I saw several people gathered around two beggars who had collapsed from heat exhaustion, one of whom might well have been dead. A more superstitious man, somebody who paid attention to the silence before the storm perhaps, might have taken it as a sign.

Leaving the city, I drove west for five hundred miles, as fast as I could, the turquoise sea on my left and nothing but an empty, shimmering blacktop in front of me. As the miles disappeared in the rear-view, it turned into one of the loneliest and most forlorn places I had ever seen until – finally – I stopped on a ridge, looked towards the horizon and saw in front of me a wasteland of parched earth, deep gorges and impassable granite cliffs, my first glimpse of Jomhuri-ye Eslami-ye Iran – the Islamic Republic of Iran.

Only a handful of US spies had infiltrated the country successfully, and even fewer had returned alive. And now, twenty miles ahead, out of sight in the wasteland, was its heavily patrolled border. All I had to do was cross it – unseen, like a ghost in the night.

4

THE MISSION HAD BEEN INITIATED, AS IS SO OFTEN THE CASE IN THE intelligence business, by a seemingly trivial event. A man, attempting to fix his car's air conditioning, had found a piece of paper – displaying nothing more than its code number and shipping details – attached to the back of a replacement part. It would have meant nothing to almost anyone on earth – except that he was no ordinary man and the square of paper, at least in one respect, was quite remarkable.

The man in question was a trusted soldier in what had become the fastest-growing terrorist organization in the world, one which called itself the New Islamic Army of the Pure and whose roots reached deep into religious fundamentalism and anti-Western hatred. There was nothing unusual about that – there were scores of such organizations – except that the Army of the Pure was the latest incarnation of probably the most violent terrorist group in modern history.

Despite what the leaders of a host of countries had claimed, the Islamic State, also known as ISIS – the brutal organization which had emerged from the ruins of Syria and Iraq – was never defeated militarily. Under constant attack, it had done what insurgent and terrorist organizations have always done. It had scattered to the four winds and the cancer had metastasized.

As a result, there were five major offshoots of ISIS and the leaders of the best of them – or the worst, depending on your perspective – branded themselves as the Army of the Pure, headed south and found safe harbour among the granite pillars, ancient villages and hidden valleys of the frontier between Pakistan and Iran. 'Why did God create the borderland?' the old joke went. 'He wanted to make Afghanistan look good.'

Satellite surveillance, industrial-scale phone hacking and all-pervasive facial recognition – the highly classified version of which can now identify people from over two hundred miles away in space – showed that the Army was attracting supporters and fighters faster than even the jaded watchers at Langley had thought possible. At its peak, ISIS had enlisted over thirty thousand foreign warriors, and a large number of them – now highly experienced – had begun to make their way along the coastal highway from Karachi or down the ancient opium trails that led out of Afghanistan to enlist in the Army's ranks.

To the thousands of men and women at Langley who, after 9/11, had devoted their entire professional lives to monitoring the shifting sands and secret currents of Islamic fundamentalism, it became increasingly obvious that they were witnessing the rise of something as terrifying as ISIS or, even worse, as deadly as Osama bin Laden's al-Qaeda. But those same analysts also knew that violent rhetoric and battalions of followers were just ornaments. Without one crucial element, any group of Islamic fundamentalists was no different to the three hundred armed militia groups operating in America – men and women who played dress-up on Friday nights and 'deployed' around the nearest forest on weekends. To be the wheat and not the chaff, adjudged genuine and not counterfeit, a terrorist group had to strike.

The harder the target, the greater the glory, and there was no target harder to hit than America. Bin Laden had succeeded in a spectacular fashion and had lit a beacon for every other terrorist group to follow. In a way, and it is not easy to say, while the site of the 9/11 attack was cleared years ago, we all continue to live among the ruins of the Twin Towers. As one historian has said – citing uncontrolled viruses, climate change, catastrophic hurricanes, massive floods and endless terrorism – truly, this is the Age of Panic.

Six hours after the agency's analysts submitted their top-secret report about the rise of the Army of the Pure – and, as a result, turned the agency's counter-terrorism signal from orange to rapidly flashing red – the CIA's huge operation in Afghanistan, Kabul Station, heard the first of what would become a drumbeat of whispers.

Sometimes, I think back to when I was relatively new to the spy trade: I was on board a freighter crossing the Andaman Sea off the coast of Thailand and, unable to sleep – nervous about having to infiltrate Myanmar to meet a group of rebel leaders – I went on deck in the small hours and stood at the railing. It was one of those evenings, the type that air traffic controllers call 'severe clear' – not a sound, sharp and cloudless, a breath of wind carrying away any pollution and the stars laid out on a crystal night.

The ship's propeller was churning, causing billions of tiny marine organisms to emit a bright glow, and I realized: I was surrounded by the phosphorescence of the ocean. With the Milky Way above and a Milky Way below, it was like travelling through a sea of candles, a perfect metaphor for the secret world. Spies also journey through strange and foreign waters, surrounded not by stars and marine organisms but by fragments of information. The trick was the same, though – not to concentrate on the candles, but to try and see the light.

After weeks of hearing the drumbeat of whispers, Kabul Station did just that – it looked past the candles and concluded that the Army of the Pure was planning a major event, an act of terrorism conceived as grand theatre that would emulate its darkest predecessors.

In the intelligence world, there is a name that is reserved for global terrorist events conducted on such a scale, and Kabul Station had no doubt that one more 'spectacular' was on its way.

5

KABUL'S URGENT REPORT – GIVEN THE HIGHEST SECURITY CLASSI-
fication and sent only to Falcon Rourke and his superior, the Director
of National Intelligence – made it clear within its first three paragraphs
that while such a devastating attack might span the Western world,
it would be focused on America.

Alarmed, the two Washington spymasters immediately deployed
every resource of the huge US intelligence network – 900,000 people
and over 2,000 government organizations, three dozen of which were
completely off the books – to the task of trying to discover everything
they could about a shapeless, barely visible plot. Both men knew that,
somehow, they had to find more candles.

The next day, a minor US asset in Afghanistan received an encrypted
message on his phone telling him to listen carefully for anything that
was blowing in the wind.

The man, an Afghan in his fifties, habitually dressed in greasy
overalls – one of several hundred CIA freelancers in the country – was
an air-conditioning technician who worked out of a mobile workshop: a rugged four-wheel-drive truck, that claimed – written on its
side in Pashto, Dari and English – that wherever you were, Doctor Air
could cure the air conditioning of any make or model of vehicle.

Throughout the borderlands of Afghanistan, Iran and Pakistan he
was acknowledged as the best of all the roadside triage specialists.
For twenty-five years, he had made a living roaming freely through
the remote villages and towns scattered across the frontiers, on first-
name terms with border patrols and officials in all three countries,
and always allowed to pass unhindered in return for a free re-gas of
freon or a simple repair.

His speciality was sourcing out-of-stock parts and, although none
of his customers ever understood or questioned why, there was a
good reason for how he did it: the CIA was flying them in from the
US and delivering them to his Kabul warehouse every month.
Recruiting him as an asset and providing everything that was necessary to make his business a success was the inspired idea of Falcon
Rourke when he had been Kabul Station chief years before.

'Hide him in plain sight – the area's an oven; everybody needs their air-con,' Falcon had said then. 'He can sit around a fire, sip the obligatory cup of tea and listen.'

The technician did exactly that: over the years, he had passed on hundreds of rumours and fragments of intelligence and he was now being asked by his handler at Kabul Station to pay even closer attention. The technician would have ignored the entreaty – he figured that the agency often sent out urgent directives just to make sure everyone was awake – but this message was accompanied by a friendly greeting, after all these years, too, from his old friend Falcon Rourke and a request to do whatever he could to help.

Ten days later, working in his warehouse in an industrial park on the outskirts of Kabul, restocking his truck with a new shipment of CIA parts, the stench from the adjacent sewage works as overwhelming as ever, he got a call from a sat phone asking for urgent assistance. There was nothing unusual about that and on this occasion it came from a man whose air-con he had fixed several times over the last few years. The customer, who seemed to do a huge amount of driving, said he was stuck in a small village over the border in Iran, near Zabol – a regional centre with the dubious honour of regularly being named by the World Health Organization as the most polluted city in the world.

In other circumstances the technician would have refused – the village was over a thousand kilometres from Kabul, there were no other requests for assistance in the area and he was looking forward to a few days' rest in the capital before hitting the road again.

The prospect of driving through the choking air of Zabol was hardly appealing; on the other hand, the man had always intrigued him. He spoke very little, travelled constantly, was an Afghan who had once been a taxi driver in Kabul and was now living in Iran with no apparent job – or at least none that he seemed willing to talk about. Maybe it was intuition born of half a lifetime in the shadow world or perhaps it was just greed, but the technician decided to make the drive. Kabul Station paid well for information and the message from Falcon indicated that it was a seller's market.

Late in the afternoon, with summer coming in hard, he crossed the border into Iran, and twenty-four hours later – having driven with barely a break – he arrived in the small village. The major cause of the area's pollution was a brown dust driven by a relentless wind, and in order to try to protect themselves from it the two men had arranged to meet in the lee of a high-walled mosque. They needn't have bothered – the wind was howling even harder than usual, boxing the compass, grabbing the smoke from cooking fires in the tumble-down houses, whipping it into a choking cocktail and turning the men and women hurrying through the alleys and streets into nothing more than ghosts in the cloud of dust.

Trying to find his way through the afternoon gloom, headlights blazing, the technician's truck crawled along the wall of the mosque and finally stopped next to an incapacitated Nissan Patrol four-wheel drive. Immediately, the driver of the Nissan got out, ran to the rear of the triage truck, wrenched open the back door and scrambled inside. He was in his late thirties, a good-looking man with skin the colour of an old bronze artefact and almost as battered: clearly, he had spent a lot of time in the sun and wind. The technician gave one of his crooked grins and pointed at the apocalyptic world on the other side of the windshield. 'In the name of Allah . . .' he said in Farsi, shaking his head.

He stepped out of the driver's seat, made his way into the rear of the truck, where he had a bed and several chairs set up amid boxes of spares, took out two cups and fired up a small gas stove. As he waited for the tea to be ready, he pointed at the Nissan.

'Another problem with the compressor?' he asked.

'There was,' the visitor replied, standing at the back of the vehicle, half in shadow. 'That was a few months ago. It came loose from the bracket, so I pulled it out and re-fitted it.'

'So – what is the trouble now?' the technician asked.

'This,' the visitor said. He was holding a scrap of paper in his hand – there were two lines of words and numbers in English printed on it – and he held it up for the technician to see. The older man didn't need a second look.

'When I pulled the compressor out I found this glued to the back of the unit,' the visitor said. 'I suppose somebody forgot to remove it.' He pushed it closer to the technician, although there was really no need. The technician knew exactly what it was: a sticker showing a code number, a group of identifying letters and the shipping details of the compressor. If nothing else, the CIA was a government bureaucracy and every part that was sent from the US was duly catalogued and marked, forcing the technician to remove every one of the stickers when the parts arrived at his workshop. Or, at least, he thought he had. He knew immediately that the numbers and letters presented no problem; that was reserved for the shipping information which showed the part had been purchased on the order of Dep.Dir.Langley for Kabul Station, benefit of Local Asset 11789.

The water for the tea was boiling and the technician told me later, when I was assembling the pieces of this narrative, that he toyed for a moment with making a grab for his old Smith & Wesson, a revolver meant for heavy-duty business lying on the passenger's seat, but he dismissed the idea; he had no doubt the visitor's right hand – out of sight, hanging at his side – was holding his own weapon, aimed directly at him.

Even though he was close to panic, the technician said he found one moment of clarity: he realized that if the meeting was just about being unmasked, he would already be dead. There didn't seem to be any point in trying to talk his way out of it, either. He shrugged. 'We've all got to eat.'

'How well do you know the Americans?' the visitor asked.

'Well enough.'

'You deal directly with the spies – or through a local intermediary?'

'Directly,' the technician replied.

The visitor lifted his right hand into view and the technician saw he was holding a Ruger GP100. He pointed the gun at the stove, mutely telling him the water was boiling, and the technician – his hands shaking hard – started to try and make the tea.

The visitor didn't take his eyes off the technician: 'In recent years we have met at over half a dozen different places – what do you think I do for a job?'

The technician spread his hands, indicating that he was uncertain. 'I never saw you with anyone, so I didn't think you were running people over the border. A gold smuggler was my best idea, tobacco maybe – although I thought you would need a bigger vehicle.'

The visitor nodded but didn't add anything to disabuse the technician of his theories. 'Do you know how much 9/11 cost the Americans?' he asked.

The technician turned from preparing the tea, so taken aback by the question that even his hands stopped shaking. 'What?'

'The Twin Towers alone – the buildings – were valued at sixty-two billion US dollars. It cost almost a billion dollars more just to clear the site.'

The technician said, no idea of the relevance, 'That's interesting.'

'Yes, it is,' the visitor replied. 'It makes you wonder, doesn't it? How much they might have paid to prevent it? Or to avoid something similar.'

The technician turned away and stared at his teacups – what was this man offering him? His heart started to pound, and he was not sure if it was from greed or from fear.

He thought back to Kabul Station's encrypted alert and the message from Falcon and wondered if the man with the roadworthy Nissan had heard something – some of those whispers on the wind the CIA was keen to hear. Maybe it was even more than whispers.

'They would pay a lot for something like that, I should think,' the technician replied carefully.

'I agree,' the visitor said. 'I asked you before, what you thought I did for a job.' He didn't wait for a reply. 'I am a courier,' he said.

'A courier?' the technician asked, not sure what that meant exactly. 'A courier for who?'

'Well, not FedEx,' the visitor replied.

6

WHEN THEY LAUNCHED THEIR ORGANIZATION, THE ARMY'S commanders made one crucial decision. They realized, despite the developers' claims to the contrary, that no civilian could buy an encrypted phone or messaging app that was truly secure.

They were right – there is no device or software the National Security Agency can't crack if the stakes are high enough. As a result, the Army's leadership decided that using human couriers was the safest method of communication and, in doing so, became part of a growing trend in the clandestine world of discarding electronics because paper can't be hacked and hand-carry can't be tapped.

Therefore, the Army selected and trained a handful of trusted, shadowy messengers to carry hidden documents and spoken messages back and forth to operatives, suppliers and financiers, but there was one aspect of their system that the Army's leadership never anticipated: the bigger the plot, the more valuable the secret, the greater the temptation to sell it.

That led to one of their couriers – a father of two young girls, a former taxi driver who had grown weary of the rigidity of the fundamentalist existence and disillusioned with much of its rhetoric, a man who saw a chance to transform his family's life and was willing to risk being executed to try and grab it – sitting in a truck in a windswept and godforsaken corner of Iran talking to an Afghan air-conditioning technician who Allah – *subhanahu wa ta'ala*, the most glorified, the most high – had revealed to him as a freelance American intelligence agent.

The courier was an amateur in the intelligence world, but it didn't mean he hadn't learned one of its fundamental rules: a secret might be worth a fortune, but if you wanted to profit from it you had to be the first to market. He knew the danger of being beaten was growing.

'Three weeks ago, people started asking questions,' he said. 'Men began to whisper among themselves – information is leaking out about what is being planned. It is why, when I called, I said it was urgent – the Americans might soon hear it themselves or somebody else could beat me to the sale.'

'A sale? You want to sell information you have to the Americans?' the technician asked. This was not a problem he ever thought he would have – he had made a living gathering crumbs. The man was a courier – the secrets he knew had to be far more substantial – and lucrative. 'Whatever information you have,' he said as he poured the tea, 'how much are you asking?'

'Twenty for me. Five for you,' the courier replied.

The technician put the pot down mid-pour and stared at his guest. He had to be sure he understood. 'Million?' he said. 'US dollars?'

'Far cheaper than 9/11. It's a bargain for the Americans,' the courier replied. 'I'll demand US passports – a safe house too, a different identity, a totally new life.'

'Twenty-five million dollars?' the technician said in awe. 'A new life – but where?'

The courier's face softened. 'Somewhere you don't need air conditioning for a start – a view of the water, a place where it rains,' he said. 'I looked on a map – Oregon or Maine, maybe. You?'

The technician shook his head – he had never thought about living in the West, or acquiring five million dollars, and had no answer. 'What do you want me to do?' he asked.

'Take a message to your handler. Ask him if they want to buy what I am selling.'

'I know them,' the technician said cagily. 'They're always looking for traps, they will want verification, proof. I don't even know your real name. What do I tell them – a man I met in Iran called Mohammad would like twenty million dollars?'

The courier shook his head, smiling. 'Tell them the information I have is about what the leaders here refer to as a spectacular—'

'A what?' the technician demanded.

'He'll understand. Tell him I am a trusted courier with the Army of the Pure and I have a good working knowledge of their plans and leadership.'

The technician reacted – the Army of the Pure? From what he had heard, they were people to be deeply feared but, then again, for five million dollars, what did he expect?

'The CIA will ask you for information, details, a host of things,' the courier continued. 'But listen – I am in control, not them. I will tell you my conditions. Are you paying attention?'

'Sorry,' the technician replied, distracted. 'I was thinking about Las Vegas – I want to see Vegas.'

7

THE TECHNICIAN SPENT AN HOUR OUTSIDE IN THE HOWLING WIND, acting as though he was repairing the Nissan's air-con in case anyone was observing them, then watched the courier drive off into the evening gloom, grabbed two hours' sleep and, in a state of intense agitation, headed back to his workshop next to the sewage works.

Once he had opened the steel roller door, was safely inside and had bolted it, he logged on to the Dark Web via the TOR network and opened a popular jihadi message board.

Describing himself as a middle-aged, poor but devout Afghan

fighter, his post – four lines long and littered with spelling and grammatical errors – was a simple but hopeless request: he was looking for a much younger wife to join him in a tiny village near the Hindu Kush. It was the latest of many similar posts by him over the years, all trying to connect with a marriage partner, and many of the tens of thousands of regulars on the board could be relied on to insult and deride him. Even in the Islamic underworld, apparently, the internet is a vicious place, but the technician knew something none of his critics did: although the message board's ownership was deeply hidden, it was controlled by the CIA.

The agency had established the site and buried it on the Dark Web as a way to monitor jihadi activity and harvest as much information as possible about its users. It also had another purpose: its message boards allowed agency assets in hostile territory to tell their handlers at the CIA that they needed a meeting, help or support. The technician's actual message was contained in the misspellings and butchered tenses. The exact combination of the mistakes spelled out that he wanted a meeting urgently.

The post attracted its usual clutch of abusive comments, but only one was of any value. Posted by a jihadi calling himself AK-47 and accompanied by an avatar of a burning American flag, it was, in fact, written by a CIA handler at Kabul Station. It, too, was in code and among its sneering suggestions about where a wife might be found or bought was embedded the time and place where the CIA would meet him.

Thirty-six hours later, one of the agency's nondescript but armoured Toyota Land Cruisers made its way past the sewage works and into a decrepit industrial park on the southern outskirts of Kabul.

The location of the technician's workshop had been chosen deliberately by the CIA; when the wind was blowing from the north, which it did for most of the year, the smell in the industrial park was almost unbearable, a fact that made it ideal for clandestine purposes. Workers ran from their cars into air-conditioned buildings, not even the smokers gathered in the shade outside their workshops and nobody had seen a casual visitor pass through its gates in years.

The Land Cruiser weaved through piles of oil drums and stopped outside a building in the most remote section of the park. The driver, an Afghan-American in his forties, one of the station's most trusted wheelmen, gave a blast on his horn and almost immediately the roller door opened. Only when it had closed tight behind the vehicle did a man sitting in the back wearing a *keffiyeh*, a headscarf covering his entire face except for his eyes, and his presence completely concealed thanks to the heavily tinted windows – alight.

Once he had removed the scarf, he revealed himself to be a handsome man in his early forties with sharp grey eyes and a two-day stubble. A native of Texas, his name was Chris Halvorsen and he was CIA chief, Kabul Station. He stretched his back – the Kabul roads were murder – the side-arm on his hip clearly visible under his denim jacket, and gave an easy smile as he saw the technician emerge.

The old guy was moving fast, shuffling a little, as he always did, wringing his hands, but that action had nothing to do with anxiety. Halvorsen knew from long experience that, more than the request for any meeting or the number of exclamation marks, the habit with the hands meant the technician had something big to report: the man could definitely see a significant pay-day coming.

8

ELEVEN MINUTES AFTER CHRIS HALVORSEN HAD BEEN DRIVEN INSIDE the workshop, he was making arrangements to leave.

The Kabul Station chief had shaken hands with his excited joe, declined a cup of tea and accompanied him to their usual debriefing post: a pair of filthy armchairs in the back corner of the structure, beside three pounding generators that made it virtually impossible for anyone to eavesdrop. Even so, the men still leaned close, almost whispering, and Halvorsen made the technician recount the entire exchange with the courier three times, trying to extract every detail, and then – satisfied there was nothing more to learn – changed all of his plans. Normally, he stayed for at least an hour to give the impression that work had been done on the air-con, but not this time.

He called to his wheelman, re-wrapped his *keffiyeh*, climbed into the back seat and told him to drive fast to Bagram Air Base where – deep within a highly secure perimeter – CIA Station, Kabul, was located. The most secure part of that sprawling, bomb-proof intelligence complex was the TEMPEST ZONE, and from inside its lead-lined walls and against the hum of white-noise generators, Chris Halvorsen – who a few months later would be captured, tortured and executed in Syria – called Falcon and briefed him on developments in the village near Zabol.

According to the agency's logbooks, it was 10.43 a.m. Washington time when the CIA director took the call. Twenty-eight minutes later he was standing in the conference room adjoining his office on the seventh floor consulting notes on his laptop, bringing his dozen closest and most senior executives up to date.

'The courier – if that is truly what he is – has conditions,' Falcon told them. 'It's understandable – if he's even close to telling the truth, he must be terrified. He says he won't commit any information to paper or a USB drive in case it falls into the wrong hands – that would cost him and, almost certainly, his family their lives.

'From his mouth to someone's ear, he says that is the only way it will work,' Falcon continued. 'That means a meeting, and he has told our intermediary that he won't risk arousing suspicion by making any changes to his routine. Any meeting would have to be on his home territory at a location that was not only familiar to him but he considers safe.' Falcon shrugged and looked around the room. 'According to him, none of these things are negotiable. He says he's prepared to walk.'

With the update complete, there was a short silence, broken finally by Bill 'Buster' Glover, one of the agency's assistant directors, a man in his late fifties who looked like an unmade bed: heavy-set, wild, unruly hair, a crumpled shirt and a permanently worried expression.

'He talks about a spectacular – did he say anything more about it?' Buster asked.

'Nothing,' Falcon replied. 'He's trying to sell it to us – he's not giving anything away for free, and that's assuming he even knows something.'

'How much?' Buster asked. 'How much does he want?'

Falcon paused, looking again at their faces. 'Twenty million for him, five for the intermediary, and the usual – passports, safe passage . . .'

He didn't finish. '*How much?*' a man's voice called from the far end of the long table, in shock. In that respect, he was acting as spokesman for the rest of the room.

'God in heaven,' a woman halfway down added. 'Twenty-five million, Falcon? This could be the grift of the century, at least as far as the spy business is concerned.'

'Yeah, could be,' Falcon replied as most heads nodded in agreement. If there was one thing that everybody in the secret world subscribed to – no matter what side they were serving – it was that the spy trade was full of cheats, fraudsters, liars, fantasists and double-crossers. 'His information might also be true,' Falcon said gently.

'You're not thinking of paying this?' the man at the far end asked, turning angry.

'Before 9/11, I wouldn't have considered it; after 9/11, I can't ignore it,' Falcon said. 'The world we live in, Jim.'

'No ... no,' Jim replied, shaking his head, joined in dissent by at least four or five other people. Within moments the room had erupted into an argument. The advocates for considering the idea were clearly outnumbered, tried to compensate by raising the volume, and the dispute grew more heated by the second.

'Okay, okay,' Buster said harshly, standing, tucking his shirt in, demanding their attention. The room quietened. 'So let's draw up the document, shall we?'

'What document?' Jim asked, aggressive. He was a big guy, smart too – a hard-driving forty-year-old with a face so rugged it looked like a long stretch of torn-up road. He was the head of analysis – the youngest person to hold the position – and someone who clearly was not planning on stopping there.

'The document we are all going to sign,' Buster replied.

'I have no idea what you're talking about,' Jim responded.

Falcon intervened. 'What Buster means is – we draw up a short note detailing who is in favour of pursuing this lead, irrespective of the cost, and who isn't. Then we all sign it.'

'Why?' the woman halfway down the table asked.

'To save time,' Falcon replied. 'After 9/11, the Commission of Inquiry found it difficult to pin down who advocated what in the months before the attack. Everybody was ducking and weaving. This way, if we are hit by another spectacular, there won't be a problem – we just hand them the document and they know precisely who stood where.'

Nobody said anything. 'Okay – who's for signing?' Buster asked.

Still there was no response. 'Things are suddenly different when it's no longer an intellectual exercise, when you have to nail your colours to the mast and sail into battle,' Falcon observed.

Everyone at the table became calmer and was now nodding: what Falcon had said was the truth. The spymaster turned back to his laptop – once again in total command of the room. 'Now, can we consider the information on its merits? If you want my opinion, I think the conditions our purported courier is demanding increase his credibility. He is acting exactly like you would expect of a man who is playing the most dangerous game on earth.'

'And the figure he wants to be paid does the same,' Buster added. 'An ask that size – he knows we are going to examine every inch of him and his story. This guy must have a huge degree of confidence.' He smiled. 'Or delusion.'

'So what do we do?' Jim asked, more collegial now. 'Ask for proof of life, so to speak?'

'Exactly,' Falcon replied. 'We say further negotiation depends on him sending a token of good faith, something to prove he is in the Army and that we are not being gamed.'

Everyone nodded. It was now up to the courier to provide a proof of life, and the executives started to relax. The meeting was over.

Buster retrieved his threadbare jacket from the floor then came to Falcon's side: 'Twenty-five million? Jeez. What a world we live in.'

'Yeah,' Falcon said. 'The world that was built by 9/11.'

9

THAT AFTERNOON, A MESSAGE WENT FROM THE SEVENTH FLOOR AT Langley to Kabul Station, was taken to the air-con workshop by Chris Halvorsen, was driven across the Iranian border by the technician, who then whispered it into the ear of the courier at a small bazaar two hundred miles south of their last meeting. The CIA wanted proof of life.

The bazaar was a mean and venal place, popular with smugglers and men preying on the constant trickle of refugees trying to reach Tehran. Sitting at the back of a deserted tea shack, the courier told the technician he had anticipated the buyers would want some sort of evidence. A few minutes later the two men went to the Nissan and, making sure they were unobserved, the technician took possession of a small token. Successfully, he carried it out of the borderlands, arrived back at his workshop and handed it over to Chris Halvorsen. At the headquarters of Kabul Station, the token – a piece of paper about the size of a business card but wafer thin – was sealed in a steel box and flown to Langley.

From there, the cropped, badly blurred photo was transported to the National Security Agency in Maryland, where, once the image experts and analysts had enhanced it, a wealth of information was revealed. With the token and the NSA's report in hand, Falcon reconvened a meeting of his closest advisers and, while none of the information in the photo was definitive, it was persuasive enough to convince Falcon and the other people present that they had to engage with the so-called courier.

Four hours after the seventh floor took the decision to meet with the courier at a time and place of his choosing in Iran, the men and women whose job it was to design the mission concluded that a Denied Access Area spy travelling alone and entering by foot would offer the best chance of success.

In darkness, at 3.22 on a Sunday morning, just minutes after Falcon had signed what is known as a Form B1706 – an order initiating a clandestine operation – the encrypted cellphone I kept on the nightstand next to my bed rang. Sleepy-eyed, I grabbed it and realized that the caller had already hung up. I had no doubt what it meant.

I looked at the list of missed calls and saw it had come from a number I recognized; a number that I knew, even if I dialled, would never answer. In the world in which I lived, the phone number itself was the coded message.

It told me a car was on the way. I was going live.

10

BY 4 A.M. I WAS IN THE BACK OF A NONDESCRIPT SUV AND WAS placing my right palm on the side of a steel briefcase that had arrived with the vehicle.

It was the latest, hi-tech version of what is known in the secret world as a lock-bag, and silently I counted to seven, giving the myriad sensors hidden in the steel enough time to measure the biometrics of my hand. I removed it and, moments later, with the system satisfied of my identity, the lid of the briefcase opened on a spring and I was looking at the screen of a specially designed laptop. A file titled 'Courier/Borderlands' was already open, telling me where, in broad terms, I was going. I felt fingers of ice creep up my spine. It had to be Iran, didn't it? By far the most deadly of all the Denied Access Area locations, and so it was with genuine trepidation that I started to read the extensive file.

By the time we passed through the guard house at Langley I was finished and I closed the lid, handed the briefcase back to the protection officer sitting in the front and looked out the window. The cool night air lent an aching clarity to the trees and – fittingly, in view of my imminent mission – a crescent moon rode high in the sky. I could not have asked for a more beautiful night to embark on what became such an ugly business.

Once I had made my way through two further checkpoints, I entered Langley's highest security zone, a vast space buried beneath the Bubble, the CIA auditorium. In the underground foyer, as I handed over the last of my possessions – phone, watch, belt and buckle – and was told to stand inside a back-scatter X-ray machine, a security officer directed me to go to the most secure of the zone's dozen conference rooms.

Accompanied by two guards, I walked through deserted corridors, listened to the hum of the generators that wrapped the exterior of the area in a wall of anti-eavesdropping white noise and stopped outside a high-security door. I swiped my pass across yet another scanner, waited while the facial recognition cameras confirmed my identity, watched the door slide open.

I stepped inside to find that the large, normally bland space had been turned into a war room. Experts in photo analysis were working at computers in one corner, hi-def screens had dropped from compartments in the ceiling, wrapping around the entire space, turning it into something like an IMAX theatre. Inside a circle of hardware, sitting at a long conference table, was a group of intelligence analysts who specialized in the borderlands, all of the mission planners and most of the seventh-floor brains trust. Falcon – seated at the far end, the ringmaster of the forty-strong circus – nodded in greeting and motioned me to take the vacant seat at the end of the table.

'You read the summary in the car?' he asked without preamble.

'I guess you got the proof of life – otherwise I wouldn't be here.'

Falcon reached to a side table for a small glass panel, handed it to an assistant and, with everyone in the room straining to see, it was delivered to me. I saw that the wafer-thin rectangle of paper – with a barely legible photo printed on it – had, for protection, been sandwiched between two pieces of shatterproof glass. It now looked like a biological specimen. I stared more closely at the paper and smiled. Falcon grinned back.

'A great trick. Ever use it, Falcon – when you were in the field, I mean?' I asked.

'I'm not *that* old,' he replied, mock offended. 'I've read about it, though.'

'Yeah, so have I,' I said.

One of the senior intelligence analysts – a woman in her fifties known for her vaping and cynicism – was perplexed. 'I don't get it,' she said. 'What's a great trick – a bad photo?'

Falcon shook his head. 'He's talking about the paper it's printed on, Margaret. The trick was how the courier got the photo safely out of the borderlands.'

'It's like a piece of history,' I said. 'The idea was dreamt up by the French resistance – the Maquis – when they were fighting the Nazis—'

Falcon interrupted: 'That's why he asked if I'd used it in the field. He was suggesting I was old enough to have been there in '42.' Everyone laughed.

'The resistance had a problem,' I continued. 'How did they pass secret information between different cells – the location of a supply drop, the time and date of a meeting – when informers and the Gestapo were everywhere? Being French, they were heavy smokers – just like in Iran – but factory-made cigarettes were expensive, so what most of them did was roll their own from loose tobacco.

'Someone in the resistance came up with the idea of writing the secret information on the inside of a cigarette paper. They would then roll it into a smoke and, if they were stopped by the Gestapo, they pulled the cigarette out from behind their ear and lit it up. Every time they took a pull, they were destroying the evidence.'

I pointed at the wafer-thin paper. 'Maybe our courier or the intermediary had read about it, perhaps they thought it up themselves.

Either way, they used a hand-made cigarette to get the token out of the borderlands. What do we know about the photo?' I asked.

Falcon indicated the IMAX screens. I turned and was astonished as the image appeared – the techs at NSA and the photo analysts in the corner had used their massive computing power and classified software to enhance myriads of pixels, turning a photo of blurred shapes and indistinct shadows into a vivid image a thousand times larger than the original. I walked forward and stared at a huddle of mud-brick houses surrounding a village square.

'No metadata?' I asked, referring to the details about time, date and GPS location that are automatically embedded into a photograph.

'No. Metadata is only included in a digital photo and we have a printed copy – but even if we had a digital version, I can guarantee there wouldn't be anything there,' Falcon said. 'As you saw from the cigarette paper, he's not stupid.'

Staring at the photo, I ran through its details: 'A shade awning strung across the square, a table ready for food to be laid out, men with their hands raised in the air, dancing, a goat they're going to slaughter tied to a stake – some sort of celebration?' I said. 'A birthday?'

'A wedding, we think,' Falcon said. 'Probably a senior member of the Army marrying a young woman from a local village.'

I looked at the twenty or so men who were visible in the photo – all of them with either their backs to the camera, too deep in shadow, or their faces cropped out to be identified. 'He's obviously made sure we can't see any faces—'

'He's not giving anything away for free. He did tell the intermediary some information to sell the pitch – he says the man in the armchair under the shade cloth is called the Emir.'

I looked at him: he was dressed completely in white, no longer young from his posture, the photo deliberately framed to remove his face. 'The title doesn't mean much, does it?' I said. 'They're always self-proclaimed.'

'Yes, but every terrorist organization needs its messianic figure,' Falcon said. 'The Emir is theirs. Probably an academic or some type of religious scholar – always invoking the deadliest interpretation of holy texts. Kill the dissenters, kill the infidels, kill the invaders. He can preach up a storm, incite others to war, but has never been in battle himself—'

'Sounds like the Pentagon,' Margaret said.

Amid a chorus of laughter, Falcon continued. 'The fighting and

planning are left to the military leader – they are always the dangerous one.' He walked forward and pointed at one section of the photo.
'Which brings us to this man.'

11

FALCON POINTED TO A POWERFUL-LOOKING SHIRTLESS FIGURE WITH
his back to the camera playing cards with three other men, waiting
for the festivities to start.

The card-playing was unusual: it wasn't encouraged in Islam, but
nor was it *haram*. Gambling is, however, and if there had been any
money we would have known the photo was fake and we could have
gone home. There wasn't. 'Who is he?' I asked.

'The courier told our intermediary he is the military commander,
apparently a strategic thinker and highly intelligent – cruel, too,'
Falcon said. 'But then you'd expect a vendor to say something like
that, wouldn't you? This time, however, he may be right.'

He paused and looked around the room and I was struck at how –
suddenly – he looked so old and careworn. He spoke quietly. 'He says
the man is Abu Muslim al-Tundra.'

I stared at Falcon – and so did everyone else. In the shocked silence,
Falcon continued to look at the card-player, thinking about him, riff-
ing on the name. 'A Muslim from the snow . . . someone from the
wasteland . . . a man out of the bleak midwinter . . .'

'Al-Tundra's dead,' I said, shocked, speaking for us all. 'The Air
Force dropped two five-hundred-pound bombs on the so-called safe
house he was visiting in Iraq.'

Falcon gave a bitter smile. 'That's the Air Force, isn't it? Like a
famous psychologist once said: if the only tool you've got is a hammer,
everything starts to look like a nail.

'After the raid, nobody could find much evidence of a house or
anything else, let alone any DNA. God help us – a thousand pounds
of high explosive to kill one man. The Pentagon, of course, announced
he was dead. They had to – they couldn't admit that the ten civilians
also in the place had been killed for nothing.'

'The forensic team that went in afterwards never found a body, but they did locate what they thought might have been a tunnel.' He looked around the room. 'So – maybe he went in the front door and straight out the back. Nobody knows – they either got him or it was a screw-up. The courier is telling us it was a screw-up.'

'If al-Tundra is still alive,' Buster said, 'no wonder the courier wants twenty-five million – he sure knows the market. What do you think, Falcon?'

'Dead or alive?' he replied. 'I don't know – we don't have any facts. If you're asking about intuition? I'd say it's Murphy's Law – anything that can go wrong will. I think it's him.'

A tremor passed through the room: al-Tundra alive was a terrifying prospect. While Osama bin Laden might have captured the world's imagination, al-Tundra had certainly earned an exalted place in the dark pantheon of terrorism.

Al-Tundra wasn't his real name, of course – nobody had ever unearthed that. Like Abu Bakr al-Baghdadi, al-Zarqawi, al-Londres, al-Brussels and a host of others, he had adopted a *nom de guerre* when he first became a jihadi warrior in what is known at Langley as 'the cauldron', the blood-soaked sweep of land between Iraq and Syria. Because the name conjured up an image of the far north, everyone figured he was from Russia, but there was no evidence to support it because nobody in the CIA, MI6 or Mossad had ever gathered reliable information about his identity and none of the thousands of field agents, local assets or informers had ever knowingly seen his face.

Constantly dressed in a *keffiyeh* and dark sunglasses, his features were always so hidden that no facial analysis, biometric algorithm or human artist had ever produced a likeness of him. Of all the prominent and secret terrorist leaders in the world, al-Tundra – the Muslim from the treeless wasteland – might as well have been a ghost.

Over the years, however, several Western spy agencies had intercepted calls and messages as other terrorists talked about him, and that had given the CIA some information; nothing more than vignettes really. Estimated to be in his forties by the time he was supposedly killed, he was reputed to have been a teenage street thug in Cairo, Beirut, Istanbul or a dozen other cities, depending on who was doing the telling. There was nothing more known about him until some scattered reports of years of distinguished military service – for what army, nobody knew – and there were some who said he was a mercenary, but they were probably just romantics. At some point in the years that followed he experienced a revelation and, like most people who find – or rediscover – their religion, he fell for it very hard. He emerged from the wilderness, the desert or wherever it had taken place as a believer in the most exacting and fundamentalist interpretation of Islam.

While there was doubt about his background, one thing that everybody agreed on was that earlier in his life he had shown a great love of tattoos. In one of the most frequently recounted stories, after his adoption of the faith he had reputedly used a box-cutter and sandpaper to perform some dry-gulch surgery and removed a dozen of them, including an ink of a naked woman on his crotch.

As a member of various terrorist groups – each one more violent than its predecessor – he became an executioner, a field commander and then one of the leaders of al-Qaeda in the Country of Two Rivers, a location better known to the West as Iraq. The Iraqi offshoot was notorious for suicide attacks on US soldiers, the beheading of American reporters, the burial alive of children and their Christian mothers and the enslavement and rape of thousands of women from several minority groups. It is a sad indictment of the traumatic history of Iraq that none of those events really registered on the Richter scale of atrocity. Except for this: out of al-Qaeda in Iraq emerged an even more brutal and ruthless organization: ISIS.

One of its leaders was al-Tundra, and that led, in a straight line, to two huge bombs being loaded on to a US plane, and a house in Iraq – which may or may not have had a tunnel – being vaporized.

With that in the forefront of my mind, I got up, walked forward and looked harder at the man on the screen. Everything except his back and part of one of his shoulders – heavily roped with muscle – was hidden from view, and I let my mind roam, imagining myself in one of the scores of unremarkable villages in the borderlands. A wedding would start soon and I saw myself appear from behind the food tables, walk past the Emir, take a seat opposite al-Tundra and wait to be dealt in to the game. Standing in a conference room in Virginia, I watched him acknowledge me with a nod, and in that moment I tried to capture something about him from his body, his posture . . . anything.

I told myself that there was no doubt of it – he was not a member of some rag-tag band or a swaggering wannabe because he had a Kalashnikov over his shoulder but somebody far more dangerous, a man properly trained in a real army. The truth about him, however, lay just over the horizon. The scraps of information we had found didn't amount to much and the shadows he inhabited were far stronger than any light the candles could cast.

'Now step back from the photo so you can see all of it,' Falcon said. 'What do you notice about his back?'

'Nothing. It's in darkness,' I responded.

'That's what I thought too, but the team suspected something could be found, and the NSA threw everything they could at it.'

The image on the screens went black – or so it seemed; then I realized I was watching the NSA's process of enhancing the image. Disturbing details started to emerge from al-Tundra's back: a leg . . . an eye . . .

'It's a tattoo,' I said, realizing. 'One he couldn't remove?'

'Right,' Falcon replied. 'The NSA recovered part of the image and extrapolated the rest. We're fairly sure it covers the whole of his back.'

More details emerged as Falcon explained. 'The experts say if it wasn't done in Japan or by monks in Thailand, it was definitely executed by someone who had studied there.'

The enhancement came to a halt and the tattoo was suddenly lit by an intense light courtesy of the technicians. Intricate and far larger than the insect it portrayed, the tattoo was rendered in different shades of black – except for its green eyes – and that, combined with the fact its wings were partly spread, made it look brooding, overwhelmingly sinister.

'A locust,' I said.

'For years,' Falcon replied, 'there is nothing, then a plague appears – unstoppable, destroying everything in its path. Maybe this is it. Maybe this is their time.'

12

FOR THE SMALL GROUP OF US LOOKING AT A BLURRED PHOTO TAKEN in a village four thousand miles away, it was a heart-stopping moment. I don't think there was anyone in that room who didn't believe that al-Tundra was alive and that suddenly the world was a vastly more dangerous place.

Consequently, there was no elation about what was clearly an intelligence coup – the CIA had discovered that one of the world's most feared terrorists had risen from the dead and had determined the broad details of his location – but, as the meeting ended and everyone filed out, the prevailing sense was of dread and anxiety.

As for me, my trepidation had been escalating ever since I got into the SUV and opened the laptop. Now, learning of the task ahead – of having to go deep into al-Tundra's web to meet a courier who said he was willing to betray him – that trepidation, accompanied by ribbons of sweat down my spine, threatened to bury me.

Aware that one of the founders of ISIS was planning what appeared to be an imminent spectacular, the preparations for my trek into Iran were accelerated and far more intense than any mission I had ever undertaken. For almost a week – punctuated only by short breaks for food and sleep – I was subjected to a whirlwind of secret briefings, conferences, doubts and expert sessions until I was close to exhaustion. By the night before I left – as tired as I was and trying not to think of the likelihood of being captured very soon by either the Iranians or, worse still, by al-Tundra and his Army – I forced myself to keep going.

I was only thirty-six, but experience had taught me that salvation often lay in the tiniest details and I was desperate to discover as much as possible about the terrorist leader. After all, my life might depend on it.

While I was supposed to be sleeping in preparation for the morning's early call and the start of my journey, I made my way instead across Langley's sprawling campus to the New Headquarters Building.

The two towers were only six storeys high, but they were like icebergs – only 10 per cent was above the surface – and I approached a bank of elevators that served only the vast subterranean labyrinth and waited while the facial recognition camera confirmed my identity. The car descended twelve floors, the doors opened and I stepped into 'the Tomb'. More properly known as CIA Archives, Langley – one of the agency's eight huge data-storage facilities – it had earned its nickname not only because it was so far underground but because its files were reputed to hold the key to where countless bodies were buried.

The information held in the facility was notoriously hard to navigate so I was thankful when I was met at the elevator by Clayton

Powell, the chief archivist. Aged in his fifties, with a purple birthmark disfiguring a large part of his face – Freud could probably have written volumes about why he had chosen to work so far underground – he was both excellent at his job and one of the most decent people I had ever met. Highly intelligent, always trying to think laterally, he shook my hand warmly and led me into the labyrinth, heading towards one of the secure cell-like rooms where a hard-backed chair, the relevant files and a computer with no access to anything except power would be waiting.

'What have you dug up?' I asked as he keyed in the access codes to the cell.

'About al-Tundra? Nothing that hasn't been pored over a thousand times,' he said, and opened the door.

Three hours later, fighting to stay awake, I was almost at the end of the rows of digital files, every one of them confirming exactly what Clay had told me: there was nothing of use in them, it was just the raw data – the muffled phone intercepts and the unreliable accounts sold by men in back alleys in Cairo – on which the Western spy agencies had built the little they claimed to know about him.

With only three files to go, I accessed the largest of them, its size being the only thing differentiating it from the others. The image that instantly appeared on the screen showed satellite footage of a man in the ruins of a burnt-out village with a score of bodies littering the street behind him. He was dressed in ISIS regulation dark glasses and his face and body were indistinguishable thanks to the *keffiyeh* and the loose-fitting robes he was wearing. He could have been any warrior in any of the war zones of Iraq or Syria.

Except, according to the research notes accompanying the footage, a highly regarded local informer, standing several hundred yards from the vehicle, heard three senior jihadis tell other fighters that the man was in fact the legendary and mysterious al-Tundra.

I sat forward, looking closely as the video unspooled, and then turned my attention to the notes. They said it had been captured by a satellite targeting the most violent part of Syria, and the date watermarked on it showed it had been taken eight months before the air strike that supposedly killed him. I paused the playback and looked again at him for second after long second. While the screen capture was of no value in identifying him – al-Tundra might as well have been playing cards – my fatigue dropped away. Once more I was in the presence of Abu Muslim al-Tundra, the man from the bleak midwinter.

I hit play, the footage showed him getting into a nondescript Toyota four-wheel drive and, once I had finished reading that section of notes, I shook my head in admiration: a very smart agency analyst had determined – thanks to the depth the Toyota's tyres had sunk into the sand – that the vehicle was carrying a lot of extra weight across its body. Under its filthy paintwork, it was heavily and professionally armoured.

The vehicle drove off and I looked at the final few paragraphs of notes: the satellite tracked it for three hours before it was lost in the labyrinth of tiny alleys and hidden garages that peppered Mosul, a chaotic city of almost 2 million people. So that was it, I told myself – one glimpse of al-Tundra, identified by hearsay, and the whole night's work added nothing to my scant knowledge of the man.

It had been a worthless exercise and even though I had two more files to look at, I knew they would be of no more value than the scores that had preceded them, and I abandoned them completely. I got to my feet, flexed my aching back and reached for a buzzer on the desk that would signal to Clay that I was finished and he could unlock the door.

I stopped – my action so sudden that my hand froze in mid-air. A thought had struck me, but where it had come from, or if it would work, I had no idea. I hit the buzzer. I wasn't leaving, though – I needed Clay's help.

13

CLAY SMILED IN GREETING AND INDICATED THE DIGITAL FILES. 'LIKE I said – thin as paint, huh?'

'Maybe,' I replied.

He looked at me quizzically and then noticed the image of al-Tundra on the screen. 'I remember pulling that file scores of times when we were searching for him, ages before he was killed.' He looked at me for a long moment. 'He's not dead, is he?'

I was surprised. 'Why would you say that?' I asked, not wanting to answer but unwilling to lie, especially to him.

'Because you're a Denied Access Area agent, because those files have been gathering dust for years and in the last twenty-four hours they have been accessed seven times and – finally – because if the Pentagon says you're dead, you are almost certainly alive.'

I laughed. 'Yes,' I said at last. 'It looks like he's alive.'

Clay didn't react to the news, but his expression told me he appreciated the honesty. 'Maybe the files aren't as thin as paint,' I explained. 'We might be able to find something deep down if you want to try. But it's right out of the box.'

He smiled. 'Well, you've come to the right place.' He walked to the corner of the cell, grabbed another of the straight-backed chairs and sat down.

'I leave tomorrow,' I explained. 'There's no time to get the seventh floor involved in this, even if anyone thought the idea might work. Do you recall what it said in the file? They followed al-Tundra's vehicle for three hours.'

'Yeah, I remember,' Clay said. 'Something went wrong, didn't it? Something weird.'

'Sure did,' I replied. 'They couldn't missile him, they had only just got a positive ID, so they wanted a recording of his voice – the notes say the NSA used every piece of technology they had. If they could just get a sample of him speaking, they could compare it to the countless recordings the satellites were harvesting every day. Once they got a match, we would know exactly where al-Tundra was and what he was talking about.'

'But they never got the recording, did they?' Clay said.

'According to the file, the moment he got in the car he fell asleep. During the entire trip he never said a word.'

Clay and I smiled bitterly. 'I remember,' Clay said. 'People mentioned at the time it was a complete bust.'

'But it wasn't,' I responded. 'They did have a voice print – it was just nobody realized it.'

'What?' Clay replied. 'You said he was asleep for the whole journey.'

'He was – but the vehicle wasn't,' I said. 'After three hours of driving they had a perfect voice print of the Toyota's engine.'

'How would that help?' Clay said, laughing, dismissing it. 'There must have been a million Toyota four-wheel drives in the cauldron.'

'But how many were fully armoured?' I responded. 'Four, five? Maybe less. The engine would have been labouring to power that extra weight, sending out an entirely different note.'

Clay was silent, looking at me. 'You want us to search the recordings from the zone but not worry about voices – we try and match the sound of an engine?'

'The technology's the same, Clay,' I said. 'Al-Tundra was a founder of ISIS and that was his battle-truck. He had to be protected; he won't be travelling in anything else. We match the sound of the car and I think we'll hear him talking inside.'

14

SILENTLY I ROAMED THE BACK OFFICE OF THE TOMB, A HUGE SPACE behind the small rooms, walking between the computers in front of forty men and women. Wearing headphones, they were listening to the occupants of a vehicle which – thanks to the distinct tone of its engine – had been identified as the battle-truck.

Clay had used AI to trawl through mountains of archived satellite surveillance of the cauldron in the period before al-Tundra was supposedly killed and our unique system had found countless instances of the armoured truck on the move. It then became a matter of listening to the men inside the vehicle and trying to work out – through the content of the conversation – who was the leader, which of them was al-Tundra.

Initially, my hopes had soared, but after two hours reality had intruded. Even hearing the occupants was problematic: the voices were often muffled; if the air-con was blasting their words were frequently indistinguishable; and then – of course – there was the sound of small-arms fire and explosions as the vehicle passed through various war zones. Worse still, the material we did hear was almost entirely trivial: gossip, complaints about food, discussions about logistics and supplies, the fastest route from Raqqa to Mosul. Talk about 'the banality of evil', I thought.

Finally, despondent, I walked over to Clay. 'Time to stop,' I said.

'This isn't going anywhere.' I had a plane to catch. Clay nodded, but before he could give the order an archivist on the far side of the room called out. 'Clay,' the long-haired guy in his twenties said in a monotone. 'You might want to listen here.'

Clay stared at him for a moment then took my shoulder and started to guide me fast towards the terminal. 'Come on,' he said. 'You may want to pay attention to this one.'

I had no idea what he was talking about – certainly there was nothing in the young guy's tone that indicated he had found something out of the ordinary. Clay saw the confusion on my face and smiled.

'There's always more than a touch of robot in Darren's voice,' Clay explained. 'Five years he has been with us, and that's the most excited I've ever heard him.' He called out to the young archivist as we crossed the room towards him. 'What is it, Darren?'

'Four guys in the battle-truck,' Darren said. 'Must have been a nice day – windows closed, air-con low, no gunfire, a long journey by the size of the file. Lot of talking—'

What a strange guy, I thought. Clay and I arrived at his side. One half of his computer screen was dominated by multicoloured bar graphs and the other half was showing a written translation in English, scrolling fast as it kept up with the spoken words. I started reading, but Darren interrupted. 'They have just left a village where a dozen families had been burned alive in their houses – intentionally or by accident, nobody is saying.'

Darren had clearly never dealt with ISIS if he thought it could have been accidental. 'What language?' I asked.

'Gulf Arabic,' he replied, as flat as before.

'Through the speakers, please.'

Darren glanced at me. Gulf Arabic is difficult to master, but I have always had a gift for languages – when I was young I started off with Russian and pretty soon hit the harder stuff – Turkish and the two most popular forms of Arabic. Over the years I had improved until I was fluent enough to withstand almost any scrutiny.

Darren shrugged. 'Whatever you say, mister.'

He brought the sound up and for the first time I heard the voices. Inspired probably by burning families alive in their homes, they were beginning to discuss other cruel things they had witnessed. I stepped closer to the screen, looking at the image of the Toyota, and told Darren to concentrate on whoever was sitting in the rear, on the passenger side.

'That's the safest seat,' I explained. 'The armour is always strongest at the back and anyone targeting them will aim at the driver and his side of the vehicle.'

Darren tweaked his controls, enhancing the clarity. The man in the safe seat started to speak, invisible behind his dark-tinted window. I closed out the rest of the world and focused on his voice. The other archivists started to gather round, but I paid them no mind; I just kept listening to the voice, going deeper until I felt like the man was talking to me.

'Whoever he is,' I said, 'Gulf Arabic isn't his native language, but he's good, very good – he's been in the cauldron a long time. As you can see on the translation, the driver is asking the men about their experiences, the most terrible things they have witnessed—'

I stopped mid-sentence as I listened to a burst of by-play between the four men, trying to imagine the body language, the behaviour, all the non-verbal things that communicate so much. Then I straightened myself and signalled to Darren to stop the tape.

I continued to stare at the frozen image of the Toyota – I was certain of it, and I exhaled, not even aware until then that I had been holding my breath. 'The man in the safe seat is him,' I said. 'You won't get it from the translation, but listen to the other three, the pauses, their tone – they are deferring to him. He's their commander, it's his battle-truck.'

For the first time ever, a US intelligence agent had heard the voice of the legendary Abu Muslim al-Tundra. I turned to Darren. 'Hit play,' I said. 'Let's listen to him.'

15

'I HEARD A STORY ONCE ABOUT A TEENAGER,' AL-TUNDRA SAID, MAKING his contribution to the group's accounts of horror. 'He was raised in a mining town on the frontier, one of those places where, as somebody said, the streets were dark with something more than night.

'It was a place of terrible winters, endless forests and a huge river. As if life wasn't hard enough, the boy and his brother – four years younger – had no mother. When they were young, the parents separated, and the mother took their two daughters and returned to Iraq where she had grown up.

'It must have been very hard, but the boys' father never faltered,' al-Tundra continued. 'He gave everything to his boys, acting as mother and father in that brutal environment, and as they grew older they not only loved him but admired him without reservation.'

Al-Tundra paused, and it took me a moment to realize that he was drinking. 'The father worked underground in one of the dirtiest and most dangerous diamond mines in the world,' he said. 'But in late spring every year, once the snow had melted, he would put his sons in his old four-wheel drive, hitch up a trailer and load it with a tent, weapons, tools and enough supplies for at least four months.

'They would drive for days through the forest until they entered an area of bogs and endless plains. When they arrived, they would set up camp and start to search for woolly mammoths.'

16

'DID HE SAY "WOOLLY MAMMOTHS"?' CLAY ASKED, SIGNALLING TO Darren to stop the tape. He laughed. 'How long have woolly mammoths been extinct?'

'Five, ten thousand years, I'm not sure,' I answered. 'I don't think the father's looking for the animals, though – he's looking for their carcasses.'

Clay and the rest of the group stopped laughing. I was forbidden from saying anything about past missions so I couldn't tell them how I knew, but as a Denied Access Area spy fluent in the language, I had been into Russia six or seven times. Once, on a train journey halfway across the country, I had heard about a strange and highly lucrative business. 'The woolly mammoth miners of Siberia are sort of legendary,' I said.

Everybody, including Clay, looked at me. 'For over five million years, Siberia was home to massive herds of mammoths,' I continued. 'The animals were born and lived in the vast landscape, and when they died their bodies sank into the earth and bogs, slowly decaying until all that remained were the ivory tusks, impervious to soil, water or time.

'That last remnant of them would have stayed there,' I said. 'Undisturbed for ever, except for the wildlife poachers of Africa. By hunting elephants and rhinos almost to extinction, they finally forced the world to act and ban the trade in ivory. The biggest casualty were the specialists in Hong Kong who made a good living carving elaborate scenes of village life into a tusk. Highly prized in China for the craftsmanship and as a status symbol, they often went for over a million bucks.

'Without any tusks, the old craft and the entire business was finished – until somebody realized that ivory recovered from the bogs of Siberia was legally clean. The mammoth tusks exploded in value and men on the frontier soon learned that one tusk could sell for the equivalent of five years' wages. If the miners were lucky and hit what they called a graveyard – a site with four or more dead animals – they could earn a fortune in a few days and escape Siberia for ever.'

I shrugged. 'The mammoth miners are real.' I nodded to Darren to restart the tape and once again we heard al-Tundra's voice.

'It was during their fifth journey into the wilderness – the boy was sixteen and his brother was twelve – when they hit it big,' he said. 'They were up to their armpits in mud, using a generator and high-pressure water guns to blast into the soft earth on the bank of a small river when the young boy saw the first tusk.

'The three of them tore and ripped at the soil with their bare hands. The tusk and its partner were huge, but that was not the best of it – within ten yards, they located four other animals. The father and his two boys had found a graveyard.

'With ten tusks, they were wealthy, and while other miners might have stayed to keep prospecting, the father was not a greedy man and each year he had seen more and more men and women roaming the wilderness. Almost all of them, attracted by the huge rise in the value of the tusks, looked like outlaws to him and he knew it was time to go.'

We heard al-Tundra pause to take another drink. 'No cops out there, I guess,' Clay remarked. 'It was probably like Tombstone before Wyatt Earp arrived.'

People laughed as al-Tundra picked up the thread. 'The family hauled the tusks back to their camp, careful not to put a foot out of line as they approached. When they had set the place up, the father adopted a practice common among the miners: he ringed their clearing with tripwires, steel-jawed bear traps and other booby devices.

'While the father loaded a shotgun and guarded the hoard, he sent the boys ten miles upstream to where they had moored a flat-bottomed aluminium skiff they had brought in with them. The father's plan was to load the tusks on to the skiff, abandon everything else and head downriver to the nearest town. What did he care about his vehicle and equipment? The family would be leaving Siberia for good.

'The boy and his brother were halfway to the skiff when they heard a faint explosion,' al-Tundra said. He paused again, but this time there was no sound of him drinking.

We sat in silence until he continued. 'The two boys were accustomed to dynamite, but this sound was different and it came from the direction of their camp. The boys ran—

'When they arrived, the tent was shredded, the remains of the shotgun were on the ground and a crumpled mess of bloody rags lay in a far corner. The tusks had been stolen and it took a minute before they realized – the mess of rags was their father.

'He was still breathing, one leg attached to his knee by nothing more than cartilage, and pints of blood were soaking his shirt and his jeans. The boys saw he had managed to tourniquet the leg – keeping himself alive – before collapsing into unconsciousness, but he could do nothing about the shrapnel that had pierced his chest in a dozen places.

'The father must have sensed the presence of his sons because he rallied and came to. As both boys lifted him on to what remained of a mattress he managed to say there were three men and a woman. They had avoided the camp's booby traps by firing a rocket-propelled grenade from the trees, hitting the cooking stove and engulfing him in a wall of metal ricochets.

'The older boy was only sixteen, but he managed to think clearly. He bound his father's wounds as best he could, used their half-wrecked first-aid kit to inject him with an antibiotic and applied pressure bandages to try and stem the bleeding.'

'He told his brother they were going to save their father's life, they would take him out by boat. Unburdened by the tusks or supplies, he figured they could get to the nearest town and medical help in two days. First, though, he had to drive through the forest and retrieve the skiff, so he grabbed his kid brother's shoulders, yelled at him to stop crying and told him to go and start the vehicle.

'As he started to prepare another shot of antibiotic the younger boy appeared on the other side of the encampment. In tears again, he yelled to his brother that the killers had not only taken the tusks. They had also stolen their entire supply of diesel.

'With no fuel for the skiff or the four-wheel drive the older boy knew they were trapped in the wilderness. There would be no medical help for their father.'

17

'THEY TOOK TURNS TO HOLD HIM,' AL-TUNDRA CONTINUED AFTER A moment of silence in the car. 'For two days they kept him alive – forty-eight hours of delirium broken by moments of clarity when he told his sons how much he loved them.

'It was the longest two days the boys would ever know, and when their father finally succumbed, the younger boy's greatest worry was how they would bury him. His brother put his arms around him and told him a burial could wait – first they had a job to do.

'He took the first step immediately,' al-Tundra said. 'He had spent a large part of his life in the wilderness so he could track a hare for miles, interpret the distant cry of a timber wolf and shoot a rifle with frightening accuracy. Tracking four marauders – a gang from the city almost certainly – presented no problem.

'The killers had travelled upstream by skiff, waited in the trees close to the camp and then one of them had crawled forward and fired the grenade. Fighting his anger, he told his brother to help him collect the six heavy-duty bear traps their father had positioned around the camp.

'Ever seen a bear trap?' al-Tundra asked his companions. 'They weigh fifty pounds and have two jaws attached to huge springs. Once an animal steps on a triggering device the jaws snap shut and rows of sharpened steel teeth drive into flesh and bone.

'With the traps on board, their marksman's rifles slung over their shoulders and the skiff's engine cut,' al-Tundra continued, 'the two drifted downstream until they found an area of churned mud and saw the marauders' skiff hidden on the riverbank.

'They waited until night and then moved through the trees and scrub, following a highway of trampled weeds. It led to three tents, a blazing fire pit and two decrepit Land Rovers that had transported the team into the wilderness.

'Using their father's field glasses, the boys looked at the occupants: there were four of them, including a woman in her forties, all dressed in various combinations of T-shirts, military fatigues and heavy boots. Under an old awning lay the ten mammoth tusks.

'The leader was a brutal man in his thirties, already gone to seed, with heavy jowls and a belly on him,' al-Tundra said. 'He had fists like ten-pound hammers and his face was inked with jailhouse tattoos – a portrait of Stalin, a skull and crossbones, tears running from his eyes, and an ace of spades, the death card, on his forehead.

'As the boys watched, the gang finished eating and began a centuries-old Russian ritual: they knocked the caps off bottles of vodka and started swilling from them with a vengeance. The boys waited for the alcohol to hit and then the final collapse into stupor.

'Three hours later, it was complete, and the boys emerged and worked fast, deploying the bear traps close to the tents, making sure they were anchored deep.

'Once it was done, they withdrew to the camp's perimeter. The woman was the first to emerge, heading to a latrine pit to relieve herself. Stumbling and reeling from the liquor, she already had her camo fatigues undone when she stepped on one of the traps.

'The jaws exploded shut, the steel teeth shattered the bones of her ankle and the woman screamed in agony. The first person to react was the man she was sharing her bed with – it seemed the men took it in turns with her,' al-Tundra recounted, 'and we heard his companions mutter a host of Arabic curses.

'That night's partner emerged from the tent,' al-Tundra said. 'He looked around in confusion and then saw her in the shadows. He lurched towards her, taking a slightly different route and triggering another trap. He howled even louder than the woman, fell in a heap and desperately tried to tear his foot free. It was hopeless.

'The remaining two marauders, sharing a tent, emerged cautiously, both armed with assault rifles, and immediately saw their two compatriots trapped by the ankle, unable to move, only their screams breaking the silence of the forest.

'The two men – one of whom was the leader – stood outside their tent, their liquored-up brains trying to compute where the bear traps had come from.

'The leader's companion – a thin man in his twenties with lank hair and a pock-marked face – moved forward cautiously. One step . . . two . . . raising his foot for the third . . . placing it tentatively – and triggering one of three traps that had been laid specifically to snare the tent's occupants. He writhed in agony, driving the steel spikes even deeper into his leg, tearing at the device and calling for help.

'The seedy man had no intention of complying. He realized their camp was under assault and he levelled his rifle at the tree-line and started to back into the tent.

'That was when the teenager, with the man already in his sights, opened fire, kneecapping him from four hundred yards, the bullet shattering the man's joint as it went through. The man's weapon went flying as he collapsed to the ground. He was not able to walk now, only to crawl or hop. The teenager waited a few seconds – until his victim had half rolled over in agony – then fired again, destroying his other kneecap.

'With all four raiders incapacitated, the boys emerged from the trees. Although the bear traps and bullets had sobered the victims up, they were still shocked – staring in disbelief – at the age of their attackers. It made them think the kids might be cajoled, bribed or harangued into helping them, but they soon discarded that idea.

'The teenager kicked the seedy man's weapon aside and told his brother to take one of the man's shattered legs. Accompanied by his screams, the boys dragged him out of the tent to a spot under the branches of a tree at the centre of the encampment.

'Satisfied, the teenager put his arm around his brother's shoulder and led him to a bench near the fire pit, and that was where they sat, waiting for nature, waiting for the smell of blood to do its work. They were waiting for the wolves.'

Al-Tundra paused, and there was barely a sound in either the car or at Langley. 'People talk about spectacular sunsets or the sight of the wind blowing across desert dunes,' he said at last. 'But they're wrong – nature isn't beautiful, nature is cruel.'

18

'THE FIRST OF THE WOLVES APPEARED AN HOUR LATER,' AL-TUNDRA said, 'his arrival announced by a pair of yellow eyes glinting in the darkness beyond the circle of firelight.

'Wolves usually hunt in packs of six and the teenager knew he was looking at the alpha male and that the rest of the pack would be in the darkness behind him. The prisoners also saw the yellow eyes and, though they were from the city, they knew enough to start screaming. Death, with its claws and forty-two teeth, was in God's house.

'The alpha male took a step forward,' al-Tundra continued. 'The animal made a guttural sound in his throat, signalling to the rest of the pack to get ready to feed. Their work done, the boys backed away until they found the track that led to the river. They turned and headed down it, planning to wait at the skiff and then retrieve the tusks and fuel once the wolves had finished their task. The tusks were especially precious to the brothers – they were their future. They had only gone a few paces when they heard the "attack bark" of the alpha male and then the first anguished scream.

'Even at a distance, the sound became unbearable to the younger boy and he began to sing a Russian folk song to drown it out. To little effect – the shrieks and cries from the other victims soon joined in as the rest of the pack attacked.

'For the younger boy, they all seemed to blend into the cries of his dying father and he started to stumble over his words, repeating parts of the lyrics, unable to move on to the next word, then tensing himself to try to force it out.'

'The night dragged on, and the cries – and the younger boy's singing – finally diminished. By dawn the silence of the forest had returned.'

His account was finished.

19

I TURNED FROM THE SCREEN AND FOUGHT TO BRING MY THOUGHTS under control. Who had told al-Tundra such a remarkable tale? I wondered and, in a moment of insight, I realized—

This was not a war story to entertain the troops. It was his own story – *he* was that sixteen-year-old boy. I turned to see that the faces of Clay and the others were still showing a mix of horror and shock. 'It was him,' I told them.

They stared at me for a beat. 'Speaking, you mean?' Clay asked. 'You said so before.'

'No, he was recounting his origin story. On a long journey, in a battle-truck with three high-ranking warriors, he was telling them – without telling them – what made him the man he is now. Hard, cruel, unforgiving, vengeful. In the tundra long ago was the moment when everything changed.'

Several of the group surrounding me looked unconvinced. 'Listen to the pauses,' I said. 'How often does he stop to drink? He was using that to hide the emotion when he was talking about his father.'

After a moment, several of them nodded. 'No, you're right,' Clay said. 'When you called, I wondered what intelligence you could get from files that were so old, but I don't think you were looking for that, were you? You were looking for insight.'

'I suppose I was,' I replied.

He smiled. 'Well, I guess that's what you got.' He started to stand the crew down.

'The boy becomes the man, doesn't he?' I said.

I turned and looked again at the truck on the screen, thinking of the terrorist in the safe seat. 'I wonder if anyone ever really escapes the mighty gravitational pull of their past?'

51

20

AN EXECUTIVE JET WITH A LOGO AND THE NAME GREENENERGY INC. on its fuselage was waiting for me outside a high-security hangar, its engines turning over in the gathering dusk.

The previous night I had returned, exhausted, to my spartan room and crawled into bed. I had already decided not to tell Falcon or anyone else about the results of my late-night research: my mission was to travel into Iran to meet a courier and any information about a car ride several years before was of no intelligence value.

Late the next day, I threw the last of my things into a bag and met the car that would take me out to Andrews Air Force Base, twenty-five miles away. Fifty minutes later, I entered the high-security hangar, walked on to the apron and boarded the GreenEnergy Inc. jet.

As the pilot completed his checks, a welcome video extolling the achievements and far-flung business interests of the corporation started to play on the screen in front of me. None of it was true. If anyone had bothered to research GreenEnergy's background they would have found a registration as a private business, a highly professional website, a head office at an expensive business park in Delaware and a list of over-qualified executives. What an investigator wouldn't have found was a working phone number or any evidence that those executives actually existed.

Like every other high-level intelligence agency – the Russians, the Saudis, the British, the Israelis – the CIA controlled a network of dozens, perhaps hundreds, of what are known in the trade as 'proprietaries': supposedly legitimate private companies that are used to acquire weapons, buy technology and implement covert operations. GreenEnergy was one of the largest of these subterranean entities, specializing in off-the-books transport.

In total, it controlled over sixty aircraft, ranging from G5 business jets – some with tailhooks that made them capable of landing on an aircraft carrier – to An-225s, the largest cargo planes in the world. In effect, Air America, the agency's private airline that had gained such notoriety during the Vietnam War, never went away; it just changed its name and moved with the environmental times. GreenEnergy wouldn't have known a wind farm if it crashed into one.

The video stopped abruptly and the cabin lights illuminated as the pilot taxied towards the runway. I looked out the window and saw the sun dropping below the horizon – it was the time of day photographers call the 'magic hour' and a golden glow spreads across the land.

When the jet turned, by a fluke of light and optics I found myself looking at a perfect reflection of myself in the window. Taken by surprise, without the chance to make excuses, I realized what a toll my work had taken on me. I am over six feet, but I no longer presented like that; there was a weariness to me, as if the anxiety of so many missions had borne down and diminished me. More than that, not even the stubble-like beard I had cultivated for my entry into the Islamic world could hide the worry lines across my forehead.

All of it, combined with flecks of grey in my dark hair and a web of wrinkles at the corner of my eyes, reminded me of what an agency veteran – a woman with a storied career who had been everywhere and seen even more – had told me once. 'It doesn't matter what it says on an agent's birth certificate,' she said. 'There's no such thing as a young Denied Access Area spy – they're all old.' That sunset, I understood what she meant.

But, continuing to look at my reflection, I knew that my romantic partner, the woman I lived with, would have had a different response. She would have told me to get over it. 'So you look older than your years,' she probably would have said. 'It doesn't mean you don't have value. Look at Stonehenge – that's a ruin too and people still like it.'

21

SHE WAS CALLED REBECCA AND SHE HAD BEEN RAISED WITHIN earshot of a freight line in West Virginia, on the outskirts of one of the scores of towns full of what she called 'the architecture of despair': boarded-up stores, abandoned houses and acres of derelict industrial buildings.

Located deep in coal country, the backwater had owed its existence to mines and steel, but when those industries disappeared it had fallen apart, like almost everywhere else in the Appalachians. As if the surroundings weren't grim enough, when Rebecca was a few weeks old her mother died – yet another victim of the opioid epidemic – and she was raised by her grandmother. Maybe it was a blessing – the older woman was a voracious reader, someone who never gave up, and it was from her that the child got her love of learning and her irrepressible spirit.

By the time I was on board the GreenEnergy jet, Rebecca McMaster and I had been in a relationship for six years. I have to say, they were difficult years – a lot of arguments, a surfeit of agency secrets and too many strange missions that could never be discussed – but somehow we managed to keep the fire alight.

One night, lying in bed naked after yet another episode of make-up sex, I asked her why she thought we kept on keeping-on. 'It's like they say about heroes,' she said, smiling. 'Glory belongs not to the fallen but to those who have fallen and risen again.'

I laughed. 'Then we should get the Distinguished Intelligence Cross or the Congressional Medal of Honor.' I looked at her in the soft lamplight and was serious for a moment. 'I want to thank you,' I said.

'Why?' she replied.

'For persevering, for making the effort. Most people would have given up long ago.'

'You're right,' she said. 'What was I thinking?'

The look on her face, the smile in her eyes, made me think of the first time we met – it was a Friday night in New York, a bar in Soho, a hip place full of sharp-elbowed people where everybody was talking and nobody was listening. Quite by chance, I came in alone, looking for a restroom, and she was in the process of being stood up by a blind date. She was sitting at a table near the kitchen door, tall and well dressed, and I noticed her immediately across the crowded room.

She was in her mid-twenties then, her long hair – highlighted with blonde streaks earlier in the day for the date that would never show – was pulled back off her face, giving her a natural look. She appeared athletic in an outdoors sort of way, but I can't tell you if she was beautiful. All I can say is with high cheekbones, a sensual mouth and eyes full of life, she was to me.

'Remember that first night in Soho?' she asked. 'What about the guy near the stairway?'

He was handsome, surrounded by a throng of people. Going by what the waiter had told Rebecca, he ran a fitness app and had five million followers.

'Remember what you said after you walked over, introduced yourself and I told you who he was? You said being famous on social media was like being rich in Monopoly.' She laughed at the memory and looked at me. 'You had me at that. I was thinking – maybe I've found a real person at last. And in here of all places.'

She trailed her fingers across my cheek. 'If I'm honest,' she said, 'I liked the look of you when I first saw that you had noticed me. There was something separate, self-contained, about you. I had the feeling somebody could be safe with you.

'There were other things that attracted me – and still do. There's your straight nose and the sharp line to your jaw – it seems to say you can be decisive and unyielding.'

Her index finger reached my forehead and circled my eyes. 'And then there's your eyes – they're deep set, so it makes it look like you're watching, always watching. It's scary – as if you know more than you'll ever say. Perfect for someone who works at Langley, I guess. Even today I find it hard sometimes to tell whether they are grey or green.'

She kissed my eyelids gently. 'They're your best feature, you know – best by a mile. Don't forget that,' she said. 'They almost make you look intelligent.'

22

I FELT THE GREENENERGY JET SWING ON TO THE RUNWAY AND HEARD the engines escalate to a roar: sunset was over and night had almost fallen.

The reflection of my face faded until all that remained staring back at me were the eyes that Rebecca had once spoken so fondly of; but they were neither grey nor green tonight, they were at the golden end of brown. To a lot of Westerners, all Arabs have dark hair and brown eyes, but I have seen plenty of blue eyes on missions that have taken me from the Western Sahara all the way to Pakistan. Nevertheless, I was entering an isolated corner of the world where my life would depend on blending in and their original colour would have brought me the one thing I didn't need: unwanted attention.

In years past, contact lenses would have been the agency's only option, but over time everyone from Russian border guards to Islamic fundamentalists had learned that all they had to do was throw sand in the face of a suspect and wait. Once the grit worked its way between the lens and the pupil, the pain became unbearable and the man or woman, no matter how good their cover story, had to take out their lenses.

Spurred on by a case in Colombia – in which the leader of a drug cartel, having realized an agent was wearing lenses to change his appearance, gouged out the man's eyes and dumped him, alive and screaming, outside the US embassy – the CIA's advanced technology division pioneered a coloured film that was surgically attached to the iris. Impervious to grit and only visible with the help of specialized equipment, it meant an agent could have whatever eye colour they needed. In my case it was a golden brown.

As I watched, my eyes disappeared from the glass – night had finally crushed the day – and for a moment, in the darkness, on the brink of yet another mission, I thought about how Rebecca would have woken up five days earlier and only then realized I had left again.

The separations had always been difficult for her, rendered even more complicated by the fact that at the outset of our relationship she had no idea what she was getting into. When we met in New York she had asked what I did for work and I told her that I was an oil industry analyst on my way to an international conference in Tromsø in Norway.

I really was flying to Norway, the conference was genuine and I was certainly registered as a delegate, but that was where the truth ran out. I was setting out on a solo mission that would take me into Russia and those elements were all part of my 'legend' – the elaborate cover story I was using.

Six months later, when it was clear that things were serious between us, I told her I wasn't an analyst and I had nothing to do with any energy business: I worked for the CIA. She stared at me, shocked, taking a long time to process it.

'And what do you do there?' she asked finally. 'Kill people?'

'I can't tell you,' I replied.

She kept staring at me, shock turning to disbelief: not only had I completely misled her but now I wouldn't even explain what my job was.

'It's not me,' I said. 'It's the agency, the policy – I'm allowed to disclose that I work there but nothing more. Nobody can go beyond that.' Still she didn't say anything – confused, the foundations of her new life shaken. 'I know it's hard,' I said. 'But that's the rule. If you want, I can show you an excerpt—'

She shook her head. 'Maybe it is policy, but I don't believe everyone follows it. There must be plenty of partners of people in the intelligence world who know exactly what they do.'

'Maybe you're right,' I said. 'There could be a lot of intelligence agents who share information with lovers or spouses, but I'm sure most of them work above ground.'

'And you work underground, is that it?' she said, seizing on it.

I realized I'd already said too much – if I hadn't crossed the line, I was perilously close to it. As a Denied Access Area spy, everything was hidden, there was no latitude, there couldn't be. 'Strike that,' I replied, more harshly than I had intended. 'I shouldn't have said it.'

She looked at me, taken aback – I think my uncompromising tone told her I had gone to the edge of something very serious. As a result, entirely by chance, I had convinced her that any more information about my work wasn't within my gift. So we sat in silence, together but miles apart, Rebecca looking at her clenched hands.

At the time we were the only occupants of the lounge at a small hotel in Maine – at Rebecca's suggestion we had driven up to look at the fall foliage – and the only sound as the seconds passed was the crackling of the fire. I could tell from her face she was trying to work out whether to go forward or walk away; caught between her heart and her head. 'I'd always had this dream,' she said quietly. 'To drive up the coast and see the fall leaves . . . with someone . . . someone I was ready to give my heart to.'

I stared at her – now I understood why she had been so keen for us to make the trip. I couldn't speak for a moment. 'I'm sorry,' I said softly.

She shook her head and tried to smile. 'Dreams can be pretty stupid, I guess.'

'The opposite,' I replied. 'If you want to live it, first you have to dream it.'

Her voice almost cracked. 'Well, I certainly dreamt it; I just don't know if I want to live it.' She paused until she had her emotions under control. 'How about you – was it always your dream to work for the CIA?' She smiled. 'Or were they the only people that'd have you?'

'Probably,' I responded, smiling back. 'No, I was a junior officer in the Navy. Submarines. The agency came later. I had skills – languages – that proved valuable, and that's what they needed.'

She stared at me in surprise; she had no idea I had a natural ability in that regard. 'What languages?' she demanded. I looked at her with regret – if she knew the languages, she would know the countries I specialized in.

'Sorry,' she said, realizing. 'The rules again?'

I nodded, a log collapsed in the fire, sending up a shower of sparks, and the silence grew again between us. I don't think either of us knew how to proceed – or retreat. 'What would you say to a drink?' she said finally.

Our eyes met and I saw hers soften. In silence she entwined her fingers with mine, squeezed them, and I started to think we might be through the worst of it.

I ordered a bottle of wine and – thankfully – we kept talking, haltingly at first but then with greater ease. Spies are taught early it's more important to listen than to speak and I was happy for her to take the lead, telling me about the trauma two years earlier when her grandmother, the only family she had ever known, had died. I learned volumes about her in those few hours and it gave her enough time to adjust to a new reality. As far as my work was concerned, she only ever raised the issue one more time.

That was months later and as I was no more forthcoming then than I had been before she seemed to realize that no amount of asking would ever change the outcome. And there things would have stayed—

23

EXCEPT SECRETS ARE HARD TO KEEP, ASK ANY SPY, AND THERE ARE probably few places more difficult than in a home you share with a lover.

A crumpled railway ticket from a faraway place, late-night phone calls from numbers that never answer, flights on private planes with no tracking data, and then the night sweats and injuries – a knife wound stitched in the field, a broken bone or muscles that have been torn apart – and it must have been obvious to Rebecca I didn't lead the life of an intelligence analyst. Underground, whatever that meant, was obviously a dangerous place.

A few months after our conversation in Maine we began living together, moving into a leafy street in Maryland where the ranch-style houses were set back from the road and you had to go out of your way to see a neighbour. It was perfect for someone like me. One Friday afternoon, with the boxes barely unpacked, I came home early from Langley, uncharacteristically parked in the driveway, and instead of entering from the back porch I came through the front door. As I walked down the corridor I could hear Rebecca in the kitchen and I was about to greet her as I stepped into the room—

She had her back to me, preparing a meal. Sunlight was streaming through the large window, casting a golden light on her hair, and I paused, just looking at her. She took a step along the bench and the sun struck the white dress she was wearing, rendering it almost transparent, revealing her slim body. I was thinking of all the times I had lain in bed and held her close, through all my secret fears and a host of dark memories, when she turned and saw me.

Alarm leapt across her face. 'You startled me,' she said.

The loving greeting that had been in my throat died. Her eyes were red-rimmed and she'd been crying. 'What's wrong?' I asked.

She shook her head, indicating it was nothing, but a week earlier I had returned from a trip to Syria: the type of mission that people in my section sometimes described as 'bring your own noose'. It turned out as badly as most of us had feared, but I counted myself lucky to have crossed the border into Lebanon with nothing more than a slashed calf and a round from a machine pistol in my shoulder.

The leg had been stitched and the bullet removed at the American Hospital in Beirut, but both wounds were still bandaged when I got home and I knew from Rebecca's behaviour – stolen glances and sleepless nights – that the injuries had been occupying her thoughts.

'No – tell me,' I said as we stood in the kitchen.

'I've barely asked about your work, not since the day when you told me,' she said. 'And I haven't said anything about your injuries this week, I just asked if you were okay,' she continued. 'But it's been hard, very hard—'

'I know, I'm sure it has,' I said.

'No, you don't know,' she continued harshly. 'You made a mistake.' I looked at her, perplexed – I had no idea what she meant. 'You went for a check-up on Monday,' she explained. 'And you brought the X-rays of your shoulder home. Unfortunately, you left them on the back seat of the car – so I looked.'

I didn't respond, I took a deep breath – some intelligence agent, I thought – and a moment later our eyes met. 'You should have destroyed them,' she said.

She was right. My only excuse was that my shoulder was hurting like hell and I was desperate to get inside and take the painkillers they had given me. Now I knew exactly where this was going. Despite her straitened circumstances but with the constant encouragement of her grandmother, Rebecca had always been a good student, and when she was fourteen – more on a whim than anything else – she had entered an essay competition asking students to describe the value of studying other cultures. For a young woman living in a double-wide trailer in Appalachia, the question must have seemed irrelevant at best, but Rebecca did her research, applied her growing intelligence and won first prize.

It was to spend a year, all expenses paid, as an exchange student in Japan, and it changed everything. She loved the culture, developed a working knowledge of Japanese and – in one of those accidents of fate – was hosted in a house where both parents worked as doctors. As a result, most weekends, she accompanied them on their rounds at the University of Tokyo Hospital – one of the best hospitals in the world – and those visits inspired her to return home with a clear idea of the career she wanted to pursue.

She worked two jobs through high school, entered college, gained admission to medical school and, with the help of several lifetimes' worth of student loans, was now in her last year of residency as an ER physician at MedStar Washington Hospital Center.

Apart from anything, it meant that she knew how to read an X-ray, and I watched as she walked out of the room.

24

SHE RETURNED A MINUTE LATER FROM THE GARAGE, CARRYING THE large envelope, took the film out and held it up to the sunlight.

'In my professional opinion,' she said, turning to look at me and holding my gaze, 'there's only one thing that causes this sort of damage. Unfortunately, I've seen a lot of it – our ER treats more gun-shot trauma than any hospital in DC. It was a bullet, right?'

I nodded – yes, a bullet. She pointed at the entry point on the X-ray and traced its path. 'An inch to the left, a little lower, you were dead,' she said. Her voice had become even quieter as she tried to keep the emotion out of it, but for a moment her eyes welled up.

'I know it was close,' I replied. 'The surgeon who took it out told me.'

She suppressed her feelings and shook her head in despair. 'Okay, I'm not going to ask you to give away any secrets,' she said coolly. 'I just want you to tell me – how will I know?'

'Know what?'

'That I don't have to keep waiting any more, that you won't be coming home? That you've been . . .' Her voice trailed away.

I finished it for her. 'That I've been lost?' I guess neither of us wanted to say 'killed'.

She nodded. 'Yeah, lost,' she repeated. 'That's a good word.'

'They have your details, Becca – they'll tell you,' I replied. 'I made sure of it a while ago.'

'Thanks for that,' she said sarcastically. 'But how? Is it a phone call, a message to visit some office? Am I taken to Langley?' There was real anger in her voice now. 'There's no way this should be a secret – I just want to know what to expect.'

61

No, that's not true, I thought. You want to know what to be frightened of; you want to know what the monster looks like. I looked out the window: night was almost upon us, and what did it matter if it was supposed to be secret? She was correct, she did have a right to know; the organization I worked for at least owed her that.

'A car will come,' I said at last. 'It will be deliberately ordinary, a four-door – one of those vehicles that are meant to be anonymous but scream "government" from every panel. It won't be travelling slowly. The occupants will know exactly the house they are looking for,' I continued. 'They will have called the hospital to make sure that you weren't working and would have done a drive-by earlier to check that you were at home.'

She sagged, shocked by the surveillance, the quiet, efficient organization of it.

'A man, probably in his forties, will get out of the car and knock on the door,' I said. 'He'll show you an agency photo ID to assure you it's official. The ID will be genuine but the name will be fake – that's standard. If you're sensible, you'll ask him in,' I continued, keeping it as matter of fact as possible. 'You probably won't want to go through this at the door. He'll say he's very sorry but your partner, while travelling overseas on government business, was killed in a car wreck, the crash of a charter flight, or something like that.'

'It won't be true, though,' Rebecca said.

'He might have a news clip, a video from German TV, whatever they've been able to create or re-purpose from other footage. It will look very real, but no – it won't be true.'

'And that's okay, is it?' she asked, her tone clearly indicating it wasn't.

I shrugged. 'It's not evil. The agency can't disclose anything about an intelligence operation in case it risks the mission or someone else's life; on the other hand, they have to account for the loss of a person's partner. What else can they do?'

'Okay – so they lie,' she said, taking a breath. 'Go on.'

'The man will be sympathetic, but his job is to make sure you accept their version of events. Ask if your partner was on CIA business and he'll say, "Yes, absolutely." Want to know what sort of business? He'll tell you he was in Germany meeting with our intelligence partners, or something just as bland. No matter what else you ask, he won't expand on it.'

'So, that's the end of it?' she said. 'If he has nothing more to say, no explanation to give – what, he leaves?'

'There'll be more conversation, and he won't rush, but yeah – pretty much,' I replied. 'He will give you a number to call if you need anything. He'll also tell you he'll be in touch if more details come to hand, not that he thinks they will – it was just a terrible accident.'

'Will he call?' she asked.

'He'll have to,' I said. 'There'll be funeral arrangements. During that conversation, he'll say as a result of the burns sustained in the accident it has to be a closed-casket service.'

She looked at me askance: it was a strange thing for me to even mention. 'Why would he say that? Burns? Why is it important?'

'Because . . .' I said. 'Listen – don't argue, you won't get them to change their mind.'

'About opening the casket?' she demanded.

'Yes. More than likely, the coffin will be empty, or it will have somebody else's body in it.'

She stared at me. It wasn't something she had anticipated, and it rocked her. Until then, despite the grim subject matter, she had been dealing with it: the tears had retreated and the deep lines of anxiety across her forehead were less pronounced. Being able to cope with death was the doctor in her, but now the reality of my work came storming back.

'It's just a sham, isn't it – the whole funeral?' she said quietly. 'Why?'

'It's not a sham. In most cases in my section – and I can't tell you any more than this – it's far too dangerous to try and recover a body. That's the nature of the work.'

'Oh God,' she said, hanging her head, her hand kneading her face. 'You were right when you said "lost" – if you die, you'll be totally lost,' she whispered.

I reached out, put my arms around her and held her. 'The casket is closed,' she said. 'Then they just fold the flag and give it to me to keep?'

'Yes,' I replied, her head leaning hard against my shoulder.

'And I'm left to put my life back together the best I can? There's nothing more?'

'No,' I said quietly. 'Nothing more.' It wasn't exactly the truth – there was one more thing, but I couldn't see any point in telling her.

Ten or twenty years later, when the mission I had been involved in no longer had any intelligence value, Rebecca would get a letter from the person who was then occupying the corner office, inviting her to attend a small and highly classified ceremony in the foyer of the Original Headquarters Building.

It is an impressive space. On one wall – etched into the stone – is a quote from the Gospel of St John, the CIA's unofficial motto: 'You shall know the truth, and the truth shall make you free'. Facing it, on the opposite wall, are rows of small stars and – on a stand below them – a book with the names of dozens of intelligence agents written in it. Rebecca would be invited to witness my name being entered and the unveiling of my star. Each name and star recorded a man or woman who had died on duty; it was the CIA's wall of honour.

The letter from the director would ask Becca if, after all these years, she wished to attend the ceremony. I had no doubt she would be married by then and have kids – she had always wanted children and it turned out to be a source of ongoing and serious trouble between us – even though we both agreed that my work didn't exactly lend itself to a stable family life.

Sitting in the plane, the engines screeching now, the illuminated runway seeming to stretch to eternity, I hoped she would find the time and the interest to go to the ceremony. More than anything, I hoped she would remember me with affection.

I looked out the window as we became airborne and saw spectacular thunderheads rolling out of the east and heading straight towards us. Riders on the storm, I thought – that's all we are and can ever hope to be. Riders on the storm.

25

THROUGH SHIMMERING WAVES OF HEAT, THE OASIS STOOD AMONG A sea of dunes, its date palms blowing in the hot wind and a broad expanse of green water glinting in the noon-day sun.

Like human rights reforms, like a new economy for a new age – like so much of life in the Kingdom of Saudi Arabia – the oasis was a mirage. It trembled and twisted on the far edge of Riyadh's King Khalid International Airport, a collection of five terminals that rose out of what could best be described as a moonscape.

The GreenEnergy Gulfstream landed on the north runway just after noon, turned briefly towards the fantasy oasis and then taxied to a highly secure section of the complex. I looked out the window and saw a dozen passenger jets with the simple words 'Saudi Arabian' on their fuselage, identifying them as part of the king's personal fleet. Closest to us was a new Boeing 737, and I wondered if it was the aircraft that had been specially outfitted to accommodate a hundred of his prized hunting falcons.

Looming behind it was an Airbus 380, still the largest passenger plane ever built, its steps replaced by a gilded escalator. It also featured, according to reports, a fountain in its entrance foyer and solid gold fittings in every bathroom. As Dorothy Parker once said, 'If you want to know what God thinks of money, just look at the people He gave it to.'

We turned and parked close to the royal terminal, not because I was an honoured guest but because it was the most discreet part of the airport. Those arrangements had been made by Falcon, who, without revealing any details of my mission, had called the head of GID, the Saudi intelligence agency, and asked him to organize for an off-the-books CIA jet to land and to then provide transport for its only passenger. There was no need for further discussion – both men knew that the radar tracking files would be deleted and the control-tower logs would make no reference to the Gulfstream. It was a ghost flight by a ghost plane: just one more mirage in a country full of them.

As the engines powered down I stared out the window. Royalty or not, it was a forlorn place; there was nobody, just the desert wind battering the huge hangars and the heat rising off a thousand acres of blisteringly hot asphalt. The pilot stepped out of the cockpit and shook his head. 'According to the gauge up front, it's 124 degrees on the blacktop.'

'But is it a dry heat?' I asked.

He laughed as I grabbed my bags and he opened the door to deploy the stairs. We both squinted out into the glare, struggling to see somebody – anybody – there to greet us. 'They're buying time to run their cameras,' I said. 'Then they'll use facial recognition to try and find a match.' I stepped back into the interior. 'No point in making it easy for them.'

The pilot smiled and pointed to one of the hangars: a mid-sized grey Mercedes emerged from its shadow, drove slowly across the apron and stopped at the steps.

Head lowered, I went down to the car – exactly the type of vehicle used by the good hotels in Riyadh to ferry their clients back and forth to the airport. The driver, coming to take my carry-ons, was dressed just like one of their chauffeurs too – except he wasn't. He was Saudi intelligence: aged in his thirties, with thin lips, a stone-cold face and dead eyes, he was typical of his kind.

Wordlessly, he waited for me to get into the back of the vehicle, slipped into the driver's seat and headed across the asphalt until we left the airport's royal precinct and hit the twelve-lane highway that circled the airport. He gunned it for a dozen miles, negotiated a cloverleaf interchange and stopped at the terminal that handled Saudia Airlines' international flights. The subterfuge was now complete: to anyone watching, I was a guest from an upmarket hotel being dropped off by one of their drivers to catch a flight. In my case it was to Karachi, the financial capital of Pakistan.

One of the axioms of the secret world is that you never leave a footprint in the sand.

26

KARACHI. WHAT CAN I SAY? CLEANLINESS PROBABLY ISN'T THE CITY'S strong suit. One of the most polluted metropolises in the world, it is also afflicted by severe flooding. Storms sweep in, rainwater mixes with an overwhelmed sewage system and diseased water surges down the city's avenues and alleyways. Year after year the rains come, and nothing changes – the outbreaks of disease escalate, the population grows larger and different terrorist groups continue to launch attacks, especially against Westerners.

Fifteen miles from the chaos of the city, on the road to Hyderabad and past a huge Pakistan Air Force base, Jinnah International Airport rises out of a flat and featureless landscape. On the day I flew in, the arrivals procedure seemed as overwhelmed as the sewage system and two hours after landing I finally stepped up to an immigration desk.

The man behind it – fifties, immaculate in his grey-and-black uniform, a sergeant's chevrons on his sleeve – compared me to the picture in the passport and slid it into a data reader.

I was travelling on a Saudi book provided by the GID, and I waited in silence while the software checked my details. I would have had nothing to worry about if the CIA had contacted the Inter-Services Intelligence group, the Pakistan intelligence agency, and told them that I was entering the country. We didn't do it because the Pakistanis – nominally an ally of ours – would have then asked for what purpose, and no matter what story we spun them, they would have followed me and tried to discover the real aim of my mission.

The truth was, nobody in US intelligence trusted the Pakistanis; not only had they been caught harbouring Osama bin Laden but that deceit only added to years of evidence that they were always walking both sides of the street. Langley was convinced that when it came to betrayal, the Pakistanis were in a league of their own. Nobody on the seventh floor believed that if their intelligence discovered my real objective they wouldn't tell the Army of the Pure about my impending arrival in order to gain some leverage with yet another terrorist group.

In Pakistan's profit-and-loss account, an agreement by the Army not to attack targets within the country would have been more than worth the death of one American spy.

The seconds dragged by. I tried not to show any anxiety, glancing at the data reader occasionally like any normal visitor, and I started to think about the worst outcomes: if either the passport or myself were flagged as suspect, I would be arrested immediately and interrogated under what are known in the intelligence world as 'extreme protocols'. People who had experienced them reported that a freezing concrete cell and a length of lead-weighted rubber hose were the Pakistanis' preferred methods.

At last the data reader started to flash. The officer scanned the screen, removed the book from the reader and looked at me with concern. He spoke in Gulf Arabic. 'I am going to have to ask you some questions,' he said.

His accent and grammar weren't perfect and I figured he was using the language to find out if I really was a Saudi. 'Sure,' I replied.

Thankfully, my Arabic was good enough to convince anyone that I was a native speaker. 'How can I help?'

'The law requires you to be completely honest,' he said, indicating a sign that explained in various languages the draconian punishments for giving false information.

'Of course,' I said, as if lying was the furthest thing from my mind.

He asked me the usual questions – place of birth, purpose of my visit, how long I was staying – until, apparently satisfied by my answers and my command of the language, he found an empty page in my passport, stamped it several times and handed it back. 'Enjoy your stay in Pakistan.'

I nodded and picked up my carry-ons. I had no other luggage so I walked through Customs, passed uniformed officers chatting among themselves and approached the doors that opened into the Arrivals hall.

They slid open and, surrounded by waves of discordant music, dozens of different dialects and the exotic aroma of spiced tea, I squeezed through a milling crowd, turned left and headed down the cavernous hall. I had never been in the airport before, but thanks to the hours I had spent memorizing its layout, I knew exactly where I was going.

I passed a group of men dressed in the traditional *shalwar kameez* – loose-fitting trousers topped by a knee-length shirt – about to enter the prayer room and then, fifty yards further, I saw a sign with a graphic identifying the bathrooms. It was what I was looking for: next to it would be a large area full of rows of luggage lockers that were available to rent.

As I had been briefed at Langley, locker seventeen was in a corner at the back, a location that had been chosen because it was the most secluded. I checked the room was empty, entered a code I had brought with me into the combination lock and opened the steel door. Inside was an envelope that had been left the day before by the CIA's station chief in Islamabad, the Pakistani capital. It contained a map of the north parking lot, the number of a bay, the ticket to insert in the pay machine and a set of car keys.

And that was how, on a Tuesday afternoon in July, a Denied Access Area spy, formerly a junior officer on a US Navy submarine, a man who had washed out of the silent service in strange circumstances and thanks to his language skills been hired by the CIA, an American citizen born in Loxahatchee, Florida, but travelling on a Saudi book, had arrived – unheralded and unobserved – at a locker in Pakistan's largest airport and was about to brave Karachi's toxic air and get in a beaten-up car he had never seen before.

The border with Iran lay five hundred miles to the west and in another ten minutes he would drive sensibly to avoid attracting attention, the road beneath him mostly flat and straight, burning like a skillet in the midsummer sun, to keep a rendezvous with a man whose name he didn't know, in a place he had seen only on maps, where the slightest mistake would kill them both.

Welcome to the rodeo, I thought as I unlocked the vehicle.

27

STICKING TO THE SPEED LIMIT, I DROVE ALONG THE LONELY MAKRAN Coastal Highway, the fastest route towards the border with Iran, boiling in the summer heat, with an old song by AC/DC playing on a loop in my head: the highway to hell, indeed.

I was at the wheel of a battered white Toyota pick-up, probably the most common – and, therefore, the hardest to track – vehicle in the Arab world, used by upstanding citizens, dope couriers, government contractors, terrorists and everyone in between.

On my left was the Arabian Sea and on the right was the Hingol National Park, one of the most remarkable landscapes in the world: rock formations as dramatic as anything in Monument Valley rose out of the desert, strange mud volcanoes bubbled on an arid plain and untouched canyon floors were green with tropical ferns.

With the waves of heat shimmering all around me, Hingol's lost world faded and I skirted a remote port called Gwadar. Barely seeing another vehicle, getting closer to the Iranian border, I stopped a few miles short of it on a ridge, looked for a long time at one of the most dangerous countries in the world for someone like me, then made a hard right and bumped down a ruin of a road. At its end was a barely known town called Mand, a collection of silent earthen-coloured houses, high walls and meandering dirt roads.

On its outskirts was a clay-brick warehouse with half its roof missing and dozens of wrecked four-wheel drives sitting among the weeds. This was Mand's auto-repair shop and the rusting vehicles were its inventory of spares. My story – if anyone should have asked – was that I was in Gwadar when the front suspension of the Toyota failed and I needed a replacement. My jarred back was a testament to the reality of the problem and there were plenty of times on the trip when I cursed Langley's attention to detail.

The suspension was the fiction; the reality was that inside a small shed used to store barrels of recovered engine oil half hidden at the back of the building, a man was waiting for me. A Pakistani in his forties – a trusted operative of our station chief in Islamabad – he had arrived the day before, driving a covered truck with three ponies hidden in the back, along with the rest of the equipment I needed.

Parking at the far corner of the property, he had approached the owner and the only other person there – the man's son – and, after the obligatory cup of tea, offered the two men half a million rupees each if they found an urgent need to go to Karachi and pick up some spare parts. He suggested that such a mission would have to take at least two days. Over the years the owner had seen it all: drug smugglers, terrorists, grifters, Pakistani security forces and – like the man sipping tea in front of him – a fair share of people he guessed were intelligence agents. He was a practical man, uncomplicated by ideology, and had dealt with them all: his only criteria were whether the money was good enough.

'Three thousand each,' he said in Urdu.

The agent shrugged. 'Sure, I offer five hundred thousand and you only want three?'

The men laughed – they all knew the owner was talking about US dollars and three thousand was a large premium over what he had been offered. The CIA operative had no information about the mission he had to help organize, but he knew nothing could be allowed to jeopardize it. He haggled for appearances' sake and then raised his hands in surrender.

The owner and his son grinned and, flush with cash and driving the most serviceable of their rolling wrecks, they set off on their unexpected journey, planning to take the opportunity to attend prayers at the white marble Masjid e Tooba in Karachi, one of the most stunning mosques in the world.

When I arrived, I parked out of sight, made my way through the workshop and stepped into the junk-strewn rear yard. Lit only by starlight, I was almost invisible, but the night was deathly quiet and the agent must have heard the Toyota approaching. I didn't realize it, but he wasn't waiting – as planned – in the shed at all; he was in the deep shadows cast by the warehouse wall, a Ruger SR40 handgun pointed at me, a weapon powerful enough to rip a crater the size of a baseball mitt in my chest. To be honest, I would have been disappointed if he hadn't been positioned and ready to shoot. It is another one of the tenets of the intelligence world: only the paranoid survive.

He waited to speak until I had walked past him so that I had no hope of outdrawing him. 'You the guy looking for a radiator belt?' he asked, using a prearranged identification.

'Front shock absorbers,' I answered, giving the correct response, leading him to step out of the darkness and put out his hand to shake.

'Welcome,' he said, and immediately pointed at the oil-storage shed. 'I've unpacked everything and laid it out inside. I'll get the ponies.'

As he headed for the truck, I entered the shed and began to examine the items he had brought: I pored over pieces of soiled clothing, checked the mechanism of an ancient AK-47 automatic rifle and paid painstaking attention to the three saddles. They were old and battered, with one of the wooden frames clearly broken and poorly repaired. Obviously, they were worthless to anyone who might have thought of robbing me, except—

Hidden in their hollowed-out wooden frames, sewn into the leather padding and concealed in the lining of the heavy saddlebags and horse blankets were four genuine US passports – one each for the Afghan courier, his wife and their two children – and fifty thousand dollars' worth of battered Pakistani *tolahs*: small gold bars with unique rounded edges that have been employed as a form of currency in the area for two hundred years.

Impossible to forge, untraceable and easily concealed, they were – as you would expect – wildly popular in the drug trade, but it was those same qualities that meant the courier insisted on them being used to transact our equally covert business. The seventy *tolahs* and the four passports were a token of our own good faith; the courier wanted to be guaranteed US citizenship for himself and his family and the gold was to pay immediate expenses; an advance against the twenty million dollars he would receive in a safe house in America once he had provided all the information he had promised.

As I used a flashlight to examine everything from the saddles to the Pakistani labels on the sealed containers of food, I couldn't find fault with anything that the CIA's specialized workshops had created: the labels were yellowing and stained, every thread of the blankets was aged, the needle holes on the saddles were torn, the leather straps of the girths watermarked with sweat and the brass buckles scratched from years of use. It was outstanding work, a testament to the skill of those involved, their efforts supervised by a woman who had once been a production designer in Hollywood: who better to create the illusion of reality than someone with two Oscar nominations?

I started to repack the equipment when I heard the agent crossing the yard, leading the pack ponies towards the shed. They were old and wiry animals, their backs bowed from years of hard work, but with their soft eyes and loose jaws they looked beautiful to me.

'I'm sorry,' he said. 'They were the best we could do.'

I got up and went towards them. I have always loved horses – since long before recorded time, they have only ever wanted to be our friends and yet we have done little except treat them badly. The leader of the team was a rich chestnut colour, favouring one front leg, and I figured he had arthritis in his knee. He also had an impressive collection of scars and nicks, part of one ear missing and a large patch on his rump where he had lost his hair. I scratched his nose and spoke softly. 'Like me, you're showing your age. Never mind, you know what the Irish say, don't you? You need an old dog for a hard road.'

He nuzzled my hand and did that thing horses do with their lips, giving a sort of smile. 'What's his name?' I asked the agent.

He looked at me askance. 'How would I know?' he replied, shrugging.

'What do you suggest?' I retorted. 'I tell that to an Iranian patrol or a group of terrorists who question me? I say the name of the leader of my pack team is a mystery?'

'Sorry,' he said, embarrassed. 'I wasn't thinking. Can we make a name up?'

I looked again at the chestnut's liquid eyes, his half ear drooping. 'I'll call him Sakab.'

'What?' the agent asked.

'It's Arabic,' I replied. 'It means a horse so graceful it moves like running water.'

28

I HAD ALMOST FINISHED CHECKING THE PONIES AND EQUIPMENT when my encrypted phone rang. Long experience had taught me that, once a mission had started, that was never good news.

It was Falcon, and he launched straight in. 'I haven't shared this with anyone,' he said. 'Six hours ago, Kabul Station reported on the latest meeting between the air-con technician and the courier.'

I certainly didn't need any more complications. 'Go on,' I said.

'The courier claims he has just learned the so-called spectacular will be launched in twenty-four weeks,' Falcon said evenly.

'Thanksgiving,' I said.

'Full of symbolism,' he replied. 'The busiest travel day of the year—'

'Might be an attempt by the courier to squeeze us,' I said. 'He gives us a date to create panic so we accept his terms and make the deal.'

'Could be,' Falcon said. 'Do you want to sign Buster's document?'

'You said you haven't told anybody?' I said.

'No,' he replied.

'Why? You don't trust them?' I said.

'Imagine if it leaked – a terrorist back from the dead, a spectacular timed for Thanksgiving, most of the Western world as a possible target and no clarity on how it might happen? The panic alone would half finish us by the end of the day.'

A deadline was just what I needed. 'Thanks for the good news,' I said.

29

THERE WAS NO MOON THAT NIGHT, AND EVEN THE STARS, NORMALLY close enough to touch at those latitudes if you were far beyond a city, were obscured by a wild storm coming out of Afghanistan.

Sakab, in the lead, and the other two ponies were skittish, frightened by the approaching weather. Keeping a firm grip on the lead rope, I was guiding them deep into the rugged mountains rising out of the scrub, following an old smugglers' trail that an eagle-eyed analyst at Langley had found in a collection of almost-forgotten paper maps. They dated from the time when the Soviets were fighting in Afghanistan and the long trail, barely used in the decades since, was overgrown and almost impassable in places.

Mand was, by then, already three hours behind us. After I had finished packing, I shared a meal with the agent and then walked to the door of the shed. I looked across the ancient landscape – night had fallen and the flat-roofed houses were barely visible, camouflaged by the dirt and sagebrush. The only sound was the splash of water from fountains hidden in mysterious courtyards. I was impatient to keep moving, and with no sign of anyone and no light, it was time to go.

The agent knew it too. He helped me load the last supplies on to the ponies and watched as I took hold of the lead rope and picked up the ancient AK-47. I checked that it was loaded, made sure the safety was engaged and slung it over my shoulder. It was a good weapon, they always had been, but this particular example was old and battered and not the sort of thing anyone would choose to take to a firefight. Still, like everything on a Denied Access Area mission – from the saddle frames to my brown eyes – the rifle wasn't what it appeared.

The agent and I smiled at one another, and you might have thought he would wish me luck or say goodbye, but those words were never used in the underground; agents thought it was too much like tempting fate. Everyone wanted to believe luck would play no role and that any parting was only temporary. Tomorrow or the day after we would meet again, raise a glass in a bar in some exotic place, and laugh about the night we had shared a meal together in a backwater called Mand. When death was like a faithful hound – always close at hand – we had to believe that there would always be a future.

So, instead of saying farewell, it had become a tradition to choose a city, any city you loved, and use that instead. 'See you in Istanbul,' the agent said quietly.

I smiled. 'In Istanbul,' I replied, and then led the ponies forward, the darkness so all-encompassing that within minutes the agent and the entire village of Mand had disappeared. Now I stopped on a section of the trail cut into the side of a mountain, looking up to where a cliff had partially collapsed years before and sent tons of rubble down to block the way. Clearly, there was no hope of getting past it.

Deadline or not, the only option was to pivot left, head down a steep and perilous incline to the valley below, find a way past the landslide and try to rejoin the trail further along: in darkness, in an alien landscape and with no landmark or even the stars to guide me.

Even assuming I could get down the hillside without injury, there was a better than even chance I would encounter another obstacle in the valley or find myself in a blind canyon. The sensible thing was to wait until dawn, but I had reasoned long before I left Langley that my greatest danger came from being seen: it was far safer to travel by night and sleep during the day.

As a result, there seemed to be no right answer: I could risk getting lost in darkness or chance being seen by daylight. Nobody could have judged which one offered the best hope of success, except for one thing – the rifle.

30

DURING THEIR INDUCTION INTO THE MILITARY, MOST RECRUITS HAVE it drilled into them that it's not the weapon that saves you, it's the training. I understand the sentiment, but I will bet that whoever coined the adage never encountered a weapon like my AK-47.

Ever since we had first made contact, the courier had been dictating the terms of our relationship. It couldn't have been otherwise – it was his life that was at stake, and we knew he would do whatever was necessary to protect himself. One of his many conditions was that he alone would decide where and how we would meet.

As a terrorist courier and, before that, a taxi driver in Kabul, he had no experience in the tradecraft of the intelligence world. And yet, clearly a smart guy, he had worked out exactly what a highly trained agent running-in-the-field would have done: he named four different locations where our rendezvous would take place. Only one of them would be genuine.

Back in Langley, we figured that the first, the furthest from the Army's possible base and the hardest for him to reach, was a throw-away – just included to make up the numbers. The second was the observation – he would lie hidden, watching through binoculars, assessing me and seeing if I had been followed. The third was the real deal; that was where we would finally meet. As with every covert plan, some unexpected occurrence was a constant threat, so the fourth location was the back-up. It made little difference, however, that we understood his plan – we still had to follow his rules.

In order to avoid any confusion or mistake, he provided – on cig-arette paper, through the intermediary – the exact latitude and longitude of the four locations. The co-ordinates of just one of them looked like this: 26°18'20.45'N 61°57'26.95E.

It meant, in total, there were over ninety numerals, letters and sym-bols. While it would have been easy for me to carry a list with me, we knew it was far too great a risk in case I was stopped and searched. Perhaps I could have memorized them, but we had to ask: was it real-istic to expect an agent in a state of heightened tension, moving fast night after night, to keep that information straight in his head? All it needed was the interchange of two numerals and everything would collapse.

Even if we found a way for me to keep the co-ordinates clear, the Afghan's plan presented another problem. How was I going to find the locations travelling overland in the wilderness? They weren't villages or towns, they were remote places: the intersection of two mountain streams, a dry well or an abandoned hut.

For all its faults, the CIA did, however, have a history of developing new technology. This was the organization that had once created the world's best encryption device, capable of making any communica-tion impossible to read. Instead of using it themselves though, they set up what appeared to be a legitimate 'proprietary' in Switzerland and sold the device to dozens of governments throughout the world. The system, having been designed by the CIA's Technical Support Division, had a secret back door that for years allowed the agency to decode every communication handled by those governments. People said that the Chinese had learned the lesson well and had been play-ing a similar game for a decade too.

Given the agency's level of expertise, creating a method – one that would allow me to accurately navigate to the four separate locations – didn't appear impossible. In fact, the year before – in a still-classified mission – technical support had helped two agents secretly enter Mongolia by going off-track and driving through the mountains of east Kazakhstan. They were travelling in a rugged six-wheel drive, so there were plenty of places to conceal a special satellite-linked GPS system, but nevertheless, it showed what could be done.

The problem with my mission was that I would be travelling on foot with three ponies – if you were looking for a solution using technology, how could you ever miniaturize or hide the equipment? The answer was delivered just after midnight, two days before I boarded the plane. The phone rang and a voice I didn't recognize asked me to go to the conference room beneath the Bubble.

When I arrived, the room was packed with technical services staff and everybody involved in planning my mission. Once I had made my way through the crowd I saw an AK-47, half stripped down, lying on the long table. I only needed a brief look to see that, despite its battered appearance, it was in perfect operating order, every moving part seemingly blueprinted and specially machined. It was, without doubt, a marksman's rifle.

Falcon, standing at the head of the table, nodded to one of the executives from tech services, a bear of a man, indicating that he should start. Once he spoke, I recognized he was the person who had phoned me.

'I'm an armourer,' he said. 'Well, a bit more than an armourer – that's where I started, but I deal mostly with technology now.' He pointed at the AK. 'Pick it up.'

I knew about weapons – as a kid in Florida I had grown up around guns – and as soon as I had the rifle in my hands, I knew it was as good as it had looked: light and beautifully balanced. 'What do you think?' the armourer asked as I examined his handiwork.

'Pretty special,' I replied. 'An iron fist in a velvet glove.'

The armourer laughed and indicated an old and scratched telescopic sight fixed to the top of the barrel. 'Take a look,' he said.

I raised the weapon, pointed it high above everybody and looked through the sight. 'What do you see?' he asked.

'Magnified target area,' I answered. 'The crosshairs, the data about range and zoom – nothing unusual.'

'But it is,' the armourer replied. 'The lens was a special order, made in Germany by the best manufacturer of optical lenses in the world. We removed their name so that it wouldn't raise any suspicions, but you won't find a better sight anywhere.'

I nodded, lowering the weapon – that was great, I thought, if I was planning to shoot somebody, but it didn't solve my navigation problem.

'Now, put your finger here,' the armourer said, taking my index finger and placing it on a special rubberized section of the trigger guard. 'Give it at least three seconds – it's reading your fingerprint so that it can't be inadvertently opened by anybody else.'

'Okay,' I responded, and even after a count of five absolutely nothing seemed to have happened. The whole room seemed equally disappointed.

'Look through the sight now,' the armourer instructed, watching as I raised it to my eye.

I cursed. The hidden function of the sight was now unlocked: the glass lens had become a full GPS and mapping system. The armourer smiled proudly. 'Pretty good, huh?'

I nodded, hugely impressed. The armourer picked up a TV remote and one of the large overhead screens displayed the view through the sight so that everybody could see it. The room burst into impromptu applause and I handed the weapon back to the armourer. 'Where's the software and batteries?' I asked.

He took several small tools out of a leather pouch and laid the rifle down on the table. Deftly, he removed the wooden stock. 'We hid the screws and other fixings, just in case some wise-ass decided to try and take the stock to pieces.'

I looked down at the cavities he had exposed, filled with lithium batteries and circuit boards. It was, undoubtedly, a triumph of design and engineering. 'It's got nothing to do with a phone-based GPS system,' the armourer explained. 'It's like a sat phone; it gets its data in an entirely different way. You're totally independent.'

I was remembering that, and thanking the stars for the armourer, as I lifted the rifle, put my finger on the trigger guard, activated the system and pointed the sight at the landslide. Instantly it gave me the exact GPS co-ordinates of the rock and rubble. I made a note of them, and now, no matter what happened in the valley below, I would never be lost. I could always make my way back to the trail, wait for daylight and search for another route.

The next step was to make it down the dizzying slope without injuring or killing myself. A little moonlight would have helped, I thought, as I took the first careful step over the lip and felt rock and dirt immediately crumble beneath my feet. In a heartbeat, I was falling.

31

THE HORSES SAVED ME. ALL THREE WERE MOUNTAIN PONIES, BORN and bred, and somehow I grabbed hold of Sakab's saddle and – sliding at his side – managed to pull myself upright.

With him in the lead, the team knew instinctively how to keep their footing in places where there seemed to be nothing but air beneath us. A dozen times their hooves struck sparks from the flint-rocks and twice the ponies behind me slid and looked like they were about to free-fall hundreds of feet to the rocks below. On both occasions, at the last moment, they found purchase and pulled back from the brink.

By the time we reached the bottom their chests were heaving, their flanks were white with foam, and I was drenched in sweat. Any case officer running me as an agent would have told me I had to keep moving: by being forced to leave the trail, I was at risk of falling behind schedule and now there was a deadline. But I couldn't do it – I had to let the horses drink and give them a chance to recover.

As soon as I had unhooked pouches from their backs and watered them, I untied the rifle from Sakab's saddle, opened the guidance system, took a reading to find the direction in which we had to travel to circumvent the rockfall and was led into the even greater darkness of the valley.

Twenty minutes later – dragging ourselves forward and with Sakab's arthritis obviously giving him grief – we crossed a dry riverbed and entered a sloping forest of parched and twisted trees. We were in a trackless and dead world: ghost-like trunks crowded in, branches arched overhead and turned the surroundings into canyons of vegetation.

The forest was unlike any place I had ever been, and the further I progressed, the deeper the silence became. I don't recall making the decision, but I started to try and move the horses forward without causing any sound. Going deeper into the unknown and guided by the gunsight, we entered a stand of long-dead saplings – killed in their prime by something – and the ponies herded closer; clearly something was worrying them.

There were wolves in Pakistan, but I knew they weren't the danger – horses are flight animals and they would have bolted the moment they caught the scent of one. No, the conviction had been growing in me that the place was to blame: I felt that something very evil had happened there and the memory, or the evidence of it, was all around us.

I kept moving forward, the horses bunched tight, Sakab pressing on despite his knee, and something from long ago rose into my head. 'Yea, though I walk through the valley of the shadow of death, I will fear no evil . . .'

As I said, I am not a Christian, but my mother was a believer and every Sunday as a child she took me to church. Some things I was exposed to then have stayed with me and probably will do so for ever. With the 23rd Psalm playing in my head, I glanced to my right and in an area of lesser darkness saw long furrows located in what, if you were generous, could be described as a field. Surrounded by trees, earth had been piled alongside the furrows, forming mounds that – over many years of wind and rain – had been flattened and in places rendered almost indistinct. Still, it all had the look of something agricultural, and it shocked me: who in their right mind would have tried to carve out a life in a place like this?

Minutes later, I led the team into a large man-made clearing. I have seen enough of the dark side to know the purpose a line of thick wooden stakes, driven deep into the ground and standing chest high, serve. Men and women are placed with their backs to them, their hands forced around the post and tied behind them, making escape and movement impossible.

I mentioned earlier that executions are horrific events, often steeped in ritual and ceremony, but not in a place like this, not in a dead forest in the wilderness. There were at least twenty stakes and it left no doubt in my mind that the clearing had been organized so that scores of immobilized prisoners could be killed as fast and efficiently as possible.

Staring at the stakes, I remembered I was close to one of the major heroin-producing corners of the world. There is so much money in that business anything was possible – the daily slaughter in the drug wars of Colombia and Mexico was testament to that. But this was too organized – it felt military, probably an operation by the Pakistan Army or the Inter-Services Intelligence group against an insurgent group that had somehow threatened the government. In both Persian and Urdu, one of the most widespread local languages, the word *stan* broadly translates as 'land' and *pak* means 'peace'. Pakistan: land of peace. Apparently not everyone got the memo.

I ran my eye along the stakes and saw the marks where bullets had splintered the wood: it was clear I was standing in the centre of a killing field.

No wonder that nothing grew in the forest. It was as if nature itself had given up. Certainly the furrows and mounds I had seen bore no connection to anything agricultural. They were mass graves, and I had seen several of those: Nazi death camps in Poland, trees hung with hundreds of nooses after the genocide in Cambodia, and the bullrings in Spain that Franco had used for a human kind of slaughter. The Germans were Protestant, the Cambodians Buddhist, the Spanish Catholics and the people who did the killing in the forest were almost certainly Muslim. If I have learned one thing about life: evil is an equal-opportunity employer.

It had only been a few minutes since I had stepped into the clearing, but already too much time had passed. But I wouldn't cross the execution ground, I didn't want to walk on that earth, and the horses certainly seemed relieved when I turned them back into the trees and made a long loop to give the clearing a wide berth.

Sakab was walking more easily and we made much better progress until, finally, the ground started to become easier to negotiate, the rocks gave way to stretches of spindly scrub and the dead trees started to thin.

We emerged from the forest on to a broad stretch of dirt and withered grass and I saw that the storm that had swept out of Afghanistan was blowing itself to pieces and the moon, pale and watery, was emerging from behind the clouds.

I turned and looked back at the cliffs we had left several hours before and by the moon's wan light I confirmed that we had bypassed the landslide. I unslung the rifle and, using the telescopic sight to scan the area to the north, I found a gradual incline that would lead us back on to the trail. As soon as I activated the GPS system I knew my exact position, and that allowed me to calculate that while we were behind schedule it could be rectified if I increased the pace and travelled fast until dawn.

I pulled out a handful of sugar cubes, gave the ponies a few each and set off for the incline. It wasn't until we had reached the trail and I looked back down into the valley and saw the miles of dead trees that I recalled that during the preparations at Langley I had seen the forest marked on the old paper maps.

I had ignored it because my route should have passed way above it, but I knew now that whoever named it had been there. They called it the Forest of Despair.

32

THE FOUR STEEL TRIPODS, OVER TEN STOREYS HIGH, STOOD ALIEN and threatening in the wilderness. Silhouetted against the rising sun, perched on a clifftop and strung with huge radar dishes, they scanned the entirety of Iran, the waters of the Persian Gulf, and looked far beyond, into the Empty Quarter of Saudi Arabia.

The site, ringed by electric fences, was Pakistan's most forward listening post: fabric balloons protected the radar dishes from the relentless wind and the steel frames supported dozens of panels that captured vast amounts of electronic communication. The entire array was flanked by low-slung buildings housing the computer systems and a dozen barracks for the large contingent of soldiers assigned to protect the site.

Probably only a handful of people had ever seen the place in person, and I stood in a small grove of trees and stared at it across a deep canyon. Any minute, once there was a little more light, I would have to turn away and start searching for my real objective: an even smaller track that was supposed to swing off to the north-east.

All through the night I had led the ponies along the old smugglers' trail, travelling as fast as I could, making up the time stolen by the detour. The plan devised at Langley called for me to be at the tripods and the intersection with the north-east track by dawn, and now, assuming I could find it, I was right on schedule. Once I had located the track, the next step was to find a secluded area, feed myself and the horses, sleep through the day and be ready to head north-east at nightfall. The agency team that researched and mapped covert routes – TripAdvisor was their nickname – had advised that camping close to the tripods would be safer than any other location: the listening post was accessible only by helicopter or by a gruelling journey overland, and that meant the area would be virtually deserted.

Furthermore, there would be little threat from random hostiles abroad in the land: the last thing a dope runner, terrorist or smuggler would want was to come close enough to the observation post to risk encountering a heavily armed army patrol.

Feeling relatively safe, I turned my back on the steel structures and began to search for the track. After ten minutes I found it, almost hidden by bushes and undergrowth. It looked impassable. While that thought was on my mind I knew there was no chance of sleep so I battled through the branches and scrub for a hundred yards and was relieved to find that the landscape changed: rock and stone encroached on the path and the foliage retreated.

The route could definitely be travelled, and I paused, looking down it. Five miles ahead was a cairn of stones that marked the frontier with Iran.

While the Pakistani border was certainly a hazardous place, Iran was a quantum far beyond it. There was only one thing that would protect me once I passed the stone marker; not the US government, not diplomatic intervention, not pleas for mercy or appeals to the Red Cross, the Geneva Convention or international law.

I was a spy, and my only protection would be my rifle and the legend I was using.

33

I WAS TRAVELLING AS A SAUDI ARABIAN FROM TABUK, A SMALL CITY in the far north of that country well known for its blood-red sunsets and as the place where the Prophet – Peace be upon Him – had once stopped to drink from the clear waters of a natural spring.

That was my home, but the reason I was in the borderlands, trekking on foot with three ponies, had to be explained by the rest of my legend: the story I would have to rely on if I was stopped and questioned by other civilians, members of the Army of the Pure or Iran's feared Revolutionary Guards.

Meeting for hours in Langley's underground bunker, myself and a group of mission planners, analysts and executives had crafted a fictional life. Almost at the outset, our creation's most important attribute – his nationality – was decided not by choice but by necessity.

The languages I had mastered over the years did not, unfortunately, extend to Urdu or any of the other Pakistani languages. I had a few phrases, but nothing beyond that. Clearly, we had to build my legend on a language that I could speak, and as I would be travelling in the Islamic world, Arabic was the obvious choice. Because the government in Riyadh could be relied on to offer any assistance – no questions asked – my invented self immediately became a citizen of the Kingdom of Saudi Arabia.

Those decisions – about language and nationality – were made within an hour so, unlike most agency meetings, progress had been remarkably fast, and that alone should have told me it was too good to last: an argument arose about Tabuk, my supposed hometown, and rapidly became heated.

A city of eight hundred thousand people, the proposal by the planners to use it as my base split the room: one group was certain that a relatively small place would reduce the chance of meeting someone who had actually lived there; the other believed that while a big city would increase the risk of encountering a former resident, there was anonymity and safety in a metropolis. The city of Riyadh or Tabuk was what it came down to.

The argument dragged on until, finally, Falcon wanted to know what I thought. As everyone turned to face me, I reminded him of the earlier mission when I had been shot and taken to the American Hospital in Beirut. 'What about it?' he asked.

I said the surgeon who had removed the bullet had been outstanding and when he visited me in recovery he reported that I would regain about 95 per cent of the movement in my arm. 'I guess my face must have shown my disappointment – I wanted a hundred per cent,' I explained. 'The surgeon said that might have been possible but over the years he had watched colleagues perform dozens of complex operations.

'One thing had struck him, he told me – how many times the doctors kept going back in, making tiny adjustments, trying to improve their work, determined to get it exactly right. On plenty of occasions he had watched those tiny adjustments unravel and the operation go completely wrong. He shrugged and told me – perfection is the enemy of good.'

'Okay, I get it,' Falcon said, laughing. 'Tabuk may not be perfect, but it's good.'

'Exactly,' I replied. 'Nobody can predict who I'll meet out there and what city or town they come from. There is no right answer – so make it Tabuk. Now that's finalized, can somebody tell me –' I looked around the room – 'what is a Saudi national, on foot with three horses, armed only with an AK-47, doing in one of the most dangerous places on earth?'

34

EVERYONE THOUGHT ABOUT THE PROBLEM, BUT IT WAS ONE OF THOSE questions few people in the room wanted to answer for fear of saying something that might harm their careers. The CIA was rife with that.

Then softly – from the far end of the room – I heard a woman's voice. It was so quiet, in fact, I couldn't make out what she had said. 'Could you repeat that, please?' I asked.

She was young – at least compared to the thirty people turning to look at her – and slightly built, with dark hair cut short, and dressed in a navy business suit. While her features were pleasant, there was little memorable about her except for the eyes. They shone with a life and intelligence that was unusual today: obviously, she hadn't spent her whole life staring at a phone.

Her name was Madeleine – though at that moment her surname eluded me – and I figured she was in her early twenties, but then I remembered when we were introduced, several hours earlier, someone had said that after Harvard she had spent three years in Europe improving her language skills. Only then did she join the agency, so I guessed she was a few years older than she looked.

During our earlier brief encounter – again speaking softly – she had told me that for the last eight months she had been running a team that was compiling a file on every terrorist-soldier our satellites had photographed as they headed towards the Army's base. It must have been exhausting work: identifying them and trying to unravel their journey through the Islamic underworld.

Now she was sitting at the far end of the room, trying to command the attention of some of the most powerful and impatient people in US intelligence. She tried to speak again, but her voice was barely any louder.

You've got thirty seconds, I thought. You have to grab 'em. Speak up, run the room—

I didn't think she could do it. I knew that among the agency's twenty thousand employees there were a host of similar men and women – shy or awkward, often downright eccentric – and it was especially true in research and analysis. I sometimes wondered what half the social misfits in America would do if there wasn't a CIA.

'I'm sorry,' she said at last. 'I'll try to speak louder. I've got a strep throat.' Well done, I told myself – a strep throat? It was pretty clear why I didn't work as an analyst.

She looked at me, speaking up: 'You asked what reason you would have – as a Saudi national – for being in such a dangerous place. I said you were looking for your brother.'

Falcon and the dozens of other men and women kept their eyes fixed on her. She was the most junior employee in the room – only there because of her knowledge of the Army of the Pure's recruits – and I didn't think anyone had a clue if the idea she was trying to suggest would have any merit.

I certainly didn't, but I also remembered what I had seen in her eyes: 'Okay,' I said. 'Deal me in. Why am I two thousand miles from home, looking for my brother?'

'Because your father is dying of cancer,' she replied. 'He's got a few weeks, a month maybe. Your brother is three years older than you and in Saudi the oldest son has special responsibilities. He will become the head of the family. Your mother and unmarried sisters will answer to him. Your father has begged to see his eldest boy – to counsel him and hold him one last time.'

The room remained silent, but it was the silence of interest now. 'And why is the older brother, the one we are looking for, in the borderlands?' This was Falcon.

'Because he joined the Army of the Pure,' Madeleine said. 'And the mother and father in Tabuk know he travelled to the border for that purpose.'

'Okay, keep going,' Falcon said. 'I'm sorry,' he interrupted himself. 'What is your name?'

'Madeleine,' she replied. 'Madeleine O'Neill.'

'I remember now. Irish,' Falcon said confidently.

'Jewish,' she replied. 'When my great-grandfather emigrated from Poland, he arrived in Boston, and I think he realized which way the wind was blowing.'

All of us laughed. 'Only in America,' Falcon said. 'Go ahead.'

'In my version, the older brother had always been devout; some said he would become an imam,' Madeleine said. 'Instead, he served Allah in a different way. He went to Syria, joined ISIS and fought from Mosul to Raqqa. We all know those were hard miles.'

Hard miles indeed, I thought. Four hundred of them, and it was slaughter every foot of the way. I recalled the civil war and ethnic cleansing carried out by ISIS, not that too much of the real horror made the nightly news. It was classified footage I had seen – most of it shot by drones – and it spared the viewer's imagination nothing. If I'd ever had any doubt about the type of people I would be dealing with, the footage unreeling in my head immediately dispelled it.

'Somewhere during that campaign, the older brother became an ISIS commander,' she continued. 'Though nobody's sure how high he rose—'

A veil lifted for me. 'This man – the commander you're talking about,' I said. 'He's real, isn't he? You're recounting the history of one of the fighters you've been researching.'

'That was quick,' she said, smiling. 'Yes, he's real, and even better – he was born and raised in Saudi. I'm marrying fact and fiction here, hoping it'll give us the best shot. The real man was a battlefield commander,' she continued. 'But pretty soon ISIS was being hit on every front. Russians, Turks, the US, Syrians, all lined up to destroy them, and the once Great Caliphate shrank to a final battle at a tiny place called al-Baghuz Fawqani. The endgame had no significance, though. By then most of the ISIS leadership had slipped away.'

Falcon held up his hand, stopping her: 'And the so-called brother was one of them?'

'Yes,' she said. 'Like other survivors, he knew about a group that was being formed – one as fanatical as he was – so he headed for the borderlands to join the Army of the Pure.'

Falcon nodded: 'Okay,' he said, starting to pace the room. 'Why doesn't the family in Saudi phone the guy? Plenty of terrorists have sat phones – why don't they report the father is dying and tell him to come home? Why send his younger brother to find him?'

Madeleine nodded. 'The older brother did have a phone and the family have tried calling it many times, but without success. It's a three-thousand-mile journey from Iraq to the Army's base. The family thinks he lost the phone or it died. They've even contacted other families, got the numbers of fighters who might be in the area and tried to get a message to him – but there's been no response.'

Falcon stayed silent, assessing, thinking, then summarized it. 'The father is dying . . . only weeks to live . . . the family have tried everything to reach the eldest son . . . by phone, messages . . . time is getting short for the father.' He looked around the table. 'They are desperate. Someone has to go and find him, don't they?'

'And the logical person,' Madeleine added, 'is to send his younger brother – our agent.'

Everyone turned towards me. I shook my head. 'There's a problem,' I said. Something had been building in a corner of my mind for several minutes, and it had just detonated. 'The brother I'm trying to find is a real person who has gone to join the Army. It's a true story, and that's the advantage of it, right?'

'Exactly,' Madeleine said.

'So, I'm chasing a real man with a genuine name and I'm in the borderlands – and let's say I run into an Army of the Pure patrol. I tell them who I'm looking for and they say I'm in luck and they take me to meet him. He immediately says I am not his brother and I'm dead.'

'That's a problem,' Madeleine said. 'It could happen – except for one thing. Your older brother, the real guy we're talking about, set out to join the Army, but he never made it to their base. I promise, you will never meet him.'

'Why?' I asked.

'Because his route took him through Afghanistan. Three hundred miles short of where the Army operates, he was picked up by a US Special Forces airborne patrol on suspicion of being a terrorist.'

I stared at her. 'Where is he now?' I asked.

'They ran him through facial recognition and ID'd him as a former ISIS commander, and he's being interrogated—'

'Where?' I demanded again.

'Morocco,' she said. 'He is in one of our black prisons at a place called Ourika. You will never meet him.'

It was a brilliant piece of work; in my opinion, the CIA had never invented a better legend and it was the sole creation of Madeleine O'Neill, twenty-eight years old, an unknown researcher, a woman wearing a plain business suit who had graduated from Harvard *summa cum laude* and – judging by the reaction in the room that day – was destined to go to the very top of US intelligence.

35

SO, MASQUERADING AS A SAUDI NATIONAL SEARCHING FOR HIS brother, I headed back along the north-east track to where I had left the horses and looked across the canyon to the tripods. Strangely, as the light grew stronger, they seemed even more menacing.

The steel supports – black and streaked with grime and rust – were thrown into sharper relief, and the only signs of life were a dozen dust devils battering the fabric balloons. Clearly visible now, however, were the burned carcasses of birds and small animals that had ventured too close and hit the electrified fences. The whole ensemble – pointless death, loneliness, the bleak and desolate landscape – filled me with a sense of foreboding and I was relieved to lead the horses out of sight of the listening post and strip them of their burdens.

Light was filling the horizon sooner than I had anticipated and it told me that I had to move fast; I only had a few minutes to spare. I was in a different world now and there was not enough time for me to grab something to eat, even though, like Sakab and the other horses, I was starving. I fed and watered them and checked my wristwatch—

The crown prince of Saudi Arabia stared back at me. Someone at

Langley had come up with the inspired idea of equipping me with one of the watches that were popular in the Kingdom: a rendering of the prince's features was engraved on the gold dial, his chin tilted up and his eyes looking with infinite wisdom into the future. I had seven minutes.

I filled a bowl with water and carefully started to perform the ritual known in Islam as *wudu*: washing my hands, face, arms and feet to prepare myself for prayer. Once it was complete, I pulled a silk mat off the pony and again consulted my watch, but it wasn't the time I was checking; the model I was wearing also came with a *qibla* compass – thankfully – which pointed precisely at Mecca and was the direction that I had to face when I prayed.

I unrolled the mat and got to my knees. As I said, I am not a religious person and I am not sure I would know what to say to God or Allah even if he or she was listening. To me, the universe is infinitely dark and each of us has to light their own candle, but my beliefs, right or wrong, were of no consequence here. I was heading into the heart of the Islamic world, dressed and masquerading as a Saudi and therefore one of the faithful. Any unseen observer – an Army of the Pure scout with binoculars or a Pakistani soldier at the listening post watching drone footage – who saw a man not undertaking *wudu* or kneeling for *Salat Ul Fajr*, the dawn prayer, at the right time would know instantly that he was a fraud.

Therefore, kneeling on a silk square in the wilderness, alone and hungry, I bowed my head, and instead of prayer I couldn't help but think of the seemingly disconnected currents that had swept through the world and were now hurling me forward down a barely marked path to a small cairn of stones.

When I estimated eight minutes had passed, enough time for a true believer to have completed prayers, I stood up. As much as I wanted to cook a meal and sleep, I had one more task to perform. I pulled out my sat phone and, making sure that none of the observation post was in the frame – the last thing I needed was to bring the Pakistani military down on me – I lined up a group of huge stone sentinels in the background and hoped that they were spectacular enough to convince any hidden observer that I was just taking a selfie.

According to the plan devised at Langley, the photo would be transmitted to a fake Saudi email account in my father's name, ostensibly letting him know that I was safe and making progress. In fact,

Langley would access the account and from the metadata embedded in the innocent image would be able to tell the time and my exact location. In effect, I was reporting to them that I was alive, it was dawn and I was at the intersection of the north-east track.

The one thing I was not telling Langley was that while my orders were to upload a photo from my route every day, this was the first and only time I would do it. I found a spot hidden from view and smashed the phone to pieces. Satisfied that the chips and circuit board were completely destroyed, I gathered up the debris and dropped it down a crevice.

In common with the mysterious leadership of the Army of the Pure, I put no faith in phones. The executives at Langley, the mission planners and the tech experts, had all assured me that the one I was using contained only an array of fake names, search history and other information to support my legend. But I was acutely aware that a fragment of incorrect data, a wrong date or an improperly deleted file meant the whole elaborate structure of my fake identity would unravel.

I had no doubt that destroying the phone would make me safer, but something else was equally certain: from now on, I really was on my own.

36

THE FIRST RENDEZVOUS PROVIDED BY THE COURIER TURNED OUT TO be a decrepit shack two nights' travel inside Iran, located near the intersection of two overgrown trails, a spot so isolated I wouldn't have had a chance of finding it without the mapping device.

The building, for want of a better word, had been cobbled together years ago out of old timber and tarpaulins by what were probably drug couriers coming down out of Afghanistan who, I guessed, had used it as a rest stop on their long trek before meeting up with freighters passing through the Persian Gulf, the next link in a chain that ended on countless streets throughout the world.

It was just before daybreak when I saw the place, nestled close to a cliff and its tarps flapping in a searing wind. It had been over two days since I had left the tripods in my wake just after night had fallen. Leading the ponies, we travelled the north-east trail without incident, moving fast, barely pausing and passing the cairn of stones under a clear sky and a spectacular star-field. Three miles further on, I crested a rise and saw a vast plain in front of me. Above it, a crescent moon was rising above Iran and I took it as an omen, but whether it was for good or ill, I had no idea.

Throughout the following days and nights I saw no sign of life: no travellers, no firelight in the night and virtually no wildlife except for early one morning when a peregrine falcon circled lazily above me, searching for prey. Given the ancient landscape and the endless miles of silence, it would have been easy to think that the falcon, myself and the three ponies were all that was left on earth.

I first glimpsed the shack across a rugged gully so I hobbled the horses, held the AK-47 at the ready and crept through the scrub. For twenty minutes I squatted in a tree-line, watching and listening.

Satisfied there was nobody lying in wait and unable to see anyone trying to keep a rendezvous, I circled the building with the rifle at the ready until, at the back of the windowless structure, I found several dozen bleached bones, scattered and picked clean by wild dogs: the remains of at least five men was my rough estimate. It appeared that they had been killed by fire from heavy-gauge automatic weapons – the sort of thing Iranian military or rival drug gangs might have used, I thought. They were years old and I doubted anyone had visited the place in the intervening time.

I approached the door and saw that spiders had spun webs over the hinges. The metal screeched as I pushed the door open, the muzzle of my rifle sweeping the room, pointing at wind-blown leaves, piles of plastic that had once wrapped bricks of opium and the blackened stones of a small fireplace. There was nobody inside.

I went back and got the horses, stripped hairs from Sakab's tail and formed it into a knot; I tied it around the door latch, inconspicuous but easily found if you knew what you were looking for. It was a pre-arranged sign; if the courier had been delayed and arrived too late, it told him that I had been there and had already moved on to the second location.

I fed the horses, tied them to a stake, went back inside the shack and lit a fire between the blackened stones. Satisfied that it would burn for a long time, I walked out, grabbed my bedroll from among the supplies and scaled the cliff. I found a dark place under a rock shelf, spread my blanket out and, with my back to the wall, I made sure that I had a clear view of the shack.

Anyone approaching would see the tethered ponies, note the smoke from the fire and leap to the conclusion that the traveller was inside. If they came closer and decided to enter, first the ponies and then the screeching door hinges would wake me, and I had chosen my sleeping place partly because it offered an unimpeded field of fire.

I checked the rifle's safety was off and settled down, confident my sleep would be untroubled. Experience had taught me something important about Denied Access Area missions: the nightmares didn't happen when you were asleep; they started when you woke.

37

ALL THROUGH THE LONG TREK SO FAR, I HAD HARBOURED A PROBABLY forlorn hope that the courier would be waiting for me at the first rendezvous. I knew if I had to embark on the second leg of the journey, the danger would rise exponentially: a far greater number of people would be on the road and I was heading much deeper into Iran.

Twenty-four hours after arriving at the shack, I had no alternative but to head to the second rendezvous. For four days, I led the ponies along trails that steadily became broader and better defined, and while travelling at night meant that I didn't encounter anybody, three times I smelled smoke on the wind and knew that I was passing close to small settlements or the campfires of other travellers.

Fighting the clock, I had been forced to push the ponies hard day after day, so it was no surprise when, on the night of the fifth, Sakab's arthritis started to give him hell and slowed us down significantly. Some people might have said the sensible thing to do would be to transfer the supplies he was carrying and cut him loose, but I knew enough about horses to predict it would have no effect. They are herd animals and they seek safety in the group: he would have just tagged along behind and, because he was the leader, the other two would have kept stopping to wait for him.

If I was being honest, I would have to admit there was another element at play. In the short time we had been together, I had come to admire his determination to keep going despite the pain and I appreciated the way his gentle eyes looked at me when I asked the impossible of him, like leading me down a mountainside. The truth was I was more than happy to keep his company.

I lightened his load as much as I could and we pressed on, but we were falling further and further behind schedule. By the time we reached the start of what was marked on electronic maps at Langley as the Plateau of White Stones, I knew that we should have already crossed it. Instead, I had to kneel for dawn prayer at its edge.

While on my knees, I decided to cross the plateau in daylight and to keep going. At our reduced pace, we were still twelve hours away from the second rendezvous, and I reasoned that if we rested I ran the risk of arriving too late and missing the courier if he was there. The danger would increase by crossing the plateau in daylight, but I had been thinking that with the tracks turning to roads and more people using them, I might arouse less suspicion if I travelled by day.

I stood up, led the ponies forward and soon discovered that it wasn't called the Plateau of White Stones for nothing. They were random sizes and shapes, forcing the horses to pick their way through them, but the strange thing was that very soon we found a flat section, overgrown with weeds and bushes – but wide and long – where the stones had been removed decades ago, leaving it completely clear.

It allowed us to travel much faster – Sakab especially found the going much easier – and it wasn't until I got to the other side and saw a broken-down pylon with a shredded windsock that I realized what we had been walking on: it was a makeshift runway, fallen into disrepair years ago and unusable now, but probably built by drug producers in an attempt to move even more product.

As I stopped beside the pylon, I looked across at a steep cliff pockmarked with caves that rose in the distance ahead. It commanded a view not only of the plateau but of the valley I had travelled along to reach it. It looked the perfect place for someone equipped with a pair of binoculars to hide – someone, like a courier, who wanted to observe me and check if I was alone and wasn't being followed.

There is a rule in surveillance – if they can see you, you can see them – and I ran my eyes along the caves and boulders, hoping to find a tiny movement, but there was nothing. I certainly didn't want to remain standing there, immobile, searching the hillsides and drawing attention to myself, so I swung the rifle off one shoulder, raised it slightly and slung it over the other.

To almost anyone watching, it would have just looked like a traveller adjusting his equipment, but to a keen observer looking through field glasses, it would have appeared that the rifle was raised in a momentary acknowledgement.

As it happened, I needn't have bothered – the courier wasn't there. He was several miles further down the road.

38

I HAVE NO DOUBT THAT I MADE A LOT OF MISTAKES ON THE MISSION – I have no doubt most agents behind enemy lines do the same – but I definitely got one thing right. I didn't cut Sakab loose and I kept him by my side. For the second time, he saved my life.

I left the broken windsock behind and, using the rifle's mapping function, struck out to the north and found the trail I was looking for. The graphic on the scope showed it would take me through lightly forested hillsides into a rugged canyon between sheer cliffs and then, ten miles further, on to a road that would lead me to the second rendezvous.

Having convinced myself the courier had seen me and would be satisfied I wasn't being followed, I grew increasingly confident that we would meet at the upcoming destination: a group of deserted hovels, roofless and crumbling, that – according to a satellite overpass – were huddled around a well that had run dry decades ago.

During the planning stage we had figured my questioning of the courier would take about twenty-four hours and, once I had finished debriefing him – and was satisfied he had been truthful – I would give him the passports, the money and an eleven-digit phone number I had memorized. Without delay we would head our separate ways: him to go home and make arrangements to get himself and his family safely across the border into Afghanistan. In that regard, there was nothing I could do to help him – travelling with me would increase the danger exponentially and, anyway, he knew the terrain and secret trails better than anybody.

Once he had crossed the frontier and was in Afghanistan, just one of the *tolahs* we had provided would buy him a phone from a drug courier or a government official. He would dial the eleven-digit number and within twenty minutes a Special Forces chopper – on standby – would pick the family up, fly them to Kabul, and ninety minutes later they would be on a plane to the United States and a full-press interrogation at a CIA safe house.

As for me, I calculated that two days from now I would start the long haul back, retracing my route to the tripods and then down to the village of Mand, where the truck was waiting for me and the horses. Without realizing it, I started to push the ponies even harder along the trail.

The sun was dipping towards the horizon and I was deep in the lightly forested hillsides when, by chance, the saddle on the pony at the rear shifted as we negotiated a rocky incline. It spooked him, and even though I made it secure I decided to take a minute to let the panic fade. Using the time to check the path ahead, I walked forward, crested a small rise, looked down the long hill and saw the entrance to the canyon – a jagged split between two cliffs – in front of me. I stopped, still among the trees with the sun behind me and, as a result, I was deep in their shadow.

While I stood and looked into the gradually darkening canyon, a thought occurred to me, and I really can't say why. Maybe it was just a professional assessment. 'If I was going to ambush someone,' I said to myself. 'That would be the perfect place to do it.'

I didn't move and continued to look carefully at the canyon, trying to see if something down there had triggered the thought but had failed to register in my conscious mind. I couldn't see anything of concern – just the wind stirring the dust and the setting sun turning the cliffs from pink to orange. Even so, I couldn't stop thinking that something in the rocks or somewhere close by must have troubled me. Most people call it intuition, but I often think it's more like a message, a faint communication from an older, far more primal part of the brain. It picks up tiny signs that have been lost to rational thought – the sort of things that might have kept us alive when we left the firelight and ventured out into the valley with nothing more than our senses and a few primitive weapons to keep us safe.

I swept my eyes across the rocks again, still couldn't find anything tangible – just a strange and distant sound I couldn't immediately identify – and shrugged: I figured that, like the pony a few minutes ago, I was spooked by nothing of consequence. I went back, got the horses and led them forward. When we reached the spot where I had stood and scanned the canyon, Sakab halted and, even before I looked, I was certain it wasn't his knee.

I tried to urge him forward, but he wouldn't move. We stood there for a long moment, surrounded by the shadows of the trees, and as I stared at the canyon I asked him something that had no sensible explanation. I have no idea why I said it or what it meant. 'What can you hear?' I asked him, thinking about the sound I hadn't been able to identify. He turned and looked at me with his liquid eyes. 'You can hear gunfire, can't you?'

I wondered if that was what had troubled me about the canyon too. Not in reality but as if some sort of echo from the future was coming down the miles to meet me. In the silence, I turned to look at Sakab – he continued to just stand there. 'I think I heard it as well,' I said at last, and smiled. 'Gunfire from the future? Don't tell anyone, okay?'

The rational section of my brain, the part with the science degree, told me that what I knew about irregular warfare was influencing my thinking. I was aware that if it really was an ambush, the hostiles would be so well hidden that the gunfire would be the first thing I would know of their presence. Assuming they wanted me alive, they would target the animals and take them out first to prevent me trying to run with them.

I stood with the horses in the gloom, trying to think, wondering if my imagination was running away with me. I had journeyed into a place older than time, where the stars stretched for ever and evil seemed to cling to a forest, a land that troubled the Western spirit and could easily evoke strange thoughts. And yet . . .

If I really believed the rational explanation, I told myself, then I should smack Sakab hard until he moved and walk with him into the canyon. At the other end of the small valley, I could laugh at myself and push on for the last ten miles to reach the road that would take me to the rendezvous. But if I believed in messages from an age when human-kind first started to walk the world or thought I could hear gunshots that had not even been fired yet, I would have to retrace my steps for an hour, cut overland and take a long loop to circumvent the canyon. Trust your rational mind or trust your intuition, that was the choice.

39

THE TERRAIN WE HAD TO COVER BY SKIRTING THE CANYON WAS FAR more rugged than I had anticipated, slowing us down and – as we were travelling by day now – forcing me to camp overnight on a windswept slope.

As a result, I didn't reach the road to the rendezvous until well into the afternoon of the following day, and all I could hope for was that the courier, probably even more desperate for the meeting than myself, would decide to risk it and wait for me there. The dirt road – when I reached it – was wide and well used, unfortunately; the last thing I needed was to run the risk, or waste the time, answering questions from people I met. But luck was with me, and I found a steep track that was ideal: not only was it deserted, but after I had climbed it to the top of a ridge, it ran parallel to the road below.

The road itself was one of the three major thoroughfares of the area, which wasn't saying much, but – according to the maps – they all intersected at a small group of structures that formed a ramshackle bazaar. The actual rendezvous lay five miles beyond it, less than an hour's travel from where I was. At last, I was within striking distance.

After the initial climb, the track flattened out and, travelling at a better pace, I glimpsed the bazaar earlier than I had expected. Encouraged by our progress, I tried to increase our speed and didn't even stop as I used the rifle's scope to check out the huddle of buildings. The major part was a group of cinder-block sheds connected by huge Army tents. The most popular trading area, as usual, was the weapons section, and I swung the sight across bazookas, countless assault rifles, handguns, rocket-propelled grenades and even landmines. Who would want them, I thought, and then I realized: poppy farmers protecting their crop.

Next to the weapons, and close behind in popularity, was an area occupied by a dozen opium traders with antique scales, chemical kits used to test the raw opium for water content – the less the better – and generator-operated presses to produce the plastic-wrapped bricks, complete with labels showing a brand name and their purity.

I kept scanning to my left, towards a general store, and still looking through the scope, I came to a complete stop. I saw the courier.

Just before I had left Langley, he had provided – through the intermediary – a photo of himself so there could be no doubt when we met that I was dealing with the right person. I knew I couldn't bring the photo with me – that would have been his death sentence if it was discovered – so I had spent time committing his face to memory.

I was absolutely certain that it was him in the crosshairs. He was right in the centre of the intersection, by far the busiest part of the settlement, six feet off the ground, his feet tied together and his arms outstretched on a heavy timber cross. He had been crucified.

40

HE WAS ALREADY DEAD, THANKFULLY – AT LEAST THE AGONY HAD come to an end. Crucifixion is more than just an execution; it is actually death by torture.

Popularized by the Romans, the practice was specifically designed so that the pain would continue for hours – days, sometimes – as the entire weight of the body, supported only by the nails, forces the hands and feet to spasm and freeze into something more like claws. Unable to move any limb, the victim, in agony, gradually becomes dehydrated and suffers from a raging thirst. Gravity, meanwhile, slowly forces the internal organs down until they begin to crush the diaphragm. Once movement of the diaphragm is restricted, breathing in can still be managed but exhaling becomes increasingly difficult, every gasp turning into endless, excruciating pain. Eventually, it is impossible to breathe out and the victim dies of suffocation.

I lowered the rifle. It wasn't just that he had been killed that had sent my mind reeling, it was the method that had been used. It said more eloquently than any sign around his neck that the courier was both a traitor to the Army of the Pure and had also betrayed his religion: he was no better than a Christian.

The intersection had obviously been chosen to ensure that everybody in the area would see or hear of it, and I knew that never again would we find anybody – either a soldier in the Army or a local villager – willing to disclose anything about the organization or its plans. If nothing else, I was looking at an intelligence defeat of massive proportions. Equally, I suspected that the courier had been betrayed by someone – a trusted friend, probably – and the first thing the leadership of the Army would have done was to torture him into disclosing everything about his arrangements. That had obviously been successful – otherwise they would still be torturing him. It meant they knew I was coming, they were aware of the rendezvous points and they had been waiting in the canyon. Gunfire from the future, indeed.

As soon as the first shock of seeing him had abated, I raised the rifle. I didn't want to look through the scope, but I knew I had to confirm something that in the first jolt of recognition I couldn't be sure I had registered accurately. If it was true, in many ways it would be even more horrific than a former Kabul taxi driver being nailed up and left to die in agony.

I put the crosshairs on the opium sellers and panned steadily to the left, bracing myself. I saw a large crowd – the men mostly wearing the *shalwar kameez* and the women totally in black, from their full *hijab* veils to their long *abaya* cloaks – milling around the intersection, wailing or quietly protesting.

A smaller number of people were gathered in front of a hillock pleading with three heavily armed men who were squatting near the top. From that position the trio commanded an unimpeded view of the intersection, and it was clear they were guards – soldiers of the Army for sure – who had been stationed there to make sure that nobody tried to release the victim or interfered with the carefully curated scene.

All three guards looked like hard men: warriors with gaunt faces and sun-toughened skin, maybe Syrians or Iraqis. They were of widely disparate ages and had bandoliers of bullets across their chests, assault rifles in their hands and a fire with a pot of tea at their side. They were chatting among themselves, ignoring the protests, not even looking at a weeping man who was virtually prostrate in front of them. Whatever he was saying, whatever he was pleading for, had absolutely no effect on them.

The distraught man was in his sixties – grey-bearded and, despite his present position, strangely dignified – and if you had told me he was a village elder I would not have been surprised. More than that, he looked like a father or grandfather.

I panned off him, continuing to move the crosshairs to the left, and though I was moving it didn't diminish the impact when I saw it. Just as I had glimpsed earlier, chained near the base of the cross, forced to sit beneath the feet of the dead body, was a woman and her two young children. I was sure it was their husband and father who was hanging above them and it was their passports that were hidden in my saddle-cloths.

I had no way of knowing if they had been forced to watch the crucifixion but, in a way, the fate that lay before them now was even worse. In the blinding heat, there was no food in front of them, just a bowl each of water. That was no act of kindness on the part of the three men squatting on the hill. A person can survive for a long time – weeks, quite often – without food, but in a place of high temperatures thirst usually kills within two days. The water was there to prolong the agony, to delay death for as long as possible: the inhabitants of the surrounding area would have to watch for days as the woman and the two children slowly starved to death.

I exhaled, trying to keep my anger under control, and then looked more closely. The mother, curled in a foetal position and dressed in her *abaya*, looked like a black puddle. Everything about her indicated she had been crushed by what had happened to her husband and the imminent death of herself and her two kids. She didn't even appear to be crying – just broken and spent. Close by her, the two children, both girls, aged about four and six, were calling for help. Initially I was surprised they weren't cuddling up to their mother for comfort, and then I realized it was impossible. All three had been chained in such a way that they couldn't even crawl to each other for touch or love. It had been guaranteed that they would die alone and uncomforted.

As for the grandfather – who wouldn't plead with the guards? – but I knew it was useless. If by some miracle the three men were willing to listen, they would say it wasn't their decision to unchain the family, they were just the jailers.

As I watched, a little boy – about eight – emerged from the crowd and, unseen by his parents, ran towards the girls. He had pieces of fruit and a wooden toy in his hand, about to give it to them. People started to yell and scream as they tried to stop him—

Instantly the leader of the guards, sharing tea with his comrades, was on his feet, raising his rifle and yelling. He was over six foot, with a muscular build and a full beard. Somewhere, he had lost a top tooth, and his most distinguishing feature, apart from the battlefield insignia on his shirt, was a gold incisor. He continued to yell at the boy, aiming the rifle. Taking into account the look of the man and the horrific tableau, I wasn't confident that he wouldn't shoot, but, thankfully, a stranger flew out of the crowd, grabbed the kid and hauled him backwards.

I lowered the scope and turned away. It was late afternoon, there were several hours of daylight left, and I could make good progress before nightfall. There was no doubt I had to go. The mission was over – there was no information about an imminent spectacular to be had here – and the rules of the CIA in such a situation were clear: I had to abort immediately and exfiltrate myself as fast as possible. I had been sent on an intelligence mission, nothing more, and whatever outrages happened in hostile territory were of no concern to me or the agency.

If I was to have a hope of getting back to Pakistan, any analysis dictated I turn around immediately. Hopefully, the Army's men were still at the canyon, waiting, but as soon as they realized I had been delayed or had taken a far less direct route to the rendezvous they would start to search. By noon tomorrow, I figured, they would be sending drones up, and my only chance was to put as much distance between them and myself as possible.

Obviously, minutes could be critical, and the only thing required of me was to put aside any thought of the horrific tableau in front of me. There are things, once seen, that can never be unseen and the sight of those two dying sisters, unable to even hold each other's hand—

I got to my feet to leave and I knew the memory of it would be with me for the rest of my life.

41

I WAS STANDING, BUT I WASN'T MOVING. IN THE TINY SPACE BETWEEN rising and walking, I started to think about flying home and seeing my homeland emerge through the clouds.

But with my only path to safety growing narrower by the minute, I stayed rooted to the spot, thinking of Becca and how much she had always wanted kids herself. In a quiet moment once, she had told me that not having a family would be a deal-breaker for her. I assumed it was because of her own fractured childhood, but whatever the reason, she left me in no doubt she would run our relationship aground if she had to.

Somebody else, a different or better agent, might never have measured their partner's dream against the reality of the two children huddled down on the road, but – as I said – I knew their image was going to live with me for ever and that reality had started already.

In those few moments of inaction, no more than several heartbeats, I was certain what Rebecca would expect me to do and – just as importantly – what I expected of myself. I was holding a blueprinted AK-47, all its parts specially machined, the entire weapon balanced like a marksman's rifle and fitted with one of the best telescopic sights in the world.

Honestly, what more could I ask for?

42

TIME DIDN'T MATTER – IT WOULD BECOME CRITICAL LATER, BUT NOT now. As I walked back towards the ponies, I looked down at the crown prince's visionary face and estimated that I had forty minutes until the setting sun was directly behind me.

For once, my interest in sunset was not related to *Salat al-Mahgrib*, the sunset prayer; I wanted the disc right behind me so that if the crowd at the intersection spun and looked at the ridge they would be blinded by the glare at my back.

I unloaded Sakab and the other two horses, grabbed the horse blanket that hid the four US passports and tore its lining apart until I found the waterproof pouches holding them. They were genuine books without photos or biographical details – they were waiting to be filled in – and as a result would be hugely valuable on the black market. Dangerous, too, if they fell into the hands of the Army or any terrorist group. I ripped out the pages and, using a long, ivory-handled knife, cut them into pieces and buried them in the scrub.

I picked up Sakab's ancient saddle and used the same knife – pointed and its edge deadly sharp – to carve a message in Arabic into the leather. I wrote that the pony's name was Sakab and that he and the other two horses had been loyal and brave beyond all hope or expectation.

'Our journey together is over. Whoever finds them, take them as a gift from Allah, the most glorified, the most high,' I wrote. 'Let them graze in a field in retirement, treat them with love and respect. God demands nothing less. In the bags, saddles and blankets you will find enough to pay for anything they need.'

Fifty thousand dollars in gold should cover it, I thought ruefully.

I stood up, loaded the ponies with anything valuable and fixed the saddle with its message on to Sakab's back. I stroked his velvety nose, looked at his gentle eyes one last time and smiled as he pulled his lips back and gave another one of his goofy grins. I then turned him around and slapped him on the rump. He looked confused for a moment and then, relieved of any lead rope, realized he was free.

He trotted forward, heading back down the track – the other two following – and, with a heart heavier than I had expected, I watched them until they were out of sight. I looked at the wristwatch – twelve minutes to sunset.

43

I HAD ALREADY IDENTIFIED THE SPOT WHERE I WOULD LIE PRONE: A flat stretch of earth ten feet above the track, a location that provided a wide field of fire, where the sun would be a blinding flare behind me and the overhanging branches of a tree would cover me in shadow.

Within a few minutes of climbing up to it I had fashioned rocks and earth into a small mound intended to support the barrel of the rifle and help muffle the sound. To help achieve that, I laid three heavy horse blankets I had kept with me for the purpose over the top of the gun. I planned to fire what are known as 'ghost' bullets – ones that nobody at the intersection would even see or hear. It meant that when the first guard crumpled to the ground, the two remaining targets would have less time to react, let alone seek cover.

Nobody, least of all me, had ever said I was the best shot in the world, but with only a moderate crosswind, shooting from a distance that was difficult but still within the weapon's accurate range, and using an outstanding scope, I figured I could do it.

The difficulty was going to be rapidly tracking from one guard to the next, locking on and then firing. I was also worried about the crowd once the first guy – and more especially the second one – fell. They would realize then that something was happening and I was worried they would start to move and get in the way.

People can certainly be unpredictable, let alone with dozens of them already in distress and the others desperate to help the woman and her kids, but I had no control over what they did and I knew I would have to play it as it came. Therefore it was with some anxiety – both about my own abilities and the crowd – that I lowered myself to the ground. I shifted myself until I was comfortable and adjusted my makeshift silencer. Only then did I jam the rifle into my shoulder, slip the safety off, look through the scope and see the scene in perfect resolution.

A wave of anger washed over me. The older sister – the six-year-old – had somehow manoeuvred herself and her chain in such a way that, spreadeagled on the ground and face down in the dust, she had reached out and succeeded in just touching her sister's outstretched hand, clearly doing whatever she could to comfort the crying girl.

The mother, too, had changed position: she was sitting up, still weeping, but gesticulating to her children, urgently trying to get them to move apart. Understandably, the younger girl wouldn't listen, refusing to let go of her sister's fingers.

Then, through the scope, I saw the reason for the mother's alarm – the guard with the gold tooth had left his hillock and, his rifle at the ready, was pushing through the crowd. Terrified, they parted and he strode towards the two children—

The mother started calling even louder, begging the kids to let go. The grandfather was on his knees, facing the crucifix, yelling to the children to separate.

As I watched, Gold Tooth took three more strides, raised his foot and kicked the younger girl's wrist hard, breaking her grip and forcing the girls' fingers apart. He picked up the chain securing the older sister and yanked it, hauling her backwards through the dust until she was completely separated from her mother and sibling.

He pulled the stake anchoring the other end of the chain out of the ground, walked closer to the base of the cross, and under the feet of the child's dead father, drove it into the earth: nobody would be touching anyone's hand any more. He checked his work, turned towards the crushed family and pointed at their water dishes, obviously ordering them to drink: there was no way he was going to let them die fast.

Watching through the scope, I saw that he had turned slightly towards me and was standing completely still as he waited for the three of them to lift their bowls and drink. The crosshairs of my scope were square on his chest. It wasn't the way I had planned or imagined it; I wanted the three guards close together so I could track between them fast and put them all down in seconds. But here we were—

Just one tiny squeeze, a fragment of time . . . ten pounds of finger pressure . . . half a lifetime of training and experience had brought me to this place and this moment . . . and I couldn't help but question if my life had been spared in the canyon for a reason . . . maybe the faint sound of gunfire was imagination . . . or perhaps, like a strange silence engulfing the world, it meant something more. It would to one family who had nothing left, not even hope . . .

I pulled the trigger.

I missed Gold Tooth's chest. Maybe the wind was stronger than I had assessed or had changed direction slightly, perhaps my finger was too tight and I jerked instead of squeezed, more likely I didn't inhale and hold my breath but was so angry I fired on the exhale; whatever the reason, the barrel must have lifted slightly.

It was enough to not only miss his chest but his throat, too. Instead, it hit him in the mouth. I don't think it was possible to observe it – it was probably just my imagination again – but I swear to God, or Allah, I saw the gold tooth explode.

A fraction of a second later, almost every organ in his head was being torn apart. Because I was firing from a point substantially higher than him, the bullet went through his mouth in a downward trajectory, severing the spinal cord and exiting out of the back of his neck. The average head weighs about twelve pounds, and now Gold Tooth's, robbed of its support from the spinal column, was hurled backwards and came to rest halfway down his back. His head attached only by shreds of muscle, he was almost decapitated by the time he hit the ground.

The crowd, in shock, stared at the falling body. The rifle hadn't made a sound, and silence fell across the intersection – nobody could understand what had happened. Everyone had been watching Gold Tooth, terrified of what he might do next when – out of nowhere – he was a bloodied mess collapsing silently into the dirt.

I was thankful to see that the other two guards weren't even aware their comrade was dead. I tracked the rifle fast, raising the elevation to pull the hillock into frame. Through the scope I saw that the youngest of the trio was still dozing under a makeshift awning, while his comrade – with his back to the intersection, making more tea – suddenly stopped and turned, probably wondering about the abrupt silence.

He registered their leader lying on the ground in a pool of blood and scrambled immediately for his rifle, which was propped against a rockface. I had to shoot fast – it was imperative I killed both of them before they could grab a phone and call the canyon for help.

By good fortune, the Teamaker had made a mistake by trying to reach his weapon – as if that was going to help when he didn't know what had happened. No matter what brutality he might have perpetrated in Syria and Iraq, it was amateurish of him. A professional would have followed the iron rule: safety first, weapon later.

His momentary delay in getting to cover gave me the chance to hold him in the crosshairs, but even so, he was still moving, scrambling, as I fired. He must have crouched – or my aim was off again – so I hit him higher than I had intended, taking a chunk out of the top of his chest and throat. From the torrent of blood spraying from his neck, I figured the bullet had severed the carotid artery, giving him about three seconds of life left.

He collapsed to the ground, but I was already swinging the sight off him to locate the guard who had been dozing under the awning. I found him quickly, but he was on his feet now. Either more experienced or far more panicked than his comrade, he wasn't worrying about a weapon, he was running for cover.

He sprinted across the tiny encampment towards a jumble of boulders, but as he passed their supplies his hand grabbed a backpack large enough to hold a sat phone, batteries and charger. I didn't panic, I had him in the crosshairs, dead to rights. I started to squeeze.

A face jumped into frame right in front of me.

It was the grandfather. Even though there had been no sound of gunfire, he had probably realized that somebody was shooting and had leapt up from his knees, about to plunge down the hill to the only thing that mattered to him: his daughter and grandkids.

His face appeared huge in the sight, directly between me and Sleeping Man, giving the terrorist cover. My finger froze just in time to avoid blowing the old man's head off.

Three relatively straightforward shots had turned into a crisis. I had maybe two seconds to kill the terrorist before he could use the phone. Throwing the blankets aside, I leapt to my feet, trying to change the angle and get a clear shot.

The grandfather was still in frame and Sleeping Man's torso was already behind a boulder, so all I could see was his legs and feet as he dragged them in behind him. It was barely a target – I had a fraction of a second, I had to take the shot. Standing upright, I fired, bracketing four rounds, and saw at least one of them blast into Sleeping Man's legs.

He screamed and sat up to grab his shattered right knee and try to stem the bleeding. A part of his torso momentarily emerged from behind the boulder—

I fired again, four more, a tight group, saw chips and sparks fly off the boulder and at least one hit him in the chest. He slumped forward, exposing more of himself, and I fired another four, then four more in tight groups, and was certain at least three had hit him somewhere above the waist.

I stopped and kept watching through the scope: there was no movement from him, and then I saw a large stream of blood emerge from beside the rock.

I lowered the rifle, breathing hard, my mouth dry, sweat running in rivulets down my face. Exhausted, I looked over at the intersection and saw that the grandfather had made his way through the crowd and was kneeling beside Gold Tooth's body.

He tore a set of keys off his blood-stained bandolier, scrambled to his daughter and unlocked the padlock securing the chain to her ankle. Tenderly, he lifted her to her feet and held her tight to his chest – he might have been elderly, she might have been a married woman and a mother, but she was, and always would be, his daughter.

Together they turned and hurried to release the younger daughter. The child fell into her mother's arms, crying, as the grandfather rushed to the older child, the one who had been so brave, and undid the padlock. He lifted her up and carried her towards her mother.

The family, restored to life, held each other, looking like a scene painted by an Old Master: the woman in black, the grey-bearded grandfather, his clothes the colour of the earth, the two children clinging to their mother, all of them forming a perfect tableau under the figure of a crucified man, the wind blowing dust across the arid landscape and the sun now just a tiny sliver above the hills.

They continued to stand motionless, and it made me worried. 'Run,' I said to them in my head. 'They'll be coming, somebody will tell 'em. Run – get to the Afghan border.'

I wondered why others weren't yelling at them too, but when I looked at the crowd I saw that nobody was focused on the family, they were staring in my direction: once I had been forced to stand, the shots had become audible and they had pinpointed my location.

I didn't know if they could actually see me – maybe there was still enough of the setting sun behind me to prevent it – but if they could, they would have been looking at a stranger, a traveller by the look of his clothes, standing alone on the ridge-line, silhouetted against the sunset, his body criss-crossed by the shadows from the branches above and cradling an ancient AK-47 in his hands. Why he had shot the three guards must have been a mystery to them and, in all likelihood, would remain so for ever.

A member of the crowd, a man in his twenties, tall and handsome with something military in his bearing – a soldier – walked towards the cross. He bent down, picked up Gold Tooth's rifle and looked up at me. He lifted the rifle past his chest and punched it high into the air.

It was a salute, and he kept it raised as all the men clapped their hands high above their heads. Standing alone in the twilight, looking down, I couldn't help but wonder if they would have felt the same way had they known the stranger on the ridge was a former US military officer and a spy for what they had been told was the Great Satan.

I like to think it wouldn't have changed a thing; that the gulf of language, culture and politics that divided us had been bridged, at least momentarily, by a common humanity.

I raised my rifle above my head in acknowledgement and discovered that, at least in silhouette, they could see me – a cheer went up from the intersection. The Soldier holding Gold Tooth's weapon lowered it and the crowd exploded into activity – heading back into the bazaars, gathering up their children and lighting the cooking fires. Among them I saw the grandfather hurry his daughter and her children to several small ponies and immediately head towards the most distant road, the one that led – eventually – to Afghanistan.

They had to start running for their lives. In a couple of minutes, I would do the same.

44

I PICKED UP FOUR LEATHER WATER POUCHES, A SATCHEL OF FOOD and the cooking implements that I had kept with me, slung them over one shoulder and the rifle over the other, and started looking for a secluded hollow. I knew that I would not be able to carry the food – I had to move fast and travel as light as possible – and it might be days before I could eat again.

It had to be done now, and fifteen minutes later, off the beaten track, deep in some underbrush, I found what I was looking for: a grove of trees surrounding a small clearing with a jumble of rocks that would mask the glow of a fire in the darkening night.

Working fast, I cooked the food – carrying prepared rations for my journey would have been a certain giveaway – and was just starting to wolf down a poor excuse for curry and rice, desperate to get under-way, when I heard footfall, little more than a fragment of movement, in the brush behind me. I kept eating, not showing by any of my actions or body language that I had heard something. Maybe it was an animal, but I didn't think so, and that suspicion was confirmed when I heard a rustle of clothing, coming closer still. It was exactly how experienced fighters, men from the Army for example, would approach a target, and I knew there would be others moving in from different directions—

I laid my tin plate down, being as natural as I could, reached un-hurriedly for a pouch of water to take a drink, ignored it at the last moment, shot my hand past it in a blur, grabbed the AK-47 with my outstretched fingers, body-rolled out of the firelight and into the undergrowth, came to a halt on my stomach and had the rifle at my shoulder, on full automatic, aiming at the location of the footfall, about to pull the trigger. When—

'Drop the gun,' a voice ordered, first in Farsi and then in Arabic, from behind where I was lying. I had been right: it was well organized and professionally done. They had approached my temporary camp from different directions in the gathering darkness, that was for sure, but what I hadn't realized was that the footfall and the rustle of clothing had been a diversion to distract me from the real danger, something that lay in exactly the opposite direction. It had not been my only mistake – I had assumed that the terrorists waiting to ambush me in the canyon would take several hours to reach the crossroads and I would be safe for that length of time; what I had not anticipated, I figured, was that there would be another Army patrol in the area or that men had been sent to reinforce the three guards at the crucifix.

I had no choice but to comply with the order, and I pushed the rifle aside.

'Roll to your right three times,' the voice behind me said, continuing in Arabic. He was making sure I was out of reach of the weapon, and I followed the instruction.

'Hands on your head and rise to a kneeling position,' he said. I scrambled on to my knees and, being unarmed and virtually immobilized, my captors did exactly as I expected: they started to emerge from the rocks and trees, about a dozen of them in all.

I stared at them, disbelief mixed with shock. Even in the wan firelight, I recognized several of them; they had been among the crowd gathered at the crucifixion.

'You can pick up your rifle,' the voice behind me said. I pivoted and saw that it was the Soldier, the man who had taken possession of Gold Tooth's rifle. He smiled. 'After what we saw you do to the guards, none of us felt like being shot when we approached. We decided we had to disarm you first – sorry.'

'No trouble,' I said, overwhelmed by relief, recovering my weapon and at a complete loss as to what they wanted.

The Soldier, clearly their leader and the architect of the visit, motioned to his colleagues to douse the fire. 'The flames aren't the problem,' he explained. 'They have dogs, though, and if the wind is in the right direction they'll smell the smoke. Just like we did.'

Dogs, I thought – that was a bad surprise. Being in an Islamic country, I hadn't considered it; for reasons concerning their religion, devout Muslims do not keep dogs as pets. But there was no restriction – as I recalled now – on using them for other purposes. Hunting, for example.

'Thank you,' I said, indicating the extinguished fire and watching as another one of the men discarded my curry and replaced it with a steaming mound of aromatic rice and several ladles of what I figured was goat-meat stew. It was, without doubt, the best food they could offer and had been carried up in special containers from their camp near the bazaar.

Two of the visitors – older men, Bedouin tribesmen maybe, highly experienced in the ways of the desert by the look of them – were filling special water skins that were far more lightweight than my leather pouches and would almost double what I could carry.

'We guessed you would have to abandon any packhorses – they are too easily seen and tracked. Your only chance is on foot and, in case you don't know it, thirst and injury will kill you very fast out here. Take off your shoes.'

'What?'

'Take them off,' he repeated, motioning a grey-bearded man forward. He was holding several pairs of sandals, identical to those which several of the men were wearing. 'They are made by a craftsman in the bazaar,' the Soldier explained. 'The best you'll ever find.

'They're meant for the rough terrain here, comfortable and impossible to destroy. You can climb canyon walls in them, and believe me you'll be doing that – to even have a chance you have to go where their four-wheel drives and half-tracks can't follow.'

I nodded; I had already thought of that. With my shoes off, Grey-Beard was fitting different sandals, selecting the best size and ready to use a long knife to adapt them. I turned to the Soldier, indicating the other men. 'You all know who I am?' I asked.

'Of course,' he replied. 'You're an anonymous traveller, a solitary man on a trail who saw a chance to help some children and their mother. Unfortunately, we couldn't see anything else, the setting sun made it impossible. Then you vanished.' He smiled again.

'Did you know him, the man they crucified?' I asked.

'Not really,' he replied. 'People had seen him at the bazaar, passing through. He was always travelling, they said, but nobody knew where or why. He was alive when they brought him here – barely. They'd tortured him and dragged him off the back of a flatbed on a blanket.

'Five of us – friends – were here with our families.' He indicated men who were ranged around the small clearing. 'We were buying supplies and ammunition when they ordered us outside and told us to dig a foundation for the cross. They had brought it with them, even heavier than the sins of a non-believer,' he said, and smiled again, gently. 'They laid the cross and the victim down beside us and we dug—'

'You said he was still alive,' I said. 'Did he talk, say anything?'

'Cursed a lot, even though he was very weak,' the Soldier replied. 'He said his cousin was also a member of the Army – he had overheard him speaking to his wife and had betrayed him.'

It rocked me – sold out and crucified by a member of your own family? Sometimes there seemed to be no end to the evil in the world.

'He kept saying that everything he had done was for his family,' the Soldier continued. 'From where he was lying, he could see his wife and daughters, and every few minutes, he would try and call out and tell them he was sorry.'

Just imagining it was harrowing enough and I forced the narrative forward. 'Did he say anything about a meeting?' I asked.

'There was a moment when he looked at us and said, if a traveller came, to tell him that everything he had told them was true. Every word.'

I thought for a moment of the photograph on the cigarette paper, the information about a spectacular and the date – all the things we had thought might be an attempt to goose the price – and I was certain that a man tortured and about to be crucified would have no reason to lie.

'He said he was due to meet someone within a few hours,' the Soldier continued. 'But that can't have been true – he must have been rambling, because nobody has arrived. We have no idea who that could be.' He raised an ironic eyebrow at me.

I smiled. 'Did he say anything about a plan, a time and place? A foreign city, or cities maybe?' I fought to keep my voice calm and measured, but I was desperate, trying to salvage anything I could.

The Soldier shook his head. 'He was close to death, then they started to roll him on to the cross. This time he really was rambling – he said there was a town in India where evil had come on the wind, a place of never-ending tragedy.'

'What?' I said, immediately alert. 'A town in *India*?'

'Like I said, he was really rambling,' the Soldier replied. 'It was nearly all about his family, trying to say goodbye. They already had him on the cross, so then they nailed his hands and feet to it and raised it upright. You saw the rest.'

'What a strange thing to say,' I said, virtually to myself. I had finished the goat stew and Grey-Beard had finalized fitting and adjusting the sandals. 'Evil had come on the wind?'

'We must go,' the Soldier said, motioning to his colleagues to pick up their weapons and equipment. 'As you are not here, we can't say farewell, can we?'

We both smiled. 'I know you are not of the Faith,' he continued, more serious. 'But allow me anyway – *barak Allahu feek*. May Allah's blessings be upon you.'

'*Wa feeka*. And on you, too,' I said by way of response. He turned, motioned to the others, and I watched in silence as they faded into the night.

Standing in the darkness, reality closed in on me: there was nothing now, no mission worthy of the name, only the words of a dying man. How could a town in India, a place of never-ending tragedy, he had said, be a target or offer any clue to a terrorist attack in the West?

45

I STARTED GATHERING MY FEW POSSESSIONS TOGETHER, THANKFUL for the decent food and the lightweight water skeins, but with nothing else to alleviate my sense of impending doom.

Deep inside one of the most hostile countries in the world, I knew I had no hope of getting back to the safety of the Pakistani border, a fact I had been aware of since the moment I had decided to try and help the mother and her children.

I would have had to travel the huge distance on foot, been forced to avoid every track and cross endless miles of arid terrain without food or water. Even worse, once the Army heard of the events at the intersection – in about an hour's time, by my guess – they would know who was responsible and would flood the zone with foot patrols, four-wheel drives, drones and now – I had learned – their dogs.

I knew enough after years of being tracked and pursued that if I was going to survive, my only realistic option was to call for help: I had to be exfiltrated as fast as possible.

A phone would have been the answer, of course; I could have made an encrypted call to the agency, but there was no point in thinking about that, I told myself – I couldn't rectify what had been done. Lacking any form of communication, as far as I could see there was only one hope of getting a message out to Langley.

To that end, I crouched down and consulted the crown prince. Because the watch was designed for the Muslim world, it had a display around the edge of the dial that indicated the time for each of the five daily prayers. It told me that dawn was eleven hours away. It meant I had twelve hours and nineteen minutes to organize everything I needed to get a message to Langley; even if I suffered no setbacks it was going to be incredibly tight.

I raised the telescopic sight to my eye, positioned my finger and activated the mapping function. Within a few seconds I found what I was looking for and saw that I had to set a course almost due south.

I was heading overland, back to the Plateau of White Stones. If I could make it there, maybe I had a chance. Twelve hours and eighteen minutes.

46

IT STARTED OFF AS A BAD NIGHT, THE WORST OF THE ENTIRE MISSION, and rapidly got worse. Running in darkness, falling and stumbling across an uncharted wasteland, I tried to stick to the ridges but countless times I was forced down into canyons and then up rugged hillsides.

Within the first hour my clothes were torn and ripped as a result of encounters with jagged rocks and, on one occasion, having to fight my way through a stretch of thorn-like scrub with the rifle. At least four times I threw myself face first into the dirt, spooked by birds I mistook for drones with night vision or thermal imaging.

Then, just before dawn, guided by the mapping, I finally saw the pylon with its shredded windsock. I dumped my water containers at its base, stripped off my shirt and – using it as a pouch – began to gather as many of the smaller white stones as I could find.

During the endless hours of preparation at Langley, I had not only seen the plateau on electronic maps but had also examined scores of satellite photos of almost my entire route, including a large number of high-definition shots of the area surrounding the plateau. All of the photographs were classified, watermarked with the NSA logo, and clearly imprinted with the details of their origin and the time and date they were taken. As a result, I knew that every day the Afghan-Axis Galileo 4 spy satellite followed a schedule determined by sunrise: it passed over the plateau and its surroundings at exactly one hour and nineteen minutes after dawn.

In normal circumstances, such spy photos might not be looked at for days, but I had one advantage. By not using the phone to upload the daily photo, Langley would have assumed something had gone wrong, and I was certain that the thousands of images from each day's satellite pass would be examined minutely and immediately to try and find either me or my body. In addition, if situations in the past were any guide, the seventh floor would have already alerted all our secret assets in the country to be on standby to try and help if necessary.

First, however, I had to send a message, and then – as they said in those parts, *insha'Allah*, if God wills it – would come the rescue. Time after time, I gathered the stones and dumped them next to the dead-flat section which I and the ponies had crossed several days earlier. When the pile was large enough, and as dawn broke, I walked back to the windsock, took my hourly sip of water and sat down to work out exactly what my message needed to say. That was when I saw the drone.

Battery-operated and silent, I would never have known it was approaching except for the fact that whoever was controlling it flew it along the eastern edge of the old airstrip and the rising sun had caught its fuselage. I was sitting partly in shadow under the windsock and it gave me just enough time to hurl myself forward as it came closer, hugging the earth, thankful that both my clothes and my shirt-less back were so filthy it was as effective as any camouflage.

Out of the corner of my eye I watched it, hoping that I wouldn't see it lose altitude and circle above me. It was with a flood of relief I saw its shadow pass the other side of the windsock and keep going. I counted to twenty and then raised my head to just catch sight of it make a hard left turn and disappear over the edge of the plateau. It didn't mean, however, that the threat was over. From its straight line, constant altitude and sharp turn, I figured it wasn't a random search flight. The unseen operator was flying a grid: sooner or later it would be back, coming in from a different angle.

Drone or no drone, I opened up the mapping function and started to search for a road where one of our Iranian assets might have a chance of picking me up and helping me to cross the border into either Pakistan or Afghanistan. Within a couple of minutes I found a back road – probably little more than a dirt track – that I could reach in two to three days' of hard trekking. In the scorching temperatures, I calculated I had just enough water for three days and nothing more.

The back road, however, connected two provincial towns, meaning that it fed into a wider and more accessible road network, allowing an extraction team to travel fast to meet me. In addition, the map also showed there was a small bridge halfway along that would act as an easily identified rendezvous. I rechecked my calculations, noted down the co-ordinates and ran for the pile of stones.

I had thirty-two minutes until Galileo 4 passed overhead.

47

THE MESSAGE HAD TO BE SIMPLE AND LARGE ENOUGH TO IMMEDIATELY grab the attention of the photo analysts and researchers who would be combing through the photos. I started by spelling out the letters S-O-S.

I had chosen the clearest part of the old runway, confident that the stark white rocks against the parched grass would be legible. It took longer than I had anticipated, though – laying out the stones chewed through the minutes and so did constantly checking the distant edge of the plateau for the drone.

I had almost finished the next part – M-A-N D-E-A-D – when I made my automatic check of the sky: with the sun slanting across the airstrip, I saw the drone approaching fast.

I threw myself down, lying prone, trying to mask as much as

possible of the message with my body and only lifting my head an inch to check the predator's progress. It was staying to the far edge of the field, flying low, just my side of the dense tree-line, looking at the forest as the operator worked on the assumption – I figured – that anybody on the run would stick to cover and never be out in open country. I lay perfectly still, the stones I had laid a few minutes before digging into my ribs and groin, making the urge to move almost unbearable, and waited to see – barely breathing – if it turned towards me.

Lying face down, watching the drone flying along the tree-line, knowing that if it was going to see me and change direction it would be any minute now, I couldn't help but think about what had happened at the intersection. I had no doubt it would have been easier to turn my back on the kids and head for the border, so I suppose it was only natural, given my perilous situation, to ask myself if it had been a mistake. With the drone coming closer, I thought about the life I had wanted to live and the Navy ships I'd always hoped to command, when I recalled something my mother had told me when I was a child. It hadn't crossed my mind in twenty-five years, but I guess it had taken root somewhere and was waiting for its moment in the sun.

Mom was not well educated, but, as I have said, she was a devout woman, and there was only one public figure she had ever admired unreservedly: Martin Luther King. She was barely a teenager when she heard Dr King speak in front of a quarter of a million people at the Lincoln Memorial in Washington and that experience had never left her; she told me about that day more times than I can recount and she knew his famous 'I have a dream . . .' speech almost by heart.

But it was a quite different address of his that she told me about one scorching day at the end of a Florida summer, sitting on the back porch with the twilight coming in and watching the fireflies, a ten-year-old boy and his mother, easy in each other's company. 'You know why I respected the reverend so much?' she asked quietly. 'Because of a simple lesson he taught. He said that if most people saw a man being attacked in the street, they would ask themselves: what will happen to me if I get involved?

'But Dr King said that was the wrong question,' she continued. 'The real question was this: what will happen to the man if I don't? I want you to always remember that.'

What will happen to the man if I don't? I recalled. No, I had no regrets about the children.

The wind was growing stronger, swirling grit into my eyes, but I couldn't blink or move. The drone was directly parallel to me, passing in and out of the shadows cast by the trees – if it was going to turn towards me, it had to be now.

It continued to fly forward. Slowly, I let myself breathe again. Its reappearance had cost me valuable time, but I didn't move until I was convinced it was out of sight. Then I scrambled up and checked my watch: nine minutes to the satellite. Running now, no time to grab a water pouch and wash the grit from my eyes, I finished the message with two minutes to spare. In the middle of the old landing strip, standing beside the white stones and their message, I quickly stripped off my headdress and the rest of my legend's outfit, getting down to just a pair of chinos. I tilted my face upwards and stared into the sky.

I had to ensure that when the satellite photographed me, they would be able to see my face and identify me, but I knew they would also lift a host of other bodily measurements from the photos. They would then run a full suite of biometrics – height, width of the chest – to make certain that I wasn't an impostor and they weren't falling into some kind of trap.

Duress, I suddenly thought in a panic – knowing how paranoid the agency was, I figured they would worry that there might be men hidden among the trees with weapons trained on me and that, unarmed, I was only acting under duress. A minute to go. I ran hard for the windsock, grabbed the rifle – and the water bags – and returned to my spot. Bare-chested, staring high into the sky, thinking about Galileo 4 spinning closer, holding the rifle at the hip, ready to fire, the safety off and the magazine loaded, probably looking like some strange prophet or – more likely – a madman, I counted down.

I hit zero. I may have made it to the appointed time, but I had no idea how long the satellite would be overhead and I wanted to give myself every chance, especially as I had no certainty that the prince was as accurate as he claimed to be.

For a further four minutes I stood there, immobile and exposed, imagining what would unfold at Langley in a few short minutes. I knew that the first thing would be an encrypted phone call from the NSA saying, in their usual understated way, that they had just received some interesting photos. Then all hell would break loose.

48

DUE TO A UNIQUE CIRCUMSTANCE, IT WAS MADELEINE O'NEILL WHO witnessed more of that night's events at Langley than anyone, and it was certainly her who gave the clearest account of them.

She told me later that she had been working late, alone in her office, that evening. With no photos from me since I had crossed the border, she had been told to drill into her files and try to find a lead on anybody along my route – apart from the Army of the Pure – who might have either killed me or was holding me captive. Kidnap for ransom was a definite possibility – apart from drugs, it was about the only growth industry in the entire region. Madeleine said that in the absence of any photos or demand for money, the view within the agency was that I had run into trouble almost immediately and was dead.

Just before 10 p.m. she heard the door at the end of the corridor outside her office open and the sound of a man running. She opened her door in time to see Buster Glover with a phone to his ear.

'They've found him. He's alive!' Buster yelled at the head of research, who was in the corridor, about to go home. 'They want you in the conference room now.' The head of research just stared at the assistant director then wordlessly turned and unlocked his door.

Buster saw Madeleine and took a moment to catch his breath. 'NSA's got satellite photos from ten minutes ago,' he said, gasping. 'He's standing on an old airfield or something.'

He turned to go but changed his mind. 'Get down to the conference room, too,' he said. 'Falcon can't locate either of his executive assistants and is screaming blue murder. He sent 'em home an hour ago, but don't tell him that. After what you did with the legend, he'll be glad to see you.'

As a result, Madeleine found herself acting as a makeshift liaison between the director, CIA departments, several of the agency's foreign stations, the NSA and the Director of National Intelligence.

She sprinted down the corridor, and by the time she entered the underground conference room the area was once again functioning as a war room with a host of personnel in place. Amid the chaos, Madeleine saw Falcon standing at the far end of the room and was

120

mildly shocked. The ever-present jacket was thrown aside, he had the top button of his dress shirt undone, the Hermès tie was loose, his gold cufflinks had been pocketed and he was rolling his starched French cuffs up to his elbows.

Margaret, the senior intelligence analyst known for her cynicism, had also just entered the room. She took a drag on her vape and stared at Falcon. 'What the—' she said. 'Any minute now, he'll kick off the Gucci loafers and put on combat boots.'

Clearly, Falcon was going operational for the first time in years, and Madeleine watched as he issued command after command, calling in support from every other silo of Washington power. In his decisiveness and coolness under pressure, she said later that she saw in him not just the highly polished intelligence bureaucrat but all the hallmarks of the courageous young agent who had floored the accelerator in Iran and earned such a huge reputation.

He turned, caught sight of Madeleine standing near the door and motioned her forward.

'Buster Glover said I might be able to help,' she explained.

'You sure can,' Falcon replied. 'First thing – find out what happened to the damn EAs.'

'You sent them home, but Buster said not to mention that,' Madeleine responded.

Falcon looked at her for a moment, surprised – I think he had grown accustomed to being treated with nothing but deference. Then he gave her a good-natured smile. 'He's a very intelligent man, Buster. You might be well advised to take his advice in future.'

Madeleine laughed, but Buster himself was approaching through the crowd, the phone once again at his ear. He stopped in front of Falcon. 'First photos are coming through,' he said. The lights dimmed and everyone turned to face the IMAX screens.

Apparently, I emerged out of the darkness in full 16k resolution, standing shirtless on the airfield half a world away, my image repeated on a dozen screens around the room.

Margaret wolf-whistled, and that brought a burst of laughter as everybody started cheering: I was alive and they had found me. Falcon called immediately for silence, not willing to take anything at face value.

He turned to Buster: 'Run the biometrics not just on his face, on his body too. Despite what Margaret obviously believes, he's got his shirt off so that we can confirm it's him. Thank God he's thinking—'

The photo on the screens was replaced by a different shot, in even better resolution, thanks to the position of the satellite. It showed me holding the rifle at the hip with one hand and pointing at the telescopic sight with the other.

'Is the safety off?' Falcon demanded of the photo experts camped out in the corner.

'Off,' one of them replied after a moment's discussion with his team.

'Magazine full?' Falcon asked.

'Breech is open, shell in the chamber. Magazine appears full,' the photo expert replied.

'Good,' Falcon said, the whole room watching him. 'He's telling us he's not under duress. He's locked, loaded, ready to fire.'

'But what's with the scope?' Buster asked.

'I think he's saying he's going to use the mapping device . . . maybe that he can find his way somewhere.' Falcon was thinking out loud. 'He needs our help . . . so he's . . .'

Buster raised the phone, listened and then: 'Okay, bring it up.' He was speaking to the control room and turned to Falcon. 'There's a message in the next batch of photos—'

Before he could say any more, it was on the screen. Everybody stared, looking at what I'd laid out in white stone. Falcon paraphrased it: 'SOS. The courier's dead. Part of a co-ordinate and then the letters SFGG.'

For the first time he looked worried. He turned to half a dozen mapping experts sitting at a group of tables with computer screens and stacks of paper charts in front of them. 'He's trying to set a rendezvous,' Falcon said. 'Is one part of a co-ordinate enough? Can you work out a location with that?'

'No,' the senior expert said. 'It's just one plotting point; we need another reference. Does he give any other information?'

Falcon shook his head, walked forward and stood right in front of the nearest screen, staring at the white stones. 'What the hell does SFGG mean?'

Nobody had an answer. The euphoria that had run through the room for the last few minutes was evaporating. Without the precise location of a rendezvous, there was nothing the agency could do. 'SFGG . . .' Falcon repeated, barely above a whisper.

'Why not just give us the whole damn co-ordinate?' Buster asked out of frustration.

'Because he's smart,' Falcon said, half lost in thought, trying to imagine what the letters meant. 'He must have figured the Army might arrive at any moment. Say he gave the whole co-ordinate, still managed to escape and they saw the message. He could never use the rendezvous. They'd just go and find him there, so he put it in code.'

'And he thought we'd be clever enough to work it out,' Margaret added.

'Maybe he got that part wrong,' Falcon said, continuing to look intently at the screen as if the letters themselves might give the answer. Everybody else did the same, ideas half forming in thirty heads and being discarded.

'If he can't use map co-ordinates,' Falcon said, 'something in the landscape, recognizable perhaps. A landmark?' He looked around the room.

'A mountain, river . . .' Buster suggested. 'Topographical?'

Falcon nodded. 'Yes, like that.' But it didn't seem to help. He was still standing in front of the screen, staring at the letters. 'SF,' he said.

'San Francisco?' Buster asked. 'It is one of his favourite cities. When we did the farewell thing, he said that's where he would see me.'

Falcon turned and looked at him. 'Maybe he thought you'd remember that.' He looked again at the letters. 'San Francisco . . . Golden Gate,' he said in triumph. 'A bridge!'

Everyone took a moment to absorb it, then Buster turned fast to the mapping team. 'Is there a bridge anywhere near the co-ordinate?' he demanded.

The room seemed to freeze as everyone waited for the group at the side tables to scan charts and enter data into their computers. 'Got it!' the leader said. 'It's two days' hike at least, maybe three, cross-country. It's wooden, over a dry riverbed, twenty yards long—'

Whatever else he said got lost as the satellite image of a broken-down bridge appeared on the screen and the room exploded into cheers. Falcon spoke above the hubbub, addressing the mapping team and the mission planners.

'We know where he is and where he's going. I need four proposals – how do we get him out?'

The dozen men and women nodded. Falcon, looking again at the photos of me and the bridge, spoke to Madeleine and Buster. 'Three days' hike,' he said quietly. 'If he hasn't got enough water, in those temperatures . . . that could be a problem.'

49

EIGHT HOURS LATER, WITH DAWN BREAKING, SITTING IN THE underground conference room, pale with fatigue, his elegant clothes crumpled, Falcon decided on the plan.

The one he chose from the four proposals featured the two hall-marks of most successful intelligence operations: it was fast and relatively simple. It also seemed, at least at the outset, to have been blessed by good fortune. That piece of luck was the direct result of the West's inability to contain the Iranian nuclear programme. As potentially catastrophic as that failure was, it meant that the CIA had more human assets inside Iran than in almost any other hostile country.

Langley had spent years assembling those networks, and while I was starting my long hike to get to the bridge, Falcon had dozens of Iranian collaborators, agents-in-place, paid informers and a wide-spread contingent of Blackwater contractors that he could use. Without them, I don't think he would have even tried to launch a rescue mission and a few months later an empty casket would have been lowered into a grave in Washington.

After listening to the planners explain the proposals and asking a series of rapid-fire questions, Falcon had stood in thought for a long moment. 'We have to ask ourselves – what are we really doing here?' he said rhetorically. 'We're launching Uber – Iran's first ride-hailing service,' he continued. 'Our agent gets picked up at the bridge and five hours later he gets dropped off at the Afghan border.

'Three of these,' he said, pointing at displays on the walls, 'are too complex; they rely on a series of events going exactly right. That never happens, at least not in any intelligence mission I've ever known.

'That one is straightforward,' he said, pointing at a plan on the screen that featured the faces of two men. 'They're both in-country and they both have jobs where they'll barely be missed for three or four days. One of them is a skilled driver who has been in plenty of tight situations and the other one has comms and computer skills that will probably be more than useful. We go with them.'

The men on the screen were both in their thirties or older, and while the national identity cards they were holding might have shown them to be Iranians, they were – in fact – foreign citizens.

'Blackwater operatives?' Margaret asked.

'Yeah,' replied one of the mission planners.

Blackwater, formed forty years ago by two Navy SEALs, was, and still is, a sprawling corporation. It is not widely known to the public because it has changed names and ownership many times, but in the secret world it is always referred to as Blackwater, a nod to the 'Great Dismal Swamp' in North Carolina where it built its first training facility.

Originally established to provide expert security for US diplomats and officials in war zones and similar locations, it eventually grew its operations by signing a contract to provide classified services to the CIA. Several years later, it expanded further – heading into much darker waters – by setting up a worldwide mercenary-for-hire business.

There was never any shortage of recruits – the huge salaries Blackwater offered attracted everyone from veterans of obscure African wars to a number of former CIA agents, Army Delta Force troops and Navy SEALs. Men – and a scattering of women – enlisted from wherever military or intelligence training was available, repre-senting over forty nations. 'You know what Blackwater is?' Falcon told me once. 'It's the French Foreign Legion on steroids.'

Like most people at the agency, he didn't like the corporation – he thought at least half their contractors were cowboys – but he particu-larly disliked the fact that both his agency and the US government spent huge amounts of time and money on training only to see many of its agents and troops leave for salaries they could never hope to match. Nonetheless, it was a testament to Falcon – and his determin-ation to exfiltrate me – that he didn't allow his feelings to affect his operational judgement. He turned to Madeleine: 'Call Blackwater and tell 'em those two are our joes now; we'll be running them for five days. Yeah, I know what their first question will be – say we'll work out the fee later.'

As Madeleine started to contact a senior executive of Blackwater, she watched as files, photographs and other classified details about the two men appeared on the screens: Falcon was calling up all the data, starting to plan the rescue mission in minute detail.

The first photo showed the man who would be in charge, the one doing the driving. The name on his passport and identity papers said he was Javid Ghorbani, forty-five years old and employed as an orderly at the Baghiyyatollah al-Azam Military Hospital in a suburb of Tehran and the go-to medical facility for officers of the Revolutionary Guard. In an alternate reality, he was James Wilkinson, son of a divorced American father and an Iranian mother, a man who had trained as a CIA security officer and whose responsibilities had included protecting travelling VIPs. A big, muscled guy with cold eyes, sharp reflexes and an aggressive personality, he showed an aptitude while driving an armoured SUV during a gig in Baghdad and soon specialized as a wheelman, completing the toughest evasive driving courses in the world.

He had ended up leaving the CIA amid accusations of domestic violence and hard drinking in bars in Dubai – places with names like the Cyclone Club and Ratsky's, where the women were only marginally more expensive than the cocktails – but with his knowledge of Farsi and Gulf Arabic, Blackwater contacted him immediately. They retrained him in intelligence-gathering, created a fake identity and embedded him in the hospital. Pretty soon he discovered how much information you could pick up – and the money you could earn – when you were emptying bedpans and mopping floors.

Madeleine, waiting for Blackwater to answer, saw on the screen that the driver's proposed wingman was Bahman Avesta, aged in his mid thirties, a skinny, highly strung man whose parents had fled Tehran during the 1978 revolution and established a new life for themselves and their young family in London.

A good student, Bahman studied computer science at Imperial College and, having been raised in a household where Farsi was the language of choice and hatred of the ayatollahs was palpable, he was an easy mark for Blackwater. They equipped him with a new identity, sent him to Tehran, and he set up his own small computer repair shop on Mirdamad Boulevard. Under that cover, he encrypted and transmitted whatever intelligence Javid and a dozen others like him acquired. If he was caught, or his equipment uncovered, he would have been just one more body dangling from a construction crane in a public square; no wonder he looked nervous, Madeleine thought.

She connected with the Blackwater executive, told him – without

126

explaining why – that the agency needed the services of the two con-tractors and hung up. Once more, she looked at the images of the two men who, in another few hours, would start a wild, thousand-mile dash from Tehran to try and rescue me.

What she didn't know, what nobody at Langley knew, was that as Ghorbani's Toyota made its way towards the old bridge, there weren't two people on board. There were three.

50

ONCE I WAS CERTAIN THAT THE SATELLITE HAD PASSED OVERHEAD, I spent fifteen minutes scattering the white stones and destroying my carefully constructed message.

As dangerous as it was to spend any time out in the open, I wasn't going to leave the Army a clue – they might have been many terrible things, but they weren't incompetent, and I knew the worst thing I could do would be to underestimate their code-breaking skills. If Langley could decipher it, so could they.

Only when the message was fully destroyed did I pick up the rifle and water pouches and head for the trees on the long journey to reach the dilapidated bridge. By any measure, it was a bad journey into that first night: I walked, climbed and stumbled for mile after mile, sticking to the cover of trees or deep shadow, the temperature hitting the century mark, the earth baking underfoot, the foliage drained of all colour and the heat rising in shimmering waves.

All through the day, even as the sun beat out its fierce tattoo, I rationed myself to two mouthfuls of water every hour, concentrating on the route ahead, trying to ignore the mirages that arose from the featureless landscape: cool oases beckoning on the edge of the hori-zon ... the ruins of Baghdad emerging out of a canyon ... the skyscrapers of Manhattan appearing behind a distant ridge. Finally, they disappeared as the sun faded, but the night brought little relief: I was travelling too slowly, and I knew it.

A few hours after darkness fell – as in every arid environment – the bone-chilling cold set in and I wrapped my clothes tight around my body, checked the GPS every forty minutes to make sure I was still on track and dispensed with my hourly drinks to save water, sipping only when the thirst became overwhelming. Although I plunged on through the night, twice I was too exhausted to take another step, found a place hard against a hillside to protect me from the wind and slept for a few hours. After the second such interlude my path took me high on to a ridge and in the moonlight, looking back across the route I had travelled, I saw a sweep of valleys and plains. Three lights, widely separated, were flickering like beacons, and the way they danced told me they were campfires blowing in the wind. In all likelihood, they were some of the search parties in four-wheel drives that had undoubtedly been sent out in pursuit. It is notoriously hard to assess distances at night, but I figured they were no more than two hours behind me.

It was even more of an incentive, as if any were needed, for me to keep moving, but it wasn't the pursuers or their dogs that worried me; it was the drones. Luckily, just before daylight, I entered an area of rugged canyons and thicker foliage that provided not only much needed shade but better cover, and while progress was gruelling, I succeeded in staying ahead of the men in the Toyotas for the whole of the day.

By nightfall, however, I was in trouble. I had travelled through the canyons far more slowly than I had planned. With the stars just beginning to appear, safe from any drone and sheltered from a wind more biting than any I had so far encountered, I opened the GPS system and calculated how far I had travelled and the distance that remained.

It confirmed my worst fears: a trek that I had estimated would take two to three days was, thanks to the unforgiving terrain and debilitating heat, turning out to be four days and, probably, five. I looked for an alternative – faster – path to the bridge. There wasn't one. Nor could I speed up; that wasn't a realistic option. Hunger was sending regular spasms into my chest and while I could deal with that, water was in a different league – thank God I had conserved as much as I had, but despite my efforts it was clear that I would drain the last of the pouches by noon the next day.

Already in a bad way, with a dry mouth and a swollen tongue, a craving for sugar and a rapid heartbeat – all symptoms of dehydration – I knew that in another twenty-four hours I would start to hallucinate, become increasingly disoriented, and then, stumbling under a merciless sun, collapse and die of thirst long before I reached the bridge. That analysis wasn't caused by panic or fear – it was, unfortunately, just maths and biology.

I looked at the map again and, as far as I could tell, there was only one alternative: a tiny hamlet tucked into the foothills of a jumble of ragged cliffs. It was so far from my predicted route, I had no information about it, but as it was the only source of water I could reach in time, that was irrelevant. I calculated that at my reduced pace the hamlet was a six-hour hike away, adding a total of half a day to the journey to the bridge.

I looked down at the crown prince and calculated that by allowing six hours for travel I would arrive at the village an hour before dawn – giving me enough time to approach the communal well, fill my water pouches and disappear back into darkness. Clearly there was no time to waste, so I scrambled out from under the rock ledge where I had been sheltering and made my way up a steep cliff, thinking about dogs again. Not those pursuing me; the ones that might be waiting—

According to Islam's second holiest text, the *Hadith* – a record of the sayings of the Prophet Muhammad, Peace be upon Him – 'angels do not enter a house which has a dog in it'. As a result, Muslims do not keep dogs as pets, but in Islam – regrettably, as far as my situation was concerned – there is no prohibition on using them outside to guard a house or village. I knew that a dog's sense of smell is far superior to a human's and I had once read that, under certain circumstances, they can detect a person from twelve miles away. I didn't know if it was true, but given that a guard dog probably presented the greatest danger of raising the alarm, I wasn't willing to risk it. I decided to stop far short of the village, circle around if necessary and make sure I only approached from upwind, keeping the breeze constantly in my face.

That was exactly what I did, but – as it turned out – within moments of finally entering the strange and dark village, guard dogs became the least of my problems.

51

I HAD ARRIVED AT THE HAMLET AN HOUR BEHIND SCHEDULE, JUST AS the eastern sky was starting to lighten.

As a result I was in far greater danger of being seen when, from the cover of a jumble of boulders several hundred yards away, I first caught sight of the huddle of earth-coloured buildings. I unshouldered the rifle and, kneeling in the dirt, looked through the scope.

Located at the base of a small cliff, under assault from wind-driven dust and tumbleweeds, the mud and brick structures were built partly into the rock; a cross between caves and houses. It probably would have appeared impoverished to anyone else, but in my circumstances, I don't think I had seen anywhere that looked more inviting.

Despite my delayed arrival, I was relieved to see there was no movement in the streets and I was confident I had enough time to get in and out unobserved if I moved fast. Crouching, darting between clumps of stunted foliage, taking advantage of the gloom, I passed the wrecks of dozens of four-wheel drives. Graveyards of vehicles were common outside villages throughout that part of the world: Toyotas – they were nearly always Toyotas – were driven into the ground and kept on the road with soldering irons and baling wire until they finally died.

Worthless by then, they were left to rot on the outskirts of the village, where they served as a reservoir of spare parts for any neighbour that needed them. Even so, there were far more of the vehicles than the size of the hamlet seemed to warrant, but I had no time to think any more about it; I had to keep moving. I took cover between two vehicles and used the scope again: there was still no sign of life, but something else took my attention. For the first time, I saw a rickety and rusted steel structure looming above several of the dwellings. Built out of what looked like scaffolding, metal vanes were spinning furiously at the top: it was a windmill, pumping water out of a deep well or an underground aquifer and sustaining the entire village.

I knew where to head now and, hoping that none of the village women were early risers and going to fill buckets for their families, I started to move through what little was left of the darkness, reaching the perimeter of the hamlet and gliding down a narrow alley between mud-brick walls. Behind one of them, I heard a shutter or door bang open and I stopped, wondering if somebody was already up and coming into the street.

Nobody appeared and I heard nothing more, just the wind moaning through the labyrinth of alleys. Maybe if I hadn't been so tired, I might have paid the silence more attention. Instead, I turned a corner and saw – in the middle of a sort of village square – a huge stone trough, the metal blades of the windmill spinning furiously high above, and clear water overflowing its sides and forming pools on the ground.

Deep in the shadow of a house, its foundations on a tilt and the shutters closed tight, I stared at the water for a moment, barely believing it, and then unslung the pouches from my shoulders and scrambled towards it, constantly looking around, worried that at any moment a voice would yell at me in Farsi to stop.

No voice came; there was just the sound of my sandals slapping in the mud as I got closer, closer. I was almost within reach and I cupped one hand, about to plunge it into the trough – and didn't move.

I looked down at the mud and the soil caked around the trough. I must have noticed it as I moved forward, but it didn't register in my conscious mind until now: there were no animal tracks in the crusted soil. Water was overwhelmingly scarce in that environment, but there were no prints from rats, wild pigs or foxes that might have crept in during darkness; nothing even from domestic goats and livestock. Or people, come to that.

Slowly, I looked around at the village – even though dawn was well past, there was still no sign of life. Just the wind and, again, a distant door or shutter banging hard in the gale. There was no washing on a line, not a child's toy in a doorway, smoke from a fire . . .

'I am a traveller,' I called loudly in Arabic. 'I am in need of help.' My voice echoed and re-echoed off the mud walls, but there was no response. It was a dead place and, I suddenly realized, had been dead for years.

I swung back to the trough and my eye fell on a sign, covered in dust, screwed to the bottom of the windmill. I put my hand in the water and started to rub it clean, but stopped – I knew what it would say even though I had barely begun. My hand was stinging and when I looked down I saw red welts and blisters already starting to appear.

The trickles of water running down the sign made the words in Farsi and Urdu legible, but I couldn't translate them. Then the water revealed one more thing: a large skull and crossbones, the international symbol for poison.

52

WITH NO WATER AND STILL – BY MY ESTIMATE – THREE DAYS' TRAVEL to the rendezvous, there was no clear way out now. Determined not to give in to fear or negativity, but unable to decide what to do, I lowered myself on to a stone bench at the side of the square.

I looked down a wide alley to where the rising sun was flooding the landscape and I saw there was no sign in the withered scrub that the land had ever been tamed for agriculture: no broken fences, overgrown fields or wrecked water troughs. Sitting in the silence, I wondered what had sustained the village before the water became undrinkable. There was only one thing I could think of. The hamlet sat deep in the shadow of mountains that were threaded with hidden trails used by smugglers and opium couriers. Water would have always been the traffickers' problem, but the more of it they carried, the less room there was for contraband. I figured that the tiny village with its deep well must have been a godsend – a place where they could re-water before the next stage of their perilous journey, a far more lucrative occupation for the village than subsistence farming.

I looked up at the mountains, still half in shadow, seemingly impassable. What a hopeless task, I thought, for any government trying to locate and intercept the contraband: it would have been a wildly expensive and losing battle until, I realized, they had found a much easier way to strangle the route. Poison the well.

Of course, it would have been devastating for the families in the village – within a few minutes of the helicopters dropping tons of poison down the shaft, they lost both their homes and their livelihoods. All that was left to mark their lives was an uninhabitable village and a graveyard of wrecked vehicles. Now I understood why there were so many of them: the opium arriving down the mountain trails by packhorse would have been transferred into a vehicle and then ferried to the coast. I recalled seeing that more than a few of the vehicles had been adapted to avoid any further government patrols by travelling overland: they were six-wheel drives with specially modified tanks to carry more fuel and—

Whatever was happening to my body, collapsing or not, suddenly didn't matter; my mind was clear. Barely realizing it, I had stood up, and now – running, stumbling – I reached the door of the nearest house, shouldered it open and started to search.

53

THE TEN WATERTIGHT CONTAINERS I HAD LOCATED – BATTERED STEEL buckets, empty plastic bottles and wooden pails lined with goatskin – were now standing among the wrecked vehicles.

I had spent three hours searching the village and the sun was high in the sky by the time I reached the SUV graveyard. Thankfully, it was much cooler once I had slipped into the shade under a Nissan Patrol, a vehicle missing its wheels and doors but conforming to the rules I had set for myself: it was one of the newer vehicles and it appeared to have a completely sealed radiator that would have reduced the chance of the fluid evaporating.

Lying on my back, I had a bucket positioned under its drain plug ready to catch whatever water it contained. All I had to do was unscrew the plug and twice, I tried, but it was corroded permanently in place.

Instead, I took hold of a water hose that was connected to the bottom of the radiator and, using the ivory-handled knife, cut the rubber. A thin, rust-coloured trickle of fluid, reeking of coolant or antifreeze, dribbled out: the radiator must have been cracked and the fluid it once contained had either leaked out or evaporated. I scrambled out and moved to the next vehicle – one of the six-wheelers, a beast of a thing converted from an old Land Rover – that was missing its rear axle but had long-range fuel tanks welded to the back. As soon as I looked under the hood I saw that it had been fitted with a massive subsidiary cooling system.

I grabbed several containers, slid under it and managed to unscrew its drain plug. Obviously far sturdier and probably better built, the radiator had remained completely sealed: gallons of rusty water – containing a proportion of coolant, but water all the same – poured out. I stared at it with overwhelming relief, felt the hours of tension uncoil a notch, and watched as the liquid continued to fill a steel bucket. When it was almost full, I dragged it aside and replaced it with a new container. In spite of my raging thirst, I couldn't even think about taking a sip – not yet.

Nearly every radiator in the world contained about half distilled water and half antifreeze, a mixture designed to keep the engine from overheating even in hot environments like Florida. The problem was that antifreeze – according to the warnings on every bottle – was made from ethylene glycol, a potent poison that was fatal in even small doses if it was swallowed. I would have been a fool to risk drinking anything that had even the slightest chance of containing it. Facing that problem, however, I had one advantage: although many times over the years I had questioned its value, I had a science degree.

It was the result of four years I spent at the US Naval Academy at Annapolis, where, given a huge assist by taking minors in foreign languages, I graduated third in my class. I then made it through Officer Candidate School and, with a commission in my hand, some money in my pocket and a future far more promising than anything I could have imagined in Loxahatchee, bought an old convertible and headed down the coast into the heart of the Old South. Until I met Rebecca, I always thought of it as the best summer of my life.

My destination was Charleston in South Carolina, yet another beautiful city with a dark history: its collection of beautiful ante-bellum mansions and oak trees hung with Spanish moss couldn't hide the fact that it had once been the largest slave port in the world. I crossed the Ashley River and arrived at the Navy's Nuclear Power School – the next step for any young officer who wanted to pursue a career in the submarine service. The status of Nuke School was legendary: it was widely judged to be the toughest course of study in the US military, even more demanding than the Top Gun flight school.

So, lying under a wrecked vehicle in the noon sun, I figured if I could understand the theory and operation of a sub's nuclear reactor, I could build a water distillation system. I would boil the contaminated water in the communal kitchen and use pipes and hoses from the vehicles to direct the clouds of steam on to tilted glass wind-shields, where it would form droplets of water. Having left the rust and antifreeze behind, the droplets of pure water would form tiny trickles and run down the slope into my water pouches.

That was my plan as I crawled out from under the beast, slid beneath a wrecked Toyota, cut the radiator hose and watched another stream of filthy fluid pour into a container—

54

WHILE MY COBBLED-TOGETHER PURIFICATION PROCESS STEAMED away, I rested on a bed I had constructed in the shade outside the kitchen, leaving it only periodically to enter the furnace-like room and refill the iron cauldron with buckets of radiator water.

Once the system had started to work I watched as the first drops made their agonizingly slow journey down the glass and into one of the pouches. Even when there was a cupful, I had to sip slowly, otherwise I would overwhelm my dehydrated organs and leach out whatever salts I had left. Caution notwithstanding, I threw up four times over the next few hours as my body tried to pull itself back to normality, but with rehydration came ravenous hunger. There was nothing I could do about that, but it was obvious I had lost an enormous amount of weight: the pants I was wearing kept slipping down my hips.

I stepped out of them and unlooped the belt I was wearing – a length of aged leather with a silver buckle, a gift from my father, according to my legend. I laid it out and, using the sharp point of the ivory-handled knife, pierced two more holes in the leather so that I could cinch it tighter; if I couldn't eat, at least I wouldn't have to keep hoisting my pants up. In adjusting the belt, however, I noticed that the buckle was breaking free from the strap and I probably would have lost it very soon. I sat down on the bed, cut a narrow strip off my T-shirt and, waiting for the water pouches to fill, used the cotton to perform some battlefield needlework.

I can't say the result was very elegant, but it worked, and though I didn't realize it until days later, that simple act of repairing the belt and buckle would have profound consequences.

55

FOR THE NEXT THREE DAYS, GUIDED BY THE AK-47, I TRAVELLED mostly by starlight, but four times, either at dusk or early in the morning, I found myself out in the open in daylight, and each time I saw black drones in the distance.

Rotors whirring and a battery of cameras slung from beneath them, they were larger and more sophisticated than any I had seen before and I was certain the Army was deploying everything in its arsenal to try and find me. Hence, it was with an enormous sense of relief that just before dawn I crested a rise and, down a steep slope, saw the road I was looking for. As I had expected, it was pretty much a glorified track with deep corrugations guaranteed to ruin any suspension and every curve covered in drifts of wind-blown sand.

I turned away from it and went back into the wilderness, looping south, towards the bridge. As I had been delayed so long, I was certain that any extraction team would have arrived days earlier, and I was equally sure that they would never have risked driving along the road more than once. It meant the agency team would have had to hide somewhere and now I had to find them.

Once I was back in the scrub and still under cover of darkness, I found a spot protected from the biting wind and opened the mapping device: I was looking for somewhere that was close enough for the extraction team to keep watch on the road but hidden enough to prevent their vehicle from being seen either from the air or the ground. After several minutes working through the possibilities, I could find only one solution – if it had been me, I would be hiding under the bridge itself.

As I set a course to run parallel to the road and started to hike through the low scrub, I imagined the team – there would be two of them; that was the protocol – listening to the passing vehicles rattling the wooden planks overhead while they sat in the shadows, jumping at any sound in the underbrush, waiting for a spy they had never met to appear.

Forty minutes later, I hit the dry riverbed three hundred yards upstream from the bridge and, though I couldn't see it, I started to move silently through the grey light of dawn towards where I knew it stood. I rounded a curve and finally saw the structure – so old it had probably been built for carts with stone wheels. It was twenty yards long, its wooden planks badly bowed and a trestle at one end close to collapse, but still more than high enough to accommodate the vehicle that was standing beneath it.

The scene that confronted me, however, was all wrong – everything about it.

56

THE VEHICLE WAS A TOYOTA FOUR-BY-FOUR AND IT LOOKED LIKE IT was undergoing roadside triage: the hood was up, tools were laid out on a tarpaulin and a jack was holding up the front wheel with the tyre lying beside it.

Maybe it was a curated scene, meant to convince anyone who stumbled on it that the driver was fixing the vehicle, but where was he – or any other adult – and who was the teenage girl sitting next to it? Certainly she wasn't a member of any extraction team.

I was standing deep in the shadow of a pile of dead trees tossed on to the riverbank during some flood, and watched as she huddled next to a gas-fired cooking stove. Allowing for how skinny she was, I put her at about seventeen, and I certainly wasn't going to move any closer until I understood what it meant. Now, as I watched, she dipped her hands into a container of water and passed them over part of her head – she was performing *wudu* to prepare for the dawn prayer. Once she had finished washing her hair, she lifted her head and seemed to look straight at me—

I withdrew deeper into the shadow of the uprooted trees, and it was only then that I realized she wasn't staring at me, she was looking at whoever was behind me: someone, from the sound of it, who was in the process of cocking a gun.

I shifted my weight slightly so that I could spin and hurl myself at him. 'Don't even think about it,' the man said harshly in Farsi. I guessed he had seen me shift my weight and knew what I was planning.

'I don't speak Farsi,' I replied in Arabic. 'I am a traveller who was robbed—'

'Sure. Very slowly, drop the rifle,' he answered, now in perfect Arabic.

I unslung the weapon and let it fall to the ground.

'Take six paces back and turn and face me,' he said.

I started to take the steps. Whoever he was, he knew what he was doing. With each step, I was moving further from the rifle, and once I turned it would be behind me, out of sight and out of reach.

I took the last step and turned. There were two of them, both at least twenty-one feet away, the distance – so the manuals say – that a man charging forward can cover in one and a half seconds. That is enough time for the person guarding them to raise their weapon and fire even two poorly aimed shots; because the distance is diminishing quickly, one of the bullets is almost guaranteed to hit. Like I said, they weren't amateurs.

I didn't think the man in front of me, aiming a Smith & Wesson Model 500 revolver at my heart, was likely to miss no matter how fast I stormed him. Aged in his mid-forties, dressed in old jeans and a stained shirt, he might have looked dishevelled but he was obviously the leader; a powerful guy, broad across the chest, with a thin mouth and cold eyes. A cruel man, I thought.

He gestured to his colleague – a guy at least ten years younger, skinny and jumpy, already balding. He was holding a Beretta 9mm, waving it around, and that worried me more than his boss: he was so hot-wired he could panic at any moment and start shooting.

Reacting to his boss's gesture, he circled behind me and I guessed he was picking up the AK-47. That was standard – get a weapon under control as fast as possible – but then he did something unexpected. He spoke in Farsi to his boss and, while I couldn't be sure, it sounded like he was calling out a list of numbers and a date. If it was the rifle's serial number and the year of manufacture – information imprinted on the barrel – Langley would have had that on file and they might have provided it to someone.

The guy with the Smith & Wesson was already speaking to me. 'What do the letters SFGG mean?' he said, short-tempered, in Arabic.

I stared at him for a moment – it had to be the extraction team and they were trying to identify me, but who the hell was the girl?

'What does it mean?' he demanded again, louder, harsher.

'San Francisco Golden Gate,' I said in English.

He had no reaction, except that he too swapped to English. 'You married?'

I shook my head. 'A partner – a woman.'

'Name?' he asked immediately.

'Rebecca,' I said.

Langley knew about that, too – Lucas Corrigan, the head of Human Resources, a man with eyes as green and cold as river rocks, was a stickler for the next-of-kin forms.

The leader, apparently satisfied, lowered the Smith & Wesson. 'Call yourself a professional?' he sneered. 'You really screwed up, didn't you?' He signalled to his colleague to hand me back the rifle.

I looked at him – honestly, I wasn't in the mood. 'Getting here late, you mean?' I asked.

'No,' he said. 'Approaching a camp without checking the surroundings. You really think we'd just be sitting there, waiting to be picked off by somebody?'

He indicated my water pouches without waiting for an answer. 'Whatever delayed you,' he said, 'it couldn't have been that bad – you've got plenty of water. Or maybe you just got lucky and found a well.'

'You're right – just lucky,' I said. 'Who's the girl?'

'How would I know?' he replied, turning and starting to walk once more towards the vehicle. I was about to explode but, just in time, he kept talking. 'She comes from a refugee camp for Afghans who fled their country – I didn't exactly make other inquiries.'

'So why is she here?' I said, ready to hit him if I had to.

'To help save your life,' he said, just as angry. 'Ours, too, maybe. She's a beard; we hide behind her. If we meet a patrol, you're a Saudi, okay? But your wife is Afghan and this is her kid sister. You came to look for her and, praise be unto Allah, you found her in a camp at a place called Iranshahr. Now we're heading back to Tehran to arrange her travel documents so that you can go back to the Kingdom and all live the happily-ever-after.

'It was the best we could come up with at short notice,' he continued. 'I got a call at 3 a.m. four days ago and was told to drive here and rescue an agent who couldn't make it out on his own, a guy that might bring down a world of pain on us all. You must be hungry, so eat.'

Sure, I was starving, but I didn't move. 'And who are you?' I asked.

'In this scenario?' he replied. 'Me and Bahman here,' – he pointed at the jumpy guy – 'we're locals who speak Arabic and Farsi so you hired us to help out, but now we've decided not to take any money. You know – because we're, like, *humanitarians*.'

He laughed, but I didn't. 'You Blackwater, both of you?'

'How'd you guess?' he replied. 'You can call me Javid Ghorbani – that's the name I live under in this shithole.'

'And she was your idea?' I said, pointing at the girl. 'You really expect a young woman, a refugee like this, to be able to stick to that story if some bad guys start interrogating her?'

'Yeah – actually, I do,' he said calmly, taking a plateful of curry and naan the girl was dishing up from the stove.

'Allah help us,' I said, shaking my head in disbelief.

'No, it was me that helped us,' he said, angry again. 'In fact, I'm damn certain she won't say anything wrong. You see, no matter what you agency guys think of Blackwater, we're not idiots. She won't say anything wrong because she's deaf and dumb.'

I stared at him for a moment, then turned and looked at the young woman – I could see now that she was even more waif-like than I had first thought. She was sitting on her haunches, dressed in black, her hair covered now by a *hijab* and her face gaunt and hollow, either from hunger or trauma. Unfortunately, I'd been wrong about her age – I would be surprised if she was more than sixteen. She turned and looked up at me and it was heartbreaking – she had the gentlest eyes I had ever seen.

'Does she know that if this goes wrong, they'll kill her?' I asked Ghorbani.

His mouth full, he laughed again. 'You think I'm crazy – she wouldn't have come if I'd told her that, would she?'

'Then why *did* she do it?'

'I offered her a new cellphone. Damn kids, huh?' he said sarcastically, and laughed again. I'd never met a man who laughed so much at things that weren't funny.

'Seems hers got stolen,' he explained. 'And typing back and forth is the only way she can communicate. So she didn't have much choice, huh? I told her we were picking up a tobacco smuggler – nothing serious, we'd done it dozens of times before – and we needed someone just to deflect suspicion.'

'What's her name?' I asked quietly, but he shrugged – either he didn't know it or wasn't interested. 'Type on your phone, will you?' I said. 'Ask her what her name is?'

He looked at me for a beat, probably trying to think up some reason not to, but then must have figured it wasn't worth it. He typed on his phone and showed it to her.

She typed something back and Ghorbani handed it to me. I was surprised she did it – in Afghanistan women are traditionally forced to keep their names secret from anyone outside their immediate family. In public they are known only as the daughter, sister or mother of the eldest male in the family. But the time she had spent in the refugee camp must have changed her because, after I had hit translate, I saw that she had typed 'Laleh'.

I called out to the other guy – Bahman, starting to put the wheel back on the vehicle – but I clearly intended it for Ghorbani as well. 'Her name's Laleh – okay? Everyone got it?'

'Yeah, sure – Laleh,' Ghorbani said dismissively.

I turned to get the food she was serving on to a plate. I smiled my thanks, and I won't ever forget the look of surprise on her face: I guessed you had to go back a long way – probably not since the last time she saw her father – to find a time when a man had smiled at her. Of course, she immediately looked away, embarrassed.

I scooped up a mouthful of the curry with the naan, and I can't say if it was really any good; all I know is that it was the best food I had ever tasted. I turned to Ghorbani: 'What's the plan? How do I get out of here?'

57

THE PLAN WAS SO GOOD, I ASSUMED IT HAD BEEN DREAMT UP BY Langley.

'We drive from here north to a small city, about half a million

141

people, called Zahedan,' Ghorbani said, still surly, continuing to eat. 'We can't drive fast; it'll look like we're running from something – it has to be completely normal. Because of that, and the condition of the road, it's about four hours away. Just outside town, there's a disused quarry – we checked it out on the way down. We pull in, give you a cellphone and—'

He pulled a heavy tarp off the back of the Toyota, revealing two nearly new dirt bikes. 'You take one of these, we wave you a fond farewell and you ride hard for the border.'

'The Pakistan border?' I asked.

'No,' he replied. 'Zahedan sits in the triangle. It's close to the borders of Afghanistan and Pakistan, about thirty-five miles from both.'

'But we own the Afghan airspace,' I said.

'Congratulations, now you're starting to think. You cross the border, make a call on the cellphone to the only number that's programmed in—'

'Whoever it is, they'll be waiting for it?' I asked, interrupting.

'Let me *finish*, will ya? Special Forces, they've been on standby for the last three days. Ten minutes later a chopper will home in on the signal and pick you up.'

While he had been speaking, I had been examining the dirt bikes. 'It's gonna be a big problem,' I said at last.

'What is?' Ghorbani asked, about to lose it.

'Ever ridden a dirt bike? They're loud as hell, especially in the quiet out here,' I said. 'Anyone searching will hear it from miles away – with drones they'll locate me within minutes. I won't have a chance of outrunning them.'

'No kidding,' he said. 'Hey, Bahman – how come we didn't think of the noise?' He turned back to me. 'They're electric.'

'Okay,' I replied. But one thing I knew for sure: this wasn't Ghorbani's plan. Like I said, it had all the hallmarks of an agency gig: I could imagine the team in the conference room, the IMAX screens jumping between maps, towns and satellite photos, somebody trying to plan an overland route and then the idea of a dirt bike emerging and a voice saying the bike would have to be electric because of the noise and Falcon saying he would never allow a couple of Blackwater guys to buy electric dirt bikes in Tehran and leave a trail a mile wide for PAVA to follow. Then an ambitious soul, probably thinking more about a career than my welfare, suggests buying them in the US and flying them overnight to Kabul and Falcon picks up the baton and tells Madeleine to contact Lord Ahmad Shah Dostum, the most powerful of the Afghan warlords, and tell him they need his best smuggler to get a shipment into Zahedan as fast as possible. In return the agency would help him with some of those plastic-wrapped bricks that were constantly flowing out of Helmand province and into Iran or the other way into Tajikistan, but in either case supplying ninety per cent of the world's heroin, and when Madeleine gets off the phone and reports that the warlord sends his warmest personal greetings to Falcon and says that it is always a pleasure to help the agency, the room explodes into activity and twenty-four hours later the bikes are in pieces and on the back of packhorses, heading for the border and then on to Zahedan or wherever Ghorbani took delivery of them. And if he wanted me to believe that the electric bikes were his idea and somehow he had conjured them out of thin air, then that was fine with me; I would take the bikes and he could have his glory.

'Battery life?' I asked, not missing a beat. 'What's the range?'

'That's why there's two,' he answered. 'We needed one for spares in case there was a problem. More importantly, while you get some rest, Henry Ford here' – he indicated Bahman – 'will finish the Toyota then take the battery out of the spare and add it to yours. With two batteries you could get halfway to Kabul.'

I swung myself on to the back of the vehicle and started familiarizing myself with the bike. 'You said about getting rest, I don't need it – as soon as he's finished we can go.'

'No, we can't,' he replied. 'Nobody travels a road like this early in the morning. No, we make it look normal. Anyway – more traffic, less suspicion. We leave at ten.'

I nodded. 'They've got drones. I've seen at least four in the last few days.'

'We've seen more than that,' he replied. 'Bahman's got it covered.' He turned and yelled to his colleague. 'Hey, Bahman, show him your gizmo.'

Bahman dragged himself up from the dirt and, as jumpy as ever, pulled a hard-shell briefcase out of the back seat of the Toyota and opened it. Nestled inside was what looked like a specially adapted laptop surrounded by black foam. 'I put it together myself,' he said proudly. 'Basically, it's a scanner, it picks up the radio signal that the controller uses to fly the drone. By following the signal and tying it into a satellite GPS system, I can tell when one is approaching.'

'What's the range? How far off can you pick 'em up?' I asked.

'About ten miles,' he replied. 'Sometimes further.'

'Okay,' I said. 'Good work.'

It was, too. Except, as it turned out, seeing drones on a screen was one thing; avoiding them in a moving vehicle was something completely different.

58

GIVEN THE CONDITION OF THE ROAD – THE CORRUGATIONS, THE DEEP sand drifts and the frequent wash-aways – the Toyota could move, slaloming through the bends and fishtailing on the curves. I couldn't stand the guy, but I had to admit it – Ghorbani was a great driver.

Bahman was sitting next to him with the hard-shell open. As he tweaked the computer and read the map – clouds of dust billowing around us and the sun a fiery disc in a washed-out sky – he could have been a navigator in the Paris to Dakar car rally.

Between checking the rifle's breech and cleaning the firing mechanism, I kept glancing over his shoulder, watching the map on the screen, desperate to make sure that, almost within sight of freedom, the small black circle that signified a drone didn't appear. Three hours to go, I told myself.

Laleh, sitting beside me, huddled in her corner – obviously uncomfortable at being in such close proximity to a male stranger – had initially shown some interest as I field-stripped the weapon but had decided the view out the window was more arresting and had her back half turned towards me. I finished with the weapon and was about to put the cleaning rod back in the tube when Ghorbani took a corrugation at speed; we half left our seats, my hand grabbed the handle above the door and, with all the mats removed, the cleaning rod clattered to the floor.

Laleh turned from the window and looked at her feet to see what had made the noise. I was already reaching for it and in that moment our eyes met. We realized the same thing simultaneously: how could she have heard the rod hit the floor if she was deaf? We held each other's gaze for a long beat, and maybe I would have said something or tried to indicate that her secret was safe, but I didn't get the chance. 'Drone!' Bahman called out, unable to keep the fear out of his voice.

I turned away from her to look at the screen: 'Where – roaming or following?' I asked.

'Following,' he said, pointing at the black dot that was swooping across the map towards us.

'How far?' I said.

He started to calculate. 'Damn, this thing is travelling.' A count-down clock appeared in the corner of his screen. 'Ten minutes, coming straight down the road behind us now.'

I was breathing hard, pulse racing, trying to work out what to do. Nobody else noticed, but Laleh was looking from me to Bahman and back again, aware that something bad was happening. Clearly, her hearing was better than okay.

'You came down this road,' I said to Ghorbani. 'I'm going to have to get out – how?'

'You don't,' he snapped. 'We've got a legend—'

'That might work with a random on the road, not guys operating a drone like that,' I said. 'It won't survive five minutes. They'll separate us and blow the story apart.'

'He's right,' Bahman said, voice cracking. 'They'll kill us on the details.'

'They're looking for me,' I said. 'You've got ID, proper papers, employment – I've got nothing. You stand a good chance without me—'

Ghorbani shot a glance at the laptop: the dot was closer, coming in hard and straight. 'We've got seven minutes,' Bahman said.

Laleh could see it too and, while she may not have understood everything, she knew enough.

'I don't know why the hell I ever got involved in this,' Ghorbani said, angry, wrestling the wheel, drifting, nearly losing the rear end but hauling the heavy vehicle back on track.

'Money?' I said.

He ignored it. 'Okay – there's a narrow cutting, an overhang of trees,' he continued, hitting the throttle. 'The drone will have to go up and over them. Eight klicks ahead—'

'Once I'm out, I'll go overland,' I said, grabbing the water bottles, making sure that the scope was firmly attached to the rifle, wrapping it in a blanket that was lying on the seat. Lose or wreck the scope and I was finished. 'I'll take a wide loop,' I continued, 'and find you on the other side of the roadblock or whatever they set up. Stop on the side of the road, fake another breakdown and wait.'

I turned to Bahman, who was working his keyboard. 'Can we beat it to the cutting?'

'No chance,' he said. 'Not the speed this thing is travelling. It's gonna be on us in three minutes. Maybe less.' He corrected himself. 'Two minutes.'

I dived to the floor – I couldn't risk them seeing that there was a fourth person in the car. Bahman, looking at the timer on the screen, started counting down the seconds. I grabbed a filthy tarp from under the front seat and pulled it over myself.

'Seventy seconds,' Bahman said.

Only my face was visible. I looked up and saw Laleh staring at me and I sort of nodded, trying to be reassuring, just hoping that she got out of this okay.

'How far to the cutting?' I yelled to Ghorbani. The vehicle took a hard curve, almost spinning, over-correcting, and then straightening and settling on its suspension.

'Six klicks,' he said, his mouth so dry he found it hard to form the words.

'Thirty seconds,' Bahman reported. He'd been right – the drone was going to reach us well before we got to the cutting.

'Where is it?!' Ghorbani yelled. 'It's gone, it should be in the rear-view—'

'I don't know,' Bahman replied, his voice cracking again. 'It must have gained altitude. I've got to reset—'

I heard him typing furiously on the keyboard, changing the mapping parameters, and for a moment there was silence – then Laleh screamed.

I pivoted to look: behind her terrified face, through the window, I saw the drone. It must have swooped down – like a hi-tech falcon – and was hovering just outside the glass, keeping pace with the vehicle, its array of beady-eyed cameras looking at her and scanning the inside of the vehicle.

I was certain it couldn't see me – not through the dust-spattered glass with only my eyes visible under the tarp – but Laleh, transfixed, was face to face with it, barely two feet away, and it seemed to be staring at her, its four rotors whirring and blurring, its black body swollen and its head sporting an array of antennas. It's like a giant insect, I thought, a massive black praying mantis.

I saw Laleh start to shake, about to cry, and I snaked my hand out from under the tarp and grabbed her ankle to calm her. Then the predator disappeared, swooping upwards.

Laleh slumped back in the seat, her body wracked by sobs. 'It's gone,' I said.

'It hasn't – it's in front!' Ghorbani yelled. 'Stay down, it's flying backwards, two feet off the windshield, cameras looking in.'

'Ditch the tracker, hide it!' I yelled at Bahman.

'I have,' he called back, voice trembling. 'It's on the floor.'

'Once we're in the cutting, throw it out the window,' I ordered. 'If they find that, you're dead.'

'One klick,' Ghorbani said. 'You ready?'

'Yeah,' I replied, even though I wasn't. I managed to shift my body enough to look down the crack beside Ghorbani's seat and see out the windshield. The cutting was dead ahead – the road, just wide enough for one vehicle, passed between two steep cliffs. Thick bushes and trees had taken root in them and were overhanging the track, some of them barely above our roof. The drone would have no choice but to go up and over—

'Thirty seconds,' Bahman yelled. 'Twenty . . . ten . . .'

The vehicle was engulfed in gloom: we were in the shadow of the overhanging trees. 'Drone's gone,' Ghorbani called back to me: the drone had soared upwards, leaving us free of surveillance for a minute, maybe less.

I felt the wind rush in as Bahman dropped his window and I caught a glimpse of the laptop disappearing out of it as I scrambled on to the seat, grabbed the rifle in its blanket, slung the water pouches over my shoulder and took hold of the door handle.

'I can't slow – they may be timing us,' Ghorbani said. 'I'll drift it into a sandbank, that might give you a chance. Four seconds . . . three . . .'

I looked at Laleh – she was crying, shaking her head, panicked to see me go. Maybe she thought I might be able to protect her, not realizing there was no hope I could do that. I glanced at Ghorbani's speedometer: eighty kilometres an hour. This wasn't going to work—

'Two . . . one . . .' he yelled, and I felt the vehicle's rear drift out as we hit the sand. 'Go!'

I threw the door open, launched the rifle out and hurled myself after it, trying to turn my body. The training says tuck your head, land on your shoulder and body-roll, but I had no time to think, let alone roll, before I hit—

My shoulder and neck took the worst of it. I felt my back wrench as I put my hand out to break my fall, smacked the ground hard with the palm of it, sending myself somersaulting through the air, hitting with my hip as I landed the second time, blasting the air out of my lungs, before somersaulting again and plunging into the ground. I rolled to a stop.

I was barely able to believe it – I was still alive. I took a tentative breath, succeeded, and took another. I sat up and looked around: it was the sand that had saved me – without any rain for years, the relentless north wind had piled it up in a huge drift of the finest, deepest powder.

The clouds of dust from the Toyota were still hanging in the morning air, obscuring the sky and providing a few minutes of cover from the drone if the operator decided to come back. I scrambled up, half limped down the road, grabbed the water pouches, found the AK-47 undamaged in its blanket and started climbing the most accessible of the cliffs.

It was critical that I got into cover as fast as possible and, when I reached the top, I turned north, staying parallel to the road, making sure that I kept it in sight. I had to reconnect with the Toyota at the first opportunity and I knew that, once I did, allowing for the rest of the journey to the quarry and the sprint on the dirt bike, I was no more than a hundred and forty minutes from freedom.

One hundred and forty minutes of good fortune – surely that wasn't too much to ask.

59

AFTER HALF AN HOUR OF HARD TRAVEL, CROSSING DIFFICULT TERRAIN and moving fast, I took cover among a set of stone monoliths perched on a ridge and used the scope to check the road ahead, looking straight down a long stretch of dusty track.

I saw the Toyota. It was right at the edge of vision, distorted by the waves of heat rising off the land. It was stopped at a roadblock, a dozen pick-ups and four-by-fours in front of it, and the drone hovering above. Horse trailers were hitched to two of the pick-ups, and it alarmed me – it meant that men on horseback were searching the ravines or gorges the drone and vehicles couldn't access. The net was closing.

Twice I lifted my eye off the scope, blinked and looked again, but I still couldn't distinguish Ghorbani, Bahman or Laleh among the people milling around the vehicle. I had anticipated they would be stopped, but I had no idea if they were just being questioned or were under arrest. Any setback now – after having come so far – would be a terrible blow, but not having any idea of what was happening made it even more difficult.

If they were prisoners, I had to know: it meant I would have to try and reach the border by myself and the journey would have to start immediately – before the Army and its drones got organized. I opened the mapping system and set a course for a ridge further down the road that would give me a far better view of what was happening at the roadblock.

Sticking to deep cover, I scrambled down from the monoliths, found a rugged gully I had identified on the map that would lead me to my observation point and started to move along its old water-course. After twenty minutes I followed it around a curve, heading deeper into the harsh terrain, and very soon I registered a strange thing about the place: there was barely any sound.

Steadily, the silence became more oppressive, the path started to narrow and the only sign of life was a bird – black with a broad wingspan, a kind I had never seen before – riding the wind high above. That same breeze started to reach down into the gully, sighing through the caves and crevices of the hillsides.

Ahead, like huge, clashing rocks, a pair of boulders almost blocked the path. I found a track that passed between them, stepped into an almost hidden place—

And there they were in a small clearing, waiting: thirty brutal men, terrorists without doubt, survivors of one of the deadliest conflicts of modern times, travellers who had crossed half a continent in their determination to build a new world.

I had walked and run for a hundred miles, I had pushed myself to the limit of my endurance, I had travelled by starlight and witnessed things most people would never see: campfires flickering behind enemy lines, mirages so real I could touch them, peregrine falcons in all their majesty, a dead man hanging from a cross.

Now, almost within sight of safety, a hundred and forty minutes on the wrong side of freedom, in a crack in the earth with no name, I had finally come face to face with the people I had hoped never to meet. I was about to be a prisoner of the Army of the Pure.

60

THE THIRTY MEN, PROBABLY A COMBINATION OF TWO OF THE ARMY'S patrols, were deployed around the clearing in a classic ambush formation. Four of them were on horseback: cruel-looking men who sat easy in the saddle, assault rifles levelled at me, wearing flowing headdresses, dark glasses and with bandoliers of ammunition strung across their chests.

At some stage I think every Denied Access Area spy imagines how the moment of their capture might unfold. I was no different, but I had never thought it would be like this. Nobody spoke, nobody issued orders to me and there was no wild shoot-out. The only sound was the wind sighing through the gully and the chatter of several encrypted walkie-talkies; old-fashioned, for sure, but as every terrorist knew, extremely difficult to track, trace and hack. The men carrying them, along with about a dozen other hostiles, were behind a group of four-wheel drives, using them as shields, while another group was ranged around the cliffs, totally in control of the tiny clearing. High above, on a bluff, was the only man without a weapon trained on me. He had a pair of field glasses around his neck, and I realized that he must have had me under observation for twenty minutes or more. No wonder they were waiting.

Facing such overwhelming odds, I made sure to stand perfectly still, not letting my hands go anywhere near the rifle. My life was clearly forfeit, but I didn't want to commit suicide by carelessness or misunderstanding.

I had always thought there was nothing to equal the fear which a spy felt behind enemy lines: to slip across a border in the pale moonlight or run through a forest strung with motion detectors, to stand on a platform armed only with a thin overcoat and fake papers, waiting to board a midnight train to Moscow or some other godforsaken place, to sit curled in a seat in the bitter cold listening to the steel wheels rolling, your nerves being shredded slowly by the sight of the security police coming through the carriage and looking from face to face, at any moment expecting one of them to bark a command, aim his weapon at you and hold out his hand for your ticket and internal passport, to pull into forlorn railway stations and stare out at the foreign crowd, trying to identify who among them were the plain-clothes cops, to be totally exhausted but unable to sleep, running on adrenaline and coffee thick enough to pave a road sold by ancient women who smelled of the earth and spoke of Stalin or some other butcher with affection, silently watching young military recruits going off to war loaded up on bathtub vodka and spoiling for a fight, and all the while heading deeper into the darkness and never forgetting that on the edge of town, just past where the streetlights ended, there was always a ditch with your name on it.

I had known all of that and more, but just before noon on a Wednesday in July, the height of summer in Iran, I learned that there was a fear far worse than any of that: it was the realization that there was no escape and hope had perished a few yards behind you. Nevertheless, sometimes you have to play even a losing hand to the end, and I spoke in Arabic, loud enough for everyone to hear. 'I am a traveller,' I said. 'I am from the Kingdom and need help. I was robbed—'

Several men laughed. One of the Four Horsemen, the rider closest to me, called over his shoulder to someone behind him, speaking in what sounded like Azeri – one of a handful of languages closely related to Turkish – and while I wasn't an expert, my Turkish was good enough to be fairly sure he had used the word 'colonel'.

Most of the soldiers, including those on the hillsides and the spotter with the binoculars, turned and looked: the horseman right at the back, half hidden in the shadow cast by the cliff, a man I had barely been able to see, rode forward. I was preoccupied, looking for a chance to convert a momentary mistake by the soldiers to my advantage, but still I felt a ripple of respect pass through the contingent – they might have been dressed like guerrillas or irregulars, but it was as though they were on parade, drawing themselves to attention. This was Death, I figured.

He was about forty, tall, over six two, lean with a lot of muscle, and there was no doubt he had what the US military likes to call 'command presence'. Arrogant and imposing in the saddle, he had a strong nose and a trimmed black beard. To that extent he was little different in appearance to the tens of thousands of other front-line fighters who had decided to wage war in the cauldron. But there was something else to him – my overwhelming sense was that his features were partly Slavic and I guessed that he had a connection to one of the Balkan nations where, centuries ago, Islam had taken root among the remote villages and wild mountains. Men grew up very hard there and produced fighters who were widely feared.

Wearing a T-shirt, faded jeans, combat boots and a cotton scarf wrapped like a turban around his head and trailing down his back, he had a tattoo along one ripped forearm. It was in Cyrillic script and probably would have meant nothing to most people, but several of the languages I had studied used the same alphabet and I saw that it was a list of dates and locations. I was perplexed for a moment and then I realized: they were battlefields where he had fought.

Whoever the man was, he had seen a lot of war.

61

AS I STUDIED HIM, HE STOPPED A FEW YARDS FROM ME – HOLDING A Glock 34 Long Barrel pistol casually in one hand – and looked down at me from the saddle. With the AK-47 still over my shoulder and the water pouches in one hand, I stood in the oppressive silence, meeting his gaze as best I could and thinking about Ghorbani and Bahman.

I doubted that they had fared any better than me, but I hoped the soldiers swarming their vehicle had spared Laleh's life. The girl was innocent, and if Ghorbani hadn't lied to her she would still have been in a refugee camp a hundred miles away. There was nothing we could do about it now, but the three of us were intelligence agents and we knew the risks we were taking.

'Robbed on the road?' the man in the saddle said quietly in pretty good English, his voice full of fake concern. 'I'm sorry to hear you were preyed on by bandits, you should have been more careful. It's a strange world and things can turn very bad out here – I'm sure you have realized that by now.'

I feigned not understanding the language; I had nothing to save me now except my legend. 'I am from Tabuk in the north of Saudi,' I said in Arabic.

'Ah, Tabuk? Beautiful sunsets, I'm told,' he replied, smiling, still in English. 'I have never been there, but several comrades I have known – Saudis like yourself – have spoken of them. It is a pity those men are not here today, you could have shared stories about home with them. That's always a pleasure for foreigners like us, isn't it?'

I shrugged – implying English was beyond me. His gaze didn't leave my face and I saw something in his dark eyes that I had not noticed before – a piercing anger, a hatred, focused on me. It seemed to be . . . it seemed intensely personal . . . I didn't know the man, I had never seen him before in my life, so for what reason – I had no idea. Because he knew I was American? I asked myself.

'Tabuk is very special—' I said in Arabic, no choice but to plough on.

'So it is,' he said. 'It is where the Prophet – Peace be upon Him – once drank from a natural spring. I am glad to discover that the CIA reads Wikipedia.'

'I don't understand English,' I said in Arabic. 'I am here to search for my brother—'

'You are? I lost a brother, too,' he continued in English. 'Unfortunately, I won't be finding mine. He was killed, shot to death. Perhaps in a minute, after we establish some things, we can help you look for yours.'

He was toying with me, but I had to play along, hoping to find an opportunity, some half-chance, that I could seize: one more minute for me, one less for my enemies, I told myself. I opened my hands as if the language didn't make any sense, but he ignored it—

'Even for the borderlands, it's been an unusual day,' he said. 'In a dry creek-bed two forward patrols find a Saudi national who's been robbed and is looking for his brother. Thirty minutes earlier we meet two men and a woman on the road who try to tell us a threadbare story about their travels. The woman is very young.' He shrugged. 'You don't happen to know anything about her, do you?'

I said nothing, but my fear ratcheted even higher at the mention of Laleh. 'No? She's a stranger to you?' he asked. With no apparent understanding of English, I just stared at him.

'She acts as if she is mute,' he continued. 'But I suspect if someone were to make her scream loud enough, she might recover her ability to speak. A miracle, you might say. What do you think? Is making her scream worth a try?'

Our eyes met and, still holding the Long Barrel casually in his hand, he swung out of the saddle and walked forward. He stopped a few feet in front of me and I would have liked to straighten up and stand tall to confront him, but I couldn't; I didn't have the strength.

'Perhaps if we can find the bandits who robbed you, we could trade her for your possessions,' he suggested. 'There's a thought – I'm sure either them, or some of the other outlaws in the area, could put a young woman, even a skinny one, to good use.'

It was no idle threat; in Syria, ISIS had sold thousands of women into sexual slavery. The silence between the terrorist and me deepened, neither the soldiers nor the four horses making a sound, and I saw the black bird again, the one with the broad wingspan, circling above us.

'A good idea, Saudi?' he asked, more menacing, more insistent. 'Make her scream or sell her to the bandits? Any preference?'

I didn't reply, continuing to watch the bird in the cloudless sky – no religion up there, nothing to hate or die for, I thought.

'Maybe we should do both,' he said at last. 'Is that what you're saying, the scream and the sale – we do both? Yes, I think so, too.'

So, it had come to this, I thought, still watching the bird. The mission didn't matter any more; launched with such high expectations and the product of so much planning, I knew it had died on the cross along with the courier. As for myself, Ghorbani and Bahman, there was no escape. Our situation would soon reach its inevitable and deadly conclusion, but I knew these few minutes would probably be my only chance to plead Laleh's case. Save what you can, I thought.

'Let her go,' I said quietly in English, tacitly admitting the truth he already knew.

154

'So you speak English?' he said in mock surprise. 'What about the sunsets, the natural spring? Could it be you're not from Tabuk at all?'

I ignored it. 'The girl was tricked, brought along to help provide a cover. She deserves—'

'She deserves nothing!' he said, spitting out the words, abandoning the mask of civility. 'What did you people say in another war – kill 'em all and let God sort it out?'

'Vietnam was a long time ago,' I replied.

'Nothing changes. I've seen what you and your allies do in Iraq, Syria, Lebanon, Gaza, Iran.' His voice hit each name hard as a hammer. 'I've witnessed schools and hospitals being bombed indiscriminately. No, the woman was old enough. She knew what she was doing. Nobody collaborates with the enemy. *Nobody*.'

'They offered her a cellphone,' I said. 'Imagine losing your life for that? It says in the Noble Qur'an: "Observe your duty to Allah in respect to women, and treat them well."'

He stared at me, probably surprised: 'And it says in your culture even the devil can quote Scripture for his purposes,' he replied.

'The girl had nobody, nothing at all,' I said. 'She's a refugee, they found her three days ago in a camp.'

He ignored it, taking a step closer. I tried to find something – anything – that might connect with him. 'She's young, she made a mistake,' I said. 'I'm just asking you to spare—'

Almost within touching distance, he spoke over me. 'You have no currency here,' he said. 'You ask for nothing and I grant you nothing – understand?' Again, I saw that terrible anger directed at me.

I continued to talk, trying to argue a hopeless case, but he ignored it, starting to walk around me. Two paces, three, and he was at my back. I didn't turn, but I could feel him behind me. I sensed him step closer, and I wondered: was this how it ended? A gunshot now from the Long Barrel or the deadly chop to the back of my neck.

I straightened myself up and imagined the gun rising and pointing at a spot just behind my ear. I felt his hand touch the side of my neck – then, a moment later, he tore the weapon off my shoulder. At last, he had decided to disarm me.

I heard the rifle clatter to the ground, felt him move away, and I had to force myself not to slump to my knees. Unclenching my teeth, I exhaled. By the time I had regained some sort of composure he was back in front of me—

'There is a town far out on the frontier,' he said, more quietly, seemingly calmer now.

I stared at him, exhausted, heart pounding, and now my mind was reeling. Why was he suddenly telling me this? And who was he – this horseman with so much command presence? I looked again at the tattoo on his forearm; over a dozen countries used the Cyrillic alphabet, including Russia, Chechnya and Uzbekistan, so it told me nothing—

But I had no time to think more about it, I needed to pay attention. 'The town is in the middle of the wilderness, hard on the banks of the Lena River. You know the mighty Lena?'

I shook my head.

'Of course not,' he said. 'Nobody from the West would. You think civilization ends at Budapest. The Lena is five thousand kilometres long, one of the ten greatest rivers in the world,' he continued. 'It's a wild thing, a never-ending force of nature – it provides food, water, transport and beauty. Death, too. Every year, hundreds of people drown during the spring melt. That's Siberia for you – the last great frontier in a world gone to hell.'

'Siberia?' I said, listening hard now. 'The frontier?'

'Yes,' he replied.

'I don't understand . . .' I said, wanting him to tell me more.

'Why I'm telling you about Siberia? You will in a moment,' he said. 'I wasn't born there – my brother and I were raised by my father. He came from the old Soviet Union, and he took us there because he had found work in one of the dirtiest and most dangerous diamond mines in the world—'

I thought of a man sitting in a battle-truck in the cauldron, telling his origin story to a group of high-ranking warriors – a man who spoke about the frontier, a mighty river and terrible winters, someone whose father worked underground and raised his two sons alone. I knew then – knew with absolute certainty – the identity of the man in front of me. I was face to face with Abu Muslim al-Tundra, the head of al-Qaeda in Iraq, one of the founders of ISIS and the military commander of the Army of the Pure.

I imagined him as a young boy gliding through the forest learning to track, hunt and survive. I pictured him, his younger brother and his father on a riverbank – full of hope – mining for mammoths. And most of all I remembered the pack of wolves.

'I spent twelve years in Pokrovsk,' he was saying, wrenching me back to the present. 'That was the name of the town and, by the grace of Allah, it made me what I am today.

'It was an outpost in the wilderness,' he continued. 'Nine thousand people were trapped between the river and a larch forest that ran to the end of the world, and the old wooden houses were built on stilts to get above the permafrost. Every morning a thick fog rolled in from the Arctic.'

I kept looking at his face. At last, an intelligence agent from the West could identify him – possibly the world's most dangerous terrorist – and I could only think of what a tragedy it was that it would never be put to any use. Preoccupied by it, I didn't see at what point al-Tundra stopped holding the Long Barrel casually. I realized later he must have tilted it up and started to aim.

'The word "wretched" didn't do the place justice, but it was where I taught myself English,' he continued. 'There was an old man, a Russian who had been educated in England; like most people in Pokrovsk, he was on the run from something.

'He had a library of books – poetry mostly, but fiction, too. *The Grapes of Wrath*, *Gatsby*, Salinger, Hemingway. For those ten years, my only companions were those books and my younger brother. He was the funniest person I ever knew, the one person who kept me sane. Him and my father were the only two people I have ever loved—'

He stopped and held my gaze. 'You asked before why I was talking about Siberia,' he said. 'I'll tell you – it was my brother sleeping under the awning at the crossroads. He was the one you shot seven times and killed.'

He pulled the trigger of the Long Barrel.

62

FROM BARELY FIVE FEET, THE BULLET TORE INTO MY LEFT FOOT, sending a broad spray of blood across the dry earth and launching searing shafts of pain up my leg and into my groin.

I reeled, felt the water pouches fly from my hand, went down on one knee first and then fell into the parched earth as a rising tide of nausea threatened to overwhelm me. It forced me to bite hard into my lip, taste the blood in my mouth and do whatever I could not to pass out; at last I understood why experienced torturers nearly always used hammers to crush the bones of a prisoner's feet.

'You must have been quite the man at Langley to be given a mission like this. Was it worth it?' al-Tundra asked as he watched me fighting for breath, my shaking hands trying to tear my sandal and sock off.

I ignored him, barely noticing him walk behind me to retrieve the AK-47 from the dirt. I managed to get my footwear off and looked down at the raw and ugly hole, pumping out blood and strewn with bone fragments. Tentatively, I felt underneath and confirmed what I had feared: the exit wound through the sole of my foot was far larger than the entry point, and I knew then that standing on it, let alone walking, would be almost impossible.

Trying to ride the surging waves of pain, I cursed myself – I couldn't have stopped him from firing, but I knew that cable-ties and hand-cuffs weren't available on the battlefields where ISIS had fought. As a result they had improvised, developing the widespread practice of shooting their prisoners through the foot, confident in the belief that no escapee ever got very far by hopping. I should have anticipated what he would do and then at least I might have been able to mentally prepare myself.

Instead, I was sitting in the dirt, trying – in the midst of a swirling fog of pain – to think about the steps I had to take to doctor myself. For me, darkness started to fall from the midday sky and I had to haul myself back from unconsciousness, forcing myself to get a grip; somehow, I had to find a way to clean, tourniquet and dress the wound.

Looking around for my water pouches, I saw that al-Tundra had already returned to his horse and was strapping my AK-47 to the saddle. I started to scramble towards the pouches when a man's voice – in Arabic, loud and hauntingly melodic – called from one of the four-wheel drives. I turned – it was a recording, playing on the vehicle's sound system, of a muezzin reciting the *Adhan*, the Muslim call to prayer: noon worship was about to start.

Al-Tundra, hurrying to fulfil *wudu*, took a ragged roll of white cotton out of his saddlebag and threw it in my direction. 'Tourniquet your leg, then bind the wound,' he ordered. 'I'm sure you know how to do that.'

He turned and headed towards the vehicles, leaving me to half crawl, half scramble across the dirt to the bandage. As grateful as I was for the strip of white cotton, I knew it had nothing to do with mercy—

It was bad news: he wanted to keep me alive, and that meant torture was coming next. I had no idea what he intended, but I couldn't help thinking – again – about bear traps and the wolves.

63

THE *ADHAN*, UNCHANGED FOR FOURTEEN HUNDRED YEARS, LASTS about five minutes and was coming to an end by the time – my hands still trembling from the pain – I had torn a strip off the cloth, tied it around my leg above the ankle and grabbed a stick lying nearby.

The stick was a crucial part of battlefield triage; following what I had been taught years before, I used it as a lever and tightened the tourniquet until it had compressed the artery and stopped the bleeding. I then picked up one of the water pouches and washed the wound as best I could before using the rest of the cloth to pack and bandage it. Given what I knew of my life expectancy, I can't explain why I went to so much trouble. Like they say, hope dies last.

Having done everything I could to treat the injury, I sat in the blazing heat and looked at my captors. The thirty of them had gathered at the four-by-fours and were using bowls of water on the tailgates to perform *wudu*. The gunmen had come down from the cliffs, and it would have provided a good opportunity to escape – for anybody that could walk. Al-Tundra had anticipated that.

As I watched, I saw him – in profile – strip off his headdress and sweat-stained T-shirt: his head was shaven, his torso even more defined than it had first appeared, and an old, badly stitched gunshot wound extended from his armpit down to his fifth rib. All around him other hardened warriors were laying down their prayer mats.

I started to turn away when, unaware that I was watching, the Colonel reached to grab a small towel and in doing so ended up facing completely away from me. I stopped – I had a clear view of the tattoo that covered his back. It was far more impressive in reality than even the enhanced version the NSA had created. As its owner stretched and moved, towelling himself dry, the green eyes seemed alive – dancing – and the wings kept rippling and flexing. It looked like it could take flight at any moment.

Running my eye down it, I saw – underneath, written in Cyrillic – what appeared to be the name of an Army regiment, but due to the angle, I couldn't read it. Next to it, though, were three gold stars and two red stripes. It meant that when he was younger, he really had been a colonel in a Russian military unit.

He turned and saw me looking at his back. 'You know what it is?' he asked, reaching over his shoulder and tapping the head of the insect.

'A pest,' I said, my voice – thankfully – sounding far stronger than I felt.

He laughed. 'That's not what the farmers say. They know when they see the first one, a plague is coming – even your Bible predicted that.'

'A plague of locusts? Yes, it did,' I said. 'But what about the rest of the story? With God's help, the plague passes and the farmers live on.'

He kept laughing, dismissing it, turning back to complete *wudu*.

'But tell me one thing, Abu Muslim al-Tundra,' I called out. It made him stop and turn back, shocked that I knew who he was. 'How much did you and your brother get for the ten tusks?'

It was probably a stupid thing to do, but it gave me the momentary pleasure of seeing him stare at me in utter surprise, completely lost for words.

PART TWO

1

AS SOON AS THE COLONEL AND HIS MEN HAD FINISHED PERFORMING *wudu* and knelt for the noon prayer in the blinding sun, I crawled across the dry watercourse, dragging my wounded foot behind me, and finally reached the shade of a half-dead tree.

With a cloud of black flies buzzing around my face, I emptied one of the water pouches over my head to alleviate the suffocating heat and tried to formulate a plan. Heroics, seizing a weapon, a wild gunfight . . . even if I could manage any of them, to what end? To fight my way back to the clashing rocks and make my escape on one foot? In my crippled state, commandeering a vehicle was my only option.

I looked at the Toyota four-by-fours scattered around the small enclave: of the ten of them, five had jacked-up suspension, special off-road tyres and were fitted with supplementary fuel tanks bolted to the back – equipment that was more than good enough for me to try and make it overland to either the Afghan or Pakistani borders. Without the AK-47 I had no mapping device, but I was confident that – given the uncharted terrain in which the vehicles operated – they would be equipped with sophisticated GPS navigation systems.

I had no idea how I could get control of one of the vehicles, but there is an adage in the spy world, 'Fortune smiles on the prepared mind', and I knew I would have no hope of implementing any plan if fever from my wounded foot took hold. Already the flesh around my ankle was hot to the touch and infection was starting to creep up my calf. Without a course of powerful antibiotics, there was only one solution—

I unbandaged the wound and, to the accompaniment of men

praying loudly, loosened the tourniquet. The blood had coagulated around the wound but now, with the pressure reduced on the artery, it started to bleed again.

I removed the last of the bandage, stretched out my foot, and the rich smell of blood attracted the flies. Within seconds, not just the wound but my entire foot was a seething, shifting, black mass of them. I lay back and tried not to think too much about it. The flies would lay their eggs in the wound and within a short time they would hatch into larvae – maggots, in other words. In order to survive, the white worms would eat the damaged flesh and, in a quirk of nature, enzymes produced by their digestion would disinfect the wound. I kept my eyes averted – trying to ignore the crawling sensation over my foot and not think about worms burrowing into my body. When I heard the prayer coming to its end, I swept the flies away and started to rebandage the wound.

I had just finished when the three horsemen, al-Tundra's lieutenants, loomed over me. They were older than their comrades, their skin the texture and colour of tanned leather, and were clearly veterans of God knows how many wars.

They forced me to hop and limp to the most rugged of the four-by-fours; the pick-up equipped with the largest supplementary tanks that I had already identified as the best vehicle to try and commandeer.

Moments after arriving at its tailgate, however, I learned that al-Tundra and his team had come well prepared. The leader of my escort ripped a tarpaulin off the vehicle's flatbed, revealing a large cage made of heavy-gauge steel mesh.

The escort leader loosened two large bolts, swung the cage door open and in Arabic ordered me inside. Without any alternative, I bent my head, climbed into the mobile cell and sat on the floor, thankful at least to get the weight off my foot. The man flicked away his cigarette, slid the bolts back into place and padlocked them.

'Hand,' he said, motioning for me to put my right hand through the mesh. One of the other guards gave him a pair of handcuffs, and he secured my wrist to the steel frame so that I was not only locked inside a cage but also virtually immobilized.

The idea of taking a vehicle, as ill formed as it may have been, was finished and any hope of escape appeared to have died with it.

2

IN MANY RESPECTS, THE HUGE CAVE WAS MORE SPECTACULAR THAN any cathedral. Firelight danced across walls that rose a hundred feet from the dirt floor to a vaulted roof, dark shadows played across ancient rock formations and from somewhere deep within the mountain I heard the sound of a commodity far more valuable than anything else in that brutal land: running water.

The narrow mouth of the cavern, commanding a stunning view across plunging gorges and a trackless mountain range, was barely wide enough for the vehicles to pass through and had offered no hint of the vast space that lay beyond it.

Staring out from the cage, I was certain that somewhere deep in the darkness out of range of the light cast by two cooking fires, past the watercourse, down tiny passages, beyond colonies of bats, nests of scorpions and the bones of animals, there were stone fireplaces dating from the dawn of time. The oldest cave paintings in the world were created fifty thousand years ago, and if someone had told me that somewhere in the hidden depths of the cavern, unmarked on any map, there were artworks of a similar antiquity, I wouldn't have been surprised.

The ten vehicles – with me secured in the one at the rear – had taken over two hours of hard driving, most of it cross-country, to reach the place. Before the convoy set off, a guard had tied the tarpaulin over the cage so that, by my guess, I was hidden from any satellite overpass, ensuring that even if Langley were lucky enough to spot the convoy, they would have no way of knowing what had happened. Imprisoned in darkness and struggling to breathe in the heat, hurled from side to side by the terrain, my handcuffed wrist almost broken every time we crossed a gully, my head constantly smacked against the steel mesh and my maggot-infested foot ablaze with pain, there were times when I thought the high-speed rough ride might finish me.

But the rugged landscape did deliver one unintended benefit – not even the tarpaulin could withstand it. After an hour's travel, while the pick-up was plunging down a steep ravine and with the suspension barely coping, two of the clips securing the tarp finally snapped, the howling desert wind roared under the heavy fabric, tore it free of the remaining anchors and sent it sailing across miles of saltbush. By that stroke of good fortune, not only was the temperature in the cage immediately lowered but, as the pick-up climbed a high ridge, it gave me the chance to look across the broad expanse of wilderness we had just crossed: I saw no vehicles, nor any telltale plumes of dust that signalled another convoy was following in our wake.

I was taken aback – a few minutes after I had been locked in the cage, and moments before the tarp was thrown over it, I saw al-Tundra and the other horsemen mount up, wheel their horses and ride south. I was certain they were heading to the roadblock where Laleh and the two Blackwater agents had been captured and I fully expected that the convoy transporting them would be in sight behind us. It wasn't, and the delay made me think of Laleh. She was a young woman, and maybe the battle-hardened men holding her had decided to treat her as a spoil of war, especially as their leader had already condemned her to death.

With that thought still on my mind, I looked past the two cooking fires into the gloom beyond: by their light, I saw that the cave had been set up as a forward operating base, hidden from satellite over-sight and ideal for launching the numerous patrols that had set out to locate and capture me. Now, with the task complete, the handful of Army soldiers stationed inside were striking camp. In the shadows off to the right – the sunlight streaming through the mouth of the cave was starting to fade and dusk was closing in – I saw a one-armed soldier working in front of dozens of tiny green lights. It looked like he was responsible for communications and was changing the batteries of a dozen high-quality walkie-talkies and a rack of night-vision goggles.

He turned and saw that I was looking at him; his dark eyes stared back, he walked close to the cage and his lip curled in a sneer. He pointed at the stump of his right arm. 'Syria. American drone,' he said bitterly in accented English.

He was about to continue speaking, but a walkie-talkie clipped to his waist buzzed as somebody miles away made contact. The connection was terrible and both men had to half shout, speaking in Arabic, to make themselves heard.

It appeared that the man at the other end – a friend, apparently – was with the vehicles that had taken Laleh, Ghorbani and Bahman prisoner. Over the screech of electronic interference, I heard that their convoy was still several hours away – stopped at an abandoned village about ten klicks upstream from the bridge – and the unseen man wanted to make sure that food would be ready when they arrived.

'What's happening with the other three prisoners?' I heard the one-armed man ask.

For a brief moment the electronic storm abated and I heard his friend laugh. 'Well, for a start,' he said, 'there's only two of them now.'

3

I HEARD NO MORE. I LEANED FORWARD IN THE CAGE, DESPERATE TO learn who was alive and who was dead, just as the cave was bathed in a searing light and I was deafened by a mechanical roar.

I turned and saw two soldiers standing next to a diesel generator; prompted by the fast-fading daylight, they had used a hand crank to start it up and set ablaze rows of overhead work-lights.

The one-armed man, the walkie-talkie close to his ear, could hear nothing against the backdrop of the thumping machine, and turned and walked towards the much quieter area near the cave entrance, out of earshot. I slumped back against the bars of my cage, frustrated, dreading what might be taking place in an abandoned village somewhere out there.

There was nothing I could do. There was nothing anyone could do. I stared at the brilliantly lit cavern, envying for a moment those people who had a religion they could find comfort in, then lowered my head and tried to sleep. Them today, me tomorrow, I thought again.

4

I WAS EXHAUSTED, BUT I COULDN'T SLEEP. FOR THREE HOURS I SAT, barely moving, chasing my thoughts, half expecting another burst of news from a walkie-talkie or the sound of engines as al-Tundra's convoy approached.

They threw food into the cage, but I had no appetite. In my world of pain, carrying the reminder of every blow, I felt the heat that had been rising from my wounded foot suddenly hit my groin, making me gasp with agony. My forehead was already beaded with sweat, but now it began to run in rivulets down my spine and I felt myself burning up. Accompanied by a piercing headache and a wave of chills cold enough to make me shake, I knew that my immune system – and the maggots, hopefully – was starting to engage in the climactic battle to try and defeat the blossoming infection.

My temperature continued to soar, and the temptation was to grab the water pouch attached to the side of the cage and cool myself by dumping it over my torso, but I knew it was a mistake; the heat of an elevated temperature was one way the body destroyed an invading pathogen, and I needed all the help I could get. Drawing my knees up under my chin and wrapping my filthy clothes tighter round my body in readiness for the next bout of chills, I felt my mind slip and start to roam across memory as a host of fevered thoughts overwhelmed me—

I saw the courier nailed to the crucifix, but he was on a hill outside Jerusalem now. Six Roman centurions were drawing lots to see who would claim the possessions of a crucified carpenter – the Nazarene – while, along the nearby ridges, brightly coloured Buddhist prayer flags flew in the wind and I was trekking through the Himalayas, heading into Kathmandu. At sunset on the terrace of a spectacular monastery, I met a Chinese dissident who had risked her life to cross the border and handed me a small incense box containing the name of a Chinese official who loved money more than his country. I looked at the incense sticks inside and I was standing in front of the statue of the Buddha in the temple at Angkor Wat. A priest in orange robes appeared and told me to light the joss sticks. 'A parent never dies,' he said. 'Not as long as their children remember them.' I lit a match, the smoke swirled, and I was crossing the Quadrangle at the Naval Academy in Annapolis, a phone ringing in my pocket—

It was my first year at the academy and I was walking with two other midshipmen, talking sports and laughing, when I saw the caller ID. My dad rarely called – he left that to Mom – and he certainly didn't do it during the middle of the day. Alarm rising, I indicated to my companions to walk on and clicked answer. The memory was so real, the vision so sharp, that I could feel the sunshine of an early East Coast summer on my back.

Dad had always prided himself on being a strong man, never given to outward signs of emotion, but I could tell immediately he was close to tears. Earlier in the day my mother had been diagnosed with an aggressive form of breast cancer and the evidence was that it had already metastasized. The doctors told them that they would do whatever they could but, in all likelihood, it would only be a matter of months.

The news hit me hard; I knew Mom had lost weight, but she hadn't even told me she was going for tests. The catastrophic development meant from that day on, every chance I got, I drove through the night and flew the redeye to Florida. As Mom's condition deteriorated, exactly as the doctors had predicted, the trip became a weekly pilgrimage. Every Friday night, always making sure I was wearing the expensive sweater she had bought to ease my passage into the preppy world of the academy, I took up residence opposite Dad at her bedside. There, surrounded by the cancer ward's unique odour of antiseptic and fear, we ended up – like most of the other inhabitants – quietly shifting all our hope from medicine to miracles. I was young, not even twenty, too young to be on a death watch, as Dad told me many times, but I had always thought that a man who didn't stand with his family – well, he wasn't any good, was he?

After the disease had reached its inevitable conclusion, all my concern turned to Dad. He and Mom had been married for thirty years and I knew that loneliness would present a serious danger to him. Although he always tried to keep his spirits up during our phone calls and he battled on with his pool maintenance business, I knew his heart was no longer in it. A few months later he quietly closed it down, drifted into retirement and busied himself with inventing home improvement jobs to keep himself occupied.

Mom's death, when it finally came, had been anything but a surprise, but Dad's was the polar opposite. Just over a year after our vigil in the hospital had ended, unbeknown to him and producing virtually no symptoms – a situation common to almost every case – a section of his aorta, the largest artery, had steadily ballooned to over three times its normal size. Known as an aneurysm, it burst as he was at a hardware megastore picking up supplies for yet another one of his make-busy projects.

Pushing his shopping cart across the parking lot in the blinding heat of a Florida summer, he fell to the ground, his blood pressure collapsing instantly and his stomach filling with blood as his heart pumped furiously to try to restore it. The bright arterial fluid then poured out of his mouth and on to the baking black asphalt. Within seconds, there was so much blood sizzling on the bitumen that a Black guy in his thirties – a contractor – who was loading pavers into his pick-up thought the sixty-year-old guy with the bright blue eyes must have been shot. Bless him, though; ignoring any danger to himself, he ran to Dad's aid, and he was the one who called emergency services and begged them to send an ambulance immediately. Unfortunately, the late-afternoon traffic was already building and there were long tailbacks on the Interstate. Maybe if the operator had sent a chopper, things might have been different but, as it was, Dad died – still lying on the fiery asphalt – two minutes after the paramedics arrived.

Throughout the long wait for the ambulance, the contractor, built like a cruiser-weight, and with a gold earring and a Maori warrior tattoo around one bicep, never left Dad's side, holding his hand and trying to comfort him as the end approached.

When I finally received the death certificate, it said that Dad had died from what the doctors termed a 'Triple-A', an abdominal aortic aneurysm. Yes, it was true that Dad had died of a damaged heart, but I didn't think it was caused by an aneurysm; I figured his heart had been broken the year before, when Mom had died.

Many months later, after I had tracked the contractor down to thank him for everything he'd done, I asked him why – despite thinking there was a chance he might be shot himself – he had still rushed to help. He looked at me for a long moment in surprise. 'Well, what did you expect me to do, leave him there?' he asked.

'Some people would have,' I replied. 'You a Christian, Dave?'

He laughed. 'In a way, I suppose I am,' he said. 'But I hope to God you never end up at my church – it's called Narcotics Anonymous.'

I grinned back, stared across at the setting sun, and asked him something that had been on my mind for a long time. 'Did he say anything?' I said. 'Before he passed, I mean.'

'He was in shock for most of it,' Dave explained, serious now. 'Then, right at the end, just one word.'

'Help?' I hazarded.

He shook his head. 'No, I think he realized it was too late for that – he knew he was on the threshold,' he said. 'Before he crossed it, he said the one word that seemed to mean everything to him.' He paused and looked me in the eye. 'He said your name. Ridley.'

And that thought was with me still, playing in my head and echoing off the brightly lit rock walls of a cave somewhere inside Iran. I looked around, as if seeing the cavern for the first time, unable to determine if I was awake or asleep, and then glanced down at my clothes. They were drenched in sweat and I realized that the fever had broken.

I would have stayed sitting there, unmoving, for hours, but from the world outside, I heard the throb of engines. I turned and looked through the mouth of the cave, seeing not only that night had well and truly fallen, but that al-Tundra's convoy was inching its way into the cavern.

I rose to my knees and leaned forward, gripping the mesh, desperate to see who among the prisoners, if any, was still alive.

5

THE VEHICLES DREW TO A STOP AT THE SIDE OF THE CAVERN, AND even though it was a long way from the work-lights, there was still enough light to throw them into sharp relief.

Staring through the mesh, I watched the soldiers, led by al-Tundra, cast lowering shadows on the rock walls as they spilled out of the four-by-fours and headed for the food tables at the rear. They were in high spirits, but that only made my task more bitter, searching among the shifting crowd and running my eye along the vehicles for any sign of Ghorbani, Bahman or Laleh.

Assuming that all three had been killed, I was about to turn away when I saw the rear door of an SUV right at the back swing open. A guard emerged and, moments later, hauled Bahman out behind him. The skinny guy, nervous at the best of times, had his ankles shackled and looked exhausted – shattered, more like it. The surge of relief I felt – at least one of them had survived – evaporated within the time it took the guard to take two steps: he was leading Bahman towards the food tables, and I knew exactly what that meant. They wouldn't be feeding him if he hadn't talked. Undoubtedly, he had told them everything they wanted to know about his network and the secret sources he worked with in Tehran.

I swung my eyes back to the SUV, in time to see a guard pull a second prisoner out of the vehicle. It wasn't Ghorbani, though, and for a moment I barely recognized Laleh. She was unveiled, her head and eyebrows had been shaved, but she was *alive*.

I allowed myself to breathe again and watched as she looked around at the vast cave, confused and terrified, and then I saw her eye fall on me. She nodded in relief: I might be a captive but at least for now she wasn't alone.

Probably thinking it was easier to supervise two prisoners in close proximity, the guard yanked the chain attached to her shackles and dragged her towards the cage. I gave her a crooked smile but said nothing; I didn't know whether al-Tundra had voiced his suspicions about whether she could hear and speak but, if he hadn't, I certainly didn't want to reveal the truth. The guard zip-tied her wrist to the cage, checked she was secure and went to eat. As we waited for him to move out of earshot, I handed Laleh the food they had thrown at me earlier, and it was clear from the way she tore into it that she was famished. Bent over, cramming her mouth with naan, I could see the congealed blood in dozens of places on her head and neck where they had cut the skin as they had shaved her.

In the West, traditionally, a woman's head was shaved to publicly shame her – I had heard once that in France, at the end of the Second World War, thousands of women who had collaborated with the Nazis were shorn of their hair in front of large and cheering crowds. In most Middle Eastern and South Asian countries, it fulfils a similar function – but, in my experience, it also does something far worse. Under Islam, it is *haram* for a woman to shave her head or eyebrows. And so it was with Laleh; the men had done it to the young woman not only to humiliate and shame her as a collaborator but also to signify that she was no longer in a state of grace with her religion. She was a woman apart and, once someone was apart, there are those who believe they can do whatever they like to them.

Laleh must have sensed that I was looking at her head. She glanced up and I saw that her eyes were filled with tears; a woman's hair is a precious thing in many cultures. Certain now that we couldn't be heard, I indicated her skull and spoke in Arabic. 'It's cool,' I said, smiling. 'It looks really cool.'

She said nothing and, worried that an English-language slang expression had got lost in translation, I asked her in Arabic: 'You understand?'

She nodded. 'You mean fashionable,' she said in English.

I stared at her, shocked. 'My father taught English in Kabul,' she explained quietly. 'Myself and my siblings were his best students. For most of the time, his only students.'

I sat in silence for a moment, thinking about what her life must have been like before, and the situation in which she found herself now.

'Thank you for the food,' she said, wiping her tears, looking at me.

I nodded in acknowledgement. 'And Bahman talked?' I asked, adjusting the zip-tie that secured her wrist, giving her a little more freedom.

'How do you know?' she said.

'They're feeding him. I'm sorry to ask,' I continued quietly. 'What happened to Ghorbani?'

She looked at me for a long moment. 'I don't think you want to know.'

6

'THEY CAME OUT OF NOWHERE,' SHE SAID, DESCRIBING WHAT HAD happened after I had thrown myself from their car. 'In less than a minute we were surrounded by a dozen vehicles.'

'I saw they'd stopped you,' I said. 'I was watching from further down the road.'

'I thought you might be,' she replied.

'They surrounded you – and then?'

'They dragged Ghorbani and Bahman out,' she continued. 'They said one of their drones had seen us camped under the bridge the day before and they knew who we were waiting for. They put guns to their heads and asked where you were, but they didn't get a chance to answer. Four men on horses rode up and said you had already been captured – well, that was what their leader, the one who was in charge, said.'

'Yeah, he was the one who shot me,' I explained. 'To the West, he is a terrorist called al-Tundra. But some of the men call him the Colonel, I think.'

'Yeah, Colonel Kazinsky,' she replied casually. 'Roman Kazinsky.'

I stared at her, rendered speechless. A waif-like refugee, a girl tricked out of a camp full of desperate people, had done what the world's most sophisticated and powerful intelligence agencies – utilizing all their thousands of covert agents and analysts – had never been able to achieve: she had put a real-world name to Abu Muslim al-Tundra. 'What?' I said finally.

'His name,' she said. 'Colonel Roman Kazinsky.'

'How do you know that?' I asked.

She shrugged; she had no idea why his identity might be important, but for the first time her face relaxed a little. In different, less harrowing circumstances, she might have smiled. 'When people don't think you can speak or hear,' she said, 'they're not very careful about what they say. I overheard a conversation between two of the men.'

The irony of the situation hit me once more – I now had the real name of the Army's military commander and, while I knew nothing of the spectacular they were planning, the information alone was a huge leap forward. But with no way to transmit it, locked in a cage in a cavern somewhere in the wilds of Iran, it was worthless – along with me, the intelligence would soon vanish into the void, never to be heard of again.

'So, Roman Kazinsky arrives,' I said to Laleh. 'What then?'

'He looked at their documents,' she recounted. 'And laughed. Then he asked what they really did in Tehran. They both had their stories. Then they told him about being paid to help a man find his wife's sister but, like you said, nobody believed it. He kept asking them about the CIA and a place or a person called Blackwater.'

I didn't correct her about Blackwater; it didn't matter. 'But they stuck to their story?'

She nodded. 'Many times, Kazinsky demanded to know what their real work was. How they communicated, who their contacts were. He wouldn't stop – I don't know why.'

'He knew they were part of an intelligence network,' I said. 'He wanted information he could trade with PAVA, the Iranian secret police – in return he would get protection, weapons, money, whatever he and his organization needed. Those two men were a gift from Allah.'

Laleh fixed her eyes on me. 'It's true then . . . what they said about you? You're a spy?'

I said nothing for a beat and then I smiled. 'Sure, but it's a secret – don't tell anyone.' This time she really did smile.

'Ghorbani and Bahman still haven't talked,' I said, drawing her back to the narrative. 'And the Colonel didn't hit them, or hurt them?'

'Not yet, not at the roadblock,' she replied.

'Where?' I said, feeling a sense of doom.

'He ordered his men to drive along the riverbed, upstream from where the bridge was,' she explained, her voice growing quieter as the memory intruded. 'We stopped at the ruins of a village, a place that had been almost washed away in a flood. Just a few houses and the old kitchen were still standing.

'The Colonel got some sort of a surgical or dental backpack, you know – one of those with a green cross on it – out of his saddlebag and, after they had thrown camouflage tarpaulins over the vehicles, he ordered everyone into the kitchen. Because of the satellites, I suppose.

'It was dark inside and incredibly hot,' she continued. 'All the men gathered in a circle and he made Ghorbani and Bahman kneel on the floor in the middle.

'He asked them more questions – well, the same questions but more times – and they repeated they were there to earn money. He focused on Ghorbani, taunting him, then he started threatening him. I couldn't understand – even I could see that Bahman was more terrified. Why not concentrate on him?'

'Because the Colonel is an expert,' I said quietly. 'You were right, Bahman was the most vulnerable, but Kazinsky was playing chess – he was sacrificing Ghorbani in order to terrify Bahman even more and make him talk. How bad did it get for Ghorbani?'

'The worst,' she said. 'The Colonel ordered his men to throw a rope over a beam that ran the length of the room. Ghorbani fought, but they had cattle-prods. I thought they were going to hang him, but they strung him up by his feet. Once they had him hanging upside down, they hauled on the ropes until his face was almost level with Kazinsky's.'

'Where were you?' I asked.

'My legs were chained, sitting against a far wall – they didn't care about me, not yet anyway,' she said ominously. 'But they dragged Bahman forward, even closer, and forced him to watch. Kazinsky opened the backpack and took out a pouch of tools.'

My heart sank. I knew what was coming. 'What sort of tools?'

'A scalpel, tongs, forceps, electrical tape . . .' she said, but she didn't know the English word for several of them so she described them in Arabic.

'Pliers,' I said. 'And dental blockers. You put them between the upper and lower teeth at the back, expand them with screws and the patient can't close their mouth. Now the dentist – or the torturer – can do whatever they like inside the victim's wide-open mouth. Ghorbani was trying to fight, I suppose—'

'He couldn't. His arms were tied, but he resisted – he wouldn't open his mouth,' she said. 'Kazinsky got one of his men to put a clamp on his nose, and then he had to in order to breathe. Once he did, the Colonel broke two of his teeth forcing the blockers in. That was when Ghorbani really started screaming—'

Laleh kept talking, but my thoughts overtook her and left her voice behind. I no longer needed her: I could picture what Kazinsky did in all its medieval horror.

7

AT THE END, SHE SAT QUIETLY, HER SILENCE AND TEARS AN ELOQUENT testament to the savagery she had witnessed. After an eternity, I asked her what had happened after Ghorbani's tongue had been cut out.

'They left him hanging,' she replied. 'I realized then why they had tied him upside down – otherwise, with all the blood, he would have drowned if he'd been standing up.'

'Kazinsky turned to his men,' she continued, 'pointed at Bahman and told them to string him up. Bahman started screaming, but I guess he had learned the lesson. He started begging Kazinsky to ask him *anything*—'

'And then, I'm guessing, Bahman gave it all up,' I said. I could almost see the cranes being assembled in a Tehran square as they rounded up his network. But I couldn't blame the man – I wondered if anyone on earth could have withstood the psychological onslaught. 'Is Ghorbani alive?'

'He was still hanging,' she replied. 'Then suddenly he made this noise – the death rattle, I suppose – and he was gone. I don't think it was loss of blood, though. A heart attack?'

'Probably,' I said. 'And you?' I asked as gently as I could. 'Did they—'

'They wanted to,' she replied. 'Not all of them, but most. Kazinsky ordered them to start driving, though – he said they might get their chance later.' She indicated the cave, and I understood why she had looked so terrified when she was dragged out of the SUV. 'Here?' she said softly. 'Do you think it will be here?'

'No,' I responded. 'They're packing up – it's a moonless night and I figure in another hour, when it's totally dark, we'll be heading out. You're safe at the moment.'

'Where are we going?' she asked.

'No idea,' I replied. As I looked at her – her fingers starting to touch her shaved head again, the shame returning – an idea struck me. I untied the bandana I had been wearing around my neck for weeks, drenched it in water from the pouch on the side of the cage and rinsed the dirt and sweat out of it.

'For your head,' I said, handing it to her. She looked at me, grateful, and I motioned for her to lean forward so that together – both of us using our one free hand – we could tie it in place. 'Now *that* is fashionable,' I said.

She smiled, but as I looked at her I saw a fresh wave of anxiety wash across her face. 'They're going to come for you, aren't they?'

'Who?' I said, confused. 'Kazinsky? He's already got me.'

'No, your people,' she said. 'The American military – they'll come to rescue their spy. I will be left alone with them, won't I?' She indicated the scores of men in the cave.

I shook my head. 'No, you won't be abandoned,' I said gently. 'But neither will anyone be coming for me. My one chance was Bahman and Ghorbani. I'm not supposed to be in-country – Washington will deny I even work for them, they'll say I'm not an American. Go talk to the British or Canadians. Something like that. There won't be any rescue.'

She slumped. 'It's over then? For both of us?'

'Not until we're dead,' I said, sounding more hopeful than I felt. 'I thought I might be able to steal a vehicle, but that was before this.' I indicated the cage. 'Even if I got a chance now, there's far too many of them. But I'm still thinking. There's always a way.'

It did nothing to lessen her fear; sensible young woman, I thought. 'If I can make it happen, though,' I said. 'If just once on this mission something runs my way, I won't leave you – I promise, I'll take you with me.'

She looked at me for a long moment, seemingly wanting to trust me but not sure. 'People say you can't believe anything Americans tell you,' she said at last.

'The woman I live with says I'm handsome,' I said, smiling. 'See – people talk crap all the time. I give you my word, Laleh.'

'*Insha'Allah*,' she said. If God wills it. And tentatively, she touched my hand through the bars.

8

AS KAZINSKY AND HIS MEN PACKED UP THE LAST OF THEIR EQUIPMENT, about to head to places unknown – seven thousand miles away, another team was also closing up its facility and turning off the lights.

In the makeshift war room at Langley, the conference room where the mission to try and rescue me had been planned, teams of technicians were removing the racks of computers and stowing away the hi-def screens. Only two people remained, waiting hopelessly for word from the Blackwater extraction team that they had collected the agent on the run and he was on the electric bike. For those two people, Falcon and Madeleine, it was word that would never come.

I know of the events at Langley because, some months later,

Madeleine told me in detail about how the agency was forced to face the failure of the mission and the loss of its agents.

'The satellite had seen you at the airfield,' she said. 'We had decoded the SFGG message and we knew you were going overland, trying to reach the bridge. Two days later we received a heavily encrypted message from Ghorbani via Bahman's computer shop. It said Lord Dostum's best smuggler had arrived with the electric bikes, they were now in the back of a Toyota and he and Bahman were leaving for the rendezvous.'

'Falcon briefed the entire team about exactly what lay ahead – three days of relentless anxiety, of checking the whereabouts of the Blackwater guys in the Toyota, getting the choppers in place, monitoring every piece of radio chatter from the zone and, most of all, scanning every satellite image for any further message from you. He said nobody could leave the building, we had to stake out a corner somewhere to sleep, and we'd be splitting into two teams so that everyone got a chance to eat and rest. Only a few people in the room had any real experience of it, he said, but we were going full-operational – twelve hours on, twelve hours off.'

Madeleine smiled at me as she recounted the events. 'Except for Falcon, of course – he worked both shifts, grabbing a few hours' rest on the couch in his office when he could, patrolling the conference room, manning an open line to the NSA, checking with the route planners and hoping the satellite would catch an image of you as you headed for the bridge.'

Her smile faded. 'But there weren't any images and the satellite didn't show any footsteps or tracks you might have left—'

'They were looking in the wrong place,' I said. 'I had to make a diversion to get water.'

'We didn't know that then,' she replied. 'We just knew the satellites were seeing drones everywhere and a hacked Pakistani communication told us the Army of the Pure was hunting a high-value fugitive. Then you missed the ETA at the rendezvous. Suddenly you were overdue – one day, then two – and that set off a huge alarm.'

'What did Falcon do?' I asked.

'What could anyone do except keep the faith? Then a codeword, a digital burst sent via a server in Kazakhstan to avoid the Pakistanis, hit a secret NSA address. It was from Bahman's computer and told us you'd arrived. You can imagine – the room exploded.'

'The news flew fast and the team that were resting emerged. Falcon told us that five hours after the Toyota left the bridge, we could expect to get the message we'd all been hoping for: you had crossed the border into Afghanistan.'

'If only . . .' I said, thinking of Ghorbani drifting the vehicle through the corners and then hanging upside down and screaming as Kazinsky's pliers touched his tongue—

'You okay?' Madeleine asked after a moment.

'Just thinking how close to the border we were, how different it might have been,' I said.

'I know,' she continued. 'That night, we heard nothing more, so we thought everything was going to plan.

'Any moment we were expecting to hear that the Special Forces had got the call, you had crossed the border and they were about to get you on board,' she said. 'But there was no call and after twenty minutes Falcon ordered the choppers airborne to see if they could put eyes on you.

'Nothing, so we kept waiting,' she said. 'Two, four, five hours. Then Buster knelt beside Falcon and told him that everyone should be stood down. Falcon nodded, and the brains trust returned to the seventh floor and all the photo analysts and mission architects shuffled out, defeated. In the end, it was just Falcon and I.'

'Keeping a lantern in the window,' I said.

'Yeah,' she replied. 'Seven thousand miles away, the Special Forces were doing the same in their helicopters. After an hour they made contact and requested permission to return to base. I thought it was obvious: of course they should. But Falcon refused, he said maybe you had abandoned the dirt bike and were crossing on foot.

'By then, you were six hours late; it would have made you a slow walker,' she said. 'I didn't buy the possibility, I don't think Falcon did either – so, politely at first, and then less so, I told him he should go home and rest.' She shrugged. 'But he wouldn't consider it, he just kept sitting in front of the row of priority phones.

'They didn't ring and we didn't move – all we could do was wait.'

9

NIGHT HAD FALLEN, AS MADELEINE LOOKED AT ME, LOST IN MEMORY
for a moment. 'How did it end?' I asked.

'I was exhausted,' she said. 'Eventually I told Falcon I had to go
home and get some sleep, so I left. But I've seen the CCTV of the
room – he sat there all night, almost in darkness.

'He looked like a broken man, and I remember thinking how
understandable that was. The mission was a bust, the courier was
dead, the two Blackwater agents were missing and you had obviously
been captured or, more likely, killed.

'Just before dawn,' she continued, 'he got up, switched off the lights
and locked the door. I guess he had finally accepted it. That was
Thursday. He came into work the next day, but nobody saw him. He
stayed up in his office, alone.'

'I'm not surprised,' I said quietly. 'As far as he was concerned – and
the agency also – it was a failure, finished. The LOCUST mission was
over and the spectacular was still on track.'

10

IT MUST HAVE BEEN ABOUT 9 P.M. WHEN THE COLONEL LED THE
convoy out of the cave in total darkness. The drivers were wearing
helmets fitted with night-vision goggles – looking like aliens in a
Martian landscape – so they didn't need their headlights, giving them
a much better chance of avoiding satellite surveillance.

Earlier, while the engines were filling the cave with blue exhaust,
one of the guards, following an order from Kazinsky, checked the
lock on my cage and then cut the zip-tie that secured Laleh to the
frame, hauled her to the back door of the vehicle and threw her
inside. He climbed in, grabbed her wrist and cuffed it to a grab handle
above the door.

As tightly secured as she was, she managed to twist her head and look at me through the rear windshield; I think it helped her to know that we were together. There hadn't been any indication – not from Kazinsky or any of the troops – about where we were going, let alone what fate they had in mind for us. Whatever it was, I didn't expect it to be over quickly or painlessly.

The only hint came when the Colonel, ready to leave, yelled to the troops above the engines: 'It's twelve hours overland,' he said, first in Arabic and then in Farsi. 'We stop only for prayers and to refuel from the drums on board. Nobody is late – time and tide wait for no man.'

He turned to me, switching into English. 'You know who wrote it?'

I didn't answer, thinking that it was a strange choice of words. Why he had used *tide*? Going on a boat? If that was the case – a boat to where? He was waiting for an answer and I pushed the speculation aside. 'No idea,' I said.

'Geoffrey Chaucer – one of the great English writers. It might be a wilderness out here, but look at us – two educated men can still discuss poetry.'

'Of course,' I replied. 'And only educated men rip out other people's tongues.'

A look of intrigue passed across his face and I immediately realized my mistake: anger had overcome my judgement. 'How do you know about that?' he asked.

I said nothing. 'I see,' he said, glancing at Laleh as she watched us through the rear windshield. 'As I suspected, our refugee is not as deaf and dumb as she claims. The men will be pleased – everyone was disappointed when they thought they wouldn't hear her scream. They say a woman's silence sort of takes the edge off the pleasure.'

He looked at me. 'You were a Saudi traveller, the courier posed as a faithful servant of ours, two workers in Tehran turned out to be Blackwater agents – and now we've got a mute that can talk. There are many secrets in play here. I can't wait to find out what the next surprise will be.' I remained silent. 'No ideas?' he asked.

'My escape?' I replied.

He laughed. 'And then you're thinking about how you will kill me.'

I said nothing, and he patted the cage. 'I'm sorry – you're going to be disappointed on both counts.'

11

THERE WAS NO MOON, JUST THE BITTER COLD OF THE DESERT AND A sweep of stars on a velvet sky, as we left the cave and headed southwest, sticking tight to Kazinsky's mysterious schedule.

Being thrown around in the cage, fighting hard to avoid smashing my head against the steel roof every time we hit a ditch, I knew that – despite what I had said to the Colonel – escape was out of the question. The handcuff may have been fitted too loosely by an amateur and the lock facing the wrong way, but even if I dislocated my thumb or broke my wrist to slip it off, then managed to open the padlocked cage and throw myself off the back, my shattered foot would defeat me. As before, my only hope appeared to be to seize a vehicle.

After five hours we made our way along a wild gorge, plunging through hidden pools, until it narrowed to nothing. The convoy jagged left and, engines screaming, crawled to the surface, and I saw the eastern sky was starting to lighten. Very soon Kazinsky would halt for dawn prayers and I was certain our on-board guard would not take Laleh out of the vehicle for the service.

I knew it would probably be my only chance. With my mind turning over every aspect of the fledgling idea, events started to avalanche. Threading our way through a landscape of huge boulders, the rim of the fiery disc appeared and Kazinsky slowed the convoy, starting to look for a space where the ritual could take place. I realized that if I broke my thumb or wrist to escape the handcuff, the injury – in conjunction with my wounded foot – would so incapacitate me I wouldn't be physically capable of another attempt: if I was going to make a run for it and take Laleh with me, the moment was now.

Suddenly I went flying – the driver had braked hard, and as I scrambled to my knees I saw that we were in a clearing and the vehicles ahead of us had already stopped. I moved back to where my wrist was cuffed to the cage and, despite exhaustion and the aftermath of the fever, I felt more alive than at any time since they had captured me. Maybe I could do this, maybe I could manufacture an escape, maybe I could deliver a surprise to a terrorist who thought he had seen them all.

I braced myself, set aside any thoughts of the agony that might be coming down the pike and reassured myself: I was trained for this. With my free hand, using all the strength I could muster, I squeezed the palm of my captive hand just below the handcuff, feeling the dozen or so bones and joints beneath the flesh start to compress, making the complex structure as small and narrow as possible. Holding my breath, pain shooting up my forearm, I started to drag my crushed palm through the metal bracelet.

The steel of the cuff bit into the flesh and I looked down and saw blood start to flow around my wrist and thumb, but the thought of whatever pain Kazinsky had in store for me concentrated my mind enormously and I crushed my palm even more, making it smaller, pulling harder, feeling the metal bite deeper—

The pick-up rolled to a complete halt and, without relieving any of the pressure on my hand, I saw that the bull bar in front of our radiator was barely an inch away from, almost touching, the side of a heavy-duty fuel carrier. Thankfully, its occupants were starting to perform *wudu* and nobody paid me any attention. Except for Laleh – she had looked out the rear window and realized what I was doing. I nodded at her in acknowledgement and looked down, bit my lip and wrenched my captive hand as hard as I could, hoping I could rip and tear it through the bracelet. The handcuff might have been poorly fitted and too loose, but it held tight.

With blood streaming down my hand, I prepared for the next option: I took hold of my thumb and got ready to dislocate it. The *Adhan* was already partway through and I had to hurry – if dislocating my thumb didn't work I had to make sure I had enough time left to break my wrist. Gritting my teeth, I grabbed hold of the thumb with my free hand, planted my foot against the side of the cage and began to twist and bend it, starting to separate the joint—

I heard an engine behind me and, worried somebody would see, I turned towards the noise: a modified Land Rover – a vehicle that had been travelling at the back of the pack – was arriving in the clearing. In a rush to join the prayer, it was coming straight towards me, the driver only braking at the last minute and sliding to a halt barely a foot from the pick-up's tailgate.

I stared at it in disbelief and then looked up and saw Laleh's face.

Like me, she had realized what it meant. With the fuel carrier broadside right in front of us and the Land Rover stopped on our tail, we were boxed in. The only way out was to move one of the two vehicles, and there was no hope of doing that in time or without being seen.

Defeated, I let my bleeding hand drop. I had little doubt that everything was lost and yet, if I had thought a little more deeply about it, I would have realized that it wasn't necessarily the case. Judging by the direction we were travelling and from Kazinsky's reference to the tide, I had decided several hours earlier that we had to be heading for the Persian Gulf.

I might have been barely able to walk, running wasn't an option, but I could swim; if there was one place where someone in my condition might have a chance, it was in the ocean.

12

OUR PRISON-ON-WHEELS CRESTED A HILL AND IN THE EARLY-MORNING light I saw a stunning beach: puffs of white cloud drifted above a half-moon bay, a sweep of dunes rose into the desert and the fine white sand was lapped by the turquoise waters of the Gulf.

By my estimate, we were about forty klicks south of the remote Iranian port of Bandar Lengeh, and while the long stretch of deserted sand could have been any one of a thousand beaches on empty parts of Australia or South Africa, I knew that three hundred miles across the water lay the brutal monarchies of Qatar, Bahrain and Saudi Arabia.

I could see that the tide was full, the sea flooding up the sand. Beyond it, out in the Gulf, the wind was picking up, corrugating the surface of the water, starting to drive whitecaps south through the narrow Strait of Hormuz, probably the most strategically important sea-lane in the world, the place where – like tectonic plates – Western sea power and the Iranian Navy ground against each other on a daily basis.

But it wasn't just any wind that was promising to create mayhem among the several dozen supertankers and warships negotiating the twenty-mile-wide choke point. As the sun rose, I was almost certain – from its direction and blistering heat – that the strengthening wind was what the people of the Gulf call the Shamal. As old as the desert itself, the Shamal blows several times a year, straight out of Syria, through Iraq, past Kuwait and down the Gulf, a nor'wester that is an ill wind for all those in its path, not least for Laleh and myself.

Even though it was still early, the sun and searing wind were already turning the beach into a furnace and as I ran my eye along it I was surprised to see that there was no boat, no jetty, no sign of anything that would have led me to think that a seaborne journey was in our future. It wasn't until several hours later, when the beach had passed its flood and the water was dropping fast, that I saw the ruins of an old wharf emerge from the sea and began to work out the tide's significance. The wooden structure must have been wrecked in a storm decades before and all that remained were half a dozen thick upright posts like a row of broken teeth.

By that time the beach was no longer deserted. Hundreds, maybe even thousands, of the Army's soldiers – heavily armed, fearsome men – had left their primary base, wherever that might be, and arrived at the beach. Among the men spilling out of their four-by-fours, bandoliers and assault rifles slung over their shoulders, I saw three equipped with hi-def video cameras and a boom mic. I should have known: executing a CIA spy and publicly releasing the footage would be of enormous propaganda value to the Army.

It was exactly what a different terrorist group had done to a man called Daniel Pearl some years earlier. He was a journalist – the local bureau chief for the *Wall Street Journal* – who was kidnapped outside the Metropole Hotel in Karachi and beheaded nine days later. I am sure Pearl was a better and braver man than me – certainly a far more innocent one – but in the hierarchy of such things a captured CIA agent would far outrank him.

Laleh had seen the camera crew too. Alone in the vehicle – our guards had thrown us each a pouch of water and had set off to join their comrades at the cooking fires – she managed, by using her teeth and her free hand, to open a sliding glass window in the centre of the rear windshield. 'What are they going to film?' she asked me through it.

'My execution,' I replied.

She paused briefly. 'Mine, too?' she asked, barely above a whisper.

There was no point in providing false hope; she would learn the truth soon enough. 'That's their plan, I think,' I said, looking out at four members of the Army equipped with drills and tool belts who had waded out and were working on two of the old wooden posts.

'Why? Why film it?' she said.

'Recruitment,' I replied, shrugging. 'I'm a trophy. Impact – to show the world and other terrorist groups they are a group to be reckoned with. In a few hours, they'll post it on YouTube. It will be banned, of course, but all that will do is generate more publicity. By tomorrow, it'll be all over social media and the Dark Web.'

She struggled to fight back the tears. 'It means my parents will see it.'

'Where are they?' I asked.

'My mother's in Kabul, with my sister,' she answered. 'Because my father taught English and wanted his two girls to work and have a future, we knew he was in danger. The Taliban had taken over the city and my parents decided he should leave. Just before midnight he boarded a bus to Kandahar and then took an overland trail into Iran. But all the following day, I worried about him – he's old and he's got diabetes.' She paused, a catch in her throat. 'I love him so much . . .'

Her voice trailed off and I turned to look at her. She was biting her lip, trying not to cry. 'That night I decided to follow him,' she said after a moment.

'Did you tell your mother?' I asked.

She shook her head. 'She would never have allowed it.'

'What happened?' I asked.

'I left a note for her, got the bus and crossed into Iran on foot,' she replied. 'Then, the following day, I was stopped by a border patrol. They were devout men and I was safe in their hands, but they took me to the refugee camp at Iranshahr—'

'And that's where Ghorbani and Bahman found you?' I asked.

She nodded. 'My cellphone had been stolen in the camp and I had no other way of getting one. I wanted to call my mother and tell her I was safe and, of course, I was desperate to hear news about my father.

'I knew if he was okay, he would come and claim me, and I could help look after him. Everything would have turned out all right,' she said. 'But a cellphone was the only way I could do it. They told me nothing bad would happen – you were carrying gold out of Afghanistan to sell in Tehran, you were just a smuggler.'

'I know,' I replied. I was sorry Ghorbani was dead, but it was difficult to have any sympathy for him: he alone would be responsible for Laleh's parents and sister turning on the news tomorrow and seeing her face just before she was executed.

'How will they do it?' she asked softly.

I knew why she was asking. She was like Rebecca, the same quiet courage: she wanted to know what to be terrified of; she had to know what the monster looked like. I shook my head – the method didn't matter, and, anyway, I had more pressing things on my mind. 'Can you swim?' I asked.

'Yes,' she said. 'Not well – it isn't very popular in Afghanistan.' She tried to smile and I grinned back. 'Why do I need to swim?' she asked. 'Can we—'

'There's a chance,' I said. 'A hundred things can go wrong, but listen – you don't have to swim well. I've been watching the bay, and there's a strong current running down to the southern spit and then into the Gulf – that'll carry us out.'

She looked past me to the water, trying to see what I meant. 'Okay – if you say so.'

'What happens once we're out in the Shamal, I don't know,' I said. 'But before we get there, you're going to have to hold your breath. *Really hold your breath.*'

My voice was hard, impressing on her the importance of what I was telling her: 'No matter how scared you are, you must stay calm – don't struggle or scream. It just accelerates your heart rate and makes you consume more oxygen. Understand?'

She nodded. 'They'll be hoping we thrash about and look terrified,' I continued. 'They want that for the video, but no matter what we're feeling, we can't. Seconds will count. A person can normally hold their breath for two minutes, but I figure we have to go three. Maybe more.'

She started to tell me she understood, but her eyes looked past me, and I saw alarm in them. I turned: the guards who had travelled with us, each holding a pan of food, had rounded a vehicle and were approaching. The one in front stared at me and I guessed he realized we had opened the glass in the rear windshield.

Cursing in Arabic, he strode forward, threw open the back door of the pick-up, hurled Laleh aside and slammed the window shut. Any communication was finished – maybe I had told her enough, but I couldn't be sure.

13

THE LATE-AFTERNOON SUN WAS ARCING TOWARDS THE HORIZON, turning the sea from turquoise to pink, when Kazinsky arrived at the pick-up, accompanied by a man dressed entirely in white, including the scarf and hood that concealed his face.

Surrounded by half a dozen bodyguards, he wasn't young; there were wisps of a grey beard straggling out from under the hood and the dark eyes that looked at me through the two holes cut in the fabric were those of a man who had seen a lot of life and probably more of death. On the remote and uninhabited beach, with hundreds of his men dressed like Bedouin tribesmen lining the dunes behind him, he looked like a vision, a prophet, from a different place and a different time. I knew it was the Emir.

Though it might not have been readily apparent, his clothes – like Kazinsky's outfit – were an eloquent concession to the modern world. The explosion of satellite surveillance combined with huge advances in facial recognition and biometric identification meant that targeted drone strikes were a huge threat. As a result, anonymity was the most valuable commodity in the terrorist underworld; it was a matter of life and death for its leaders, and the man in front of me was not taking any chances. The hood and loose-fitting clothes meant nobody would be running facial recognition or biometrics on him any time soon.

He took a step closer and looked at me through the steel mesh, inspecting me like a lab animal. I ignored him, speaking to Kazinsky: 'So,' I said. 'I also get to meet the Emir.'

Determined not to show any surprise this time, Kazinsky merely nodded.

The Emir had arrived at the beach an hour earlier, travelling in a convoy of five off-road vehicles, all of them masquerading – according to the muddy logos on their doors – as part of an organization called the Central Asian Wildlife Survey. The largest of the so-called Survey's vehicles was the most remarkable, a cross between a luxury SUV and a truck that I had only ever seen before in the wealthy oil states of Saudi Arabia and Qatar. Made by the AMG division of Mercedes, it was a twin-turbo, six-wheel drive, built on a military chassis and capable of crossing even the most forbidding terrain. They were wildly expensive – hence you never saw them outside of the Gulf states – and because this one was carrying Pakistani licence plates I figured it had to have been provided by either a wealthy donor or, more likely, by PIA, the Pakistani Intelligence Agency. It was always helpful, I thought, to have reliable allies in the fight against international terrorism.

The Emir continued staring at me through the mesh, but I was looking past him to where the film crew were approaching, focusing on Laleh's frightened face. Even though she crouched down and tried to hide from the lens, one of the men leaned through the window, grabbed her by the throat and forced her to look into the camera. I could just imagine her parents and sister having to watch that. Once the cameraman was satisfied, he panned and moved in to film my face and the Emir's unwavering gaze. As the tape rolled, the man in white – right on cue – turned to Kazinsky and spoke in Farsi through the mask. 'Carry out the sentence,' he said.

Having approved the execution, he turned and, accompanied by his bodyguards, headed towards a group of shade umbrellas and an armchair – the same one I had seen in the courier's smuggled photo – that had been set up for him on top of one of the dunes.

'Uncuff 'em and get them out,' Kazinsky said in Arabic to half a dozen guards.

While Laleh was dragged out of the back door of the vehicle, my ripped and bleeding hand was freed from the steel bracelet. The door of the cage was unpadlocked by one of the horsemen and I crawled out, my legs so cramped that as soon as I put any weight on them, they buckled and I fell. I grabbed hold of the tailgate, clenched my teeth against the pain as the circulation returned and hauled myself up.

Kazinsky turned to the guards. 'Get them ready for the posts.'

I saw Laleh look at the wrecked wharf: low tide had passed several hours before and even though the water was running a long way up the beach, the broken teeth were still exposed. Kazinsky, meanwhile, was pulling off his headdress, neck scarf and T-shirt in preparation for wading out through the water with us.

Once again, I saw the locust tattoo on his back, the three gold stars and two red stripes of a colonel and – clearly now, in Cyrillic script – the name of the unit in which he had served. It was the 3rd Spetsnaz Brigade, a Special Forces group that was steeped in brutality and

Russian history: it had been the first into Berlin during the Second World War, campaigned twice in Afghanistan and saw action – among other theatres – in Kosovo, Chechnya, Ukraine and as unbadged troops in the endless dirty war in Syria.

I was still looking at the tattoos when he turned to his men and pointed at Laleh and me. 'Okay, take off their clothes,' he ordered.

I panicked: in all my planning, it was one thing I had never anticipated. The guards smiled, looking at Laleh, already mentally undressing her. She tried to step back, but other men were already moving behind her, more than happy to help.

I had no time to worry about her modesty – I was desperate. Somehow I had to keep my clothes on—

14

'NO, COLONEL,' I SAID TO KAZINSKY. 'DON'T HUMILIATE US. ESPECIALLY the girl – she's a teenager. Take her life, but let her keep her dignity, leave us dressed.'

He stared at me as if I was deranged. 'You saw the camera crew?' he asked. 'You know why they're here?'

'For YouTube,' I answered.

'Yeah, for recruitment, and you know who we want? Young men. We could post long sermons on the web; that's what the devout men want. Or we can put rap music on it, strip the girl and take her out to the pylon. Which do you think is going to get more hits?'

I was looking at him but barely listening, trying to think of any argument to keep myself dressed. He turned to walk away. 'Do it,' he said to the guards. 'Naked – now.'

As they moved in on Laleh and me, my mind was racing, willing to grab anything, thinking suddenly – for a reason I didn't understand – about the 3rd Spetsnaz Brigade and the row of tattoos on Kazinsky's forearm that listed the battlefields where he had fought. I had seen the name Aleppo, the city in Syria, and a date – and I wondered why that engagement was sticking in my memory. It was a well-known battle, famous for a particular reason, I realized, and seemingly out of nowhere, a memory of a box that had once held apple tea surfaced in my mind; I knew what I had to do. 'Colonel,' I said loudly in Russian.

Kazinsky, walking away from me towards the water, stopped in mid-stride. He turned—

'Permission to speak to the commanding officer of the first regiment of the 3rd Guards Spetsnaz Brigade – sir!' My Russian was close to perfect, and I was addressing him in the way all their soldiers were taught.

He stared at me. 'Now you speak Russian? If it's not one thing with you, it's another.'

The guards, the camera crew and Laleh – everyone else was as shocked as Kazinsky about the language I was using. 'What do you want, soldier?' he asked in Russian, just like the officer he had once been, indicating to the guards to stop grabbing at our clothes.

'I was in Aleppo in northern Syria on the seventh of May,' I replied.

For the second time in as many seconds, he was taken aback. 'Bullshit. It was years ago – what were you doing there?' he said.

'Fighting, sir – before I joined the agency, I was in the Marines,' I lied. 'I had a skill the 75th Rangers needed when they went in there. The local language was Arabic, our allies were Kurds who spoke Turkish and we knew the Russian Spetsnaz were on the other side. I was fluent in all three so the Pentagon thought I would be useful.' I shrugged as if it made perfect sense. None of it was true – apart from knowing the languages – but I had never been to Aleppo and my military service was in nuclear submarines, about as far from the Marines as you could get. Believe me, if there was a better plan, I would have used it.

I had one advantage, though: the engagement of 7 May in Aleppo, the one where Kazinsky had fought and had memorialized on his forearm, was well known in US intelligence circles. While for three days the 75th Rangers and the unbadged Spetsnaz engaged in a deadly firefight around the medieval castle in the centre of town, I was working as a young intelligence officer at Langley. Shortly after the engagement was over, because of my knowledge of the languages, I was brought in to help translate numerous accounts from all sides.

'You fought there?' Kazinsky asked in Russian.

'Near the northern wall of the citadel,' I lied.

'Bullshit,' he said again, but there was no conviction to it and I figured he was testing me.

'If you say so – sir,' I said, shrugging as if I didn't care.

'Go on,' he ordered.

'There were six of us, part of a light infantry unit,' I said, recalling one graphic report I had read. 'Just after dawn on the first day we saw about twenty-five of the 3rd Guards leading a force of Syrian troops up a route to the citadel that nobody had anticipated. We wanted to withdraw, but the only way out was across open ground so we engaged them,' I continued. 'You could barely see for the incoming, but we managed to delay them so that a defensive line could be set up. Four of us went down wounded in thirty minutes, and if you were there, you know every hour it was like that in hundreds of engagements across the city.'

Kazinsky stared at me, unsure. 'What happened when the battle was over?' he asked.

'After the air strikes had forced the Syrians and Spetsnaz to withdraw?' I asked. 'We went out and brought in our own dead and buried yours.'

'Why ours?' he said.

'A tribute. Respect. They were brave soldiers; we'd all seen acts of heroism. We thought your fallen deserved more than the wild dogs.' What I was saying – about burying the enemy – was true; it really had happened: all of the accounts had mentioned it.

'And what did you do as you were burying them?' Kazinsky asked, still probing.

'We collected everything we could from the bodies,' I said. 'Jewellery, dog tags, photos, journals, anything that might mean something to their loved ones.'

'And then?'

'We put it in a box, gave a Syrian we had captured a white flag and sent him over to your lines to deliver it,' I said.

Kazinsky looked at me for a moment. 'What sort of box was it?' he asked, cunning.

There had been numerous reports about those terrible days – several of them in military journals with a lot of detail – but I was sure none of them had said anything about personal items being returned or the type of box. Only somebody who had fought there – on either side – would have known about it. Praise be to any god that existed, I thought, that it was described in at least one of the eye-witness accounts I had read.

'A senior sergeant found a cardboard box in an old pantry in the citadel,' I said. 'It had once contained Turkish apple tea – there was a painting of an orchard printed on the lid – and we used that.'

Kazinsky said nothing. Then he turned to the guards. 'Leave the American dressed,' he said. 'Let him die like the soldier he once was.'

'The girl?' I asked, pressing.

'Underwear,' he replied. 'Now get them out there.'

15

ESCORTED BY KAZINSKY AND THE GUARDS, THE FILM CREW CIRCLING and filming us – Laleh in her briefs and bra, using her hands to try and preserve her modesty – we were shoved and herded through the shallows and out to the poles.

By the time we reached the broken teeth, the water was up to our waists, the tide was rising swiftly and I could feel the current pulling at my calves much harder than I had anticipated. That, at least, was good news: it meant that if we managed to escape we would be swept down the beach and around the spit of land very fast.

Three times while we were being hustled through the water, Laleh had caught my eye, silently pleading for some explanation about what was going to happen. I didn't respond, not giving her any comfort: I was frightened that either Kazinsky or one of the guards would realize that I wasn't intending to go quietly into the night. With my jaw set and eyes staring ahead, I worked hard to make them believe that I was a study in stoicism.

Only once, as Kazinsky waded ahead to check the special steel collars that his workmen had attached to two of the posts – and with the film crew splashing along in his wake – did I get a chance to say something, under my breath, to her. 'Remember – when the water reaches your chest, don't scream. You'll need every second of oxygen you can find.'

She nodded, and I could see that knowing there was still a plan calmed her a little, but that was the last of our contact: the guards started hitting us with their weapons, making us wade faster towards the posts, closing their ranks around us.

I looked past the men in front of me and saw clearly Kazinsky's version of a death chamber: two slime-covered posts were standing side by side, each one featuring a metal collar. The collars were made of toughened steel and the workmen had screwed them so deep into the wood they were unmovable. Each of them was in two parts, hinged at the back, and in less than a minute Laleh and I would be forced to stand with our spines against a post – facing the beach and the cameras – while the collars were clamped around our necks and padlocked at the front. Our feet would be on the sand, but the beauty – if that was the right word – of the collars was that while we had no chance of escape, our feet and arms would remain completely free. We could scream, writhe, thrash, flail our arms or kick our legs as the incoming tide raised the seawater higher and higher until – eventually – our noses submerged beneath the rising tide.

Execution by the inch, drowning in slow motion in front of the Emir and the men gathered on the dunes and captured in high definition for a worldwide audience. That's entertainment, I guess.

Splashing through the water, we both stumbled at least once in the strong current before we reached the poles. The guards immediately spun us around and shoved each of us until our backs were hard against the wood.

Kazinsky himself did the honours, looking into our eyes as he clamped the steel collars tight around our necks – first Laleh and then me – and turned a key, locking them closed with old-fashioned, heavy-duty iron padlocks.

He looked at me one final time. 'Goodnight, America, and all the ships at sea,' he said before joining the guards and leaving us to the rising water and our deaths.

16

VOLLEYS OF GUNFIRE TORE THROUGH THE LATE AFTERNOON, SENDING a flock of gulls swirling into the air and forcing packs of rats to break cover and scurry through the scrub and across the dunes.

With the water climbing up our chests, the metal chokers biting into our necks and the current pulling at our legs, Laleh and I watched as the hundreds of men silhouetted along the dunes lowered their weapons, moved closer to the Emir and sat down to watch us die.

The three film-makers had left the execution posts behind them, shooting Kazinsky and the guards as they splashed back to shore. With the beach flooded in the golden light of the setting sun, the wild troops on the dunes looking like a Bedouin army straight out of the desert, the hooded Emir seated under his umbrella as if he was a medieval potentate, and the black locust on Kazinsky's back rippling and threatening to take flight, I had little doubt it would all account for thousands of new recruits. Whatever you might think of their ideology or methods, it was impressively staged.

I needed to speak to Laleh and explain our one chance to escape, but even though the film crew and everyone else was now out of earshot, I suspected the boom mic was sensitive enough to pick up sound over a long distance and I wasn't yet willing to take that risk.

Laleh – her body shaking with fear, her arms wrapped around herself as if in protection – tried to speak, but I shook my head as best I could, motioning her into silence. As a result, we stood there with our backs rigid against the posts, each in our own private terror, fighting to stay calm and control our breathing, arms at our side, monitoring the seawater creeping up towards our shoulders, staring at the men ranged on the dunes.

Finally, the film crew and their mic were halfway up the beach and I turned to speak to Laleh. Worried that the men on the shore would see me talking instead of screaming and jump to the conclusion that I was planning something, I bowed my head, put my palms together in front of my face in the Christian gesture of prayer and spoke quietly.

My words were drowned out by a massive roar from the dunes – the spy knew that he was about to die, the spy was terrified, the spy was trying to make his peace with God. I looked at them from under hooded eyes and – across the rising tide – saw Kazinsky smiling from the beach. With the crowd falling quiet, I continued with my prayer. 'We've only got a couple of minutes,' I told Laleh. 'Just listen, don't look at me, stare straight ahead.

'We've had one piece of luck,' I said. 'You are standing slightly higher than I am – that means your nose will be out of the water and you'll be able to breathe a few seconds longer than me. It might be the difference between life and death.

'When the moment comes,' I continued, my palms still together at my face, 'and the water is over your lips, take the deepest breath you can through your nose. Fill your lungs. But don't hold it, breathe out a tiny amount at a time. That will help keep the panic at bay.'

She couldn't contain herself; I don't blame her – the dread must have been paralysing. 'Where will you be?' she asked, her voice cracking.

'By the time the water has covered your nose – I'll be below you, underwater,' I replied. I had absolutely no certainty it was true, but what else could I say? The prospect of me escaping and freeing her – the relief – was almost too much for her, and she started to turn to look at me. 'Don't turn this way,' I said harshly.

'Now listen,' I continued. 'When the water is almost at your eyes, raise your arms and thrash about. Try to pull yourself up through thin air – no matter what I'm doing underwater, act like you're drowning.

'With your arms raised, clench your fists then let them fall – limp. You have to make them believe you're dead. Your face will be under-water, they won't be able to see you, so they'll believe it if you do it right.'

She nodded, and I looked down at the water: it was up to my shoul-ders already and a ragged piece of chop washed through from the rising Shamal, hit the steel collar and splashed into my face. Through the spray, tasting the brine on my cracked lips, I looked at the beach—

Several of the Bedouin had their rifles raised and were using the telescopic sights to examine my face, the Emir was leaning forward expectantly in his padded chair and smoke was rising from the fire pits. Only Kazinsky was completely still, kneeling on one knee on the beach, apart, his eyes fixed on me at the gloaming of the day, waiting for the tide – and death – to finally swallow me.

The water rose over my shoulders, and I knew the time was close. Underwater, I lifted first one foot and then the other, kicking off my sandals. I dropped my hands from the prayer position, heard whistles and cat-calls from the Bedouin and – with my hands hidden by the water – unfastened my belt and un-looped it from my pants. Far too big for me, they fell down to my ankles and I stepped out of them.

Gripping the leather belt tight in one hand, I used the other to locate the silver buckle and checked that the needlework I had undertaken at the poisoned village was holding tight. Satisfied, I manoeuvred the prong of the buckle so that it was between my thumb and forefinger and then looked down at the water. In another few seconds, it would cover the heavy iron padlock and I would be able to start.

17

WITH THE BELT IN ONE HAND AND THE PRONG POSITIONED IN THE other, I watched as the seawater covered the metal collar, swamped the padlock and hit the underside of my chin.

I saw the Bedouin and even the Emir rise to their feet: the water was close to my mouth and nose; the moment was almost upon us. Surely, I would break and start screaming in desperation. Instead, I focused my eyes dead ahead and tried to give the impression of being unyielding. Defiant to the end.

Beneath the water, though, my fingers were working furiously. It had been years – during basic training – since I had been taught how to pick locks, and the instruction certainly did not include trying to do it underwater.

I felt the prong of the buckle enter the keyhole and I applied pressure to it, bending it into the necessary shape that would make it function better as a pick. Continuing to stare straight ahead, trying to keep my breathing as deep and regular as possible, feeling the water cresting my chin and starting to spatter my lips, I saw Kazinsky rise to his feet and take a few steps closer to the water, his eyes unwavering, fixed on me. I couldn't tell if he was just preparing for the moment when water would swamp me or if he had seen something that made him suspicious. Despite my best efforts, I felt my heart rate spike and I spoke to Laleh through gritted teeth, barely moving my lips—

'I'm worried about Kazinsky,' I said. 'Divert him. Start pulling at your collar. Scream, kick your legs – give him something to watch instead of me.'

'Terror?' she replied, her breath coming in short gasps. 'I won't be acting.' In other circumstances, I would have laughed. She started yelling with desperation, pulling at the collar, trying to grab the pole above her head to gain every inch of height, but the slime on the wood prevented her fingers from getting a grip and her hands slid back down.

Kazinsky barely paid her any mind. He stepped closer to the water, staring, at me.

I kept working underwater: the bent pick deep in the keyhole, working by touch and thanking divine providence that the padlock was old-fashioned and the locking mechanism was relatively simple. The water hit my mouth and I estimated that I had two breaths left before it covered my nose. It was now a race between my knowledge of lock-picking and the gravitational pull of the moon. While Laleh continued to scream and claw, not giving up, I kept my stare unaltered and I saw Kazinsky take another step closer to the shallows, seemingly worried by my unexpected stoicism.

I tried to ignore him, forcing myself to concentrate, and I finally felt the pick engage part of the mechanism. Without a tension wrench – one of the classic lock-picking tools – I now had to improvise, trying to guide the pick through the mechanism.

I refused to look at Laleh, but I could tell from the panic in her voice that there was no element of performance now: it was terror for real, and I guessed the water had hit her mouth.

I jerked my head up, just enough to get my mouth out of the water: 'Stop!' I told her. 'That's enough. You need to breathe regularly again, don't let the panic in. We're going to get there.'

'Okay,' she said, and I heard no more. I just had time to grab one deep breath before I was inundated. The water covered my nose and there was no way to take another one. Two minutes, three at the most, I told myself. After that I was either free or I was dead. I felt the current swirling around my face: I was effectively underwater, trapped by the neck.

With only my eyes still above the surface, I saw the Bedouin start firing their weapons into the air in celebration of my imminent demise and Kazinsky turn and yell up the dunes. He wasn't celebrating, though: he was signalling for something.

Still working the pick, I glanced at Laleh: I was right, the water was covering her mouth and in less than a minute it would be over her nose. I was just starting to try and communicate encouragement with my eyes when the pick found a channel and slid deep into the mechanism.

I had to focus my mind – the next few seconds would be crucial. With sustained pressure I twisted the pick one way, trying to turn it, and met complete resistance. Letting out a little of my precious breath, knowing that very soon I would be on empty and with my lungs already starting to ache, I turned the pick the other way.

There was more resistance, and then – suddenly – none at all. I twisted harder and a moment later the re-fashioned belt buckle tripped the mechanism. I felt the padlock open. If I hadn't been underwater and drowning, I would have yelled in relief.

Making sure I kept a grip on the buckle and belt, I slipped the padlock out of the clasp that held the two parts of the collar together: the device fell from my neck. I was free.

But I couldn't move – I had to stay where I was, desperately trying to hold my breath, otherwise Kazinsky, or anybody else watching me through a scope, would realize that I was no longer trapped by the collar, and everything would be lost. Only when the water covered my head completely and I was hidden from view would I be able to plunge down, come up under Laleh, risk grabbing a breath of air if I had to, and start to try and free her.

With the water lapping my eyes, I looked at the beach and saw what Kazinsky had been signalling for: a soldier delivered a pair of binoculars, and the Colonel raised them, training them directly on me. We stared at one another; Kazinsky trying to see if anything was amiss and me with no other option but to hold my breath and wait.

I tried not to think about the screaming pain in my chest or imagine what was happening to Laleh. Behind me, the sun had almost sunk into the Gulf, darkening the surrounding waters, lengthening the shadows across the dunes and making the beach look even more beautiful. It was magic hour – and then it was gone. The rising seawater had filled my eyes and I lost sight of everything. I estimated it would take ten seconds for my head to be covered and I started to count. After eight, I could see I was underwater. I grabbed hold of the post, my lungs on fire and feeling like they would explode, and went down as deep as I could without letting go, leaving the deadly collar behind.

By now the water would be over Laleh's nose and I was terrified she might not have been able to eke out her oxygen and had already drowned. I half scrambled, half swam, along the sandy bottom, moving as fast as I could to get to her, and then saw the post that was holding her. I approached it from the seaward side, made out the shadowy outline of her body, launched myself towards it and grabbed her ankle.

For a moment there was no response and a surge of panic hit me as I started to think that she was already gone. Then there was a small kick – she was alive.

I crawled up the post, determined not to run any risk of breaking the surface, and saw that she was completely underwater, her eyes staring at me wide with panic; she was clearly at the very end of breath and life.

I had no choice – keeping the bulky post between myself and the men on the beach, using it to try and mask my presence, I surfaced and dragged a huge gulp of air into my mouth and nose, filling my lungs.

I had no idea if I had been seen by Kazinsky or anyone on shore but dived back below the surface as fast as I could. One tiny stroke and I was beside Laleh again, her head lolling and her mouth slack – almost gone.

I pulled her head towards me so that her ashen face was up against mine, our noses touching, and locked my lips on hers. I blew a lungful of air into her mouth and kept my lips sealed on hers in case she opened them and started to swallow water. Her eyes suddenly sparked as the oxygen hit her bloodstream and she stared at me.

They say you never forget your first kiss . . . well, I can guarantee that a young Afghan woman, underwater, on the shores of the Persian Gulf in Iran would probably never forget hers. I surfaced again, grabbed another lungful of air and gave her mouth-to-mouth again, staying with her until I was satisfied the panic had passed, her lungs were full and she could hold her breath. Only then did I take the buckle and start to pick the lock.

Facing the keyhole, being able to see what I was doing – even through the seawater – should have made it easier, but the padlock was more battered and corroded than the one that had secured me and it was a much tighter fit for my makeshift key. Unwilling to for-cibly twist it – if I broke the prong we were doomed – I made myself work slowly and three times I was forced to go to the top and replen-ish our air.

On the second trip I saw, in the gathering twilight, that Kazinsky had waded deeper into the water and was no longer staring at the poles – almost totally submerged now. He bent down and started to pull something out of the water.

I had no idea what it could be – at least not until the next time I surfaced. Eyes peering from just above the water level, half concealed behind the post, I saw him brandishing something above his head, showing it to the hundreds of men gathered on the dunes and starting to scream orders. My discarded pants had floated in with the tide.

They must have confirmed his suspicions; for some reason, I had wanted to keep my clothes on. He started to splash forward, searching for any sign of me or Laleh.

I sucked in as much air as I could, dived back down, 'kissed' Laleh again and returned to my frantic task. Ironically, Kazinsky flying into action was the incentive I needed: there was no time left to be cautious and I decided to turn the prong to the left again, forcing it much harder this time. After a moment's resistance, I felt it slide through the mechanism: I had guessed right. I kept twisting it harder, hoping against hope that the prong wouldn't break, felt the corrosion give way and sensed the prong engaging – the lock opened.

Unwilling to risk taking another breath, I clenched my teeth against the roaring pain in my chest, released the padlock, opened the steel collar and set Laleh free.

She collapsed into my arms and I held her close, making sure we both remained submerged, and even though our lungs were red-lining I let the current, running as strong as ever, start to carry us down the beach.

All we had to do was survive the next few minutes; if we did, I was confident that in the deepening gloom, we would be able to surface as often as we needed until we were swept past the sandspit and out into the Gulf. Except—

Laleh, in my arms, started hammering my shoulder, forcing me to look at her: she couldn't hold on without air any longer and was pointing to the surface. I had no choice; together we rose up, broke the surface, gulped a breath – and were bathed in light.

I had underestimated Kazinsky – as soon as he had grabbed the pants and concluded we had somehow escaped, he must have realized that the growing darkness would be our best ally and his greatest problem. He must have screamed an order up to the men on the dunes and ordered them to sprint for the vehicles parked on the crests and turn on their headlights. Most of the pick-ups had spotlights mounted on their roll bars and now they were manoeuvring them to add to the blaze of light.

It was flooding the bay, stretching into the darkness of the Gulf, concentrated on the area between the execution posts and the spit of land. Kazinsky, binoculars raised, was moving at speed along the beach in the shallows, heading towards the sandspit, obviously aware what way the current was running. Already, men on the dunes were raising their assault rifles.

I didn't have to tell Laleh – she understood what was happening and ducked back underwater as fast as I did. With our forearms clasped together, frightened we might lose each other in the darkness, we gave in to the current, allowing ourselves to be swept along and crabbing our way out to deeper water to make sure we cleared the sandspit.

Only when our lungs were screaming did we put our heads up again to breathe. This time, though, Kazinsky had guessed where we might surface and had concentrated the lights on that area. We heard a roar go up from the dunes when they saw our heads, followed by the muzzle flashes of scores of assault rifles. We dived again, pushing hard with our legs—

Next time we surfaced the soldiers would have a better idea of the range and would be much more disciplined. Even if they weren't, one lucky shot from weapons that can fire six hundred rounds a minute on full auto would finish us. We held on for as long as we could and then surfaced again into the deadly light, staying as submerged as much as possible, only our nostrils above the water, dragging in air fast and deep, hoping that the wind-driven chop would hide us. It didn't.

By good fortune, though, the current had gathered pace and we were further down the bay than either the shooters or Kazinsky had anticipated, leaving him – still sprinting along the beach – further behind us and forcing the men in the dunes to adjust their aim.

Even so, the water between us and the shore was peppered with a hail of bullets, at least a score of them close enough to hear the red-hot metal sizzle as it entered the water. Three bullets hit directly in front, making us both flinch, but it was the water that saved us – it is eight hundred times denser than air and a high-velocity bullet that strikes it is rendered harmless within three feet. A direct hit on the head would still have been fatal, however, and Laleh and I both plunged back down into the dark undersea. In those few moments on the surface, I had grabbed a look at the sandspit and estimated that one more trip to the top would be enough to carry us past it, into the Gulf and out of harm's way.

I had underestimated the speed of the current, though, and when we surfaced we were at the very tip of the spit, forty yards offshore, being swept fast. Due to the geography of the bay, the vehicles and their lights had not been able to travel with us. Nevertheless, a broad ladder of silver light still enveloped us, this one hauntingly beautiful. A full moon, huge in the clear desert air, was hanging just above the horizon. By its light we saw that Kazinsky was standing alone, unarmed, on the sand, searching the water for us.

He must have seen us because he suddenly stepped forward – unable to reach or harm us, and while Laleh submerged herself, I stayed where I was for a moment, pushing with my legs against the current, facing him.

And so, the mysterious Abu Muslim al-Tundra – a boy who had grown up and learned English in the Siberian wilderness, became an officer with the elite Spetsnaz Brigade, saw action in the cauldron of Aleppo, wandered into the desert and embraced a brutal form of Islam, was pronounced dead in the ruins of a safe house in Iraq, was secretly resurrected and born again, took command of the military operations of the much feared Army of the Pure and was now identified by his birth name of Roman Kazinsky – he and I found ourselves on an un-named spit of land in Iran, somewhere south of Bandar Lengeh on the Persian Gulf, holding each other's gaze across a hundred feet of moonlit water.

How long was it – a dozen heartbeats? More? I cannot say except it seemed to last for ever and then, unable to fight the current any longer, I raised my hand in ironic farewell and was carried into the waters of the Gulf and the roaring teeth of the Shamal.

Even then I had the overwhelming belief that very soon we would meet again.

18

'YOU MUST HAVE BEEN TERRIFIED OF THE SHAMAL,' THE MAN SAID, his voice quiet, his manner totally professional. 'Did you have any idea how you might survive it?'

'None,' I said. 'That's what I told Laleh when we were in the water and she asked the same thing. I said it didn't matter, anything had to be better than the beach.' I smiled. '"When you ain't got nothing, you've got nothing to lose."'

'And what did she say to that?' the man asked.

'"Bob Dylan,"' I answered, laughing. 'She knew a lot about Western music – she'd listened to it at home illegally.'

I was sitting in the office of Lucas Corrigan, the CIA's head of Human Resources – the man with eyes as green and cold as river rocks. My files and medical reports lay on the desk in front of him and the question of whether I was fit to return to active service hung in the air between us. Any agent who had been in rehab as long as I had was required to undergo an assessment by Human Resources and, given my experience with Lucas Corrigan in the past, I knew it wasn't going to be easy. Though I changed my mind later, at the time I still subscribed to the common view that there were only two kinds of people in the world; those who couldn't stand Corrigan, and those who hadn't met him yet.

Aged in his sixties, he was a spectral figure – tall and thin with a shaved head, pale skin and a face dominated by the large green eyes. A doctor of medicine who had switched disciplines – gaining a fistful of postgraduate degrees in psychology – he also had a long relationship with the CIA: his father had been station chief in Saigon in '75 when the city fell to the North Vietnamese. It was during the last hours of the war that his father, amid the explosions and tracer fire, refused to leave the embassy until the last moment. While choppers were evacuating US diplomats from the rooftops and North Vietnamese tanks were smashing through the compound walls, the station chief – surrounded by piles of steel boxes – stood alone in a courtyard and fed millions of dollars in US banknotes into an incinerator to prevent the CIA's huge slush-fund from falling into enemy hands.

It was little surprise then that his son had found a home at the agency and – given his outstanding academic qualifications – that he had risen to his present executive position.

'I suppose it was ironic,' he continued. 'In the end it was the Shamal that saved you, wasn't it?'

His voice conveyed very little, and the remark was casual enough, but the role that the wind, or anything else, had played in my survival wasn't the purpose of the meeting. Far from it. Corrigan's job was to look through people – to get deep into the subtext of their physical condition and try to assess their mental and emotional state.

As the head of the department, the most highly qualified and experienced of its hundreds of employees, he always handled the most difficult cases, the ones concerning the spies, the men and women whose stock in trade was deflection and deceit.

'Yes, it was the wind and the girl,' I replied evenly. I had heard of skilled agents who had been in fit-for-service meetings with him and had only realized too late that they were playing chequers and he was playing chess. I had to be very careful; because of the unique nature of the agency's work, I knew my job was on the line—

An adverse report, or even an area of concern, would sideline me for months and require another assessment at the end of it. If that went badly, it was almost certainly a desk job in research and the end of my career. The last thing the agency needed was a loose cannon over the border somewhere.

As I watched him leaf through the files – as if to remind himself about Laleh, although I was certain he was completely familiar with their contents – I knew how it was going to play out: he would take me through the events, getting me to describe and explain them, all the time watching my reaction, probing whatever facade I might be presenting, looking for any sign of stress or avoidance that he could prise open.

'Shall we dance?' I asked.

'Dance?' he said.

'Just an expression,' I replied. 'Do you want to start?'

He looked at me hard. 'Yes, let's do that. You said the girl helped save you?'

I nodded. 'The fever from my wounded foot had broken in the cave, but it had weakened me. The events at the beach had also taken a toll and, some time after midnight, trying to stay afloat, I realized I was starting to slip into unconsciousness. That was deadly, of course, but Laleh – who was a better swimmer than she had acknowledged – managed to get her arm under my neck and kept me afloat. I had blacked out again when she saw it – rising up a swell.'

'The fishing skiff?' Corrigan asked, pulling up a photo on his computer screen.

'It was half submerged,' I said. 'I guess the wind had torn it free of a mooring somewhere up north and carried it down the Gulf. Laleh had the sense not to leave me and try to swim towards it – she would never have found me again in the dark. Instead, she dragged me until she was close enough to grab the rail.'

'How long were you unconscious?' Corrigan asked.

'I don't know. I came round to find her clinging to it and supporting me. Once I could hang on, she got aboard. Like all small boats, there was a bailing bucket and she started trying to clear the water. But the planking must have been split and she couldn't make any progress so in the end we just clung to the edge of it and used it as a flotation device. Laleh was thinking all the time, though; she took the rope off the bucket, lashed it around my shoulders and tied it to a bracket at the stern—'

Corrigan interrupted: 'To stop you drifting off into the night?'

'That's right. And I did pass out again, but I was as safe as she could make me.' I paused for a moment, thinking about her and what she had done. 'I may have saved her life earlier,' I said. 'But she paid me back a hundred times over. I wouldn't have made it without her.'

'I guess not,' he said, without emotion, just as a fact. 'And now – today – that night comes back to you often?' he asked. 'You re-live those feelings?'

I guessed it was a trap – denying it would only tell him I was lying. 'It was a big event,' I replied. 'Of course I think about it – it's only natural. Nothing anybody would call out of the ordinary, though.'

He was silent, then he nodded, seemingly agreeing. 'What then? You were roped to the boat and had passed out.'

'Just before dawn she started shaking me, and it brought me back. She was trying to tell me there was a sail on the horizon. The wind had fallen and the sea was calmer. I looked and, in the grey light, through banks of low-lying cloud, I couldn't see anything in the direction she was pointing and I started to turn away.

'Then the cloud cleared and I saw the top of a huge, ghostly sail. Laleh yelled again, I stared and then we hugged each other. The sail wasn't a boat at all. It was a building a thousand feet high – a fifty-storey exclusive hotel, the Burj Al Arab – built to look exactly like a sail that was full and drawing in the desert wind.

'"Iran is on the other side of the Gulf," I said to her. "Dubai is in front of us – we're safe."'

Corrigan had no reaction; he pulled a photo out of the files and handed it to me. 'Do you know this man?'

19

THE PHOTO SHOWED A MIDDLE-AGED ARAB GUY WITH AN OPEN, uncomplicated face dressed in the uniform of a maintenance worker.

'No,' I said.

'His name is Mustafa Aksoy,' Corrigan replied. 'A Turkish national whose job was to manicure the sand in front of the Burj Al Arab's beach club at dawn. He was the man who found you lying at the high-water mark. You were drifting in and out of consciousness and Laleh was little better, unwilling or unable to speak. You don't recall any of this?'

I shook my head.

'Well, he ran up to the beach club,' Corrigan continued. 'And called hotel security. Two minutes later they arrived, saw the wrecked boat with an Iranian registration number on its stern, took one look at you, saw the mess you were in and called the cops. They had you taken to hospital, where you were put in a room under guard and ended up being rigged up to monitors and drips.'

'I remember that. It's where I came round,' I said. 'I was in a bad way physically and they started running a lot of tests. Almost immediately things got out of control. Because my eyes were badly inflamed from the polluted water in the Gulf, they were worried about permanent damage and called in an ophthalmologist.

'He examined me and told the cops it was something he had never seen before – I was wearing special, surgically attached lenses to change the colour of my eyes. Add that to the gunshot wound and an Iranian-registered boat – well, to say the cops were alarmed doesn't come close. The senior cop went out into the corridor and began making phone calls. Twenty minutes later members of State Security, the UAE's intelligence agency, arrived.'

'They have a bad reputation,' Corrigan said. 'Very brutal. What was your reaction?'

'I didn't have any – I wasn't panicking, if that's what you mean. I had a plan. Until then I had barely said a word, and that was only in Arabic, but I switched to English and that took them aback. I told them I was an American citizen and I wanted to see my ambassador immediately. Which, of course, they didn't do.'

'They wouldn't, would they?' Corrigan said. 'They were a spy agency. They weren't going to call anyone until they knew exactly what they had and if they could trade it to their advantage.'

'That's what I anticipated – they might call themselves our allies, but they aren't much better than the Pakistanis – but calling for the ambassador put them on notice and bought me some time while they sent it up the chain of command.'

'Then you got lucky,' Corrigan said, flicking through the files, showing me a photo of a man in his sixties dressed in a crisp light brown uniform. 'This guy is a lieutenant colonel now, but he had once been a minor asset of the CIA, working in the Dubai Police communications department. He used to hear a lot of things and he'd pass on titbits about drunken diplomats, compromising situations, secret visits by Iranian officials – you know, small stuff for a bit of extra cash.

'Well, he went dark about seven years ago – probably got worried about being caught and figured the money wasn't worth it. Apparently, he rose through the department, got to his present rank and, while you were trying to avoid being interrogated, he happened to be in charge of police communications that day.

'He heard that the boat was Iranian, you'd been shot and he realized that the fake eyes almost certainly identified you as an espionage agent. He was also aware you were demanding to see the US ambassador and that meant you were an American spy.

'It seems the cop was a bit like me,' Corrigan said, and I thought for a moment he was going to smile. I stared at him but, thankfully, he suppressed the urge, and the Earth maintained its orbit. 'He hated throwing things away. He managed to find an encrypted cellphone hidden in his garage – one that hadn't been used for the seven years – powered it up and slipped in a burner SIM card.

'He entered a series of numerals, not knowing whether the number he was calling was still active, and listened while it connected. There was no voice at the other end, but that didn't surprise him and he sent a transmission burst that lasted a fraction of a second. It was a text, two codewords he had been instructed to send years ago if something big happened. He had been told somebody would contact him, but he had no idea if there was anybody at the other end.'

'*Phoenix rising*,' I said. 'I heard that was the two-word text he sent.'

'Right,' Corrigan replied. 'The phone number that received it was a long-dead contact drop, but the NSA always maintains them; they are never retired. The specialists at Fort Meade dug through the archives and found that the phone and the code were genuine – from way back, a CIA asset was calling, requesting an urgent contact. Nobody knew, but maybe something big *was* going down.

'The CIA station chief at the US embassy in the UAE then called the lieutenant colonel on the encrypted phone. The Dubai cop told him that a man, almost certainly an American spy, was in a heavily guarded room on the ninth floor of Rashid Hospital, demanding to see his ambassador, but his only visitors so far had been four senior members of State Security.

'Twenty minutes later, after the station chief had promised ten thousand dollars to the cop if the information panned out, the ambassador entered the hospital unannounced.'

I smiled. 'It was chaos at the entrance to my room,' I said. 'They wouldn't let the ambassador in, State Security was calling for back-up and the cops were totally confused. They only relented when the ambassador threatened to call the sheikh who runs Dubai.

'So the ambassador walked in – he clearly had no idea who I was – told me his name and then introduced a man who was accompanying him as the embassy's military adviser. I had never met him, but I was certain he was the CIA station chief.

'The ambassador ordered everybody out,' I continued. 'But the doctors, the cops and State Security all refused, and I certainly wasn't going to say anything while they were present. I called over the "military adviser", motioning him as close as possible, and muttered so low that nobody else could hear: *Tell Langley the man from Tabuk is alive.*

'The station chief nodded, humouring me probably – of course he had no way of knowing whether it was important or not. Maybe I was just some fantasist or one more fraudster. He told the ambassador he was going to their car to make a secure call.

'I slumped back and only sat up when I heard feet running down the corridor. The station chief was back, and he was taking no prisoners. He told the cops and State Security that the US Secretary of State was on the phone right then to the sheikh and they were to back off and leave the room immediately.

'They looked at him in shock. Once they'd left, the station chief told the ambassador and myself that a military air ambulance from the huge, secret US base in Saudi was on its way and would medevac me back to the States immediately. We'd head for the airport in ten minutes.'

'But you wouldn't leave, would you?' Corrigan asked. I might have been wrong, but his tone seemed to have changed; there was a hint of respect to it.

'Not immediately,' I replied. 'I told the ambassador and the station chief: "There's a girl. I don't know what state she's in or where they've got her. She's an agency asset, too. She's coming with us, okay?"

'The two men didn't say anything,' I continued. 'Where had this girl come from – who was she and why hadn't Langley asked about her?'

'It wasn't true, was it?' Corrigan said without rancour. 'She wasn't an agency asset, was she?'

'She was to me,' I replied.

'You couldn't leave her, was that it? Not after what she did in the Gulf.'

'There was that – but I also knew there would be something State Security wanted and they'd trade her to Iran for it. When they finished with her, they would probably return her to the Army of the Pure.'

'I hadn't thought of that,' Corrigan said. 'The report from the station chief said that he was about to go and find her when one of the doctors intervened. He said she was on the seventh floor, in the women's ward.'

20

I MIGHT HAVE BEEN SITTING IN CORRIGAN'S OFFICE, BUT I COULD have been back in the hospital – I could clearly recall the sound of voices speaking in Arabic as they approached my room.

The ambassador and the spook turned towards the door, one of the doctors opened it and I heard a young woman telling two female orderlies she no longer needed the wheelchair.

Laleh stepped inside through the door, and I saw her: bathed and fed, dressed in a long white hospital smock and loose-fitting white trousers, her head covered in fresh bandages that had been fashioned to look like a tightly wound headscarf and concealing the fact that her hair had been shorn. The last time we had been together I was lying on the beach, half dead, and now she grabbed my hand, bent her head and murmured something in Arabic that I couldn't quite hear but sounded like a prayer of thanks that I was alive and conscious.

For a long moment, we ignored the doctors and everyone else and looked at one another: nobody else knew what it had been like back there and it had forged an unbreakable bond between us. I saw the two men staring at us in puzzlement or shock. The station chief recovered first: 'Your daughter?' he asked tentatively.

'Do I look that old?' I said, still croaking. Both of them nodded, and they weren't joking.

I motioned for Laleh to turn. 'Laleh,' I said. 'I'd like you to meet the United States ambassador to the United Arab Emirates and—' I paused, catching myself in time and just avoiding blowing the spook's cover. 'And a senior embassy official.'

She looked at them shyly – unveiled – completely unaccustomed to having her given name volunteered to strangers. 'Mr Ambassador,' I said. 'Would you mind if Laleh used your phone for a few minutes?'

The diplomat was confused for a beat then reached into his pocket. 'Well, sure,' he said.

Laleh had her eyes fixed on me, not quite believing. 'Go ahead,' I said. 'Make the call. She's been waiting a long time.' Fighting her emotion, Laleh took the phone and dialled a number, waited for it to answer and started to speak softly, haltingly, in Arabic.

I turned to the doctors and the two officials: 'She's calling her mother in Kabul,' I said. 'Laleh's been lost for quite a while – now she's telling her she's alive and safe.'

Then I saw Laleh trying to get the words out to ask the question that had occupied her thoughts for so long. I glanced at the others: 'Her father had to flee Kabul and crossed the border into Iran. As we all know, that's dangerous territory and she's trying to find out if the family has had any news.'

Laleh was silent, listening to her mother, and I saw that she couldn't hold the tears back any longer. Her shoulders heaved and she tried to catch her breath. She kept listening – and crying – then tried to speak but was so overcome by emotion it took two attempts. 'My father is safe—' she said finally in English. The room erupted into applause. Laleh, still on the phone, tried to smile through her tears of relief.

'He was robbed,' she said. 'But he made it to Tehran and he's working as a translator. He's been trying to find me for months – fearing the worst. My mom says she'll call and tell him the news as soon as she gets off the phone.'

I turned to the ambassador. 'Laleh saved my life – and the mission,' I told him. 'She can't go back to Kabul, it's too dangerous. It's impossible for her to stay here and she's wanted as a collaborator in Iran. That's why I would like you to arrange—'

'I understand,' he said, turning to the station chief. 'Rich, from what you were told on the phone, do you have a problem with us helping the young lady?'

'Not at all,' Rich replied, and smiled at me. 'The organization was very—' He searched for the words. 'Well, they were pretty overwhelmed when I gave them the message that the man from Tabuk was alive.'

The ambassador turned and saw that Laleh had finished the call and was about to hand him back his phone. 'Laleh, is it? Laleh, I can issue an emergency authorization,' he said. 'If you want, in ten minutes there's a seat on a plane to America.'

Laleh looked confused – it was the last thing she had expected. The idea of America brought huge cultural, religious and historical baggage for a young Afghan woman. So many wars, so much hate on both sides, so many broken promises. I think she needed some form of reassurance and, continuing to look at the ambassador, she indicated me in the bed. 'Would I be travelling with—'

She paused, realizing. 'I don't know your name,' she said sheepishly, not understanding that spies don't have names – or at least none you can rely on. I smiled – I didn't want to tell her that the two officials didn't know what to call me either. 'Sadiqaa,' I said.

She grinned back and the doctors laughed. The station chief turned to the ambassador, translating. 'It means "my friend" in Arabic.'

213

21

CORRIGAN PUSHED HIS CHAIR BACK, AND THE SOUND OF IT SCRAPING on the floor wrenched me out of my reverie. I realized I was staring out through the armoured-glass window of his office, looking at night beginning to fall.

'Then you both flew to America on the same plane?' he asked.

'Yes, I deteriorated on the flight,' I said. 'Twenty supertankers a day pass through the Gulf and they dump their trash overboard – "hepatitis on a stick" is what somebody once called the waterway. Either the bullet wound or the cuts on my wrist acted as a gateway to bacteria. It took hold slowly, then just made itself at home—'

'And very soon you got discoloured patches of skin,' Corrigan said. 'Difficulty breathing and confused thinking? Sepsis?' he asked.

'That was the diagnosis,' I replied. 'Thankfully the plane had good doctors and facilities, but by the time we landed at Andrews, I was in pretty bad shape.'

'I'm sure you were,' Corrigan said. 'Sepsis hits fast. You can go from no symptoms to death within forty-eight hours.'

'I was rushed to hospital from Andrews and spent several days in ICU,' I continued. 'That led to three months of rehab, and here I am. As I told the people out there – ready to go.'

Corrigan nodded. 'Yes, you certainly present like that.' He paused and looked at me for a long moment. 'But the hospital they took you to wasn't the one that was planned, was it? Why have you tried to avoid talking about it?'

'I haven't avoided it,' I replied. 'I just didn't think it was important.'

'Oh, my mistake then,' Corrigan replied evenly. 'I think you were originally meant to go to Walter Reed Army Medical Center. By any measure, an outstanding hospital—'

'Yes,' I replied, 'and as you know, because it's military, it would also provide the best security for an intelligence agent.'

Corrigan nodded. 'But on the day you and Laleh arrived, Washington had been hit by huge electrical storms. Is that correct?'

'It was chaos. When we landed there was widespread flooding, road closures, numerous power outages and seemingly endless accidents and injuries – you name it,' I said. 'I didn't find out until later, but apparently the area around Walter Reed near Bethesda had been hit hardest and, as a result, the hospital was running on generator power and dealing with a huge number of emergency admissions.

'Once the rain stopped, the hospital expected a surge of cases and the administrators just hoped that the emergency power supply would hold on. We were still several hours away from US airspace – I was either asleep or unconscious – when Langley decided to change arrangements and send me to a much larger hospital, half an hour to the south, in an area less affected by the rain and power outages.

'Given my condition, it was a minor adjustment, and with me still thinking we were going to Walter Reed, Laleh and I were transferred to a helicopter for the last leg.'

I remembered Laleh sitting in the chopper, staring out at America wide-eyed, more than a little fearful. As for me – I was flat on my back, watching the interior of the chopper twisting and distorting and the thunder cells rolling across the capital morphing into the past until I found myself looking at a peregrine falcon floating high above the Iranian wasteland. I felt the chopper – or the bird – pitch and yaw violently as we battled the winds, driving rain and unrelenting turbulence. Finally, the pilot managed to put the craft down on the hospital's helicopter pad, the landing so hard that it made Laleh scream.

I recalled that a team in waterproof ponchos were waiting for us. They immediately unloaded the two gurneys from the helicopter, hard-plastic bubbles were dropped over the stretchers to protect us against the driving rain, and I lost sight of Laleh as I was wheeled fast across a broad expanse of concrete and through a set of swinging doors.

Somewhere en route a clear oxygen mask was clamped over my mouth and, breathing easier, I stared out through the plastic bubble and saw a mass of people in a large waiting room. The two attendants guiding the front of the gurney started yelling that it was an emergency and for everyone to make way and the crowd twisted and changed, and then I saw a group of four people in suits pushing through the crowd trying to get close to me. I wasn't sure if they were real or not and then we went through another set of swing doors and left the waiting room behind.

We were deeper in the hospital, in a white and brightly lit space, but it was only marginally calmer. An admissions nurse was speaking loudly above the din: 'Is that him – the guy the NSA called about?'

Nobody seemed to know, and she spoke again, even louder, keeping pace alongside the fast-moving gurney. 'I need a name.'

One of the attendants at the rear of the gurney, a big guy providing most of the propulsion, grabbed a clipboard that was attached to a stand holding a drip, looked at the patient details and called back, 'Sadiqaa Khan. Is that the guy?'

'That's him,' the admissions nurse said, relieved. Who the hell was Sadiqaa Khan, I thought. What a strange name. As I said, I certainly wasn't thinking clearly.

'Bay three,' the admissions nurse directed us, and the four attendants were almost running now. We pushed through a white pull-along curtain, and I was flying out the door of a four-by-four, hitting a sand drift with my shoulder, knowing immediately that I was hurt.

Thankfully, as I rolled to a halt on the road – not far from a broken-down bridge somewhere in the badlands – three white-coated doctors and several nurses leaned over me, anxiety creasing their faces, starting to yell orders. How did they get to Iran, I wondered, and why were they speaking English? I looked up at them through the hard-plastic bubble, still spattered with rain, and for a moment I imagined I saw Rebecca's face looking down at me.

I couldn't help it, the tears began to flow – I missed her so badly, there had been so many hard times and I just wanted to hold her. Soon I would, I told myself, soon I would be home. Maybe I was there already, maybe I wasn't in Iran any more—

Wanting to touch something solid to find out what was real, I slipped my fingers under the bubble and a woman's hand took hold of them. I imagined it was Rebecca, staring down through the bubble at my brown eyes, my breath rasping in the oxygen mask.

'It's all right, Mr Khan,' the woman said. 'You are very sick. You've got a bad infection. I'm not sure you can understand English, but we are going to do everything to help, you are going to be fine.' The woman even sounded like Rebecca, and I felt the tears flow harder.

'It's okay,' she said. 'It's okay.' Whoever she was, I thought, she was a kind person.

'Bubble off,' someone called. The plastic slid away, the faces of the doctors and nurses continued to look down at me, the woman who sounded like Rebecca reached down and removed my oxygen mask, I put out my own hand. I wanted to touch her face—

The woman froze, stared at me and then reeled back in alarm. The reaction was so unexpected, so *un-medical*, I sat up, momentarily shocked into reality. I stared at the woman, her hands up to her face, staring back at me. It was Rebecca. I turned and looked at my surroundings. 'Where the hell am I?' I said.

A senior nurse, a slightly built guy, a bundle of energy, replied: 'ER, Mr Khan.' The other doctor and the nurses were trying to get me to lie down, nobody knowing what was going on, especially in regard to Rebecca, who looked like she was about to collapse.

'ER where?' I demanded, my voice weak and sounding very distant, even to me.

'MedStar Washington Hospital Center,' the slightly built nurse replied.

I couldn't speak. MedStar Washington was where Rebecca had done her residency and now worked as an ER physician. I looked over – it really was her. I tried to swing my legs off the gurney, desperate to go to her, but several pairs of hands restrained me. A female senior ER nurse was at Rebecca's side, holding her by the shoulders, trying to tend to her.

'What is it, Rebecca – what is it, girl?' the female nurse was saying.

'It's . . . it's my partner. The man I live with . . .' Rebecca said, pointing at me.

'Holy shit,' the nurse said. 'What's wrong with you, girl? You don't live with no Sadiqaa Khan.'

'That's not his name,' Rebecca said, freeing herself from the nurse and coming to my side. I wouldn't let the doctors push me back down – through the fever and sepsis, I just stared at her.

Rebecca reached out, took my hand in one of hers and, with the other, touched my face – loving, wanting to know if it was real. She started to cry, her body wracked. 'Look at you,' she managed to whisper, anguished. 'They've hurt you; they've hurt you so much.' Then she noticed: 'What have they done to your eyes?'

The other doctor who had been hovering over me and who I now realized was probably the head ER physician – a man in his fifties with a shaved head – reached across to an instrument tray and grabbed an ophthalmoscope. He looked into my right eye. 'I can't be sure,' he said to Rebecca, trying to reassure her. 'I think his eyes are okay. But a prosthetic film has been attached to them, maybe to change their colour.'

Rebecca nodded, relieved, and somehow not surprised. Everyone

217

else was. A prosthetic film to change the eye colour? The head physician had no time to worry about it. He put down the instrument, ordered two nurses to check my vital signs, adjusted the drips feeding into the cannulas in my arms, stripped the Dubai bandages off my wrist and foot, examined the wounds, grabbed my medical history that had accompanied me from Rashid Hospital and started issuing another flurry of orders.

Rebecca put her hands on my shoulders and made me lie back down. I allowed her to do it, but I wouldn't let go of her hand. I heard one of the attendants behind us – the big guy responsible for propulsion – speak to his colleagues nearest to him, confused. 'Why would anyone have the colour of their eyes surgically changed?'

'Because he's some sort of fucking spy, RainMan,' the slightly built guy said. 'That's why the national security people called ahead, it's the reason he's here under a false name and it's why those four people in power suits are outside in the waiting room.'

A dozen eyes looked at Rebecca and me: the young doctor's partner was a spy, a man who – to judge by his injuries and the secrecy – had obviously just come back from – well, where on earth, nobody knew. Rebecca didn't notice – she had hold of the file containing my medical history from Dubai and was reading it furiously, trying to get a handle on my condition and any other injuries.

'C'mon, everyone!' the head physician ordered, putting an end to it. 'There are scores of other patients. Someone call ICU and get Mr Khan or whatever he's called up there now.'

The room dissolved into a flurry of activity, the gurney was pushed towards the elevator and Rebecca kept hold of my hand, refusing to let go.

22

INTENSIVE CARE WAS A WORLD APART – A CLOISTERED PLACE OF DIM light and soft footsteps, of muted colours and whispered conversations, all of which disguised the turbulence beneath.

Down in emergency, the doctors there, including Rebecca, had realized that my condition had deteriorated on the flight and I would very soon be suffering from what was clinically diagnosed as severe sepsis if it wasn't treated immediately. Certainly, I was exhibiting all the symptoms: difficulty breathing, mental confusion, erratic heart-beat and exhaustion.

The danger was that I would at any moment flip into the next stage of infection, a full-on medical emergency. As the attendants wheeled me into an ICU bay, I heard the physician-in-charge talking to Rebecca, who was walking fast at my side, still holding my hand. He was saying something about the figure being over fifty per cent. In my confusion, it took me a moment to understand: more than half the cases of septic shock ended in death.

'What's his platelet count?' the physician asked.

'We took bloods as soon as he came in,' Rebecca replied. 'We haven't seen the results. It's chaos down there.'

The physician turned to an ICU nurse and said he needed the results immediately. As the nurse left, Rebecca slipped her hand inside my hospital gown and put it palm first on my naked chest. It was one of the most touching things she had ever done, I thought, until – in a moment of clarity – I realized it had nothing to do with affection; she was gauging how erratic my heartbeat had become.

She also realized how much my body was shaking and, alarmed, turned to the physician. 'The chills are worse and his breathing is going south too.'

The physician nodded. 'I'll increase IV fluid and change the medi-cation that's supporting his blood pressure.' He looked at her, his tone and face softening. 'They told me downstairs – he's your partner. Sepsis isn't a mystery illness, Rebecca – he had good treatment in Dubai and on the flight. They got it fast, we know what has to be done and he's in one of the best hospitals in the country. He's not leaving us – except to go to high-dependency and then on to rehab.'

I looked up at Rebecca, her hand still on my chest. Her determin-ation to be professional over-rode the worry I could see on her face, however, and she tried to smile, grateful for the reassurance.

'Sorry – but you're no help to us here,' the physician continued. 'You can do a lot of good down in emergency. I'll call you the moment anything changes.'

She nodded, understanding. Another nurse was already introdu-cing a sedative into the cannula and I could feel myself slipping away.

Rebecca leaned over and I felt her lips on mine and I wondered for a moment if it was another fever dream.

'God protect you,' she whispered, almost in tears. I knew then it had to be a dream – I mean, Rebecca didn't believe in God.

23

I DIDN'T SEE HER GO – I HAD SLUMPED ON TO MY SIDE AS THE sedative flowed into my bloodstream – and I watched myself start to float and realized that somehow, miraculously, I had been transferred to another hospital.

I was standing upright now, travelling in an elevator that took me up to a white ward where, unlike the intensive care unit, every medical battle had already been lost. I walked down an empty corridor, pushed open the door to one of the rooms, and my mother, lying frail in the bed, turned to look at me as I took my usual seat opposite Dad: I was revisiting a past I would never leave. Finally, thankfully, the drug-induced darkness enclosed me and my last thought was of being a child, safe in their arms again.

Rebecca, on the other hand, was very much in the real world. She told me later she had walked out of ICU, turned a corner and saw the four people in suits, three men and a young woman, sitting inside a small, glass-walled waiting area. Outside, through the windows, the storm was getting worse – a thunder cell of black clouds, accompanied by flashes of sheet lightning, was approaching across the parking lot and, even though it was early afternoon, it cast the waiting room into semi-darkness.

Rebecca had never met any of the four visitors, but she could tell from the oldest man's authoritative stance and elegant clothes that he was one of those people who ran with Washington's big dogs.

Dressed in her scrubs, afforded only a fleeting glimpse of them in the dim light, she kept walking, heading back to ER.

'Excuse me, Doctor,' a voice called from behind, and she turned to see the elegant man had stepped out of the waiting room. His colleagues were also at the doorway, looking anxious.

Rebecca stopped and, from down the corridor, called back. 'Yes?'

'I think you admitted Mr Khan down in ER,' the man said. 'They told us he'd been brought up here – we were wondering what the situation is?'

'And you are—' Rebecca asked, starting to walk towards him.

'Friends of his,' the well-dressed man said.

'I see,' Rebecca said. 'If you don't mind me asking – do you always wear suits, especially in a weather emergency, to visit a friend in hospital?'

'More like work colleagues, actually,' the man said, smiling, charming.

Rebecca was halfway towards him when the thunder cell hit – the darkness deepened thanks to the black clouds and sensors in the corridor reacted as if night had fallen. A series of overhead lights came on. For the first time, Rebecca saw the man clearly and immediately berated herself. Had she not been so preoccupied with what they would be doing in ICU, she would have recognized him from the news photos she had seen and realized it was Falcon Rourke.

In that moment, she told me, she was overwhelmingly angry – at him and the agency – but she cranked it down. 'Work colleagues,' she said, and indicated their dark suits. 'Where's that? Bank of America?'

The well-dressed man looked at her, not sure whether to laugh or be offended, but he said nothing. 'It's strange you should mention work,' Rebecca continued. 'The other doctors and I were just talking about that. You may not know it, but Mr Khan has a bad wound on his wrist.'

'Does he?' Falcon asked, surprised.

'Yes, it was mentioned in a report we got from the team who had treated him in Dubai. One of the physicians there said it looked like it had been caused by a metal bracelet, almost as if he'd been trying to escape from a handcuff.' She looked around at the group. 'I know – it's weird. But he's also got a partially dislocated thumb, which seems to support the idea. Any idea what that might be about?'

All four shook their heads. 'No? Then there's the bullet wound in his foot—' Rebecca said.

The visitors didn't respond; a bullet wound? 'He was shot a few days ago,' Rebecca said, 'and somebody – Mr Khan, we guess – used maggots to try and stop the infection. As a treatment, that was popular a thousand years ago and it was a good idea. But we don't see so much of it now. Well, more accurately, we never see it – mainly because people who get shot go to hospital and, if they survive, an infection is treated with antibiotics.'

Rebecca, according to her account, shrugged and maintained her seemingly reasonable tone. 'After looking at his foot, the team on the plane did a full-body assessment. That's standard. Apart from sepsis and widespread sun damage, as if he'd been in a very harsh environment for a long time, those two things – the wrist and his foot – are his major injuries.'

'That's bad, I suppose,' Falcon said. 'But it could be worse.' He and the others looked relieved, but before they could make more inquiries, Rebecca corrected herself—

'I should have said major *current injuries*. They noted an ugly scar from what they thought was an old knife wound in his lower thigh. It was stitched years ago – I can't say by an amateur – but definitely not by a cosmetic surgeon.' She paused, smiling.

Neither Falcon nor the others smiled back; they knew that wound came from the Libyan mission.

'A long scar on his shoulder was a far different animal, though,' Rebecca continued. 'Dubai pointed out that it was really professional work; it had to be, they said – it was a very serious injury. From the X-rays in the file, it looked to me like the entry wound from a medium-calibre bullet. In case you're wondering – we have a lot of experience with that here. Unfortunately, most Washington hospitals are world experts on gunshot wounds.

'The bullet probably shattered when it hit a rib. Most of it stayed inside and had to be removed, but a part of it created an exit wound on his back,' she said. 'You can still see the old staple marks from where it was stitched. Dubai identified the staples that had been used, and they are not available in the US. Interestingly, they're mostly confined to the Middle East. In my opinion, if the bullet's path had been an inch to the left and a little lower, your Mr Sadiqaa Khan would have been dead.

'So,' she continued. 'A knife wound and hit by a bullet. One injury patched up by a veterinary assistant and the other treated by a good surgeon who worked in Syria, Lebanon, Israel maybe . . .' Her voice trailed off, but none of her audience said a word.

'It leaves me with a question,' she continued. 'Where the fuck do you people work? The post office?'

Falcon dropped the pleasant tone. 'Thank you, Doctor,' he said. 'I think we can terminate any discussion about Mr Khan's past or his work right now. I just want to know what his prognosis is.'

That was how all the big dogs barked, Rebecca thought, but she was too angry to be intimidated. 'Of course,' she said evenly. 'So I'll give you my assessment.'

'Please,' Falcon replied, apparently relieved.

'I would say people like yourselves,' she admonished, letting all the fury she felt about the injuries I had suffered – past and present – start to slip the chain, 'send young men and women into some dark place and they come back like *that*.' She pointed down the corridor towards the ICU ward. 'If they return at all, that is.'

Falcon and the other three stared at her, unaccustomed to such vehemence. 'Like him, they're damaged, ripped apart,' she continued. 'Fighting for their life. They've been shot, knifed – tortured, for all I know – and it's not just once. The old wounds tell anyone with a brain you send them out there time after time.'

One of the men at the rear – a guy in his fifties with a high forehead and a permanently worried face – started to object, but Falcon stopped him. 'It's all right, Buster – it's okay,' he said to the CIA's assistant director.

Rebecca barely heard it. 'You wrap it in the flag,' she said. 'You tell yourselves and each other that it is all for the good of the country and conveniently forget about the loss, the anguish, the devastation that follows behind it.

'You never think about the men and women who wait at home, not hearing a word, living with fear every minute, hoping a nondescript car never comes down the road, dreading a knock on the door when a man they don't know, and will never see again, gives them the worst news imaginable and then sends them an invitation to a funeral at Arlington, where, more than likely, an empty casket will be lowered into the grave.'

The four visitors were shocked – who the hell was this doctor? How does she know about that? Rebecca met their gaze, her breathing hard and sharp.

'I'm telling you,' she said. 'There are people who might love that man, whose lives would never recover if he hadn't come back from whatever hole you sent him to. In fact, he's still not back, he's still got a chance of dying in there.'

She looked from one to the other of them. 'You got it? That's my assessment. I hope it has been helpful.' She turned on her heel and walked away.

A moment passed, then Falcon called after her. 'Doctor?' She kept walking. 'Doctor,' he called louder. 'What's your name?'

She slowed and turned. 'Rebecca – Rebecca Khan, Mr Falcon Rourke,' she said. 'I am Sadiqaa's partner, although when we're in bed I usually call him a different name.'

She wheeled and left. Nobody from the CIA said a word and they watched until she was a small figure disappearing into the depths of the hospital.

'Whoa,' Falcon said at last, and smiled – or so Madeleine told me later. 'That's a helluva person. It's a long time since I've been spoken to like that.'

24

'SO, YOU ARRIVED AT ANDREWS, THOUGHT YOU WERE GOING TO Walter Reed but were admitted to MedStar instead,' Corrigan said, watching me closely from behind his desk.

'Why didn't you want to recount it?' he asked. I paused – trying to gather my thoughts – but he didn't wait for me. 'You were worried that your partner's attitude to the agency would be a problem? Obviously, she's not an enthusiastic supporter of your work.'

I looked at him, surprised. 'Partly,' I said. 'Frankly, I wasn't certain you'd heard about it.'

'I understand,' he said. 'As you know, there were four people from the agency at the hospital. Falcon, Buster, Madeleine – and I was the fourth one.'

'Oh, shit,' I said, and took a breath. 'I was right, though,' I continued. 'You didn't hear about it, you witnessed it.'

He got up, stretched his long legs and went to a coffee pot brewing on a hot plate in the corner. 'You said "partly" a moment ago. I think you were also happy to skip telling me about the reunion with Rebecca – you didn't want to talk about that either, did you?'

'Not particularly,' I responded.

He lifted the coffee pot in my direction, silently asking if I wanted a cup. That was a first – Lucas Corrigan trying to be a good host – and I wondered if it was an awkward, unsociable man's tentative attempt at friendship, or at least cordiality. Taken aback, I shook my head to the coffee.

'Why?' he asked.

'It was very personal, between the two of us – I thought it should stay there. The whole thing was very raw,' I said. 'It still is – and probably always will be.'

'The reunion with her was that difficult?'

'Of course it was,' I said. 'Seeing Rebecca, being able to touch her. There were so many times when I didn't think I would come home. Over the past few weeks, I made myself say goodbye to her a thousand times. I was overwhelmed.'

'Too much emotion for one person?' Corrigan asked. 'The same thing even when you sit here and have to recall those few minutes?'

'Pretty much,' I answered. 'It was a unique time, hard to recall. Emotionally.'

'Do you think . . . how do I say it? . . . sort of breaking down in emergency doesn't reflect well on you?'

'Probably,' I replied. 'We all know what Falcon says – emotion is a spy's worst enemy.'

'Falcon, yeah,' Corrigan said, carrying his coffee, returning to his desk. 'There's an expert on human relationships.' Again, he almost smiled. 'Even so, his first reaction in the hospital was to give you the time and space to recover and process it all. That was the human being speaking. The spymaster had to get to your bedside immediately.

'We were still in the waiting room, the four of us,' Corrigan continued. 'Rebecca had just headed back down to emergency, and we didn't know what you'd been through, but she had said you'd been shot in the foot and – according to Madeleine – that was a classic ISIS move. Combine it with the wound from a handcuff and clearly you'd been taken prisoner by the Army of the Pure.

'Falcon figured you had more than likely put eyes on the Emir and the guy with the locust tattoo – but even if you hadn't, you would still have serious intelligence. We knew from your rescue message that the courier was dead. The priority was to debrief you. It had to be done fast, though – before the Army had a chance to relocate or evade the satellites.'

Corrigan gave a rueful look. 'Falcon said it was unfortunate, but the information was the priority; your recovery was secondary. I told him he was a great spymaster, but it didn't matter what *he* wanted, the physician in charge of ICU would never allow you to be interviewed. Falcon said he would once he got the phone call.'

Phone call? I thought. What phone call?

'Yes, I was as confused as you,' Corrigan said. 'Then Falcon turned to Madeleine and told her to get the president's chief of staff on the line.'

'The White House Chief of Staff called my physician?' I asked, shocked.

'No,' Corrigan replied. 'The president made the call himself. Minutes later the physician was in the waiting room handing out gowns and gloves to the other three. Apparently, Human Resources wasn't needed in there—'

'A pity,' I said, grinning. 'I'm sure you would have protected my welfare.'

'Don't be crazy,' he replied. 'I know how to get ahead here.' And this time he really did smile. Against every expectation I had ever held, Lucas and I laughed, enjoying the rank cynicism of it.

'The doctor told us that you should be debriefed immediately; he and his team had already started treating you with drugs to reverse the sedatives,' Corrigan said. 'So, once everyone was suited up, he let Falcon and the others into ICU.'

25

RIGGED UP TO IVS, LYING IN BED IN ICU, ALONE IN AN ISOLATION room, I felt myself veering between a twisting, distorted reality and a strange, drug-induced sleep.

I was riding waves of total confusion when the door opened and three people dressed like surgeons entered. It didn't fool me, though – I was rational enough to know their presence in the room was drug-induced. Falcon Rourke was no doctor.

Smiling under his plastic shower cap, he approached the bed and fist-bumped me with a gloved hand. 'There were a lot of times when I thought we'd never see this day,' he said gently. 'Welcome home.'

I knew it wasn't real, but that didn't mean it wasn't comforting. 'Thanks,' I said, my voice sounding like it was coming from some faraway place. 'I'm surprised, though – your gown looks like it's off the rack. I thought if you were a doctor, Falcon – at least it would be specially tailored.'

He laughed, and so did the make-believe Buster and Madeleine behind him, everybody pleased I was in such good spirits.

This wasn't so bad, I thought. Despite my exhaustion, I started to warm to the exercise. I pointed at his neck. 'Not sure about the tie, Falcon.'

He looked down at it. 'What's wrong with it?'

'A bit loud,' I replied. As far as I knew, nobody had ever questioned Falcon's taste to his face, and I was enjoying it; I made a mental note to get the name of the drugs.

Falcon was starting to look at me quizzically, but it didn't matter, it was only make-believe. 'You're the only person I know who makes everyone else feel like part of the Third World,' I continued. 'I'm just suggesting, the tie lets you down.'

He, Buster and Madeleine exchanged a look. 'You don't understand,' Falcon replied. 'I have taste; most people have appetites.' It was well put, I thought, and laughed.

Meanwhile, Buster seemed to have understood something and, catching Madeleine's eye, started laughing and shaking his head. Falcon was staring at me and started to nod, as if he too had understood something very deep. I had no idea what it was, but it didn't worry me. 'And Buster – why not use a belt instead of some rope?' I said.

'I only use rope on dress-down Fridays,' he replied.

Suddenly I felt completely exhausted, and slumped back, expecting the fantasy version of reality to finally give way to the drug-induced sleep. Except it didn't. Falcon and the other two make-believe doctors stayed stubbornly rooted to my bedside.

'I'm tired,' I said. 'It's been fun, but you should leave. Come back later as Elvis, huh?' They didn't move. 'Go on, back into the ether,' I encouraged.

I kept looking at them. The fatigue started to lift as fast as it had hit, but the situation in front of me didn't change: my three colleagues were still there, visiting a room in ICU, dressed in their anti-infection outfits, becoming increasingly real by the second. We all looked at one another. 'Shit,' I said.

'I think the rope thing was a bit out of line,' Buster said.

'Sorry,' I replied.

'Well, now you're back,' Falcon said. 'You up to it?'

'To what?'

'Debrief,' he replied, taking out his encrypted phone and activating the recording function. Apparently, the proposal wasn't open to negotiation.

The other two followed suit and, with three phones about to record every word, we were ready to start. Drugs or no drugs, I told myself, I had to be on guard – there were aspects of the mission I had to avoid discussing at any cost. At least being exhausted, on medication and in ICU was an advantage: it meant I had every reason to keep it short and it would allow me to swerve around areas that were definitely better left unexplored.

'The message you wrote on the airstrip said the courier was dead,' Falcon said.

'Yes,' I said. 'He wasn't at the first rendezvous, and I was running late for the second—'

'Why?' Falcon wanted to know.

'I didn't go through the canyon that was on the proposed route,' I said. 'Once I got there, it looked far more dangerous than on the sat photos. To me, it was a perfect place for an ambush.' I said nothing about intuition and Sakab's reluctance to move forward. Any mention of gunfire from the future and they would have had me committed for sure.

'Okay, so you bypassed it,' Falcon replied. 'And then?'

I described the crossroads, the weapons bazaar, the heat and the dust. I recounted that I had seen the courier: 'There was a large wooden cross in the centre of the intersection,' I said. 'They had crucified him.'

'Crucified?' Falcon said. He and Buster had dealt with more than their share of horrific events, but it shocked even them.

'They tortured him first,' I continued. 'I can't be sure, but from a bloodstain I think they might have cut off his genitals.' My voice conveyed how I was feeling: I was weary, no doubt of it, but it was a weariness of the soul too.

'The crucifixion was for impact, I take it,' Falcon said. 'A big crowd?'

'A few hundred, maybe more.'

'The family – the ones we provided the US books for?' he asked. 'Any sign of them?'

'I couldn't tell who they were,' I lied. As I said earlier: any deviation from the mission, or involvement in other events, was a breach of every CIA rule. I had done what I thought was best and, somehow, I had made it home. What did it matter? It was in the past. I just had to keep it there.

'Once I knew he was dead, I burned the books and got rid of the gold,' I continued. 'I had just finished and was getting everything together when I heard someone outside my camp.' Thankfully, I was on firmer narrative ground now.

'I grabbed the rifle, body-rolled and was about to shoot when I saw him – a man I recognized from the crowd in front of the cross.'

'How did he find you?' Falcon asked immediately.

'The horses – something had spooked them earlier and two of them kept neighing,' I said, inventing it on the fly; I couldn't say they had seen me shooting. I would have preferred to forget about anyone visiting my makeshift camp but, professionally, I couldn't ignore the courier's dying words. Even though I did not understand them, it might be valuable intelligence, and there was no question – it had to be reported.

'The man had been a close friend of the courier's,' I said, extemporizing. 'He was one of five men forced to dig a base for the cross, and while he was doing it the courier – lying nearby, barely alive – said if a traveller arrived, to tell him that everything he had disclosed was true. Every word of it.'

'You're sure?' Falcon said, interrupting. 'That's exactly what he said?'

I nodded – at least that part was the truth. 'I asked him if the dying man had said something about a time, the name of a city – cities, perhaps – anything specific.'

'And did he?' Falcon asked, leaning forward, trying to find some way forward.

'Not really,' I replied, pausing to catch my breath. I was in bad shape. I tried to sit up straighter to ease my breathing then continued as best I could: 'My visitor said that when they rolled the courier on to the cross, just before they nailed him to it, he really started to ramble. He said there was a town in India where evil had come on the wind, a place of never-ending tragedy.'

'What?' Falcon demanded. 'A town in India? Not Indiana?'

'No, India,' I replied. 'According to the informant, they were the exact words. But, like he said – the courier was rambling by now, mostly about his family.'

'Even so,' Falcon said, turning away, thinking. 'It must mean something . . . it's not like a man in his situation would . . . obviously he thought it was important. ' "Evil had come on the wind . . . a place of never-ending tragedy," ' he repeated, unable to fathom it. 'And then, after you had spoken to the visitor?'

'I ran,' I said, relieved to leave the events at the crossroads behind. 'I figured they had only crucified him when they were certain he had revealed everything about our plans to meet.' I shrugged. 'I knew they would already be looking for me.'

'And they captured you?' Falcon said. 'Madeleine says the wounds indicate it.'

'Yes, I had the pleasure of meeting them,' I said.

'Which ones?' It was Buster, but I was sure the question was on all their lips.

'Mainly our target with the locust tattoo,' I replied.

'Al-Tundra?' Falcon said, close to disbelief. 'You spoke to al-Tundra?'

'His real name is Roman Kazinsky,' I said, and the three of them stared at me, totally shocked now. 'Colonel Roman Kazinsky. Don't thank me, though,' I continued. 'Thank the young woman who I brought back with me.'

Nobody could speak, not even Falcon – the restless spymaster, the man always pushing forward, the former agent always asking the next question, was like al-Tundra himself: lost for words.

'Kazinsky served with the Russian 3rd Spetsnaz Brigade,' I continued, my voice faltering. 'He's a decorated soldier, a veteran of a host of battles including the famous firefight in Aleppo. He grew up in a village on the Lena River. You know the Lena?'

They all shook their heads. 'What's wrong with you?' I asked. 'Do you think civilization ends at Budapest?'

They had no idea what I was talking about. I laughed. 'That's what Kazinsky told me when he asked me the same question.' I realized my voice was starting to falter and my breathing was becoming even more laboured; the memory of Kazinsky probably didn't help either. 'The village on the Lena was called Pokrovsk.'

Falcon continued to stare at me in astonishment. His joe, the one he had been convinced was dead, had – seemingly – turned a disastrous mission into a success.

'The father came from the old Soviet Union and raised his two sons there,' I continued. I stopped, and I think they figured I was done, but I wasn't – not quite. 'I found this out about the time Kazinsky strung Ghorbani up by his ankles and removed his tongue.'

There was silence for a long moment, and it gave me a chance to gather some strength. 'The base?' Falcon asked eventually. 'Did you see the base?'

'No,' I said weakly. 'I only saw . . . there was a cave, some sort of forward camp, abandoned once they caught me.'

'Other people?' Falcon continued. 'Names, descriptions, structure – leadership?'

I shook my head – nothing. 'The Emir?' Buster said, pressing also.

'Saw him. A mystery – covered head to toe,' I replied, my voice so weak by now that they had to lean closer. 'Facial recognition won't find him.'

I saw the disappointment on their faces. 'How do we find 'em in time?' Falcon asked, angry at the situation. 'Where do we look—'

'Search . . .' My voice trailed off. 'Search for . . .' I said, trying again. 'An AMG . . . six-wheel drive, Pakistani plates.'

'Go on,' Buster said. Like Falcon he was leaning close, making sure he heard.

'Central Asian Wildlife Survey . . .' I said. 'Locate the vehicle – you'll find the Emir . . . he'll lead you to the base.' I looked up at Falcon. 'I don't think I've got anything more.'

'Sleep,' he said. 'Brilliant work.' He gently pushed on my shoulder, forcing me to lie down. 'Absolutely brilliant.'

Maybe it was good work – maybe he was right. But it still ended up costing me my job.

26

LONG IS THE WAY AND HARD, THAT OUT OF HELL LEADS TO LIGHT – SO SAID
the blind English poet John Milton three hundred and fifty years ago.
He might as well have been describing the agency's desperate search
for Kazinsky, the Emir and the Army's base.

As soon as my three visitors had left ICU and were back in the
waiting room, Falcon was on the phone launching a full-court press
to find the AMG. Three hours later the NSA had hacked into the sales
data at Mercedes headquarters in Stuttgart and discovered that, with
fewer than a hundred of the six-wheel drive vehicles ever sold, there
was only one candidate that could logically be roaming the borderlands: one that had been bought by a shell company associated with
a wealthy Pakistani businessman based in Islamabad who had long
been suspected of helping to finance terrorist organizations.

The deep-dive NSA hack then provided the exact date the vehicle
was delivered to the financier, and that information, combined with
the agency's ability to deploy a massive amount of artificial intelligence, allowed them to hone in on millions of old spy-satellite
photographs and endless miles of archived footage. Less than twenty-
four hours after I had told Falcon about the Emir's ride, the CIA had
found satellite footage – captured two years earlier – that showed the
brand-new six-wheeler leaving a Mercedes facility in Islamabad, being
driven across the Pakistan border and handed over to four mysterious
men at a warehouse outside Shiraz, a city in the south-west of Iran.

'No question it's the vehicle,' Falcon said to Buster, Madeleine and
the other analysts and executives who had gathered in Falcon's office
to review the footage. 'I want to see every frame or photograph of it
between the handover in Shiraz and now. Two years' worth. We know
it was goofed up with the logo of the Central Asian Wildlife Survey,
and that should help. Buster, grab whatever resources you need.'

With fifty additional analysts and researchers called in from home,
the greatly expanded team worked round the clock and succeeded in
pinpointing the vehicle in numerous locations – they had several hundred sightings of it on the first pass alone – and three days later Buster
met with Falcon and the seventh-floor brains trust. Just as night was

falling, he stood up and – flashing images on a large video screen – took the group from one archived image of the vehicle to the next until – finally – he brought up the last sequence of the huge number of stills and video footage he had at his disposal.

'This is the last place we can track it,' he said. Falcon and the others watched as an 8K image of a rugged and uninhabited landscape appeared on the screen. In its centre was a canyon pock-marked with a complex of mountain caves – some of the openings as large as hangar doors, others so low you would have had to bend double to enter.

The executives stared at a hidden world: verdant trees lined an old watercourse; pools of deep shade lay beneath their branches and the tracks of gazelles were visible in a sweep of dirt and grass. The opening into the largest cave was almost a perfect arch, sculpted by the wind over millennia. Nowhere in the limitless landscape was there any sign of mankind or his works. The secluded caves, in all their grandeur, seemed to hearken back to a far more primal time—

'What's it called, this place?' Falcon asked.

'Nothing. It doesn't have a name,' Buster replied. 'Isolated, too little known.'

'Not even on an Iranian battlefield or secret maps?' Falcon asked.

'No,' Buster said. 'One team started calling it Tora Bora West, and that sort of stuck.'

'Tora Bora West?' Falcon said.

In Pashto, *tora bora* means 'black cave', so the name was ideal for the landscape Falcon and the others were looking at: the surrounding valleys and gorges seemed to be in permanent shadow. More than that, though, the name referenced the original Tora Bora caves, hundreds of miles to the east in Afghanistan, once the stronghold for Osama bin Laden and al-Qaeda.

'We went back through the data from NSA's low-orbit satellites,' Buster continued, bringing up a host of data and charts on the screen: thermal imaging, screen grabs, motion detection. 'Until recently, the caves had barely seen a visitor from one year's end to the next. A few hunters, a couple of smugglers.'

Then he pointed at a new data stack. 'And now? A massive influx of people – getting bigger every day as more fighters arrive.'

Falcon said nothing, nor did anyone else, but they were all convinced now – even though our inside man had been nailed to a cross, a terrified Blackwater agent had sold out his network to try and save his life, a wheelman had been strung up by his ankles and had his tongue ripped out, a young woman was left to drown and a spy presumed to be dead had been washed ashore alive – that the agency had achieved the impossible: they had managed to locate the Army of the Pure's base.

27

FALCON ENTERED THE LOBBY OF THE WEST WING OF THE WHITE House, took the elevator down one floor, stowed his electronic devices in a lead-lined cabinet at reception and entered the situation room, the most secure area in the entire building.

Seventy-two hours had passed since he had first seen the caves at Tora Bora West and, in that time, he had insisted that every frame, every data stack and every assumption be checked and re-checked: the people who would be listening to him were not known for their generosity of spirit or tolerance of mistakes.

Six of them were waiting inside the room, four men and two women, all occupying positions at the very highest levels of the US government. Falcon had barely stepped through the soundproof door, nodded a greeting to them and was about to engage in the small talk he hated so much when the door behind him opened again.

Everybody rose to their feet. Clifford Montgomery was a tall and imposing man then, still in his late sixties, and not frail and shrunken by the colon cancer that would take his life a few years later, the first president to die in office – apart from by assassination – in almost a hundred years. While Falcon didn't agree with him politically – they were an ocean apart on many issues – he certainly admired the man's work ethic and intelligence, his decency and directness. His sense of humour didn't hurt either.

'So, Falcon,' the president said. 'What news from the front line at *Vogue Homme*?'

Several of the participants smiled, the two who couldn't abide the spymaster sniggered, and Falcon laughed. 'French cuffs will be big this winter, Mr President. Apart from that, the Army of the Pure poses a larger threat every day.'

He nodded to a National Security Council staffer sitting in a control booth at the back, the lights dimmed, and six large video screens flicked on hi-def footage of the cave complex. With the satellite reprogrammed to zero in on the location, the images were vastly more comprehensive, capturing huge numbers of people, weapons and vehicles on the move, ammunition and explosives bunkers built into a hillside, fighters discharging high-velocity rounds on a sophisticated firing range and, on the back of a truck, what appeared to be a type of limpet mine – an explosive device – which, if attached to the hull, was capable of sinking almost any ship afloat. Clearly, the canyon was no longer a haunting and ancient place, it was dangerous and violent, inescapably a part of our era.

'We found it several days ago,' Falcon explained. 'This is the Army's base, now known as Tora Bora West.'

Nobody at the conference table could hide their reaction. 'That was fast,' the president said, impressed, much to several people's chagrin.

'Pity we didn't do the same with al-Qaeda – we should have found 'em sooner and hit 'em, socks and jocks, out of the gate,' the Secretary of Defense said. Jose Pereira was a huge man, so big in stature, he had once been described as a danger to shipping.

'As you know, we believe the Army are in the final stage of planning a spectacular, details unknown,' Falcon said, ignoring him. 'The question has always been – are they capable of it? For several reasons, we now believe they are—'

He motioned to the staffer in the control room and a photo of a middle-aged, bespectacled man appeared on the screen. Dressed in an expensive Western business suit, he had a full head of dark hair, a deep olive complexion, an aquiline nose and the haughty expression that often accompanies people of great wealth. Power, too. As the control-room technician changed the images on the screen, the people gathered at the table saw him at Davos posing with the heads of three international banks, at a palace in Saudi Arabia smiling at the side of the crown prince, in the owner's enclosure at Royal Ascot . . .

'I've met him,' President Montgomery said, surprised. 'At a climate conference in Abu Dhabi or somewhere. A huge dinner, I remember. What's his name?'

'Yusuf Faheez,' Falcon answered. 'Third richest man in Pakistan, very close to the prime minister and their intelligence services. People say he secretly holds over a billion dollars on behalf of the six most powerful members of the ruling political party.'

'A top athlete or something when he was young,' the president said. 'I recall the English were all over him.'

'A cricketer,' Falcon replied. 'He's a national hero in Pakistan.'

'So why is he significant?' Pereira asked.

Falcon motioned again to the control room. 'He purchased an expensive vehicle and gave it to the leadership of the Army.' Spy-satellite footage of the brand-new Mercedes six-wheeler leaving Islamabad and being handed over at the warehouse in Iran started to play on the screens. 'We have now looked at his opaque financial records – we are convinced he has been funding the Army. If he hasn't done so already, it is almost certain he will be the lead financier for the spectacular. To a man of his wealth, it won't mean a thing. The attacks on 9/11 cost al-Qaeda less than five hundred thousand dollars while the War on Terror has cost the US over ten trillion dollars. What is a million or two to Faheez?'

The sobering analysis was met by silence, finally broken by Falcon. 'Yusuf Faheez gives them the funds. This man gives them the ability—'

The images of the Mercedes AMG disappeared and were replaced by the courier's photo of the men playing cards at the village celebration. 'What's that on the man's back?' the president asked, looking hard at the enhanced photo.

'A locust,' Falcon replied. 'You're looking at the only photograph in existence of Abu Muslim al-Tundra.'

'Al-Tundra? Why are you showing us him?' Pereira asked.

'It was taken in Iran, about a month ago,' Falcon replied.

'Bullshit,' Pereira said sharply. 'It couldn't have been – al-Tundra is dead.'

'He isn't. He's very much alive,' Falcon replied.

'You're wrong,' Pereira countered. 'You know what happened – he was killed in a bombing run on a house in Iraq.'

'The Pentagon *said* he was killed in a bombing run. There was no forensic evidence.'

'Sure – and you know it's him because a satellite or something took a photo of some guy's back?' said Pereira, blustering, puffing himself up even larger.

'No – because a few days ago one of our agents spoke to him in

Iran,' Falcon said evenly, allowing time for their stunned reaction. 'That's right – spoke to him and discovered his real name is Roman Kazinsky.'

He signalled to the control room and photos and information from a military record – all in Russian – appeared on the screens. In the centre was an image of Kazinsky as a much younger man – shaved head, less weather-beaten, but even more handsome, his eyes as arresting and cruel as ever. 'The NSA hacked Russian military records and got a copy of his file,' Falcon said. 'This photo was taken on the day he was promoted to Colonel in the Spetsnaz, the Russian Special Forces, one of the youngest to ever hold the rank.'

Not only had al-Tundra returned from the dead, but at last the US could put a name and a face to him. Images of Kazinsky – in various uniforms, on a host of far-flung battlefields – continued to play on the screens, but Falcon turned his back on them and addressed the room. 'The nominal leader of the Army of the Pure is a man known as the Emir – because of his devotion to the harshest version of Islam and his knowledge of the Holy Qur'an, he gives the group weight in regard to religion. But experience shows that a terrorist group's military leader is always the most dangerous—'

'And the Army's military commander,' the president said quietly, 'is al-Tundra, now identified as Roman Kazinsky?'

'Yes,' Falcon replied. 'One of the founders of ISIS, a highly trained soldier and probably the most formidable military leader we have had the misfortune to encounter. Al-Qaeda included.'

'And you're sure about this?' the president asked. 'You're certain al-Tundra isn't dead?'

'Certain,' Falcon confirmed.

'You said an agent spoke to him?' the president said. 'You have confidence in this spy?'

'Total,' Falcon responded.

'How did he manage it? What happened to him after he found Kazinsky?'

'I can't disclose that, Mr President.' In response, Montgomery nodded, understanding – he knew it was not because Falcon didn't trust him; it was because the CIA director didn't believe others in the room wouldn't gossip or leak. It was Washington, after all.

The president looked away, processing the information, trying to measure its reliability, probably thinking about the Army of the Pure and past spectaculars. As a much younger man, Montgomery had been three miles from Wall Street on 9/11.

Falcon, watching him, remembered what he had told him once about what it was like to occupy the Oval Office. 'Every day you climb a wall of worry,' the president had said. 'The only thing that separates one day from the next is the height of the wall.'

Falcon told me later that, from the look on the president's face, in those few minutes the wall was very high indeed. 'So, they have the funds,' he said finally, turning to Falcon and the others. 'And they have the military leadership. What do we know about the plan?'

Falcon nodded to the technician in the control booth and a map of India appeared on the screens. 'This is the only clue we have.'

'India?' Pereira asked scornfully. Falcon didn't dignify it with an answer. In silence, everyone else in the windowless room stared at the map as tiny electronic pinheads started to appear: dozens at first, rapidly multiplying into hundreds, then thousands until almost the entire country was dense with them.

'What are they?' the Chairman of the Joint Chiefs, a close professional and personal friend of Pereira, asked.

'Towns – or at least places that might fit the description,' Falcon explained. 'Twenty-six thousand of 'em. And one of them is a place where "evil came on the wind, a town of never-ending tragedy".'

'That's it? That's the clue? Poetry?' Pereira asked. 'A town of never-ending tragedy? I've been to India – if you ask me, that's the whole fuckin' country.'

Falcon just shrugged – what can you do? 'Yes, that's the clue. We had a source inside the Army. His cover was blown and he was crucified—'

'You mean metaphorically?' the president asked.

'No, I mean for real,' Falcon replied. 'The statement about a town in India was among the last words the man said. He might have been rambling; it's also possible he was trying to tell us something.'

'A town – and there's twenty-six thousand?' said the chairman. 'Not exactly helpful.'

'Not helpful at all,' Falcon agreed. 'Except Kazinsky's military record provided one piece of additional information. You know better than anyone, General – the endless civil war in Syria was one of the dirtiest ever fought.'

'Sure,' the chairman replied.

'We were all there, taking sides – ourselves, the Russians, the Kurds, militias, tribal leaders, mercenaries. The only sensible ones were the Chinese – they stayed out,' Falcon said. 'Chemical weapons were used everywhere – chlorine, mustard gas, sarin, anything that would kill and maim. All banned, of course, but when has that ever stopped anyone except us and the Brits? At one stage, early on, there was a wild engagement involving the Russians in an area surrounding Kafr Zita, a town of about thirty thousand people. The battle was going badly for the outnumbered Russians but nearby was a broken-down chemical plant whose major activity was turning liquid chlorine into a gas.

'The Russian commander,' Falcon continued, 'gauged the direction of the wind, waited until it turned to the south, then sent a team into the plant to blow up the huge steel storage tanks. Using time-delay fuses, the tanks were torn apart, the chlorine gas was released in a huge cloud and the wind did the rest.

'It wasn't just that the gas killed indiscriminately, there was another, equally important effect. Because you can smell chlorine before it becomes lethal, it induces panic as people flee. That was what happened – villagers, opposing troops, townspeople and even the animals ran for their lives. As a result, the Russians managed to snatch victory from almost certain defeat.'

Falcon paused, and nobody, not the Secretary of Defense, the Chairman of the Joint Chiefs, the Secretary of State – an elderly woman with a Ph.D. in engineering and one of the smartest people in government service – said anything, imagining the battlefield scene, the deadly clouds of approaching gas, and the panic as the town emptied.

'Of course, the Russian commander saw first-hand the devastating effects of a crude chemical weapons attack,' Falcon said. 'His name was Roman Kazinsky.'

28

IN THE MISERABLE SILENCE THAT FOLLOWED, FALCON STARED AT THE screens, lit only by the red pinpoints. 'I can give you another example of a chemical plant being destroyed – there was no war on this occasion; instead it was one of the worst industrial accidents in the world.'

'One night just before Christmas, several miles outside of a large city, a huge steel tank holding a deadly gas used in the production of pesticides started to overheat. Because several fail-safe measures had not been maintained properly, the temperature grew exponentially until a series of valves ruptured and the tank spewed almost fifty tons of the toxic chemicals into the atmosphere.

'In less than two hours, over five hundred thousand people living nearby were exposed to at least some of the toxic agent.' Everyone stared at Falcon: five hundred thousand people – could this be true?

'The people running away on foot – because they were engaged in intense exercise and breathing hard – inhaled more of the chemical than those who tried to escape in cars,' Falcon continued. 'The gas was heavier than air, so it sank, and its greatest concentration was closest to the ground. That meant children, being shorter, inhaled more than adults. To say life and death was random that day would be an understatement.'

The details had the unmistakable ring of truth, and even the sceptics were chastened. Falcon kept going. 'The region's entire health-care system collapsed that night. Within seventy-two hours every tree in the area was stripped of its leaves and the fields and valleys were littered with the bloated carcasses of livestock and pets. The human toll has never been established – even today, nearly fifty years later – people are still dying from the effects. Everyone agrees; however, it numbered in the tens of thousands—'

'Falcon – where did this happen?' the Secretary of State asked quietly.

'India,' he replied, turning to the map.

'Bhopal,' the president said, realization dawning. 'The Union Carbide factory. My father had just been made Secretary of Commerce. I was in my first year at college and I remember Dad saying Union Carbide – an American corporation – was the ugliest face of capitalism he had ever seen.'

Falcon pointed at the map. 'That's right, sir – Bhopal,' he said, and the red pinpoints started to vanish until only one, close to the centre of the huge country, remained. 'Known as the City of Lakes, with a population of over one and a half million people, the surrounding national park is stunning, inhabited by tigers and leopards. That was what Union Carbide almost destroyed.

'Maybe our source, the man who was crucified, had heard of the Bhopal gas disaster, or perhaps he was just rambling, but one thing is certain: you could not find a better example of a town where "evil came on the wind".'

Falcon looked directly at the Secretary of Defense. 'Was it poetry? Or was it a clue?' he asked rhetorically. 'Personally, I think it was the latter – mainly because of this.' The map of India faded from the screens and was replaced by highly detailed satellite photos of specific areas at Tora Bora West. Falcon picked up an electronic pointer and indicated several large craters and bombed-out vehicles.

'In an adjacent canyon we have identified what we believe is the aftermath of high-yield improvised explosive devices. That means the Army has a bomb-maker, and the evidence we have points to an elusive man called the Somali – he was trained by al-Shabab, the jihadi terrorist group in Yemen, and later became the chief bomb-maker for ISIS. He is generally considered to be the best in the business.'

Falcon shifted the pointer to indicate a small convoy of vehicles heading into an explosives bunker. 'On the back of the first truck is a crude limpet mine. Crude, however, doesn't mean it won't work.'

'Limpet mines are used against shipping,' the chairman interrupted. 'We're talking about tanker ships now?'

'You're right about the use, General – but no, not tankers,' Falcon said. 'As you know, a limpet mine is attached to the hull and can take down any vessel afloat. They are specially designed because most large ships are double-hulled – the explosive has to destroy a thick section of metal, blast through an air void and then penetrate another metal skin. Apart from ships, there is one other type of vessel that is double-hulled—'

'Storage tanks for chemicals and gases,' the Secretary of State said, her voice reflecting her rocketing anxiety.

'And it gets worse,' Falcon said. 'Our surveillance and experience tells us the bomb-maker is not interested in designing a state-of-the-art limpet mine. He's making a device that can be assembled from materials readily available everywhere in the world.

'He designs and tests the weapon at Tora Bora West and then uses an encrypted app to send instructions to individuals or terrorist cells working anywhere – a storage facility in Queens, an auto-repair shop in Van Nuys or a garage a couple of miles from here. Those irregular "agents-in-place" buy a pressure cooker and everything else they need to build the device. And that's just the people here. Then there is Berlin, Paris, London – you know the list.'

'There must be a primary target?' the president said, the wall he was climbing growing higher every minute. 'Any visibility?'

'Targets, plural,' Falcon replied. 'They're talking about a spectacular – multiple, coordinated attacks, we think. Like 9/11. Those targets are all around us. Over a hundred highly dangerous chemical agents are used in manufacturing in this country, and they are stored somewhere; no, strike that – they are stored everywhere.'

He brought a chemical formula up on the screen followed by a graphic showing its molecular structure. 'Hydrogen cyanide,' he said, 'is one of the most widely used industrial chemicals, involved in mining and the production of a host of items including plastics, pesticides and iron and steel. Over a *billion pounds* of it are produced every year in the US alone.'

The red pinpoints reappeared – but this time they were on a map of America, multiplying fast. 'Those are sites where that chemical is stored,' Falcon continued. 'As you can see, there are facilities – in many cases, a number of them – on the outskirts of most major cities. New York, LA, Chicago, New Orleans. And that's just one chemical – there are another hundred. If I brought those up, the map would look worse than the towns in India.'

The president stared at it as the number of chemical storage sites continued to explode. 'I know it's just an example, but is hydrogen cyanide as bad as it sounds?'

'You don't hear much about it any more,' Falcon replied. 'But there was a time when it was well known. A German manufacturer marketed it under the brand name Zyklon-B – it was what the Nazis used in the gas chambers at Auschwitz. So, yes, Mr President, you could say it is very bad indeed.'

29

'ENTIRE CITIES TURNED INTO GAS CHAMBERS, MILLIONS DEAD AND countless Bhopals – or even worse – emerging overnight? Endless panic and children dying first because they're smaller?' the president said, and looked around the table.

'Bill Clinton thought bin Laden was an isolated fanatic, a crazy man living in a cave,' he continued. 'We won't repeat that mistake with Kazinsky. Let's light this candle – what do we do?'

The Secretary of Defense straightened himself in his chair; he had been waiting for his moment and his large frame appeared to expand. 'We have no choice – the CIA has located their base: we destroy them.'

'How?' the president asked.

'Target Tora Bora West with a bombing campaign. Half a dozen MOABs will take out even the deepest caves,' the Secretary of Defense replied. MOABs was shorthand for the 'Mother of All Bombs', a thirty-foot-long air-burst bomb that was, apart from nuclear devices, the most powerful weapon in the US arsenal.

'That's a good strategy,' the elderly Secretary of State said. She was from a wealthy family in the South and her voice was like cut glass. 'If you want to start World War Three.

'In case Jose hasn't noticed,' she went on, 'Tora Bora West is in Iran, home to the eighth-largest army in the world. They can put a million trained personnel under arms – almost the same number as Russia – and one third of them are elite Revolutionary Guards. This isn't Iraq or Grenada, Mr President, this would be a real war with huge casualties.'

'There won't be a war,' the Secretary of Defense replied. 'They'll make a lot of noise, but they won't strike back. We bomb and missile them and it will be over in seventy-two hours.'

'The Pentagon's bombs worked well with al-Tundra's house in Iraq,' Falcon said. 'I can't imagine why anyone would think it wouldn't work now.'

The Secretary of Defense wheeled to face him. 'You know what's wrong with this country, Falcon? We're great at handling disasters, we just never listen to warnings. Read the damn 9/11 report. We act today; yesterday wouldn't have been soon enough—'

The Secretary of State started to fire back, but the president raised his hand, stopping her mid-sentence. 'Falcon?' he said.

'Surgical, like the Israelis,' Falcon replied. 'A targeted strike against the leadership; it's the only way it will work without blowing up the whole Middle East. It's also the only way we'll know for sure we have killed Kazinsky, the Emir and anyone else near the top of the pyramid. The Army can stay in their cave. A snake without a head is no threat to anyone—'

'Okay. Then how do you do it?' the president asked.

'We know where they're based; it's inaccessible except by four-wheel drive,' Falcon replied. 'We identify the leadership and when we see them on the move, we missile the vehicles.'

'Missile them from over the border? That's ridiculous,' the Secretary of Defense intervened. 'We can't penetrate the Iranian air-defence shield. We would have to destroy their entire system first, and it's among the best in the world. They'll shoot your half a dozen missiles out of the sky as soon as they approach the border. It will never work.'

'Jose's right,' the chairman added. 'Their air-defence system was provided by the Russians to prevent exactly this: any form of American attack.'

'Nothing can evade it,' the Secretary of Defense continued. 'The Army of the Pure is safe behind the Iranian shield. That's why we launch a bombing campaign – we destroy the air defences, then take out the caves.'

Falcon shook his head. 'There is a way to beat Iran's air defences,' he said. 'We can eliminate the Army leadership with a targeted missile attack and avoid the risk of a major war. It would be surgical and impossible for anyone to detect how it was done.' He looked around at their faces. 'We know what I am talking about, don't we?'

There were only seven other people in the world who were privy to one of America's most closely guarded secrets. All of them were in the situation room that day, and none of them spoke; they were acutely aware, so I learned later, that on a Thursday afternoon in Washington they were face to face with history—

Without doubt, implementing Falcon's suggestion would change the nature of warfare for ever.

30

THE SILENCE DRAGGED ON UNTIL IT WAS FINALLY BROKEN BY FALCON: 'We can't do it without your authorization,' he said to the president.

'I know,' Montgomery replied, his face averted, deep in thought. He turned towards them. 'So it's up to me. This is it, then – Julius Caesar has reached the Rubicon.'

Falcon tried to smile. 'But will he cross it?' he asked, doing his best to hide his pessimism: he and the Secretary of State were outnumbered by those supporting the Secretary of Defense and the Chairman of the Joint Chiefs, and he had always thought of Montgomery as the consummate politician, not known as a risk-taker. A conventional bombing campaign, with all its nightly television appeal, would probably be attractive to him.

He looked at Falcon for a long beat. 'Julius says he wants to think about it.' He got to his feet and headed to the door.

31

PESSIMISTIC AT THE ANTICIPATED OUTCOME, DESPAIRING AT THE thought of the country risking another unwinnable war, Falcon left the situation room, retrieved his electronic devices, exited the West Wing and – so he described to me later – encountered one of the most spectacular sights he had ever seen: wildfires had been burning in Virginia that year and the wind-blown smoke meant that a huge blood-red sun, shooting the horizon with streamers of purple, was edging the horizon, starting to set.

In a fluke of atmospherics and timing, the city was dark around the edges but the great monuments of Washington were bathed in a fiery glow. For a long moment he didn't move: it reminded him that in a world full of broken promises and lost dreams, of dark secrets and soul-sapping cynicism, there were still things worth fighting for. Their symbols were all around him, burning like beacons.

He started to walk fast; he had work to do. While he was deeply worried the president would decide to start a full DEFCON One conflict with Iran, he knew the wheel of fortune might turn in his favour. If it did, he had to be able to identify the Emir and Roman Kazinsky with absolute certainty. There was only one American that he was aware of who had ever laid eyes on them.

Falcon reached his black SUV, waiting in one of the campus's prime parking spots. 'Some light show, huh?' Falcon's driver, Will, who also served as his primary close protection officer, said as the director got into the safe seat in the back.

'Sure is,' Falcon said. 'It probably looks like the sky after Krakatoa.'

The driver looked at Falcon in the mirror. 'Come again, Director?'

'A volcano in Indonesia erupted in the late 1800s,' Falcon said. 'It was one of the loudest natural sounds in the history of the world – people living four thousand miles away heard it. Ash rocketed three hundred thousand feet into the sky and clouds of smoke and debris circled the Earth. That's the point – for months afterwards London experienced eerie sunsets of purple and green, just like today.'

Will smiled. 'You think it's an omen?'

'I hope not,' Falcon replied.

'Langley?' Will asked, heading towards the White House security gates.

'No,' Falcon said. 'Washington MedStar Hospital. As fast as you can.'

32

I HAD BEEN LUCKY – THE DECISION BY THE DOCTORS IN DUBAI TO start a course of potent intravenous antibiotics immediately, followed by the skill of the team on board the air ambulance, meant the worst consequences of sepsis never took hold.

I was young and fit, or so the physician-in-charge of ICU told me, with no underlying medical conditions and – thankfully – they found no evidence of any organ damage. As a result, I was discharged from their care and sent to a private room several floors below. Because of my covert job and the agency's determination to prevent me from being exposed to scrutiny from other patients, I found myself as the sole patient in an area reserved for people suffering from highly infectious diseases. The previous occupant of my room had died from Ebola, so it wasn't as if anyone made social visits. If a visitor, patient or an unauthorized member of staff did make it past the three security barriers, they were met by two armed Marines stationed outside my door.

It was one of them, apparently, who Falcon sent to find a wheel-chair. I didn't know anything about his visit – I just saw the door open and, expecting dinner, looked up instead to see him enter. He took a seat next to the bed and asked how I was feeling. I knew then something was afoot – he was receiving frequent updates on my condition by phone, so it was just filler. 'What's happened?' I said.

'We've located the Army's base.'

I reacted, surprised – it was faster than I could have imagined. 'The Mercedes?' I asked.

'It led us to a series of caves,' Falcon continued. 'We've targeted them with satellites for days, and we've also searched the archival footage. We have seen hundreds of people there – thousands, probably – but we have a problem.'

He paused. 'It has to be a surgical strike, and that means I need positive ID. You're the only one who has seen them – Kazinsky, the Emir and the three lieutenants you've spoken about. I need you at Langley to identify them.'

'I don't know if I can help,' I said, shaking my head reluctantly. 'A lot of them were hooded or masked. As I told you, I never even saw the Emir's face—'

He nodded. 'I met a movie star once,' he said, seemingly apropos of nothing. 'Scottish guy, drove an Aston Martin on screen – he'd played a spy years before and he came out to Langley for some PR visit or something. He was waiting in the conference room and I saw he'd had great work done on his face, neck and the back of his hands. He looked ten or fifteen years younger than his age.

'Then he stood up and came forward to shake hands – and he walked like an old man. No amount of plastic surgery in the world could hide what he really was. I am telling you because our bodies give away more than our faces. You have spent a lifetime looking at details because your life might depend on it. You may not realize it, but you can help.'

I didn't know if I was even physically strong enough. 'You said it was going to be surgical. How?' I asked, playing for time, trying to judge.

'We wait until they leave the cave in vehicles and we'll missile them on the move.'

'Missile them where?' I asked, perplexed. 'Are they driving into

Afghanistan? They'll leave the Iranian air-defence shield behind? Jesus, they'd have to be crazy.'

He looked at me hard. 'I want to missile them in Iran.'

There have not been many times in the secret life when I have been left speechless. That moment, lying in bed in an infectious-disease ward in Washington and listening to the director of the CIA's plan, was one of them. 'And how are you going to get missiles through the Iranian air defences?' I asked.

Falcon looked at me, our eyes met, and I knew, as mysterious as the plan was, there was no point in asking any more questions; he was the consummate spymaster and he wasn't going to tell me.

'I know you haven't recovered and I know it's unfair, but I need you to come with me now. It's a few days – we have a full medical suite in the Original Headquarters Building and I can arrange all the support you need. We'll take the doctors from here if we have to. Yes?'

'I get tired . . . medically, maybe it's possible,' I replied. 'But I start rehab tomorrow. It's my foot and it's going to be a long haul – I still can't put any weight on it.'

'I just happen to have arranged a wheelchair,' he said, smiling.

'Okay – but there's one more thing,' I said.

'You're worried about Rebecca?' he replied.

I nodded.

'I don't blame you – having met her, I would be too,' he said ruefully.

We laughed. 'How much can I tell her?' I asked.

'Explain you are looking at photographs, tell her it is a matter of national importance. Say that if I could, I would bring the photos and footage here, but the security risk is too high – I'm sorry, but Mohammad has to go to the mountain.'

Then he paused. 'No, better still – tell her she can come to Langley. I'll prove to her that you are not operational, that you're safe.' He smiled. 'She can be certain there won't be an empty coffin at Arlington, not this time.'

I stared at him, uncertain of what he was going to do, but – for the first time – I realized how much his plan needed me. Before I could say any more, one of his three cellphones rang—

It was the red one, the phone he never turned off, the one used only for emergencies or the highest-priority messages.

33

BY THE TIME FALCON FINISHED SPEAKING, WE WERE IN THE BACK OF his SUV with the soundproof glass between us and the driver raised, a pair of crutches next to me and the wheelchair stowed in the trunk, heading to Langley.

'Remember the Pakistani tripods where you camped the night before entering Iran?' Falcon asked. 'The call was telling me that the listening post has harvested a phone call using the heaviest encryption you can find.'

Will – the driver – exited the hospital and hit the vehicle's blue flashing lights.

'The call originated at a villa owned by a Pakistani billionaire called Yusuf Faheez who has a lot of form funding terrorist organizations. He was the man who bought the AMG Mercedes for the Emir,' Falcon said. 'The recipient of the call was located in Iran, but Faheez was always contacting terrorists and radicals. Because he was close to the government, the calls were of no interest to Pakistani intelligence and they never bothered marking them for decryption.'

'So how did we get hold of it?' I asked.

'Because of the Mercedes, we had flagged the guy. We still would not have been able to get the recording of the call out of the Pakistanis, except the US had provided the equipment being used at the tripods—'

'And the NSA had arranged for a back door to be built into it,' I said, guessing.

'Yes,' Falcon replied. 'The Pakistani yield was automatically downloaded to the NSA facility at Fort Meade in Maryland. It took one of their analysts less than a minute using geo-tracking software to find that the recipient of the call was at the Army's base.'

'The code-breaking has begun, and I suppose the seventh floor is starting to read the decrypted conversation now?' I said. 'That's why our blue lights are flashing?'

34

FALCON LED THE WAY DOWN INTO THE VAST HIGH-SECURITY ZONE beneath the Bubble. Like a fool – or a typical male, as Rebecca would have said – I had let my pride get the better of me and had refused the wheelchair once the SUV had parked.

Hobbling along on the crutches, I soon realized that I had badly overestimated my physical condition and I was half exhausted as we negotiated the X-rays, the iris scanners and biometric cameras and entered the conference room where – seemingly so long ago – I had first seen the photo of Kazinsky's back and the locust tattoo.

The white noise hadn't changed, nor had the grey steel door, but as it slid open, I saw that everything else had been transformed. Dividing walls at either end of the already large space had been activated and had vanished into the floor, revealing raked, stadium-style seats, a large command console, endless computer monitors and almost triple the number of analysts and specialists at workstations. It was clear that the conference area was now command central for one of the agency's largest-ever missions: to hunt, identify and destroy the command pyramid of the Army of the Pure.

Falcon motioned me towards the centre console and, as I limped towards it, the buzz of normal conversation ground to a halt. In silence, I paused on my crutches and saw everybody turning to look at me. I recognized many of them and gave a nod in greeting, confused about why there appeared to be such a shocked silence.

Then I realized: they were taken aback by my appearance, shaken at the sight of me. Only a few weeks had passed since a young and fit agent, highly trained, had sat in the same room with many of them. Now he had returned and, while virtually none of them had any idea about what had happened, they must have been certain by looking at me that nothing had gone according to our elaborate plans.

I had lost almost a quarter of my body weight and the jeans and T-shirt Rebecca had brought me from home several days before only helped accentuate it, hanging off what looked like a skeleton. To add further to my ghostly appearance, my face was gaunt and drawn, the skin stretched tight, my cheekbones jutting out and my eyes sunken and rimmed by shadows. The injuries were even more obvious – my head had been shaved in order to stitch and clean several cuts, my hand was bandaged, my strained wrist splinted, my foot encased in bandages and protected by a moon boot and my breathing was fast and laboured from fatigue.

For everyone in the room, it was probably the first time they had seen the consequences of the missions they orchestrated. Like Rebecca had told Falcon – while the problems the agency worked on were seemingly intellectual, the costs were human and maybe the people at the desks saw that now. The silence which accompanied the sight of me might have dragged on for minutes had it not been for Falcon guiding me to the console, taking the captain's chair and immediately getting down to business.

'Where are we, Buster?' he said to the assistant director, who was sitting at a desk in front of us.

'We're decrypting the phone call, but there is no way of knowing the exact identity of the two men speaking,' Buster replied. 'It could be the Emir himself and it is certainly either the financier or one of his aides. Although it was encrypted, they are talking in riddles, mixing a range of languages, but we think they are trying to organize a meeting—'

'A meeting?' Falcon demanded, even more alert. 'What have you got on it?'

'Not much at the moment,' Buster replied. 'It was mentioned at the top of the call. Right now they're discussing the details, the final payments of something,' Buster replied. 'I would say if they are going to strike us, it's going to be soon.'

'Okay – the meeting first,' Falcon said. 'They said nothing more about it?'

Buster shook his head. 'Not that we've heard – the translation from the different languages is taking time.'

'Wherever it is, it won't be in Afghanistan or Pakistan,' Falcon said. 'Far too dangerous. They'll stay behind the Iranian air-defence shield—'

Margaret, the woman who wore her vaping and cynicism like a badge of honour, interrupted, urgent. 'You're right, Falcon,' she said. 'It's not in either of those Stans.'

She was staring at her computer screen: one half showed the transcript of the conversation – decrypted – but in Punjabi, Farsi and several very obscure dialects; on the other side of the screen was the English translation. 'I'm ahead of you, I'm getting the first feed from the translators. It's in Casablanca,' she said.

'Bullshit – they're not going to Morocco,' Buster said.

'I'm just telling you what the transcript says,' Margaret replied.

'Casablanca?' Falcon said, perplexed. 'At least it would make it a lot easier to hit them – Morocco is Muslim but the government would play ball with us.'

Buster, looking at his screen, had also started skipping ahead. 'No, you can strike Casablanca. The financier's side is saying they have a twenty-four-hour drive from Islamabad in order to get to the meeting.'

Falcon turned to the room: 'Map of Iran now – how far can you drive from Islamabad in twenty-four hours?'

'Seventeen or eighteen hundred klicks,' a male analyst, sitting in the gloom at the back of the stadium section, an expert in the geography of the region, called out. 'The roads are sketchy – so even driving hard, that would be the limit.'

'Give me a cone showing eighteen hundred klicks from Islamabad,' Falcon ordered. Then, before one of the technicians could get the graphic up on the overhead screens—

'Falcon!' It was Margaret again. The director turned to face her. 'Whoever is at Tora Bora West says there's greater safety and anonymity in crowds. He is telling the financier the location is highly urbanized—'

'Good,' Falcon responded. 'We're looking for a heavily populated town in Iran no more than eighteen hundred klicks from Islamabad—'

'Zahedan,' I said, as loudly as I could. 'I know that part of the world,' I continued. 'It's where I was going to cross the border on the bike. There's no other place in the area that you could call "urbanized".'

The cone appeared on the screens and Zahedan was by far the largest dot. 'Okay, everybody,' Falcon said. 'We've got a theory – there's a meeting in Zahedan.'

'Population of seven hundred thousand,' the geography expert added, displaying a series of images on the screens. Judging by the chaotic traffic, the small city was certainly urbanized. In addition, its crowded streets were lined with small shops, washing hung from balconies, in the centre was a large souk with hundreds of tiny stalls, large umbrellas shaded barrels of spices and sacks of vegetables, food

252

hawkers lined the pavements and veiled women manoeuvred past men pushing handcarts laden with fruit.

'Casa Blanca,' I said to anyone that could hear. 'The white house?'

Falcon turned and smiled at me. 'That's what I was thinking.' He spoke to the room at large. 'Until we get something more definitive, we're looking for a white house in Zahedan. Yeah – I know, nearly every house in Iran is white.'

People smiled, booting up their laptops. 'It's teams of three,' Falcon continued, 'split the city into sections, pull up the satellite images and go street by street, house by house. A white house or building. We can narrow it down – it has to be secure and probably have grounds big enough to get a group of vehicles off the road. A dead-end street with no passing traffic would be on my wishlist too if I was organizing it.'

Several of the younger analysts – almost certainly the most ambitious men and women – had already started searching, and Falcon had barely returned to his seat, starting to zoom in and examine the satellite images himself, when a voice called: 'Director?'

We turned. It was a young guy – Dylan Watson, according to the ID card around his neck. 'There's a possibility at twenty-nine degrees, thirty minutes . . .'

He continued to give the co-ordinates and the image of Zahedan on the screen started to grow larger and larger, highlighting a stark white building standing in one of a matrix of narrow dirt roads little wider than alleys. 'It's on a dead end,' he said.

'A mosque?' Falcon said, looking at the building. 'Not much privacy for a crucial meeting, especially if you're planning something as big as a spectacular.'

'It's got a house, and there's a large area inside a wall at the back where a few dozen vehicles could park,' Dylan said nervously, not accustomed to being the centre of attention but forging ahead. 'The house is probably a residence for the imam; it shares a courtyard with the mosque. Pretty private, Director.'

Falcon walked up to a large screen as a technician zoomed in on the cluster of buildings. The house itself was a traditional old Arabian home: low built with a flat roof and, as always, there were no windows on to the street. Everything was turned inwards and looked into a series of lush and private courtyards, while every door – especially those accessing the road or leading from the guest areas into the family part of the home – was offset so that there was no line of sight and therefore no risk of strangers glimpsing the unveiled women of the household.

'Mohammad Jannati is the name of the imam,' Madeleine, consulting a database on her laptop, called out from her perch halfway up the raked seats. 'Interesting man, late thirties, doesn't travel much – he's on almost every terrorist watchlist in the world.'

'Always preaching *jihad* and advocates attacking the Great Satan,' Falcon said, his voice world-weary. 'Over the last few years, I've seen references to him many times – neutralize one hate-preacher and three more like Jannati emerge to take his place. It's worse than whack-a-mole.'

He stared more intently at the windowless house, concentrating on the private courtyard, which was virtually hidden by a pair of over-arching date palms. It featured, barely visible, a constantly bubbling fountain that would make it almost impossible to eavesdrop on any conversation. 'A good place for a covert discussion,' he said, almost to himself. He turned to the room. 'Okay, I'll buy what you're selling, Mr . . .'

'Watson,' Dylan replied nervously.

'Well done, Mr Watson,' Falcon said. 'All right, we have a putative location for a meeting, but I want everyone to keep searching. I want to be certain there are no other possibilities.'

As the men and women at the workstations turned back to their screens, Buster spoke into the quiet. 'I think we might have a date,' he said. 'Five days.'

Everybody looked at him, bewildered by how he had arrived at the suggestion. 'What?' asked Falcon.

'Go back to the beginning,' Buster instructed. 'Near the top of the transcript.' I had been wondering why Buster had been so quiet, and now I understood – instead of searching for a white house, he had been trying to unravel what he knew would be the next problem: the date.

'I thought at first, it was just casual conversation,' he said. The transcript and translation appeared on the screens and Buster used a cursor on his laptop to highlight a sentence. 'There,' he said. 'The guy in Tora Bora West is laughing – he asks if the financier is going to be in good enough shape for a meeting. The financier laughs backs and says he will have had three days to recover.'

'Recover from what?' I asked.

'That's what I just realized,' he replied. 'We're almost at Eid al-Fitr. For those who don't know, it's a festival which marks the end of Ramadan, Islam's holiest month. As it happens, it can fall in any month. Its date is a very complex calculation. The highlight of Eid is a feast, a huge event in the Muslim world. I figure the financier is saying he will have had three days to recover from the feast—'

Falcon addressed everyone, urgent: 'Okay, when is the feast?'

'Wednesday,' somebody called out.

'Three days to recover afterwards – that makes it Saturday,' Falcon said. He looked around the room. 'Until it is proven otherwise, there is a meeting on Saturday at a white house attached to a mosque in Zahedan.' He paused, and it was clear there was no doubt in his own mind. 'Congratulations, everyone.'

The room broke into applause. Falcon turned and scanned the raked seats until he found Madeleine, and spoke over the clapping. 'Call the White House – our White House, I mean,' he said, smiling. 'Tell the Chief of Staff I need to speak to the president.'

Everybody knew why Falcon was calling. The director would tell the president they had a location and a date for a meeting, and it was now possible to destroy the leadership of the Army of the Pure. Given the magnitude of the threat, and the urgency, few people had any doubt about what the commander-in-chief would decide.

'It's going to be war, total war,' Margaret said sadly to Buster, voicing what several people must have been thinking. 'We can't hit Zahedan without taking out the Iranian air defences, and the ayatollahs won't suck that down. We do that, and we give the terrorists what they want. They will have dragged us into another unwinnable war, just like Afghanistan. The fundamentalists don't have to win – they just have to wait until we are exhausted and give up. After thousands of lives have been lost, we'll do what we always do – declare victory and go home with nothing to show for it.'

Just because Margaret was cynical didn't mean she wasn't right, and I was one of the few people in the room who knew why her sadness ran so deep: she had lost her brother in Iraq, another unwinnable war. She was an outstanding intelligence analyst – scary-smart and highly intuitive – but she might not have had enough information. Maybe a huge war wasn't inevitable, I thought, recalling what Falcon had said about a surgical strike against the Army's leadership and his refusal to reveal how the air-defence shield could be penetrated.

It seemed to me that a far different solution was being planned for the men who would be travelling very soon to a secret meeting at a white house in Zahedan, but I had no time to think about it.

Falcon had checked his watch, picked up his phone and was speaking to someone who I assumed was one of his executive assistants: 'Call my driver,' he said. 'Tell him to bring the wheelchair to the Bubble.'

Without explanation, he stood up and led me towards the grey door.

35

I WAS SITTING IN THE WHEELCHAIR, ALONE IN FALCON'S OFFICE, looking out at the moon rising above the surrounding forest, when I heard the door behind me open. The director himself had wheeled me out of the Bubble, up to the seventh floor, and had left almost immediately, telling me he had to deal with a visitor.

I turned to see him return; the visitor was with him and she smiled at me. Fashionable but understated, she was elegant and very attractive – at least to my eyes.

'I think you know each other,' Falcon said, smiling.

'Of course,' Rebecca replied. 'How are you, Sadiqaa?'

'A lot better if I'd received some decent medical care,' I said. She kissed me on the cheek.

Falcon moved behind his desk and spoke to Becca. 'I'm sure you know this is very important, I certainly wouldn't pull anybody out of hospital if it wasn't. Unfortunately, we have only one person who can identify a small group of individuals.'

He swung his computer screen around so that Rebecca could see it. 'I wanted you to come here so that you could see there is absolutely no danger.' He entered a command on his keyboard—

A still photo of the high-security conference room appeared on the screen, showing Falcon and me sitting at the command console surrounded by the large hi-def screens and the stadium-style seating.

'What is this?' she said, taken aback. 'Mission control for a moon shot?'

'Pretty much,' Falcon replied. 'Just a little more complex in my view.' He smiled again. 'As you can see, this is where we're working—'

He was about to continue, but his speaker phone dinged. 'The president is returning your call,' a voice from his outer office said. 'Thirty seconds and he will be on the line.'

Falcon looked at us apologetically. 'Sorry,' he said, and walked to a doorway that led into a small, even more private area, probably the most secure on the campus.

'That's impressive,' Rebecca said to me. 'The president calling your boss just as I got here.'

'Yeah, we did it for your benefit.'

'I figured that,' she replied.

She turned and looked at the photo of the conference room on Falcon's screen. In the background of it, information and images being displayed for the benefit of everyone in the stadium seating were visible on the overhead screens. They were indistinct, but not completely so—

She pointed at the photo of the Emir, Kazinsky and the others playing cards at the wedding. 'Terrorists?' she asked.

'Yes,' I replied. 'Very bad terrorists.'

'Where is it?' she asked, pointing at another blurred image of an incredibly bleak and forbidding landscape. I shook my head – I couldn't tell her that.

'But you were there, in that environment?' she asked.

'Nearby,' I said.

'On foot?'

'Mostly.'

She looked again at the arid landscape, close to disbelief. 'Holy shit, how did you survive?'

'With great difficulty,' I said, smiling. 'You saw the result.'

'How long will it take?' she asked. 'To identify these people, I mean – or is that classified?'

'A few days,' I said. 'If it gets too much and I run into difficulty, we have a full medical suite a couple of hundred yards away.'

'I know – Falcon organized for me to see it when I first arrived. A man called Lucas Corrigan showed me around. From how he talked, he was probably a fine doctor before he turned to psychology. I was surprised to find him working here – he seemed like a really decent guy.'

I stared at her. 'You're probably the only person who has ever said that.'

'Really?' she replied. 'Maybe that explains a lot about US intelligence.'

'You could be right,' I said, and looked over her shoulder to see Falcon exiting the secure room. Rebecca turned, and we watched him, preoccupied, walk towards us.

He looked up and shrugged. 'It's hard to believe – a politician has just done the right thing.' He went to his desk and clicked on his speakerphone.

'Phone the Secretary of Defense,' he said into it. 'If he's not there, leave a message. Tell him Julius Caesar just crossed the Rubicon.'

36

THE MISSILES THAT MIGHT, CONCEIVABLY, EVADE IRANIAN AIR defences – probably the most secret and advanced armament in the world, weapons that were now intended to prevent a devastating attack on the West – were loaded, ten hours after the president's decision, on to a US Air Force Globemaster III freight plane in Troy, Alabama.

The missiles themselves were nothing special – not yet, anyway – but the plane itself was unusual: its registration letters and numbers had been painted out, its flight plan had never been filed and its crew were all wearing US Air Force uniforms although they were, in fact, CIA employees with the highest possible security clearance. Even that didn't mean they had any knowledge about what was occurring.

Once the Globemaster was airborne, the route it followed was so circuitous that anyone tracking it would have soon realized it wasn't in the same zip-code as normal. They would never have been able to follow its path, though – the transponders that relay real-time flight information to the ground were turned off as soon as the freighter left US airspace. The other clue to the crew – and any other observer – that something very strange was afoot lay in the fact that the huge plane, capable of carrying one hundred and seventy thousand pounds of cargo, only had four six-foot-long missiles on board. Altogether, with their packing cases, they weighed nine hundred pounds.

The type of weapon, known as Hellfire missiles – had first been developed over fifty years earlier and, due to their success on the battlefield, had been produced in tens of thousands. The facility responsible for manufacturing them was a Lockheed Martin factory in the small city of Troy, from where, usually, they were loaded on to eighteen-wheelers and flown to different wars across the world. Not tonight. They were destined to make an eleven-thousand-mile haul to one of the most peaceful places on earth: a joint British and American military base located in the middle of the Indian Ocean.

The tiny atoll, nothing more than a speck on a vast expanse of sea, was called Diego Garcia and, without doubt, it was one of the most remote places in the world. Not only did it house a large US military base and the site of a long-denied CIA black prison, it was also – if the rumours were correct – the place where some of the country's most advanced and experimental weapons were developed and tested.

As inaccessible as the island was, and with Navy patrol boats constantly circling its rocky shores and sandy beaches, there was an area within its confines that was even more tightly controlled; off limits to almost everyone stationed there. As a result, nobody knew for sure what happened beyond the concrete-and-razor-wire fence and the three guard towers that protected the northern section of the sixty-mile island; the forbidden zone on Diego Garcia was one of the most secret and secure places on the planet.

Just after dawn on a Monday – with another tropical rainstorm sweeping in and bending the palm trees lining the miles of untouched beaches – the Globemaster came in low over the narrow ring of land that enclosed a spectacular lagoon and landed on one of the two runways built to take the heaviest bombers in the US Air Force. On the asphalt apron, the four metal transport boxes holding the missiles were loaded on to the trucks of a small convoy that made its way along the rim of the atoll. Heading north, with the lagoon on one side and the ocean on the other, they were in fact travelling along the highest point of a vast underwater mountain range, the water around them so clear that the truck drivers could see rays and schools of tropical fish from the cabs of their trucks.

The convoy passed an abandoned coconut plantation, its British colonial residence long fallen into ruin, and approached the gates of the secluded and forbidden area at the north end. Passing through the checkpoint and far inside the steel gates, the trucks skirted a massive concrete building protected by a breakwater and an artificial reef. Its roof and walls were heavily camouflaged and the building itself stretched far out into deep water. I didn't see the structure until some time later but, given my career before I entered the shadow world, I knew exactly what it was: a submarine pen.

To most people who stepped on to the isolated atoll, the mystery would have been this: why would the submarine pen – a massive, windowless structure with walls twenty feet thick and lined with lead – have been built in such a location? Modern nuclear-powered subs can circle the Earth at will – able to operate for almost forty years without the need to surface for fuel, water or oxygen – so why station a single submarine so far from any conflict zone? Almost anybody would have thought that the pen seemed to serve no practical purpose. Of course, that was wrong.

Beyond the pen, almost obscured by a squall of rain showers, the convoy approached a cluster of concrete, block-like buildings. The most remote of them, not even identified by letters or numbers painted on its side, was surrounded by stretches of rocky outcrops, a sweep of white sand beach and several groves of palm trees.

The missiles in their transport cases were unloaded, taken through a huge hydraulic door once the air pistons had hissed it open, put on a conveyor belt and carried into a glass-walled airlock to be sanitized and rendered dust free. They were then lost to view as they passed through a heavy stainless-steel shutter—

The other side of it was a cavernous space – sterile and pure white. With huge generators, air handlers and refrigeration units constantly working deep beneath its floor, the temperature in the room was kept at a never-wavering seventy-four degrees Fahrenheit and the humidity at precisely 41 per cent. The air was held at positive pressure to make it impossible for dust or other contaminants to enter and the dozen men and women working at steel benches were dressed in antistatic DuPont seamless coveralls and hoods fitted with glass eye-slots. The 'clean room' to end all clean rooms.

Once the four missiles had been removed from the transport boxes they were attached to robotic arms, suspended in mid-air – making it appear as if they were floating – and bathed in high-intensity light. The techs starting to work on them recognized them as the very latest generation of Hellfires, weapons that had profited enormously from the stunning advances in battery technology and weight reduction.

Until recently the missile – launched either from drones or Apache attack helicopters – had a range of about ten kilometres, but the version floating in mid-air at Diego Garcia could, according to its top-secret specifications, hit a target more than four hundred kilometres away. But the men and women at the workbenches knew that an increase in a weapon's range was evolution. The special, enormously complex casings they were fitting to the missiles – ones that had been designed and manufactured on the island – were a total revolution.

As members of the team used hand-held devices to control the robotic arms and others manipulated remote instruments, they deftly removed the black outer shell of each missile and exposed the five discrete sections containing the warhead, guidance and propulsion systems. Now, they replaced the outer shell with something extraordinary: a casing made of millions, possibly billions, of dazzling white tiles, each one little larger than a pinhead.

By virtue of the high-intensity light, the tiles glimmered and shone like a myriad diamonds, making the missile look completely futuristic and strangely ominous. That was the exterior; on the inside, each of the countless tiles was connected by a fibre-optic thread – a fraction of the width of a hair – to a control box that had been fitted at the rear of the long tube. The fibre-optic threads were so fine, wrapped so tight and so numerous, they made the inside of the casing look as if it was covered in gossamer.

As difficult as the team's work was, they had one advantage: none of the missiles were fitted with explosive warheads. Instead, their armament consisted of a device colloquially known as the 'sushi bomb', which was a direct descendant, and a far more advanced version, of the 'ninja bomb'. The peculiarity of both 'bombs' was that they didn't actually explode; they were designed to kill the occupants of moving vehicles without any blast so that innocent bystanders were not maimed or injured. The way they did it was best indicated by the name – sushi is thinly sliced with a razor-sharp knife.

In a dark and twisted way, the sushi bomb was a brilliant invention, and history indicated that the intended victim would never escape: the ninja bomb, which was nowhere near as sophisticated or as deadly as its offspring, had been deployed at least twelve times and had taken out eighteen prominent terrorists in five countries without ever missing or injuring anyone outside the vehicle.

In silence, concentrating, they finished fitting the last of the four glittering cylinders and used the robotic arms to reload the weapons into their original transport boxes. Twenty hours after they had arrived at Diego Garcia the specially adapted missiles were loaded back on to the Globemaster and given a suite of documents that masked that they had ever been at the atoll. They were then transported, like countless Hellfires before them, to Bagram Air Base – the centre of all renewed US operations in Afghanistan and a location not too distant from a white house in Zahedan.

If all went to plan, Kazinsky and the Emir's lives were almost over.

37

AT THIRTY-FIVE THOUSAND FEET OVER PAKISTAN, ANOTHER ELEMENT in probably the most secret operation ever undertaken by US intelligence was moving into position. Three people, hitherto unknown to each other and from widely disparate backgrounds – all young but highly skilled – were on board a G5 jet that had made the long haul from America, crossed the Arabian Sea and would soon land at Bagram.

Combined, the trio was known as a 'strike cell', and the two men and a woman were all elite United States Air Force pilots – even though none of them had ever occupied a cockpit. Instead, their skill consisted of sitting in front of a bank of computer screens and using a keyboard and joystick; it would be their job to remotely pilot the four glittering-white 'smart' missiles to their targets.

As they sat in the high-altitude darkness and silence, two of them were asleep and the third had a laptop open in front of him, examining the basic specifications of a weapon he had never seen before. It looked like a Hellfire missile – one of the new-generation long-range iterations – but its weight, interior layout and, most of all, its circumference were dramatically different. It was as if an entirely new casing had been fitted to it.

Like his colleagues, he was well equipped to dig deep into that kind of data. All three had graduated from highly ranked colleges with degrees in engineering or science, and had also completed a host of courses in advanced aviation. There was a time, not long ago, when they would probably have topped the class at the Top Gun flight school, but fighter pilots were now about as useful to modern warfare as infantry with muskets. The three young pilots flying towards a mission that they – as yet – had no understanding of, were people who had grown up surrounded by gaming and coding, a place where the line between a screen and reality had almost ceased to exist. Without anyone realizing it, Silicon Valley had quietly prepared them for a future as digital warriors in a digital world.

The young man focused on his laptop was Connor Bryant, a twenty-four-year-old surfer from Huntington Beach, southern California, the youngest of four children, and someone who had never been an outstanding student at any of the three high schools he had attended. He was blessed, however, with a remarkable degree of eye–hand coordination and a preternatural ability to instantly process vast amounts of visual information. As a result, he seemed to be born to pilot drones – and missiles now – especially in extreme battlefield situations; more importantly, he could remain calm and unpanicked through it all. Research by the Air Force had shown that failures by pilots were never about their skill; it was always about the stress. In that regard, Connor was in a league of his own.

As Falcon told me later, maybe it was the drugs: while none of the three pilots knew anything about Falcon Rourke, he knew everything about them and, given the highly secret nature of the mission, it would have been derelict of him not to have done so.

He knew that it would have been more surprising if Connor – growing up at a hip beach in California, in an era when medical marijuana had taken off and the laws prohibiting its use were being rapidly liberalized – hadn't spent a lot of time kicking back and blazing weed. The guy was a non-drinker – thank God, according to Falcon, because plenty of the men and women pilots were well on the road to alcoholism – but Connor still found getting buzzed as enjoyable as ever. Not on deployment, though – he would never have jeopardized any mission, or his career, for that – and Falcon was enough of a realist to know the world was changing so fast that his skills far outweighed his private behaviour.

With dawn flooding the eastern sky as the G5 approached the border between Pakistan and Afghanistan, it was likely the young drone pilot looked out the window and saw the vast expanse of wild terrain unfold beneath him. Although he didn't know it, very soon he would pilot a missile across a similar landscape and attempt, in total secrecy, to violate the airspace of Iran, a feat that had not been accomplished by any nation in over fifty years.

In more ways than one, a new day was dawning.

38

NO SOONER HAD FALCON TOLD THE SECRETARY OF DEFENSE THAT the Rubicon had been crossed and the mission launched than the mood at Langley turned very sombre, very fast.

As the pilots and their missiles progressed on their long journey to Afghanistan, even the optimists in the conference room – led by Buster – soon realized that while the date and place of the meeting had been discovered it was clear that the task was far more challenging than just missiling some cars in a distant city. What if there were a dozen cars in the convoy? Or twenty? As Falcon had said, it had to be surgical: Langley now had to identify the Army's leaders – the primary targets – and know what vehicles they were travelling in.

We also had to know the information well ahead of time because the Apache helicopters that would launch the missiles needed three hours to get close to the Iranian border, the weapons themselves – once they had been launched – would take another forty minutes to be piloted over the frontier and into Zahedan, while the vehicles containing the Emir, Kazinsky and other members of the leadership group had to be monitored second by second to judge exactly when they would be grouped together in the narrow street on the way to the meeting. All those disparate and volatile threads had to be drawn together – the progress of the vehicles, the helicopters and the release of the four sushi bombs would have to be timed to perfection.

'The first element,' Falcon said to the room. 'If we are going to track the leaders, we have to identify them.' He looked at me. 'We have one advantage – at least we have someone who has seen them.'

Up to a point, I thought.

Falcon and Buster then ordered up thousands of hours of satellite footage of Tora Bora West, both archival and recent, that the agency had assembled. The cave complex was the location where the terrorists were congregated and – so the thinking went – would provide us with the best opportunity to identify the Army's leading members as they moved around outside.

Starting to look at it, I began heading into memory, trying to visualize every moment I had spent with the Army, hoping to find some detail I had overlooked. The process was distressing, but the worst of it was the fatigue from my injuries – having to fight every moment in my chair at the command console to stay alert and present.

Once the satellite footage had been split and distributed to scores of three-person teams, Buster handed out physical descriptions of the Emir, Kazinsky and the three other leaders that I had provided: height, weight, tattoos and anything else that might distinguish them. The teams were about to start making the first cull, discounting anyone who clearly did not fit our broad criteria, when I sat upright, fully awake. My memory had drifted back to the forward staging post, the place where I was waiting to see if Laleh had been killed, and I started to think about the man with the walkie-talkies. It suddenly struck me that a group of men in a number of vehicles travelling to a crucial meeting in Zahedan without cellphones would need someone in charge of comms. From there I leapt to when Laleh and I were boxed in by vehicles on the way to the beach and I had seen the face of the man driving the refuelling truck. I wheeled in my seat and looked at a nearby screen showing the distance between the Army's base and Zahedan and I knew instantly that the distance was too great: they would have to refuel on the way.

'We've made a mistake,' I called to Falcon. 'We've only been thinking about the leaders – the support staff are critical. They'll be accompanying them: drivers, a one-armed man in charge of comms, a short, overweight guy – a keg on legs – responsible for refuelling their vehicles who is probably in charge of all logistics.'

Falcon cursed himself. 'I should have thought of it. Anyone else that you recall – add their descriptions to the list.'

Four hours later, it was clear that I wouldn't recall anyone else. Scores of possible hits had been relayed to me for further identification but, as I had warned Falcon earlier, most of the prospects were hooded and masked, their loose-fitting robes, trailing scarfs and shapeless tunics making it difficult to even define body shapes. An hour after that, still with no hint of success, I suspected a group that disavowed mobile phones was also more than wary of satellite surveillance; it seemed to me that whenever they were outside, their anonymity was deliberate. I called to Falcon.

'You okay?' he asked as he approached. 'You look terrible.'

'Don't we both,' I said, noting the grey cast to his face, the crumpled clothes and the deep weariness in his every step.

'It's not working, is it?' he said, indicating the images of various terrorists on the screens.

'Not even close,' I agreed. 'They are disciplined, they know how good the satellites are – the leaders especially aren't taking any chances. I've seen three different men, dressed very similarly, outside at the same time – any one of 'em could be Kazinsky. But listen—'

'Is it an idea?' Falcon asked. 'I hope so, because I'm fresh out of 'em.'

'If you thought you might be under surveillance, but you had to drive to a crucial meeting – what would you do?' I said.

Falcon thought for a long moment, turning it over in his head, doing what he had always done best: thinking laterally.

'I'd send every vehicle out,' he said at last. 'I'd flood the zone, I'd play the biggest shell game the world has ever seen. I'd have hundreds of vehicles on the move but provide no indication which of them contained the five or six leaders.'

'I'd do exactly the same,' I said, smiling. 'Early in the morning, use every vehicle I could find and overwhelm any surveillance. I'd surprise us and make it impossible to keep track of them all. In groups of two, three, a dozen, I'd have them head to every point of the compass, double back, turn around, split apart and send us on a huge wild-goose chase.'

'We have one advantage,' Falcon added. 'Something they are not aware of – we know their ultimate destination.'

'That's right,' I said. 'The hero vehicles will rendezvous before they make the final run to Casa Blanca, and if we are following everyone, we'll see them do it—'

Falcon turned to address the room. 'Forget trying to identify the leaders,' he called out. 'The morning of the meeting they will try to bury us – hundreds of vehicles will leave the base. But we will be ready, we follow every one of them until – finally – those with the leadership will rendezvous for the last run to the mosque. This is going to exhaust everybody. Get some rest – go home now. There's nothing you can do until then.'

As they filed out, he looked at me. Even a man accustomed all his professional life to masking his emotions couldn't hide his concern. 'You too,' he said.

'I'll sleep on the plane,' I responded.

'A plane?' he said, as if he had no idea what I meant. 'Why – you going somewhere?'

'There's no choice, is there?' I replied. 'Once the vehicles leave the rendezvous and head for the mosque, everything will happen in a rush. We know what these things are like – if it's not mayhem, it'll be a first. The hero vehicles will probably arrive late, there might be ten or more for all we know, the drive to Casa Blanca could be quick – our window might be very small and closing fast. The launch choppers will have to ditch any extra weight and be refuelled and the travel time of your mysterious missiles might have to be reduced – and you're going to have to co-ordinate it all and I'll have to identify whoever I can on the run. There won't be time to send messages half-way round the world and risk confusion – we are going to have to be in the room, standing next to the strike cell.'

'Yeah, I figured hours ago I'd go to Kabul,' he said. 'But are you strong enough?'

'Me?' I replied. 'Never fitter.' Given the anxiety, it was good for both of us to find something to laugh about.

'Rebecca?' Falcon asked.

'That'll be difficult,' I replied, thinking about her reaction to me telling her I needed to fly to Afghanistan when – according to her – I shouldn't have even left hospital.

'You don't have to tell her,' Falcon suggested. 'You can speak to her a few times a day, tell her you're in a security lockdown, still here at Langley.'

I thought about it. It was true – I could. I wasn't happy about it, but she would never know.

DEEP IN THE GRAVEYARD SHIFT, TWO MEN AND THREE WOMEN – ALL senior air-persons – rode electric scooters through a massive US supply warehouse at Bagram Air Base, checking inventory and identifying items for the forklifts.

Earlier, at the start of the shift, the team had received that night's job sheet and the fifth item on it directed them to unpack four Hellfire missiles that had – according to their documentation – arrived from Alabama twelve hours earlier, check them for damage and then convey them into the adjoining high-security hangar.

The task was assigned to the most junior member of the group, a newly pinned young woman from Colorado on her maiden overseas tour, who – surrounded by towering racks of military equipment – forklifted the boxes to a large work-table. Working single-handed to check them, she unscrewed the heavy wooden transport boxes, attached a missile to a robot arm – and started yelling.

The other four members of the team, scattered throughout the huge building, reacted; nothing ever interrupted the night's monotony until the 3 a.m. coffee break, not even the regular rocket and mortar attacks on the base. They were confined to daylight and early evening, but suddenly the young woman was calling for them to come quick.

The first to arrive was the team leader. Tall, with gangly legs, he turned a corner, looked past the discarded packaging and stared almost in disbelief at a glittering white missile, half out of its box, suspended on a robot arm. 'What the—' he said, moving closer, staring at the weapon all a-sparkle under the warehouse's rows of metal-halide lights. He had never seen anything like it.

The other three team members, only moments behind him, came to his side and had the same response: 'What is it?'

'According to the box, it's a regulation, latest-generation Hellfire,' the young woman from Colorado said. 'I don't know about you, but I've seen dozens of them, and that sure ain't regulation anything.'

'Where'd it come from?' the team leader asked.

She pointed at her tablet computer and bar-code scanner. 'The production manifest, waybill number and tracking details all say direct from Lockheed Martin in Alabama.'

The team leader walked forward to look more closely. For some reason he couldn't explain, the sleek weapon chilled him. 'Check the tech details and order form,' he told her.

'I have,' she replied, indicating the tablet. 'It says it's a special order for the 425th Expeditionary Force – whoever they are – mission-specific camouflage.'

'Yeah?' he said. He'd been around combat zones long enough to have seen MS-camouflage on several occasions and he knew it was generally used on helicopters. It was a specially designed paint job, a complex series of colours that would exactly mimic the terrain the choppers would fly over and lessen their chances of being detected. As a result, it was research intensive and hugely expensive; SEAL Team Six, for example, which flew into Pakistan to kill Osama bin Laden, had used it on their helos.

There was no reason it couldn't be used on a missile, but he shook his head. 'Makes no sense. Somebody can put whatever crap they like on a form. White MS-camo on a missile? If you ask me, that's disinformation—'

'It's what?' another member of the team, standing at the back, asked. A hulking, friendly twenty-two-year-old from Chicago, he had joined the military to get an education but so far nobody had worked out where to start.

'I said it's disinformation – military for bullshit,' the team leader explained, circling the weapon, running his hand over the tiny ceramic tiles.

'You don't know it's bullshit,' a ripped woman, the oldest of the group, a hard-ass who made a habit of butting heads with everyone, said. 'Maybe they're gonna use it over snow.'

'Sure,' the team leader replied, taking a step, flicking a switch and turning off the overhead lights. In semi-darkness, through a set of huge barn-like doors, the world outside the enormous space suddenly became visible: forklifts were driving across an apron, ranks of jets and choppers stood outside maintenance sheds and teams of refuellers and weapons techs were busily preparing two AH-74 Apaches, the most advanced attack helicopters in the world. Had the warehouse team looked more closely, they would have noticed the two choppers had no markings, had been stripped completely to lessen their weight and were now being fitted with long-range fuel tanks.

The team leader pointed past the helos and the rows of planes to where a full moon was shining on a ring of snow-capped mountains. 'It's late summer,' he said. 'That is the only snow in Afghanistan – on the high peaks. It don't matter which mountain range it is – Hindu Kush, Koh-i-Baba, the Safed Koh – they're all the same, the worst and loneliest places in the world. You go days, weeks, and you don't see another dude – if you're lucky, just a few ruined buildings.'

He pointed again at the missile. 'They send a missile fitted with a special warhead – one that don't explode. A regular Hellfire kills within sixty feet, but not this baby, this is a sushi bomb – it don't harm anyone outside the vehicle. It was designed for crowded places, so why they gonna use it over snow, on some mountain you couldn't find a civilian even if you wanted to? No, this sure ain't no MS-camo for snow.'

'What's the story, then?' the young woman asked. 'Hellfires like these have a range of four hundred klicks – maybe they're not for Afghanistan.'

'Where then?' the hard-ass woman asked. 'Pakistan? Iran?'

The team leader shook his head. 'You don't need no missiles in Pakistan. Special Ops and SEALs go in and out – they didn't missile bin Laden, did they?

'And it's not Iran,' he said. 'Nobody's that dumb, not even the Pentagon – they ain't gonna start firing missiles into Iran. No chance.'

40

'YOU KNOW THE BIGGEST DISAPPOINTMENT ABOUT BEING HERE?' Connor Bryant, the surfer dude from southern California, asked an hour after the strike cell had arrived in Kabul.

They were sitting together – as I found out later – in the deserted canteen of what had once been the headquarters of the first US task force to enter Afghanistan thirty years earlier and now, after being superseded by vastly larger facilities, had been repurposed as the command centre for one of the most remarkable military attacks ever mounted.

'The food's no good?' the young woman – Mila – who had grown up next to the Gulf of Mexico in Florida and had the sun-streaked hair and the tan to prove it, said, looking around at the forlorn room.

'Yeah, that too,' Connor replied, watching the other two sipping on Coronas, everybody getting to know each other. 'No, what I meant was we're only a few hundred klicks from a small city called Balkh but, because of the security situation, it's unlikely we'll get to see the Mosque of the Nine Cupolas.'

Spencer Wilson, the third member of the team and a strait-laced career officer from the east, lowered his beer and stared, taken aback. 'The what mosque?' he said.

'Nine domes; it's the oldest Islamic building in Afghanistan,' Connor continued. 'Very strange vibe, people say – sort of mystical.'

'I'm surprised,' Spencer said. 'I know we've only just met, but looking at you, I wouldn't have guessed you were interested in that sort of thing.'

'Yeah, a lot of people underestimate me,' Connor said happily. 'I love all that cultural stuff.' He lowered his voice, drawing them in, making them lean closer, conspiratorial. 'By coincidence, Balkh also produces the best weed in the world. Now, if you want to go shopping in the Stan here – forget woodcuts of camels and all that hand-woven rug crap – Balkh is the place to go.'

Mila laughed.

'I'm going to talk to one of the helo pilots the first chance I get and tell him about my interest in mosques,' Connor continued. 'See if we can't hitch a ride out there – an hour on the ground, tops, do a quick buy then get out of Dodge. What do you say, Spence – a plan?'

'Just so there is no confusion,' Spencer replied, looking hard at Connor. 'I have no tolerance for recreational drugs.'

'That's interesting,' Connor said good-naturedly. 'Very interesting. Out of curiosity – ever heard of anyone dying because they couldn't get a hard-on?'

Mila nearly spat out her beer. Way to go, Connor, she must have thought.

'Erections? What are you talking about?' Spencer asked him.

'Viagra. If that isn't a recreational drug, I don't know what is,' Connor replied. 'It sure ain't life-saving.'

Spencer stared at him but couldn't find an argument to counter it. Connor smiled his surfer-dude smile and shrugged. 'World's changing,

Spence. A lot of people want to get laid and just as many want to get high.'

Mila grinned. 'Well, I just want to do both,' she said, defusing the situation but also catching Connor's eye. Spencer, looking from one to the other – and even as straight up-and-down as he was – couldn't help but recognize an invitation when he saw one.

Before Spencer had time to think any more about drugs or sex, the door opened and they turned to see one of the four high-ranking officers they had met on their arrival enter. A major general from Special Ops, introduced to them as their briefing officer, he was a muscular, powerful man with buzz-cut hair and a swagger in his step. It meant there was little to distinguish him from hundreds of other senior officers – not even his name-tags. They had been removed. The strike cell had noticed it earlier, but none of them had said anything – the braid and insignia were enough – and now, with him standing in the doorway, they leapt to their feet.

'At ease,' he said. 'Two people are arriving from stateside – they are an hour away at the moment. As soon as they land, the briefing will start. Understood?'

'Sir,' the pilots said in unison, waiting for him to leave and then getting back to their beer and food. 'Even more brass, I guess,' Mila said. 'Like we need any – have you ever seen so much?'

'Another few officers is fine,' Connor said. 'It's when the CIA turns up you know it's gonna be a screw-up.'

41

ANOTHER DAY, ANOTHER MISSION, I THOUGHT AS I LOOKED OUT THE window of one more GreenEnergy jet and saw the mountains of the Hindu Kush – grim and ominous – on the horizon. I could not help thinking about what a blood-soaked landscape lay beneath me, and I recalled what somebody famous once wrote: 'Afghanistan is where empires go to die.'

The British, the Soviets and the United States had all chanced their hand at the gateway to India and, through it, to the rest of south Asia, and they had all left defeated and diminished. The thought of so much wasted life and effort did little to lift my mood.

Twelve hours earlier, despite Falcon's suggestion, I had called Rebecca just before I left Langley and told her about my imminent departure, and that had turned out to be an even more difficult conversation than I had anticipated. She felt, of course, that Falcon and I had planned the flight all along, and it was hard to convince her otherwise – after all, the organization I worked for was renowned for its subterfuge and cunning. My refusal to tell her my destination only amplified her concerns about the risk to my health.

'Am I missing something here – weren't you just in intensive care?' she had said, her tone clearly indicating she was fighting hard not to lose her temper. 'You're still so weak you can barely walk, the rehab hasn't even started and you're flying somewhere which probably ain't the Maldives? When you were admitted to MedStar we missed something. We should have tested your mental health.'

'It's my job, Becca – you know that. You think I'm going anywhere without medical support?'

'Put 'em on – the doctors,' she demanded, sceptical.

Thankfully, Falcon had organized for us to be accompanied by a doctor and two nurses and I put the doctor on speaker. It was a woman and, doctor to doctor, she updated Rebecca on my condition and told her about the plan for the next three days. I could tell from Rebecca's reaction she was relieved it was a short trip and when the doctor told her that my fatigue and injuries meant it would be impossible for me to leave the room where I would be stationed, I realized that – quite inadvertently – she had swayed Becca into believing I would not be in any danger.

The doctor may not have completely won the battle, but at least an armed truce was declared, and Rebecca asked to speak to me privately, gave me a shopping list of things to monitor about my health and – finally, quietly – told me she loved me. Nevertheless, exhaustion had left me sapped by the time I boarded the flight and just as I began, at last, to drift into sleep I was wide awake again – heart pounding – with a sense of imminent death. While it had happened several times since I had returned, I had not told anyone about the feeling of panic. It will pass, I told myself.

So, instead of resting, I sat and thought about the man at the vortex of everything, someone who knew what Bhopal really meant, the terrorist we were on our way to try and kill. And maybe I would not have said anything to Falcon about the Colonel or my misgivings except that the pilot told us we were fifty minutes out from landing and the director, who had been sleeping a few rows in front of me, walked past on his way to take a shower.

'Get any sleep?' he asked.

'Not much,' I replied.

I guess the tone of my voice alerted him and he looked at me for long enough to show he knew that something was troubling me.

'He won't be there, Falcon,' I said. 'Kazinsky won't be part of any convoy.'

'You're wrong,' the director replied.

'I can see him standing on the beach,' I said. 'One of the things I remember most – he had real command presence. But on the spit, I could see how he felt as I waved goodbye. He *knew*, Falcon – he knew if an American spy made it home, they were finished. He only had to think about what I had seen and what he had told me – yeah, he hoped I would be drowned by the Shamal, but he couldn't be certain of it and he would never know the truth. He had to assume the worst. He had been a colonel in the Spetsnaz, he understood strategy and danger – he knew the moment I vanished into the Gulf I was an existential threat, that there was a good chance the Army was blown.'

'No,' Falcon replied. 'The Army is only weeks away from a spectacular. They won't run, not now. Would bin Laden, would al-Zawahiri, would any of them run? You're giving Kazinsky more credit than he deserves. He's like the rest of them – just another terrorist commander. We've seen dozens of them, haven't we?'

'Not like him,' I replied, thinking about the first time I saw him riding towards me like Lawrence of Arabia. 'Not like him – I was a prisoner long enough, I know him.'

'You don't, Ridley,' Falcon said harshly. 'We never know any of them. We can't. There is no common ground on earth any more – we're a group of different tribes forced by circumstance to inhabit the same cave. That's what has happened to the world – everything divided. "Things fall apart; the centre cannot hold."'

I looked at his careworn face. 'God save us – poetry now, Falcon?' I said, smiling. 'Yeats?'

He grinned back. 'Yeah, I thought I'd slip it in. "The Second Coming" – one of the best. "Anarchy is loosed upon the world . . .

innocence is drowned,"' he quoted. '"The best lack all conviction, while the worst are full of passionate intensity."

'That's us,' he continued, the smile gone. 'Our governments lack all conviction.' He pointed at the hi-def images of the Army's base open on my laptop. 'And the terrorists are full of passionate intensity.' He held my gaze. 'Kazinsky has the passion,' he said. 'He'll be in the convoy. You'll see – we'll find his body in the wreckage.'

'Maybe,' I said. '*Insha'Allah*.' If God wills it.

42

BAGRAM WAS ONE OF THOSE LANDING STRIPS WHERE ONLY A FOOL would have ignored the pilot's instruction and not fastened their seatbelt.

Located on a high-altitude plateau, it had always been a terrible place to land and the wreckage of military aircraft lying beside its runways was a testament to its wild winter snowstorms and searing summer gales.

With a massive dust storm darkening the horizon, the Gulfstream came in low over the surrounding mountains, fought the treacherous downdraughts and hit the runway so hard that the doctor and one of the nurses exclaimed in shock. It was a blistering summer day and as I looked out the window the hangars and endless rows of buildings were barely visible through the shimmering waves of heat.

Apart from a handful of people, nobody was aware that Falcon and I were even in-country and there was no high-ranking officer or CIA station chief to greet us. Backlit against that eerie scene of red dust and snow-capped mountains, we made our way – my crutches slowing us down considerably – across the baking asphalt towards an SUV driven by a grunt who had been told to pick up two civilian contractors who would be arriving on a private jet.

I had only been to the base once before – on assignment early in my career to help interrogate several terrorists held at a black prison hidden in its most remote corner – and since that visit a decade ago, the huge base had been closed and reopened half a dozen times. Depending on who was in the White House and what they considered to be in America's best strategic interests, US forces were regularly being wound down, surged, minimized, maximized, withdrawn completely and then redeployed. As Falcon and I scrambled into the rear of the SUV, the base was in the midst of another massive build-up.

By any estimate, our ride was a strange vehicle, fashioned for survival more than anything. Even after years of war, the base still came under rocket and mortar attack, with only the identity of the insurgents wielding the weapons changing – one year it was the Northern Alliance or the Taliban, then, a decade later, a re-born al-Qaeda, ISIS-K or the Pashtun rebels – and the SUV, like most other vehicles, had to be heavily protected. But Bagram was part of a hugely expensive deployment, the budget was supposedly tight, and there wasn't the money for transports like the SUV to be professionally armoured at the factory. Instead, thick sheets of rusting scrap metal had been bolted and riveted to its frame. Known as 'hillbilly armour', the makeshift metal made the SUV look like something out of one of those post-apocalyptic movies.

Sitting in the back of the vehicle, we made our way towards what people on the base called 'downtown'. Little had changed over the years: it was still the only base in a combat zone where you encountered traffic jams. The place was a boomtown. The main drag featured crowded fast-food outlets – all the usual suspects – chain coffee shops with queues halfway down the dusty street, stores run by locals known as *haji* shops doing a roaring trade in everything from sunglasses to under-the-counter bongs and rows of stalls selling some of the best Indian street food in the world. Without doubt, Bagram base was one of the liveliest and most exotic small towns I had ever visited; certainly the only one with regular incoming artillery fire.

At the end of the strip, we headed down a long and empty road towards a heavily armed checkpoint set in a high wall.

Topped by cameras and motion sensors, the wall enclosed the base's most sensitive facilities and, five minutes later, having had our identity checked by half a dozen different methods, the SUV stopped in front of the command centre for the missile attack. The sandstorm was still clinging to the horizon, thankfully turning away from the plateau but still managing to throw it into a strange half-night. Falcon took my arm to help me and I limped up to a door manned by two Marine guards.

We took an elevator down three floors, walked along a brightly lit corridor and entered a room lined with monitor screens, computers, a host of satellite feeds and complex GPS data. Three workstations were set against a wall and each of them was a cocoon of even more technology: more computer screens, a keyboard and a professional joystick that would have been at home in the cockpit of the most advanced fighter jet.

Sitting in the captain's chairs in front of them, facing the major general who was serving as the briefing officer and four other generals, were the three missile pilots, waiting for the briefing to start.

43

WHILE THE LOADING CREW MANOEUVRED FORKLIFTS, TAKING THE unpacked missiles into the high-security hangar, and the unmarked Apache helicopters were being checked and rechecked, the three pilots sat in complete silence. The briefing was over, but none of them moved – they remained sitting in their hard-backed chairs staring at the huge interactive screen in front of them. They were silent, in a state of shock.

It wasn't because they had been shown the glittering white casings on the missiles – they had no knowledge of those at all; nor was it the fact that they would be piloting new-generation armaments and not the drones they had spent several years commanding. They were more than comfortable with their ability in that regard.

The explanation for their silence was on the screen – for the first time, they had seen the proposed destination of the missiles they would be piloting. The three of them had only just met, but because they were so experienced, they knew exactly what the others were thinking: they were being asked to do the impossible.

I was as perplexed as they were – I had no idea how the missiles were going to evade the Iranian air defences and destroy the convoy, and while I had looked questioningly at Falcon several times during the briefing he had studiously avoided giving any answer.

'It'll be the surfer, he'll be the one that'll start asking the questions,' Falcon said softly. 'He's a smart kid.'

A few moments later, Connor stood up and asked the briefing officer for permission to speak. Appropriately deferential to a major general, even one without a name-tag – he said that on the flight to Kabul he had read dozens of reports on drone flights in the north of Afghanistan. 'Those missions stretched all the way from the border of Pakistan to the frontiers with Tajikistan, Uzbekistan and Turkmenistan,' he said quietly. 'A lot of those flights reached the edge of Iran.

'Every time they did, Iranian air defence locked on and tracked them until they turned away,' he continued. 'The Iranians didn't miss one, not in the past five years, no matter how low and fast the pilots were flying or how good they were.'

'You're right,' the major general replied. 'Iran has a state-of-the-art surveillance and defence system supplied by the Russians. It can pick up anything a hundred miles this side of the border – so yeah, it's very good indeed. Go on—'

'And even if the Iranian system missed it, sir,' Connor continued, 'or the men and women controlling it were napping, the Pakistanis have four tripods at a forward listening post that sweep the entire region. That system was supplied by the US and, according to the reports, it doesn't give anything a pass. I'm no expert, but I figure they'd tip off the Iranians about any incursion just to win credit with them.'

The major general laughed. 'I'm sure they would,' he said.

'To be honest, General, we'll do our best,' Connor said, before looking at Spencer and Mila; they both nodded in agreement. 'But I can't see any way we can get a missile through an electronic wall.'

'I understand,' the major general said, more reasonably than any of the three pilots had expected. 'What about the vehicles, though?' He pressed a button on a remote control for the interactive screen, bringing up satellite images of various vehicles on the move: Toyota pick-ups – of course – Nissan Patrols, modified Land Rovers and other four-wheel drives. 'Can you hit any one of 'em?' he asked. 'No margin for error. Are you certain?'

Connor, Mila and Spencer nodded in assent – they had done exactly that hundreds of times either in reality, on the simulator or on dummy runs.

The major general may have been satisfied, but Falcon wasn't and he picked up his own remote. 'Even here, in Zahedan?' he asked. As the images changed on the screen, I leaned forward and just managed to hear Connor mutter to his comrades.

'Like I said – once the suits arrive it's trouble.' I couldn't tell if Falcon had heard or not, but two of the generals definitely did: they both had to suppress their laughter.

Images of the sprawling city appeared on the screen; until then Zahedan had just been a name and a dot on the map. After looking at image after image: 'I don't think it would be a problem. We've been in worse places,' Connor said.

Falcon nodded and brought up a specially created CGI video showing various vehicles weaving through the town's crowded streets and then climbing a hillside laced with narrow alleys, old earth-coloured houses and a stark white mosque. 'What if the vehicles are travelling at speed down narrow, crowded alleys?' Falcon asked. 'You're confident you can do that with absolute precision?'

All three pilots nodded. 'With no civilian casualties and especially no damage to the mosque?' Falcon said, pressing.

'Yes,' Connor replied. 'Using sushi bombs, it's what we've been trained for.'

'Okay,' Falcon replied, hitting the remote and turning off the screen. 'You let the suits worry about penetrating the Iranian air defence, and you can worry about the targets.'

44

'NOW IT STARTS,' FALCON SAID, KEEPING HIS VOICE COMPOSED, BUT not even a man as skilled at concealment as he was could hide the undercurrent of anxiety. We had left the briefing room and were walking slowly into the high-security hangar adjoining the supply warehouse.

Despite the arid and windswept environment, the yawning space was spotlessly clean and, while there was room under its roof for fifty helicopters, only the two unmarked Apaches were currently occupying it. They had been moved inside for secrecy's sake and now specialist technicians were stripping plastic dust covers from the four missiles, ready to fit them to the firing rails under the choppers' bellies.

I stared at the missiles – white and stark and all a-sparkle as their billions of tiny tiles acted like the facets of countless diamonds under the high-intensity electric light. And while I had never seen them before, or anything like it, I knew then that I was standing on the threshold, that in some way it was a watershed moment.

I looked at Falcon – his face was inscrutable, and to this day I do not know if it was the first time he had seen them or not. Certainly, though, he understood the implications. 'Welcome to the future,' he said.

'Twelve hundred years ago, there was a Chinese alchemist,' he continued, his eyes fixed on the weapons. I had no idea where he was going, but I was happy to let him run. 'The alchemist was trying to create the mythical elixir of life so he combined three elements into what he believed was a remarkable medicinal compound. In a way he was right – it was remarkable, just not medicinal.' He smiled, but there was no humour in it – more sorrow, I thought. 'What the alchemist had done, completely by accident, was invent the first chemical explosive. Within a few decades, bows and arrows had been abandoned, clubs and spears forgotten – all replaced by bombs or projectiles fired from some tube or other. The compound he had created was gunpowder, and warfare would never be the same. There was no turning back for humanity either: overnight the world had become a different place.'

He indicated the missiles. 'Right now, you and I are standing in the twenty-first century's version of the alchemist's lab. Mark it well.'

The automated steel doors that opened from the high-security hangar out on to the concrete apron began to slide back and through the towering opening I saw the sandstorm had dissipated completely and the sun was shining down on the ring of surrounding mountains: it was three days since the festival of Eid al-Fitr had come to an end, the Saturday when – *insha'Allah* – a group of vehicles would converge on a white mosque to keep an appointment they would wish they had missed. 'Where do the Apaches fly to?' I asked.

'Rise to a ceiling of six thousand feet, turn south-west and pick up National Highway One,' Falcon replied. 'They follow the blacktop and pass over Kandahar, the Taliban's home base, and twelve minutes beyond it, they put eyes on the Kandahar River. They track with it for seven minutes until they reach a town called Garmsir. It translates as "hot place" so that pretty much tells you all you need to know. Forty klicks south of it, in the desert, they land next to three all-wheel-drive tankers that are already in place, refuel and wait.'

'It's as close as they can get to the border without being picked up by Iranian air defence?'

'Right,' he said. 'The choppers will be in Afghanistan but ten miles on the safe side of Iran's cone of surveillance. At my order, they rise vertically, launch the missiles—' He shrugged. 'Then it is up to the strike cell to guide them to Zahedan and hit the target.'

'You left out the most interesting part,' I said. 'The bit about them flying through Iran's electronic shield.'

'Did I?' he replied. 'I can't understand why.' He smiled. 'Okay – here they come.'

He pointed through the automated doors, and I saw two armoured Jeeps were coming straight towards us. In normal circumstances, dozens of vehicles would have been arriving and leaving the apron, but the entire area was deserted this morning, cleared by Falcon's order of everyone except the most essential personnel. As a result, myself and the director were two of the only people who saw the three women and a man in flight suits, carrying helmets, step out of the Jeeps.

All of them paused on the apron and looked around: it had turned into a brilliant day with a sky so clear it was almost crystalline, a surprise given the fierce sandstorm; it was as if the endless waves of swirling grit had scoured the country clean. If only.

Falcon and I watched them walk into the hangar. 'They are all veterans of Iraq, Syria, Kuwait, Yemen – every war that has destroyed half of the Middle East,' he said. 'If I told you they knew what they were doing, it would be an understatement.'

I nodded. Backlit by the sun, their faces in shadow and half hidden by dark glasses but their uniforms and helmets in sharp relief, they seemed larger than life.

They were about to climb aboard the Apaches when the hum of motors and a mechanical rattle made us look up: the entire roof was retracting, allowing light to flood in. It meant that with only blue sky above, the choppers could take off as secretly as possible, lifting off the concrete floor, powering up, rising vertically and soaring away before anyone outside had a chance to register the payload they were carrying.

With the helicopters, the missiles and the refuelling tankers in place, Falcon led me through the hangar, out of the automated doors and on to the concrete apron; from there we would be able to watch the aircraft until they made the turn to the south-west. As we waited in silence I saw him look past the edge of the plateau and across a rugged valley to the towering mountains and the wilderness beyond. He had told me once how much he loved the wild places, the desert especially. Unnoticed, I kept watching his face and saw the yearning—

'Your childhood?' I asked quietly.

'What?' he replied, turning to look at me.

'Where was it you grew up – New Mexico? Out west in Nevada?' I said. 'Is that why you love the desert? None of the biographies ever mention your parents or where you were raised.'

'You think that was an accident?' he said with a smile. 'I realized years ago it wouldn't play well in some circles. No, I guess I was like Lawrence of Arabia – I grew up a long way from what I came to love. He was from Wales, I was born in a small whistlestop in the bayou – a part of America where the entertainment of choice was the banjo and you could still meet men who had worked on the chain gang.'

He must have seen the look of surprise cross my face and he laughed. 'I was an only child,' he said. 'And I never knew my father. When I was about four my mother lit out for the bright lights somewhere and I was raised by an older aunt and uncle. They had no kids of their own and they did their best, but love was never on the agenda.'

I glanced at him and again he was looking at the mountains and the desert – something out of reach, I guessed. I wondered why he was telling me about it; maybe he knew the old world was passing and he was happy to talk about his past, maybe it was simply nobody had ever asked.

'In the way of things, I grew up ambitious – God, was I ambitious,' he said. 'And I wanted to travel, but what hope was there? I hadn't heard from my mother in twelve years, then a strange thing happened – she turned up. Or at least a letter from a lawyer in New Orleans saying she had died did. I never knew her, so I didn't know what to feel. Just regret at what might have been, I suppose. She was thirty-five, cervical cancer, but apparently she had remarried well, a much older man who had predeceased her.

'She left no will herself and, as the only descendant, I found myself the owner of a large house draped in Spanish moss in New Orleans and three bars near Bourbon Street. I sold them all, looked after my aunt and uncle, and knew that I would start dressing better.' He laughed. 'Then I would travel and eventually go to some Ivy League college.'

'Yale,' I said.

'Yale,' he replied. 'Is there anything more establishment than that? So there it is – like most good spies do, I created myself. Just like you did, I invented a legend and called it my life – you ran track for the Navy, you live with a doctor and you move easily through the fashionable restaurants and bars of Georgetown. But your father cleaned pools in Florida and your mother took in sewing work if she could find it. Buster presents himself as dishevelled so people will underestimate him. He knows better – his father was head tailor at Brooks Brothers. Look at a young woman in her power suits – but until she went to college, Madeleine O'Neill, the Irishwoman who is Jewish, shared a bedroom with four siblings. Lucas Corrigan doesn't want to be a terrified child in the chaos of Vietnam so he turned himself into an emotionally distant, highly educated, controlling man.' Falcon shrugged. 'That's why those of us in the secret world can adopt legends so easily – we're used to wearing someone else's clothes.'

The scream of powerful engines made us turn: the pilots were on board the Apaches and the rotors were turning as they started to warm up. Five minutes, I thought and – if Falcon was right – the future would be upon us. 'And the wild places, the desert?'

'Like I said, I'd always wanted to travel,' he replied, eyes drifting back to the mountains and the land beyond. 'I wasn't out of my teens, but I had the money so I wandered, always restless, searching. In a way, I guess I was born a drifter, and I ended up in Egypt, visiting one of the great monuments of antiquity – the temple at Dendera, far in the south on the banks of the Nile.

'I was alone, driving an old Land Rover, and I approached it from the north. It was the end of the day and there didn't seem anything remarkable about the place. I was about to give up on it when I walked towards a tall, relatively modern cinder-block wall guarding the site. There was nobody around, I opened a gate, stepped though it – and I'd passed through a wormhole: I was on a different planet.'

He smiled at the recollection. 'I was a kid from the bayou, a small town nobody has ever heard of, and I had never seen anything like it. I walked past the sacred lake and entered the Temple of Hathor, saw the stone reliefs of Cleopatra on the walls and stared at the pastel colours of the countless hieroglyphs. The place was two thousand years old, built by the Pharaohs to last for ever.' He indicated the jets and transport planes on the runway. 'So yeah, tell me about Western civilization.

'It was getting dark,' he continued. 'And I walked out the back of the temple and there, on the banks of the Nile, was a tribe of Bedouin with their tents, cooking fires and camels. It was timeless beyond belief.

'The next morning,' he went on, 'I changed all my plans and decided to keep driving south, heading for the border of Sudan with the vague idea of visiting Khartoum. As the day wore on, the road I was travelling diverged from the river and the landscape became increasingly sparse. At one point in the late afternoon, I pulled to the side of the road and climbed a steep bluff to get my bearings.

'I looked west,' he said. 'And saw an ocean of rolling dunes spread out before me. There was no footprint or vegetation anywhere, just the setting sun turning the dunes every shade of red and orange. The wind, combing the sand from their crests, made it look like the desert was in constant motion. The only sound was the moaning of the wind. It was then I realized – I was standing on the edge of the Sahara.' He paused, remembering that first glimpse. 'I remained there for ages, long past nightfall . . . somehow I felt like I belonged in that forbidding and empty place, and I don't know why.'

His voice trailed off for a moment and then he continued: 'I guess it's why I have always felt at home in my work. Is there anywhere more forbidding or morally empty or inexplicable than the secret world?'

It wasn't a question that needed an answer, but I could not have replied anyway. The sound of the engines in the hangar was rocketing up into a deafening roar. I saw the blades of the Apaches' main rotors blur into invisibility as the two craft lifted off and disappeared through the roof. Falcon and I, still on the apron, saw them emerge above the building and climb so rapidly that the sunlight glinted off the four white missiles for no more than a second before they banked hard and made the turn.

'We had better go,' Falcon said. 'If we're right about the shell game, half the Army should be on the move by now.'

'And if we're wrong?' I asked. 'Head for the desert?'

He laughed. 'Why not? At least I'll be happy.'

45

IN THE COMMAND CENTRE, CONNOR, MILA AND SPENCER WATCHED AS Falcon and I took our seats in front of a wall of screens. The dozen monitors, fed by a satellite transmitting in real time, all showed different angles of the Army's base at Tora Bora West.

Neither the strike cell, the briefing officer or the other four military brass – standing at the rear of the room – had any idea what Falcon and I were hoping to see or the reason for our anxiety. We saw that the screens were showing no sign of any mass movement at the base; a few Army soldiers, their faces and bodies well hidden, were moving between various bunkers and caves, three men on the firing range were blasting away with little purpose and even less skill, and a group of mechanics was working on several vehicles under the shade of a large tarpaulin. On several occasions, vehicles – either in ones or twos – arrived or left, but they certainly didn't constitute anything exceptional. To all intents and purposes, it was a normal day in the wasteland.

I kept glancing up at the digital clock in a corner of the video wall and seeing one minute click over to the next. Falcon didn't – or wouldn't – check the time, but I knew him well enough to look down at his left hand: he was clenching and unclenching it as he always did in moments of extreme stress. I am sure he was thinking exactly the same thing I was: what if we had got this entirely wrong? Would he call the president and tell him to prepare for a devastating attack we had no idea how to stop?

'What exactly are we looking for?' Connor asked, watching me as I kept glancing at the clock, clearly bored and wondering how long the silent vigil might continue.

'Vehicles,' Falcon answered quietly, continuing to monitor the screens. 'Scores of them, Mr Bryant, maybe several hundred.'

'Why would that many vehicles suddenly leave the caves?' Connor asked.

Falcon turned to look at the young pilot and was about to reply when I grabbed his arm and indicated the screen: four vehicles were driving out of the arched opening of the largest cave.

Both of us stared, hoping against hope that more would follow, aware that four vehicles did not constitute anything. There could have been any number of explanations for it. 'Come on . . .' I said under my breath. 'Come on.'

The digital clock continued to tick away the minutes and hope was dying when a cloud of dust appeared in the archway: three vehicles emerged. They had barely cleared the entrance when two more followed; then another five came out of an ammunition bunker.

'We're on,' Falcon said, turning into a whirlwind of activity – shrugging off his bomber jacket, enhancing some images on the screen and hitting a command on the remote. Watched by the strike cell and the military brass, a large image of the war room at Langley appeared at the top of the video wall. I heard a sharp intake of breath and murmured comments from behind: I doubted that any of them had seen the inside of a war room at CIA headquarters, let alone one on this scale.

'See 'em, Buster?' Falcon asked as the agency's assistant director stepped into frame.

'Got 'em,' Buster replied, looking even more scruffy than normal: he had been monitoring the caves all through the night.

'How many vehicles can you follow?' Falcon asked.

'As many as they can throw at us,' Buster replied. 'Any more than four hundred might be a problem.'

Four hundred? I said to myself, shocked at the scale of it, and watching as Buster stepped aside and allowed the camera to pan and capture the entire space. It was far larger than when I had sat at the command console a few days earlier: more walls had been retracted and more workstations crammed into the stadium seating. The myriad screens now hanging from overhead tracks all showed the same images as our video wall in Bagram: dozens more vehicles were leaving the cave complex and heading in different directions across the wilderness.

'Can you see how many are leaving now?' Buster asked. 'They're really going for it, aren't they? We're not just using our personnel here to track them, though – we're employing satellite and surveillance bases in Pine Gap in Australia, the big array in the Andes, Misawa in Japan, Menwith Hill in the UK and half a dozen others.' Lights in the shape of beacons lit up on the map, illustrating the secret facilities he was listing. 'We've got eyes on the whole of southern Iran, monitoring not just the visual but communications and everything else we can think of.'

'Good work, Buster,' Falcon said. 'It's up to the Army now – there's nothing more we can do. We wait until their high-value vehicles head for a rendezvous.'

'That, or we discover they've gamed us,' Buster replied. 'Gamed us completely – there's no meeting and the leadership are all sitting in their cave laughing.' He was smiling, but that didn't mean he wasn't serious.

'Moscow, maybe,' Falcon said. 'Moscow might pull a gag like that, but not these guys, not today.'

Three hours later – with the brass and the strike cell slumped half asleep in their chairs and me little better in mine – Buster appeared on the feed from Langley, and it was his voice that roused me. 'We've got two vehicles from very different directions, both driving towards Zahedan.'

I was awake instantly. Falcon was already staring at two separate screens, each one featuring a four-wheel drive that Buster had marked with a red flag. 'Assuming they're not decoys – let's say they are the real thing – can we guess at a rendezvous point, Buster?'

'Not really. The trackers are working on it, doing projections,' Buster replied. 'It could be the airport, they say, but nobody's sure. Does that worry you?'

'The airport? No, they're not flying anywhere – not even Casablanca,' Falcon said, smiling. 'But the car park would be ideal for them – a lot of traffic, people coming and going, confusion. How many vehicles left the caves?'

'Two hundred and seventy-four.'

'Jesus – that many? Apart from these two, how many other candidates do we have that might be genuine?' Falcon asked.

'We've discounted most of them,' Buster replied. 'We think there are another twenty-three good possibilities.'

'Twenty-five vehicles,' Falcon said, worry and anxiety once again writ large across his face. 'They're not screwing around. If they decide to send ten of them up the street to the mosque, we've got a big problem. Four missiles means we have to know exactly which cars to hit.' He turned and looked at me—

'Yeah, I know, Falcon,' I replied. 'We have to know who is in what vehicle.' I spoke to Buster directly: 'Bring the twenty-five vehicles up live, will you? If the windows are down or the glass isn't tinted, I might be able to identify somebody. We might as well start.'

As I waited for the screens to spark up, I realized that the strike cell, the high-ranking brass and the briefing officer were all staring at me. How could I identify any of them, they must have been asking. Who in hell was I?

Falcon, too, saw that they were all looking at me – propped up in my chair, my body battered, my skin grey with fatigue and the doctor and nurses waiting outside the door – and he turned to them. 'I'll only say this once,' he told them. 'The man whose name you will never know is one of the bravest people I have ever worked with. You would be well advised to forget that you have ever seen his face. Am I clear?'

Nobody said a word. I swallowed the embarrassment and continued to watch the images unspooling on the screen: they showed the twenty-five vehicles travelling through vastly different areas of wilderness. Assisted massively by classified satellite technology that was able to look at the vehicles not just from above but at least partly side on, I quickly found the few among them – four in all – that either had their windows down or where the glass was untinted. Although I examined the occupants as closely as possible, I soon concluded, as you would expect from such carelessness, that none of them were part of the leadership group.

I turned to the more problematic candidates, those vehicles with glass so heavily tinted that it was almost black, and I had worked through five of them when I stopped. I kept staring at the rear passenger window, the safe seat of a battered green Nissan Patrol, a vehicle that was as nondescript as all the rest.

'What is it?' Falcon asked.

I pointed at a list of technical, subsidiary information collected by the satellites and worldwide ground stations that was scrolling down the side of the screen next to each vehicle: speed, direction of travel, type of engine and a host of other metrics. 'There's a heat signature in the back seat,' I said.

'Of course, somebody is sitting there,' Falcon replied. 'It's reading their body heat.'

'No, it's too intense. Concentrated on one spot,' I explained. 'The person is smoking.'

'Well, it's Iran – they're years behind the research. Everybody smokes.'

'Yeah, but what do a lot of smokers do when they finish. They throw—'

I didn't get any further; Falcon – realizing what I was about to say – was already on the direct line to Buster at Langley. 'Vehicle numeric fourteen on the video grid. Green Nissan. Close on the rear passenger window and hold on it.'

Within seconds Buster must have relayed the information to the NSA and somebody immediately made the adjustment. From four hundred miles in space, the target window sprang closer and into sharper focus.

Nothing happened. The vehicle continued barrelling across the rugged terrain and I started to despair; just our luck, I thought, we had found an environmentally conscious terrorist who was using the ashtray. Then the tinted glass started to drop. The whole room leaned forward.

The window continued lower, and we saw a man sitting there, unmasked so that he could smoke: he was elderly and I could see his face in profile as he took one last drag on the cigarette.

Then he turned to throw the butt out of the window, and I saw him clearly. 'It's him,' I said to Falcon. 'It's the Emir. That grey hair, the penetrating eyes, the way he lifted his hand. It's him.'

Falcon, his face breaking into a grimace of relief, was back on the line to Buster. 'Positive for fourteen, the green Nissan. It's the Emir.'

Buster must have had his mic open because Falcon and I – and everyone else in the bunker – heard the cheer that went up from the war room in Langley. 'Follow the Nissan,' Falcon continued to Buster. 'Don't worry about the others, the Emir has just invited us to the rendezvous.'

Then he turned to the strike cell. 'Get ready.'

46

AS SOON AS THE SATELLITE IMAGE OF THE OPEN-AIR CAR PARK AT Zahedan International Airport hit our screens, it was clear that it was the perfect location for a clandestine rendezvous.

The old and crumbling complex was a major regional hub serving a host of cities in Iran and, as a result, was large enough to be extremely busy but too small to have anything that might be called a traffic management plan. The car park and the roads were a chaos of cars, buses and milling crowds.

The satellites, ground stations, hundreds of people at Langley and all of us in the bunker at Bagram were looking at it from on high, and we had no problem following the green Nissan as it twisted and turned through dozens of other pick-ups and four-wheel drives. It told us, unequivocally, that the car park was the rendezvous point. We watched the Nissan mount the sidewalk to avoid the huge line waiting to take a ticket at the pay-station and then drive through a collapsed section of wire fencing into the car park. Who was going to argue with men who might answer with Kalashnikovs?

I leaned forward in my chair, watching the Nissan drive to a corner of the lot and park under a broad expanse of canvas sails designed to protect the cars and pedestrians from the blistering sun. Despite my doubts about his presence, I could not get Kazinsky out of my mind and I wondered – hoped was more like it – whether he had travelled with the Emir and at any moment he would get out of the Nissan to stretch his legs. Nobody got out; in fact nothing happened and one minute turned to ten and then thirty.

I exchanged a glance with Falcon, who – equally perplexed – opened the mic to Buster: 'You got anything—'

'We've got no idea what he's doing,' Buster replied, tersely. Clearly, the strain was telling at Langley as well. 'Wait,' he said, even more sharply, quickly followed by a flood of relief in his voice. 'Three candidate vehicles just turned into a road that accesses the airport.'

I felt my shoulders relax as the tension eased. Then Buster gave another update: 'Two more candidates, different direction but not far behind.'

'Six vehicles, including the Nissan – not four, damn it,' Falcon said.

'Something's happening,' Buster interjected. 'North corner, near the hangar—'

Falcon, myself and everyone else in the bunker immediately looked at the screen on the video wall that Buster was referring to.

'That's smart,' Falcon said bitterly as soon as he saw the eight parked vehicles that had suddenly left their distant spots in the parking lot and were converging on the Nissan.

'They've got vehicles already in place,' he continued, 'stashed there over the last few days. Get ready, targets are going to start transferring between vehicles. Now we've got fourteen rides in all. God help us if they all go to the mosque.'

I had come to the same conclusion and, deep in concentration, I watched an elaborately choreographed ballet unfold: the eight approaching vehicles parked close to the Nissan, the five candidate four-wheel drives arrived, joined the chaos under the sail cloth, vehicle doors began to open until, suddenly, flames and black smoke billowed from a pick-up parked forty metres away.

Eyes flying between screens, Falcon clicked open his mic and spoke to the war room at Langley, commanding everyone: 'Diversion,' he said loudly. 'Eyes on the game—'

That was what I was doing – trying not to allow myself to get confused. I saw, half obscured by smoke, one of the eight approaching vehicles – a nearly new and much cleaner Toyota Land Cruiser – stop in a vacant spot right beside the battered Nissan. As women and children, driven by the burning pick-up, fled across the asphalt and men rushed to try and extinguish the blaze, the Emir – his face completely hidden again – got out of the Nissan, took two steps as an unseen hand threw open the back door of the Land Cruiser and was inside the vehicle with the door closing behind him in less than three seconds.

Nobody else emerged from the Nissan – he was obviously the only passenger. I turned my attention to the other vehicles, hoping to catch sight of Kazinsky. Immediately I saw two men who, despite their head coverings and robes, I was sure were part of the leadership team who I'd seen on horseback. Then I recognized the one-armed guy and the refueller and I flagged one other man I thought I had seen next to the Emir in his armchair at the beach. They were all part of a milling mass of men transferring between vehicles. As I called them out to Falcon, he relayed the information to Langley and within moments red targets were superimposed on each of the vehicles they were stepping into.

But, of Kazinsky, there was no sign. In two minutes, maybe less, the dance in the car park was over, by which time the fire on the back of the pick-up was still growing larger and the Land Cruiser with the Emir inside was pulling out of its bay. Other vehicles started to follow, and Falcon and I watched them head not for the exit but for the broken-down wire fence where the green Nissan had first entered.

'Five vehicles, including the Land Cruiser,' Falcon said. 'You see any others?'

'No,' I replied. 'There are still nine back in the parking lot.'

He nodded. 'So, five for the final run – not perfect,' he said. 'But it could be worse.'

Worried, he turned to the strike crew. 'Can you hit two vehicles at the front and the two at the back almost simultaneously?'

Connor thought for a long moment. 'I don't like it much, but we could get close. Why?'

'Each missile has reservoirs of highly flammable fuel,' Falcon said. 'The reservoirs are set to ignite a hundred and twenty seconds after the weapon strikes the target—'

'Ignite? Liquid fuel?' Connor asked, taken aback. 'I thought the missiles were electric.'

'They are,' Falcon replied. 'The fuel is there to destroy the missile once it's blown so that the tech doesn't fall into the wrong hands. In a narrow street wedged in between four blazing wrecks – it might just be enough to KO the vehicle in the middle.'

Connor looked at his two co-pilots, silently canvassing their opinion: can they take out all four vehicles almost simultaneously, setting off a firestorm? Mila and Spencer shrugged. 'Hitting 'em will be hard enough – you wouldn't try it by choice,' Mila said. 'But I guess that's one thing we don't have – choice.'

'Not today,' Falcon replied. 'Not in these circumstances.'

Grimly, he looked at the vehicles as they bumped over the sidewalk and on to the road. 'Just our bum luck,' he said to me. 'Kazinsky will be in the middle vehicle and we'll miss it.'

'Or he won't be there at all,' I replied. 'I didn't see any sign of him during the transfer.'

'We didn't see any sign of most of the occupants,' Falcon retorted. 'Believe me, he left Tora Bora West days ago, he'll be in one of the stashed vehicles. That's what you would have done, isn't it?'

'No – I wouldn't be there at all,' I replied, smiling but not joking.

'Of course he will be. He's not thinking about missiles,' Falcon said. 'They think they are safe behind the defence shield.'

'Maybe. But there are roadside bombs, IEDs, Mossad – the Israelis once used a remote-controlled gun activated by a cellphone to ambush a car full of high-ranking Iranians outside Tehran. You yourself went into Iran to destroy nuclear centrifuges—'

'Yeah, and that went well,' he countered. 'Kazinsky will be in one of those vehicles. If he's as smart as you say, it will be the second from the back, the safest in any convoy.'

I looked at a silver RAM pick-up with dual cabs he was pointing at – a big vehicle in good condition, built on a sturdy frame and fitted with off-road tyres and a jacked-up suspension. Maybe Falcon was right, logically, maybe Kazinsky was in it, but my heart said he wasn't. 'How long to drive from where they are now to the mosque?' I asked.

'We just calculated it looking at the traffic,' Buster replied from Langley. 'Thirty-seven minutes, give or take.'

'How long to get the choppers up, launch the missiles and have them in the street?' I asked Falcon.

'Thirty-five minutes,' Connor Bryant replied instantly, looking at the maps on the video wall and running calculations on his laptop.

'He's right,' Falcon added. 'So we've got two minutes to spare – you know, just in case things aren't tough enough.'

47

THERE WAS BARELY A BREATH OF WIND SO THE SMOKE FROM A campfire rose straight up until it vanished into a sky so bleached of colour that it was more white than blue. That was how hot it was at the end of summer in the desert south of Gamsir, one of the hottest places on earth, on the afternoon when four missiles were about to be launched from Afghanistan into Iran.

The fire had been lit in a steep-sided gully by three men, dressed like Bedouin, whose business meant they always tried to avoid open spaces. They were smugglers – drugs, gold, any sort of contraband – and they had travelled for sixty klicks along the gully when the rear axle on one of their three four-wheel drives finally gave up. With the vehicle up on jacks, the wheels off and a spare axle ready to be fitted, they had lit the fire to brew a cup of tea and rest during the worst heat of the day. They were sitting on rocks, cups in hand, when a hurricane of dirt and sand, accompanied by the sound of mighty engines, swept across the top of the gully.

The men, fearing the imminent arrival of their most-feared adversary – airborne elements of the Afghan Army – scrambled for their assault rifles and grenade launchers. They were going to fight it out, not because they feared arrest – decades in the smuggling business had taught them that the Afghan Army would steal the contraband and then execute them to avoid any unwanted complications.

As the men took cover, hoping to catch any attackers in a withering crossfire, the storm of dirt and sand continued and the engines showed no sign of abating. With panic subsiding, the oldest and most experienced of the smugglers – a man in his late forties with one eye patched and a deep scar from his temple to his neck – climbed the steep incline to the top of the gully, found protection between a group of jagged boulders and stared across a stretch of baking desert and withered scrub—

For some reason he couldn't fathom, two Apache helicopters without any markings had landed beside three equally anonymous refuelling tankers. What the helicopters were doing in one of the most blighted landscapes on earth and where they were going – certainly not into Iran; everybody knew that was impossible – he had no idea. He turned at a sound behind him and saw that his two colleagues, emboldened by the fact that he hadn't been shot, had followed him up the incline.

They took cover beside him, saw the anonymous craft, and the youngest of them was about to start peppering their leader with questions when the whine of the engines became louder. The choppers had refuelled quickly and were lifting off. Half shielding their eyes from the grit and glare, the three men watched them rise higher, turn slightly, catch the sun directly on their skids and reflect off four missiles attached to their underbellies. The weapons were so dazzling with their millions of diamond-like tiles, so unlike anything the three men had seen before – and they had seen every conceivable weapon during countless decades of war – that they stood up to try and get a better look.

But the choppers were rising so fast, banking hard to hit their pre-arranged launch point, that the missiles were lost in shadow until the craft themselves became barely visible against the bleached-out sky.

The three men started talking animatedly, little knowing how minutely they were being observed. Our satellite feed had been initiated to monitor the helicopters refuelling but had inadvertently picked up the interlopers. While their presence had initially caused alarm among myself and the Army brass, Falcon waved it away. 'What does it matter? What have they seen? Two unmarked helicopters and some unusual missiles. They're smugglers, for God's sake. What they gonna do? File a fucking report?'

Everyone else continued to watch the choppers rising higher and higher, getting close to the point when the helo pilots would hit their triggers, send an electrical charge to the firing rails and launch the four missiles in plumes of white smoke.

Falcon had his eyes fixed on the screen, speaking to me but loud enough for everyone else to hear. 'It's about fifty years since Jimmy Carter launched Operation Eagle Claw and deployed US troops to rescue dozens of Americans held hostage at the embassy in Tehran. Fifty years . . . that was the last time US assets attempted to enter Iran's airspace.'

'And that mission was a god-awful disaster,' I said. 'Let's hope we have a better result.'

48

THE SATELLITE FEED OF ZAHEDAN SHOWED THE CONVOY HAD LEFT the traffic chaos near the car park, passed the ugly jumble of industrial buildings that seem to surround every airport in the world, and hit a two-lane road that led directly into the city.

With every passing minute, the traffic became lighter than we had anticipated and the five vehicles, with the Emir's Land Cruiser in the lead, sped past a collection of fast-food joints. The situation was deteriorating fast enough for Buster's face to appear on one of the screens connecting Bagram to the war room at Langley: 'They're making much better time than we expected—'

'How far ahead of schedule are they?' Falcon asked, interrupting.

'Three minutes,' Buster replied.

'And they're barely a quarter of the way there,' Falcon said, anxious and frustrated. 'At this rate they'll pick up twelve minutes and we'll have no hope of getting the missiles into the street to meet them. The leadership will be inside the house—'

'Or the mosque,' I said. 'Totally out of reach.'

'Damn,' Falcon cursed, clenching and unclenching his left hand faster than I had ever seen. 'How do we slow 'em down?'

Nobody said anything, but in my experience, on every successful mission there is always a stroke of luck or good thinking; I don't know what it was that day, but I said: 'Traffic lights?'

Falcon looked at me for a second then opened the mic to speak directly to Buster. 'How many sets of traffic lights between the convoy and Casa Blanca?'

Buster only needed a second. 'Three.'

'Get hold of NSA now,' Falcon ordered. 'Tell 'em to hack Zahedan's network and take control of every traffic light in the city. We don't have time to be choosy.'

'Turn 'em all red?' Buster asked.

'No,' I interjected. 'Drivers will get frustrated and crawl through the intersections. Turn 'em green – crashes will slow them down more.'

'Green it is,' Falcon said to Buster. 'Go.'

'Choppers are in position,' Connor reported to Falcon, pointing at a screen showing a satellite image of the two helicopters in stunning detail. A circle beside them was flashing green, indicating they were at the correct altitude and the right GPS co-ordinates.

The strike crew turned to their own screens and controls, getting prepared: once Falcon gave the order to fire, the chopper pilots would launch the missiles and Connor, Mila and Spencer would immediately start to 'fly' them.

'You have three minutes from the time the helicopters launch to when you hit Iran's cone of surveillance,' Falcon told them. 'Pilots ready?'

'Sir,' the strike crew snapped in unison.

Falcon picked up a mic connected to the helicopters. 'Fire,' he ordered.

49

THE LAND CRUISER – WITH ITS CONVOY IN LINE BEHIND – PASSED A bus in the slow lane and, well ahead of schedule, drove at speed towards a large intersection.

The traffic light was green and several cars ahead of the convoy accelerated in order to beat the light before it changed. The signal remained green, the cars – followed by the Land Cruiser and its convoy – entered the intersection – and they all made it across without incident. The Zahedan traffic light system was still operating normally.

A mile further on, the convoy – with at least a dozen vehicles in front of it – approached an even larger intersection. A badly dented grey Mercedes saloon saw it had a green light, rushed to get through it, surged ahead of the vehicles around it, entered the intersection – and was broadsided by a white Ford van on the right that had also been speeding through on green. The NSA hackers had done their job.

The Mercedes, the far lighter of the two combatants, spinning like a top, struck a glancing blow against a station wagon, hit a minivan head on and ground to a stop. Behind it, three vehicles that had been on its tail had no chance even to brake.

They tried to swerve, but that only increased the chaos, barrelling into cars that had also come through on the green from either side, hitting them so hard it sent two fenders and a hood flying through the air. The airborne hood took out a pick-up's windshield, the driver ducking instinctively and immediately losing control, sending him into the path of—

A swerving, hard-braking water tanker. The two vehicles hit, the water tank ruptured, its contents flooded the street and both vehicles came to a screeching halt, blocking the intersection.

The driver of the Emir's Land Cruiser braked hard, swung on to the sidewalk, destroyed several parked motor scooters and just managed to avoid entering the blocked junction. The other four vehicles in the convoy followed in its wake, inching along to avoid a gathering crowd of locals.

Watching on the screens, Falcon and I saw the convoy stick to the sidewalk, slowly skirting the debris and wrecked vehicles, until at last they reached the far side of the intersection and were ready to hit the clear road ahead.

The screen with the Land Cruiser's ETA in the street leading to Casa Blanca showed the disabled traffic lights had done the trick. We were back on schedule.

50

CONNOR GLANCED AT A HOST OF DATA AND THEN A DIGITAL CLOCK on one of the two screens in front of him. 'Forty seconds and we hit the air-defence cone,' he announced, his eyes not wavering from the displays.

He had the responsibility for piloting two missiles, and as I watched him work the twin joysticks, enter commands on the keyboards and highlight information and co-ordinates with his trackpad, I was reminded of a classical music concert Rebecca had taken me to during one of her periodic attempts to 'civilize' me. It featured a performance by a virtuoso pianist and I saw in Connor that same combination of total control and absolute freedom, the sense that he could not only skate on thin ice but could do it for mile after mile. By contrast, Mila and Spencer – as good as they were – seemed to be much closer to the edge of panic or disaster.

'The moment of truth,' Connor said quietly, probably meant for Mila's ears only. 'The Iranians will lock on first, then the Pakistani tripods a moment later. Ten seconds now before they see us.' He raised his voice, addressing the room at large: 'Nine seconds.'

The military brass moved closer to the video wall and I could sense their apprehension behind me. I shifted slightly and only then realized how tense I was. I glanced at Falcon's left hand, fully expecting to see it rapidly clenching and unclenching, but he had both hands in his pockets. Whether or not that indicated a whole new level of anxiety – hitherto unseen – I had no way of knowing.

'Seven seconds,' Connor announced.

I looked at one of the screens on the video wall and watched the four missiles, white and beautiful in the sunlight, travelling fast, about to hit a computer-generated cone of red, pulsing lines.

'Four seconds.'

The strike cell, acting in unison, made an adjustment and the four missiles straightened course, ready to hit the cone head on. The pilots sat more upright in their high-backed chairs, as if they were bracing themselves for the Iranian and Pakistani surveillance to lock on.

'One second,' Connor said, his voice not betraying anything.

The four weapons hit the pulsing red lines. 'Now!' Connor said.

Nothing happened. The missiles continued to fly straight and even. There was no sound, no flashing alerts in any of the strike-crew cocoons. Connor and the other two continued to fly the weapons, but they were staring at their screens, clearly shocked.

'What's wrong with the Iranians?' Connor asked after checking his data. 'Are they asleep?'

I have to admit I, too, was taken aback, but at least I had a little foreknowledge. Nobody else in the room had any warning. The missiles were penetrating deeper and deeper into the cone of surveillance and yet there was nothing to mark it.

'Where the hell are the Pakistanis?' Connor said, sort of scared, searching for an answer. Finally, he surrendered. 'It's stealth . . . got to be . . . the missiles . . . they've got some sort of stealth on steroids.' He looked hard at Falcon, hoping for a hint of confirmation or, better still, an explanation.

The director said nothing and continued to watch the missiles and their rapid progress. Connor continued to stare at him. 'Just fly, Mr Bryant. You need to concentrate.'

Connor looked back at his screen, and his professionalism finally overcame his bafflement. 'We're through the cone of surveillance,' he reported as the missiles exited on the far side of the pulsing red lines. 'Crossing the border . . . *now*. We are in Iran!'

It was the first time an American pilot had been able to say that in over fifty years. The military brass applauded and we heard a muted cheer from Langley. The only person who showed no reaction was Falcon; I don't think he had ever harboured any doubt that while the mission could always fail, the missiles – at least – would prove successful.

The military brass stepped forward to congratulate him but got no further. Connor was looking at his data and GPS—

'Twenty-five miles to target.'

51

A FIVE-YEAR-OLD GIRL LAUGHED AS SHE FLEW THROUGH THE AIR, floated for a moment, waved her hands in joy and dropped back to earth.

She was on a battered trampoline in an empty lot, surrounded by parents and other kids waiting their turn in a makeshift playground on a narrow street. At one end of the road, past houses crowded together, where veiled women were hanging washing from balconies, was the white mosque. All of the houses had been built long before there was any need for garages and cars were parked haphazardly on either side of the street, forcing pedestrians on to the road.

Among a large group of them was a man in a wooden wheelchair. Wearing a baseball cap featuring the logo of Manchester City, an English football club, he wheeled himself up the incline and barely broke rhythm as he waved to the kids at the trampoline.

As I watched him on the video wall, I thought about the price of devotion: five times a day he wheeled up and down the arduous street in order to pray. And he wasn't alone – groups of other men, and quite a few women, were also making their way up the hill to the mosque, passing a group of teenagers playing football in the street, men sipping tea outside a hole-in-the-wall café and old women in black *abayas* carrying their shopping home. If the strike could be executed without civilian casualties, it would be a miracle.

I glanced past the man in the wheelchair and looked down the road to where a delivery truck was driving slowly, searching for a parking place. It found one, pulled into it and—

Revealed the white Land Cruiser entering the street behind it.

52

AS IT APPROACHED, I SAW THE OTHER FOUR VEHICLES WERE BUNCHED close behind it and, though I stared hard at the tinted windows of the pick-up second from last – the silver RAM with the dual cabs – it was impossible to tell how many passengers were on board, let alone if Kazinsky was one of them.

'You see them? All five vehicles?' Falcon asked the strike cell.

'Got 'em,' Connor replied. 'Traffic lights did the business: they're eighty seconds behind schedule – we're good to go.' He looked at Mila and Spencer for confirmation and they nodded; it was time for them all to start really flying now.

I looked at the video wall, and the satellite showed that the four missiles, low over Zahedan, were separating in order to approach the street from different angles. 'Confirming the strike plan,' I heard Connor say. 'Fifty-four seconds and I take the Land Cruiser head on. It will stop the convoy dead. Spence?'

'I hit the Toyota in the rear and trap the rest of them between the two wrecks,' he said.

Mila had her eyes fixed on her screen, making tiny adjustments with the joystick. 'I take out the second in line. Forty seconds.'

'I'll blow the RAM pick-up with my second missile as fast as possible,' Connor said. 'Thirty seconds now. With luck, the middle vehicle will incinerate. Okay? Let's go.'

There was complete silence as the three pilots concentrated. I looked up at the digital clock: twenty-nine seconds. I glanced at Falcon – he was in his own zone, every ounce of attention fixed on the video wall and the four screens, each showing one of the missiles.

I looked at the screen featuring Connor's first missile, the one that would – if everything worked in twenty-seven seconds – obliterate the Emir's Land Cruiser and all of its occupants. The glittering white missile skimmed several rooftops and was heading straight for the street.

The Land Cruiser was continuing up the road, slowing for pedestrians, but right on course for the mosque. It seemed inevitable – the missile was going to hit it straight in the centre of its windshield. Twenty-two seconds.

The face of the little girl on the trampoline suddenly appeared on the screen – she was taking another bounce. Connor made a rapid adjustment with the joystick and the six-foot-long missile, pure white, travelling at eight hundred miles an hour, skirted the trampoline completely and continued on its course.

I stared at the screen. So did Connor and everyone else. A remarkable thing had just happened—

Nobody in the vacant lot had reacted; not the little girl, nor the parents or the other kids. It was as if they hadn't seen anything; like the missile wasn't even there. Certainly it was travelling fast but, even so: a blur, a flash, a sweep of white movement – surely, something should have grabbed their attention and registered. It was as if . . . as if . . .

The three pilots, myself and everyone except Falcon said a similar thing: 'What the . . .'

'Quiet,' Falcon ordered.

Spencer, clearly mastering his surprise, was piloting his missile uphill, straight along the centre of the road, barely four feet off the ground, aiming to destroy the Toyota at the rear of the convoy from behind. He passed the men sipping tea at the hole in the wall, avoided the footballers and the man in the wheelchair. Again nothing – no reaction, no recognition.

Just like the kids and parents in the vacant lot, nobody in the street showed any fear or panic; nobody pointed or screamed.

'They can't see 'em,' Connor said, echoing my thoughts. It was the only explanation. 'Nobody can see 'em,' he said, all but repeating himself, his voice conveying his utter shock. 'They're cloaked, completely—'

'Keep flying!' Falcon demanded.

Connor did as he was ordered, his eyes focused only on the first missile under his command, watching the weapon hurtle, front on, straight at the Land Cruiser. 'Three seconds,' he said. 'Two. One.'

Although we were hundreds of miles away, I felt everybody in the room brace for impact.

'Now,' Connor said. The missile hit, the windshield shattered and the warhead was automatically deployed. It was the sushi bomb—

53

I KNEW EXACTLY HOW A SUSHI BOMB WORKED – I'D SEEN A demonstration of it just before one was deployed in Yemen against a brutal warlord who I'd helped find.

Like the Emir, he too was at his most vulnerable while travelling in an armoured vehicle, but the problem was that he rarely left Aden, a densely populated port city of a million people, a place where any explosion could be guaranteed to kill scores of bystanders.

Invited to the US Army's Aberdeen Test Center in Maryland, I watched as the circular bomb smashed through the glass and toughened steel of a vehicle occupied by four crash-test dummies. Moments later, once inside the car, a dozen long, scythe-like knives – made from tempered steel and sharpened to the finest edge – unfolded from the spinning ball.

In the US Army's graphic simulation, the knives – each over two feet long – whirred and rotated blindingly fast, immediately slicing through the driver's neck, beheading him, cutting apart the leather seats, headrests and doing the same thing to the man sitting next to him.

The ball of knives, slowing dramatically, continued through the vehicle, into the next part of the cabin, and hit the two rear-seat passengers. A blade scalped one of the men before the rest of the knives – still whirring – destroyed the rest of his body, the seats and the man in the adjoining seat.

In the bunker at Bagram, a long way from Maryland, I watched it for real. For a fraction of a second, captured by satellite through the shattered windscreen, the wall of video screens showed the Emir – unmasked – screaming in the safe seat. The image disappeared in a huge shower of blood as he, the driver and the other occupants were cut to pieces.

The Land Cruiser, now with a dead man at the wheel, rolled to a sudden stop and the vehicle travelling close behind crashed hard into its tailgate.

At the rear of the convoy, the driver of the Toyota, realizing something was wrong ahead, braked hard, screeching to a halt – inadvertently providing Spencer with a stationary target. The pilot worked the joystick quickly, adjusted his aim and we watched on the video wall as his missile slammed into the Toyota's rear windshield.

In a shower of glass, the weapon entered the cabin, the knives deployed, and the four unidentifiable men inside might have just had enough time to scream before their viscera wallpapered the inside of the vehicle's tinted glass, hiding the carnage from the satellite's roving eye.

I glanced at the screens monitoring the street and saw that the men at the café were staring at the Toyota in bewilderment while several of the footballers – confused, intrigued – approached the stalled convoy. Then they saw the slaughterhouse inside the two vehicles and started to yell, just as the women on the balconies were leaning over to try to find out what was happening. But nobody was running or screaming in terror – the entire street knew something was going on, but what it was, nobody could explain. Apart from smashing windshields, they had seen or heard nothing.

In the midst of their confusion, Mila's missile hit the windshield of the vehicle that had rear-ended the Land Cruiser, taking out the three men inside in a millisecond. Four of the footballers were showered with glass and were close enough to catch a spray of blood. That was enough for them; they turned and ran, almost knocking aside the man in the wheelchair. He had realized death had come out of nowhere and was gesticulating at the children in the vacant lot to stay back.

Mila, her work done, drenched in sweat from the intense pressure, glanced at the remains of the three wrecked vehicles before looking at the footage of the crowd spilling into the street. 'What's wrong with them?' she said. 'The missiles are six feet long. Why don't they see 'em?'

'They can't,' Spencer replied, his work also finished, shaking the tension out of his hands.

'Of course they can. They're right there, on the screens—' Mila said, pointing at the fourth missile, being flown by Connor, as it dropped down out of the clear blue sky and started to hurtle down the middle of the road.

'Sure, something's on the screens – we're looking at a computer rendition, an avatar, an *electronic representation* of a missile, call it what you like. One thing is for definite – on Iranian radar and on that street, those weapons are not fucking visible.'

Mila stared at him. What sort of weapon was it? She turned to Falcon and looked like she was going to ask a question, but she stayed silent when she saw the director was still concentrating on the screen that was displaying Connor's second missile.

Mila turned to watch and saw that the fly-boy she had slept with the night before was quite the pilot: the narrow street was filling with a crowd of confused civilians and in order to hit the silver RAM, he had to go high—

He had one advantage. Even though it was second from the back of the convoy, the RAM's big tyres and jacked-up suspension made it clearly visible. I leaned forward, watching intently: if Kazinsky was in the convoy, the RAM was almost certainly his ride.

Connor's missile, having gained altitude, was closing in on the vehicle fast. Time seemed to compress as it plunged down towards the street, avoided the crowds of confused bystanders, levelled up just behind the bloodied and wrecked Toyota, rose a little higher and skimmed its roof.

It hit the RAM, and this time half the people in the street screamed. As the rear windshield vanished in an explosion of glass, I just saw the outline of three men in the vehicle before the knives deployed and tore the man sitting in the safe seat in the back to pieces. Was it Kazinsky? It would almost certainly have been the seat he would have occupied, but trying to see through the flying glass and blast of blood was impossible. Whether it was him or not, I had no idea.

I stared at the wreckage of the RAM and felt nothing, nothing at all – certainly not success – just curiously flat, and it was in that strange state of mind that I heard Mila speak quietly to Connor. 'Stealth on steroids, you said. Is that what it is?'

'I think it's much more than that,' he said, exhausted, picking up a bottle of water and splashing it over his face. He was about to offer some further thought, but he didn't get the chance—

The Land Cruiser erupted in flames as the three reservoirs of specially designed fuel – engineered to burn at a far higher temperature than either gasoline or jet propellant – ignited, the white-hot flames rapidly consuming the interior of the vehicle. The glass windows and rear windshield blew out from the heat, shooting flames high into the sky. As everyone in the street scrambled to a safe distance, the reservoirs in the other three vehicles were also blown. The heat was so intense from the four-vehicle blaze that even the women on the balconies were forced to withdraw and the men in a Nissan Patrol in the middle of the convoy, up to now shocked into inaction – and the only one that had not been missiled – tried to wrench open their doors.

But it, too, had been rammed hard in the rear during the initial chaos of the attack and, though none of its four occupants had realized it until then, its frame and panels had been twisted out of shape. The doors were too badly buckled, or the automatic locking mechanism had been triggered. Either way, the men were trying to force the doors open as flames leapt on to the vehicle from front and back, instantly liquefying its blue paint.

As the men screamed for help, the flames hit the oil sump under the engine, causing the front of the vehicle to erupt in red flame and black smoke, forcing the crowd back even further. Nobody was getting out of there alive.

Falcon rose to his feet – weary – put on his bomber jacket and exchanged a look with me. 'Bhopal – you know what the word signifies now?' he asked. 'Nothing – a city in India nobody has ever heard of.'

He looked at the strike cell. 'Thank you, pilots,' he said. 'None of this ever happened. We'll talk about that in detail at a meeting tonight. Get some rest.' Then he turned to the briefing officer. 'General, take possession of all the material. Notes, mission plans, video. A mobile three-tier burn box will be here in twenty minutes.'

He headed for the door and the pilots started to pick up their jackets and water bottles, leaving me to look at the smouldering wreckage of the RAM and wonder about the identity of its occupants.

54

I FOUND HIM WELL BEYOND THE COMMAND CENTRE, A SOLITARY figure standing on the escarpment, his hands pushed deep into his pockets, looking out across flat and arid plains towards the mountains. With the sun low in the sky and no sign of human settlement, it was easy to imagine that you were in the desert. Egypt, maybe.

He turned at the sound of my approach. I was walking slowly, the crutches making heavy weather of the uneven terrain.

'You shouldn't be out here,' he said. 'Do the doctors know?'

'No,' I replied as I stopped beside him. 'They're probably out looking for me now,' I said with a smile. I indicated the empty landscape stretching in front of us. 'Quiet, isn't it? A good place to think, I suppose.'

He didn't say anything.

'That was pretty overwhelming in there, Falcon.'

Again, he didn't reply.

'They were just symbols on the screen,' I continued. 'Nothing more than a graphic representation of the missiles.'

'Were they?' he said with mock innocence, turning to look at me.

'Damn right they were – we all saw the missiles were invisible to everyone watching. There wasn't a person in the street who saw them.'

He nodded. 'Yes, you're right – I'm sure we witnessed exactly the same thing. I'll tell you what I saw – terrorists planning a spectacular attack against the West, men on their way to a meeting, a well-executed military strike and a world that is safer today than it was yesterday.'

'I saw that, too,' I replied. 'One of the pilots also said it was stealth, stealth on steroids.'

He thought for a long moment and then shook his head. 'No, it wasn't – that doesn't do it justice. Use stealth on a plane and it retains a signature – radar can find it. You could never get that through the Iranian air-defence shield. This is called cloaking technology, and it's been decades in the making.' He paused. 'It is going to change warfare – and the world – for ever.'

I thought he had finished, but he continued. 'Imagine a battlefield with four hundred tanks in position. They're not camouflaged, they're not hidden, they're attacking, but the enemy can't see them. They have no idea of their presence because they're cloaked. The first the enemy know of their existence is when the shells hit them.'

'How does it work?' I asked.

'The underlying science, they tell me, is fairly simple. We only see an object because it reflects light – stand in a room full of furniture and then black it out completely. The furniture is still there, but we can't see it because it doesn't reflect any light.'

'Cloaking technology,' he continued, 'is the idea – the science – of bending light around an object. If no light hits it, it can't be reflected and the object appears as if it isn't there. It's invisible.'

'The tiles?' I asked.

'Yes,' he replied. 'They manipulate and bend the light – you saw that they formed the entire casing of the missile, all controlled from a special compartment behind the warhead.'

'And this was the first time it's ever been used?'

'The first time,' he repeated.

'What are the plans for it – are other weapons systems being fitted with it?'

He smiled. 'You know I can't discuss that.'

I nodded, understanding. 'There is something else we have to talk about, though—'

'You're gonna have to hurry,' he said, looking over my shoulder. 'Here comes your ride.'

I turned and saw a Jeep with the doctor and one of the nurses on board kicking up a cloud of dust and driving straight towards us.

55

THE CONVOY OF THREE SUVS, ALL WITH THEIR HILLBILLY ARMOUR, stopped close to the GreenEnergy jet and the two nurses helped me out of the last vehicle and up the air-stairs.

We were giving the strike crew a ride home, and they – along with Falcon and the doctor – had gone ahead and were already in their seats by the time I made my way down the aisle.

The nurses started ushering me towards an empty row, but I stopped them, indicating Falcon sitting isolated at the front. 'I'll sit next to the director,' I said.

Falcon looked at me quizzically. 'It's about Kazinsky,' I said.

'What is there to say about him?' Falcon replied. 'He's dead.'

'He's not, Falcon – he wasn't in the convoy.'

'Just like you predicted? To play Sigmund for a moment, you

don't think the need to be right might be clouding your judgement here?'

'No, I don't,' I said.

'Simply because we didn't see his actual face when the missiles hit doesn't mean he wasn't in one of the vehicles,' Falcon continued. 'How many men were in them – twelve, fourteen? I don't think I could make out any specific faces.'

'It's not about seeing him. If he was there and had died, I think I would . . .' My voice trailed off.

'Have felt something?' Falcon asked, and smiled. 'A disturbance in the force – something like that?'

I didn't reply. He was right – it sounded ridiculous. 'You're tired – it's been a helluva few days. Worse for you – you're injured, you were exhausted before we even started. It'll seem much different when we're home and you're in rehab.'

I sat in silence, thinking, then I spoke quietly. 'Remember when you debriefed me in ICU?' I asked. 'I said how I had taken a different route to avoid going through the canyon?'

He looked at me. 'Sure I do. What's your point? You said you thought it was the perfect place for an ambush so you changed course. It was the sort of thing any good agent would do.'

'I heard gunfire,' I said.

'No wonder you avoided it, then,' he said, smiling. 'I would have, too.'

'No, this was like a premonition, Falcon. Gunfire from the future. It wasn't real,' I said.

He kept his eyes fixed on me, realized I was serious and the smile vanished. 'From the future? Gunfire?'

I nodded.

'This is scaring me,' he said.

'Me too,' I replied. 'I don't know what it was. An intuition? Some small, weird rip in time. Whatever it was, I heard it and I knew not to take that path.'

'Because you heard these sounds? Jeez,' he said, turning, looking down the body of the plane and starting to signal.

'No,' I said forcefully. 'I don't need a doctor.'

'Yes, we do,' he replied. 'I shouldn't have brought you – the stress, the fatigue. You were wounded. It was too much. I'm sorry—'

'No,' I repeated. 'Tell the doctor to go back.'

Our eyes met – two strong-willed men – and I think he realized I wasn't going to climb down. Finally, he raised his hand again, signalling the doctor to return to her seat.

'I was right,' I continued. 'The Army's soldiers *were* waiting in the canyon. That instinct or whatever it was that saved me – it was a hundred per cent correct, and I have the same feeling now, Falcon – Kazinsky's not dead. Not even close.'

He kept his eyes on me, a mix of concern and alarm. 'I knew it was a risk bringing you, but I had no choice. We're going to forget this conversation ever happened, okay? We say nothing to nobody. As soon as we get home, you go back to hospital, talk to Rebecca. We can sort this shit out.'

I shook my head – I wasn't mentally ill, at least not in my own mind. Then again, crazy people never think they are, do they?

'Listen,' he said, unwavering but trying to calm me. 'The Iranians will be at the strike site now. They'll try to identify the victims and then they'll contact the Russians – either for dental records, DNA or to inform them of Kazinsky's death. The NSA will hack the communication and that will prove he died. I want you to go back down, find a seat and get some sleep.'

'DNA testing and Iranians contacting the Russians will take months,' I replied. 'And who says the messages will be accurate? The Russians or Iranians might want us to think he's dead. It could be total disinformation—'

'In the name of God, Ridley!' he exploded, keeping his voice low. 'What the fuck else can we do? I want you to talk privately to the doctor now. That's an order.'

We stared at one another, then he turned and started to arrange his pillows. I had no choice, he had ordered me to leave, so I got to my feet and was about to head down the aisle when my visit to the Tomb stepped out of my memory.

'Voice-print him,' I said.

'What?' Falcon replied, frustrated, barely listening.

'You asked what else we can do. We voice-print him. Today,' I said.

'Look, just go and sleep, for God's sake.'

'No,' I said, risking pissing him off even more. 'Buster said the ground stations and satellites were grabbing data from the vehicles. Everybody in the convoy would have been talking as they drove from the airport – it means those conversations were recorded. What did you say – a dozen or so men? We listen to them, compare their voices to Kazinsky's, and if we get a match we will know he was there and he's dead.'

He stared at me.

'If not – I'll talk to the doctors and they can try and straighten me out,' I said.

'Don't be ridiculous,' he replied, caught between anger and pity. 'How do we get a match? What do we compare the voices to? We have never managed to capture even a few seconds of Kazinsky talking. How can you voice-print anyone without an original?'

'No,' I said. 'There is a recording of him. We do have an original we can match to—'

'What recording? We damn well don't,' Falcon said, still arguing, but with less conviction.

'The night before I left Langley to rendezvous with the courier,' I said. 'I didn't have a chance to tell you. I went down to the Tomb, and I heard him.'

'How?' he said tersely.

'I didn't try to voice-print him; I voice-printed his armoured vehicle.'

Falcon looked at me for a long beat – maybe I wasn't crazy after all. 'You voice-printed the vehicle and then followed it through the cauldron? At some point, you heard him?'

'Yes,' I replied.

'Why wasn't I informed?' he said icily.

'The recording was from years ago,' I said. 'It had no intelligence value.'

'I make those decisions, not you,' he snapped. 'Tell me what he said.'

I took a breath. 'What do you know about mammoth mining?'

'Large-scale stuff? Iron ore, coal, open-cast – that sort of thing?'

'No, *woolly* mammoths,' I replied.

'Elephants?' he said, staring at me – clearly I was back in the crazy category again.

56

CLAY POWELL, THE CHIEF ARCHIVIST, HAD EMERGED FROM HIS subterranean lair and, armed with digital drives containing a huge amount of video and audio recordings, was waiting for us in the conference room adjoining Falcon's office.

The director and I had talked throughout the long flight and, as a result, we were in a sombre mood – despite the seeming success of the attack in Zahedan – when we greeted Buster.

Falcon had called him from the plane, told him about the possibility of voice-printing Kazinsky, and the assistant director had organized the rest. As we took our seats, the wood panelling at one end of the room slid open to reveal a wall-sized hi-def video screen, the lights dimmed, and we were back in the narrow street in Zahedan.

Clay, a remote in his hand, was acting as ringmaster. 'From the audio recordings captured by the satellites, we identified sixteen different voices in the five vehicles,' he said. 'The men were in high spirits, talking excitedly about some form of spectacular, although it was clear that the individuals we marked as drivers and bodyguards had no knowledge of what it actually was. Still, we voice-printed everyone just to be thorough.'

The image on the screen changed to the scene from several years earlier: Kazinsky's battle-truck driving into the sunset as the arid landscape surrounding it turned into a blaze of red and orange. 'This is what we took as a reference,' Clay said. 'It was in the middle of him talking about a wolf attack. We then compared the sixteen voices travelling in the convoy to this voice—'

'And—' Falcon said.

'No match,' Clay said. 'Kazinsky was not part of the convoy on the way to the mosque and he didn't get missiled.'

Falcon drew a deep breath – he was too tired to try to hide his disappointment. I didn't say anything. In such instances there is no joy in being proven right. 'There is one other possibility,' Falcon said finally. 'He might have been asleep, or not talking—'

I abandoned my vow of silence. 'What – he suffers from some form of narcolepsy, Falcon? Every time he gets in a vehicle, he passes out?

If we want to silence him, we don't need to missile him – just send a taxi.'

The director had the good grace to smile. 'Okay, I agree,' he said. 'It's not likely—'

'It's impossible, Director,' Clay said.

'Why?' Falcon asked, surprised at Clay's certainty.

'When there was no voice match in the convoy,' Clay replied, 'I looked at the rest of the vehicles that had left Tora Bora West that morning – maybe Kazinsky had broken down or there'd been a change of plan.'

'Two hundred and seventy-four vehicles,' Buster reminded us.

'It was a big trawl, a lot of overtime, Director,' Clay said with a smile. 'I had forty people working on it, but after five hours we had listened to hundreds of voices and were getting nowhere, so you can understand – I was ready to abandon ship. Then we got lucky – one vehicle started to stand out. There were no voices accompanying it, nothing at all, and I finally realized – the driver was travelling alone. Out of two-hundred-and-seventy-odd vehicles, he was the only one. Most of the others had at least two passengers, so we started to focus on our loner—'

Clay hit the remote and the footage of a heavily modified Toyota pick-up with long-range fuel tanks and subsidiary water drums welded to its back appeared on the screen, kicking up a long plume of dust as it sped across an empty landscape. Despite my fatigue, I tried to look at the driver closely, but on the two or three occasions I glimpsed him through the heavily tinted glass I could see only that he was wearing a *keffiyeh* and dark glasses. It could have been anyone.

'If he had nobody to talk to, how did you hope to voice-match him?' Falcon asked.

'No idea,' Clay replied. 'But having no passengers was so unique we continued to dig through, pull up the footage of the vehicle and follow his route. Then it got weirder. After four or five hours and several hundred kilometres from the base, as the other vehicles were starting to loop for home, our guy kept going. Two more hours, then he stopped.'

'Where?' I asked.

'In the middle of nowhere,' Clay said, hitting the remote again. 'At one of the Army's long-range fuel and supply bunkers.'

Satellite footage of the Toyota pulling up to a man-made cave – built into a hillside, deep in shadow and protected by a heavy steel door – started to play on the screen. The driver didn't get out, he didn't do anything – he just stayed in the car – while, all around, the silence of his vast and desolate surroundings was broken only by the hum of the vehicle's air conditioning.

'For thirty-two minutes, he sat there,' Buster said. 'Then he took a call on a sat phone. In total, he spoke for twelve seconds – just long enough for us to run the software and compare the driver's voice to Kazinsky's.'

Falcon and I said nothing, waiting for the verdict. 'I'm sorry to tell you, it was him,' Clay said. 'Kazinsky was several hundred kilometres from the convoy in Zahedan.'

Falcon kept looking at the screen, probably thinking about how, for the second time, the US had failed to kill the so-called al-Tundra. Then he turned to me: 'You called it,' he said. 'I owe you an apology. I should have listened to my agent.'

I shrugged. It was a hollow victory. 'When did the sat call come through?' I asked.

'Eight minutes after the attack,' Buster replied.

'He had a spotter in Zahedan,' Falcon said, angry with himself for not anticipating it. 'Of course he did. After you escaped, he figured the Army's leadership was going to be targeted – exactly like you told me – so he had some joe, somebody, anybody, to tell him if there was an attack. That was who called him.'

I nodded – I was certain he was right. 'What did Kazinsky do after the call?' I asked Clay.

'Got out, unlocked the steel door, refuelled the Toyota, filled all the subsidiary tanks – wherever he was going, it was a long way – and drove out of the gully like the devil was on his back.'

'North?' I said, looking at footage Clay had brought up showing Kazinsky getting back into the Toyota, not even bothering to relock the bunker: the Army wouldn't be needing any of their supplies now; they might as well be left to the smugglers and the wild dogs.

'North for a while,' Clay said. 'Then he was gone – the satellite surveillance had finished with him and the other vehicles; everything was concentrated on the aftermath in the street in Zahedan. We don't know where he went.'

'Tehran,' I said. 'It's almost two thousand klicks, and for security he'd try and stay off-road – that's why he needed so much fuel.'

Tehran? The three of them looked at me, wondering why I was so sure. 'A city of ten million people,' I continued. 'Easy to get lost in. He'll burn his papers, go down to Nowshahr, the nearest port, and bribe a freighter skipper to take him across the Caspian. We know what's on the other side—'

'Russia,' Buster said.

'He's going home,' I replied. 'The safest place he knows – it's hard for us to enter and almost impossible to operate in. He'll regroup and raise as much money as he can. He'll have a plan – Bhopal, or something worse. Chemical or biological, if the past is anything to go on. Then he'll emerge again and we'll find him in the cauldron. Nobody's safe or ever will be—'

'Men change,' Falcon said. 'They get tired. He's military, and he might have finally decided he's done his duty and retire. He's in the Rodina, secure in the motherland, maybe he wants to slip quietly into the night.'

'No, he's really got something to prove now – not just to himself and to God but to us. We beat him, Falcon. He won't be giving up. Not today, not ever.'

We stood in silence – we had no way of knowing what he would do; only time would tell – and in the gloom of the late Sunday afternoon, I thought of him standing on the deck of an old freighter as it crossed the Caspian Sea. Then, out of nowhere – like gunfire from the future – I heard a distant howl.

In the vast machinery of the United States intelligence community, there was only one Denied Access Area spy who spoke the language of the Rodina, was well acquainted with its dangers and had seen Kazinsky in the flesh.

I knew then I would be going to Russia – I could already hear the wolves calling to me.

PART
THREE

PART
THREE

1

WHATEVER KAZINSKY'S PLAN MIGHT HAVE BEEN WHEN HE LEFT THE borderlands is a mystery and will remain so for ever. One thing was certain, though – the path he took was still potentially devastating.

Once Clay had proved that the Colonel was still alive, Falcon motioned me into his office and slumped into his chair. He may have prevented a deadly spectacular, but it had little currency with him; ultimately our elaborately orchestrated attempt to kill Kazinsky had been a failure. We had certainly been out-thought and there was no point in dwelling on it. It is better to light a candle than curse the darkness: 'Three or four months, the doctors estimate,' I said.

'For what?' he asked.

'Rehab,' I answered. 'We use the time to find him, then I go into Russia and finish it.'

'Nobody's going into Russia,' Falcon said wearily, lifting his hand to staunch my objections. 'We track him, put him on the watchlist, we do whatever it takes to make sure he never emerges but, until we see any different, he's finished—'

'No,' I said angrily. 'You think Kazinsky has given up? That he won't try to lay half the world to waste the first chance he gets? Bhopal may just be the name of a city, but it's so much more than that: it's an ideal, a mission, a desire.'

'Maybe you're right – maybe he'll try,' Falcon retorted. 'That's what he *wants* to do, but where are the means? The Army's finished and he's left the field. You'll say "not for long", but we can't target everyone who is *thinking* of doing us harm. That list would be endless. No, we concentrate on the groups with a plan, not men with a desire.'

I shook my head, on the other side of a great divide, but there was little point in trying to change his mind, not when failure was our companion and despair was in the house. 'Like I said,' Falcon continued, trying to put it to bed, 'we monitor him and, right now, the priority is for you to get into rehab. Have you called her?'

'Not yet,' I replied.

'Then do it, tell her you're on your way to Saratoga.'

2

I SAT IN THE FOYER OF A GRAND VICTORIAN MANSION – ALL TURRETS and domes – waiting for a rental car to enter the estate through tall gates adorned with gilded eagles and then negotiate the long drive past the ornamental lake before stopping at a front door large enough to accommodate the Hindenburg.

I had travelled to reputedly the best rehabilitation clinic in the country by chopper – leaving Langley, flying low along the Hudson Valley, looking out at the breathtaking foliage and following the river as it shone silver in the moonlight. Then the chopper banked hard, crossed Saratoga Lake, and put down on what had once been the croquet lawn of, arguably, America's most magnificent nineteenth-century mansion.

Built by one of the era's great robber barons, it was a remarkable place with countless barns, secluded guest houses, servants' quarters and a bathing pavilion all set among acres of manicured lawns. What do they say? Behind every great fortune lies a great crime? Although the plaque next to the front doors didn't mention it, the estate was in fact funded by one of the largest securities frauds in US history. Unfortunately, it meant that when, after several generations, the money ran out, the house – horrendously expensive to maintain – quickly fell into disrepair and seemed to be heading for the wrecking ball. It was only saved when the Mayo Clinic stepped in, spent yet another fortune and turned the four hundred acres into a world-class rehab centre.

As a result, on a Sunday evening I was sitting in a wheelchair in a foyer panelled in matched Cuban mahogany, a spectacular chandelier glowing overhead and electric logs lit up in a monumental fireplace, waiting for Rebecca. I had spoken to her as soon as I had left Falcon's office and she immediately arranged to fly to Albany and get a rental car to drive to meet me.

Just after 9 p.m., a set of headlights didn't, for once, head down to the modern buildings scattered among the trees but kept coming towards the house. I got up and limped through the doors.

Rebecca was already out of the car by the time I reached the bottom of the stone entrance steps, and I was so pleased to see her that I didn't register she wasn't alone. It was only when we had kissed that I looked over her shoulder and saw that someone had stepped out of the passenger's side and was standing next to the vehicle. Rebecca smiled. 'Guess who I found?' she said.

It was Laleh.

Shyly, she walked forward, unsure of what to do or how to react to me. They were strange circumstances, indeed – the last time we had seen each other was on the flight from Dubai. We stood and looked at one another and then, obviously learning Western ways very fast, she put out her hand to shake.

Instead, I reached out, and she half stumbled and fell into a hug. I felt her frame wrack with sobs.

I untangled Laleh's arms, stepped back and looked at her: the dark circles under her eyes had vanished, and rest and good food had taken the edge off her haggard frame. She looked like what she was – young, attractive, full of life – and while her hair hadn't grown much, a base-ball cap covering an almost-shaved head and a pair of boyfriend jeans gave her an unmistakably hip look that I was sure she didn't feel.

I smiled gently and swept my arm across the mansion. 'What do you think of our country cottage?' I asked. From her face, it was obvious she thought for a moment I might be serious.

'Don't listen to him,' Rebecca said. 'He's an idiot.'

Laleh laughed. 'Mom says the same about Dad.'

'There's a fire inside,' I said. 'Tea and coffee are on a trolley.'

She walked up the steps and, looking around in awe at the grand-eur of the place, was swallowed by the huge doors.

'One of the nurses told me a young woman had been brought in with you,' Rebecca explained. 'Once you were stabilized, I went and found her and then asked Norma if she wouldn't mind helping. Laleh has moved into her place.' Norma, a friend of Rebecca's, was a fellow intern and the daughter of one of DC's wealthiest families. 'They have a guest apartment over the garage and Norma and I have been taking her on night rounds – now she's decided she wants to be a doctor.' Rebecca laughed. 'Remind you of anyone?' She paused. 'She told me about the beach.'

'She shouldn't have,' I said.

'Classified?' Rebecca asked.

'Of course,' I replied.

'What are you gonna do? Arrest me?'

'Maybe,' I said, taking her hand in mine. 'I'll have to get some handcuffs.'

'Promises, promises. Anyway, it doesn't worry me. I'll call my buddy Falcon.'

I laughed. 'Oh yeah, I forgot how close you two are.' I turned serious. 'Did Laleh tell you about the refugee camps and crossing into Iran alone to look for her father?'

'Yes, she did,' Rebecca replied.

'Did she tell you that, out in the Gulf, she saved my life?'

'No, she didn't,' Rebecca said, taken aback.

3

'WILL THERE ALWAYS BE SOMEONE THERE FOR YOU, SOMEONE LIKE Laleh?' Rebecca asked after I'd told her about how we reached Dubai. We had walked down from the house, found a bench and were looking out at the lake.

'Someone to save my life? I'm sure there won't be. With any luck, I won't need it.'

'Maybe you're right, but what about the future? How long do we live like this? How long do I wait for that car to come down the road?' she asked, more in sorrow now than anger.

'Two more years – that's all I need. I'll be three months at least in rehab, maybe longer – they told me at MedStar I have to be able to run twenty miles a day before they'll even consider declaring me fit. So – it leaves twenty months of active service.'

'And then?' she said. 'What – another twenty months? Then another twenty?'

'No,' I replied. 'In two years, Buster will take early retirement – he says he'll recommend me for the job and I'm sure Falcon will agree.' I turned her face to look at me. 'Assistant Director, and I get to use my experience to run other agents in the field. But I won't even be considered for the job if I ask for a reassignment now. It's an investment, twenty months – then we settle down and raise up a family.'

'Twenty months?' she replied. 'It's not that long.'

'It's not,' I said, encouraged.

'And how long does it take to kill a man, even someone as highly trained as you? A second? Let's be generous and call it two. How many two seconds are there in twenty months?'

What was there for me to say?

'You've been lucky so far,' she continued. 'You know the trouble with luck, though? It runs out.' She held my gaze and I could feel her heart beating hard through her jacket. 'You want twenty months, and you can have it. But you give me something in return.'

'What?' I asked.

'We try for a family now,' she answered.

I was shocked, and it took me a second to reply. 'You're willing to do that – to take the risk that you might have to raise a child alone?' I asked.

She shrugged. 'It's not much of a risk. Once you hold a baby in your arms, I think you're going to change your mind – there's a reason why DNA is built like a chain.'

4

FALCON CALLED REGULARLY AND, THOUGH HE WAS CHECKING ON MY health, it soon became clear from our conversations that he was as good as his word: he was using as much of the agency's resources as he could spare to try and locate Kazinsky.

It was a fruitless exercise; we had virtually nothing to go on – my belief that the Colonel had driven north and made a run for home was nothing more than conjecture – and when, after six weeks, three agency teams had found no trace of him, Falcon decided to pull Clay Powell out of the Tomb and hand the task over to him and Madeleine O'Neill.

The decision reassured me – Kazinsky might have disappeared, but it told me Falcon was far more worried about him than he had ever said.

Ten days after they took on the assignment, I got a text on a Saturday morning from Clay saying that he and Madeleine were coming to see me. I tried to contact them, but they were already underway, and so it was without any knowledge of the reason for their visit that I greeted them at the front doors. They had flown in on an agency jet with two close protection officers and it was soon apparent that they had already made at least one unusual arrangement: the normal Saturday movie marathon for patients and staff, held in the mansion's old ballroom, had been cancelled.

With me limping – I still hadn't been allowed to even start trying to run yet – we headed towards the converted theatre as Clay told me that Falcon had suggested he and Madeleine come to Saratoga to give me an update. I knew nobody in the agency was *that* thoughtful but, beyond it, he didn't offer any explanation.

Once the protection officers had checked the nearby rooms for civilians and had taken up positions to prevent anyone walking in, we settled into our seats and waited while Clay started to project images and videos from his laptop on to the movie screen. The first of them showed a Caspian port ringed by mountains: it was Nowshahr, the Iranian port where I had suggested Kazinsky would have boarded a freighter to take him north.

'Using the footage of his face when he was refuelling at the bunker, the first teams searched whatever CCTV of the docks they could find, looking for a match,' Clay said. 'When that was unsuccessful, they tried a port to the west called Bandar-e Azali. No luck there either, but that didn't mean he hadn't found a boat – it just meant they couldn't identify him from the footage.'

'So they attacked it from the other end,' Madeleine explained. 'They drew up a list of every boat that had sailed from the two ports in the ten days after the Zahedan attack. Then they checked their routes and tried to see if they could find him disembarking at one of the three Russian ports on the Caspian.'

'Still nothing?' I asked. They shook their heads.

'So the analysts and agents started thinking that maybe he never got on a boat and they needed to look further afield,' Madeleine continued. 'A big job got even bigger until, finally, Falcon lost patience and we got involved.'

'We went back to square one,' Clay said. 'We looked again at the port at Nowshahr—'

'Then, after ten days of zero success, Clay had one of his moments,' Madeleine said, interrupting. 'He asked: what if Kazinsky was on a boat that had left Nowshahr but it didn't make it to its destination. Say something happened and it had to make an unscheduled stop and he got off. It wouldn't be in any of the footage or data we had seen—'

'A breakdown, an event like that?' I asked, leaning forward.

'Yeah, maybe,' Clay replied. 'Or even this.'

He projected an image from a weather satellite of a storm system sweeping across Iran and over the vast expanse of the Caspian Sea. It was an impressive sight – the Caspian is the largest inland body of water in the world and the storm blanketed almost all of it. Apart from its size, the sea is also unique in another respect: if you travel north, Europe is on the left bank and Asia is on the right; you literally sail between two continents.

'Rough gales had been brewing for days,' Clay explained. 'This one hit two days after the strike in Zahedan – just enough time for Kazinsky to make the drive, get on board a boat unseen and be in open water.'

'The meteorological reports showed that the wind had been blowing hard from the south all day,' Madeleine said, opening her briefcase and pulling out a sheaf of papers. 'Then, at nightfall, it really ramped up. With every hour the waves grew wilder and the troughs steeper. By midnight it was a storm for the ages.'

'The maritime records showed there was one boat that ran into real trouble,' Clay said. He brought up an image of an old freighter with rust streaks down her hull and black smoke belching from her funnel. 'Her name was the *Caspian Legend*.'

'Not the sort of vessel you'd want to be on board in a storm,' I said.

'Built in '74, she should have been scrapped years ago,' Clay said. 'The skipper had the same opinion as you and says so in his report – she was barely seaworthy in good weather, he claimed.'

Madeleine produced another document, handwritten in Russian, and gave it to me. I skimmed the captain's account and it told me enough to realize what a nightmare it must have been on board – every old steel plate shuddering and moaning under the onslaught of the elements, the water from her plunging bow coming aboard like a black wall, the rusted deck struggling to emerge from the flood and her foghorn blaring not for any apparent reason other than to shout defiance in the face of terror.

According to his report, the *Legend* was carrying a heavy cargo of used mining parts out of Tehran, heading for the Russian port of Makhachkala, when – at 3.14 a.m. – part of the load in the hold broke free and shifted. It would have capsized almost any other vessel but, reading between the lines, she was clearly under the command of a master mariner. You would never have guessed from his unprepossessing appearance on the attached photo that it was his skill that dragged his ship back from the brink.

As the storm reached its climax – with the twelve-person crew cowering in the companionway, fully aware that there was no hope of launching the lifeboats, let alone surviving in them – the helmsman saw some distant lights of buildings on the European shore.

'Baku,' he yelled to the skipper, and pointed. The faint glimmer was coming from LED screens covering the Flame Towers – a trio of weird, pointed skyscrapers – and it gave the crew a chance to identify exactly where they were.

Baku, the capital of Azerbaijan, sits at the end of a peninsula and – guided by its lights – the skipper and helmsman managed to crawl and wallow towards it, around the point and limp into the city's port.

I laid the document aside and looked at Clay and Madeleine. 'So,' Clay said. 'We had a ship that had left Tehran heading for a Russian port but had made an unscheduled stop in Baku. Unless you looked at the detailed records, nobody would have known.'

I nodded. 'But was Kazinsky on board?' I asked. 'Did he get off in Baku?'

5

'NOT ACCORDING TO THE CREW LIST OR THE SHIP'S MANIFEST,' CLAY replied.

'But he wouldn't be included on either, would he?' I said. 'It was against every law or maritime regulation to take on board an undocumented passenger.'

'Of course – but for the right amount of money, it might happen,' Clay said, smiling. 'So we searched every piece of footage we could find of the port from the time the *Legend* arrived in Baku until the moment she left.' He brought up on the screen grainy, fractured video of the docks, the warehouses and the ship. 'But it was hopeless; the storm had destroyed most of the port's surveillance cameras and the place was in chaos.'

'No sign of him at all?' I asked.

They shook their heads. 'Then Madeleine asked me how much I thought he would have had to pay the ship's skipper for the ride,' Clay said.

'It was idle chit-chat, but that got me thinking,' Madeleine said. 'Guys like Kazinsky are terrorists. They don't carry wallets with wads of paper money or have credit cards and bank accounts – how did he pay for it? Physically pay?'

'*Tolahs*,' I said, realizing.

'That's right,' she replied. 'Highly valuable, easy to transport and hide – he would have had no folding money, but he probably had a bag full of them.'

'I can see where this is heading,' I said. 'There's a street in Baku, narrow and lined with stone buildings, close to the old walled city, right?'

Madeleine and Clay turned to one another, surprised. I didn't tell them, but I wouldn't have been able to make the leap except that, many years before, early in my career, I had been to Baku.

Not many Westerners had back then. A city of two and a half million people, it was remote and little visited. Bordered by Russia to the north, it was the site of a handful of skyscrapers and scores of anonymous apartment blocks. At one time, however, a hundred years ago, it was the wealthiest city in the world, home then to the Rothschilds and other wealthy European notables. With extraordinary mansions, camel races with trained monkeys as jockeys, opium dens and desperate men and women selling jewels – and a whole lot more – on the streets around the casino, it was probably the most exotic too.

Alone, I spent five nerve-wracking but memorable days there. I had flown in as an oil-rig technician looking for work, but my real purpose was to meet a middle-aged communications expert at a nearby Russian naval facility, a sad-eyed woman – or so the photos of her indicated – who was willing to exchange a raft of valuable codes for enough money to feed a gambling habit she could no longer contain.

On the last night of my mission, after waiting for a coded message from her that never came, I realized that she had either won really big at the tables or had been unmasked by the FSB, the successor to the KGB. Incapable of sleep in case it was the latter and my own life was in danger, I walked to the waterfront to wait for my flight out the next morning. It was there, well after midnight with a long swell breaking on the shore and an electrical storm rolling in – a huge show of lightning but no rain – I saw something that was extraordinary, almost impossible for a young guy not long out of Florida to believe.

About a hundred and forty years ago Baku was the centre of the world's first, and greatest, oil boom; the source of its original wealth. A newly invented fuel called kerosene had suddenly replaced whale oil for lighting houses and businesses, and no place on earth had more oil – the raw material from which kerosene was derived – than Azerbaijan. Its newly minted oil barons and the endless caravans of wildcatters who arrived overland from Turkey and the Middle East barely had to even drill a well; in Baku, oil literally bubbled out of the ground.

In what seemed little more than the blink of an eye, the great businessmen of their era had converged on the walled city and lined the streets with grand mansions, half of which appeared to be French chateaux-by-way-of-Baghdad with limestone facades, glass cupolas and numerous minarets. Restraint didn't seem to be in anyone's vocabulary – least of all the city fathers'. They only constructed one great public building, but it wasn't a hospital or a university – it was an exact replica of the Beaux Arts casino in Monte Carlo. More than anything, it seemed to capture the tenor of their times.

Then, at the height of its pomp, death came to the Baku of old. Oil was much too precious a commodity for its northern neighbour to ignore. In 1920, shortly after the Russian Revolution, the Red Army rolled towards the city walls and the Rothschilds and their kind fled. Baku quietly slipped into a coma but, even so, some vestiges of the city's earlier life remained: now and again you could stumble on opulent mansions with overgrown gardens and, in a few scattered places, oil still seeped from the ground.

Most commonly it was from underwater fissures that quietly opened up, and there were times – apparently – when you could stand on the windswept shore and see oil spread across the surface of the water. On rare occasions it caught fire. That night, I saw it.

A shaft of forked lightning had hit the water, igniting the oil, setting the sea close to the shore ablaze. As the waves rolled in, other people came down to watch and we stood in silence. To this day, I, for one, have never seen anything that filled me with so much wonder and primal fear as the fire-surf of Baku.

It was no surprise then that I had never forgotten the city, and perhaps that was why I could recall, even after a decade or more, a crooked street with several blind alleys where sharp-eyed men – traders – sat inside old stone buildings and motioned for me to enter. 'We're talking about "the Street of Gold" – right?' I asked Madeleine and Clay.

They laughed. 'You got it,' Madeleine said. 'Forty shops – maybe more – where you can buy and sell gold without too many questions asked. If he was in Baku, that's where he would go and change at least some of his *tolahs* for Russian rubles. I mean, the skipper would have taken *tolahs*, but you can't exactly buy a sandwich with a gold bar, can you?'

Clay pulled up footage of the street, which was exactly as I remembered it. 'Because of the value of what is traded there,' Clay said, 'it is under constant CCTV coverage.'

He started to play a grab from one of the cameras, a wide shot of the street, and there – among scattered groups of pedestrians – I saw Kazinsky. The *keffiyeh*, the sunglasses and the dust-covered clothes were gone and in their place were a dark-blue reefer jacket, jeans and work boots. With his beard trimmed and his military tattoos covered, he could have been any one of hundreds of seafarers passing through the port.

'We know from the time code on the CCTV,' Clay continued, 'that he was in the street after the *Legend* had left to resume its journey north. So he stayed in Baku.'

'And now?' I asked.

'We don't know. After he left the gold dealer, we lost him,' Clay said. 'We tried voice-printing, but there are almost 3 million people in greater Baku, and that got us nowhere. So we turned to Friday prayers at the most fundamentalist mosques. We got a grab on him – just a few sentences – but we couldn't track him. He's gone again.'

I cursed quietly.

'That was why Falcon suggested we see you,' Madeleine said, explaining their visit at last. 'He thought you might have some idea . . .'

Originally, he was heading for the port of Makhachkala. But why? I asked myself. There were other Russian ports much further north. He had bought a ticket to Makhachkala, but that was probably because the *Legend* was the only boat that would give him passage. He had ended up in Baku by accident.

'He was far south in the largest country in the world,' I said. 'Two thousand klicks from Moscow and five thousand from Siberia; he could have gone anywhere.'

Madeleine and Clay nodded – they had run into the same wall.

'You said you got a voice grab from him in a mosque. What was it?' I asked.

'He was speaking to the imam,' Madeleine replied. 'Kazinsky told him he'd been at sea during the storm. At the height of it, the boat was only moments from destruction, but the Colonel said he was certain that Allah – *subhanahu wa ta'ala*, the most glorified, the most high – was protecting him. He said he had no doubt his life was saved for a reason.'

I sat up straighter. 'And did he give him any idea what that purpose might be?'

'He may have,' Clay replied. 'But it was a big mosque, the call went up for prayers to start and we lost the rest of the conversation in all the voices.'

Like Rebecca had said, luck runs out. Beyond that, without any ideas, I couldn't be of any help to them; I was in rehab and all I could do was start to run.

6

IT WAS A FEW PAINFUL PACES IN THE GYM AT FIRST, THEN THROUGH the mansion's grounds as I grew stronger – the trees of the Hudson Valley turning into an even greater riot of gold and copper as the weeks passed – and finally along the streets surrounding our home.

I would wait until Rebecca went to work – she was on the

graveyard shift at MedStar – and very late, while the world was sleeping, I would pound down the empty roads, pushing my legs harder, building the muscle, forcing myself to overcome the stiffness and recurring pain in my foot. I ran with anger and determination, but I was never alone; I ran with my memories.

Week after week I would push the distance a little further, and I was close to the twenty-mile goal when, late one night, the trees around me were suddenly illuminated from behind me. I turned and saw a car – an unusual sight on that route so late – coming slowly towards me. Its headlights were on high beam and too dazzling for me to identify anything about the vehicle.

Old habits die hard, I guess, and so I stepped aside, deep into the shadows, keeping several thick-trunked trees between myself and the vehicle, all the while cursing that in my naivety and foolishness, I hadn't brought a pistol with me.

The car slowed but was still approaching, and it was only when the headlights were almost passed and I was out of their glare that I recognized the car and saw who was at the wheel. It was Rebecca, and I stepped out of the shadows, looking at her in relief and exasperation as she lowered the passenger window.

'Sorry, I didn't mean to scare you,' she said.

'I thought you were at work,' I said, feeling relief wash over me.

'They made a mistake and doubled up on the roster. I got to leave early so I went home, and when you weren't there, I thought I'd come find you.' She looked around at the all-enveloping darkness. 'When you run, where do you go?' she asked.

'It changes,' I said. 'Usually it's another six miles down this road and then, when I—'

'I didn't mean that,' she said. 'I meant in your head.'

In the gloom, we looked at one another. 'Why don't you get in?' she continued. I climbed in, and she started to drive. 'Is it the same every night?'

'The thoughts? A lot of it,' I replied.

'You go back there – to the beach? Places like that?'

I said nothing. She swung left, down a narrow track, and I knew she was heading for a secluded nature reserve with huge ponds and overhanging willows. Just as we stopped, a wedge of wild geese heading south for the winter came into land in the bright moonlight. They looked magnificent, and, quite by accident, the sight of them was enough to take the edge off the strained silence between us. Rebecca reached out her hand and took hold of mine.

'I asked if you went back to the beach?'

'Other places. A canyon, mostly. I hear things, Rebecca,' I said, still looking at the geese. 'I don't know why, but sometimes I sense things about what lies ahead.' I turned and saw she was looking at me sceptically. I sort of smiled. 'Yeah, I know . . . but it saved my life.'

'Was this with Laleh?' she asked.

'No, before that,' I replied. 'I went to meet a man and, on the way, I was heading into the canyon when I got a sense of men opening fire. I took a different route and found out later that there was an ambush specially laid for me. It wasn't imagination – I already knew it, Rebecca.'

She stared at me. 'Afterwards – did you find the man you went to meet? Did he tell you it was an ambush?'

'No, I found out another way. When I got close to the rendezvous, the man had been crucified. His family were chained nearby, and I wondered if my life had been spared so that I could help his wife and their two little girls.'

'Did you?' Rebecca asked. 'Help them?'

'I'm not sure what happened to them afterwards, but I gave 'em a chance,' I said. 'It was long range, but I had a marksman's rifle and I sometimes think maybe that was part of some grand design, too. I shot their three guards.'

'Killed them?' she wanted to know.

'Yes. One of them must have been quite something as a kid – when he was twelve, he and his brother had nursed their father for days as he lay dying in the wilderness. Then they carried him out and gave him a proper burial.' I paused. 'I shot him half a dozen times, I had to, but sometimes I ask myself – how much evil a man like me has to do so that good can prevail.'

'Quite a bit, it seems,' she replied coolly. I felt her hand tighten in mine. 'What about now – do you still hear things?'

'Sometimes I hear wolves,' I said. 'They tell me I'm going to Russia.'

'What else?'

'Ruins. I've been seeing ruins. No detail; just a city, I think. There's a large sign on a wrecked building: "Be—" and a lot of missing letters. Then "Good—" and more spaces. *Be Good*, but there's death all around it,' I replied.

'Yours?' she asked, taking a breath, clearly fearing it was.

'No,' I said simply, and kept looking out into the dark night. 'Yours.'

7

I TURNED BACK TOWARDS HER AT LAST AND WE HELD EACH OTHER'S gaze, but nowhere in her face – unlike my own, I am sure – did I see any fear. Just sadness and a profound concern for me. 'Do you think,' she said gently, 'you might be suffering from some form of – I'm talking as a doctor here – post-traumatic stress disorder?'

I smiled just as gently; there was no doubt she had a great bedside manner. I shook my head. 'No.' Then I thought about it. 'On the other hand, I don't suppose anyone suffering from PTSD realizes it, do they?'

'Often not,' she said, trying to grin back. 'But you'd be a perfect candidate for it.' She shrugged. 'And I'm judging by just what I know about. I'm sure there's more.'

'Definitely more – and maybe you're right,' I responded. 'But all I know is this – I heard things, but not with my ears, and because of it I didn't die. What do you call that, Becca – an illness or a blessing?'

'I think you're wounded, Ridley,' she replied, avoiding the question. 'That's all I'm saying. Deeply wounded.'

'It might be a good thing,' I said. 'You know what they say – a crack is how the light gets in.'

8

WE SAT TOGETHER, MOSTLY IN SILENCE, UNTIL DAWN HIT THE PONDS. I had my arm around her, both of us thinking, I am sure – in totally different ways – about the danger that threatened the person we loved more than anything in the world. That wasn't an exaggeration – we had both lost our parents and there was no other family in our lives; we only had each other.

'Home?' she said.

'I'll see you there.'

'You're going to run?' she replied, shaking her head and smiling.

I nodded – I couldn't explain why, but I had a feeling that I had to be fit if I was going to have a chance of saving her.

She drove off and I fell into a loping rhythm, picking up the pace, pounding the asphalt harder and starting to think, as I always did, about Kazinsky: the crackling hatred, the desperate desire for personal revenge for the killing of his brother, the cold-blooded cruelty, the command presence, the vast military experience and the profound belief that he was the elect of Allah. All that electricity and no plug, was what I kept telling myself. God help us when he found the connection.

I ran even faster and, once again, I imagined him on the deck of the *Caspian Legend*, watching the storm clouds gather, feeling the wind build, and I wondered: did he regret he'd had no choice but to bribe his way on to a ship that was barely seaworthy?

I slowed suddenly as a thought struck me and I found myself standing motionless in the middle of the road. But he did have a choice. He hadn't been forced to buy a ticket on the *Caspian Legend*. He had no reason to believe that he was being tracked by us; sixteen men had died in the missile attack and he could have been any one of them. It was only the voice-printing that had proven otherwise, and he had no idea we could do that. Instead, he must have thought he was safe at the port. There was no pursuit, as far as he knew – he could have waited days for a ship, weeks if he had to, but he chose to travel on the *Legend*. It meant he *wanted* to go to Makhachkala. There was nothing random about it.

Why Makhachkala? I asked, starting to run again, newly energized, drawing up a mental image of a map of the North Caucasus. As if I was clicking on Google Maps, I kept pulling back from the city, expanding my field of view. Then I saw it: there may have been nothing for him in Makhachkala, but there certainly was two hundred klicks away.

I launched into a sprint, heading down pedestrian-only lanes, coming out on to another country road and pounding across a kids' playground. The shortcut took me to a wider road, where I saw the red tail-lights of a car waiting at a stop sign. I picked up the pace and hammered on its trunk as it started to take off.

Rebecca, startled, looked in the rear-view, saw that it was me and stopped. I opened the passenger door, gasping. 'Change your mind?' she asked. 'Decided you want to spend the morning in bed with your wife?'

'Langley,' I said, sweating hard, barely able to breathe.

'Where else?' she said, shaking her head in despair.

9

ONLY THE NIGHT CREW WERE WORKING, SO CLAY, MADELEINE AND I had no difficulty finding a group of desks in a quiet corner of the Tomb to set up as our base.

Calling Clay from Rebecca's car, I told him that I believed Kazinsky had been en route to Grozny – the capital of Chechnya – when the storm hit the *Legend*, forcing them to dock in Baku. Clay had instantly suggested the three of us meet in the Tomb and – given that the most common language in Chechnya was Russian – he called in Darren, the long-haired archivist with the robotic voice, who was also fluent in the language.

Footage of a bombed-out cityscape was already playing on our computer screens as he took off his backpack and his bicycle helmet. 'What's that?' he said in his usual monotone.

'The heart of darkness – even for Russia,' I replied. 'Grozny.'

'Capital of Chechnya,' he said, like he was reading a grocery list. 'You've been there?'

I smiled and shook my head. 'I can't tell you that.'

'I understand,' he said, and indicated an apocalyptic scene playing on one of the screens, smoke billowing from buildings. 'Vacation, I guess.'

I turned and stared at him, taken aback – he couldn't be serious.

'That was a joke,' he said flatly.

'Yeah, I got that.' I looked at him anew, starting to warm to him. 'Don't tell anyone, but I went there for intelligence work a long time ago,' I said as he sat down.

'It is in Russia, but it's Islamic,' I continued, starting to brief him. 'It has more than a few radical mosques and a lot of the go-hard guys from Spetsnaz were Chechens. The man we're looking for is the guy you heard talking about wolves in the battle-truck. My guess is he knows somebody in the city.'

'You were there during this?' Madeleine asked, indicating the carnage on the screens.

'No, before my time,' I replied. 'That's just after the Soviet Union collapsed. The Russians – the province's former overlords – started fighting groups of wild Chechen separatists, and the Chechen warlords fought each other, and the Islamic fundamentalists fought everybody. Peace deals were eventually signed, promises were broken and yet another war broke out: the same players, but with different allegiances and better weapons. The undertakers were the only winners, though – out of a population of little more than one point two million, up to three hundred thousand died.'

I pointed at the piles of rubble and the occasional shell of a forlorn building. 'According to the United Nations, it was the most wrecked metropolis on earth. It might as well have been Stalingrad in the Second World War.

'By the time I got there, the city had been rebuilt – which made it a kind of strange experience. There was no history there, not a building or a house; its past only really existed in the hearts and minds of its people.'

I couldn't tell them, but I had been in Grozny on my way to Baku to meet the gambler-cum-spy with the naval codes and I had spent several days wandering the miles of housing blocks and its clutch of nondescript skyscrapers. Thankfully, it meant I knew something of its geography and layout.

'So, how did Kazinsky get to Grozny from Baku?' I asked.

'There are flights,' Darren said, having moved ahead, bringing up data on his screen.

'He probably destroyed his papers,' I said. 'He wouldn't have been able to board a plane. Even if he could, he would have known passenger lists are notoriously easy to hack – he wouldn't have taken the chance.'

'No point in him taking another boat to Makhachkala,' Madeleine added, looking at an electronic map. 'The port is still a three-hour drive from Grozny. He might as well—'

'Have gone from Baku by road,' Clay said.

I nodded. 'Hitch a ride and pay some truck driver not to see a stowaway in his cargo trailer. What are the road connections like?' I asked, but Darren was already marking them on the electronic map.

'Grozny is six hundred klicks from Baku – eight or nine hours,' Clay said. 'The coastal route, the E119, is the only realistic option.'

'I can't see how it helps,' Madeleine said. 'If we are right, all we know is that he was on a long stretch of highway. So what?'

'Gas stations,' I said. 'That distance and eight hours on the road – the driver is going to have to stop for fuel and food.'

'We try to find CCTV footage of every gas station? That won't be easy,' Clay said.

'We've got an advantage,' I replied. 'How many gas stations on the highway?'

'Ten,' Darren said, before anyone else could finish counting them on the map.

'It could be worse,' I replied. Although years had passed, I was confident that one thing hadn't changed: as it wound its way north, the E119 passed four large Russian military bases positioned to protect the country's southern border. It meant the area was strategically important, and that led to another consequence—

'Don't ask me how I know,' I said to the others, 'but the road is under constant US satellite surveillance; so, inadvertently, are those ten gas stations.'

10

THE TASK OF TRAWLING THROUGH MILLIONS OF FEET OF ARCHIVED satellite footage of ten service centres was made infinitely easier because we knew exactly what day Kazinsky had been in the Street of Gold.

Because of the way he had ended up in Baku, there was no reason for him to delay his departure, so we targeted that day and the three that followed. Clay immediately called up the footage, we split it among ourselves and started reeling through endless scenes of the highway and its pit-stops.

We had stopped for food and coffee – but nothing else – when Madeleine started on the footage of the seventh fuel station. Halfway through it – her eyes glazing over at the sight at another long-haul truck and coastal delivery van – a white eighteen-wheeler entered the parking lot, its trailer emblazoned with a group of penguins sitting on an iceberg. Apart from that there was nothing to distinguish it from the hundreds of other big-rigs we had seen.

Madeleine watched the driver swing out of the cabin and head for the bathroom. Moments later, as she was about to turn away, the passenger door opened, a man got out and a high-pitched alert shattered the calm of the room. The artificial intelligence that Clay and Darren had set up to assist in the search – or at least its facial recognition software – had found a potential match and we all gathered around Madeleine's desk.

Only a fraction of the guy's face was visible. No human would have paid it any mind and it was possible the artificial intelligence had got it wrong. The four of us stared at the man's ear and jaw, hoping more would be revealed. A second passed, and then another, until he turned to look at a group of fast-food joints and faced us—

Against overwhelming odds, we had found Kazinsky.

In the shadow of the big-rig, he scanned the food outlets, the fuel pumps and the store; all of them had CCTV cameras on their rooves, covering the surroundings except for the parking bays, and the terrorist – as smart as ever – must have decided not to approach and risk being taped. Instead, he stayed in the shadow of the rig, pacing up and down.

It is strange how history can turn on the smallest thing: Saloth Sar, a young Cambodian studying in Paris, was crossing the road one afternoon when an out-of-control vehicle travelling at high speed grazed his thigh. Bystanders at the time, this was in 1950, said that another inch and he would have been dead. He survived, returned to Cambodia, adopted the *nom de guerre* Pol Pot and more than two million Cambodians died. An inch to change the future, that was all.

In Baku, it was more than likely that Kazinsky had planned to travel in the cargo trailer of a big-rig and, had he done so, he would never have got out to stretch his legs, the satellite would not have captured his image and we would have lost him. But the vehicle he was travelling in never gave him the option to remain hidden: the penguins were the logo of a company that sold frozen fish and Kazinsky had to travel up front because the trailer was a mobile freezer. Twenty minutes inside it would have killed him.

Once again – nothing but an inch in it.

11

AS SOON AS CLAY AND DARREN HAD RE-PROGRAMMED IT, THE software had no difficulty in following the white rig. It wasn't as if there were dozens of penguins on the road.

Surrounding Madeleine's desk, we watched the footage of it leaving pit-stop seven, then travel through an increasingly industrialized area south of Grozny and then pull to the side of the road opposite a railway station. 'Don't get on a damned train,' I said.

Instead, Kazinsky jumped out of the cabin, sprinted across the road – dodging the traffic – and reached a taxi rank adjoining the station. If you have seen how people drive in Russia and its satellite republics, it would come as no surprise to learn that the late-model cab had both fenders missing and a large dent in the driver's door. Again, this made it easy to follow.

The taxi pulled into the traffic and headed towards the centre of the city, travelling down a wide road that had once been known as Lenin Prospekt. It passed the city's grand mosque – one of the largest in Europe and built on the site of the bombed-out presidential palace – and ten minutes later reached the main artery of downtown. Its name told you more than any history book about who had eventually won the decades of conflict in Chechnya. It was called Vladimir Putin Prospekt.

Finally, we saw the taxi enter an area dense with scores of housing blocks, every building as anonymous and poorly constructed as the next. As good as the satellite imagery was, it had no chance of showing which apartment doorbell – among the dozens on the panel – Kazinsky pressed and was buzzed in by so it was impossible for us to identify his contact or friend.

Instead, Madeleine called in the NSA and we spent hours searching through footage hacked from three CCTV cameras that were covering the block's various entrances. Of course, the surveillance state is a terrible thing – until it's past midnight and you are trying to track the most dangerous man in the world.

Thankful for the lack of privacy, we saw Kazinsky emerge from the apartment block three days after he had arrived. Exactly what he had done or spoken about during that time will never be known, but early in the morning he walked out with a man who looked like he had been carved out of granite. Bald and bullet-headed, he was in his forties with broad shoulders, a lot of muscle in his arms and an untrimmed black beard.

Madeleine immediately opened her laptop and accessed her database, but while she couldn't face-match him to any former ISIS fighter, one aspect of his background was evident. On a bulging bicep, just visible under his tight T-shirt, I saw that he had a tattoo of the Grim Reaper who instead of carrying a scythe over his shoulder had a Russian assault rifle. The inked image was almost mandatory among the Spetsnaz.

We watched as the two men got into an old Lada and, with his companion driving, headed out of the city. They entered a heavily forested area and followed the blacktop for twenty miles. This was all captured by a satellite targeting a nearby chemical factory, closely aligned to the Russian military, said to be producing industrial chlorine but, quite possibly, something far more sinister. At an abandoned roadhouse facing a large intersection, its overgrown surroundings still littered with old shell casings, they turned left and followed an electrified fence that separated the forest from a huge expanse of flat land completely free of any vegetation. It was a military airfield.

The car slowed and turned towards a set of steel entry gates dominated by a concrete blockhouse and guarded by a dozen Russian soldiers. We stared at the footage, with no idea what Kazinsky was doing.

'You know this place?' Clay asked me.

'No,' I replied. 'But it's military, and we're dealing with one of the world's leading terrorists. It's not a good combination.' I stopped the tape. 'Call Falcon. He needs to see this.'

12

THE DIRECTOR ARRIVED TWENTY MINUTES LATER, AS IMMACULATELY
dressed as ever, even though it was long before sunrise. The four of us
had been staring at archived footage for almost twenty-four hours
and the strain was starting to show.

'You look wasted,' he said to us as he approached, before pausing
and shooting me a loaded glance. 'And what the hell are you doing
here? Aren't you supposed to be in rehab?'

'Yes, technically, but you might find this is worth it.'

'Why? What have you got?'

'We're not sure – but it's interesting.'

He stopped at the computer screen, nodded a greeting to Clay and
Madeleine, and then looked at Darren. I handled the introduction
and, as it turned out, it was almost worth staying up all night to
witness.

'Darren James – this is Falcon Rourke, the CIA director,' I said.

'Hello, Mr Rourke,' Darren replied in his standard monotone. 'I
have seen your photograph in the paper, sir. It is an honour to meet
you.' He extended his hand.

Falcon shook it, keeping a wary eye on Darren. He'd probably
never actually heard anyone speak like Darren did before. 'No need
to be nervous – we're just trying to unravel something here.'

'Oh no, Darren's not nervous,' Clay explained. 'He's always like
that.'

Falcon looked like it was the first time he had ever encountered one
of the agency's more unusual employees.

'Darren speaks Russian,' I said.

'Interesting,' Falcon said. 'Where did you study, Darren? Yale,
Harvard?'

'In my basement,' Darren replied. 'I did it on Google Translate.'

'I didn't know you could do that,' Falcon said evenly.

'It's not hard,' Darren explained. 'You enter phrases, read the translation, then go online and work out the pronunciation. It was slow at
first, but I can be pretty thorough – I'm on the spectrum, Mr Rourke.'

'Really?' Falcon replied.

'Quite a long way along it, according to some people.'

'Well, what do people know?' Falcon asked. 'Most people like cage fighting – are we going to listen to them?'

Darren shook his head.

'Darren found the battle-truck that led to Kazinsky's voice-print,' Clay said.

'That was great work,' Falcon replied. 'I am very happy to have you on board.'

'Thank you, Director,' Darren replied. 'I'll tell my dad – he says you are one of the most evil people in America.'

I tried not to laugh. 'Well, you never know, your father may be right,' Falcon replied, and decided it was time to move on. 'You said it was interesting?'

I hit play and we watched the Lada enter the gates and – escorted by a military vehicle – head deep into the base. It swung into a car park attached to an isolated hangar and found a space among dozens of other similarly battered cars. A long line of men in civilian clothes and – unusually, for Chechnya and the Russian military – a few women was creeping towards a door. Leaving his companion behind, Kazinsky got out of the car and joined the queue.

'What the hell is this place?' Falcon asked.

'Military airfield outside Grozny,' I replied.

'Jesus . . .' Falcon said, and pointed at the queue. 'What are they doing?'

'We're not sure. Processing?' Madeleine offered. 'Recruitment, maybe?' She turned to another screen and brought up an agency surveillance map of the area. 'No help from the database,' she said. 'The hangar is marked as abandoned.'

I pointed at something on the screen. 'The woman, fourth from the front,' I said. 'She's reading a piece of paper. Some of the others have got 'em too. Zoom in, Clay.'

The document loomed larger and larger on the screen, blurred at first but coming into focus. A title across the top – a few words, in Cyrillic script – was just visible.

'It says *Special Regulations Concerning* . . .' Darren and I translated in unison. 'I think it is the name of a place,' I continued. 'A city, maybe? Begins with a "B". I can't see.'

'What about the other people holding it?' Falcon said, and turned to Madeleine. 'Call NSA and see if they can tell us the rest of the sentence. If they can find a locust out of nothing, they should be able to do this.'

'Special Regulations,' I repeated, looking at the woman. 'Somewhere restricted . . . a place where you can't visit or live without special permission maybe? A ZATO?'

'Could be,' Falcon said, thinking. He saw Madeleine, on hold to the NSA, looking across at us. Her expertise was in Middle Eastern terrorists, not Russia.

'A Russian acronym,' Falcon said. 'It means a closed city where foreigners are banned and travel, residency and communications are controlled by an iron fist. In some of them, you can't even have a cellphone.'

'There are forty ZATOS,' Darren said in his monotone, not needing his screen or notes. 'I read about them when I was studying on Google. Very interesting. There is only one that starts with the letter "B". Like Severomorsk, the home port of the Arctic Fleet, or Vector, the biological weapons lab in Siberia, it's a Category One. The most secure.'

The rest of us were staring at him in surprise. 'So tell us,' Falcon said patiently. 'What's the ZATO that starts with a "B"?'

'Baikonur,' he said.

Falcon and I exchanged a look. 'Baikonur Cosmodrome?' I said. 'If Madeleine's right and the hangar is a processing centre – why the hell is Kazinsky going there?'

'No idea,' Falcon said. 'But strange things happen at Baikonur. Because it's a ZATO, it's almost impossible to find out exactly . . .' He shrugged, as if dismissing it, but I knew him better than most: I glanced down and saw that he was clenching and unclenching his fist. He knew enough to be worried.

13

'WHAT SORT OF THINGS?' I ASKED.

'We're not sure – research, bioweapons, chemical warfare, a lot about space,' Falcon said. 'I guess that's only natural – it's the largest and most historic space facility in the world. The rocket carrying Yuri

Gagarin – the first human to ever leave the Earth's atmosphere – was launched from Baikonur. A single orbit, just a hundred minutes, but it was the starting gun for the space race.

'They had Gagarin,' he continued. 'So we put Armstrong on the moon and sent *Voyager* way past Neptune. Now – researching the origins of the universe apparently – the Russians are using remote craft to bring back samples from every asteroid they can find.'

'Aren't we doing the same?' I asked.

'Everybody is – the Europeans, the Chinese – but to nowhere near this extent. The Russians have a big interest in off-earth mining.'

'Cool,' said Darren.

Falcon smiled. 'Yeah, cool – and whoever gets it right will lead the world on to the frontier. It'll be like a goldrush—'

'Bigger than Baku?' I asked.

'It will make Baku look like cents on the dollar – bigger than the Klondike, bigger than Silicon Valley, even bigger than AI. It'll be the biggest in history. But there is something far more important than money. Look at rare earth minerals – seventeen of them, used in everything from cellphones to stealth bombers. These days you can't build a car, a computer or an electronic device without them. China controls over ninety per cent of their mining and processing. Apart from Beijing, who thinks that is a good idea?

'Go out and look at the moon,' he continued. 'We planted a flag and never went back, but our closest neighbour has a huge concentration of those minerals – and that is only one celestial body. There are millions of them with gold, magnesium, nickel and everything else on the periodic table. That's the Kremlin's interest.'

'And that's why even the mention of Baikonur makes you anxious?' I asked.

'Anxious?' he replied, shaking his head. 'Me?'

I looked down at his clenched fist. He followed my gaze and laughed. 'What did I always say? You can tell a lot about a man by the way he moves.'

I smiled back while Clay and the others just looked at us, confused.

'Baikonur's a mysterious place, and Kazinsky is probably the most dangerous man on earth,' Falcon said. 'I'm always anxious about anything I don't understand.' He indicated the computer screen showing Kazinsky in line outside the hangar. 'Just tell me what the hell is he doing there?'

As we all stared at the Colonel, Darren put up footage of Baikonur on another screen. Whatever the season, it looked like a post-apocalyptic world: dust storms howled across a flat and arid landscape, blizzards of snow covered the parched bones of animals while the sepia tones of old prison buildings, swarms of rats and rows of lonely graves emerged through a howling wind.

'Baikonur is on the Great Steppes, the prairie that stretches all the way down to Central Asia,' Falcon said. 'It was founded a hundred years ago as a prison camp, part of Stalin's Gulag, and now it is a town of a hundred thousand people. It's seen a lot of death – first the prison, then the casualties in the early days of rocketry and finally with the space programme. It still holds the record for the most deadly launch accident ever. Maybe what they say is true – evil can cling to a place. Baikonur has a lot of mysteries, but one thing is certain – it's home to several radical mosques. I don't like it. I don't like that combination one tiny bit.'

'Nor me,' I said. 'They have a saying in Russia: "Everyone shares what they are rich in."'

'And we know where Kazinsky's wealth lies,' Falcon added. 'Damn! Why didn't we kill him in Iran? How far in front of us is he?'

'Far enough,' Clay replied. 'The footage from the recruitment centre is from a couple of months ago.'

Falcon nodded and then, obviously looking into the future, looked at Darren. 'What security clearance do you have?'

'Not very high, not like everyone here,' Darren replied. 'But you can trust me, Mr Rourke.'

'Yes, I think I can,' Falcon said, smiling. 'Your father – probably not so much.'

'Definitely not him,' Darren confirmed.

'Okay – you're in,' Falcon said. 'It's a team. You've got five days. We're hoping for the best, planning for the worst, but we may have to go in after him. You do the historical stuff – get me everything you can on Baikonur.'

Things were moving fast, and I sighed with relief – as I had antici-pated, it looked like I was heading for Russia. I turned to Clay, taking command. 'First,' I said, 'we need a private work area—'

'What are you doing?' Falcon asked.

'Getting organized,' I replied.

'No, no, you're getting fit. That's your job.'

'My job is here – Baikonur,' I said.

'We don't even know if Kazinsky's there yet, and if he is, why. Whatever it is, it's almost certainly just a stop along the way. Think about it – he might have already been and left. If you want to help, finish the goddamned rehab.'

14

I HIT THE TWENTY-MILE TARGET EVERY NIGHT FOR THE NEXT FOUR days and, as a result, was confident enough to present myself at Walter Reed early on a weekday morning to be examined by a panel of doctors whose objective, it soon appeared, was to consign me straight to the scrapheap rather than authorize any return to active service.

They put me through such a battery of physical and medical tests that I started to think that the depredations in Iran weren't so bad after all. Nevertheless, by early evening I managed to complete the Illinois Agility Test and they finally surrendered, passing me fit – physically at least.

The following day, I sat in Lucas Corrigan's large office looking through the four-inch armoured glass at the lawns surrounding what is known as the Original Headquarters Building, as he read the medical reports. 'Pretty impressive,' he said, smiling at me.

It was going to be okay, I thought. We looked at each other for a handful of beats, but the river rocks didn't waver for a second. 'So, tell me about the panic attacks,' he said.

I took a moment. 'What panic attacks?' I said, trying to sound more confident than I felt.

Corrigan wasn't buying what I was selling. 'After what you experienced, if you weren't suffering from a panic disorder I'd be checking for a pulse,' he said levelly.

We continued to look at each other. It was the old story – if you're in a hole, it's a good idea to stop digging. I said nothing.

'You know what I'm talking about,' he gently rebuked me. 'The anxiety, the night sweats, the racing heart and tingling hands. When we get past that, tell me about the feeling of being out of control, recount the fear of death – of either yourself or someone you love – of not wanting to close your eyes because you know where the dreams will take you. Do you want me to go on?'

What could I say – it was frighteningly accurate. Especially the part about fearing the death of someone you love. Rebecca in the ruined city, I thought. Then I looked at Corrigan and something struck me about his description: his account was too good, too on the money, that it couldn't have come from any textbook. 'You've been there, haven't you?' I said.

He stared at me. 'Iran, Pakistan, the Persian Gulf?' He laughed. 'No, I'm not crazy – I've never been anywhere near them.'

'Not the places. I meant lost behind enemy lines, some place like that,' I replied.

I saw his forehead knit with concentration. 'Congratulations,' he said quietly. 'Yes, you're right – we both know what it's like.'

15

'I WAS SEVEN,' HE SAID. 'LIVING IN WHAT WAS THEN SAIGON. MAYBE you've heard that my father was the station chief in Vietnam during the last years of the war.'

'Sure, people talk about it,' I said. 'Especially the part about five million dollars in US bills going up in smoke.'

He shrugged. 'The war wasn't going well, but in late '74 Saigon wasn't in any apparent danger, so my mother, desperate for us to be a family, packed a bag for myself and her, locked our house in the Washington suburbs and moved to the embassy compound in what was once the most elegant city in Asia.

'By April of the following year, the number of refugees was ballooning, but you wouldn't have known it – the boulevards with the fashionable shops were crowded, the girlie bars were booming and the analysts at Langley said we were safe for at least another nine months. That didn't turn out to be accurate.' He smiled.

'Five days later, the North Vietnamese launched a major offensive and, before we knew it, a hundred thousand enemy troops had surrounded Saigon. Our military immediately panicked and launched a plan to evacuate a huge number of Americans and loyal South Vietnamese on planes flying out of Tan Son Nhat airport. Which was fine until the airport came under artillery fire. A few hours later it was abandoned completely when a South Vietnamese pilot, flying a fully laden bomber, defected in mid-air and destroyed the only runway still operating.

'So there was only one option,' Corrigan continued. 'The generals in charge initiated the largest helicopter evacuation in history. It was April, but the Armed Forces radio started playing Bing Crosby's "White Christmas" and I was really excited. I thought Santa was coming early – until Mom explained it was a pre-arranged signal to all US citizens to make their way to the nearest evacuation point.

'One of the locations was the US embassy, but with the Vietcong coming into the city and the reprisals starting, thousands of South Vietnamese were also heading for the compound. Within hours it was bedlam – Air America choppers operating off rooftops, Americans trying to enter the embassy, Vietnamese parents with young kids climbing the fifteen-foot walls, ten thousand people gathering in the street outside, Marine guards fighting to keep the crowd at bay – it was chaos.

'Meanwhile, in the embassy garden, the Company's agents were burning files and lists of informers. More sensitive material was sent to the industrial incinerator,' he said. 'That was manned by Dad and was where he burnt the five million bucks.'

Corrigan paused, and I saw how much colour had drained from his face; there were still aspects of the story that took him back there. 'Dad . . .' he said quietly.

'Anyway, night fell,' he continued. 'The weather added to the sense of doom – there were these tropical downpours and rolling thunder – as Mom carried me from our residence across the compound. I don't recall being scared. That came later – I was with Mom and it all seemed like an adventure. We had a close friend, the wife of a US diplomat, with us – a woman in her sixties who was in poor health and exhausted – carrying a small suitcase holding her most precious possessions.

'At the embassy gates, Marines with weapons levelled were trying to keep the crowds at bay while, inside the walls, thousands of people were scrambling to get to the open-air car park. The centre of it was surrounded by embassy vehicles with their headlights on, turning it into a landing pad. Sitting on it was a Sea Stallion heavy-lift chopper. Even above the sound of its engine, everyone could hear two more helos circling overhead. A rumour swept through the crowd in the streets that they were the last planes out, which caused an even wilder rush to scale the walls and reach the car park. As it happened, the rumour wasn't true, but it was that kind of night.

'Mom – still carrying me – and the diplomat's wife eventually made it to the edge of the car park. Mom plunged forward, leading the way through the crowd, and finally elbowed her way the last few yards. Thank God, one of the Marine guards recognized her and he used his rifle to push the crowd aside, clearing a path to the edge of the landing pad. Mom was so relieved – we had made it.

'Only then did she realize that in the chaos the diplomat's wife, the woman who was her closest friend in the country, hadn't managed to keep up.'

16

LUCAS RUMMAGED IN THE BOTTOM DRAWER OF HIS DESK, PULLED out a framed and faded colour photo and handed it to me. It showed a young, tow-haired boy with green eyes standing near what was probably the Saigon River holding hands with a handsome, athletic woman – his mother – who had her arm draped around a much older and frail-looking woman.

'The friend?' I asked. By the look of her, it was little wonder she got left behind.

'Mom scanned the crowd behind us but couldn't see any sign of her,' Corrigan continued. 'All around, evacuees – showing passports or visas to the Marines – were racing across the parking lot towards the huge chopper. At its doors, a guy wearing coveralls who looked like he was stoned – a load officer – was performing strange dance moves and bustling them aboard.

'There was no doubt how Mom would deal with the situation – she was the daughter of a Marine general, after all. She turned around, and I recall her putting me on the ground and crouching down to look at me. "Run, Lucas," she said. "You understand? Run to the helicopter. Mommy's gonna get Mrs Lawford. I'm two minutes behind you."

'I must have nodded, but it was the first time I remember feeling scared. Mom turned me around and told me later she watched me join the swarm of people crossing the parking lot. Certain I was on the way to the chopper, she plunged back into the tide of people behind her, determined to find Kathy Lawford and get back to me as fast as possible.'

Corrigan shrugged. 'What she didn't know was that, getting more frightened, I turned around halfway across the parking lot and tried to rejoin her. None of the adults, desperate to get on board, probably even noticed.

'I made my way back to the young Marine who'd cleared the path for us, but he didn't register me, he was having an argument with an aggressive Vietnamese guy. Anyway, I passed him, went into the crowd and started calling for Mom. It didn't occur to me that she had no chance of hearing me over the noise. I headed deeper into the chaos and passed three Marines, who, at gunpoint, were making two senior South Vietnamese military officers unlock two suitcases they were dragging towards the landing pad. Even the crowd fell quiet as the bags were upended and all these gold bars spilled out.

'It was about then I started to cry. I discovered later that somewhere in the parking lot Mom found Kathy, sitting on a wrecked wall, her small suitcase beside her. She had her fist pressed to her chest, and Mom cursed herself: she knew Kathy suffered from angina but in the panic hadn't given it a thought. No wonder the woman couldn't keep up.

'Mom helped her to her feet and told her they had to move as quickly as possible. Kathy picked up her suitcase and almost fell from the pain in her chest.

'Mom said she told Kathy gently,' Corrigan continued, 'that they would have to leave the suitcase, they could move faster without it. Kathy agreed, but then Mom saw her eyes fill with tears and, though she tried, the elderly woman couldn't let go of it. That was when Mom realized what was inside.'

Corrigan looked at me and shook his head. 'Almost sixty thousand young Americans died in Vietnam,' he said. 'One of them, killed during the siege of Khe Sanh, was Kathy's son, her only child. In the period between being drafted and when he died, he had written to his mother twice a week; the letters, and an album of photos, were all she had left of him and they were in the suitcase.'

Lucas and I held each other's gaze and I thought of the old lady in the photo – trying to flee in the middle of a pitched battle, choppers overhead, the rain beating down and the constant sound of gunfire. What a nightmare – and all she wanted was to hold on to a suitcase. 'What happened?' I asked.

'Mom said she picked up the bag. Angry at the war, angry at the waste of life, angry at men like her father who insisted on thinking there was glory in it, she took Kathy by the elbow and managed to reach the line of Marines. Holding up their US passports, they were allowed through and saw the load officer starting to close the Sea Stallion's doors ready for lift-off.

'Mom hurried Kathy forward and they squeezed on board with only moments to spare. The doors closed and, in the darkness, Mom dropped the suitcase at Kathy's feet, turned and looked for me.

'The Sea Stallion was built to take forty combat troops, but nobody knew how many evacuees – most with just the clothes they were wearing and two of them relieved of their gold bars – the chopper was holding. A hundred – maybe more – were crammed on board, heading for a US aircraft carrier waiting offshore. Given the over-crowding, it wasn't surprising Mom couldn't see me.

'She struggled through the crush and started calling my name, but the pilot had powered up hard and as the skids left the ground the evacuees gave a huge cheer, drowning out everything.

'Mom kept yelling for me, but there was no reply and the chatter between the evacuees, mostly in Vietnamese, faded as they realized something was wrong. Mom pleaded with them to find her son but, of course, I wasn't there.

'The only response was a murmur: he's not with us. Mom had to admit what had happened – I didn't get on board.

'She saw the load officer and got hard in his face. "Go back?" he said to her. "No can do, lady. He'll have to catch a ride on the next lift." "He's seven, you idiot," she replied, and pointed at his headset. "Tell the pilot – he has to turn around!"

'The load officer reported back. "He can't, there's a chopper on the pad and he ain't circling. He says he's gonna contact people on the ground, tell 'em to look for him."'

Corrigan shrugged again, fatalistic. 'Mom knew that even if the pilot could contact anyone at the car park, who would do the looking? Would they even care, with the embassy on fire and the North Vietnamese at the gates?'

17

I WATCHED CORRIGAN BEND TO THE DRAWER AGAIN, IMAGINING what it must have been like for a boy alone, lost behind enemy lines.

He handed me a yellowing paper folder and I saw it was an old CIA file, probably retrieved by him from the Tomb years ago. In it was an account of the final moments before the embassy fell. I couldn't be sure, but I suspected it was written by the agency's then station chief, Walter Corrigan – the father of the man sitting opposite me. I started to read.

It said that smoke from the fires in the embassy garden swirled up the side of the six-storey building and across its roof. Located up there was the ambassador's private helipad and the document said a silver-and-blue Huey – a Bell Iroquois – chopper operated by Air America, the predecessor of GreenEnergy Inc., was on the pad with its rotors turning, ready for a quick escape.

The pilot was a twenty-eight-year-old maverick called Pete Wrigley – call sign Eagle 420 – who had all his attention focused on the door opening on to the roof. He saw it burst open and the CIA head of station and his five remaining agents came barrelling through. Two of them immediately swung behind the .50 calibre door guns, flicked off the safeties, and the chopper lifted off and swung hard across the embassy compound.

The seven men on board looked down at the crowd swarming the parking lot to try and board another overloaded Sea Stallion while – outside the perimeter wall, it was far worse – the mass of people was huge, someone had found a garbage truck and was using it to smash a hole in the wall, and the Marine guards, carbines at the ready, were setting up a defensive ring around the chopper.

Walt Corrigan, in the co-pilot's seat, looking through the windscreen, had once seen the Irrawaddy River in full flood and miles of jungle turned into a moonscape by Agent Orange, but that didn't compare to a city in its death throes. 'Jesus,' he said.

'I guess the Viets must have heard,' Wrigley yelled back.

'Heard what?' Walt asked.

'Two more up-lifts, then it's Americans only.'

'Says who?' Walt asked, shocked.

'Kissinger. Twenty minutes ago. For the South Vietnamese, it's now or never.'

'Didn't we say we were never going to abandon them?' Walt asked bitterly.

Wrigley laughed. 'You believed that shit?'

'I did once,' Walt replied. 'I thought that was what we were fighting for.'

'I guess we've all done grown up,' Wrigley replied. 'What does it say in the Bible: "For now we see through a mirror, darkly; but then face to face." We see the truth, ain't that what it means?'

Walt turned and stared at him: he had known Peter Wrigley for four years and he had never thought of him as someone who could quote the Bible.

The young pilot pointed to a broad swathe of darkness below. It was the Saigon River with what looked like hundreds of fireflies on its surface. 'Sampans and their lanterns,' he said. 'They're sailing out to try and find the Seventh Fleet. Sampans in an ocean in the middle of a storm. God help 'em—'

He suddenly held up his finger for silence: a message was coming through his headphones. His face turned ashen. 'Roger,' he said, and clicked off. 'Hold on!' he yelled at the door gunners and executed a stunning combat roll and headed back towards the city.

'What the hell are you doing?' Walt yelled, trying to catch his breath.

'Going back.'

'Back? Why?'

'Someone's been left behind, some kid,' Wrigley yelled.

'Shit,' cursed Walt, and then, a second later, a huge orange fireball lit up the horizon as the entire Long Binh ammo dump exploded.

'You know that Saigon's finished – we could die back there?' Walt asked.

'I know,' Wrigley replied.

'Whose kid anyway?'

'Yours,' Wrigley said, pouring on the power.

18

'I WAS SMALL FOR MY AGE,' CORRIGAN SAID ONCE I HAD LAID THE old agency file down.

'Before long, the crush of people trying to reach the choppers meant that I was trapped in a courtyard near the parking lot, trying hard not to cry. I had called for Mom so often my voice was hoarse and I had given up. Meanwhile, my polo shirt was torn and that had upset me badly – the shirt was new and Dad always got mad if I didn't look after things.' He smiled.

'The crowd kept surging, pushing past me, but somehow I reached the safety of a frangipani tree in the corner of the courtyard. I stared into the crowd and tried calling for Mom again. People ignored me, but I knew she'd come. In my seven short years of experience, that's what mothers always did.

'I would have kept calling, too, except that very close – on the other side of the perimeter wall just behind me – there were several explosions and, a second later, the sound of people screaming in agony. Years later, when I read the files, I learned that two men on motor-scooters had driven into the crowd outside the gates, throwing hand grenades. Whether it was at the South Vietnamese they figured were US collaborators or to clear a path for themselves into the compound, nobody ever discovered.

'The rain swept in harder, drenching me, and – trying to avoid the worst of it – I grabbed an American flag somebody had dropped and put it over my shoulders. In the air, Wrigley told Dad that Mom had said she thought I would probably be in the car park or close by, searching for her.

'Wrigley turned on the chopper's searchlight and bathed the parking lot in white light. The mass of people were scared, trying to back away, and almost immediately a Marine officer on the ground called through to the chopper, yelling at Wrigley to turn the damn light off: "I don't need some idiot in a chopper attracting a hail of incoming," he said.

'Wrigley lied like a champion: "No can do, Major. Priority uplift – direct order of Flag Officer, Seventh Fleet. Talk to him."'

'Dad was barely listening, trying to find me among the crowd. He had no success and realized that with the surging mass of people, a Sea Stallion on the pad, and buildings surrounding the parking lot, the Huey – with a rotor measuring fifty feet across – was going to have a problem. He shouted to Wrigley: "You can't land. Put her on the roof. We'll go down on foot and find him."

'Wrigley told Dad to keep looking. "Find him first. Let me worry about the rest." Dropping lower, he kept the craft moving across the car park, approaching a small courtyard. Then, on a night that had seemed cursed in every way, a piece of luck—

'The rotor-wash from the descending helicopter blew deeper into the courtyard until it reached the frangipani tree, blasting the leaves and blooms off the branches. Dad, searching the crowd, glanced across at the flying foliage—

'Through the stripped branches, in the back corner, huddled under the tree, he finally saw me. "Got him!" he yelled, pointing.

'Wrigley shouted to the guys in the rear: "Gunners ready. Safety on." He sure as hell didn't want anyone getting shot. "Now aim at the crowd."

'He hovered over the courtyard and spoke into his headset mic. Loudspeakers on the chopper's skids broadcast his voice in English and Vietnamese: "Stand back! That is an order. Stand back! We will open fire"—

'The crowd saw the guns swinging into position and ran. The war had been so crazy for so long, nobody doubted what Americans in an unmarked chopper were capable of.

'Dad spoke softly: "God help us", as he realized – Wrigley was going to bring the chopper down in the narrow space between the buildings and land it in the courtyard.

'An even wilder rush for the exits began; the crowd were terrified that the chopper's main rotor was going to touch the walls and send ten thousand pounds of metal, engine and jet fuel plunging to the ground on top of them.

'In the cockpit, Wrigley focused on the space between the walls, trying to judge the wind and rain gusting across the rooftops, ignoring the screaming people on the ground, picking his moment.

'He dialled back the power and guided the helicopter between the buildings. Dad, looking at the tips of the rotor, didn't think they had a chance, but he dragged his eyes away and saw that I had stood up, staring – like everybody else – at the chopper descending into the courtyard.

'Dad's fear was that, not recognizing the unmarked chopper as American, I might run. "Stay there, Lucas. Stay there," he said.

'Without warning, the chopper lurched as a violent blast of wind that meteorologists call a "roll eddy" came over the top of one of the buildings and hit the craft, but Wrigley worked the rudder and stick fast as hell and brought the machine back towards the middle of the gap: my God, Dad always said, the guy could fly.

'Wrigley took a breath; the immediate danger had passed. "No go, weather's turnin' bad," he said to everyone. Then he spoke to Dad: "Ever ridden a hook?"

'Dad realized immediately it was the only hope. "Once," he replied.

'Wrigley laughed. "Good, so it's not like you're inexperienced." Dad scrambled into the main cabin as Wrigley hit a switch. A crane swung out from the side of the craft.

'I watched from the ground, and it looked surreal: a helicopter hovering in mid-air, towers of storm clouds rising above it, rain squalls hitting the buildings, the searchlight's cone illuminating a frangipani tree and – dropping down the facade of the burning embassy – a guy in a flak jacket standing on a hook, being lowered to the ground.

'In the rain and searchlight's glare, I didn't recognize my father. It wasn't until the man started yelling that I realized who it was. "Run, Lucas! Run!" he called.

'Finally, I saw his face. "Dad!" I called, and ran fast across the courtyard, through the cone of light and into his outstretched arms. I felt him hug me, so tight it was as if he was never going to let me go.

'He secured the harness and called "Set!" to the men above. The cable tightened and the winch started to lift us.

'The crowd on the ground watched Dad and me – still draped in the flag – rise towards the chopper. As it started to gain altitude, we were both dragged on board.

'Wrigley killed the lights and Dad leaned forward and put his hand on the pilot's shoulder. "Thanks," he said quietly, unable to say more in case his voice broke.

'Wrigley shook his head. "Just tell your boy to remember me. Tell him at least Pete Wrigley did one decent thing in this lousy war."'

'He banked the chopper hard towards the river. The fireflies were thicker than ever and we followed them out towards the Seventh Fleet, where Mom – standing on the deck of the USS *Blue Ridge* – was keeping vigil. At dawn a rating told her a chopper had just signalled it had her husband and son on board. Staring across the South China Sea, she saw the helicopter appear over the horizon and then, a few minutes later, land on the deck.'

Corrigan shrugged, his account over, and I looked at him in amazement. 'Quite a man, your father,' I said after a long pause. 'We all know what would have happened if the North Vietnamese had captured the CIA station chief.'

He nodded, not saying anything. 'But that's parents, isn't it?' I continued. 'It's like Rebecca told me – there's a reason why DNA is built like a chain.'

Corrigan stared at me. 'She's a smart woman – probably too smart for us,' he said.

I was relieved to see he started to smile, and I grinned back. 'Remarkable story,' I said. 'I guess the other hero was the pilot – not bound by blood, he did it out of decency.'

'Yeah – a great man. Two weeks after the night in Saigon, Mom and Dad and I were at home in Washington when Dad got word about Pete. He had flown into the Mekong Delta on what was meant to be his last Air America mission – to bring out a South Vietnamese intelligence officer and his family who had been hiding out in one of the floating villages.

'I've looked through the files, and it wasn't clear whether it was an intelligence leak or even if the officer was still alive, but shortly after nightfall as the chopper came in to land at an old coconut plantation, it was hit by four rocket-propelled grenades from a well-laid ambush.'

Corrigan paused. 'Peter Michael Wrigley,' he said, 'twenty-eight, the son of a pastor out of Possum Trot, Alabama, a young man who once said he liked dogs more than people, died as a secret soldier in a land he loved, on a flight to pick up a man who may have been already dead, on a mission that never existed.' He shook his head in sadness. 'That's the secret world for you, isn't it?'

19

I KEPT LOOKING AT CORRIGAN, LOST FOR WORDS.

'You seem surprised at the story – you didn't expect it?' he said, laughing. 'You've gotta remember – this is the CIA, it's full of secrets.'

I smiled and kept my eyes on his face; I couldn't help but think that, stripped of his armour, he looked like one of the loneliest men I had ever met. He indicated my medical files. 'Yes – as you suspected, I know about panic; so tell me – how often do you get the attacks?'

After the story he had recounted, I couldn't see any point in evading it. 'Once a week maybe, sometimes less.'

'Given what you went through, I had expected more. You should consider yourself lucky. Problem is, in your position, panic attacks present a risk. To you.'

'And to other people?' I said. 'By that you mean you're worried I might go postal?'

'Stronger people than us have,' he said. 'There are always triggering events, and psychotherapy is considered the best way of controlling and treating them. But that's not going to happen for someone sworn to secrecy, is it? I don't see a spy sitting in group therapy. I could prescribe serotonin uptake inhibitors, but I don't think you'd take them.'

I shook my head – no, I didn't want to do that.

'It leaves one thing. As soon as the feelings of panic, the physical sensations – the elevated heartbeat and all the rest – become more familiar, they are usually less threatening and the attacks diminish. In other words, familiarity makes it fade. With a resilient person, time and rest—'

'What do you mean, time?' I asked, alarmed. 'I don't have much of that, Lucas, I'm in the middle of . . . I mean, we're tracking a man who is one of the most dangerous—'

'I know what you're doing. Falcon told me,' he replied. 'But you and I have discussed the symptoms – we know you're suffering from a panic disorder. Okay, it's not serious – not yet. But the Company's guidelines are clear, I can't allow you to return to active service.'

'No,' I said, starting to object, but he rode right over it.

'What do you want me to do, ignore the diagnosis? Forget the guidelines? I would never ask an intelligence agent to be unprofessional, and you can't expect it of me either, okay?'

I ran my hand through my hair, but I could tell there was no use; the man wasn't for turning. 'How long?'

'Best practice says we should reassess in six months. For you, I'll call it three.'

Three months on the sidelines? I started to object loudly, about to slip the chain, but I came to my senses: Lucas was trying to help me. 'I'm sorry,' I said. 'It's not your fault, I appreciate what you're doing. It's good of you—'

He smiled. 'Thanks. Sounds like you might be the exception.'

'Exception to what?' I asked.

'You know what they say,' he continued. 'There are only two types of people in the world. Those that hate Corrigan and those who haven't met him yet—'

'Who says that?' I asked. 'I've never heard that.'

'Thanks for lying,' he replied, laughing.

I laughed back. 'They'll put you on light duties,' he explained. 'Working on something from the past, most likely.'

'I can still go to meetings?' I asked. 'That counts as light duties?'

20

I WAS ALREADY TEN MINUTES LATE AS I SAID A HURRIED GOODBYE TO Corrigan and rushed out of the Original Headquarters Building heading for the Bubble. I pulled my cellphone out mid-sprint.

As I expected, Rebecca – keen to hear the outcome of the meeting – picked up immediately. She didn't even bother trying to hide how happy she was when I told her that I would be spending at least the next three months on the inactive list.

'Didn't I say he was a good doctor? Hopefully he'll find reasons to extend it.'

'Why not call him and suggest it,' I replied. 'By the way – thanks for the support.'

'You're welcome,' she said, but then her tone changed, serious: 'Are you okay?'

'Pretty much,' I said, equally seriously. 'It wasn't like I had a choice, he got me cornered – Lucas knows more about life behind enemy lines than I would have credited.'

'Did you tell him about the wolves?'

'No.'

'You should have,' she said. 'Are you still hearing that stuff?'

'Not so much,' I lied, worried she would feel – as a doctor – that she had to inform Corrigan or Falcon. 'Anyway, I can't talk, I've got to hand my cellphone in.'

That much, at least, was true. I had arrived at the Bubble's entrance and the uniformed guy behind the security desk already had his hand out—

21

RUNNING LATE, I SLIPPED INTO THE BACK OF THE CONFERENCE ROOM as quietly as possible and – in almost total darkness – came face to face with Kazinsky.

It was footage of him unspooling on the IMAX-style screens and I recognized its provenance immediately; thank God for the Street of Gold, I thought. For the first time, as he walked down the narrow road, we had captured a distinct image of his face. Greatly enhanced by the NSA, it gave us at least a reasonable chance of continuing to try and track him.

I took a seat in the rear row – unnoticed and far removed from anybody – and allowed my eyes to grow accustomed to the darkness. Falcon had given Madeleine, Clay and Darren five days to pull together everything they could find in the Tomb about Baikonur and its dark history. And this was the result.

Except I saw that – in my absence – the scope of the report had grown significantly. Buster was there and so were two members of the seventh-floor brains trust, Margaret was sitting to one side – keen to escape and have a vape, I was sure – and I recognized two people from the elite Russia Desk. Along with several researchers and an expert on satellite imagery, there were about twenty people, and the presence of such a diverse group told me something very important: just how deeply worried Falcon was about Kazinsky.

A typical spymaster, I thought – never show your hand, never show your fears or deepest anxieties. Not to anyone, not ever.

Right now, he was standing in front of the screens, about to drop a bomb on at least some of them.

'This is the man we have to find,' he was saying, pointing at the seafarer in his dark blue reefer jacket. 'For most of you, unaware of recent developments, he probably looks like just another anonymous face in a crowd.

'But in fact you know volumes about him. He is one of the founders of ISIS, for years the most wanted terrorist in the world – this, at last, is the mysterious Abu Muslim al-Tundra.'

Most of those in the room were surprised; at last – after so many years – the agency had managed to put a face to the name.

'The footage was taken several months ago in Baku,' Falcon said.

Surprise turned to disbelief. Recorded a few months ago – how could that be? He was dead, wasn't he? The room was filled by a rising murmur of conversation—

Falcon spoke over it: 'No, he is very much alive, I am afraid. Buster is now sending you the codes to access a file. You will see the name on it is Roman Kazinsky.'

There was a flurry of activity as several dozen laptops were opened. 'Attention, please,' Falcon continued, his tone making it clear it was an order. 'I want to know where Kazinsky is, everybody he has met with, what his plan is.'

Footage of Kazinsky and his companion driving through Grozny, passing the abandoned roadhouse and approaching the guard house, played on the screens.

'This is where we last saw him,' Falcon said. 'Two months ago at an airfield in Chechnya, where he entered a supposedly abandoned hangar.

'Seven hours later a convoy of ten buses drove out of that building and travelled to the large complex at the centre of the base. As far as we can tell, Kazinsky stayed out of sight in a barracks until five days later—

'When an even larger number of buses left the barracks and

conveyed several hundred men, and at least two dozen women, to the apron adjoining the runway.'

The screens showed the buses stopping next to three ungainly looking Ilyushin Il-76 military transport planes, stubby four-engine flying whales, each capable of carrying a hundred and forty people and – remarkably – landing on dirt runways. They could fly – and land – almost anywhere.

'Due to the short time they spent on the asphalt,' Falcon said, 'we have been unable to identify Kazinsky among the passengers, but we believe he was processed at the barracks and was then among those boarding the Ilyushins. In line with most Russian aircraft, it is a piece of junk – on average, two of them crash every year.

'Unfortunately, not this time; it would have made our task a lot easier. The transponders on the planes were switched off mid-flight to mask their route but, as some of you are aware, we have classified tech that can overcome that. This is where we believe he went—'

Images of a vast and flat landscape dominated the room. The moonscape was relieved only by small areas of marshland and one other element – stretching to the horizon were the hulks of scores of freighters, fishing boats and oil tankers. Herds of camels, battered by swirling eddies of dust, wandered among the craft as vultures perched on the rusting superstructure. It appeared to be a huge graveyard of rotting ships, marooned in the middle of nowhere.

'This is the Aral Sea – a spectacular testament to the ultimate ecological disaster,' Falcon explained. 'Sandwiched between Uzbekistan and Kazakhstan, it was the fourth largest lake in the world until it was destroyed by the upstream irrigation policies of the old Soviet Union.'

I stared at the images of the sea – according to Falcon, it was once dotted with over a thousand beautiful islands, a breeding ground for a vast array of wildlife – and I couldn't help but think of a line from the poem *Ozymandias*: 'Look on my works, ye Mighty, and despair!'

'One of the two rivers that fed into it was the Syr Darya,' Falcon continued. 'On its banks, in 1955, the Soviets started to build this—'

A new image appeared. A massive industrial complex – like the wrecked ships before it – was marooned in the vast, desiccated wasteland. 'Welcome to Baikonur Cosmodrome,' Falcon said.

I sat forward and looked harder at the footage. Somehow, I knew I was going there. Despite what I had told Rebecca, in my head the wolves were howling louder.

'Baikonur?' a voice I recognized – that of a sixty-year-old veteran from the Russia Desk – called out. He had a reputation as a difficult man, but everybody who had dealt with him – me included – agreed that he really knew his stuff. 'That's a ZATO?'

'Yes,' Falcon replied.

'And you want us to find the formerly dead al-Tundra in a ZATO?' the veteran asked, incredulous.

'You didn't get the memo, Antonio?' Falcon replied. 'I never said it was going to be easy.'

22

I BARELY HEARD THE EXCHANGE BETWEEN FALCON AND ANTONIO – I was concentrating on the satellite images of the Cosmodrome playing on the screens. To virtually anyone it would have looked like any other huge, polluted, industrial complex. But I had a different perspective—

From past missions, I knew the colour coding the agency used to identify the most highly classified buildings in Russia and their probable function: the secret research facilities, the weapons development bunkers, the hidden biological labs and the chemical warfare production sites. Baikonur had more of them flagged than any other place I had ever seen except for Vector, the notorious smallpox and virus facility in Siberia.

I stared at the forest of red and yellow markers scattered across twenty launch pads, a massive refinery for propellants, a power-generating station, five hundred kilometres of railways, twelve of the biggest structures on the planet – rocket and space-shuttle assembly buildings – and a run-down city of a hundred thousand people. Covering it all was a dirt-coloured haze – a deadly combination of smoke and toxins spewed out by the various facilities. It should have been left to the rats and wolves, I thought.

Falcon drew everyone's attention to three military-grade runways – each five thousand metres long, twice the length of their commercial counterparts and built to take the heavy-lift cargo planes that delivered components for rockets and spacecraft – but I found myself staring at the miles of scrub and the shimmering heat waves surrounding them. Something tugged at my memory – it reminded me of somewhere, but I couldn't place it. Then the mental file opened: 'Paradise Ranch,' I said to myself.

The ranch was a small part of the Nevada Testing Site – the US proving ground for scores of nuclear explosions – and I had gone there to be briefed on a mission to Amman in Jordan that ended up being aborted moments before I got on the plane. Nevertheless, it meant I spent three days in Nevada.

Baikonur had that same desolate landscape, the identical feeling of a huge complex adrift in the wilderness. The ranch was also next to a body of water – Groom Lake – and the similarities didn't end there. Paradise Ranch, too, was a highly secret place, and entry to it was also strictly forbidden without a raft of authorizations. In popular culture it usually went by a different name. It was known as Area 51.

Everything at the ranch was divorced from ordinary life. At the time, I thought how anything could happen inside its vast perimeter and nobody would know – they wouldn't even find the body. And that was my *homeland*. I tried to imagine a Russian spy accessing Area 51 and started to realize the magnitude of the task that lay ahead of me. Penetrating the Cosmodrome seemed impossible but, in a corner of my mind, I started to plan a mission that did not even yet exist.

I lifted my eyes to the screen and looked again at the three huge runways – just as giant pillars of light illuminated the desolate landscape. Captured as night was falling, they were beaming up from the landing strips, piercing the sky and fading into the heavens; both beautiful and strangely ominous.

'What the hell is that?' I asked from the darkness at the rear of the room.

Falcon took a moment to locate me. 'You again,' he said good-naturedly. 'They use unmanned craft – like freighters – to gather material from space,' he continued. 'The pillars help ground control guide them into a landing. The Russians say an element in the light helps sanitize the craft – similar to UV – but it's probably bullshit. This is one of the freighters—'

The footage showed a vehicle that was like a grim version of the space shuttle – a dull black exterior, windowless, overwhelmingly brutalist in its design – strapped to a rocket on the launch pad. It seemed, like everything else at Baikonur, run-down and diseased.

'Everything is robotic,' Falcon explained. 'The ship lands on a target – an asteroid – automated equipment scoops up material, and then it returns. The craft are turned around fast and reused, pretty much disposable, which is just as well. This was a few months ago—'

A lick of flame suddenly appeared in an electrical box on the gantry supporting the rocket. Almost instantly the flame became a cloud of fire and smoke as a leaking gas ignited, hit the fuel tanks and the whole ensemble – freighter, rocket, gantry, cranes and support vehicles – were enveloped in a cataclysmic explosion.

Everyone in the room reared back as, on the screen, men and women near the pad ran for their lives. They had no chance of out-pacing the flames and we watched as the fire engulfed them. 'Rocket fuel – nothing could survive it,' Falcon continued quietly.

'The Russians said that because the craft was unmanned, there were no casualties, which was true – if you ignored the twenty-six technicians and labourers on the pad who got barbecued.

'But the gold medal for disaster at Baikonur actually goes to us.' Falcon stopped the footage on the massive fireball and turned to face the audience.

'Strategically, we are in deep trouble,' he said.

23

'FOR MONTHS – YEARS,' FALCON CONTINUED, 'THE AGENCY HAS BEEN warning at secret congressional hearings and during private meetings that the Russians – world leaders in rocketry ever since Gagarin – have been way ahead of us in planning to discover, mine and recover off-earth minerals. Did the politicians listen? Do they ever?'

People murmured in agreement, but Falcon didn't pause. 'Now we've learned that four days ago, this craft returned and brought with it one of the richest deposits of rare earth minerals ever found.'

Falcon indicated a black freighter dropping down the columns of light and about to land on one of the runways.

'As you know, China controls the entire supply of rare earth minerals on our planet. Now the Kremlin, once they get fully online, will be totally independent. And where are we?'

'Strategically adrift,' the legend from the Russia Desk – Antonio Silva – said. 'As everyone here knows, that's technical talk for "up shit creek".'

'Antonio's right—' Falcon said, but he was forestalled by an elegant, athletic-looking woman in her fifties. She was a researcher whose primary task was to collate information from the world's leading futurists. As a result, she was one of the few people to predict that drones would change the face of warfare and Russia would invade Ukraine, four years before the first tank even crossed the border.

'It's not only rare earth elements,' she said in a voice straight out of the Mississippi Delta. 'It will apply to every other precious metal imaginable. That is what SpaceX, Boeing, Galactic and their competitors are really reaching for – they plan to be the first commercial mining operation to hit the mother lode.'

'And what are we reaching for?' Antonio said into the silence. 'It used to be humanity's greatest dream, didn't it? To explore the universe, to boldly go where no man or woman has ever gone before, as Captain Kirk would say. Now space is just a strategic and corporate opportunity. Taking tourists into orbit ain't the half of it, for Chrissake! I know I'm old, but do you ever wonder what happened to us?'

24

NOBODY SAID ANYTHING, BUT FOR A MOMENT THE AIR SEEMED TO leave the room, dragged out by a sense of resignation and defeat. Antonio Silva was right: so many dreams had come to nothing.

Then the lights on the screen suddenly became even more brilliant, forcing everyone to look – apart from the pillars, one runway was now illuminated by powerful lamps on either side of the asphalt.

The black freighter with its historic cargo approached and hit the strip, throwing up puffs of smoke from its tyres before taxiing to a stop beside a construction crane. Dozens of men and women in coveralls, ghostly figures against the blaze of light, surrounded the craft and attached steel cables hanging from the crane to brackets on the side of the freighter. Only then was it clear that the back of the freighter was a removable pod containing the material that had been mined from some distant asteroid. The crane winched the pod off and deposited it on a huge transporter, its balloon tyres dwarfing the ground crew swarming around to secure it.

'That is just the landing crew,' Falcon said. 'The project is in its infancy. How many people will they need once they scale it up – support teams, refuellers, mechanics, workers in the processing plant, drivers and loaders, the whole system working three shifts a day, seven days a week? Thousands of people. Maybe that is why Kazinsky and all the others have been recruited.'

The images on the screen changed to show Kazinsky in the line at the Grozny airfield and I realized what a perfect candidate for the job he would be: he had grown up within sight of the dirtiest diamond pit in the world, worked in terrible conditions as a teenager mining for ivory in Siberia, spent most of his adult life in the cauldron – a place far more austere than anything on the Great Steppes – had served as one of the hard men of Spetsnaz and had shown he was a commanding leader; all of which meant he would have had no difficulty passing the security checks. Of course, they would have grabbed him.

'Does it pay?' the woman from the Delta asked. 'It says in the file we just received that he might have gone to Baikonur to raise money to fund a new terrorist organization. Is that possible?'

'Yes – it's possible, Alice,' Falcon replied. 'If they're not offering huge salaries and bonuses, how else do the Russians attract people to a closed city, the last stop on the line, where it hits over a hundred in summer and forty below in winter? The profits from rare earth minerals are so huge, money would be no object. With plenty of radicalized men willing to support a cause and several very wealthy mosques – well, you can see where it leads. Abu al-Zarqawi established al-Qaeda in Iraq with two hundred and fifty thousand dollars in seed money from bin Laden. That's always been the problem – terrorism is warfare on the cheap.'

'Once the material has landed, what happens to it?' I asked.

'The pod is taken to the processing plant,' Falcon replied. 'But the material is not removed until it is in a supposedly completely sealed environment. It is all robotic – kept isolated behind tempered glass – to prevent any contamination of Earth's environment.'

He summoned new footage on to the screens. I had experienced hell on earth in many different guises in my career, but I had never seen anything like the off-earth processing plant at the Cosmodrome.

Converted from an old industrial building, the dark interior was dominated by a dozen blast furnaces spewing bursts of smoke and red-hot flames and throwing twisted shadows across the towering brick walls. Enclosed conveyor belts criss-crossed the huge space, transporting piles of rock and ore into massive machines that crushed the raw material to powder. You could almost smell the air, fetid and thick with dust, feel the unbearable heat and hear the deafening machines.

Flowing through the entire structure – a chaos of scaffolding, pipes and machinery – was a stream of molten metal, promising an agonizing death to anyone who fell from the maze of rickety overhead walkways. It looked like the River Styx, the mythical boundary between the Earth and the underworld.

Certainly the scores of men toiling among the clouds of smoke – stripped to the waist, silhouetted against huge showers of sparks and breathing in the toxic air – looked like the inhabitants of another realm.

'As you can imagine, the monthly pay for working in such an environment is huge,' Falcon said. 'But the real money comes if the crew hits the monthly production target – the bonuses, in Russian terms, are off the charts. That's why a lot of recruits apply for the facility but only the toughest men are ever chosen. Not to be sexist about it, but you won't find any women here—'

'Too fucking smart, that's why,' Margaret said. 'Not to be sexist about it, of course.' It brought a peal of laughter from around the room, including from Falcon.

'The plant was built seventy years ago,' he continued. 'It was used to forge the steel used in the Soviet's fledgling rocket programme, but even then it must have seemed like a throwback to the darkest days of the Industrial Revolution – the deadly mills of Baltimore and Detroit. It has now been repurposed with the addition of this—'

He pointed at the screen as footage of a distant section of the plant, emerging through sparks and flying debris, came into focus. The camera moved close enough so that we could look through glass walls into a totally white, sealed environment: the freighter's cargo pod had negotiated an airlock, and now, inside the huge chamber, its cargo hatches opened automatically and robot scoops unloaded the off-earth ore on to a stainless-steel conveyor belt.

The belt transported the raw material into a series of sanitizing baths and under high-intensity lights that were designed to destroy any foreign organisms. As an added precaution, clearly in case of any sudden environmental emergency, huge industrial nozzles were ranged along the steel ceiling, ready to flood the sealed chamber with either a sterilizing gas or antiseptic spray. Once it had been cleansed, the conveyer belt carried the ore into a crusher. Pulverized, it emerged into another airlock and finally out into the plant for further processing.

Nearly everyone in the room was focused on the huge glass isolation chamber, but I was looking at something else entirely—

25

ONCE THE MEETING WAS OVER, I WAITED UNTIL ONLY FALCON remained. I made my way down the steps towards him: 'Can you tell me?' I asked quietly. 'How did you do it?'

'Do what?' he replied, turning.

'You've got an asset on the inside at Baikonur.'

'Do I?' he said innocently.

'The Aral Sea, the landing strips, the launch pads – I get all that,' I said. 'It was taken by satellites or spy planes flying at the edge of space. But what about the footage inside the processing plant? There was no other way – someone with a camera just fucking walked in there.'

We looked at each other for a long moment. Falcon didn't say anything, but he wasn't denying it. 'How the hell did they do it?' I asked. 'You can't just wander about a facility in a ZATO waving a camera around.'

'A miner's helmet,' Falcon said at last, breaking into a tight smile. 'You know – with a headlight on the front of 'em.' He pointed at his forehead. 'This one had a little more – hidden in the light was a 4K camera with a tiny gyroscope to keep the image steady. Wherever the person walked, it was shooting footage.'

I shook my head in admiration. 'But how did you even get an asset into Baikonur?'

'I didn't,' he replied. 'My predecessor did. She was a brilliant woman – she saw the future and acted on it.'

I didn't know her, she was before my time, but that was what everybody said about her. Falcon was her deputy and there were stories about the two of them, but I don't think anyone knew the truth. Perhaps the rumours continued to be whispered – even today, so many years afterwards – because on the rare occasions when he spoke about her it was always with a respect bordering on reverence. Sorrow too. A few months before her forty-seventh birthday she was diagnosed with a virulent form of breast cancer. She was gone six months later.

Her passing opened the door for Falcon, and here he was, still working with strategies she had put in place. 'Fifteen, twenty years ago,' he continued, 'she realized the newly resurgent Russians would pour money into their rocket space programme. Finding a source of information became her highest priority, and that led her to a man stationed at the Cosmodrome whose wife had never been able to join him – she had a chronic illness that required constant and expensive medical care in the outside world.' He shrugged. 'It was the old story – not everybody is a traitor, but everybody has a weakness.

'He became our asset and when he died unexpectedly his wife was still alive. With no real means of supporting herself – another member of the family, a doctor, took on the role.

'When it started, it was basic, smuggling out written accounts on microdots hidden in Christmas and birthday gifts. Incredibly inefficient, but it was the best we could do. Eventually everything changed, and if I can claim credit for anything, the miner's helmet was my idea – although it took two years before the asset could take possession of it while visiting the invalided relative at a hospital on the Black Sea.'

'Who is it – the asset?' I asked.

Falcon looked at me with something close to pity. 'You know better than that.'

'But the asset is looking for Kazinsky now?' I said.

'No,' Falcon replied.

'For fuck's sake, Falcon,' I said, my voice rising.

'Listen to me!' he shouted back. 'The asset is highly restricted in their movement – everybody is, it's a goddamn ZATO, ferchrissake! It was just coincidence that a visit to the processing plant coincided with the freighter's arrival. That was our luck. Be thankful for it.'

'Sorry.'

He nodded, accepting it. 'Anyway, I'm not sure what you are doing here. I spoke to Lucas Corrigan just before I arrived – he said you weren't on active service now; you were on light duties.'

'That's true,' I responded. 'Whatever "light duties" means.'

'I'm sure I can find something.'

26

IT HAD BEEN TWO WEEKS SINCE MY MEETING WITH CORRIGAN – TWO weeks that I had spent cooling my jets in the office, trying to adjust to the hours of inactivity – when I heard a tone from my computer indicating that a high-priority message had just hit my inbox.

Jacket already in hand, I was about to head out of my office to try and beat the rush at the busiest Starbucks in the world. I unlocked the computer and saw that the message was from Falcon. As I opened the first of the attached files, a strange silence seemed to engulf the world. Some people might have said it was the universe marking the moment when the stars aligned but, as I mentioned earlier, I was not one of them.

I paid the silence no mind, saw the codename Magus on the title page and realized it was what Falcon had meant when he said he'd find something for an incapacitated spy to work on. It had been my intention to take only a cursory glance, but I ended up pulling up a chair and reading the files until night fell. When I finished, I called Clay in the Tomb and asked him for all the raw material on which the files were based. By then I had decided it was my way back in. Even Lucas Corrigan's concerns about my panic attacks would carry far less weight with Falcon if such a difficult issue as the Magus's betrayal in Tehran could be resolved.

I also asked Clay for a favour. I needed him to look the other way so that I could take everything home and work on it over the weekend to prepare myself for the dawn meeting with Falcon on Monday.

As I had expected, the archivist – good man that he was – waved me and the files through and, at home, in a bedroom converted to an office, I worked far into the night, making copious notes. After a few hours' sleep I got up before sunrise and continued, scattering paper files on the floor and having a host of different files open on my three screens. It wasn't what anyone would call an important intelligence operation so, for once, I had left the door unlocked.

Listening through headphones to an interview with the motor-cycle taxi driver who had helped the Magus make his rapid exit from the Espinas Hotel, it was only when I took the cans off that I realized Rebecca was in the doorway, waiting for me to finish. She had just arrived from work: sweat-stained, hair pulled back and exhausted. I smiled as she picked her way through the papers on the floor and kissed me.

'It's 5 a.m.,' she said. 'I never sleep because young residents aren't allowed to – it's a rule, apparently. But you do it from choice, and that's sort of crazy. I'm talking as a doctor here.' She smiled and looked at a photo of the Magus on one of the screens.

It showed a tall and lean man, in his late forties when the photo was taken, handsome with dark, wavy hair and tanned skin, but already showing evidence of a dissolute life: the jowls starting to sag and the eyes discoloured from too many late nights drinking in Dubai.

'Another bad guy?' she asked.

'Yeah, he was one of our most trusted assets until we found out he was batting for the other team. Of course, because he did it to us, he's a traitor; if he was Russian and did it to them, we'd call him a hero. Confusing, right? Someone who once had Falcon's job described the secret world as "a wilderness of mirrors".'

'What happened to him?' she asked, indicating the man on the screen.

'Disappeared. The agency has been trying to find him for years. The theory is I might have a chance because I know how to hide. Apart from that, they need to give me something to do.' I smiled.

'Getting close?'

'Not really. You start with the family or the lover, the things people find the hardest to leave behind – but for twenty-five years he worked in the covert world, so he knows our approach. Long before he went rogue, he would have set up some form of communication system with his wife or mistress that we can't uncover. Probably encrypted messages on a board on the Dark Web – similar to a method we use in Afghanistan.'

'Friends?' she suggested. 'Not everybody can be using a secret message board.'

'Most of his friends are dead.' I pulled out a series of photos of the ten bodies hanging from cranes in Tehran. 'Our traitor and four of his closest friends were part of an intelligence network,' I said. 'That's what happened after he revealed their names to the Iranians.'

'He sold out his friends?' Rebecca asked, shocked. 'What sort of person does that?'

'Only four were friends,' I said. 'The other six who were executed were just colleagues so I guess they were expendable. What sort of person does it? Someone who loves money.'

'That part makes sense,' she said. 'He's got expensive taste.'

I looked at her. It was a strange thing to say, given the small number of pictures, videos and documents she could see. 'Why do you say that?'

She picked up a newspaper clipping showing him on a bridge over the River Spree in Berlin twenty years earlier. It was a winter's night and the story said a woman had thrown herself into the freezing water and would have died if a passing motorist had not stopped, dived in and dragged her to shore. I think I said earlier – the Magus was a brave man.

Accompanying the story was a photo from the scene and another shot in which he was smoking, looking into the camera. 'He's driving a Mercedes,' she said. 'The overcoat he threw off before he dived in didn't come off the rack, and there's the cigarette,' Rebecca said.

'What?' I asked.

'The cigarette,' she said. 'Look at it – we always think of cigarettes as white, but I don't think this one is. Maybe it's the shadow, but there is one type that's black and has a gold band at the filter. Sobranie Black Russian – they're unusual – and very expensive.'

'And you know this – how?' was my next question.

'They're popular among some wealthy, elite groups in Japan,' she explained. 'When I went on the rounds with my exchange hosts there was a patient in the hospital who was a senior lieutenant – a *saiko komon* – in the Yakuza. He had them delivered every day.'

I stared at her, my mind racing, and I started to rifle through the files until I found a photo taken from the CCTV footage of the night the Magus betrayed us. He was sitting at the table in the bistro of the Espinas Hotel, his raincoat hanging over a chair and the ashtray holding the crumpled credit-card receipt and the butts of two cigarettes.

'See – a grand hotel. I told you he likes luxury,' Rebecca said.

'No – look at the cigarettes stubbed out in the ashtray,' I said.

She took a moment. 'It's difficult. Even the ends of them are crushed – maybe . . . maybe they're the same.'

I picked up a closely typed report written several years before. 'The research report says they're cigarillos – thin, small cigars – probably Cuban. No marks, untraceable.'

'That might be right,' she replied, examining the photo even more closely. 'I guess the casing of a cigarillo is really dark too – but look, that could be a tiny corner of gold. If it is, I bet they're Sobranie Black Russians.'

I was already half lost in thought. 'It's possible some researcher might have been mistaken or made an assumption. The files show the agency tested everything – the DNA on the butts, the make of the raincoat, every last detail of the credit-card receipt – but maybe nobody ever questioned the belief that they were cigarillos.'

Rebecca smiled, pleased to have contributed. 'Well, I guess I'm done,' she said. 'I'm going to bed. If Langley needs any more help, you know where I am.'

'It would mean he's been smoking the same cigarettes for over twenty years,' I said to myself. 'What are the chances he would change brands now?' As Rebecca headed out the door, I picked up my phone and dialled.

27

IT WAS STILL EARLY ON A SATURDAY MORNING AND I COULD TELL immediately I had woken Madeleine up. It came as a shock, and I don't really know why, to realize from a muffled voice in the background that she was in bed with someone.

As she asked me to hold for a moment I heard her putting on some clothes and then the voice spoke more clearly – it was a woman, volunteering to get them both a coffee.

'It's brand new, our first night together, so your timing was impeccable,' Madeleine said as she walked into my office an hour later, took off her jacket and put down two coffees and a bag of bagels she had bought us for breakfast.

She opened her laptop and showed me an enhanced image of the cigarette butts in the ashtray. 'It's from NSA twenty minutes ago,' she said. 'You can see there is a fragment of gold band on one of them. It's meaningless – unless your "confidential source" is correct and they are Sobranie Black Russians.

'I assume the source is right, and I have told my friends at NSA I need help tracking a terrorist. I've asked them to try and access the distribution and sales information from Japan Tobacco—'

'Japan Tobacco owns the brand?' I asked.

'Ultimately. How much do you know about Sobranie?'

I shook my head. She went on.

'At one stage they were cigarette suppliers to almost every crowned head of Europe. The Black Russians – the top of the tree – are still made in Ukraine and the gold-banded filter is embossed with the imperial crest of the czars.'

'The czars? Very fancy,' I replied. 'Thank God they're special – if you could buy 'em at a gas station we wouldn't have a prayer. Let's hope your buddies at NSA can help – what we need is a list of the distributors and shops that sell them.'

'I know,' Madeleine said. 'But London, Paris, Tokyo or New York – cities like that – they won't be much use. There will be thousands of customers.'

'I don't think that's where the Magus is hiding,' I said. 'We're looking for something unusual – somebody living in the Australian outback who gets ten cartons on a special order.'

'Assuming we can find something like it, when do we need it by?'

'Six a.m. Monday,' I said. I didn't tell her, but I wanted to blow Falcon's immaculate silk socks off.

28

I ARRIVED AT FALCON'S EMPTY OFFICE A FEW MINUTES EARLY AND waited for him in his anteroom, looking at the photos and awards hanging on what he called his 'wall of shame'.

They showed him as a young man in combat fatigues in the Middle East and South America, posing in the Oval Office with three presidents, standing alongside the heads of state of countries stretching from New Zealand to Sweden, visiting a battlefield in the Balkans and in various gilded mansions with half of the world's worst tyrants.

I heard the door behind me open and I indicated a clutch of war zones. 'Afghanistan, Syria, 9/11, Iraq, the War on Terror, Ukraine,' I said. 'Does it ever end?'

Falcon stood beside me. 'It's like Lenin said: "There are decades when nothing happens and weeks when decades happen."' He laughed. 'I got the latter. Did you read the files?'

'Yes,' I replied as he buzzed himself into his office, and we sat down at his small conference table.

'We have to get a list of ideas to at least explore,' he said. 'Anything we can think of. I don't hold out much hope, everything has been pored over—'

I opened my briefcase and laid out sheets of data. 'What's that?' he asked.

'A list of distributors and sales points from Japan Tobacco.'

'The cigarillos?' he replied.

'Except they're cigarettes. Very exclusive – the crowned heads of Europe and the Yakuza have more in common than we thought. They both like Sobranie Black Russians.'

Falcon stared. 'And this is what he was smoking at the hotel? How do you know?'

'A tiny fragment of gold on one of the butts. He's been smoking them for twenty years,' I said. 'Remember the photo on the Berlin bridge? Same cigarettes.'

'And you think, wherever he's holed up, he's still smoking them?' Falcon asked.

'I don't know, but why stop now?' I replied. 'There are two places that are relatively remote where the cigarettes are delivered to. This is the island of St Kitts in the Caribbean.'

I laid out photos showing rugged mountains, palm-fringed beaches and beautiful resorts. 'Plenty of expensive homes, about a thousand packs of Black Russians sold at the exclusive wine shop every year,' I said. 'Maybe a resident or two smokes them, but St Kitts is also popular with oligarchs on their mega-yachts. They probably love cigarettes embossed with the crest of the czars.'

'Seriously – the royal crest?' Falcon said as he leafed through photos of half a navy of huge boats riding at anchor in the island's marinas and ports. 'And the other place?'

I showed him satellite images of a chain of tiny islands. 'Barely on the map. Located halfway between Greece and Turkey, right where the Aegean meets the Mediterranean.

'Some are uninhabited, others are home to fishing villages and the large estates of people who value privacy above anything else.'

I showed him photos taken by the FBI several years before of several estates with stables, multiple swimming pools, private beaches and one with a zoo featuring a pride of lions. 'One of the smaller islands is owned by a "Sicilian family", if you get my drift.'

'And there are shops out there?'

'On some of the larger ones,' I replied. 'Basic stuff mostly, and there are a few beach restaurants. The most interesting place is a sort of trading post – it was set up to supply the yachts that sail the Greek and Turkish islands during spring and summer.'

I pulled out photos of the store and slid them across the table. They showed a boatshed-style structure at the end of a wharf. Painted white and blue, it seemed to almost float on the sparkling water. 'The guy running it has a good business – boats cruising the area send in an order for wine and food, whatever they need, well ahead of time; he imports the goods from the mainland, packs it in fancy boxes, they pick it up and he charges a hefty premium.' I paused. 'Every three months he gets a hundred packets of Black Russians from the distributor in Istanbul.'

Falcon looked more closely at the photos of the trading post. 'A hundred packs – one a day for somebody with a twenty-year habit. Or it could be the owner orders them for the vacationing boats. There must be plenty of wealthy people coming through.'

'It could be nothing; maybe you're right,' I replied. 'But it's also a chance.'

'No, it's more than that. It's the best lead we've had. I'll send people out to have a look.'

'No,' I replied.

'No?' he said.

'You send me.'

He held my gaze for a beat. 'What am I not getting here? Aren't you grounded?' I couldn't tell if he was serious or toying with me. 'Of course,' he continued, 'there might be an agent who thinks that by doing a great job I might be persuaded to countermand Lucas and put them back on the active service list.' He was toying.

'You think somebody would try such a thing?' I asked.

'I know, it's hard to imagine,' he replied.

'But now you mention it,' I said. 'A few night sweats don't indicate much at all. You could say they're a rational person's response to being taken prisoner in Iran.'

'Funny,' Falcon replied, 'that's not much different to what Lucas said privately.' He picked up the images showing the tiny chain of islands and leafed through them again. 'We don't even know if he's there, do we? Okay, you go – but first thing, you run your own reconnaissance. See how it plays. If you find him, you call for back-up – he's dangerous – I have ten people hanging from cranes to prove it.'

29

BECAUSE OF MY WORK, I HAVE LIVED A VIVID LIFE AND BEEN TO A number of extraordinary places, but I have never seen anything quite like the trading post at the end of the universe.

A weather-beaten wharf, the colour of driftwood, ran out from a small and deserted beach, its arc of golden sand protected by pure-white cliffs. On top of one of them, its ragged cloth sails turning slowly in the wind, was a Turkish windmill with a thatched roof. Framing it all, stretching to the horizon, were the sparkling turquoise waters of the Aegean and the aquamarine of the Mediterranean. Perched at the end of the wharf, painted pale blue and a brilliant white, seeming to float between water and sky, was the old boatshed-turned-store. The structure was fronted on three sides by awnings and pergolas, and a Tibetan prayer flag on a tall pole fluttered in the breeze, silently blessing the surrounding landscape.

I first caught sight of it from the bow of a broken-down inter-island ferry I had boarded in İzmir in Turkey – rust streaking its decks, an old diesel engine thumping so loud below I had doubts about whether we would make it out of the port. The whole wreck was so badly designed, it was one of the only times I have ever actually listened as a deckhand, this guy long past retirement age, gave us a run-down on where the flotation jackets and life rafts were located.

There were only five of us taking passage: myself and four American college students backpacking through Europe and planning to stay at a small hostel on one of the myriad islands' hidden beaches. They were determined to start a conversation but, thankfully, my command of Turkish – seemingly my only language – managed to make it so difficult that they soon admitted defeat and retreated to the benches at the stern to share a spliff. To the three deckhands, I was a businessman from Istanbul going to tidy up the affairs of my father, who had died a few days earlier. As a result, between the language barrier and my grief, I managed to travel in silence – by far the best option for an intelligence agent without any legend to speak of.

I saw the deckhands prepare the mooring ropes, felt the wind change direction on my face as we rounded a long isthmus of pine-covered land and watched the wharf and the trading post come into view. I opened my backpack, pushed aside the two weapons and their spare ammunition clips, and pulled out a pair of small binoculars, the sort of thing any well-organized traveller might carry.

I tracked from the prayer flag, past the café tables and found the owner on the wharf, ready to help tie up the ferry. The fifty-year-old guy looked little different to the photos that the Drug Enforcement Agency had provided: squat and well muscled with slicked-back dark hair and even darker eyes. According to the DEA, he had done time for stabbing a rival drug dealer almost to death in Istanbul and now supplemented the provision of foie gras and other gourmet trifles with a more lucrative sideline: cocaine and ecstasy. Apparently the demand among the wealthy yacht owners was high enough to warrant the drug agency's interest, but every attempt to prosecute him had failed to gain traction with the Turkish police; apparently quite a few of the boat owners were very well connected.

With my backpack over my shoulder, casually dressed, I disembarked the ferry and then, as it headed off to its next destination, I entered the shop. The owner, Yusuf Kaplan – commonly known as Tiger since his days running crack houses in Istanbul – smiled from behind the counter and asked if I wanted a coffee and where was I headed.

'Coffee'd be great,' I replied in Turkish. 'And a pack of cigarettes.'

'Marlboro, Benson & Hedges, Chesterfield – name your poison,' he replied.

'Sobranie Black Russians,' I said, changing to English.

He looked at me hard. 'We don't have those,' he said, his eyes suddenly alert. I was standing opposite him with only the oak-topped counter between us.

'You don't stock them?' I asked.

'No,' he replied, and I knew then I had come to the right place. Why would he lie about carrying them? Before I left Langley, I had figured that if the Magus was in the islands, he would be paying the store owner a retainer to alert him if anyone started asking difficult questions.

'I think you're mistaken,' I said. 'Can you check for me?' I saw his right hand slide out of sight below the counter. A knife or a gun, I wondered.

'I don't know who you are,' he said. 'But I told you I don't stock 'em. Now I am going to give you some advice. Pick up your pack and get out of here.'

'Strange,' I said. 'You don't get a hundred packs every three months from the distributor in Istanbul?'

His right hand reappeared fast. It was a gun. But already he was screaming – my hand had shot out and grabbed him by his hair while my left chopped down hard on his forearm, sending the gun flying. My fingers twisted his hair, making him yell louder, and I drove his head down, smashing his face into the counter.

Blood was streaming everywhere and, though it was not strictly necessary, I smacked his face down hard on the counter again and spread his nose even further. I have to admit it's a small prejudice of mine: I've never liked drug dealers.

Tears were streaming from his glazed eyes and I raised his face up so that he could look straight at me. 'Who are you?' he asked.

'Not the sort of man you ever want to meet, Tiger. How do they get to the smoker?'

He said nothing, either from shock or reluctance. I tightened my grip on his hair and he knew he was about to visit the countertop again. 'How are they delivered?' I repeated.

30

I SAW THE LITTLE FREIGHTER APPROACHING THE WHARF AT DAWN THE next morning. She was old and sturdy and, though she must have seen plenty of heavy weather over the years, her hull was well painted and the brightwork polished and glinting in the sun.

From what Yusuf Kaplan had said through his broken teeth, the skipper – an Egyptian, a fourth-generation sailor out of Alexandria – made a living by delivering supplies to the villages and estates scattered among the islands.

Kaplan himself was handcuffed, one wrist and one ankle, to heavy bolts – a useful legacy of the boatshed's past – set into the floor of its bar area. There was no hope of him escaping – or contacting anyone for that matter; I had destroyed the three mobile phones I had found and had fitted him with a ball gag I had brought with me specially for the purpose. The last thing I needed was for him to start yelling to attract the attention of any visitors.

As it happened, there were only three instances of that – crew members of large yachts that were passing through on their way to İzmir or Bodrum – and on each occasion they had left after reading the sign I had attached to the door in Turkish and English: *Closed due to unforeseen medical emergency.* Now, as the small freighter approached, I removed the sign and waited for the door to open.

The skipper was a short and lean man, in his sixties, still fit thanks to the hard physical work and with a spark in his eye that would not have been out of place in a much younger person. He called out as he entered, looked around the interior, saw Kaplan with his crushed and bloodied nose handcuffed to the floor, and then registered me with a

Sig Sauer 9mm pointed in his direction. He nodded at me: 'Under new management, I see.'

I laughed – he was certainly showing grace under pressure and I liked him immediately.

'How can I help you?' I asked.

'I was hoping to fuel up,' he replied.

'We're running a special promotion today,' I said. 'Introductory offer – free fuel.'

'I like the new management already,' he paused. 'What do I have to do?'

'You deliver Sobranie cigarettes to a man. Take me there.'

He looked from the pistol to Kaplan's bloodied face. 'I think I can do that,' he said evenly.

31

THE SKIPPER SQUINTED AGAINST THE GLARE OF THE SUN AND POINTED out the island as I raised the binoculars, steadied myself against the roll of the deck in the long swell and followed the direction of his outstretched arm.

I saw the wreck of an old boat lying on a reef with half her steel sides hollowed out and her exposed propeller turning in the breaking waves. The skipper saw what I was looking at. 'It's bad water,' he said. 'A sailor has to know what he's doing when he comes here.'

'Maybe not just a sailor,' I replied, keeping the glasses raised, looking beyond the wreck to hidden coves and dangerous beaches carved out by strong currents.

'You see the villa?' the skipper asked, intermittently shouting orders to his two disinterested Sudanese deckhands. 'Look for the red bougainvillea.'

I found the splash of colour and concentrated hard. It was as if the large house – which must have had spectacular views – was camouflaged. Set into the side of a hill, with foliage tumbling all around it and covering the roof, not even someone with a pair of high-powered field glasses would be able to see it unless they knew exactly where to look.

'How do you access it?' I asked.

'There's a boatshed and a track through the pine forest on the other side of the headland.'

'And you leave the propane, cigarettes, food and other supplies in the boatshed?'

'Yes,' the skipper replied. 'There's an intercom, and I buzz and tell him it's waiting.'

'How long before he picks the stuff up?'

'Depends,' he said. 'Sometimes that day, sometimes three or four days.'

It was critical that I got close enough to identify him because it was possible – not likely, but possible – that by some terrible fluke the man on the island was not the Magus but just some other fugitive or recluse with a taste for expensive cigarettes. Before I had left Langley, I had thought of downloading file photos of him and showing them to the likes of Yusuf Kaplan, but then I realized: the work the Magus had paid for at Gstaad or Villars would have changed his appearance so dramatically that any earlier image of him would have been useless. As for me, I had met him several times in a different life, and I was reasonably confident – if I could get close enough to observe him – I would be able to see through the cosmetic changes. The problem was, I had neither the supplies nor the resources to wait four days until he came down to the boathouse.

I had little choice but to approach the villa. 'He's alone?' I asked.

'Yeah, always alone.'

'What does he do – how does he pass the time?'

'Travels a few times a year. I pick him up, take him to the trading post and he catches the ferry to the mainland,' the skipper said.

'Any idea where?'

'No, he's not what you would call talkative – but I guess you know that.' He looked at me, trying to open up the conversation, but I held his gaze until he averted his eyes. 'Then again, nor are you.'

He went to take the wheel as the freighter rounded the headland and a few minutes later I saw the boatshed tucked into the corner of a cove, a small wooden structure barely visible in the shadows cast by the trees and cliffs. I doubted if any passing boat had noticed it in years.

'Are you one of those sailors who knows what he's doing?' I asked the skipper as I saw a plume of water splash up close ahead as a swell hit an underwater outcrop of rock.

'I hope so,' he said wryly. 'How about you? You ready?' He indicated the two Sudanese guys, who were lowering a small aluminium skiff with an outboard from a jib.

I reached into my jacket, pulled out a thick wad of US dollars and tossed it to him. 'There's five thousand,' I said. 'The same again if you're still here when I get back.'

He stared at the money. Ten thousand was probably more than he made in a couple of years. 'How long will you be?' he asked.

'If I'm not here by nightfall, go. I won't be coming,' I said, shouldering the backpack, sliding the action on the Sig Sauer and checking the ammunition clip.

Yes, I was ready.

32

THE TOTAL SILENCE WAS THE MOST STRIKING THING. I HAD WADED ashore from the small boat, watched the Sudanese guys make their way back to the mother ship and entered the boatshed through an unlocked door.

It was cool inside, the water surging under the floorboards, with a long set of railway tracks extending through barn doors. It allowed a rubber Zodiac inflatable sitting on it to be launched almost immediately. Maybe it was just someone's recreational craft or maybe it was a hunted agent's fast escape vehicle.

Along one wooden wall was a desk, a row of bookshelves and numerous files and bills. Light spilled through a long, cantilevered window and I could imagine how pleasant it would be to work with the window open, the sea breeze blowing in and the whole structure shaded from the worst of the sun. A hammock was slung from two poles and near the desk was a large wastebasket full of discarded bills and files, waiting to be shredded. People only do that with confidential material and I made a mental note to scoop it all up when I left.

I put the backpack down – I didn't want to be encumbered by it – and opened the refrigerator. It was stacked with different craft beers and, given how hot it was already, I was sorely tempted. I took a large bottle of water instead.

It was fortunate I did. The track that led to the villa was much steeper than it had first appeared and, for once, I was pleased about the battery of tests I had undergone to prove myself fit. Running to minimize my time in what I had to assume was hostile territory, I still had to stop twice to drink and give my calves a rest. On the last occasion, I turned to see the way I had come, and paused: the view was extraordinary. Through the slender branches of a stand of cypress trees I saw a vast sweep of shimmering blue water and two gulls – the only sign of life – skimming the swell. In the overwhelming silence I stood for a long moment, taking it all in – it would have been hard to imagine a scene more distant from a square in Tehran and ten bodies dangling from cranes.

With that in mind, I returned to the task at hand and started to climb the track again, keeping even closer to the shadows as I came within sight of the villa. I stopped and lifted the binoculars to my eyes: there was no sign of life. The gardens and grounds were totally overgrown, long ago having returned to nature, while the house itself was virtually inaccessible thanks to the cliff behind it and a series of tall and unscalable walls. They were either covered in vines or thorn-laden bougainvillea and the small patches of plaster and brick still visible were crumbling and water-damaged. Any casual observer – or satellite analyst – who knew nothing about the trading post and the boatshed would have said it was just an abandoned house on a remote island.

Yet, from my vantage point – slightly above the house and assisted by the glasses – there was something about the whole appearance of it . . . something hard to describe . . . almost like the house was too perfect a version of being abandoned, as if it had been curated.

I moved forward, circling the structure, cautious about motion detectors or concealed pressure pads, but there was no easy way in – just a heavy basement door. But it was my only option and better than risking the thorns on the bougainvillea – the next best option, to my mind – so I approached slowly, stuck the Sig in the waistband at the small of my back and had both hands free to work the lock picks and tension wrench I pulled from my pocket.

It was a good, well-maintained lock, totally out of character with a derelict house, and very difficult to pick. Finally, I felt the action trip and I opened the door. It was a small storage area: drums of chemicals just visible in the gloom, a collection of aluminium poles, half a dozen large pumps in a corner working almost silently and – on the far side – a set of stairs with a door at the top. I closed the one behind me, decided against using a flashlight, and in total darkness crossed the room and climbed the steps.

Sig in hand, I listened for a long time and then slowly, silently, pushed open the door.

33

WHAT I FOUND WAS REMARKABLE, BEAUTIFUL EVEN. AN INDOOR swimming pool shimmered in semi-darkness, the mellow brick walls were softly lit and reached up to a vaulted ceiling aglow with tiny stars. A marble Medusa's head, half submerged in the pool, spouted water as classical music played on hidden speakers. If I closed my eyes a little, I might well have been in a Roman bathhouse or the famous water cistern in Old Istanbul.

Slowly, I walked around the pool and came to a set of glass doors opening into a lounge area with a sweeping staircase. I went through the doors and climbed the stairs, worried less that a voice might call out in alarm than that the last thing I'd hear was the cocking of a pistol and the sharp retort of a bullet firing.

As I moved carefully, gliding – every shadow a threat – the rest of the villa unfolded around me. It was even more remarkable than the pool. Wide corridors led to sumptuous living rooms, a wood-panelled library opened on to a vast terrace and I passed half a dozen hidden courtyards full of terracotta pots, white awnings and luxuriant ferns. Fountains and antique waterspouts bubbled in nooks and a koi pond dominated a walled garden; no wonder there were so many pumps in the basement.

From somewhere deep inside the house, I heard a man's voice – soft, just a fragment of sound – but with the Sig held high and ready, I followed its direction and entered a family-style dining area. On the far side was a large kitchen and a man standing in front of a gas hob – flames leaping, going full blast – sautéing shrimp in a pan, singing quietly to himself in Italian.

He was taller than the Magus and the hairline was markedly different, as were the nose and cheeks, but that could have been shin implants and surgery. Standing in the shadows, I watched him: picking up a plastic bottle of oil, adding it to the pan, reaching past a small kitchen fire extinguisher and adding salt from a bowl. There was something in the way he held himself – the tilt of his head, the habit of running his hand through his hair as he took a step – that made me believe I had found him.

I kept watching though, wanting to make sure, and then I saw him hesitate for a fraction of a second. He was looking at the stainless-steel cooking hood, and I realized: he had seen my reflection in the polished metal. He didn't panic like any normal person, and that spoke volumes about his identity, and then all my doubts evaporated as he spoke; it is strange that people can spend a fortune to change their appearance but they pay no attention to their voice. I had heard him in the flesh and listened to numerous recordings of him, so I knew from his first words that, after so many years and so much effort, the agency had finally found its man.

'I wondered when somebody might come,' he said sadly, without turning. He shrugged and sort of smiled, indicating it was all over, seemingly resigned to his fate. 'They always do, don't they?' I felt no sympathy, just thinking about his betrayal.

He turned to face me, his left hand went to switch off the gas, I registered his greatly altered features and for the briefest moment his right hand was hidden from view. It all exploded at once, he wasn't resigned to his fate at all—

His left hand spun the gas higher, the flames shot upwards, his right hand swept the bottle of cooking oil on to the hob, the plastic melted instantly, the oil hit the flame, plumes of fire roared up, the exhaust fan in the hood dragged it to the ceiling, I slipped the safety off the Sig and aimed, but he was diving, stretching full length, grabbing the fire extinguisher as he hit the ground and combat-rolled—

I fired through the billowing clouds of black smoke and flame, but I was vying with what experts call the 'startle effect' – reeling from a burst of sudden and unanticipated events – and the three shots, sounding deafening in the silence, missed him by an inch or more.

Adjusting my aim, expecting to be hit by a blast of chemical foam from the extinguisher and blinded at any moment, he hurled it instead. Not at me – into the roaring flames on the cooking hob. I had never thought that a fire extinguisher could be a lethal weapon – and certainly it had never been mentioned in any of the training sessions about improvised explosive devices I had ever attended.

The Magus must have invented it on the fly, realizing that under the right conditions a pressurized container could serve as an effective bomb – and the conditions that day were about as perfect as possible. As I learned later, at 175 degrees Celsius the pressure inside a fire extinguisher becomes uncontainable. A gas hob – and the one in the villa was part of a four-alarm fire – can burn at almost *two thousand* degrees Celsius.

The Magus was still rolling, seeking shelter against the heavy benches, when the laws of physics and chemistry took over. The fire extinguisher exploded, sending a hail of metal shrapnel straight at me. The chemical powder inside it vaporized and turned to rolling white clouds, engulfing the kitchen, giving him cover, as I hurled myself aside. It was a brilliant piece of tradecraft—

I hit the floor as the blast passed overhead, then I felt a searing pain in the back of my left shoulder and smelled the reek of burning flesh; a piece of red-hot metal had just hit the soft tissue. By the time I had scrambled to my feet and was getting ready to open fire again, the agonizing pain had passed and I knew that it was bad; with burns, you want the pain to show the nerves are still intact. I had no choice but to ignore it and tried to see through the fire, smoke and vapour. There was no sign of the Magus and – knowing that he'd in all likelihood already accessed a weapon – I upended an oak table and crouched behind it. I fired three brackets of three at the base of the kitchen benches, but there was no reaction so I slid the magazine out and replaced it while I could.

Fully loaded, I ducked and weaved into the kitchen, ready to shoot if I saw any movement. There was none and, as the roiling smoke and vapour thinned, I saw a door into the walled garden swinging on its hinges.

I sprinted through it and registered someone's shadow on the far side of the koi pond. Behind a trellis of climbing roses was an earthen ramp leading to the top of the wall, and the Magus was already going over it. Although I knew I had little chance, I fired off two rounds, hoping that even if I didn't hit him, the same startle effect might make him fall. It didn't.

By the time I had followed him to the top of the wall, jumped at full reach, grabbed the branch of an overhanging cypress tree and swung to the ground, he was gone. The Magus – a magician indeed. Except I had one asset: I was certain he would be calculating his options as he ran. He knew, with his identity and location blown, I would call in support and within hours of the choppers landing his island would no longer be a refuge but a prison and he would be hunted down. He had to get off the island fast and head to another bolt-hole or a boat he had on standby. His only option was the Zodiac with its big outboard and long-range fuel tank. I wheeled and started to run—

Plunging through the pine forest, trying to intersect with the trail, going downhill was far more challenging than the climb to the villa. Every hidden root or outcrop threatened to send me into a headlong crash. More through luck than skill, I stayed upright, sped past where I had stopped to admire the view, turned a bend and saw that the large barn doors of the boatshed were already open.

I accelerated, hoping to get close enough to fire once the Zodiac emerged. The trail took a hairpin, but I went overland, saving myself precious seconds and, with growing confidence that I would make it, I reconnected with the path, took a switchback, lost sight of the boat-shed and came round a turn, only to see that I had failed.

He was further ahead of me than I had thought and the Zodiac was already on the rails, slipping out of the shed and into deeper water. I saw the Magus standing at the stern, starting the outboard, and while I could see him I couldn't stop him: he was out of range of the pistol.

As I plunged on, I saw tendrils of smoke spilling from the boatshed window and I wondered if the Magus had set the building alight; if he had and my backpack was going up in flames, everything was lost.

By the time I burst into the shed, drenched in sweat with blood trickling down my back from the burn, the Zodiac was weaving through the treacherous water, making its way towards the open sea. I only had two minutes at most, but at least the shed wasn't on fire. Instead, he had set alight the wastebasket containing the papers, trying to destroy anything important before he left.

His attempt hadn't been very successful, the basket was only smouldering, and as I grabbed the backpack I decided, in case we had to track him later, to stamp out the fire and save what I could. I raised my foot then stopped with a second to spare. Something was wrong—

He was too thorough to leave clues lying in a wastebasket and I stepped back. It was human nature to stamp out a fire and perhaps that was what he was relying on. I looked at the base of the wastebasket and gave a grim smile – my God, he was a piece of work.

I turned, pulled the second gun out of the backpack, the one I thought I wouldn't need, and ran for the barn doors. The weapon was an MCX Rattler, the world's most compact rifle, only sixteen inches long but able to fire a .300 Blackout round – larger than the standard-issue NATO cartridge – and as a result could hit as hard as many much larger weapons.

I unfolded the stock, braced myself against a timber pole and saw the Zodiac negotiating the last of the choppy water, driving hard against a strong current. With the craft bucking and weaving wildly, the Magus crouched in the stern trying to hold on and steer. It was going to be a difficult shot even without the plumes of spray being thrown up by the outboard.

No time for niceties, I played the percentages and fired at the Zodiac's thick rubber skin to deflate it. At the sound of the first shot, the Magus dived headlong into the belly of the inflatable – if not entirely out of danger, at least out of sight. Those vessels were built like rhinos and the first four shots seemed to have no effect on it. I fired two more and saw the second of them rip a large hole in the rubber near the stern and then a tongue of flame shot out. The projectile, travelling with a muzzle velocity of two thousand feet a second – and glowing red hot – must have gone straight through the inflatable tube and hit the fuel tank.

Moments later the combination of an almost sealed container, gasoline, oxygen and flame caused what scientists call a self-perpetuating reaction – an explosion, in other words – that tore the Zodiac in two and launched a massive fireball.

I searched the shards of rubber and metal hurtling skyward for the Magus's body, almost certain I would see it cartwheeling thirty feet into the air – surely nothing could survive the explosion – but I saw no sign of him or any body parts.

There was no sign of him in the maelstrom of foam and flying spray or the surrounding water, so I was fairly confident that he must have been killed by the explosion or drowned. I turned and walked inside. I had found him, cornered him and destroyed his only method of escape. There was nothing more I could do.

In the boathouse, I saw the smouldering wastepaper basket and picked up a lead fishing weight lying by the door. Standing back, I landed it in the basket, and it did exactly what a stomping foot would have done – it triggered the anti-personnel mine welded under the container. It blew it to the roof and scattered debris across the room. I figured the Magus must have prepared the device years before and had it ready, just in case. Like I said, he was a piece of work.

Fortunate to be alive, I turned and looked out at the fiery carcass of the Zodiac, pulled an encrypted phone out of my pocket and dialled Falcon.

34

I WALKED INTO HIS OFFICE FULL OF OPTIMISM – I WAS ALMOST certain the Magus was dead and, as a result, I had resolved one of the agency's most intractable cold cases – but I still left twenty minutes later a half-broken man.

On the island, I rejoined the freighter and gave the skipper his extra five grand on condition he take me to İzmir on the Turkish mainland, the site of a large airport, and from there I hitched a ride on a GreenEnergy jet to Washington.

There were half a dozen wild boys on board – Marine Raiders – who had been into Belarus, near the Russian border, to sabotage a small biological research facility. The plane was still on the apron, but they were already making good use of the courtesy bar. 'Agency?' one of them, an arrogant guy, asked as they watched me pass.

'Me?' I said, laughing. 'No, flight crew relocating.'

'Stewardess?' the guy asked. His colleagues laughed as I sat down, but at least I was spared the necessity of spending the entire journey listening to their war stories.

It was only when we landed at Andrews and a nurse came on board and checked the wound in my shoulder that they decided to look at me more closely. Their curiosity spiked even further when the pilot ordered them to remain in their seats while I disembarked.

A black SUV was waiting to meet me and, as a close protection officer opened the door, he indicated the faces of the wild boys staring out the plane windows. 'Buddies of yours?'

'No, the circus left town, but the clowns stayed behind,' I said.

He laughed, and thirty minutes later Falcon was shaking my hand and guiding me towards a chair facing his desk. Strange, I thought – we always sat on the sofas, and there was a formality in his manner that I hadn't seen before or expected now. 'Like I said on the phone, it seems like it was a success. Congratulations,' he said, without much emotion.

'You searched the island?' I asked.

'Five minutes after you called, I had six teams of ten people on their way by chopper.'

'And?' I asked.

'No sign of him. We couldn't find a body either, but that's not surprising – those currents and tides could have carried it anywhere. The thought is he'll be washed ashore after the next big storm.'

I nodded, but I had my doubts. I thought of the booby trap in the wastebasket and how much forethought that must have taken. Somebody capable of doing that was capable of anything. He was the magician, after all.

Falcon could see the scepticism on my face. 'You worry too much,' he said. 'Congratulations.'

I nodded and smiled my thanks.

'I suppose we should talk about your future,' he said – again, strangely formal.

'That'd be good,' I replied, perplexed.

He picked up a manila folder lying on his desk. 'A strange thing happened in Afghanistan two days ago,' he said.

'What was that?' I asked. There was nothing alarming about it – strange things were always happening in Afghanistan – but I had no idea why Falcon was telling me about it or what was in the manila folder; I assumed he was starting to explain a new mission.

'We had a walk-in at Kabul Station,' he continued. 'Elderly man, he'd crossed over from Iran a few months earlier and finally made his way to the security gates at the compound.'

I mentally shrugged – people were always arriving out of the blue at agency stations and US embassies, mostly telling tall tales or trying to sell non-existent information.

'He had no apparent intelligence value,' Falcon said. 'His age and his respectful manner meant he didn't fit any profile the guards were used to, so he was turned away. Three days in a row he came back – nicely turned out, a little bottle of water and some food – and squatted under a tree on the far side of the road to wait for a summons that never came.

'On the fourth day, one of the guards walked over and told him that there was no point in continuing to turn up. She said he should stay home and enjoy his days. He said home was in Iran and he missed it very much – he had been highly respected in his village and now he was just another one of thousands of refugees. The guard believed him and asked how long he intended to keep coming back. He said his concern was that he had very few clothes and how cold it would be in winter.'

I stared at Falcon – winter was months away. Falcon nodded. 'Yeah, I know. So the guard called inside and begged either the embassy or the agency to send someone down so that they didn't end up with a dead body under the tree. Finally, a kid came down – the third assistant secretary for something or another – and listened to the old man.

'The story was so interesting he told his boss and the old man was asked inside and spoke to the Kabul Station chief. His report ended up with me,' Falcon said, indicating the manila folder.

'Why was it so interesting?' I asked. 'What did he have?'

'A pretty bad experience,' Falcon replied. 'He, his daughter and her two kids were grabbed from their house one day by a group of terrorists and taken to a crossroads.'

A crossroads? I stared at Falcon, whose gaze was already fixed on me, but I said nothing. My heart was suddenly camping out in my throat.

'The woman and the two children were chained to the ground and left to die while her husband – a courier for the Army of the Pure, betrayed by his cousin – was crucified next to them.'

I remained silent – I knew what was coming, but what was there to say?

'The grandfather had come to the embassy because he wanted to pass on his thanks to the man – an American spy, he was told – who had killed three guards dead and allowed his daughter and her two kids to escape. He said he couldn't understand how a man who was a running dog of the Great Satan could also be a servant of Allah. Surely, he said, God works in mysterious ways.'

Falcon opened the folder, pulled out a large photo and showed it to me. It was taken in an embassy office, but the last time I had seen the man's face was when he had suddenly appeared in the crosshairs of my telescopic sight. I laid the photo back down, dreading what was coming.

'You lied to me,' Falcon said. 'Not only personally, but in the debrief.'

'I didn't want to, Falcon. I knew if I reported it, I was finished, so I took the risk.'

'There's no way out, you know that,' he said. 'No way back.'

I nodded, acknowledging it. Perhaps because I wasn't arguing or protesting, the stiff formality disappeared and Falcon's anger and disappointment broke through. 'For God's sake, Kane! The agency's rules leave no latitude for interpretation. You knew that. You had to abort. Whatever else was happening was not our mission or our responsibility. You walk away.'

'I made a decision about the family,' I said. 'I knew what I was doing.'

'Of course you did, but it's a tragedy all the same.'

'Not for those kids,' I replied.

'Damn kids! Why did they have to be there? Why then? Why you?'

'I don't know,' I said. 'The Muslims would say it was God's will.'

He stared at me. 'Then God doesn't know what the fuck He's doing!'

We continued to look at one another. 'I withdraw that,' he said quietly. 'About God.'

'They were given water,' I said. 'They were going to starve to death, that was the intention, it was planned to drag on for days. When one of the kids tried to comfort her sister, they were re-chained so that they couldn't touch each other.'

'Jesus, children . . . how old?'

'Four? Six? Young, for sure.'

He shook his head in despair. 'I just thank God I wasn't in your shoes. I'm sure a lot of people would have done what you did; maybe I would have, too. Did you think about the mission, your career?'

'Not really,' I said.

'Then you're a better man than me.' The anger in his eyes had been replaced by an overwhelming sadness; we had known each other for so long and been through so much together. 'I can let you resign,' he said quietly. 'It's the best I can do. I have no choice – you understand?'

'I understand,' I replied, trying to tamp down the loss.

'I never thought it would end like this,' he said. 'I always thought it would be a funeral.' He tried to smile.

'In the darkest moments, me too,' I said. The silence grew between us. 'I guess there's nothing more to say . . .'

He shook his head. 'Only to thank you for all the years you gave – not just to me or the agency, but the country too.'

'And all the good ones you gave me,' I said, and put my hand out to shake.

He took it, but I guess he didn't think it was enough and he drew me into an uncharacteristic embrace. Then he stepped back and looked at me. 'You were lying in ICU; it was straight after Iran,' he said. 'You'd shown so much skill and courage. You know what I told myself?'

I shook my head.

'Envy the country that has heroes,' he said.

I smiled. 'No, that's not it: pity the country that needs them,' I replied.

35

I ARRIVED HOME IN A TAXI – REBECCA HAD NOT SEEN ME SINCE I HAD left for a so-called routine surveillance operation on a sun-drenched Aegean island, and she met me on the porch, happier and more relaxed than I had seen her in years. I was too preoccupied with my own troubles to wonder why and was pleased to just put my arms around her.

'Nice vacation?' she asked. 'Plenty of beach time?'

I nodded, not feeling exactly light-hearted, and she knew instantly something was amiss. 'What's wrong?'

'They fired me,' I said. 'Falcon – out of decency – allowed me to resign, but that was what it was. I wrote the letter an hour ago, handed in my cellphone and badge, and two security guards escorted me off the campus.'

She stared at me, unable to process it, her brow furrowed. 'Why?' she asked finally.

'Remember the two girls and their mother – what I told you about giving them a chance? It broke all the rules, Becca. The mission was over, finished, you don't get involved, you exfiltrate immediately. Then, even worse, I never reported it.'

She untangled her arms and looked at me, eyes blazing. 'For that? They fired you for helping those kids? Fuck 'em,' she hissed. Rebecca never swore, and it was an eloquent indication of her anger. 'Fuck them and their rules. I am proud, incredibly proud, of you. You think I'd be with somebody who turned their back on that? Would anybody?'

'People at the agency, I suppose,' I replied with a bitter smile.

'I mean in the normal world. Not crazy-town. Can you appeal?'

'In the spy business? Where everything is secret? I was in Iran – Washington would say I wasn't even working for them. Who would listen? Where do you find that sort of judge?'

We were still standing on the porch, hand in hand. 'You want a beer?' I said, not waiting for a reply, steering her into the house.

'So there's no way back in?' she asked.

'A national emergency, a presidential pardon maybe,' I said with a laugh. 'No, there's no way back.'

'Have you thought about the future?' she asked gently.

'Not yet,' I replied. 'That's for tomorrow.'

We stepped into the kitchen. I opened the refrigerator, pulled out a beer and held it up, offering it to her. She shook her head and I turned and reached for a bottle opener. I paused as a thought struck me. 'You sure?' I said.

'No, I'm fine,' she replied.

I looked at her and our gazes met. 'I can't, not now,' she said. 'Not for a while . . .'

I don't remember who reached out to the other – I guess we both did at the same time – but we ended up in each other's arms. 'You okay?' she asked. 'Shattered by the fact you're going to be a father?'

'No, no,' I replied, holding her even harder, kissing her neck.

'But happy?' she was desperate to know.

'Of course.'

'So what's the matter?' she asked.

'I wanted to be with you through it all,' I said.

'And why won't you be? Especially now you're unemployed,' she replied, and then, growing alarmed, pulled away a little so that she could look at my face. 'The wolves?'

'I'm sorry – I wasn't honest with you when I told you they were fading,' I said.

'It's all right – I didn't believe you, anyway,' she replied. 'How bad is it?'

'Pretty bad,' I said, trying not to display any emotion, hiding the chill creeping up my spine. 'They're getting louder, closer.'

'And you think it means you'll be going soon?' she asked.

'Yes,' I replied.

'Except that it doesn't mean that, honey. I'm not saying you don't hear 'em, of course you do – you experienced a series of traumatic events, you get panic attacks. But the sounds are a symptom, not reality – they will fade. You watch, you'll be here with me.' She smiled. 'Anyway, how would an agent escorted out of Langley get sent to Russia? Who would do that?'

36

'IT WAS THE BEST OF TIMES, IT WAS THE WORST OF TIMES ... IT WAS the spring of hope, it was the winter of despair.' So somebody wrote over a hundred years ago, and they might have been talking about Becca and me.

There was nothing unique about her being pregnant, of course – 200 million women a year are in the same situation – but it was still a wondrous thing. Maybe all first-time parents felt like we did; it was hope and love and a sense of immortality all bundled together. Looking at Rebecca aglow in the morning or stepping out of the shower and seeing her unconsciously touch her belly, I was amazed that a collection of cells, as yet unborn, could dig a well so deep that it would never run dry.

At the same time, however, I was making calls, chasing down rumours, looking for a job I didn't want and being rejected by a corporate world I didn't understand and which didn't know me.

Less than twenty-four hours after I left Langley for the last time, as I expected, Blackwater called. Three of their most senior executives made a time to come to the house and spoke eloquently about career opportunities, offered me a boatload of money and showed me where to sign. I couldn't do it.

I had enlisted in submarines through a sense of duty – of greater purpose, I suppose – and had been washed out of the service by order of a rear admiral I had never met, drifted over to the West Coast, found work in a warehouse in Los Angeles where every day I struggled with my sense of failure and was walking down a street in a bleak place called the City of Industry early one morning when two men who said they were from the FBI but turned out to be lying stopped me and asked if my Russian and Turkish were any good.

'Not as good as my Arabic,' I replied, no idea what the Feds could want with me.

They escorted me to a parked car which seemed to have lost its licence plates and I wanted to know if I was under arrest; they told me I would be if I didn't get in. They drove me through miles of anonymous warehouses and business parks to an old book depository that, according to the sign on the heavy metal gates, had been converted into a graphic design studio. I remember thinking at the time that the huge workshop must have specialized in very valuable commissions; I had never seen so many cameras and motion detectors. 'By Appointment Only,' it said under the sign.

In a bland conference room, I met a panel of three people who questioned me, rapid fire, in the different languages, swapping from one to the other, testing me, asking about my education, work experience and my time in the Navy. They kept demanding to know if I had Russian or Arab friends and tried to lead me to think that it was part of a national security investigation, but I didn't believe them. Apart from exploring my language skills, it felt to me more like a job interview, where I wasn't allowed to ask any questions. Finally, the leader of the panel – a woman close to retirement age whose clothes were pretty sharp, certainly more East Coast than West, and whose mind was better honed still, dismissed her two colleagues, inquired if I had already had breakfast, called down for croissants and coffee, and asked if I had ever considered serving my country in a more *unconventional* way. I said having left the Navy under a cloud meant that job opportunities were limited and I had been more concerned with serving myself in the most *conventional* fashion possible: like paying the rent and eating.

She smiled, said I was sitting in a satellite facility of the CIA and, after a pause while I digested it, explained that I had a set of skills – the *languages*, primarily – that the agency was looking for. Would I be interested in being trained as an agent?

What did I have to lose? I joined her department, and she was the woman – the one who had been everywhere and seen even more – who told me there were no young Denied Access Area agents; they were all old. She was Buster's predecessor as assistant director and had run the unit, to great acclaim, for over a decade. When I was a young agent, she taught me more about the secret world than anybody else and had instilled in me a sense of the agency's true mission. Like Falcon, she despised Blackwater and, as a result, I wasn't ready yet to join the people she called guns for hire when she was in a good mood, and the dogs of war when she wasn't, and I showed the three suits trying to enlist me to the door.

Rebecca, in the den, had listened to the conversation, heard the annual salary they were offering, waited until they had left and walked in, shaking her head. 'Not many people know what they're really worth,' she said. 'Wow.'

We both laughed; she knew me so well she had never doubted I would reject their offer but, following that, there were only depressing interviews with so-called think tanks and visits to featureless offices where pleasant young people offered me bottled water and showed me into meetings with men and women who ran firms specializing in what they called 'defence analysis', whatever that might have been, and it quickly became apparent that if I worked hard enough I might eventually graduate to a cubicle next to the window.

The bleak employment landscape was relieved only by a call from a colleague who had left the agency a decade earlier to set up a high-end security and threat prevention service for rock stars and celebrities. He said he had just been contracted by a movie star – a guy who had made a career out of huge action movies and had always boasted about doing his own stunts – and he was calling to offer me a well-paid job running a team that would be responsible for fulfilling the contract.

When I told Rebecca she smiled. 'He's the dream, and you're the reality – probably best if you each stay in your own lane.'

After that it was more hours of sending out résumés, of lowering expectations, of the days growing longer and the nights more troubled. Kazinsky had disappeared as if he never existed and there was no hope of me ever finding him – and yet, strangely, the wolves still called to me.

And then at 3.38 on a Sunday morning I got the call.

37

I HAD RETURNED THE AGENCY CELLPHONE, BOUGHT MY OWN, AND I no longer kept it next to the bed – what was the point; there would be no calls from numbers that would never answer – so I had to scramble down to the living room to find it.

I grabbed the phone off the coffee table, half expecting it to be a wrong number. Instead I heard a man's voice which I didn't immediately recognize. Because my new phone was not encrypted, the caller was using an end-to-end scrambling device to keep the conversation secure and it took me a moment to realize it was Falcon.

Sounding like he was talking from the biggest bathroom in the world – all echoey, his words as harsh and brittle as ice – he told me: 'Get in your car and drive,' he said.

'Where?' I asked.

'Not Langley,' he replied. 'I'll tell you when you're on the road. Head towards Capitol Hill. Wait for a call.'

38

EVERYTHING WAS WHITE AND COLD: THE MARBLE OF THE STATUE, THE moonlight on the water, the floodlit fountains. It was still dark, very early Sunday morning, and the only thing that broke the silence was the distant roar of someone taking a sports car out for a blast on empty roads. The high-pitched scream was unmistakable; to anyone who loves cars, the sound of a Ferrari engine is like God speaking.

The location of the meeting was deserted, just a dozen United States Park Police standing near the long, reflecting pool, within sight of the colossal statue of the man variously known as the Great Emancipator and the Saviour of the Union: Abraham Lincoln, seated centre stage in a Greek Doric temple nineteen feet high, weighing one hundred and sixty tons and dwarfing the man waiting on the steps near one of the entrance pillars.

The park police paid him no mind and I had the feeling Falcon was a familiar sight to them, that he often came to the shrine in the early hours and, like Lincoln himself, sat in silent contemplation. He once told me he was not paid to work, he was paid to think – and it would have been hard to find a better place for such an exercise.

I made my way towards him, walking the length of the reflecting pool, hands in my pockets, shoulders hunched against the chill, and saw him come down the ceremonial steps to meet me. Somebody observing us would have said it was a perfect time and place for a meeting between an intelligence agent and his spymaster: the stillness of the water, the illuminated statue, the emptiness and loneliness of the site and two solitary men walking towards each other in the moonlight.

A woman at the agency had once told me they thought I was like the son that Falcon had never had and I wondered what the purpose of our meeting was – a reconciliation, a new hope, some voice or betrayal from the past?

'Kazinsky?' I said as we shook hands.

'Forget about him for now,' he said. 'I want you back. I always wanted you back – and now I know how to do it.'

I stared at him, my mind leaping – I couldn't fathom what path Falcon was taking; he was throwing me a lifeline, and that was all that mattered.

'Go on,' I said, but he looked past me and I glanced behind to see two park police – doing their hourly round – coming towards us. Falcon steered me away; in the stillness and the chill of the night, voices would carry across the water and he wanted to make sure we were out of earshot of anyone before he got down to business.

The location of the meeting and his behaviour told me that the subject was far too secret, or sensitive, even to be discussed at Langley, and I was not surprised that he went off at a tangent as he walked us into an area of greater privacy. 'I was here that day, you know,' he said.

I had no idea what he meant so I said nothing.

'I was standing at this spot – we were lucky, we had arrived early,' he continued. 'I was very young; my aunt and uncle had brought me. Dr King was on the first tier of steps and the crowd stretched down to the Washington Monument—'

He turned and pointed at the stone obelisk in the distance. 'I read later that we were a quarter of a million strong. The monument is over five hundred feet high, the tallest building in the world when it was first constructed, but it looked almost insignificant against so many people. It was ironic – Dr King's speech was about racial equality, but there we all were, standing in the shadow of a memorial to the first president that slaves had helped build.' He smiled. 'That's America, isn't it – full of contradictions.'

'You were here?' I asked. 'I've heard about that day a thousand times. My mother came too. She said it was one of the greatest moments of her life.'

'See – I knew we had a lot in common,' he said with a grin, then checked on the cops, who were finally almost out of earshot. He looked along the reflecting pool to the statue of Lincoln.

'I doubt your mother knew back then,' he said. 'I don't think anyone did. Maybe Dr King realized just how deep the racial divide ran. We didn't understand that the more one group was lifted up, the more the anger would grow among another part of the country. God, the hatred that's out there now. It's like Antonio Silva said the other day: whatever happened to us?'

'My mom knew his speech backwards,' I said.

'Same with me.' He turned and looked at me. 'The two of us, standing in this place – it seems like a night to talk about the past.' He checked the cops were out of hearing. 'Why did the Navy wash you out of submarines?'

I was taken aback. An event from years ago – one of the most painful episodes of my life – was the last thing I had expected to be asked about. I didn't immediately respond.

'Go on,' he said.

'Authority with the crew, that's what they said,' I replied at last. 'I'd just graduated as a junior officer and had returned from my first tour at sea. I was called into an office and was told that, following observations on board, I lacked the necessary "command presence".'

'And did you?' Falcon asked.

'What did it matter? It was the Navy – the chain of command was the only opinion that counted.'

'Devastating?' he said.

'Serving on subs had been what I'd wanted to do since childhood. Something about the solitude, the thought of transiting the world unseen, that appealed to me. Then to be accepted into the programme, to go through Annapolis, to graduate from Nuke School – and have it taken away in a ten-minute meeting.' I shrugged. 'It was hard, worse than flunking, in a way – I hadn't failed, I'd been rejected.'

'I guess some people just didn't think you were suited for that job.'

'No shit,' I replied. 'The Navy didn't tag me as a future skipper of a boomer, that was for sure.'

'I wasn't thinking about the Navy,' he replied. 'Other people didn't think you were suited – I meant their opinion.'

What did that mean? 'What people?' But I didn't get a chance to ask—

He ignored my question. 'You remember the name of the man who cashiered your career?' he said. 'What was he – a rear admiral?'

'Yes. Wilberforce. Rear Admiral Nathan Wilberforce. Tough man. He gave me less than an hour to pack my kit and get off base.'

Falcon took a sheaf of papers – about five pages – out of his jacket and handed it to me. 'What is it?' I asked.

'A list of all flag officers for that year. It's alphabetical,' he said.

Perplexed, no idea why he was showing it to me, I leafed through it, found the spot, checked it again and looked up at Falcon. I was totally confused.

'You can't find him?' he asked. 'No Wilberforce?'

'No, there's no flag officer of that name,' I said, my pulse starting to accelerate. For years I had lived with a sense of past failure, and now ... this? Who had fired me, and why? There was only one answer I could think of. 'The agency?' I asked.

Falcon nodded. 'Not me, if that's any compensation. My predecessor. She contacted a retired flag officer so he knew how to act the part. The agency always wanted you—'

'Why not just fucking ask?!' I half shouted, the sound carrying across the water. There had been so many years ... so much bewilderment and hurt. I felt myself about to explode, but one thing kept the pin in the grenade – I had lived so long in the secret world that surprises and betrayal were nothing new. As I said: we lived in a wilderness of mirrors. Just one more piece of fractured glass, I figured.

'Why not ask?' Falcon repeated. 'And if they had – what would you have said? They knew you were committed to submarines.'

I thought for a moment, and I realized he was right, I would never have agreed, and that helped take some of the air out of the balloon.

'They'd been watching you for almost three years,' he said. 'They'd seen your command of every language they needed, the academic achievements and the desire you mentioned – to transit through the world unseen. Believe me, that phrase belongs in the manual of the spy world.

'Apart from that, they knew you,' he continued. 'Maybe better than you knew yourself. Their psychologists kept saying that running a boomer was off the table, you would never skipper a nuclear-armed sub. You were too independent, too much your own man to follow each and every order—'

I was shocked. I knew the responsibilities of an officer. I could have succeeded; I would have knuckled under. I started to argue—

'Tell me again about the crossroads,' he ploughed on. 'What the hell happened to those orders?' I could offer no answer, and he continued. 'My predecessor was convinced she was right – you were made for the secret life even if you didn't know it yourself. All they had to do was get you into a position where you would embrace it.

'So they washed you out of the Navy, and embrace it you did,' he said. 'Look at your career, look at what you've done. I don't care what you think: you may not want to admit it, but she made an outstanding call – she saw something in you and led you to your destiny. Be thankful – how many people ever find that?'

He said no more, and in the cool moonlight I found myself thinking about fate and divine providence and an unseen structure to our lives. I thought about silence falling on a world and snow that never came, about a canyon where an ambush was waiting, of being armed with a marksman's rifle when a family's life depended on it, of hearing timber wolves when I was far from any forest. But most of all I thought about the ruins of a city and a vision of Rebecca dying.

'Why are you telling me this now?' I said at last.

'I've thought for years you had a right to know,' he replied. 'Tonight, I'm offering you the chance to mission-out on a submarine, so it seemed like the right time.'

'Mission on a sub where?' I asked.

39

NOW LIFE HAD COME FULL CIRCLE. THAT WAS WHAT I THOUGHT AS Falcon guided me into a pool of shadow, far out of Lincoln's gaze, and found a wall for us to sit on.

In one of those random acts of childhood, a boy in Florida had been fascinated by submarines, went to college, joined the silent service, got cashiered out in strange circumstances, was recruited by the CIA and was now being asked, after a fifteen-year absence and while no longer working as a spy, to step aboard a sub once again.

'You asked where the mission would go,' Falcon said. 'It doesn't really matter. The important question is – what sort of submarine?'

'Okay,' I replied. 'I'll play – what sort of boat?'

'If the technology works – it's out of the future.'

'That's not helpful,' I replied. 'Subs are always changing, they're in a constant state of evolution – in a way, they've always been boats of the future.'

'Not like this. You've already seen the idea. Remember the missiles in Zahedan?'

I was confused. What was he talking about? 'You mean a submarine equipped with that type of missile?'

'No, I mean a submarine fitted with that sort of technology.'

'Cloaked?' I said, suddenly having to catch my breath.

'Yes, completely cloaked, invisible,' he replied. 'Unable to be detected by anyone or anything.'

I was astonished – so much so, I couldn't respond. I thought about the missiles – white and glittering, mysterious and menacing – and how they had penetrated Iran's electronic wall and continued their journey down the narrow street, completely silent and invisible to everybody. I thought of the six-foot-long projectile skimming past and nobody even turning to look. It was as remarkable in memory as it had been in reality.

If it worked, Falcon had said. But that didn't stop my mind from making the leap. A modern submarine, already the most lethal weapons platform in existence, clad in countless billions of the same tiny white tiles and being able to pass completely unseen and unheard through the waters of the world. It could enter Vladivostok on the Sea of Japan – the home port of the Russian Pacific Fleet and one of the most target-rich sites in the world, with over seventy ships and eighty submarines in its docks. None of its defenders – either human or electronic – would be aware of the sub's presence until the attack began. Like Pearl Harbor multiplied by ten. There would be no time to do anything; it would be all over in the time it took the sub's missiles and torpedoes to travel the few kilometres to their targets.

It would be the same in Severomorsk, the base for Russia's Arctic Fleet, or in half a dozen other huge facilities serving the second largest Navy in the world: they could all be eliminated within minutes by a handful of fully cloaked submarines. I was so lost in the implications, it took me a moment to realize that Falcon was looking at me.

'Some possibility, huh?' he said.

'Extraordinary,' I replied.

'Frightening, too, by the look on your face.'

'For sure,' I said. 'Nothing ever prepares you for the shock of the new.'

'I felt the same when I first heard about the missiles. But they were never going to be the main event,' he explained. 'They were always the warm-up act. It was always intended that the technology would be scaled up. The sub is the first attempt.'

'Does anyone know if it works?' I asked. 'On something the size of a sub, I mean?'

'No, it's about to undertake a sea trial to discover its potential.'

'And why am I on board?'

'There's been a fire,' Falcon said.

'In reality, or is this part of some legend?'

'In reality. It burned out a supply building adjacent to the sub, but it could have easily gotten right out of control and exploded – the building was full of chemicals. The cause was almost certainly electrical, but everybody – the president, the Director of National

406

Intelligence and, God help us, the Danger to Shipping – decided that with a project as critical as this we couldn't take a chance. It was possibly an attempt at sabotage.'

'And you convinced them they needed an intelligence agent?'

'Of course,' Falcon replied, smiling. 'I told them if we were serious, we needed the best, someone accustomed to very difficult situations. A Denied Access Area spy, for example. If he or she was qualified in submarines, even better.' He splayed his hands. 'I made sure there was only one agent steeped in subs, one person who fitted the bill. I told them we had no choice – you had to be brought in from the cold.'

'And they agreed?'

'What choice did they have – not even the Danger to Shipping could argue,' he said.

I turned away and took a breath; my sense of relief was almost physical. I didn't realize until then how deep my anxiety had been running, how adrift I'd felt, without work or purpose. I swung back and faced him. 'Thank you,' I said simply.

He waved it away. 'Remember the air-con tech in Afghanistan? That's you on the sub. Like him, you sit with people, sip the obligatory cup of joe or whatever, and listen. I don't have to tell you how to follow leads. Personally, I don't think you'll find anything, but if you do, that's outstanding. And if you don't, the precedent is set – I bring you back to Langley.'

'What do I go on board as – what legend?' I asked.

'A late replacement. Oak Ridge National Laboratory has one of seven observer slots on board. Unfortunately, their guy has been taken ill and you're going in his place. Oak Ridge's work has always been so secret – it's where the atomic bomb was developed – so nobody on board will know him. Or you.'

'He's sick? What happened?'

'Food poisoning,' Falcon replied. 'Sudden and pretty serious, I'm told.'

I nodded but kept my gaze fixed on him. 'And . . .' I said.

'So sudden, apparently, he felt fine until he got a phone call from me. Right now, he's on an all-expenses-paid vacation in Hawaii.'

Both of us laughed. 'You have a file on him?' I said. 'Just in case anybody asks.'

He shrugged and spread his hands innocently.

'When do I leave?'

'Tonight,' he said. 'The sea trial starts in four days. Get a few hours' rest then come to Langley – we'll do a run-through, and we'll have a stack of files waiting for you. You'll love it.'

He stood up and stretched his back. I looked past him and saw that dawn was breaking. 'Does it have a name, this boat?' I asked.

'How can it have a name – it doesn't exist,' he said with a grin. 'But it's got a working title – the USS *Leviathan*.'

I nodded. 'The monster from the deep,' I said, got to my feet, and thought no more of it.

40

EARLIER, REBECCA HAD REGISTERED ME STUMBLING DOWN TO THE living room to answer the phone in the dead of the night and had listened as I started the car and driven off. As a result, even though it wasn't yet 6 a.m., she was waiting near the back door when I walked in.

'Falcon?' she asked.

'What could possibly make you think that?' I replied.

'Who else calls at four in the morning and thinks it's normal?'

I laughed. 'I'm back,' I said.

She stared at me, not certain that she understood. 'Back? In the agency?'

I nodded, and she looked at me, confused and conflicted. As much as she was distressed by my work, she had also seen what I had been going through over the past few weeks. That must have led to some sense of relief but – she was also pregnant – and that brought its own burden of fears and anxiety.

'What do they want you to do now?' she asked warily. 'The Badlands? Russia? Where now?'

'A submarine,' I said.

For the second time in as many minutes, she was taken aback. 'Are you serious?' I had spoken to her many times about what that part of my life had meant to me. 'How many years is it?'

'Fifteen,' I replied.

'How do you feel about it?'

'Nervous. Hopefully I won't like it too much – I don't want to spend the rest of my life thinking about what might have been.'

'Dangerous?' she asked, broaching the subject that was never far from her mind.

'No, a US sub – watch and listen. I'll be gone about nine days total.'

Her shoulders slumped with relief and she turned and found a stool.

'Will you be okay?' I asked.

'Of course,' she said. 'But thanks for worrying. I had a little bit of news—'

'What?'

She shook her head, changing her mind. 'Actually, it doesn't matter. It can wait – you look exhausted. I guess they want you at Langley as soon as possible?'

'Nine a.m.' Her news remained a mystery I didn't try to solve. If I am being honest, and to my eternal regret, my mind was elsewhere.

'Get to bed,' she said.

I nodded my thanks and headed towards the door. I was almost through it when she spoke—

'I know it's a submarine,' she said. 'But where is it taking you? Why?'

I turned back, looked at her for a moment, and shook my head; I couldn't tell her, there was nothing I could say or explain about something so highly classified.

'I was really hoping we'd moved past that,' she replied at last, the disappointment and hurt showing on her face.

'I can't tell you, Becca – not with this, not this time.'

She met my gaze and held it. Then she must have seen there was no way I was going to change my mind, and she gave up. 'Go to bed,' she repeated tersely. 'I'll be heading to work myself in an hour. I'll see you when you return from wherever you're going.'

I would have gone to her and embraced her but, justifiably disappointed in me and angry, she turned away and busied herself with breakfast. That small moment, insignificant in a way, was to haunt me for days beyond reckoning.

Later I thought of an old song that could have been written for that moment, and its line 'I always thought that I'd see you again' – one of the saddest collections of words ever written.

41

I WOKE BARELY FIFTEEN MINUTES BEFORE THE CAR THAT WOULD TAKE me to Langley was due to arrive and – in a flurry of activity – began throwing the sort of nondescript casual clothes that I thought a scientist from Oak Ridge might own into a kitbag.

For once there was no need for me to invent an elaborate legend and make sure that everything I was carrying conformed to some fictional reality – I was an American working in eastern Tennessee, about to travel on a US sub, where nobody was going to be asking any questions. Given the time constraints, I was thankful for that.

I picked up the kitbag, grabbed my phone and wallet off the nightstand and headed for the front door. Rebecca had already left and I saw the agency car waiting in the driveway when I realized – my wallet. What was a guy from Tennessee doing with a Maryland driver's licence and half a dozen credit cards in a name I would certainly not be using?

I turned at the door and went straight to the nook in the living room that Rebecca used as a makeshift office. I opened her desk drawer and was throwing in anything that would identify me when I saw a flimsy square of paper lying inside.

I recognized it immediately and picked it up: it was a printout of an ultrasound. I smiled – her first scan wasn't scheduled for another five days but obviously she hadn't been able to resist seeing the baby. The previous evening, she had been working in emergency and she must have found time to have one of the technicians carry out the procedure.

I took my first look at the baby and didn't move. I was not a doctor, but I knew enough to see that the ultrasound had revealed something interesting: two heartbeats. That was the news she was going to tell me.

My instant reaction was to call her at work, but I realized it would ruin her surprise so I pulled my driver's licence and other things out of the drawer, dumped them on top of the desk, grabbed my kitbag and ran towards the waiting car.

For once I didn't spend the journey worrying about an upcoming mission. All I could think about was what life would be like with twins.

42

I LANDED IN DIEGO GARCIA JUST BEFORE SUNSET. THERE WAS NO breeze. A complete stillness had fallen on paradise, and the only movement was the long swells of the Indian Ocean – as well ordered as the ranks of any military parade – marching in and surrounding the atoll with a ring of white surf.

Clouds on the western horizon were turning crimson and gold while the profound blue of the world's second deepest ocean was streaked with silver. On the shore, clusters of palm trees were throwing long shadows across beaches of pink sand and I couldn't help but think if the submarine worked, what an idyllic place for warfare to be changed for ever.

Myself and half a dozen other stragglers had flown in from the States on a Galaxy freighter, one compartment of which had been converted some time earlier into a troop transport. Obviously, it had been done on the cheap – there was nothing that could even be charitably described as seats. Instead, there were metal frames fitted with webbing running along each side of the fuselage; maybe it had been installed for paratroopers. From my point of view, however, the set-up had two advantages: first, with so few passengers, it meant I could stretch out full length and sleep; second, it prevented anyone from sitting alongside and engaging me in conversation – something I wanted to avoid given how little time there had been to prepare a legend for the mission.

That was the plan, but it didn't deter – two hours into the long-haul flight – a man in his early sixties who could have passed as a retired boxer from pulling up an empty plastic cargo box and lashing it to the rings on the floor next to me. It was clear from his gait that he had undergone hip replacement surgery, and his knees probably weren't too far behind.

'Baxter Woodward,' he said, putting out his hand, introducing himself. It was a total surprise – not that he wanted to make conversation but that his face, which seemed to carry the marks of so much physical and emotional pounding, was in such sharp contradiction to his warm and gentle voice. That, combined with a ready, crooked smile, certainly made it hard to dislike him. I felt I had no choice but to take his hand.

'I saw the passenger manifest – Daniel Greenberg?' he asked.

I nodded. Somebody at Langley, realizing that I would need a new driving licence, credit cards and other identity documents had been tasked with creating them while I was asleep and, overnight, I had been transformed into Daniel Raymond Greenberg.

'The manifest said you're from Oak Ridge,' Baxter continued. 'I guess you're one of the advanced-material scientists – cladding, that sort of thing? I'm a physicist, and I do the same at Los Alamos – nanotech mostly, electrical pulses and light. How about you?'

I was instantly alarmed – engineering billions of little white tiles was far beyond my pay grade – and I tried to think fast. 'I can't say anything about it, Baxter,' I replied. 'The manifest shouldn't have even said where I worked.' I shrugged. 'You know how it is.'

He looked at me, seriously impressed – *that* secret, huh? 'No – no, sorry,' he replied, and I thought it might end the conversation. 'Ever been on a sub before?' he persevered.

'A few times,' I said. I didn't really want to engage, but he seemed like such a decent person I felt I had to continue. 'How about you, Baxter? Are you an old salt?'

'Never,' he said, trying to laugh. 'Always in the lab.' He turned serious. 'My wife died a couple of months back. Forty-three years of marriage. It's like somebody said – don't be sorry for what you've lost, be thankful for what you've had. It's good in theory, hard in practice. I applied for the observer post – I've worked on stealth for years and I thought it might be just the shake-up I needed.' He gave one of his ready smiles. 'Now, thinking about being a thousand feet underwater, I'm not so sure. You got kids, Daniel?'

It took me aback, and I thought about it. 'Yes,' I said, not entirely dishonestly.

'We never had any,' Baxter replied. 'We got close, four miscarriages. How many?'

'Twins,' I said, smiling.

'Lucky you,' he replied, genuinely pleased. 'How old?'

'Young,' I responded. 'Very young.'

'A lot of work, huh?'

I warmed to the subject. 'Plenty. Luckily, I've got a partner but, even so, we spend our lives exhausted.'

'I'm not surprised,' he said sympathetically. He indicated the other passengers and lowered his voice: 'I know it's a submarine, but what exactly will we be observing?'

I smiled enigmatically and saw my chance. 'I was just about to say, Baxter – for a new parent, there's only one good thing about flying ten thousand miles in a freight plane.'

'What's that?' he asked.

'Uninterrupted sleep.'

He laughed. 'I can believe it,' he replied. 'I'll let you turn in.'

'Thanks.'

'Maybe we can catch each other later,' he continued, standing. 'When you wake up.'

'That'd be good,' I said as I turned over. Strangely, it wasn't a total lie. Like I said – he was a hard man to dislike.

43

THE FIRST BLAST OF TROPICAL HEAT HIT AS THE DOOR OF THE GALAXY opened and the seven of us started to make our way down the steep stairs to the military bus waiting on the apron.

Perhaps it was the shock of the stifling heat, or maybe I had been right and his knees were shot, but Baxter – on the step in front of me – stumbled suddenly and started to pitch forward head-first.

I had spent half my life relying on my reactions; I dropped my kitbag, threw out my left hand, just managed to grab his shirt collar as he became airborne, and caught him around the waist with my right arm. It wasn't elegant, but it succeeded in stopping his fall and he turned, panting hard – scared – and tried to thank me. I dismissed it with a smile, but I knew then that any chance of us not being para-dise buddies was well and truly gone.

Once we were all on board, the bus drove north with Baxter and I sitting together in silence – he was still badly shaken – looking out the window. Within minutes, the ocean appeared on one side and the lagoon on the other – a view that was so spectacular it would have calmed anyone, and I was relieved to see the colour starting to return to my companion's cheeks.

As we travelled on, the setting sun turned the sky into a riot of pink and gold and we passed deserted beaches where surfers were still out, picking up the last waves of the day. I saw tiki torches burning among the ruins of the abandoned coconut plantation and dozens of men and women in uniform holding beers and relaxing on the broken-down verandah, watching fellow military personnel barbecuing under the palms.

Just beyond them, looming large, was the concrete and razor-wire fence that protected the high-security area at the northern end of the island. As cameras and guards observed us from their three watch-towers, security personnel checked our papers, took an iris scan of everyone and eventually waved us through.

Under constant surveillance, the bus headed deeper into the forbidden zone – a deserted landscape of palm trees, long stretches of sea-grape and drifts of wind-blown sand – until we slowed down, turned hard at a thick grove of mangroves and found ourselves facing the burned-out shell of a large supply building.

Even though the blaze had been extinguished several days before, crews of military firemen and women and construction workers in full hazmat suits were still clearing the site. We slowed as we approached four fire trucks half blocking the road and I stared at the charred remains of the structure. While there was no doubt it represented a stroke of good fortune – it had opened the door for me to re-enter the secret world – I was thinking less about luck and more about fate. It felt as though unseen wheels were turning, propelling me forward. I had the creeping sense that somehow I was meant to be there. I shrugged and tried to shake it off – it had been a long flight and I was tired.

'Is that it?' Baxter asked.

I broke free of my reverie, but I wasn't sure what he meant.

'Danny – did you hear?'

I dragged my eyes away from the burnt-out warehouse and looked in the direction Baxter was indicating. Past a jumble of dormitories for a legion of resident workers, beyond their basketball hoops, open-air cinema, machine shops and rows of coffee wagons, was a massive concrete structure. Low slung and flanked by a breakwater and an artificial reef to protect it against the incoming swell, the building stretched far out into the deep waters of the ocean.

'The pen? Yeah, it has to be,' I replied, although it was far different to any submarine pen I had ever seen.

'You've been on subs – the pens always this size?' Baxter asked. He wasn't the only one intrigued – everybody else on board was craning to see it too.

'Not even close,' I said. 'Apparently, the walls and roof here are reinforced concrete, twenty feet thick, and that's sandwiched between three layers of a Kevlar-style material that's denser than lead.'

'To make it missile-proof?' Baxter asked.

'No,' I replied. 'To stop new-generation penetrating radar from seeing inside the structure or other satellite sensors recording voices or computer keystrokes. The whole building is electronically impenetrable—'

I didn't mention the only reason I knew about any of it was because of the files Falcon had given me at the CIA run-through a few hours before I got on the plane.

'Seems like overkill,' Baxter said. 'A hostile satellite will see the sub as soon as it leaves the pen.'

'That's why the structure is so long,' I replied. 'The boat submerges *inside* the pen and there are underwater rails to guide it out into deep water. The sub is never allowed above the surface.'

The bus squeezed past the fire trucks, sped up, and was now fast approaching the entrance to the pen.

'What about the large black boxes in the water, going out past the breakwater?' Baxter continued, pointing.

'Oxygen generators,' I replied. 'A sub is safest from detection in turbulent coastal waters – the currents and bubble clouds help defeat sonar and other devices. The generators simulate those conditions. In addition, the boat will throw out billions of pieces of tiny metal strips as it leaves the pen, confusing any attempt to photograph it even underwater.'

Baxter smiled. 'I guess you've spent quite a bit of time on subs.'

'No,' I lied. 'I've always been interested in them, that's all.'

The bus stopped at a security checkpoint attached to the pen and we had our eyes and documents checked once again. We deposited everything we were carrying in lockers, then approached a group of whole-body X-ray machines.

As I passed through, I felt the excitement rising, trying to imagine what the sub would look like. I was at the front and, once the X-rays had proven to be all clear, we walked through an airlock and into what I knew would be a vast pen. But – there was nothing to see, we were in total darkness.

44

BUT NOT QUITE AS DARK AS I'D THOUGHT WHEN MY EYES ADJUSTED to the gloom. We were obviously in the concrete cavern, where it was far cooler than outside; I could hear water lapping somewhere below and the overwhelming scale of the place became apparent.

As my vision improved, a row of pinpoint blue lights appeared in the floor, marking a path, and I followed it with Baxter close behind and the rest of the group in his wake. I stopped when the lights ran out, managed to make out a railing in front of me and decided we were on a type of platform.

Out of the gloom, I heard the rumble of heavy engines starting up. I tried to trace its source and saw, in the distance, a vertical crack of light appear. It grew wider, and daylight began to intrude. The engines were opening a set of massive steel sea-doors at the far end of the pen.

The doors opened further, and the Indian Ocean was revealed as a sheet of gold, a blood-red sun balanced on the horizon, flooding light into the pen, illuminating the most remarkable craft I had ever seen. Hard edged, angular and powerful – over six hundred feet in length and the equivalent of seven storeys high, no longer built for outdated stealth but for unbridled underwater speed – she was unlike any submarine I had ever encountered.

And she was shimmering – white, almost pearlescent – every inch of her covered in tiny white tiles. Ordinarily, seaborne war machines were the grey of the ocean and had been for generations, but this was a boat for another time, another era.

I had seen the missiles that targeted the convoy in Zahedan and had convinced myself I was prepared for what I would encounter on

Diego Garcia; I wasn't. The size, the beauty, the power and the sheer threat of the sub was overwhelming. Again, I was reminded of the night I witnessed the fire-surf of Baku – I had that same sense of boundless wonder and deep fear, intertwined and inescapable.

Standing on the platform, looking down at her from barely thirty yards away, was a remarkable experience for me. But for Baxter and the others, with no forewarning or preparation, it was obviously staggering: they were standing in stunned silence, several unconsciously putting their hands to their faces, others – wide-eyed – rooted to the spot.

'That's a submarine?' Baxter asked finally of nobody and everybody. There was no response and the group probably would have remained immobile except for a high-pitched whistle which cut through the still air to shake them from their reverie.

I recognized the sound and realized that the boat's crew were 'manning the rail' – standing on the hull, lining her sides – as part of a formal ceremony. The boat's captain and the other senior officers had appeared on shore-side, stepped on to the gangplank and were being piped aboard.

The piping stopped – the skipper was aboard – and I saw that the huge sea gates were finally open. The USS *Leviathan*, a submarine that didn't exist, a craft that had been designed to disappear, was ready to set sail for waters unknown.

45

A FULL MOON HAD RISEN BY THE TIME THE THREE ILYUSHIN TRANSPORT planes crossed the desiccated Aral Sea, approached the huge pillars of light and begun their final descent towards one of Baikonur Cosmodrome's military-grade runways.

The passengers, illuminated by the brilliant pillars, stared out and saw one of the black and battered space freighters returning to earth. It must have seemed like a vision of the future, and I'm sure more than one of them – having just seen the armada of ghost ships marooned in the Aral Sea – would have thought that humankind, guilty of pillaging and polluting its own planet, was now intent on doing the same to the rest of the solar system.

According to a passenger list hacked by the NSA, Kazinsky was in a window seat close to the front of the first aircraft and, therefore, would have had a stunning view of his new field of operations – the largest space facility in the world, a place where for eighty years, rockets and ballistic missiles had been tested, whose millions of acres were littered with craters, missile debris and spent rocket stages. It must have looked like a cross between a junkyard and a museum.

What Kazinsky's thoughts were, of course, we have no way of knowing, but thanks to an endless debrief of our asset in the miner's helmet and a series of other hacks by the NSA – including a huge cache of CCTV footage of Baikonur, unusually complete with audio, a remnant of Russian paranoia probably, that was stolen from KazakhTelecom – I have no doubt that this is the most accurate account of the events at the Cosmodrome during those few months as there ever will be.

Once the plane had landed, nobody moved – the passengers had been ordered to remain in their seats while three officials from the Cosmodrome climbed the air-stairs and came aboard. The leader of them, a tall Chechen in his late forties, had the look of a man who had spent too much time in the gym: corded muscle rippled through his old combat shirt, even his fatigues bulged at the calves and he had hands the size of meat hooks. Located above a full beard and a pock-marked face, his dark eyes were set closely together under a monobrow.

A merciless former soldier, his name was Aslan Kadyrov but, thanks to having the same initials as the AK-47, the most widely used shoulder gun in the world, he was universally known as Rifle. He was in charge of assigning new recruits to their jobs in Baikonur's fledgling off-earth mining enterprise and his team was on board to relay that information to the new arrivals. Rifle himself, however, had little interest in most of them; he was looking for one man in particular.

Consulting a clipboard, he walked down the aisle and passed half a dozen rows before he stopped and looked at a man in a window seat staring out at a huddle of buildings on the side of the apron, his back towards him.

'Colonel?' he inquired respectfully.

Kazinsky turned and saw him standing in the aisle. The terrorist commander rose to his feet, his face broke into a smile and he reached out to embrace him. 'When was the last time, Rifle?' Kazinsky asked. 'Aleppo?'

'Yes, Colonel. I was commanding the north flank when you ordered the regiment to take the citadel—'

'And you were the first to breach it,' Kazinsky replied. 'The best second-in-command I ever had.'

Rifle smiled. 'Not sure about that. You probably don't recall, but I didn't even know I'd been shot until I came round and you and a stretcher-bearer were carrying me into the field hospital.'

'Of course I recall,' Kazinsky said. 'Many harsh words were exchanged about your weight.'

Rifle, laughing, pulled up his combat shirt to show several ugly scars extending from his shoulder all the way down to his six-pack. 'I just wish you'd found a surgeon instead of an upholsterer – he stitched me up like a cheap sofa,' he said, before turning serious. 'The war moved on; I never got a chance to thank—'

'Thank me? For doing my duty? The Spetsnaz look after their own, they always do, you know that,' Kazinsky replied.

'I know,' Rifle said. 'That's why, when I got the message from my brother in Grozny that a commander from Aleppo had come to the apartment looking for me, I managed to get hold of a phone and called him immediately.' He dropped his voice: 'Why Baikonur, Colonel?'

'To do Allah's work, whatever it may be,' he replied. 'Possibly to raise money, to start over – perhaps, God willing, we'll raise the black flag of ISIS again. I saw on a message board that you were here, and I knew Allah was calling me to this place.'

'My brother said the Army of the Pure had been defeated – I thought you might have retired.'

Kazinsky smiled. 'A man's not finished when he's defeated, you know that – he is finished when he quits.'

'You'll find plenty of quitters here, sir. It's a harsh place. As long as you can pass the security check, nobody cares about your past, a criminal record or your education – it means we're trapped on the steppes with the dregs of Russia. When you step outside, smell the air. The stench of filth is everywhere.'

'I've been to plenty of bad places,' Kazinsky said. 'And what does it say in the Holy Qur'an? "Be grateful to Allah for our hardships. Each one is a test, every suffering a challenge."'

'That's exactly what you told us in Aleppo!' Rifle replied, and the two men laughed. 'At least there, we didn't have to contend with the rats.'

46

PEOPLE SHOULD HAVE PAID MORE ATTENTION – TO THE RATS. THEN again, in hindsight, it's always easy to see the writing on the wall.

Rifle had collected Kazinsky's belongings from the overhead locker and led him off the plane first, down the air-stairs and – ignoring a fleet of broken-down buses – up to his personal ride: a repurposed armoured personnel carrier. Its machine gun had been removed and rough windows cut into its sides, but its steel tracks, identical to those used on a tank, were intact. Rifle could go anywhere without having to worry about the site's cratered and dilapidated roads.

By moonlight, with Kazinsky sitting beside him in what had once been the vehicle's command turret, Rifle left the airstrip, drove down Karl Marx Prospekt and headed into the town, passing the Sputnik Hotel and, finally, a monumental statue of the head and shoulders of a young Colonel Gagarin in his peaked cap, staring up, fittingly, at the sky.

Once the vehicle had travelled beyond the last of the decaying apartment blocks, they encountered a railroad track and ran alongside it, keeping pace with a *motovoz*, one of the old diesel-powered trains that shuttled workers between the town and the Cosmodrome's launch pads and industrial plants. Despite the hour, the carriages were crowded with workers ready to start an overnight shift – dead-eyed, hollow-cheeked men and women, staring straight ahead. In the silvery light, wreathed in the locomotive's billowing clouds of black smoke, they looked like ghosts.

For miles, the two vehicles travelled in tandem until Rifle let the train pass, crossed the tracks behind it and headed deep into the wilderness. He crested a rise and slowed almost to a walk. Out there, far from the town, surrounded by the Great Steppes that stretched all the way to Mongolia, the starfield was astonishing in its brilliance, the Milky Way shimmering and pulsing like a living force.

Rifle gestured to where a launch mount – the tower that supported a rocket during take-off – rose out of the flat landscape, silhouetted in the moonlight, and pointing straight at the constellation of Orion. 'Site Number One,' he said with reverence. 'That was Gagarin's pad. It hasn't been used for years – out of respect for his memory. He came back a hero and was dead at thirty-four. Sometimes I come out here and just sit – I look at it and then up at the stars, and you realize, right here, we are standing on the shores of the universe, the mystery of life and death and space all around us.'

'Yes, all around and stretching to eternity, with only God to light the path. Where are we going?'

'Siberia – it's what everyone calls the most remote corner of the site. As of tonight, you're in charge of the midnight shift at what is becoming Baikonur's most important facility. Honestly, you were a godsend. It needs a lot of work, Colonel—'

'The plant and equipment?'

'No, the people.'

47

FIRELIGHT FROM THE FURNACES AND SMELTERS PLAYED ACROSS THE interior walls of the plant as it processed the off-earth minerals, illuminating faded eighty-foot-high murals of Stalin, Lenin and heroic Soviet workers staring into a golden future that had yet to arrive.

The murals would have been invisible had it not been for the flames, but it turned them into something haunting; like Egyptian hieroglyphs, the barely understood reminders of a distant past.

CCTV footage that was recovered later showed Rifle lead Kazinsky through a door into the building and the Colonel stop on the threshold to stare at the paintings. After a minute, he shifted his eyes and ran them across the hellscape before him: the huge and forbidding interior, the roaring blast furnaces, the incessant clattering conveyor belts and the river of molten metal. The diamond mine of his youth must have seemed like a jewellery boutique by comparison.

He walked on, continuing to examine the facility until he reached a circle of forty bare-chested men – tough and bearded – cheering and yelling in a mix of languages ranging from Kazakh through Russian to Uzbek and Arabic. Gathered in the shadow of a massive ore-crushing machine, the men – almost the entire shift, at least half of them bearing scars and burns inflicted by the equipment around them, were throwing handfuls of rubles and *tolahs* on to the ground inside the circle. Kazinsky looked questioningly at Rifle—

'Gambling,' he said with disgust, shouting above the roar of the machinery.

'On what?' Kazinsky yelled back.

Rifle motioned his former commander to a set of steps leading up to one of the overhead gantries, walked along it and stopped at a platform that allowed them to look down into the circle, where a fight to the death was underway—

The two biggest rats Kazinsky had ever seen; far larger than anything he had encountered in the wilds of Siberia. It wasn't just their size, though, the rats were unique in other ways – their blue eyes were shot through with gold and their blood-spattered fur was such a pale shade of brown that it had an almost ghostly sheen. The way their coats laid meant that it joined in a raised crest running the length of their spine, as if their hackles were permanently raised in anger.

'Who's ever seen rats like that?' Kazinsky asked, shocked.

'Nobody much – the men say they're rare but getting more common,' Rifle replied.

'What are they called?'

'Ridgebacks, the men have named 'em,' Rifle said.

'Ridgebacks?' Kazinsky said, continuing to stare at the rodents: ripping and clawing at each other, their prominent teeth – more like fangs – continually going for the throat of the opponent. 'Am I right – they've got canines?' he said. 'They're used for combat – rats don't normally have canines.'

'Yes – but the most startling thing about them isn't their teeth, it's the aggression,' Rifle replied. 'Nobody understands why or where they developed – it's another one of Baikonur's mysteries.'

Suddenly a huge cheer went up from the crowd: the smaller of the two rats had its teeth in its opponent's rear leg, had thrown it on to its back and, blood spurting, was trying to rip the limb from the torso. As Kazinsky and Rifle watched, the larger rat – instead of screeching and trying to escape – just continued fighting, almost oblivious to the damage being done to it.

'It's hard to tell,' Rifle said, 'but the men say they have a much higher threshold to pain.'

'It doesn't look like they have any threshold at all,' Kazinsky replied, turning away from the rats and the howling men and looking around the dark interior. 'Who's in charge here?'

Rifle pointed to a glass-walled control room at the end of one of the walkways commanding a view over most of the complex. A balding, overweight man in his thirties was leaning back in his chair, smoking and watching TV. 'You see the problem?' he said.

'Yes, I understand entirely,' said Kazinsky, the man who had once laid bear traps for his enemies and waited for the wolves to arrive. 'I think I can take it from here.'

48

KAZINSKY WATCHED RIFLE CLIMB INTO THE ARMOURED PERSONNEL carrier and head out into the barren landscape. He stood alone in the shadow of the building, lost in thought for a moment, until the silence was broken by a tiny alarm from his watch.

He glanced at it, and then looked at the eastern sky – dawn was breaking. He walked back into the gloom and fury of the processing plant, picked up his kitbag and bedroll and looked for a place to perform *wudu*. It led him – unnoticed by anyone – past the gamblers and into a cafeteria and kitchen.

He stopped near a pile of old electrical cabling and a row of fire extinguishers fixed to the wall and called out in Russian to a sweating short-order cook, working a dozen gas burners to prepare breakfast for the workers. 'Water, please.'

The cook shrugged and indicated a trough-like basin used for washing dishes. Kazinsky stripped off his jacket and shirt and started to wash. The cook, about to turn away, stopped and stared at the stranger's back. 'Why a locust, my friend?'

'They swarm – and when they do, they stop for nothing. Where I come from, wise men fear them more than wolves.'

If the cook had looked more closely, he would have also seen Kazinsky's other tattoos, and that might have given him pause. Instead, he lifted up a meat cleaver and laughed: 'No, this is what men fear.'

Kazinsky didn't argue – time would tell – and, having finished *wudu*, he untied his prayer mat from his kitbag and walked back into the processing plant. He looked at his watch to check the direction of Mecca, laid his mat down and, as he sank to his knees, saw that he was not alone: a few other devout men, scattered throughout the huge space, were also kneeling in subjugation. The *Adhan*, the call to prayer – playing through speakers but barely audible over the roar of the machinery – was almost finished, but it did nothing to disturb the betting circle, which seemed to be growing larger and louder by the minute.

The CCTV footage showed that the smaller rat had proven victorious and was being returned to his cage, as his dead opponent, covered in blood and his pale fur drained of all colour now, was lying in the centre of the ring. The ringmaster – the organizer of the event and the last word in settling any betting disputes – ordered two assistants to haul away the body. 'What do I always say?' he called out. 'It's the size of the fight in the rat that matters; not the size of the rat in the fight.'

He gave a huge belly laugh and Kazinsky looked at him from under lowered brows with loathing. In his early forties, shirtless, he was a hulking man, so broad across the chest and shoulders that his neck seemed to have been swallowed whole. He had large, arresting eyes, but they were cold and without pity; what people in Russia call 'prisoner eyes'. He motioned to another two helpers to bring in a pair of cages, ready for the next bout.

As the ringmaster started to list the new rats' statistics, the crowd began to lay their bets. Several of them glanced in Kazinsky's direction and nudged each other, sneering at the devout newcomer. He'll learn, they seemed to say.

If Kazinsky had registered it, he paid no attention. When his prayers finished, he rolled up his mat, walked quietly back into the cafeteria and started to sort through the pile of old and discarded electrical cabling. Selecting a length of finger-thick, highly pliable cable wrapped in a weave of fabric and metal, he weighed it carefully in his hand.

'Cleaver,' he called to the cook. The sweating man, his back to the room, was not aware the bare-chested Kazinsky had returned and turned to face him, saw him with the cable in his hand and then spread his hands in confusion: 'What the—'

Something in the stranger's manner, the way he looked at him, warned the cook not to argue. 'Cleaver – now,' Kazinsky repeated, and the cook found himself handing it over without objection.

He watched as Kazinsky laid the cable out on a table, assessed the correct length, weighed it again in his hand, raised the cleaver and sliced the cable with one blow. He returned the implement to the cook and the man watched as Kazinsky formed a loop at one end, wrapped it around his right fist and, trailing the rest of the cable behind him, walked out of the canteen and into the plant.

In one of those quirks of fate, the ore-grinding machine had seized up moments before – not that any of the workers cared; equipment was always seizing up – and a relative silence had fallen over the area, broken only by the low thrum of the conveyor belts and the gamblers cheering wildly as the two new rats went at each other tooth and bloody claw.

Crack! Kazinsky's makeshift bullwhip, clearly audible now that the ore crusher was silent, sounded like a rifle shot as it flew through the air and snapped back on itself.

The end wrapped around the legs of a snarling, skinny man elbowing his way forward to throw down his bet. Kazinsky yanked on the whip, and the man's legs flew from under him, bringing him crashing to the ground.

Kazinsky hauled him backwards across the concrete and through the metal debris littering the floor as the other gamblers turned to look, shocked. The skinny man, roaring with rage, untangled himself, rose to his feet and launched himself towards the tattooed stranger with the whip—

There was another rifle shot as Kazinsky quickly drew the cable back, whipping the man clean across the face, the metal ripping open his nose and cheek and sending bright blood spurting in an arc.

The man crashed to the ground again – not to get up this time – as the other men in the circle roared, confronting this new threat. Who was this guy? Forgetting the rat fight, they swarmed towards him, but Kazinsky was ready—

He whipped the closest man hard around his bare torso, the cable tearing into the skin and whirling him around until Kazinsky released the tension and sent him, bleeding, careening into half a dozen of his comrades. Men went sprawling, but already the whip was cracking again—

This time it hit a big, tattooed man. The metal cable cut him from his left temple all the way down to his right jaw, probably taking out one of his eyes; it was hard to tell because the man was stumbling, clutching his hands to his face and reeling into the gloom.

Kazinsky stepped back to give himself and the whip more room and he snapped it again, skimming it across the top of men's heads, driving them back. More rifle shots rang out – again and again – taking down another three gamblers. The others quickly got the message and retreated even further—

It was clear from the CCTV footage what Kazinsky's strategy had been – to open an approach to the ringmaster, still hovering at the back. With a clear path, the whip flew out again, cracked in mid-air, snaked its way forward fast and wrapped itself around the hulking man's chest. Kazinsky dragged him forward and released him, bringing him to his knees.

The ringmaster leapt at his chance and hurled himself towards his attacker, but Kazinsky was already whirling the whip around his own head, rodeo-style, and flicked it out hard. There was another rifle shot, but this time the whip coiled around the man's calves and Kazinsky ripped his legs out from under him, sending him sprawling.

Unravelling the whip from his legs, the ringmaster tried to clamber to his feet, but he wasn't an agile man and all Kazinsky needed was a moment. He drew the whip back and with the gambling boss struggling to his knees the Colonel let fly again, half the length of the metal and fabric striking the victim on his exposed back. A huge, bloody welt appeared instantly and the flesh split apart—

The ringmaster screeched with pain and collapsed forward on to his chest. Kazinsky took a step forward, planted his feet wide and whipped him again. Time after time, he tore into him with all the rage of the righteously devout. 'Haram,' Kazinsky hissed. 'You understand that? Under Allah, gambling is haram.'

Flesh can be easily flailed, and within moments the ringmaster's back was turning to pulp. Even the cook, who had come to the doorway to witness whatever the stranger had in mind, turned away, but Kazinsky kept the rifle shots coming – hitting the man's buttocks now, shredding the fabric of his filthy jeans, exposing the white flesh beneath and turning it to the colour and texture of ground beef.

Except for the machinery and the gurgling cries of the ringmaster, silence had fallen across the workforce – both the gamblers and the religious. His chest and back streaming with sweat, Kazinsky stopped. He pointed the whip at two random workers watching. 'Pick him up,' he said.

The men hesitated, fearful after what they had just witnessed. Kazinsky raised the whip and started to coil it, as if in preparation. 'I gave you an order,' he said, barely bothering to look at them.

It didn't take any more encouragement; the men moved forward, grabbed the ringmaster under the arms and looked at Kazinsky for instructions. 'Throw him out,' the Colonel said, indicating the doorway into the wilderness. 'Let him crawl to find help – maybe he'll survive, *insha'Allah*. Or the wolves and rats will have him.'

He turned to the glass-walled control room and saw that the supervisor had abandoned the TV and was standing on the walkway, looking down in astonishment and fear at the mayhem. Kazinsky called to him: 'With that much flesh on you, my whip will really cut you up. Or you can get out now and never return.'

Moving surprisingly fast for his size, the supervisor grabbed his jacket and headed down by a different set of stairs, giving the whip the widest possible berth.

Kazinsky turned to the rest of the men, motioning the devout to also come closer. 'Listen hard,' he said. 'There was once a great prophet revered by the Christians. He went into the temple in Jerusalem, overturned the tables of the money-changers and cast out the wicked. Why? He was doing the work of God. I am not a carpenter from Nazareth, but I am truly blessed by Allah and I, too, do the work of God.'

Nobody said anything. 'Who am I?' Kazinsky continued. He pointed to his tattoos and recounted their meaning. 'Spetsnaz . . . a colonel . . . the battlefields where I fought . . . the black flag of ISIS I marched under . . .' A ripple passed through the ranks – they were accomplishments to be feared. Kazinsky half turned so that they could see the locust, slick with sweat and flecked with the whipped men's blood, on his back. 'And the locust – a plague sent by God to cleanse the Earth. You will call me the Emir.'

He walked away and ripped a sheet of filthy canvas from a set of tall windows, letting light penetrate the darkness. A few men at first, and then the others, joined him and started to strip away more of the sheeting.

As they moved aside, one of the CCTV cameras had an uninterrupted view through the glass walls of the sealed environment. Inside the huge chamber, the remote-controlled scoops were loading the unsanitized off-earth ore on to conveyor belts and, for a moment, lit by a single shaft of light coming through the grime-stained windows – more than likely never observed in the gloom of the facility – the camera captured something strange.

A host of pinpoints of light were floating in the air around the ore, glowing and hauntingly beautiful. They looked like the smallest dandelion clocks in the universe and were smaller than the diameter of a human hair.

49

IN TIME – VERY SOON – THE SPORE WOULD BE GIVEN THE NAME *SIBER*. While the identity of the person who coined it will never be known, they got it right: *siber* means 'the sleeper' in Russian.

God only knows where it came from – some galaxy far away, probably, carried by the cosmic wind until it landed on an asteroid, where it would lie, seemingly asleep, for millions of years – just the blink of an eye in a universe formed fourteen billion years ago.

And there the spore would have stayed, not alive but not exactly dead either, until an unmanned vehicle from a depleted and extravagant planet began to mine for rare earth minerals. There is no doubt the spores were not a virus, they were something far more mysterious than that, but they were close enough to remind me of a definition I had heard when I was studying for my science degree. 'A virus is a piece of bad news wrapped up in protein,' the Nobel Prize winner Sir Peter Medawar once said. 'No virus has ever been known to do any good.'

As the sun climbed higher over Baikonur, that shaft of light shifted and the fragile *siber* disappeared from view. As a result, only one other thing of interest remained in the sealed environment of the glass-walled chamber – a rat.

By nature, they are burrowing animals, and they can squeeze through a space the size of a coin. Perhaps the chamber wasn't completely sealed after all, because a normal-looking rat emerged out of a tiny fissure in the floor, looked around with curiosity, rose up on its hind legs and stared out at the processing plant.

Of course, it breathed in the dust, the air and anything else that happened to be floating inside the forbidden zone.

50

THE RECORDS OF THE HARBOUR MASTER AT DIEGO GARCIA SHOWED that the *Leviathan* slipped her mooring, travelled down the underwater rails and was free of the oxygen bubbles at 3.21 p.m. on a day no one will ever forget.

As it headed, unseen, into clear water, I was standing behind the other six observers in the sub's command centre, watching the skipper and his team – the navigator, officer of the deck, the pilot, the sonar and communications techs – follow the cardinal rule of all submariners no matter which flag they sailed under: to run silent and to run deep.

To that end, the depth finder showed we were diving fast, and that helped create the other-worldly feeling I remembered so well – of being alone in a windowless world, of plunging into a twilight zone surrounded by a silence so complete that there wasn't a sound as the officers moved from one workstation to the next; in common with all subs, everybody was wearing special rubber-soled shoes that allowed the boat's complement of one hundred and sixty-eight men and women to pass through the corridors without even a muffled footfall. For submariners, noise has always been the enemy of stealth.

The sub's command centre was in semi-darkness with only the glow from computer screens and the tiny LED lights on racks of equipment to illuminate the faces of the crew. The gloom was deliberate – numerous psychological studies had shown that the brighter the light, the greater the anxiety and fatigue among the sailors and officers.

And there was plenty to worry about in the Indian Ocean – underwater currents that plunged into apparently bottomless canyons with the force of huge waterfalls, unmapped mountains, hidden wrecks, trans-ocean communication cables and abandoned fishing nets – all compounded by travelling in zero visibility at almost forty miles an hour with just the instruments and a thin skin of metal to protect you. Outside that fragile barrier, the water pressure was deadly – if the *Leviathan* fell through the two thousand feet mark, it would reach 'collapse depth', where the pressure of the seawater, over sixty times higher than at the surface, would be so great the craft would be crushed like an aluminium can in a giant fist.

At least in such a situation death would be instant. On the other hand, any accident or catastrophic equipment failure that resulted in near-freezing water flooding in or caused the nuclear reactor to shut down would mean the crew's chances of survival or rescue would still be negligible. If any of them did manage to seal themselves into a watertight compartment, they would face the prospect of the craft icing up as the heating elements failed and the air becoming increasingly poisonous once the oxygen generators began to run out of cartridges.

It wasn't theoretical – a few decades earlier, the nuclear-powered Russian sub *Kursk*, with a crew of one hundred and eighteen, was badly damaged when a faulty torpedo exploded while the vessel was submerged in the Barents Sea. Twenty-three sailors took refuge in a watertight compartment and managed to hang on for hours in a waking nightmare, banging on the hull, praying for rescue, before their oxygen finally ran out. As in nearly all the other instances of a nuclear submarine sinking, nobody survived.

It was little wonder then that the *Leviathan*'s skipper, Commander Rick Martinez, a good-looking guy of thirty-eight, with olive skin and dark eyes, was leaning over the electronic plotting table and its huge map, his face creased with worry. Born in the buckle of the Bible Belt, just south of Memphis, Tennessee, he had by virtue of hard work and superlative academic scores made his way from the streets of the barrio to the shores of Chesapeake Bay and the historically WASP-ish environment of the US Naval Academy. His achievements did not stop there, though – out of the 350,000 people on active duty in the Navy, he had become one of the elite seventy-four, the men who commanded a nuclear-powered US submarine.

Only when he was certain that his craft was on course and travelling through safe water did he turn to the observers. 'A submarine is different to a surface ship for one primary reason,' he said. 'When things get really bad, the skipper can't throw himself overboard.'

He smiled and we laughed; a commander of any boat has almost unbridled authority and it was good to be in the company of someone who didn't appear to take himself too seriously.

'And it will get bad,' he warned. 'You have probably seen on the plotting table that our destination is New York. It isn't – that's a notional destination entered to initiate the navigation computers – but we still have a long way to travel into very difficult waters.'

He turned to the large table – an electronic slab – tilted it towards us so that we could see the map clearly and circled an area of ocean south of Australia and South Africa.

'We're heading to a vast and empty stretch of water, home to the Roaring Forties and the largest whales in the world. As you may know, we will be testing a revolutionary form of stealth technology. Once the experiment begins, it will be our mission to avoid detection and the task of the best assets the US military can muster to try and find us.'

He was right about the assets that were being sent to locate us; I had seen them. While he was explaining the scale of the pursuit to the rest of the room, I thought of sitting in the briefing room at Langley and watching a live feed of the huge number of sub-hunters racing to rendezvous with us. I saw two of the country's eleven aircraft carriers – both surrounded by their battle groups of a cruiser, two destroyers and ammunition and supply ships – plunging through the heavy swells of the great southern seas. Even the carriers, a thousand feet long and with a crew of five thousand – one of them boasting its own McDonald's – were doing it the hard way, their bows throwing up huge sheets of spray and sending them on to the flight decks sixty feet above. On one of them, a Poseidon – a submarine hunter aircraft – was catapulted off the pitching runway and, as the launch team stared in horror, veered abruptly to port, barely managing to get airborne.

The Poseidon was just one of the seventy-five aircraft on board each carrier, all of which could be used to find the *Leviathan*. To that end, they would be aided by the seven hunter-killer submarines accompanying the fleet, the two satellites which had been repositioned for the mission, the underwater microphones dropped by the Poseidons that would listen for a sub's propeller or an unmuffled footfall and teams of data analysts and strategists working at the NSA. By any reasonable standard, sub-hunting experts would have said that the craft codenamed the *Leviathan* would have had no chance of avoiding detection.

There was just one problem, though: none of those experts had seen what had taken place on the sun-baked streets of an obscure town called Zahedan.

51

IT WAS WELL BEFORE DAWN – THE STREETS OF WASHINGTON WERE almost deserted and a leaden sky was pressing down on the White House – when Falcon got out of his SUV and walked briskly towards the entrance to the West Wing.

Any experienced observer would have known that something serious was afoot: the director's shirt was crumpled and it clashed with his jacket, as if he had grabbed the first clothes that had come to hand.

He deposited all of his electronic devices in the lead-lined box and entered the situation room to find that the president, the Chairman of the Joint Chiefs, the Secretary of Defense, the Secretary of State and the few other cabinet members privy to the secret cloaking technology had already arrived. 'Apologies,' he said. 'I was out running when I got the message. What's happened?' For a beat, nobody answered—

Four days had passed since I had stood in the *Leviathan*'s command centre and listened as Rick Martinez briefed us about the mission. During that time, the sub had sped beneath rolling seas, heading for the waters surrounding the French Southern and Antarctic Lands, a group of uninhabited islands scattered across a huge expanse of water, home to colonies of penguins and the breeding ground of wandering albatrosses, the largest birds on earth, the lonely voyagers that ancient mariners thought were the souls of lost sailors, a belief that had convinced them that killing one would curse the ship and its crew. I never got the chance to ask if anyone on the *Leviathan* had brought one of the majestic birds down, but maybe I should have.

I had spent the four days roaming the sub and allowing myself to sink into a host of memories. As revolutionary as the *Leviathan* had looked from dockside, she was based on what was called a 'Block Seven' Virginia-class fast-attack sub – an updated version of the craft on which I had served and close enough in its layout to feel familiar to me.

During all those explorations I was barely ever alone. Baxter – not a sailor but a lost soul himself, someone whose grief was not close to touching bottom – was my companion and, because I had never considered myself a particularly kind person, I was surprised at how much pleasure I found in helping him keep his loneliness at bay.

Together, Baxter and I started at the rear of the sub, close to where the pump-jet propulsor – a more modern and silent replacement for a conventional propeller – was powering us fast through the silent underworld, and we slowly made our way towards the bulb at the front that served as the *Leviathan*'s eyes – its hugely complex system of sonar arrays. As we climbed, squeezed and crouched from one compartment to the next, I discovered a quality in my companion that I had always admired in people: despite his age, he was endlessly curious, and I soon realized that it was one of the primary reasons he was such an outstanding physicist. Just how outstanding I didn't discover until we were in the secondary command post when he mentioned – just casually – that he had been nominated three times for the Nobel.

I nodded as if I knew all about it – I didn't have a choice, I was supposed to be working in a similar field at Oak Ridge – and it was only later, thinking back, that I realized he had looked at me with something bordering on curiosity. Suspicion, even.

Instead, I concentrated on the secondary command post. It was something I had never seen before – an innovation for the *Leviathan* – that meant if the primary command centre was damaged or inaccessible, members of the crew would have a chance of controlling the vessel. Mentally, I filed the new development in the same category as the sub's three escape hatches: included more for comfort than practicality.

From the secondary command post we made our way through the

galley – a chaos of activity – and into the wardroom. Like everywhere else I had been on the boat, I sat quietly and listened or engaged the crew members in conversation and seemingly innocent questions. During that time I neither heard nor saw anything that could remotely be termed a security risk or hinted at a plan to sabotage the vessel – not even among the two people who were of Chinese heritage and who the agency, in time-honoured fashion, had immediately racially profiled. I had quickly come to share Falcon's view that the fire at Diego Garcia was an accident and any other explanation was dead out of gas.

On the third day of the journey south, Baxter and I entered a deserted area that I was unfamiliar with. I soon realized that the Virginia-class hull had been extended by a hundred feet in order to include what was known as a multi-purpose platform. Judging by the equipment, it was earmarked – once the *Leviathan* was operational – to accommodate a contingent of Navy SEALs. Several Zodiac inflatables were stacked against a wall, brackets to hold weapons were bolted nearby and behind a dozen narrow bunks were large blast-proof cabinets for explosives and grenades. Far more impressive than any of those things, even more remarkable than the high-powered jet-skis clamped to the floor, was a SEALs special delivery vehicle: a mini-sub.

Twenty-eight feet long and able to carry eight SEAL combat divers and a crew of two, it occupied a circular section of flooring that would lower the craft hydraulically into a lock-out chamber below, allowing it to be launched – underwater and unseen – within minutes.

As Baxter and I circled it, intrigued, I glanced across and saw four state-of-the-art decompression pods standing in a bay crammed with monitors, gauges, valves and dials. Bright yellow, the machines were startling in the white, antiseptic environment. The chambers were the only way to save lives in a medical emergency – one that was caused when divers surfaced too quickly and nitrogen bubbles entered their bloodstream.

'To treat decompression sickness?' Baxter said. 'The bends?'

I nodded. 'It can kill or paralyse you.'

I watched as Baxter, ever curious, walked over to the pods. 'Some equipment,' he said admiringly, running his hand along the steel side, pointing first at the airtight perspex domes that covered a single bed and then indicating a host of inlets and monitors located inside the futuristic cylinder. 'A totally independent oxygen supply, its own power source – huge batteries, by the look of it – precise temperature regulation, IV drips for fluids . . . who designed and built it? NASA?' He was kidding.

'That's what they say,' I replied; I wasn't – kidding, I mean.

He stared at me, about to respond, when a watertight door into the area opened and three men and two women – junior ratings – entered. They nodded a greeting and as they conducted a daily maintenance check on the equipment and Baxter continued to examine the pods I found myself alone and watching them. More diverse in gender and race than any naval group I had ever encountered, they worked like a machine – familiar and totally at ease in each other's company.

More than any other branch of the military, at least to my mind, the warriors who fought in the underwater battle-space were a true brotherhood – a sisterhood now, too – and as I stood quietly six hundred feet below the surface, I realized something about myself. Call it a small epiphany, if you will. I did not belong in that world.

Being washed out of submarines when I was young had cut me to the bone, a wound that had never completely healed, but I saw clearly now that I was someone best suited to walking alone. Maybe it was because I was an only child, but whatever my skills were, I certainly was not suited to being a member of any team.

I had returned to submarines in unusual circumstances and I could say now that I had no regrets about what might have been; I was blessed – I had found my place in the world – but no credit was due to me. Strange as it was, the CIA had known me better than I knew myself.

52

I LOOKED ACROSS AT BAXTER, WHO WAS STILL PORING OVER THE pods, and managed a smile: 'You know why the crew says we always go round as a pair?'

'No, why?' he replied.

'Specialization. One of us can read and the other can write.'

He laughed, and the maintenance crew joined in. 'You want to keep going?' I said, indicating the exit.

We left the multi-purpose platform, passed ranks of empty missile launch tubes and climbed a steel ladder that led to the heads and the laundry. Beyond it was an area that housed giant spools of cable for what was called the towed sonar array and, in semi-darkness behind it, I found what I was looking for: a set of wide watertight doors protected by electronic locks, a facial recognition scanner and a host of CCTV cameras. 'Entry forbidden' was painted on the doors in large letters.

I keyed in the code for the lock – given to me at Langley – and waited nervously while the facial recognition scanner identified both Baxter and myself. I figured I would be authorized but I was not sure about Baxter, so it was with some degree of relief that I heard a dozen electronic bolts slide back. I pushed open the door with no clear idea of what I would find but, hundreds of feet below the surface of the ocean, Baxter and I entered a wonderland.

An entire wall of the large space was made up of a computer system that had nothing to do with the normal operation of the boat: scores of identical black cabinets with steel-mesh doors held countless processors, circuit boards and hard drives. The entire array flickered and glowed, a myriad dancing lights playing along the cabinets as the computer performed a staggering number of operations.

I dragged my eyes away and registered the white metal floor, interspersed with stainless-steel grids, beneath which I could see a matrix of colour-coded high-pressure pipes. I listened, and in the all-enveloping silence I just managed to tune into a bass-like thrum. I tilted my head to catch it more clearly and realized something was flowing through the pipes – apparently the computer's processing power was so huge that it had to be liquid-cooled.

I looked again at the array and saw a small nameplate on the front of one of the cabinets. It identified the computer as a system and model number manufactured by Cray, the legendary company responsible for the world's most advanced supercomputers.

Baxter had followed my line of sight and saw the nameplate too. He shook his head in something close to shock. 'I didn't know a second Aurora Four had been built,' he said. 'I'm not sure anybody does.'

He walked towards it and stared at the cabinets. 'It uses over twenty million cores,' he said. 'Each cabinet has sixty-four blades and there's only one hop between any two nodes. Fastest computer in the world by a country mile – it performs over five billion billion operations a minute.' He smiled. 'But I'm not telling you anything you don't know, you must recognize it – Oak Ridge has the only other one in existence.'

I smiled in apparent acknowledgement and nodded my head – I had no choice; an Aurora Four? If you say so. I watched as he drew his eyes away from the cabinets, looked around at the other walls and the high ceiling and opened his palms in an expression of silent awe—

He had turned his attention to the even more remarkable aspect of the room: we were in the middle of a glowing, gossamer web. Countless fibre-optic threads – the ones smaller than the width of a hair, identical to those on the missiles – connected each of the glittering white tiles on the exterior of the sub to a row of control boxes wired to the Cray computer. The threads, billions deep, wrapped the walls and coiled across the ceiling with a glimmer of light – as fast as a blink – passing along each one, indicating to a technician that the connection was operating and live.

That pulsing, golden light played across our faces, and I thought of starlight and the Milky Way again and the vastness and mystery of the universe. Baxter, who was no stranger to mysteries himself, found his voice first. 'And this?' he said, indicating the glowing threads. 'They connect the tiny white tiles to the control boxes and computer?'

'Yes. I'm glad you could see it – I'm sure they used a huge amount of your research,' I said, and smiled. 'I doubt you got the three Nobel nominations for nothing.'

'To render the sub invisible, isn't it,' he replied, more as a statement than a question. 'That's what the skipper meant when he said a "revolutionary form of stealth"? It's cloaking technology?'

I nodded.

'A vision of the future . . .' he said almost to himself, looking at the glowing threads and the dancing lights. 'To me it was theoretical . . . and now we're standing among it . . . I hope they know what they are doing.' He turned and looked at me. 'How did you get access to this?' He indicated the doors with their electronic locks.

'I can go most anywhere,' I said. 'I've got the highest security clearance. It's like I told you, I do pretty secret work at Oak Ridge – it's why I know more about this than most people.'

He nodded and then spoke quietly, without a hint of aggression. 'Yes, you sure know a lot about it, but no matter what the flight manifest says – you're not from Oak Ridge, Danny.'

'I'm not?' I said, as coolly as I could muster.

'No – I never received three nominations for physics.'

'I'm sorry,' I replied. 'I was sure that was what you told me – my mistake.'

'Yes, that was what I told you, but I only ever got one Nobel nomination. It was the year I won it.' He shrugged. 'I think a leading physicist at Oak Ridge – someone with the highest security clearance – would know about my history and the prize, especially as we work in the same field.'

He had outsmarted me, but I don't suppose I realistically stood a chance – my legend was paper thin and the guy had won the Nobel for physics; he had even set up the three-nominations trap to test me. There was nothing for me to say, and the silence stretched between us.

'The way you know your way around,' he said finally. 'I take it you served on submarines?'

I nodded. 'Nuke School.'

'So – would you like to tell me who you really are?' he asked.

I paused for a long beat. 'No, I wouldn't,' I replied.

We both began to laugh. We got no further – an illuminated panel on the wall started to flash at the same time as special bands on our wrists vibrated, alerting us to an urgent command. 'General Quarters, all hands,' the message on the light panel said.

'What does "General Quarters" mean?' Baxter asked.

'It's a modern term,' I said. 'It used to be called "battle stations".'

53

FALCON, DRESSED IN HIS LESS THAN ELEGANT ATTIRE, WAS STILL waiting for someone to tell him why the most powerful men and women in Washington had been summoned to the situation room at such short notice.

'The hunters have found the *Leviathan*,' President Montgomery said.

Falcon looked at him, shocked. 'So fast? No wonder I couldn't finish my run.'

'At least it proves a point,' the Chairman of the Joint Chiefs said. 'We launch a state-of-the-art submarine with the best conventional stealth technology, and what happens? It barely gets close to the fleet before it is detected. In a shooting war, it would be at the bottom of the ocean now. That's how good anti-submarine warfare has become. This is where we are now—'

He called through a command to the technicians in the control booth, the lights dimmed and a video update appeared on the large screens. 'Four days after leaving Diego Garcia, the *Leviathan* entered the exclusion zone near the French Southern and Antarctic Lands.

'To maintain the integrity of the experiment,' the chairman continued, 'none of the carrier groups or other assets were aware of the *Leviathan*'s existence. As far as they were concerned – the press and public, too – they were engaged in a long-planned open-ocean war game. They were completely in the dark—'

'Then, less than twelve hours after the *Leviathan* entered the zone – north of a chain of islands called Îles Crozet – a patrolling Poseidon anti-sub aircraft dropped a sequence of underwater microphones. One of them picked up the faintest sound, but something the analysts on board the carriers and subs determined was too regular to be an anomaly.'

'Any idea what it was?' Falcon asked.

'Probably an irregularity in one part of the *Leviathan*'s pump-jet propulsor,' the chairman replied. 'Tiny – but enough to convince the listeners it was mechanical, and the entire fleet had no choice: this was so serious they focused every piece of tech on tracking and identifying the unknown craft. This came through fourteen minutes ago—'

A series of sonar displays, computer-generated images and other data showed a remarkable grey mass moving through the underworld, meaningless to any civilian, but not to Falcon. 'So, they know it's some sort of submarine,' he said. 'It's in the middle of them, and we know what the on-board techs did next—'

'Grabbed the Navy's secret list,' the Secretary of Defense added.

'And they found that the data they had about the intruder,' Falcon continued, 'didn't match the sound signature of any known submarine – not ours, our allies' or foes'. To the fleet it is a mystery, an unknown apex predator on the prowl. I imagine they are freaking out.'

'Freaking out doesn't do it justice. To them, this wasn't part of any war game,' the chairman replied. 'They immediately sounded General Quarters.'

The screens showed footage from the on-board cameras of the surface vessels in the fleet: sailors stripping protective covers from deck guns, missile ports opening, damage-control crews grabbing fireproof suits, blast shields deploying, fighter jets rising up elevators on the carriers and planes hurtling down pitching flight decks. Even at such a huge distance, there was something terrifying about twenty or thirty thousand men and women moving to battle stations.

'You can run as many tabletop exercises as you like,' the chairman said. 'This is as close to a real conflict as you can find without launching. The fleet will keep tracking the sub and the *Leviathan* will do everything it can to evade—'

'But the sub hasn't got a chance,' Falcon said. 'Not in reality. Like you said, the contest between stealth and detection is totally in favour of the hunters now. What's the plan – try and make the *Leviathan* disappear?'

'Yes, let's see what forty billion and fifteen years of research can do,' the president said.

54

'TELL ME – WHICH ONE CAN READ AND WHICH ONE CAN WRITE?' Martinez asked, very relaxed, as Baxter and I, summoned to General Quarters, entered the *Leviathan*'s command centre.

Baxter was quick on the uptake. 'I do both,' he responded over the laughter of the officers and specialists. 'Danny is a good guy, but he's pretty slow, if you follow me.'

'Oh, I'm following. From Tennessee, isn't he?' Martinez said. 'Can you explain to him that despite the most advanced stealth capability of any boat afloat – conventional stealth, I mean – the sub-hunters found us fifteen minutes ago.'

I had suspected it when I entered: the sonar techs were leaning into their screens, concentrating hard, and the data and maps on the displays in front of them showed that the *Leviathan* was being 'pinged' by active sonar from several different directions.

'An anti-submarine destroyer got the first hit on us with their sonar,' Martinez said. 'Then, of course, it started to avalanche.'

No wonder he'd ordered General Quarters, I thought – half a dozen attack assets were converging on him – and I realized that in the fifteen minutes it had taken Baxter and I to make our way for'ard, all the mechanical systems were stopped and the crew had scrambled to their posts without a sound. Martinez had used every strategy at his disposal to escape the fleet's tightening electronic net.

Even now, as we stood with him in the command centre, I could tell from the information streaming across the ship control panel in the middle of the room that Martinez was continuing to try and duck, slip and dive his way to freedom. Just like in chess, he was still playing the endgame, even though he probably knew it was checkmate.

As if in confirmation, he indicated the plotting table that was displaying computer-generated images of where the two carriers and all the other hunters were believed to be located. 'They're doing a good job, a credit to the US Navy – they've got us boxed in.

'The commanders would have loved the idea of a huge war game,' he continued. 'It's a great opportunity to show the Pentagon just how capable you are. But a skunk has turned up at the picnic, and I bet they are not liking it – they're going to move fast.' He indicated the latest movements on the plotting table. 'Any minute, our sonar will hear their torpedo shutters open – that is a warning from them – the last step before they decide to fire.'

'So – what now?' I said, something no member of the crew would have had the temerity to ask the skipper.

'Wait for orders from the White House,' he replied. 'And pray that no one is trigger happy.'

I looked over at the communications officer sitting in front of his wall of screens. An order from Washington for the *Leviathan* to activate the cloaking would come via Deep Siren – the codename for one of the Navy's most closely guarded secrets. A remarkable achievement, it was the method by which the Pentagon did the seemingly impossible: it could communicate with submerged submarines thousands of miles away without being overheard or revealing the sub's location.

Brilliant as the method might have been, Deep Siren remained silent. Surely Washington had to know that the approaching craft were readying themselves to fire.

Along with everyone else in the cramped space, I kept glancing at the plotting table to check on the hunters' progress. Closer and closer—

'Torpedo shutters opening,' the sonar tech said.

'That's the final warning,' Martinez said. 'They're set to fire.'

I looked at a screen showing our surroundings: we were ten thousand miles from home, six hundred feet below the far Southern Ocean, on board a huge and futuristic craft that was almost adrift, the engine drawing just enough power to provide steerage way, all the rest of the systems in a virtual coma, the silence becoming increasingly oppressive, a long swell rolling overhead and an unnamed underwater mountain range lying not far off to port. To say that it was not an ideal situation in which to be under imminent threat—

A man's soft voice, polite and weirdly threatening, emanated from a speaker. 'Alert the commander,' it said. 'Please open the channel now.'

The communications officer sat straighter, alert, while the rest of us turned to look. Deep Siren was finally making contact.

The comms officer opened a data channel and moments later a printer spat out a series of codes. He handed them to Martinez and the skipper picked up his small tablet computer and entered them. He read his orders quickly and then, from the movement of his eyes, read them again to be sure.

He turned to the *Leviathan*'s pilot: 'Set half speed ahead,' he ordered. 'Go to full cloaking. Maybe this skunk is trickier than they thought.'

55

IN THE WHITE HOUSE SITUATION ROOM, FALCON AND THE REST OF the cabinet members were silent, waiting for the president's order for the *Leviathan* to go to full cloaking to take effect.

'Everybody,' the president said. Falcon, looking down at the floor, turned to see Montgomery pointing at the screens.

The *Leviathan* had appeared: gliding silently through the underwater gloom, startlingly white, seven storeys high, overwhelmingly modern and unlike any underwater craft ever seen before, especially not like this, on the loose in its natural habitat as the tiles began to glow, long and sharp edged.

It only took a moment for Falcon to realize that the flood of data being provided by the surface ships, the submarines and the satellites had in the last minute or so allowed the NSA to compose a computer-generated image of the *Leviathan*, remarkable in its accuracy and detail.

'Now I am become Death, the destroyer of worlds,' Falcon said, his eyes fixed on the image, reminded of another pivotal event in the development of warfare: the explosion of the first atomic bomb.

Other images of the Southern Ocean appeared on several of the screens. The first showed the leading aircraft carrier smashing through the swell at over thirty knots. The second was from inside the carrier's bridge and staffed by the vice-admiral commanding the fleet, the captain of the carrier and the other officers and crew charged with handling the massive ship. They were all staring at the same NSA feed that had appeared in the situation room, the first time any of them had seen the *Leviathan*. Or, indeed, anything like it.

'What the fu—' the vice-admiral said, stopping just in time. 'What the hell is that?'

Nobody on the bridge could answer. Even though an incredibly lethal weapons platform was under the sea in front of them, they were as dumbfounded by its shape, size and presence as their admiral. Similar scenes of confusion and astonishment were being repeated – so it was revealed later – on board the rest of the surface fleet, in the prowling attack subs, the circling AWACS radar planes and the NSA monitoring centre.

On the bridge of the leading carrier, the executive officer was the first to recover. 'It can't be anything of ours,' he said. 'It's not in any of our databases.'

The shock of the initial sighting was passing and the executive officer realized they were face to face with a threat of unknown proportions. He looked at the admiral. 'Do we fire?'

'Not without a direct order from the Pentagon or the White House,' the admiral replied.

'It's fading, sir,' the sonar tech reported, his eyes focused only on the image of the white boat on his screen.

'What do you mean,' the admiral said, 'it's fading?' He turned to look. 'Well, get the link back up!' he ordered.

'It's not the computer, sir,' the sonar tech replied evenly. 'Everything is running fine. NSA is seeing the same decay—'

'It's the sub,' the officer of the deck intervened. 'It's the sub that is disappearing.'

'In front of our eyes?' the admiral said. 'That's not possible.'

In the situation room, the president, Falcon and the others were looking at the same image, watching the sparkling white tiles start to turn dull and fade, but their reaction was vastly different – a tremor of excitement, bordering on triumph, was rippling through the room.

At the same time, deep in the furthest reaches of the *Leviathan*, in the Aurora 4 wonderland, the stainless-steel grids on the floor were now atremble as the liquid in the high-pressure pipes was forced through faster to cool the supercomputer. Behind the mesh doors of the cabinets, a symphony of flashing lights was playing out as it handled an ever-escalating number of operations; across the ceiling and down the walls, the pulsing lights of the gossamer web were ablaze, and electronic graphs on the wall showed that the entire array was approaching its peak operating level.

In the sub's command centre, a computer-generated image of the *Leviathan* appeared on a screen. It showed waves of light were being diverted, swerving around the giant craft. Baxter and I stared – it was as if the submarine was travelling in its own impenetrable cocoon.

As we all watched, the sub's hull and angular shapes rapidly became a patchwork of missing sections. It looked like a half-finished painting, and it was obvious – the *Leviathan* was disappearing fast.

Aboard all the other assets, the image from the NSA was also showing the *Leviathan* vanishing from sight. On the bridge of the leading carrier, the sonar operator started furiously keying in commands, adjusting dials, forgetting about the NSA, trying to use his own resources to keep some form of the *Leviathan* in frame. It did nothing; the technology he was confronting was in a realm far beyond anything he could muster.

'It's going, sir,' he reported. Everybody on the bridge just stared. Then he corrected himself: 'It's gone,' and he slumped back in his chair.

He was right: there was no sign of the *Leviathan* on his screens or on the feed from the NSA. In an instant, before their eyes, the boat had vanished. To them, and everyone else in the fleet, it was a ghost ship; a modern version of the *Flying Dutchman*.

'What the hell was that?' the captain said at last, deeply shaken by what he had just witnessed.

'A mirage?' the pilot offered.

'Underwater?' the admiral responded, disbelieving.

'An optical illusion?' the executive officer said.

There was no reply; nobody was buying that either. They all knew they had seen it, it was real, and now it was gone; but that didn't mean it couldn't come back. They all stared at the screens, alarmed now.

56

BY STARK CONTRAST, THE MOOD IN THE SITUATION ROOM WAS CLOSE to euphoric. The missiles of Zahedan were one thing, but a submarine was a universe apart. All that time, all that research, and now all the opportunities for power and influence in a world reconfigured.

It must have been a heady experience: they had witnessed a world-altering event. The president, however, seemed to sag – the tension, the anxiety, of the experiment had taken a toll and now, as the adrenaline drained, the fatigue washed in. Maybe, too, the cancer that would eventually kill him was already staking its unseen claim.

Nevertheless, he continued to stare at the vacant screen where – until moments ago – all six hundred feet of the *Leviathan* had been fully visible. 'Jesus Christ,' he said quietly.

His reaction, muted as it was, broke the spell, and a hubbub of exuberant voices exploded. One cut through it all: the Secretary of Defense was in full flight, swelling with success. 'I said last night – if this doesn't work, I'd chew glass.'

'That can be arranged,' Falcon replied.

The room was rocked by laughter, evidence of the high spirits overwhelming the occupants. Even the Secretary of Defense managed a bitter, thin-lipped smile.

57

IN THE *LEVIATHAN*'S COMMAND CENTRE – INDEED, ACROSS THE ENTIRE boat – the silence was deeper and more pervasive than anything I had ever known on a submarine.

The reason for it, according to a screen showing a virtual-reality rendering of our surroundings, was lying off to our port side. Hidden, but still slightly visible in the foothills of the underwater mountain range, lurking close to what is called a hydrothermal vent – a fissure in which saltwater penetrates the ocean floor, hits boiling magma and gives off clouds of steam and debris, making it, essentially, a hot spring – was the US attack sub *SSN-849*.

Whoever was in command of the craft knew their business. The hot spring, known as a 'white smoker', offered far better cover than the turbulence produced by coastal waters or bubbles generated by machines inside a reef at Diego Garcia. As a result, it was the perfect position in which to lie in wait and attack the *Leviathan* should it return.

As a result, all eyes in the command centre of the *Leviathan* were riveted on the screens showing the attack sub and its makeshift smokescreen. I watched as we crept slowly towards the sub, suddenly alarmed as I realized we were going to pass within a few hundred yards of it; less than an air-kiss in the world of underwater warfare.

If the cloaking cocoon started to break down . . . well, God help us. The attack sub already had its torpedo hatches open – there would be no warning this time, just a few seconds for Martinez to identify his boat and avert instant destruction. I assumed the skipper's secret orders were to test his craft's stealth ability in the most aggressive fashion possible, but I couldn't help thinking that this rendered us chillingly vulnerable to panic or malfunction.

I looked around the barely lit room and could see on the other faces that I wasn't the only one whose heart was in their mouth. Together, we watched in silence as the distance to the attack sub diminished metre by metre—

I admit even I could feel the tension. But the attack sub didn't move at all, not even when we were right alongside it. Surely, though, it had to sense something. There was nothing – its torpedo hatches, clearly visible, showed no tremor or pulse of pressure as they were cleared for firing. *SSN-849* was as motionless as we were invisible.

Within hailing distance, against the backdrop of the underwater mountains with their craggy peaks, schools of fish darting through the foothills and climbing the escarpments and the white smoker spewing out endless debris, I watched as the two submarines – one from the past and the other from the future – passed each other.

I kept my eyes fixed on the screen until we had passed the sub and were heading, unseen and invisible, into the limitless and trackless world of the planet's great oceans. I turned away from the screen and my eye fell on one of the navigation computers fixed to the bulkhead. 'Skipper,' I said, 'you've got a malfunction on the nav computers—'

Martinez turned. I don't think he liked having civilians on board – what Navy commander would? – and, God knows, the last few hours had been stressful, probably the most intense of his entire career. 'What?' he demanded.

'The nav computer,' I said. 'It says we are much further west in the Southern Ocean—'

He glanced up at the bulkhead then turned and saw the same anomaly displayed on the screens at the navigation workstation. He turned to the navigator: 'Can we get that back online?' he ordered, starting to head towards the coffee machine in the corner of the room.

He didn't make it. 'The clocks,' Baxter said, pointing at several displays on screens and a digital clock over the plotting table. Hours and seconds were reeling through erratically: flipping, pausing, launching forward in leaps and bounds—

'Computers rely on an internal clock,' Baxter continued, alarmed. 'They use it to synchronize their functions. It's essential, without it they can't—'

'Keep your thoughts to yourself if you don't mind, Professor. It's a malfunction, that's all.' Martinez's voice was curt.

'We're in trouble,' Baxter said, almost to himself.

'There's a problem with sonar, sir,' the operator said, forgetting for once to keep his voice even and calm. 'The internal clock can't keep up. Time isn't stable or something—'

'Skipper! Forward Compartment Nine,' the officer of the deck, focused on the ship control panel, reported. 'Burst high-pressure pipe—'

I looked at the panel and saw a number of alarms glowing red. I knew the compartment was close to the reactor, and I imagined one of the pipes – high pressure meant steam – blasting out a torrent of super-heated vapour. As a result I only just registered Martinez calling out orders, enforcing a sense of control and calm with his own behaviour and voice.

Fire and flooding are the two accidents – any untoward event is called a 'casualty' in the silent service – that pose the greatest threat to a sub, and I looked immediately at the CCTV coverage of the crew quarters to see that a damage-control team had already grabbed a box of temporary gaskets and several chain-wrenches to repair the broken pipe.

As they ran for Compartment Nine, a tremor followed by a deep rumbling began to shake the hull of the submarine. Everyone in the command centre stopped. We felt it pass through us, gathering strength, until a metal panel covering a host of electrical connections flew off the wall, crossed the room and struck the sonar operator on the forehead. Now there was a real casualty—

I looked at the CCTV to see two panels in a companionway explode towards the damage-control team, barely missing them. Then the rumbling subsided and was replaced by creaking from the steel bulkheads.

Martinez's voice cut through the groaning metal and the reports coming in from different departments – he was on the PA, ordering a medic to come immediately to the command centre: blood was pouring from the sonar operator's head.

The communications officer was already starting to kneel next to him, but he didn't have a chance to staunch the bleeding. The officer of the deck, concentrating on the ship control panel, called out, 'Code Red, laundry.' Code Red meant fire, and the communications officer was back at his post in seconds.

The Code Red had barely been sounded before other warnings – different colours – appeared on the ship control panel, showing even more casualties, but whether they were human or mechanical, I had no way of knowing.

I looked across and caught sight of Martinez's unguarded face – wrought with anxiety, or maybe fear – and saw his eyes narrow with concentration as he looked from one workstation to the next. A fire, a water leak, a cascade of other alerts. 'Emergency blow,' he ordered.

Baxter, frightened, looked at me and his eyes said it: a what?

'Ditch the ballast, get to the surface as fast as possible,' I said, surprised at the tremor in my own voice.

I looked up and saw, according to the navigation screen on the bulkhead, that we were approaching the bottom of South Africa and would, within hours, enter the southern Atlantic Ocean – except it was patently not possible to have travelled that distance. Meanwhile, the clocks were still scrolling through seconds and minutes while more casualty alerts were piling up on the ship control panel.

I braced myself to hear the massive high-pressure pumps kick in as thousands of tons of seawater – the ballast – started to be pumped out, and I wondered if we could possibly get to the surface in time: we were eight hundred feet below, locked in a cocoon of cloaking, invisible to every military asset the United States could muster, with a boat suffering a rolling series of failures and a cauldron of water above us—

'Ballast pumps unresponsive,' the executive officer reported. 'Cannot void ballast.' We weren't going to the surface after all.

Martinez paused for a moment, fighting to take stock, then continued to issue command after command to try and get the situation under control. Baxter turned to me. 'What's happening?' he asked, his face pale and a nerve in one cheek quivering.

'I don't know,' I said. 'Not sure anybody does.'

'You think the clocks are the clue?' he replied, having to speak louder to overcome the sound of alarms, voices on the intercom and a constant stream of orders from Martinez.

'Making the computers malfunction?' I replied.

'No,' he said. 'Deeper than that. Worse. I don't know ... in these conditions ... maybe if you start bending light ... you fool with time,' he answered. 'Divert one thing and you twist another?'

I stared at him, not willing to dismiss what he said; the man had won the Nobel Prize for physics. Despite the onslaught of damage reports and a sense of burgeoning chaos, Martinez turned: 'Is that a theory?' he interjected, desperate for information. 'Or a fact?'

'A theory,' Baxter replied. 'But not mine entirely – more like Einstein's.' He looked up at the spinning clocks. 'Who knows what happens when you bend light at this scale? Nobody has ever tried it – at this depth, in these temperatures ...' His voice trailed off and he shrugged, lost to his thoughts.

Martinez turned away, looking at the data and alerts surrounding him. He was trying to save the sub, he had to make decisions, and wild Einsteinian speculation wasn't helpful. He turned to the officers and operators. 'There's no guaranteeing the integrity of this space,' he said, indicating the command centre, speaking even louder to be heard above the escalating noise of the intercoms, alerts and ventilation vents. 'I need at least one officer to man the secondary command post – just in case, a failsafe.'

The executive officer indicated the avalanche of information and alerts: 'With respect, skipper, we're all needed here. This is where we can save the boat.'

Nobody contradicted him – he was probably right. Martinez was about to order one of the officers to head out when I spoke up: 'I can go.'

They all turned. Martinez shook his head. 'I admire your courage, the desire to help, but I need someone who, in an emergency, can organize the command of the boat.'

'I'm qualified in submarines,' I said.

He – and everyone else – looked at me, confused. The only one who didn't was Baxter.

'In submarines? Qualified? What? You're a scientist from Oak Ridge,' Martinez said.

'I don't work at Oak Ridge. I graduated from Nuke School in Charleston, third in my class.'

'Then where the hell do you work?' Martinez asked, understandably alarmed at who he had on board.

'The CIA,' I said. Nobody said a word. Not even Baxter.

'What do you do there?' Martinez asked, looking at a fresh set of red alerts. 'Hurry!'

'An intelligence agent,' I replied quickly.

'A spy?' he said. 'What sort of fucking spy?'

'A Denied Access Area agent,' I said.

Martinez indicated his crippled boat. 'Well, you've come to the right place.'

'I wish I hadn't,' I said.

'You and me both. What's your name – I'm damned sure it's not Greenberg.'

'Call me Kane,' I said.

58

THE EUPHORIA IN THE SITUATION ROOM HAD SETTLED INTO A QUIET but still intoxicating excitement. The president, still pale and careworn, had no doubt about what had been achieved.

'Congratulations to everyone here, of course,' he said. 'If it wasn't so early, I'd say we all deserve a drink.' Everybody laughed; he was a well-known teetotaller.

'As commander-in-chief, there's another group I want to thank personally,' he continued, signalling to the technicians in the glass booth and speaking into a desk-mounted microphone in front of his chair. 'Put me through to Captain Martinez of the *Leviathan*,' Montgomery said. 'Ask him to make sure my comments are broadcast to the entire crew.'

As the technicians set to work, the president started moving around the table, shaking each person's hand, saying a few private words of appreciation, patting backs, making everyone feel like they were the most important person in the world. My Lord, he was – at least by Falcon's account – the consummate politician, a person who never stopped campaigning.

As it turned out, he never got as far as Falcon. Quite by accident, the CIA director was last in line, and he spent his time waiting to have his private moment with Montgomery by watching the techs prepare to announce that Deep Siren, once again, had made contact.

Falcon's brow furrowed as he watched them turn from their screens, engage in a hurried conversation and enter more commands. Anxiety mounting, he walked forward and opened the soundproof door. He immediately heard the computerized voice—

'Please alert the commander,' it was saying in its faintly menacing tone. 'Captain Martinez is required online now. Please alert . . .'

Falcon spoke to the senior of the three operators: 'How many times have you tried?'

'Five,' the woman replied. 'No response.'

Falcon turned on his heel and was barely through the door before he spoke: 'Deep Siren can't contact the sub.'

It was greeted by a stunned silence, broken only when the Chairman of the Joint Chiefs shrugged: 'It's just new technology for this sub; everything on board is in the same category – they'll get it fixed.'

'Cloaking is new technology; this isn't,' Falcon replied. 'Deep Siren has been used for decades, constantly upgraded and refined. It was tested dozens of times on the *Leviathan* before the boat went to sea.'

The Secretary of State – the wealthy woman with a voice like cut glass – spoke quietly. 'How many times has Deep Siren failed in the past?'

'None,' Falcon replied. He turned and looked through the glass at the three operators in the booth. He could see the senior of them leaning her head forward in an attitude that looked close to despair.

Falcon told me later he couldn't help thinking of another hugely complex American craft – an equally impressive technological achievement – that had also suffered enormous, life-threatening damage. He looked at the others—

'Houston, we have a problem,' he said quietly.

59

TWICE IN MY LIFE, BOTH ON FOREIGN MISSIONS, I HAVE FELT DEATH'S hand on my shoulder. The first was in the abandoned village with the poisoned well in Iran. The second was on board the *Leviathan*.

As the damage to the sub continued to cascade, threatening to overwhelm Martinez and his team – a crisis made worse because nobody could identify its cause – I motioned to Baxter to grab a headset mic-and-earphones off the wall, did the same myself and led him out of the command centre into the controlled chaos of the submarine.

I had no idea what I would find in the secondary command post – or even if it was still operational – but if it became necessary for me to try and get the *Leviathan* to the surface, I knew that I wouldn't be able to monitor the avalanche of graphs and alerts and enter the computer commands alone. Baxter might not have had any experience in submarines, but I figured a Nobel Prize-winning physicist would be no slouch on the uptake.

Almost immediately, we ran headlong into a team of men and women unreeling hoses, ready to connect them to portable submersible pumps. It meant there was water entering the sub, and I wondered if the hull had been fractured. I yelled at a mechanic's mate doubling as the water evacuation leader. 'The hull?'

'No,' he replied. 'The tremor or whatever it was broke a seal on a torpedo tube – it's taking water, but they're fitting a new one.' He tried to smile. 'It could be worse.'

I nodded, not believing it. Baxter and I squeezed past and headed deeper into the belly of the beast. It was clear the boat's computers were saving power and directing it to the most critical areas. Apparently, the corridors and companionways were not on that list.

We hugged the walls, passing more damage-control teams and saw, up ahead, shadowy figures moving quickly, carrying small portable generators and toolboxes with them. At one junction, I saw Baxter looking around, alarmed by the level of chaos around him: pipes hanging from brackets, collapsed electrical conduits and doors torn off storage closets.

'It's not as bad as it looks. A lot of it is superficial,' I said, hoping I was right. 'At least, if the ventilation is anything to go by, the fire in the laundry has been extinguished.'

He nodded. 'Are you as frightened as me?'

'No,' I replied, smiling. 'I was in Pakistan as a young agent working out of the embassy when it was stormed by a huge mob. In my opinion, if there aren't five thousand armed men coming over the wall to kill you, then it's not an emergency.'

He laughed, and we climbed to the next level. There in front of us, crouched in the passageway, was a two-person team doing double duty as medics. They were tending to one of the nuke engineers who had either fallen or been hit by something: his right arm was hanging limp, clearly broken.

The medics waved us through, but I stopped. There was nothing either Baxter or I could do, but I indicated the tool belt and flashlight clipped to the man's waist. 'Can I?' I asked.

'Be my guest,' he replied through gritted teeth. 'No use to me.'

I took the belt and headed into the gloom.

60

TWENTY THOUSAND MILES ABOVE THE EARTH AN ORION SATELLITE – tilted on its axis, its huge parabolic antenna fully deployed and a forest of cameras focused directly on the great Southern Ocean – was spinning through the vacuum of space.

Its images were playing on one of the screens in the situation room. Alongside was footage of the aircraft carriers superimposed over a grid, a dozen Poseidon sub-hunters in the air and an attack submarine running deep, trailing a towed sonar array for miles behind it. They were all searching.

Falcon hung up a phone connected to a landline. 'Anything?' the president asked.

'No sign of it,' Falcon replied. 'Not from the NSA, Langley, the National Reconnaissance Office or even the weather service – we're trying anybody with satellites or planes aloft.'

'What are you telling them we're searching for?' the Secretary of State asked.

'I said that an unidentified submarine is monitoring our open-sea war game and we need help tracking it. If we say we can't contact one of our own subs, it'll leak and we'll have a hundred news organizations chartering planes and wanting a crew list.'

'Anyway,' the Secretary of Defense said, 'we don't know anything is wrong – we just can't contact them is all.'

'It's not like that,' Falcon said. 'The skipper'll be waiting to hear from Deep Siren . . . apart from anything, he needs orders. When he doesn't get them, they will try to contact us. Standard operating procedure.'

'Maybe they can't reach us – for the same reason, we can't contact them. A technical fault,' the Danger to Shipping replied. 'I'm telling you, it's the most likely—'

'Then why don't they go to periscope depth and contact us through conventional means?'

The Secretary of Defense had no answer.

'Should they have done that by now?' the Secretary of State asked. 'Periscope depth?'

454

'Wouldn't any of us?' Falcon replied. 'My guess is they have suffered some sort of failure – possibly catastrophic. But what do we do? How do we help them? The vessel is fully cloaked—'

He looked around the room. 'How the hell do you find an invisible submarine?'

61

BAXTER AND I WERE MOVING AS SWIFTLY AS POSSIBLE DOWN A companionway between the crew's tiny bunks when the next tremor hit.

Pulse rocketing, I felt it first through my feet: another ominous shudder, accompanied by the same deep rumbling, started to pass through the hull of the sub, but this time it didn't stop – it just grew in intensity, until the whole boat seemed to suddenly twist hard on its axis. I swung fast in the companionway, trying to grab a handhold to brace myself for whatever might be coming next. Baxter did the same and succeeded, but I was too late—

The bow of the huge craft plunged downwards into what felt like a freefall. My feet left the deck and for seconds I felt weightless – like an astronaut floating in zero gravity – as I hurtled across the confined space.

I hit a bulkhead hard and only my outstretched hands prevented me from cracking my skull. I fell to the deck, thinking I was at least safe for a moment, but a stack of large steel storage boxes broke their lashings and came smashing through a cupboard door ten feet away.

The heavy boxes hurtled towards us, brushing past Baxter, who was still clinging to his handhold, and narrowly missing me. But the tremor had also ripped apart the shelving holding the boxes and long shards of metal were flying through the air right behind them. I yelled a warning to Baxter and he spun out of the way, but . . .

A piece of metal shelving, two feet long, as sharp and narrow as a spear, flew straight towards me. Only seeing it at the last moment, I tried to hurl myself aside, but didn't have the fraction of a second I needed. It hit my left shoulder, burying itself deep, just stopping short of pinning me to the wall.

Clutching at the wound, trying not to pass out, I felt the tremor pass and the *Leviathan* straighten out: it had at least arrested its downward plunge. Gasping for a few moments, trying to master myself, I tentatively probed the entry point and took hold of the spear, trying to judge how firmly it was embedded.

Baxter scrambled to my side. 'We have to get it out,' he said, kneeling, taking hold of the metal shaft.

'No!' I yelled through the pain. 'Pull it out and the wound will open wide. I'd lose too much blood—'

'Well, we can't leave it in!' he said.

'No – but we need to be ready to pack and dress the wound,' I gasped, worried now that I was about to lose consciousness.

'How?' he demanded. 'Where in God's name do I find a first-aid—'

'Don't bother . . . we've gotta get to the control post,' I said. 'Find where the women sleep.'

'The women?' he replied.

'Foot lockers are at the end of the beds. There's a storage area under the mattress. I need tampons and sanitary pads.'

'Okay,' he said, looking around, overwhelmed—

'Go!' I said, propelling him into action.

As he headed towards the bunks and started ripping curtains aside, I took hold of the shaft. From the angle of the steel and the movement, I was fairly certain the spear wasn't lodged in bone, which was a blessing. It wasn't going to be easy, but removing it was at least possible.

Baxter returned holding a handful of tampons and a packet of sanitary pads.

'Good,' I said, and told him to get a tampon out of its packaging.

I took a firm grip on the spear and spoke as I tried to breathe deeply. 'It's a battlefield strategy for gunshot wounds. You get the projectile out, plug the tampon deep into the cavity, it absorbs the blood, starts to expand and supports the walls of the wound. It stops them from collapsing. As many tampons as we need, then we pack and dress it with the sanitary pads.'

Baxter shook his head in disbelief. 'Neat trick – so CIA spies don't just kill people?'

'You can't kill anyone if you're dead – the first rule of espionage,' I replied, bracing myself for what was coming.

'Truly?' Baxter asked, staring helplessly at the shaft and blood. 'Is that really the first rule?'

'I just made it up,' I said, feeling my face contort with pain as I started to exert pressure. It was now or never—

I planted my feet against the bulkhead and hoped to hell I didn't pass out. 'Now!' I said. The spear resisted and I felt the first waves of pain start to engulf me, but I knew I couldn't stop – if I did, I wouldn't have the energy or the mental strength to start again.

Baxter was holding my other shoulder to offer emotional support. 'More,' he said, and I kept pulling; the darkness was closing in, but I felt the spear start to give.

A feeling of warmth started coursing down my chest and I knew it was my own blood, but I didn't look; concentrate on the spear, I kept telling myself. Another wave of pain hit me, but I pushed past it and after a moment's hesitation I felt the metal start to glide—

I pulled harder, and the blood flowed more freely. I could sense the metal coming out of the wound and at last heard it clatter to the deck.

I opened my eyes. Baxter was ready and pressed a tampon into my hand. Instantly I reached into the slippery wound, felt the blood pulsing out and pushed the white cylinder in as far as it would go. Already I felt it expanding as it filled with blood.

I withdrew my fingers and Baxter had another tampon ready. The flow of blood started to slow and the final two tampons went in far more easily and barely started to expand.

I slumped back, reached down and grabbed a roll of electrical tape out of the tool belt. 'Sanitary pads,' I said, but Baxter was ahead of me. He had them waiting and started to pack and bandage the wound as I wrapped the dressing tight with the tape.

Five turns around my shoulder and we were done. We looked at one another for a moment and I tried to smile my thanks.

'Ready?' I asked. 'Now for the easy part – let's see what we can do about this boat.'

62

MY INJURED SHOULDER MEANT THAT MY LEFT ARM WAS NEXT TO useless on the ladders between floors, but I strapped the flashlight to it, leaving my good hand free and allowing us to see the path ahead and move as fast as we could.

We were heading a long way aft and saw fewer and fewer members of the crew. Nevertheless, on three occasions, we encountered teams with extinguishers heading to trouble spots where men and women with gaskets were working on ruptured pipes, blocking the path ahead. It forced us to double back, climb at least twice through the sub's four decks and find an alternative way forward.

That meant negotiating the steel ladders, which I was forced to climb by grabbing each rung one-handed.

Finally, having just negotiated another series of ladders, I was about to stop and try to reorientate myself, wondering if – in the confusion and gloom – I had somehow ended up on the wrong deck and had missed the secondary command post.

At that moment, down a long companionway, I saw a glow of light far different to any of the emergency LEDs that were illuminating the gangways.

It grew stronger as we approached, spilling out of a doorway: at last, we had found the secondary command post. Perhaps if I hadn't been so determined to learn what was wrong with the boat, I might not have moved so quickly.

Maybe then I might have paid attention to the tiny drops of water pooling in places on the floor, the beads of moisture around the joints of a large pipe set into the wall or the high-pressure hum it emitted.

Instead, closely followed by Baxter, I entered the secondary command post and immediately clicked open the headset mic, hit the channel for Martinez and the command centre and tried to report that I was on station—

There was no answer. Four times I tried, and only once did I hear something apart from static: a muffled voice, someone calling in distress, and then . . . nothing. Baxter and I looked at each other for a long moment. He tried his best, but not very successfully, to keep the fear out of his voice. 'What do we do now?'

'No choice – we gotta try and launch the emergency blow.'

I looked at the screens above the workstations and saw, thank God, that more than half of them were still showing streams of data. Directly in front of me, the navigation screens were displaying our position and the computers attached to it were recording every detail of our course. If I could get the sub to the surface and activate one of the conventional communication systems, the computer would immediately give our position when I started transmitting Mayday.

More encouragingly, the ship control panel in the centre of the room was still operating, its expanse of glass aglow with columns of red-flashing data I didn't understand, fast-scrolling updates from scores of systems that were accompanied by pulsing yellow and orange triangles and – in the middle of the kaleidoscope of alarm – a single element had been given more prominence than any other. A large, flashing alert said:

INITIATE EMERGENCY BLOW NOW

The computers running the sub had distilled the data into the most dangerous threat and offered the best strategy to save the boat. I touched the alert and the screen immediately brought up a menu of prompts that would lead me through the authorization procedure. I was confident that I remembered more than enough from my time in the Navy to handle it successfully and rapidly began tapping 'yes' to them—

The dimmed overhead lights in the ceiling suddenly flickered. I glanced up and then looked at the computer screens in the workstations. They turned black – momentarily – and then came back to life. The overhead lights flickered again, and it wasn't as if I needed any further encouragement—

I turned to Baxter. 'If we lose power, we don't have a chance. Thirty metres back, there's a closet marked "Electrical". Inside is a battery-operated generator.' Baxter nodded. 'Wheel it here – it'll give us enough juice to keep us running. We're only gonna need a few minutes.'

He turned and moved as fast as his knees would allow into the companionway and I continued scrolling through the commands. I completed four entries on the screen—

The high-pressure hum that I had barely registered was changing tone. I looked at the far wall – from the sound, the large pipe was located behind it – just as the hum suddenly flew up the scale and became a high-pitched scream.

I straightened up and started backing towards the door. My foot was still in mid-air when the pipe burst with a shattering force, blowing a hole in the wall and sending a large chunk of metal flying through a workstation and across the room.

The debris was followed by a torrent of water that shot across the space and hit me in the chest, hurling me off my feet and across the room.

I heard Baxter yelling in alarm from partway along the companionway. 'Kane! Kane—'

'The generator,' I replied, scrambling to escape the torrent of water. 'Get it here now!' There was nothing Baxter or I could do about the burst pipe, but without power we were doomed.

Gasping, I clambered to my knees. Due to the diameter of the pipe and the pressure under which it was operating, the floor was already inches underwater and rising. Somewhere in the chaos I had the presence of mind to realize the water was fresh and not salt, which meant it was coming from within the boat and the hull hadn't been breached. If that had been the case, it would have been all over within minutes.

I had to get back to the ship control panel and finish launching the emergency blow. Ignoring an alarm that started screeching overhead, I sloshed as fast as I could to the screen, only to see that it was a wasted effort. The damaged power cables hanging from the wall and the rising water meant that all electricity to the control room was being shut down. I watched the panel die. Only then did I turn to the screeching alarm: a sign above it was flashing the single command:

EVACUATE

A display indicated there were three seconds to go before something happened; I guessed what that would be, and then I saw Baxter running towards me, hauling the small generator behind. 'No!' I screamed. 'Stop – get back!'

He had no idea why, but he stopped just short of the doorway. I scrambled towards the door myself – four paces, five – but I was slowed by the water swirling around my calves. One second to go, the display said—

I had no choice if I didn't want to be sealed in a watertight coffin. I dived headlong for the doorway. In mid-air, I heard—

Two explosions of compressed air from the bulkhead above ring out like gunshots. They activated a heavy steel slab – a watertight door – which immediately plunged down from a cavity in the roof.

I was flying through the opening and the slab was right above me, dropping like a stone. My body and thighs managed to get through the diminishing space, but my legs were trailing, about to be hit.

I pulled them up to my chest, forcing the air from my lungs in a final effort, and at last felt the slab graze the soles of my sneakers as it passed.

I landed in a heap on the other side of the doorway just as the slab hit the surging water and locked into a channel on the floor with a shuddering crunch. It would without doubt have cut me in half.

I looked up to see Baxter standing with the portable generator, just staring at me. Panting, I tried to smile. 'Don't just stand there, Baxter. We've gotta go.'

63

SILENCE HAD SETTLED OVER THE SITUATION ROOM LIKE A LOW-pressure trough. The occupants had waited for Deep Siren to make contact with the *Leviathan* or for the sub to surface, but nothing had happened. Even the sighting of a floating debris field would have been a blessing; at least it would have told them where to send help.

Finally, the Secretary of State looked at the president. 'Without any contact, I think Falcon's right,' she said. 'They must have suffered some sort of massive failure.'

Others nodded their heads. Not even the Secretary of Defense was ready to argue.

'We're going to have to make an announcement,' she continued. 'An address from the Oval Office, something like that?'

Montgomery shook his head. 'I think we can delay, give ourselves more time – nobody even knows the *Leviathan* exists.'

'I'm sorry, sir – I don't think waiting's an option. We are supposedly running a war game, and with that concentration of US forces, half a dozen foreign satellites are watching. They'll know from the fleet's behaviour something is wrong. Their analysts have either worked out now – or will very soon – that we are conducting an underwater search. They won't know it's the *Leviathan*, but that doesn't matter. Do we want the Russians or Chinese to tell the world that the US is looking for a lost submarine?'

Montgomery seemed to slump.

'That's a recipe for a disaster,' the Secretary of State said. 'There are missing US personnel and the government didn't move immediately to try and save them? We've waited several hours for contact; that was prudent – but it can't last. We have to launch a search and rescue mission.'

The president thought for a moment. 'What is the depth of the ocean that far south?'

'Its deepest point is twenty-three thousand feet,' Falcon replied. 'The average is twelve thousand.'

'And what is the collapse depth of the *Leviathan*?' the president asked.

'Roughly two thousand feet,' Falcon answered.

'Good God,' the president said, slumping further for a moment before getting to his feet. 'The poor bastards don't have a chance.'

64

THE CHYRON RUNNING ALONG THE BOTTOM OF THE SCREEN OF THE twenty-four-hour news channel was short and precise:

Breaking News – US submarine missing north of Antarctica

Its sound down, the television was fixed to the wall of a ward at Washington's MedStar Hospital. None of the four male patients were watching, nor was the doctor doing his rounds – but the keen young refugee who attended the hospital three days a week, doing informal work experience, taking blood pressure and checking drips, glimpsed the screen and stopped to stare.

'Do you mind, Doctor?' she asked. 'Can I turn it up?'

The doctor smiled. 'Not my TV, Laleh,' he replied. 'Ask the gentlemen.'

Nobody objected, Laleh turned up the volume and an image on the screen of the aircraft carriers in the far south of the Indian Ocean was replaced by President Montgomery in the White House press briefing room.

She walked closer as the president announced that a search mission had been launched for an 'experimental' US submarine which had been participating in the well-publicized war game being held near an uninhabited French territory called Îles Crozet.

'With a total complement of one hundred and forty-three men, eighteen women and seven scientific observers . . .'

With the doctor and the patients all discussing what was on the screen, Laleh had to concentrate to hear. 'I have ordered the immediate suspension of the manoeuvres,' the president continued. 'The commanders on site are now doing everything possible to locate the vessel. In addition, I have authorized two specialized submarine rescue ships, both with deep-submergence vehicles, to proceed . . .'

Laleh, unnoticed – so she reported later – moved to the back of the room, took her cellphone out and made a call.

'Rebecca,' she said quietly when it was answered – she was not supposed to know anything about my work but, given our history together, Rebecca had felt justified in telling her the broad details of what I was doing. Even so, she didn't want to broadcast it. 'Turn the news on. It's about a submarine that's gone missing—'

Rebecca, working in ER, headed into the public waiting room, retrieved the remote from the nurses' station and lifted the volume on one of the four TV screens serving the area.

A cold fear crept over her as she listened to the broadcast. Only then did she realize that Laleh was still talking. 'There are seven subs in the area, the president said, so don't panic. I just thought you should know.'

'Seven submarines,' Rebecca said, grappling with what she was seeing on the screen. 'But only one experimental one.'

65

BREATHING HARD, BAXTER AND I HAD LEFT THE FLOODED compartment and were trying to make our way – half in darkness – through a chaos of destruction, back to the primary command centre. We hadn't heard from Martinez or the rest of his team and, though it might have been a failure of the communication system, I was expecting the worst.

Having lost the flashlight and assisted by nothing other than random flickering lights, we had climbed a ladder on to the next deck when we heard voices yelling from behind. We turned and saw two women with headlamps on their helmets, carrying fire extinguishers.

'Stand aside, Code Red, coming through!' they hollered.

We let them pass and then followed close, thankful for the light provided by their headlamps. The women, like Baxter and I, were exhausted – their breathing laboured and shallow – and I put it down to stress and exertion but, as they stopped near a large trash compactor, I soon realized it was something far more serious.

Illuminated by their headlamps, we saw wisps of smoke drifting out of an electrical cabinet, and the taller of the two women immediately pulled open the cabinet door: low flames were quivering and jumping from a dozen different connections.

Her colleague raised a heavy-duty carbon dioxide extinguisher and was about to blast the cabinet when I yelled: 'Stop.'

The women looked at me: 'What?' they both said. 'It's a fucking fire.'

'The flames,' I said, pointing, catching my breath. 'Look at them – it should be a full-alarm blaze. Why are they just flickering?'

The women paused and looked anew at the fire.

'The oxygen,' Baxter said after a moment. 'There's not enough oxygen. It's why it is so hard to breathe.'

The taller woman quickly entered commands on her tablet computer. 'The oxygen generators are failing,' she reported. 'I don't understand – those things are supposed to last for decades—'

'Well, they're not lasting now – it's like the boat is ageing, way beyond its years,' I said.

'No oxygen? We are going to . . .' the woman with the extinguisher said, wide-eyed with terror. 'How long have we got?'

'An hour, less maybe,' her colleague replied. 'We've gotta get them restarted.'

'It won't be possible,' I replied. 'Not if they have aged out. Those things can collapse very fast, we have to reach the multi-purpose platform—'

'No,' the taller woman said. 'We have orders – put the fire out, then go to the wardroom. Everybody is assembling to launch a rescue plan.' She nodded to her comrade: 'Ella,' she ordered, and the younger woman blasted the electrical cabinet with the gas, almost drowning out our voices.

'A rescue plan won't help,' I yelled. 'Not if the oxygen generators are finished. Nothing will. If we get to the platform, we might have a chance—'

Ella had put out the flames and killed the extinguisher. 'The wardroom,' the taller woman said, adamant. 'You coming or not?'

I shook my head. She tried to smile. 'Okay, good luck. See you in heaven if you make it there.'

Baxter and I watched them sprint away until their lights were swallowed by the gloom.

'Why the multi-purpose platform?' Baxter asked, trying to keep his voice firm. 'We going to use the mini-sub?'

'No, the mini-sub's a deathtrap,' I replied. 'At this depth we'd be crushed in seconds. But the reactor is still running; you can feel it under your feet. They're built to last forty years, so there may be life in the boat yet. Like I said, we might have a chance—'

66

AFTER TEN MINUTES OF MOVING AS QUICKLY AS POSSIBLE, NEGOTIATING ruined companionways and climbing stairs – our breathing becoming more strained as the oxygen depleted – we reached the entrance to the multi-purpose platform.

It was in total darkness and we had no flashlight. Attempting to catch my breath, I waited on the threshold for a long moment, calling up from memory the area as I had first seen it: the Zodiac inflatables, the brackets for weapons, the blast-proof cabinets and the mini-sub. I imagined the direction it was pointing and then thought about the maintenance crew checking its systems.

'Kane? We've gotta hurry,' Baxter said, gasping.

'It's going to be difficult, we need to find the energy—'

'For what?' he asked as I led him towards the rear of the mini-sub.

'We have to turn the sub on its axis,' I said. 'I'll tell you when to stop.'

Shoulder to shoulder, with Baxter trying to ignore his dodgy knees, both of us extracting what we could from the rapidly depleting air, putting every ounce of strength we had into the process, we started to swing the twenty-eight-foot-long sub, inch by inch, into position.

'Stop,' I said finally – gasping – when I estimated we were in the right place. I didn't have the breath to explain, so – in silence – I opened the sub's hatch and, just as I had seen one of the maintenance team do earlier, I slipped inside.

'I thought you said we weren't—' Baxter said, struggling to breathe, barely audible.

'We're not,' I replied. 'Give me a moment.'

It took me three attempts to find the right switch. When I did, the large headlight, battery-operated, on the front of the sub illuminated the room, pointing directly at the four yellow, state-of-the-art decompression chambers in the corner. I indicated them to Baxter—

'We've got light,' I said. 'Now we've gotta get 'em running before the oxygen runs out.'

But Baxter barely heard. He was moving towards the chambers, talking half to me and half to himself: 'Of course – independent oxygen supply, temperature regulation, its own power supply straight from the reactor, battery back-up, unlimited water.' Impressed, he turned towards me. 'We can survive—'

'Maybe. Just as long as the reactor keeps running. It might buy us enough time for them to find the sub and to either enter or raise it.' I shrugged. 'The best we can do.'

He was about to turn back to the machines, but I kept my eyes on him. It was the first time since we had left the flooded command post that there had been enough light to see him clearly. He was so pale now, and his lips were thinly drawn and tinted blue – maybe from the lack of oxygen – or possibly from some chronic circulatory problem.

'Are you okay?' I asked, holding on to the mini-sub for support. I hadn't realized how exhausted I was. 'What's up? Your lips are discoloured. Why are you holding your shoulder?'

'A bit of pain,' he replied. 'Angina. It comes on worse when I exert myself. It'll pass.'

I had my doubts. He was downplaying it and I pressed the issue. 'You got your meds?'

'No,' he said. 'I left 'em back at the bunk. I brought my wallet, though.' He tried to smile. 'You never know when you'll need a credit card on a submarine.'

For either of us to go and retrieve the medication was impossible. 'Okay,' I said, more fatigued than I could have imagined. 'There's not much time – we have to try and fire up the chambers.'

'I saw the electrical control when I was looking earlier,' he said, and headed to an electrical box on the wall. He opened it, flicked a series of switches, and two of the decompression chambers sprang to life: interior lights glowed through their perspex domes, illuminating the single beds and a row of monitors, gauges and dials. A large screen above the bed announced:

READY FOR SET-UP

Baxter turned to a computer screen next to the electrical box and booted it up. It must have been on the same dedicated power supply as the pods – thank God – and the screen came alight. As fatigued and blue-lipped as he was, Baxter started to enter commands, adjust dials, set values—

'I'm glad you know what you're doing,' I said.

'I wouldn't say that,' he replied.

'Oh, yeah,' I answered. 'I heard you had a Nobel Prize and half a dozen degrees.'

'Don't let that fool you,' he responded. 'A fellow winner once said: "Never confuse education with intelligence – you can have a Ph.D. and still be an idiot."'

I laughed, and we heard the hiss of gas as oxygen started to flow into the pods. The large screens inside them changed to read:

We looked at one another, both of us coughing. 'No reason to wait,' I said. Our eyes didn't waver. It was time to say goodbye. Neither one of us knew what we would find on the other side – or if we would emerge at all.

I put my hand out, but Baxter hesitated. 'Make sure you survive,' he said softly.

'You, too,' I replied.

'No, it's different,' he said. 'I'm glad Sophie went first. When you are in love, the one left behind does it the hardest. You're trapped in loneliness; you can't find anything to live for – day after day you're just kind of waiting. Don't let that happen to your wife and the twins. Whatever it takes – get home, Kane. Do whatever you have to. Don't leave 'em behind like I was.' He took my hand and started to shake it.

'Thank you, Baxter,' I said. 'It's been a privilege.'

'No,' he replied. 'The honour's all mine. Can you tell me – what's your real name?'

I paused. 'Ridley,' I said. 'Ridley Walker.'

'Ridley,' he repeated softly. He dropped my hand, reached out, and we embraced for a long moment. Without another word, we turned and each climbed into a pod. I pressed the button to lower the canopy, heard his shut and lock and sealed mine.

I laid down on the bed, drank in the pure, filtered air and felt the fatigue close in. I was about to fall asleep when a light outside the pod flickered to life. I sat upright, looked around the multi-purpose platform and saw that an air-quality monitor on the far wall was working. It must have had a back-up battery and was issuing a final warning; of the seven bars on it, six of them were red.

As I watched, the remaining bar turned from green to red: there was no oxygen left in the boat. The truth was inescapable: everybody else on board was dead or would be in two minutes; Baxter and I were the only survivors.

With the grim reality crushing down, imagining bodies lying in the wardroom where the crew had been ordered to assemble, I slumped back. The only light that remained came from the mini-sub's headlight, and it took me a moment to notice that the beam was dancing as it hit the far wall, like it was trembling—

I knew what that meant. I grabbed hold of the pod's frame and braced myself as the tremor hit. It was immediately clear that it was bigger, stronger and more violent than either of the previous ones – it roared through the boat from bow to stern, ripping two jet-skis from their brackets and hurling them across the room.

I watched one of them pass through the headlight's beam and smash into the mini-sub as metal plates on the floor buckled, panels and conduits were torn from the ceiling and my pod threatened to tear itself free of its steel moorings. If it did, tearing apart the lines providing the independent power and oxygen supply, I was a dead man.

The tremor appeared to hit a crescendo, a moment where I doubted if the hull could survive, but this time the boat didn't plunge in a freefall or twist on its axis. It seemed to take a giant shift sideways, a massive leap, and I had the unmistakable feeling . . .

Even to this day it is imprinted deep in my memory . . . that the sub was like a railroad car that was jumping a track.

And then it stopped: the pod hadn't broken free, and I had the sense we had entered calmer waters and were floating. I lay for a long time, expecting another tremor even greater than the last, but it never arrived and the coiled tension across my chest started to unwind.

The battery that powered the mini-sub's headlight finally faded and failed, leaving me in utter darkness, no idea where we were or where we were going.

Sail on, I told myself once again, and I imagined an ocean of candles with the Milky Way above and a Milky Way below. Maybe the journey never ends, I thought. The journey of life, I meant – did it ever really end?

PART FOUR

1

A PROFOUND DARKNESS – THE EVIL KIND, NOT THE ONE THAT ARRIVES with the night, a wave so large it could drown the whole world – came to Baikonur on a Friday, during a period known on the Steppes as the season of fog.

Its arrival wasn't unheralded. A hundred miles away, three men and a woman – nomads scavenging for copper they could sell in Tashkent – were camped among the wrecked ships marooned in the desert when they were woken by the sound of pounding hooves.

Long thought to be extinct, the wild horses of the Aral Sea had emerged from an unmapped gully and, ghost-like in the fog, thundered past the rusting hulks in the pale moonlight. A hundred strong – manes flying, their flanks flecked with foam, clouds of dust rising in their wake – they were heading north, fleeing from something. Whatever it was that had spooked them, they knew its nature.

The four scavengers scrambled out of their tent and stared at the animals. Nobody would have believed their account except that the woman grabbed her phone and photographed the black stallion and his herd. She posted the photos on social media, and I have seen them – downloaded by a NSA team monitoring any mention on the web of western Kazakhstan.

There were other events – rain in the Sahara falling so hard it sounded like a thousand hands a-drumming, forked lightning in clear skies above Patagonia and the night sky over Paris shot through with what looked like a rain of fire.

But horses, even those of the Aral Sea, are easily spooked and, along with everything else – the rain, the lightning and the meteor showers – their behaviour could be easily dismissed or subject to rational explanation.

The wolves were a different matter.

On the far side of the three-thousand-square-mile complex, a Russian boundary patrol was helping to protect Baikonur's nine launch complexes from a land-borne attack that would be astonishing if it ever happened; Genghis Khan had been the last invader to sweep across the Great Steppes.

Nevertheless, every night a crew of nine would clamber aboard their broken-down BMP-3 – a Soviet version of an armoured personnel carrier – and head out to ride a sector of fence so dilapidated it was barely worthy of the name.

Bumping through the desolate landscape of spinifex and scrub, following the tracks of countless earlier patrols, the vehicle powered up a high drift of sand and ploughed to a halt.

The driver had seen five wolves – big and powerful, all muscle and teeth – loping through a dry watercourse ahead. Nocturnal predators, they were on the hunt, passing under high-voltage electricity lines and ignoring the high wind singing in the wires.

According to a report filed by the young officer in command – and hacked later by the NSA – the BMP-3 was downwind and, having never seen a wolf pack before, he decided to follow them.

He ordered the seven conscripts, perched on top of the vehicle, to be silent and they tracked the pack along the watercourse and through the shadow of several high-voltage towers until the alpha male crested a rise and stopped—

The officer found a similar vantage point and, together, the men and the wolves stared across the wasteland to bursts of orange flame leaping high into the night. The flames were coming from the blast furnaces part of the off-earth processing plant. For a long moment the only sound in the wilderness was their distant roar and the lament in the wires—

Then, without warning, a man's scream split the night. The officer and his men reacted, lifting their field glasses to their eyes. The piercing cry originated in the processing plant, and they focused on that.

The wolves did too – any creature in trouble meant food – but this time it was different. The alpha male stared at the plant, listened intently for a moment and raised his hackles. He howled, turned and fled, leading his pack into the vastness of the Steppes.

The scream ended as abruptly as it had begun and the men heard no more but, perhaps, the wolves had realized something – maybe they knew it wasn't quite dark yet but the darkness was coming.

2

INSIDE THE TOXIC PLANT, THE SCREAMING MAN WASN'T IN TROUBLE any more; he was already dead.

Closed-circuit footage found later showed that – against the background of the roaring blast furnaces – the man's heavily tattooed raised right arm was visible, seemingly in a last futile appeal for help. The rest of him was submerged in the broad stream of molten metal flowing through the building as it carried him towards a giant cast-iron mould, fifteen feet high.

All around him – on the gantries, sprinting across the concrete floor – scores of men were yelling, trying to organize a rescue; not for him, he was dead the moment his body hit the boiling river, but to try and save a brawny man named Anton – to go by the men who were calling his name – dangling by one arm from a half-collapsed walkway thirty feet above the molten liquid.

The CCTV footage showed that he – and his dead companion – had been pushing a steel cart laden with scrap metal along the walkway. One of its spans buckled, snapped free of its rusted brackets and tilted downwards. The cart and the about-to-be-dead man went careening down the sudden slope. He tried to grab hold of something, found only air, was hit by the plunging cart mid-fall, and followed it head-first into the river, sending up a huge spray of molten metal, hitting four workers nearby and sending them screaming to the floor.

Acting on instinct, Anton managed to grab hold of a pipe carrying high-pressure steam running alongside the walkway, burned his hand badly, but bought himself just enough time to grab hold of part of the collapsed railing with his other hand.

Now he was hanging directly above the molten river, unable to use his burnt hand to help support himself as the wrecked railing slipped and threatened to break apart under the stress of his weight.

Down below, there was more chaos as men and women rushed to help the four victims splashed with the liquid metal; they were writhing on the ground, trying to tear the scorching material from their skin and succeeding only in ripping off their own flesh.

Other workers were swarming up gantries and stairs to reach Anton. The first rescuer – a tough guy in coveralls – put a foot on the half-collapsed walkway and started to move along it. The walkway lurched lower, the remnants of the railing almost broke free, when a voice yelled: 'Stop! Get back—'

It was Kazinsky, bursting out of the supervisor's glass-walled control room; his office now. There was no way the half-collapsed walkway could support a rescue operation.

'Hurry,' Anton screamed. 'I can't hold—'

'Get the crane!' Kazinsky yelled to the men below, pointing to a travelling crane with a hook attached hanging from an overhead grid. A worker grabbed a remote control from a rack, hit a command and launched the crane down a track towards Kazinsky.

As he waited, the Colonel looked at the prostrate men and called to a muscled man helping to restrain one of them: 'Call Rifle, tell him to bring the medics—'

The muscled guy abandoned the victim and sprinted for the so-called 'Emergency Centre' in the cafeteria, which consisted of a battered first-aid kit bolted to the wall, one red electricity kill button, another to summon urgent medical help, a row of fire extinguishers and a built-in intercom. He hit the call button, issued a stream of instructions, then ripped the first-aid kit off the wall and ran for the injured men.

The crane and its hook were flying down the overhead track as Kazinsky climbed on to the railing outside his office. He was timing it—

The hook raced through a huge cloud of smoke and sparks and the men below watched as Kazinsky crouched. His feet left the railing as he tried to leap across twelve feet of clear air—

He flew through space, his arms reached out – the distance to the hook seemed to be too far; it was travelling too fast when he lunged forward – and caught the hook. Everybody below gasped and Kazinsky shouted at the worker with the remote control: 'Now!'

The man, with the remote, used a joystick to make the hook change direction. Anton, his face stricken by pain and terror, watched Kazinsky swoop towards him. He looked at the lava—

'Hurry . . .' he begged as his hand, clutching the wrecked railing, started to slip.

Standing on the hook now, Kazinsky – gripping the chain above him with one hand, reaching out with the other – was directly above the molten river too. He came closer and closer—

Anton was fighting desperately to hold on as the wrecked railing finally pulled free of its last anchor. The metal and Anton, screaming, fell—

Kazinsky's hand lunged out, his fingers grabbed the collar of Anton's shirt and held him in mid-air. The Colonel yelled with the sudden wrenching pain of it—

Anton, suspended by the shirt collar and staring in terror down at the river of metal, was screaming as the worker with the remote hit a command and swung the joystick hard, flying Kazinsky and Anton across the deadly metal river. Once the Colonel saw they were finally clear he let go of the chain with a cry of relief. He and Anton hit the concrete floor and tumbled towards the four injured men.

Several workers were already kneeling beside them, ripping off burnt T-shirts and jeans, exposing their wounds. Kazinsky, managing to get to his feet, struggling for breath, looked around. Nearly everyone else was staring at him, taken aback by what they had just witnessed. Whatever else they thought of him, they knew courage when they saw it.

Kazinsky saw what he was looking for: Rifle was running through the door with a woman doctor and two medical orderlies. The workers surrounding the victims parted and the doctor knelt beside the four victims.

She was in her late twenties – blonde, with few of the Slavic characteristics that were common at Baikonur: she had been born and raised in the far north, in that part of Russia bordering Finland, and she was as tall, fair and self-sufficient as the men and women who lived on the other side of the electrified fence. Her name was Tatyana Zhukov, educated at a prestigious university in St Petersburg, a young woman who graduated from med school near the top of her class and who, much to everyone's surprise, decided to succeed her father as medical chief at the godforsaken ZATO of Baikonur after he had died unexpectedly.

She called to one of the orderlies for syringes filled with ketamine, a popular battlefield painkiller, and plunged a needle into each of the injured men.

The drug worked fast and Dr Zhukov turned to the most seriously wounded man, who had a gaping hole in his chest, bleeding profusely, where a huge glob of liquid metal had burnt through almost to his ribs. There had been no hope of any of his co-workers applying a tourniquet to the wound and he had all the telltale signs of enormous blood loss.

She yelled for QuikClot dressings, bandages infused with a chemical that stimulates the body's own natural clotting. As the orderlies dug into their backpacks, the heavy cart laden with scrap metal had been carried forward by the lava river and now was dumped into the almost-full mould. A tidal wave of molten metal surged over the lip of the giant container and swamped a doorless cupboard holding a bird's nest of electrical connections, shorting out the whole production line in the process and plunging half the complex into darkness. Green lights over the emergency exits, the CCTV monitoring and several of the huge extractor fans were the only things that still appeared to have emergency power.

'Back-up generator – where is it?' Kazinsky yelled.

'There isn't one!' Rifle hollered back from the gloom. Kazinsky cursed and called for flashlights, but Dr Zhukov had already grabbed her backpack and pulled out a miner's helmet with a headlight on the front. She didn't bother putting it on, sitting it on the ground instead and aiming it at the hole in the man's chest.

As one of the orderlies handed her the QuikClots, Kazinsky picked up the helmet and held it so that it gave her a much better light to work by. Alarmed, she watched him look at the helmet carefully – it was well made, probably not Russian, he must have thought, and he started to pay even closer attention to the headlamp.

The doctor continued shooting him anxious glances, but there was nothing she could do except finish dressing the wound as fast as possible. As soon as she did, she smiled – forcing herself to act casually – took the helmet from his hand and put it on her head.

'A gift from my family,' she said pleasantly. 'My father used to work here. He was a lucky man – he knew Gagarin.'

She turned to the next patient, trying to unknot her stomach; every day she must have worried that somebody would discover the camera inside the headlamp and she would be unmasked – for whatever tragic family reasons – as a United States' intelligence agent-in-place. What happened then – well, it was far better for her not to think about.

3

IT WAS LATE AFTERNOON, SUNLIGHT FILTERING THROUGH THE TREES lining the quiet street in front of our house in Maryland, when Rebecca's phone started beeping with alerts.

She was in the kitchen, trying to force herself to eat something, her face grey with fatigue and relentless anxiety – she had barely slept since she had heard the news of a missing submarine – and now she stumbled and almost fell as she rushed across the room to retrieve her phone.

The alerts were from half a dozen news sites and after glancing at the screen she called out: 'Laleh, turn on the TV. The Navy is giving an update.'

Without anyone suggesting it, the young woman had moved into the house immediately after she and Rebecca had heard the news at the hospital.

Now she emerged from the bathroom, ran to the living room and started flicking through the channels. Rebecca was at her side by the time she found the live briefing from the Pentagon. In the dry tones adopted by all the grey-suited men and women tasked with handling national emergencies, the spokesperson read a prepared statement and then tried to roll with the tidal wave of questions from the press pack.

Rebecca didn't hear any of them – one term the spokesperson had used had struck terror into her heart. She turned to Laleh. 'They're saying it's a recovery mission—'

'Yes, I heard,' Laleh said, looking at her friend's face. 'Why is that bad?'

'They're not saying it's a "rescue mission" any more,' Rebecca replied. 'It means they don't believe anyone is alive, they're just trying to find and raise the boat. *Recovery*.'

Gasping for breath, she continued to look at the screen, reading a chyron running along the bottom of it. 'They're releasing the names of the people on board,' she said, suddenly clinging to the desperate hope I wasn't on the list, mixed with the dread that I was.

She and Laleh turned to the laptop open on the desk in a corner of the living room and Rebecca found the Pentagon website. The list was in two sections: Navy personnel and observers.

'Which list?' Laleh asked. 'Observers?'

'No,' Rebecca replied. 'Ridley is qualified in submarines. Navy.'

Choking from anxiety, she scrolled through the names of the crew, looking at their pictures, scanning the mini-biographies. Only when she got to the end of it with no match, her breath returning, did she look at the observers list. Another bald column of names, nearly all the information redacted for security purposes, and none of them meant anything to Rebecca, especially not the one that read: Daniel Raymond Greenberg, Oak Ridge, Tennessee.

Relieved, she took a long moment to settle herself and recover. Finally, she turned to see Laleh grinning at her. Rebecca smiled with her—

'I told you,' Laleh said. 'There are six other submarines in the area. He must be on one of them.'

Rebecca nodded – Laleh had to be right. She got to her feet, frightened her legs might collapse under her, and walked out on to the front porch. Looking at the world as a lifetime of hope and love reopened, thinking constantly of the two new lives growing inside her, she sat on the front steps, watched in wonder as the dappled sunlight spilled through the trees, and let the warmth of life renewed flood through her.

She had been sitting for an hour, daydreaming, when she heard the car approaching.

4

NORMALLY THERE WAS TRAFFIC ON THE ROAD – NOT MUCH, BUT enough to make a passing car unremarkable – but some intuition made Rebecca turn.

She saw a four-door sedan coming towards the house – its colour and style so anonymous that it had to be from the government – and her heart dropped like a stone.

She didn't move as it stopped out front and a man in his forties in a dark suit, as anonymous and unremarkable as the vehicle, walked towards her. I am certain that she recalled the conversation between us when neither one of us was willing to say the word 'killed'.

'Lost' was the word that we had substituted, never realizing how perfect a description it would become. For Rebecca, my epitaph would be like the inscription on war memorials the world over; beside the list of names, so often, was the simple entry: 'Lost at Sea'.

Laleh watched through a window as the man gave a name and showed an agency ID with a photo. 'Perhaps we should go inside,' he suggested, but Rebecca declined.

'Now my partner is . . . gone,' Rebecca said, not willing to listen to his scripted preamble, refusing to give in to deceit. 'I want the agency to know that he took the best of me with him, and left the best of himself behind. Tell Falcon I'm pregnant.'

The agency messenger, taken aback, nodded. 'I can't give you any details but rest assured—' he said, attempting to get back on track and deliver the pre-ordained script.

'It'll be an empty casket, I assume,' she said, struggling to hold back the tears.

Under the assault of her obvious knowledge, the man probably couldn't see any point in pursuing the deceit. He nodded.

'Did you know him?' Rebecca asked.

'No,' the messenger replied. 'People say he was a brave man. Very brave.' He paused. 'At the moment, I don't suppose that is any consolation.'

'A brave man?' Rebecca asked rhetorically. 'Yes, I think he was. A lonely man in many ways – a slave to duty. They fired him, you know? But when they called, he went back. If he hadn't, he'd still be alive today. Right up to the end, he served the agency.'

'His country, too,' the messenger added, correcting her.

'What is that worth to my unborn children?' she asked. 'Can you answer that? Can anybody? You were right, though – none of it is any consolation.'

She turned, walked into the house and left the CIA and its messenger on the doorstep. She closed the door, saw Laleh and collapsed into the young woman's arms—

'Shut the shades,' Rebecca managed to say. 'Close the shutters and lock the doors.'

I suppose she was thinking, in her anguish and pain, that if the world didn't intrude, the loss might not exist.

5

THE DAMAGE TO THE OFF-EARTH PROCESSING FACILITY WHEN THE molten metal engulfed the electrical box and killed most of the power was far greater than anyone had first assumed.

Given the age of the building and the poor materials that had been used to carry out repairs in the past, the plant was offline for two days as a team of electricians worked to rewire whole sections of the site.

Earlier, as soon as Dr Zhukov and her orderlies had transported the injured to hospital, the men employed in the plant were stood down – much to their satisfaction, as technical failures meant they would still receive full pay – and Rifle, responsible for staffing the plant, designated Kazinsky as the person in charge of supervising the repairs.

As a result, the Colonel and his former comrade were the only two people – apart from the electricians – in the plant when the switch was thrown and the lights and machinery emerged from their two-day coma. Even the blast furnaces, using a separate, dedicated power supply to prevent them from cooling and failing completely, began to throw off sheets of sparks.

While the sleeping dragons came alive, and with the rows of naked work-lights flickering and then holding and moonlight filtering through the closed glass of two massive cooling vents in the roof, Rifle walked towards the door, heading for his vehicle: the job was done; all that Kazinsky had to do now was contact the night crew and get the process restarted.

The two men were at the door, about to shake hands, when another screeching alarm cut through the gradually escalating roar of the rock-crushers and furnaces.

'Not again!' Rifle exclaimed, about to start cursing, before remembering how much his former commander hated blasphemy. 'I'll call the electricians back.'

'No,' Kazinsky replied. 'It's not electrical – it's mechanical.' He was looking through the smoke, across the spark-filled expanse, to the glass-walled chamber.

Inside the huge, seemingly sealed environment, the pod of an off-earth freighter – filled to the brim with a rich haul of ore from the distant asteroid – had already passed through the airlock, automatically opened its wide cargo doors and had been in the process of depositing its load when the power failed. As a result, the four robotic arms and their huge scoops had frozen mid-swing.

Once the power was restored, however, they had resumed their endless, mindless work. Not for long; on the second sequence one of the robotic arms had swung too low on its downward arc and had become wedged under the bottom lip of the pod.

The crippled arm immediately seized up, causing the alarm to sound. Inside the chamber the lights dimmed and the whole unloading process came to a grinding halt.

Kazinsky and Rifle crossed the lava river and approached the glass wall. At a command console, Kazinsky turned a dial and the lights immediately reached their maximum operating level, flooding the chamber with light.

'Stop,' Rifle said abruptly, perplexed, anxious—

'Why? What is it?' Kazinsky asked, turning to face him.

'I saw something,' Rifle replied. 'In the dark, back there just as you turned up the lights.' He walked forward, moving closer to the glass.

'Saw what?' Kazinsky said, confused. He hadn't seen a thing.

'Something glowing, tiny – just for a moment.'

'Tiny? A tiny what?'

'I don't know – floating in the air – like a spark,' Rifle said.

Kazinsky looked at him, frowned, then turned the lights in the chamber back down. The two men pressed their faces almost to the glass and stared in at the white chamber, the giant pod and the mounds of ore, searching for a small, glowing—

Smash! The tempered glass in front of them shattered into a web of fractures and almost broke as it was hit by something very powerful, sending them leaping backwards.

Half crouched as if poised in combat, they looked back into the chamber. They stood up, took a step closer, and then Rifle pointed to a large chunk of ore lying inside the glass, just below the impact point.

'Who the hell threw that?' Rifle asked.

Kazinsky turned to the control panel and dialled up the lights again. He scanned the chamber, looked at the crippled arm and laughed. Rifle followed the direction of his gaze – the robot arm had broken free of the lip at the bottom of the pod, then must have flown upwards, spun on its axis, and the abrupt motion had hurled a piece of ore lying in its scoop halfway across the chamber and into the glass, cracking it and scaring the two men witless.

They exchanged a rueful smile. The glass had protected them, but the arm was now jammed under the pod's *upper* lip. Nowhere inside the chamber was there any sign of a tiny, glimmering light – not a spark or anything like it. Rifle must have figured he had been mistaken.

Kazinsky entered commands in the control panel and manipulated several joysticks, trying to get the jammed arm working again. He successfully manoeuvred the other three robots, but the fourth arm remained stuck fast.

'I'll call the technicians,' Rifle said.

'The equipment's fine; it works perfectly,' Kazinsky replied. 'The arm just needs to be freed from the lip and, according to the diagnostics, the lower joint checked and adjusted.'

'Yeah – sounds simple, but we still need the technicians,' Rifle said, starting to move towards the intercom in the so-called emergency centre.

'And how long before they arrive – three days?' Kazinsky said. 'Then they'll empty the chamber and use the overhead nozzles to flood the place with antiseptic spray.' He pointed at the large devices hanging from the steel roof. 'They'll wait for it to dry, then use the same nozzles to blast the chamber with sterilizing gas. Because nothing can survive it, they'll have to put on spacesuits and break for a cigarette before they go inside. On top of the two days we've already lost, it'll take another six days to be back online, maybe more.'

Rifle said nothing: the Colonel was probably right; the technicians were notoriously slow. 'All that for a few minutes' work,' Kazinsky continued.

'Yes, but there is a protocol, a system—' Rifle replied.

'When did we care about systems? Did we follow the rules in Aleppo? At the chlorine plant? Anyway, it's a system that doesn't work – three days for them to even start?' Kazinsky said, his tone brooking little opposition. 'We will have lost any chance of reaching the monthly target. There goes the bonus, and we all know that's where the real money—'

'Yours especially. I have my job to think—' Rifle responded.

Kazinsky stared at him. 'Money? For myself?' he spat out. 'You think that? For years I have been fighting, planning – doing God's revolutionary work, never a day too long or a target too far. I have waited for His call and I know I was brought here for a reason. Yes, the bonuses are a gift from Allah, they enrich the local mosques, and every good mosque knows where its obligations lie—'

'You still can't go into the chamber. The area is fully automated because the ore hasn't been sanitized. Anyway, the computers—'

'Log every aspect of it,' Kazinsky replied. 'Including entry. I know. I'm sure every day there is an avalanche of reports about the Cosmodrome – but who reads them? Even if they do, there's been a power failure here; so what – the log shows an incorrect entry? It was an error, another glitch. The plant is full of them. We were both here, nobody entered the chamber. Who is there to contradict us?'

Rifle did not reply, his resolve wavering.

'Six more days' delay?' Kazinsky persevered. 'For something I can fix in five minutes?' Still Rifle said nothing, and Kazinsky knew his silence was tantamount to acquiescence. He entered a series of commands into the control panel: he was powering down the system and, while the lights inside the chamber stayed on, the robot arms froze.

'How do I get inside?' Kazinsky asked.

'Through the airlock,' Rifle said quietly. 'There's a maintenance hatch near where the pods first enter. Eight screws, and you'll need a pneumatic screwdriver. You have to be quick – nobody's going to believe a five-minute glitch.'

As Kazinsky went to get the tool, Rifle turned and looked again through the glass into the brightly illuminated chamber – there was no glimmer of light or anything remotely spark-like.

Then again, if the missiles of Zahedan or a revolutionary submarine had proven one thing, it was this: just because you can't see something, doesn't mean it isn't there.

6

THE MAINTENANCE HATCH WAS A SUBSTANTIAL STEEL PANEL SET INTO the wall, secured by eight large industrial screws. Kazinsky – in coveralls with a tool belt around his waist – used a heavy-duty pneumatic screwdriver to start to release the hatch. Even then, the screwdriver, powered by two large battery packs and turning at several thousand revs a minute, made hard work of it.

Rifle – leaning forward – continued to watch through the glass as Kazinsky finally released the last screw, lifted the heavy panel aside and stepped into the airlock. Rifle's face was devoid of expression, but his fist was drumming on his thigh. It was clear that no matter what the Colonel said, he was still worried about the whole exercise.

Inside the airlock – one set of heavy doors closed and sealed behind him – Kazinsky stopped at the sliding doors that led into the pure-white chamber. He hit a button on a wall panel and after a moment's delay, accompanied by a hiss, the doors slid open.

A digital clock on a wall of the chamber was clearly visible on the CCTV footage. It showed that at exactly 1.16 a.m. on a Sunday the Colonel entered the chamber and wrote a date in history. The darkness was almost upon us.

He waited for the airlock doors to close behind him and then – passing alongside the battered pod, looking inside its cavernous interior – he moved towards the crippled robot arm. His progress was slower than he had anticipated; he had to scramble over mounds of already unloaded ore, almost falling at one point, while his work boots kicked up clouds of dust. Without a space suit, breathing in the unfiltered and unsanitized air, he might as well have landed on the asteroid itself.

Forty seconds later he reached the crippled robot. Taking a screwdriver from his belt, he made an adjustment to the arm's lower joint and then by brute strength pulled it from the pod's upper lid. The arm, spring-loaded, suddenly flew upright, spun blindingly fast on its axis and sent its heavy steel scoop hurtling straight towards his head. He glimpsed it, managed to duck with only a moment to spare and watched it return to its correct position.

While he was breathing hard – recovering, letting the adrenaline dissipate – the unexpected whirlwind tripped a safety switch on the arm and any remaining power to the chamber was immediately cut.

As Kazinsky groped for a flashlight in his tool belt, Rifle was staring through the glass with rocketing alarm.

In the gloom, myriad tiny sparks were floating everywhere, including in the air around the Colonel's face and his mouth.

Rifle began hammering on the glass, gesticulating wildly, making Kazinsky look up from his tool belt. Suddenly the Colonel saw the small, glowing spore: at close range, they were even more beautiful, just minuscule pinpoints of light, so fragile and incandescent that they were like the tiniest filaments from countless sparklers. They looked almost magical.

Kazinsky stared at the *siber* spore for a beat as Rifle yelled through the glass: 'Hurry! Just get the fuck out, will ya?!'

Realizing the thick, tempered barrier was killing any sound, Rifle spun round to the control panel, hit the power-on button, activating the unloading system, restarting all four robotic arms and bringing the brilliant lights back up, the illumination swallowing the tiny sparks and allowing Rifle to broadcast his voice into the chamber.

He grabbed the mic, but said nothing. Kazinsky, galvanized by the equipment roaring into action, was already moving. Surrounded by the roar of the unloading, ducking the robotic arms, climbing over mounds of ore, he headed for the airlock, hit a button on the wall and stepped through as the doors slid open.

He was out of the chamber, sprinted towards the access hatch, and by the time he had emerged, re-screwed and sealed it behind him, Rifle had arrived.

They looked at one another. 'You see those fragments?' Kazinsky asked. 'Incredible.'

'I told you there was a spark,' Rifle replied, looking intently at his colleague.

'Yeah, you were right,' Kazinsky acknowledged.

Rifle continued to look at him closely – the Colonel appeared fine, completely unaffected by the experience apart from breathing hard from exertion. He had been inside the chamber for no more than two minutes and Rifle started to relax. 'What do you think it was?' he asked.

'Mineral dust,' said Kazinsky. 'Fluorescent or something; it seemed to react to the light.'

'Yeah – a mineral makes sense. Probably one of the rare earth elements. You should still take a shower, scrub yourself, burn the clothes and boots. Just to be safe.'

'Of course,' Kazinsky replied. He indicated the interior of the chamber, where something seemingly far more important to him was occurring: the four robots were working perfectly, the ore was being loaded on to the stainless-steel conveyor belts, the sanitizing baths were full and the crushers were pulverizing the rocks. 'The system's working fine,' he said, smiling. 'That's six days we've saved, Rifle.'

Satisfied, without waiting for an answer, he turned and – accompanied by Rifle – headed through the deserted plant towards the showers.

7

CLOUDS OF STEAM BILLOWED ACROSS WALLS COVERED IN BILIOUSLY green old tiles, almost obscuring a naked Kazinsky, alone and standing under one of a long row of showerheads as he scrubbed himself under a torrent of water.

He had his back to a CCTV camera – installed to prevent theft from scores of lockers in the changing area – and while the angle was oblique it still managed to capture him at a distance, and that, combined with the steam and the shadows thrown by two hanging bulbs, made it appear as if the locust on his back was rippling, alive with movement.

A casual observer scanning the footage probably would have paid it no mind and moved on, but it wasn't a trick of circumstance or an optical illusion. The locust really was moving, or at least something under Kazinsky's skin was—

Small and barely noticeable, emerging from his lungs, more than likely, it appeared reptilian as it crawled up his spine and made the skin above come alive.

The movement slowly grew larger and stronger as it spread across his back, flowing and bulging beneath the flesh until it started to cover his shoulder blades. He was not in any pain – he didn't even notice – and then he glanced down at his six-pack and saw the defined muscles of his stomach begin to swell and contort.

He kept staring and then glanced at his arms. The veins were visible, growing more prominent by the moment, while the flesh and muscle beneath the surface started to knot and protrude, driven on by the same unseen and alien force.

Tentatively – alarm written all over his face – he reached out and touched his twisting stomach. He immediately pulled his fingers back – his skin was burning hot to the touch but, perhaps even stranger, there was no blistering or redness to it.

He didn't know it – nobody did then – but the changes that were

488

affecting every cell of his body were throwing off a huge amount of energy – far more than the normal mitochondria ever did – and that was being converted to heat. Unnoticed under the escalating onslaught, his skin – the largest organ in the body – was already changing and toughening, acquiring a far greater tolerance to damage and pain.

Kazinsky staggered out of the shower, inadvertently coming closer to the camera and breathing now in short, anxious gasps. He spun around and saw – in a corner, surrounded by shadows, defaced by graffiti and barely ever used – a perspex-walled sanitation shower with water jets lining its interior and a large barrel of some type of antiseptic on its roof. He stumbled towards its door; maybe it would stop whatever it was that was overwhelming him—

Halfway there, he suddenly stopped, tried to take a step, fell to his knees, his hands scrabbling at his throat. Whatever was hijacking his body – a raging virus, a sequence of code, a fragment of foreign DNA, a strange infection, the genome of something from a place far away – had travelled out of his lungs, up his spine, across his shoulder blades, and had now reached his throat.

He tore at his neck as – deep inside – the rings of cartilage that made up his trachea also started to swell and bulge, restricting the airflow, effectively throttling him.

His eyes protruded, his face contorted as he grappled to free himself from a deadly, invisible fist and somehow grab a breath. The veins and capillaries across his forehead suddenly appeared in huge detail, forming a remarkable map as they distended; his carotid arteries – running up either side of his neck – pulsed wildly and visibly with every panicked heartbeat, and his larynx rattled hard as the small amount of air that could gain passage rippled over the swollen cartilage.

Still gasping, he managed to regain his feet. He seemed to be growing bigger, stronger, filling out his frame as the musculature became more pronounced and his skeleton and spine better defined. It was difficult to countenance – but not to anyone who had seen the rats in their cages or one of their kind inside the chamber, breathing in the spore.

In desperation, he grabbed hold of the door to the sanitation booth and wrenched it open. Half falling, grabbing a tap for support, he dragged himself inside, hit a button to activate the jets on the walls, flooding the space with antiseptic, and twisted the tap to maximum.

It was the hot-water control – scalding hot, spewing steam – but, as with the antiseptic, Kazinsky did not react at all. Instead, standing upright, his body twisting and wrenching, he clung to two of the nozzles, facing out, arms outstretched, and pushed his face, contorted in silent anguish, close to the perspex. The blinking red eye of the CCTV camera watched it all.

Kazinsky's own eyes – dark brown, wild and unblinking – glinted with flashes of brilliant gold, his body gave an almighty twist, the hair of his beard shrivelled and arterial blood exploded out of his mouth and nose, clearing his passageways and splattering the perspex, almost obscuring him. His hands fully outstretched, he sprang free of the nozzles and fell to the floor.

He drew his legs up to his chest, curled himself into a foetal position and opened his mouth in some sort of elemental scream. He lay there with his chest heaving, eyes dilated and staring wide, until the spraying nozzles, clouds of steam and the hard rain of scalding water covered the perspex and hid him completely.

Whether he was dead or alive, no observer would have known.

8

I AM NO BIOLOGIST, BUT IT SEEMS TO ME THAT IT IS THE VANITY OF our species to think that evolution stopped with us, that humankind is – and always has been – the final destination. The truth is far more inspiring and much more terrifying: the process of evolutionary change never ceases.

Frequently, it comes out of nowhere, without warning; 60 million years ago, the planet was ruled by the dinosaurs. The massive explosion they heard? That was an asteroid – six miles wide – hitting just off the coast of modern-day Mexico. So much debris was thrown up into the atmosphere it has become known as the 'impact winter'. Within a short period of time, 70 per cent of the life-forms on earth were dead – and the modern world was born.

On the Great Steppes, minute after minute passed until – inside the sanitizing booth – Kazinsky's hand and forearm, hairless and incredibly pale, emerged from the steam and tried to grab hold of the door handle. He was alive.

It may have already been past midnight on a Sunday on a moonlit night, but utter darkness had truly arrived.

9

IN THE VAST AREA BEYOND THE LOCKER ROOM, RIFLE WAS SILHOUETTED against a wall of red and white flame, checking a row of oil-stained gauges near the open door of blast furnace Number Four.

It was a fearsome place – toxic fumes swirling, the massive chimney looming overhead and sheets of sparks flying out of an overhead vent, as Rifle turned towards a small control panel with a row of buttons and switches.

He hit a red button and activated a large stainless-steel tray loaded with slag and scrap metal. The tray immediately tilted up – almost vertical – and poured the load through the door and into the roaring flames.

Now empty, the tray – highly polished and completely slick – returned to the horizontal and Rifle looked at the gauges again. Satisfied, he shouted over his shoulder.

'That's the last of 'em – all four furnaces are up and running.'

He waited for a response and, getting none, turned and scanned the deserted facility. 'Colonel,' he said. 'Did you hear me?'

Still there was no reply. 'You can't still be in the shower,' he said, half to himself, frustrated.

Watched only by the dead eyes of Stalin and Lenin, he walked beneath the murals towards the locker room. 'Colonel?' he called as he entered.

Again, no response. He looked in at the row of showerheads and then saw the graffiti-covered sanitation booth in the corner, its door swinging slowly on its hinges. Steam was rising from the floor and one of the nozzles had not shut down properly. A drip like a heartbeat was the only sound—

'Colonel?' Rifle said again. He may have been alone and walled in by silence, but he was a big man; he had survived brutal wars in Chechnya and had come out alive from Aleppo. Fear was not something that easily afflicted him. Even so, he hesitated, starting to move cautiously.

'Hey, Colonel – come on,' he said. 'Are you all right? Where are you?' He opened the door of the booth and looked inside. Empty.

He was about to turn away when a shadow fell across him. He stopped, his hand still on the door handle, and he realized: somebody, looming large, had appeared out of the pools of darkness behind him.

'Why didn't you answer?' Rifle asked.

'Is something wrong?' Kazinsky replied quietly.

Rifle, relaxing, turned, and even in the patchwork of deep shade, the camera captured his expression: Chechnya and Aleppo notwithstanding, a profound and terrible fear had finally found him.

'In the name of God,' he whispered.

Kazinsky had grown in stature – his frame was larger, and he seemed far heavier. All of it was muscle, though, and the tissue – along with the rest of his body not hidden by a pair of jeans – was covered in a hairless carapace so pale it was almost translucent. The ghostly sheen was frightening enough, but when Rifle glanced across at a mirror on a wall facing them, he saw something even more terrifying: the skin of the Colonel's back had creased and converted. It had formed a hard ridge down his spine.

Rifle, barely able to breathe, said nothing for a moment, but then whispered: 'Ridgeback.'

'What?' Kazinsky asked, not catching it.

'We need help,' Rifle said more audibly, a little of the shock abating. He started to head towards the emergency centre and its intercom.

'No,' Kazinsky said, coldly and without rancour, but his eyes flashed, arresting Rifle.

The process of seroconversion was complete – every cell of the Colonel's body had been co-opted and changed, including his irises. They had turned green, shot through with streaks of gold, and – like the spore itself – were irresistibly and deceptively beautiful. They also indicated something else, and Rifle probably should have recalled the gladiator rats' unchecked aggression—

'What do you mean, "no"?' he replied, panicked and confused. 'Whatever this is, it wasn't mineral, it was . . . we need to get you help.' He gave up and turned to go to the intercom to summon someone, anyone.

Kazinsky took two strides, hugely athletic. His hand flashed and grabbed Rifle's shoulder; the big man winced in pain and Kazinsky pivoted him so that they were facing each other.

'I walked out of Aleppo,' the Colonel said pleasantly. His larynx had recovered, but it too had been co-opted – his voice was deeper, more commanding. 'I survived, just like you, Rifle. How many men that missioned in with us can say that?'

'A few hundred,' Rifle managed to reply, looking into the green eyes, terrified.

'Three times since then I have been saved from what would have been certain death,' Kazinsky continued. 'Once in Iraq, when I stopped a car miles from a safe house, sent a bodyguard ahead in my place and watched two American bombers roar overhead. The next, I escaped a missile attack in a town called Zahedan, and – finally – I was on a freighter sinking in the Caspian Sea. Why, against all logic, was I spared, Rifle?'

'The will of God,' Rifle answered softly – more by fear than conviction.

'Yes,' Kazinsky replied. 'After the Caspian, out of nowhere, I was led here for a reason.' He swung them both around so that they could look at him in the full-length mirror. 'Now we know why, don't we?

'None of those things was an accident,' he continued. 'Nothing was random or happened by chance. Even the world's greatest scientist would agree. "God does not play dice with the universe."'

Kazinsky turned to Rifle and looked into his eyes. 'God was waiting, he met us in Baikonur,' he said. 'Of course, it had to be here – it's the end of the world and the highway to the stars. You said it yourself – we're standing on the shores of the universe.' Like every apocalyptic prophet since time immemorial.

'Life and death all around us, with only God to light the path,' Rifle said quietly, remembering what Kazinsky had said those weeks before.

'That's right. I am nothing more than an agent of God's will,' Kazinsky responded, pointing over his shoulder to the tattoo. 'Look at this – the locust, a plague sent to cleanse the Earth. I was twenty-two when I had it inked – everything was written a long time ago, wasn't it?'

'The will of God,' Rifle repeated, nodding. 'I can see that now.' He started to edge away.

'Come with me,' Kazinsky said, taking him by the shoulder, leading him out of the locker room and looking across at the glass-enclosed chamber. He picked up the pneumatic screwdriver and handed it to Rifle. 'You'll need this,' he said.

'Why?' Rifle replied, his throat dry and his voice cracking with fear.

'Go inside the sealed chamber,' Kazinsky said. 'It's simple – all you have to do is breathe.'

Rifle nodded, tried to smile, but didn't reach for the screwdriver. 'Yes, simple,' he said – and tore himself free of Kazinsky's hand.

He bolted towards the bridge crossing the river of molten metal, hoping to get to the other side and hit the nearest emergency switch to summon help. He was a strong man and he seized a cart of metal ingots, spun it fast and drove it into a row of wheelie-bins, sending them flying, straight into Kazinsky's path.

Trying to if not hurt then at least delay Kazinsky, he was disappointed on every front. The Colonel took three powerful strides, dropped the pneumatic screwdriver, leapt high – over the bins – and swung on a group of pipes attached to the underside of a walkway.

Rifle, terrified, looking over his shoulder, saw what he was doing and ran faster—

Hanging one-handed, Kazinsky ripped one of the pipes down and broke it: super-heated steam blasted out. The pipe itself must have been red hot, but Kazinsky's hand and skin remained completely unaffected.

He directed the torrent of steam, which arced through the air, hitting the fleeing Rifle square in the back.

He went down screaming, somehow scrambling to his feet, but Kazinsky launched himself from the pipes and landed behind him. Rifle made a desperate lunge to escape—

Kazinsky's hand shot out, grabbed him by the scruff of his shirt and hauled him upright. He spoke cheek to jowl: 'You're frightened, Rifle – I understand. It's the shock of the new, the first glimpse of the frontier.'

Rifle twisted his face and looked at him. Then he nodded, held so tight he must have felt he had no other choice. 'Yes, frightened,' he said, conciliatory. 'I'm sorry.'

'And you were frightened when you stormed the citadel in Aleppo, weren't you?'

'Yes, Colonel.'

'I wasn't,' Kazinsky replied. 'I knew I was destined for something more.' He turned and walked Rifle back towards the cart of metal ingots.

'I read something when I was growing up in Siberia – some men are born great, some find greatness and some have it thrust upon them. That is where we are now, isn't it?' He picked up the pneumatic screwdriver. 'The world is going to be rebuilt,' he continued. 'This is destiny, whether we like it or not.'

'Yes, I understand – I can see that now,' Rifle said.

'Of course you do,' Kazinsky replied.

'You have been destined to lead us.'

'Wasn't I always?'

'I saw that – we all did.'

'It means so much to me that you have seen the light,' Kazinsky said. 'To be my comrade again, to walk together into the future.'

'Exactly, companions on the journey.' Rifle's eyes darted around. 'What a fool I was,' he said.

Kazinsky smiled and shook his head. 'Forgiveness is available to all men, though.'

He extended his left hand, put it on Rifle's right shoulder and kissed him, first on one cheek and then the other. Rifle looked confused – in Islam a kiss is used as a greeting – and then realized: it was a farewell.

'But not this time,' Kazinsky said sharply, full of anger.

Rifle struggled, but Kazinsky's left hand held him tight while his right hand lifted the pneumatic screwdriver and hit the power switch.

Rifle heard the screwdriver roar to life and fought even harder – panicked – as he felt its end of hardened steel bite into the back of his neck. He screamed—

'Liar,' Kazinsky said, and kept drilling at three thousand revs a minute.

Blood, bone and flesh sprayed across Kazinsky's hand as Rifle spasmed helplessly.

Kazinsky – his face impassive, devoid of compassion – kept increasing the pressure. The screwdriver plunged deeper into Rifle's neck – whose arms and legs stiffened, losing all movement. The tip of the screwdriver had hit his spine, severing the nerves and paralysing him.

He continued to scream, unable even to move now, the sound mixing with the high-pitched whine of the screwdriver's motor as Kazinsky pushed harder.

Rifle slumped, his eyes glazed over and he was dead. Kazinsky released his grip and let him fall to the ground. Without a glance, he turned away and looked across the space to the sealed chamber and the piles of unsanitized ore.

He stood there for a moment, then walked forward, shifting his gaze. His eyes were fixed on the two huge cooling vents in the roof.

10

ASTEROIDS MAY HIT THE PLANET AND OFF-EARTH MINING ENDANGER the world, but the biologists say one thing never changes: the most elemental driving force of every organism is to survive and procreate.

In the gloom of the processing plant – lit only by the glow from the furnaces – Kazinsky leapt up, grabbed a small handhold and started to scale one of the grime-covered walls. Finding hand- and footholds, he climbed higher and higher until, forty feet from the ground, he reached his objective – a clutch of heavy-duty pulleys and chains.

They were supposed to operate the cooling vents above him but had somehow become tangled among themselves. Hanging by one hand, he used his new strength to take the pressure off one thick chain and unloop it from the pulley it was twisted around. Suddenly, restored to its proper place, the chain flew upwards, a group of other pulleys flew into action and the entire mechanism sprung taut, unjammed.

Kazinsky climbed halfway down, leapt to the floor, grabbed a brake lever and pulled it hard, plunging the counterweights down. Chains rattled through the pulleys and, high above, a small electric motor kicked in.

The two glass cooling vents slid open, revealing the stars, the moon and the clouds. The combination of heat trapped within the massive brick walls and a high wind whistling out of the Steppes immediately created its own weather system: as Kazinsky watched, a spiral of dust and ash swirled up and dissipated out of the vents into the darkening sky.

The procreation was almost done—

11

THE OVERHEAD CRANE MOVED STEADILY ALONG ITS RAILS, AND THE hook – carrying one of the huge buckets used to transport molten metal – passed over the blast furnaces, the lava river and the supervisor's glass-walled office.

Kazinsky was standing in its doorway, remote control in hand, guiding the crane and its load through the facility, towards the steel ceiling that spanned the walls of the sealed chamber.

He stopped the hook above the ceiling. The huge bucket – loaded with tons of scrap metal – was silhouetted against the murals of Lenin and the heroic Soviet workers. It hung there for a moment—

Kazinsky pressed a button on the remote and the huge bucket was released. It plummeted downwards and hit the ceiling, which buckled and tore apart, the girders supporting it shattering and the glass walls of the chamber bursting in a massive wave of translucent fragments. Instantly the lights in the entire facility failed once again.

Across the facility, flooding out of the obliterated glass chamber in a continuous stream – dancing in the firelight and gloom – were visible billions of minuscule glowing lights, just as beautiful and otherworldly as ever, which joined the vertical spiral of dust and ash, rose upwards and started to stream out into the world.

CCTV footage later showed that, according to the clock on the wall, it was exactly 1.28 and 22 seconds on Sunday, the second week in July, when the spore was let loose on the world. Nobody may have known it then, but that date and precise time would become critically important.

12

THE PREVAILING WIND IN BAIKONUR DURING THE SEASON OF FOG is from the east. That – combined with a huge storm sweeping out of

China and over the Steppes – meant that the spore was efficiently distributed to Ukraine, Germany, France, Britain and the rest of Europe, before crossing the Atlantic and hitting America's East Coast and beyond.

Even assisted by the Earth's rotation and the strength of the jet stream, it was still hard to credit how quickly such tiny fragments of genetic material could travel; except that some years earlier another viral fragment called Covid-19 that had either escaped from a Chinese research lab or had jumped species in a wet market – depending on whether you believed Beijing or not – had been found in remote parts of Africa and South America within days of the first patient in Wuhan being identified.

Among a myriad other places, the *siber* spore hit a leafy street in Maryland within hours. It was twilight local time – men and women were just coming home, dogs were being walked and the kids weren't inside yet for the evening.

Lights were on everywhere – except in one house, whose doors were locked and shutters closed. It looked like a place where life had already departed and, in a way, it had.

In the attic guest room, Laleh was about to make a video call to her mother in Kabul when she heard voices calling from outside. It was unusual enough for her to cross to the dormer window and raise the blind.

Looking out the closed window, she didn't move, staring in astonishment at thousands of the most delicate, tiny pinpoints of blue-hued light falling from the sky, backlit by the setting sun. In the street, people were staring, kids were trying to catch them. Doors in houses everywhere were opening and drivers were stopping on the side of the road. It was magical.

A foreigner in a foreign land, Laleh thought she had an idea of what it was all about. She turned and called to Rebecca, who had barely left our bedroom since the news that I would not be coming home. 'Becca – come and look.'

There was no reply. 'Rebecca, it's beautiful, you should come—'

'What is it?' Rebecca said from the doorway. She had emerged – her face was drawn and pale, the dark circles under her eyes were a testament to sleepless nights and she had clearly lost a lot of weight.

'It's sort of lights,' Laleh replied. 'Your festival, Christmas, is coming very early – it must be part of that.'

Rebecca joined her at the window and looked out. She put her palms against the glass, taken aback by the downpour of luminous filaments and the number of people gathering in the street. 'No,' she said. 'Not this early. It's nothing to do with Christmas.'

'What is it then?' Laleh asked.

'I don't know,' Rebecca replied. She turned, walked to the end of the bed and turned on a TV. It was already tuned to a twenty-four-hour news channel and a montage of the glowing spore falling like rain over Paris, London and Washington was playing—

'A White House source said initial studies by the National Oceanic and Atmospheric Administration showed the phenomenon originated in either Kazakhstan or central China,' the anchor was saying. 'Minutes ago, the Chinese government denied any knowledge of the source of what is now being described as the "symphony of lights". The NOAA is presently trying to determine the exact point of origin.

'Meanwhile, in Canada, the professor of forestry at the University of British Columbia said it almost certainly resulted from the premature germination of spores from the northern hemisphere's vast conifer forests. Because they are immature, he said, they absorb moisture and appear to glow. He was confident they presented no danger to anyone but advised people with asthma or severe pollen allergies to remain indoors.'

Laleh looked at Rebecca. 'We don't suffer from either of those,' she said brightly. 'Let's go outside – it'll do us both good.'

Rebecca looked out the window. The voices were louder, more animated, and the falling spore – if anything – had grown more intense. Laleh pleaded with her. 'Please.'

Rebecca continued to look out the window. 'No,' she said finally. 'I don't understand any of this. I've got babies to think of.'

Laleh stared at her, crestfallen, and had she not been a guest she would almost certainly have argued. 'Close the blind,' Rebecca said.

Laleh reluctantly did as she was asked, and it was that small decision – not to go outside – that saved both their lives, although it was, in many ways, a pyrrhic victory; very soon the living would envy the dead.

13

JUST BEFORE MIDNIGHT REBECCA WAS ROUSED BY AN UNUSUAL flickering light creeping around the edges of the closed window blind.

She was tired and she tried to ignore it. Surrendering at last, she went to the window and – half asleep – pulled the blind aside. And stared.

The luminous spore had vanished, but houses all along the street were ablaze, sending up an eerie orange light. The sky and distant horizon were aglow and filled with smoke. Devil's Night, Rebecca thought with a spike of fear, recalling the annual ritual, years earlier, when marauding gangs in Detroit would set thousands of derelict buildings on fire.

In Maryland, it certainly looked like a vision of hell. Irrigation systems across countless gardens had been turned on and were pumping out fountains of water. Then Rebecca saw the first of them—

Shadowy figures – three men and a woman, powerfully built – appeared amid the smoke and spray, thrown into sharp relief by the flames from a burning house behind them. Their bodies were almost colourless, their hair missing, and Rebecca, grasping for any explanation, thought they might be burn victims, although she could not understand how they could be walking so purposefully. But then one of the men turned his back and she saw the skin had formed a hard ridge down his spine. In all of her years of medicine, Rebecca had never seen anything like it.

Reeling, Rebecca looked more closely at the woman. Her body had changed and her facial features were more brutal, but aspects of her were still familiar; Rebecca recognized her as a neighbour, a woman who had always been unfriendly, and last seen dancing with her partner – taking a video selfie – as the shower of tiny lights had fallen all around her.

Trying to walk the nightmare back, to shake herself into an awakening that would never come, Rebecca grabbed a remote and switched on the TV. She heard the sound of piano music – 'As Time Goes By' – and saw that a classic black-and-white movie was playing, a desperate fragment of normality. She was momentarily relieved until she suspected the broadcast was on some sort of auto-play. She changed channels a dozen times and all she found was static or white noise.

Fear rocketing, she looked out the window again to see the four ridgebacks, or whatever the hell they were, approaching the house, the only one in the neighbourhood that was not yet alight. One of the men had an assault rifle and the woman was carrying a baseball bat.

In a moment of strange lucidity, Rebecca guessed the weird snow-flakes were somehow responsible and that fire and moisture were instrumental in effecting some kind of transformation. She pulled on her jeans, yelling for Laleh and heading for the door: somehow she had to survive, the twins had to survive. The two women met at the bottom of the stairs—

'Did you see them?' Laleh asked, wide-eyed.

'Yes,' Rebecca replied, throwing her a set of car keys.

'Who are—'

'No time,' Rebecca said. 'Turn on the watering system and get in the car. Don't open the garage door, not yet—'

Laleh nodded. 'What about you?'

'I'll burn the house. If they think we are like them, it might buy us time.'

She swung to a window and lifted a corner of the blind – the four ridgebacks had just started to cross the neighbour's lawn, coming closer. Rebecca looked at the military-grade rifle with a scope on the barrel that one of them was carrying and, from her work, knew exactly what sort of damage that could do.

She ran for the kitchen, turned on the gas burners and dumped a bottle of cooking oil on them, leaping back as flames exploded and started to consume the entire wall.

A moment later, the sprinklers outside burst to life and, with the kitchen already ablaze, she grabbed a flashlight and a hammer from a drawer and ran for the downstairs spare bedroom that served as my office.

She threw the door open, crossed to a filing cabinet and used the hammer to smash the lock until it broke. Using the flashlight, she searched the drawers, flinging out files and notebooks. I had never told her about it, she had no way of knowing, but she was confident she would find what she needed. In the bottom drawer, she tossed aside stacks of photos, old railway tickets and journal pages ripped from logbooks – the detritus of a life lived in the secret world – and knew she was close.

Hidden underneath she found a pistol – a Sig Sauer M17, the best combat side-arm in the world and a weapon that I kept at home for our protection. Rebecca didn't know how to shoot, but she was ready to learn, and she grabbed a box of ammo sitting beside it, killed the flashlight and headed out of the office—

There was a sudden crash as the glass in the front door shattered and Rebecca heard a male voice on the porch: 'Maybe she already left—'

'She hasn't. The place had been closed up for days, the husband – or whatever he was – got himself killed,' the woman said. 'I never saw her outside tonight. I think she's fired up the house and turned on the sprinklers to fool us. She was always clever.'

Rebecca, in the hallway, looked across at the front door: the woman's hairless and colourless hand and arm came through the shattered glass and groped to unlock the catch.

Rebecca raised the Sig, thinking in her panic about shooting, but realized she didn't have the skill to take out four of them. She didn't know then – nobody did – that their skin was a carapace, almost as good as body armour. With only a few seconds before they were inside, she ran for the kitchen and the back door, which was well alight, with flames roaring up the walls and across the ceiling.

She heard the intruders pounding down the hallway behind her. No time to hesitate – she grabbed a kitchen towel, held it over her mouth and plunged into the inferno.

It was the best thing she could have done: the intruders arrived at the kitchen moments behind her but, engulfed by smoke and flame, couldn't see her.

Only when she ripped open the back door, allowing a blast of air from outside to enter, did the intruders realize she had been only yards ahead of them. They would have followed instantly except that the whirlwind of fresh air hitting the enclosed, super-heated space caused what firefighters call a flashover. The kitchen and the entire side of the house exploded in flames, forcing the intruders back—

Rebecca sprinted across the yard to the garage, the sky all around her aglow as more buildings were torched, where Laleh was waiting for her.

'It was the spore? Breathe it in and—' Laleh called to her.

'That's what I figure.'

'They're gone now,' Laleh said, indicating the sky. 'It's clear.'

'Thank God,' Rebecca replied. 'It seems like they're finished once they land. They must need to find a host.'

The two women ran for the side door that led into the garage.

'I got the car started,' the young woman said.

Rebecca led the way. 'Open it,' she said, indicating the large electric door. As Laleh ran for the control, Rebecca scrambled into the driver's seat of the small SUV. With the garage door still rising, she put it into gear.

When Laleh dived into the passenger's seat, Rebecca, pedal to the metal, realized that she had forgotten to release the emergency brake. She hit the button, taking the brake off, and the car launched backwards, exiting the garage at speed—

Directly in its path, the female ridgeback tried to dive. The rear fender hit her full on, breaking one leg and sending her crunching into a small retaining wall.

Rebecca, driving at full speed backwards, barely in control, sent the vehicle careening across the lawn, heading towards a low picket fence.

The male ridgeback with the assault rifle scrambled to his feet and raised the weapon, but by the time he adjusted his aim Rebecca had smashed through the fence, blasted across a nature strip and hit the asphalt. She swung the wheel wildly and, tyres screeching, headed south-west.

'Where to?' Laleh asked.

'The freeway.'

'It's not safe,' Laleh replied, alarmed, desperate, pointing at a shopping mall ablaze with scores of pale figures roaming the car park, torching vehicles. 'Nowhere is.'

'One place might be.'

14

A LATE-RISING MOON – BLOOD RED FROM THE SMOKE AND FLAMES burning across the world – was casting a pale light over the waters of Chesapeake Bay.

With Rebecca hunched over the wheel and the Sig in her lap, the SUV – its rear fender missing and two tyres shredded – sped down a deserted four-lane blacktop, swung into a side road and accelerated hard.

Up ahead, a pair of metal gates blocked the entrance to a large marina – scores of expensive boats were bobbing at a complex of quays. A huge shed with slipways provided maintenance facilities, and a sleek office and café extended out over the water. On a normal summer's day, it must have been quite the place.

But at 5 a.m. on Devil's Night, a high wind was rattling the rigging on the yachts. Like the motor cruisers moored nearby, their hatches were fastened and tarpaulins had been deployed to protect the decks and running gear from a wild summer storm that was heading up the coast.

Without pausing, Rebecca continued to accelerate, smashing into the metal gates, tearing them apart and then barrelling into the parking lot. The two women scanned their surroundings and, to their relief, could not see any ridgebacks, but unfortunately neither had they seen any other survivors during the miles of chaos they had driven through.

Ahead, Rebecca saw the entrance to the marina office, but instead of slowing, she spun the wheel and drove straight at it, ploughing the SUV across the foyer and into a shop selling supplies and nautical artefacts.

Rebecca hit the brakes and, Sig still in hand, leapt out of the vehicle. She headed at a sprint towards an inner office, where there was a steel security cupboard fixed to the wall behind the manager's desk. It was exactly what she was looking for.

She raised the Sig, spent a moment to find the safety, slid the action to cock it and aimed at the cupboard's lock. It took her three shots – their retorts echoing sharply in the silence of the marina – before she scored a direct hit and the cupboard door sprang open.

Inside, hanging on a board in neat rows and numbered to correspond to their berths, were the keys to all the boats.

15

CARRYING THE BOARD WITH THE KEYS, REBECCA STOPPED AT THE doorway and grabbed a pair of binoculars hanging on a coat rack.

Laleh, towing a cart piled with batteries, flashlights, wet-weather gear and everything else she had pillaged from the shop, stopped beside her.

'What are we looking for?' she asked.

'The right sort of boat,' Rebecca replied, scanning from vessel to vessel. 'Not a party palace, something serious, a big engine, built for heavy weather—'

She pointed across the marina to the waters of the bay, which, lit by moonlight, were covered in whitecaps and wild spray from the wind. 'Once we leave the shelter of the bay,' she continued, 'it's going to be rough out there. Will you be okay?'

Laleh smiled. 'It can't be any worse than the Persian Gulf.'

Rebecca grinned back. 'Sorry, I forgot.' She kept the glasses fixed on one boat. 'Red zone,' she said. 'Berth thirty-four.'

Rebecca grabbed a set of keys off the board from the steel cupboard and ran. Laleh followed, jogging along the wharf, towing the cart behind her, before they both stopped at berth thirty-four.

Moored at it, surrounded by other far bigger and more impressive boats, was a sixty-foot sport fishing boat; deep hulled and with a wide beam to provide stability, sleek and low enough not to be battered by the wind, she had five large outboard engines on the back to provide enormous power. She had the look of a boat that could go anywhere. Heaven only knew how much she was worth, but Rebecca had already taken possession, ripping off the tarpaulin that covered the wheelhouse and using the keys to open the door.

Inside, Rebecca used the ignition key to turn on the electrical system. The gauges and screens came alive; but only one instrument interested her—

'Thank God,' she said. 'She's fuelled up.'

Minutes later, the big outboards rumbled to life and, with Rebecca trying to learn to control the vessel, the *Lonesome Dove* – as she was called – smashed into the bumpers on either side of her berth, scraped noisily along the side of a ninety-foot sailing sloop and finally reached the channel outside the marina. Heading into the bay and turning south, Laleh asked: 'And now?'

'Open water,' Rebecca replied. 'Twenty miles out, we should be safe for a while – then we can try and decide what the hell we're going to do.'

Laleh made no reply. Instead, she was studying her friend closely. Despite their terrifying circumstances, she was reassured – for the first time since Rebecca had heard the news of my death, she was ready to fight.

16

DAWN WAS BREAKING AS THE *LONESOME DOVE*, HEADING SOUTH, approached the eighteen-mile-long Chesapeake Bay Bridge and Tunnel that crossed the mouth of the bay and marked the entrance to the Atlantic Ocean.

With the wind howling from the north, the tide was running hard behind them, a steep swell churning the ocean into whitecaps beyond the bridge. Battered by the constant wind and spray, Rebecca fought the wheel, keeping the engines throttled back, her face a picture of fierce concentration as the bridge loomed ever closer.

With Laleh watching anxiously, she brought the boat's bow around slightly and steered for the centre of a gap between two of the bridge's huge pylons. The sea was surging between the concrete structures, the water hitting their bases with enormous force, turning into a riot of white foam. The darkness of the sky and the deep shadow cast by the roadway above made the gap seem even more threatening, ominous.

'Have you seen the—' Laleh asked, glancing up towards the roadway nearly two hundred feet above them. It was littered with burning cars, and several dozen ridgebacks were leaning over the railing, looking down at the boat.

'I saw them,' Rebecca said, not shifting her gaze from the gap between the pylons that was approaching faster than she had anticipated. Within seconds, the craft was almost in the gap. As the water swirled faster around her hull, the vessel was inexorably pulled into the maelstrom—

Rebecca felt the wheel jump and spin hard in her hands. The bow veered towards the left – and, by misfortune, the looming slime-covered concrete of the closest pylon. One hit and the boat would be at the bottom within seconds.

She had no idea how to slow the boat against the power of the elements. Counter-intuitively, at the last moment, she realized she had to take command. She hit the throttle. The five big outboards roared up to full power, bringing the *Lonesome Dove* alive, her bow raised up. Though she flew faster towards the pylon, the wheel felt suddenly far lighter in Rebecca's hands—

She spun it hard. The pylon was almost on top of them. The boat turned on its heel and the left side of the hull skimmed the slime and slid past the pylon. They were through the gap.

Above them, the ridgebacks, racing across the roadway, watched the boat emerge from the shadows, blasting out the other side of the bridge and straightening up on her course.

Rebecca, drenched in sweat, rested her forehead on the wheel. Laleh lifted her friend's chin up, put her arms around her and they held each other, trying to stop shaking.

Laleh spoke quietly in Arabic. Rebecca drew back and looked at her. 'What is that?'

'A prayer,' Laleh replied.

Rebecca paused for a moment then reached out, took Laleh's hand and bowed her head, not comprehending a word of what was being said but certain that if somebody or something was listening, they would understand.

Laleh finished and Rebecca opened her eyes: all that lay in front of them was the limitless grey ocean with a heavy swell rolling through it and the wind whipping the tops off the whitecaps. Even though the sun was at last rising, it brought Rebecca no joy and even less hope.

She pushed aside the despair and told Laleh: 'Go below, check what food and water we have. There'll be a communications set – see if you can get the nav system working. Even if we don't know where we're going, we have to know where we are.'

Laleh nodded and headed downstairs, leaving Rebecca alone. The sense of hopelessness came crashing back, worse than before.

Looking out at a colourless world, the grey sea merging into the lowering sky, she saw a symmetry to it: a father drowned on a submarine and a mother and their two unborn children dead on a sunken boat. It meant that the only true family she had ever known would be reunited at last – lost at sea.

She tried to force the black dog back into its kennel – she knew she couldn't give up, she just couldn't – and it took her a moment to realize that Laleh was yelling for her. 'Clamp the wheel,' she was saying. 'Come quick.'

17

THE VOICE WAS TOUGH AND AUTHORITATIVE – A MAN WHO SOUNDED like he had grown up in Louisiana, Rebecca thought. She was staring at an audio speaker beside a rack of equipment and computer screens in the *Lonesome Dove*'s communications and navigation area.

Laleh was trying to explain. 'I didn't know what I was doing – just trying stuff. I managed to get two screens to work – one of them was the GPS system and it told me where we are and gave me the option to enter a destination. I was about to come up and tell you,' she continued, breathless. 'Then I turned on this bank of equipment and started twisting dials—'

Rebecca looked at a blue cube and saw the brand name 'Iridium' on its front-plate followed by a model number and the words 'Satellite Communicator'.

'I thought I heard something, very faint, but it took me a while to find the volume—'

Rebecca interrupted, holding her hand up, signalling for her to stop. The man from Louisiana had started to speak again and Rebecca realized it was on a loop, the same message being repeated and probably broadcast on a wide range of frequencies—

'*We are fighting. The resistance has begun. There are survivors in Paris, London, Sydney and Buenos Aires. In America, we are clearing and defending the island of Manhattan. Try to reach New York. We are fighting. The resistance has . . .*'

Rebecca and Laleh looked at one another. They were in a boat, they had a navigation system and they were four hundred kilometres from New York. The voice told them something more important than any of that, though:

They were not alone.

18

I WAS LYING IN THE POD IN TOTAL DARKNESS, NOT SURE IF I WAS DEAD or alive. I could hear nothing, but I felt it—

It must have been what had made me stir: a subtle change in motion, the slightest tremor passing through the submarine's massive hull. Then the lights in the multi-purpose platform flickered, illuminating the other decompression chambers.

Then they were gone, swallowed by darkness, until – moments later – they returned, only to disappear almost immediately. Again and again it happened, strobing, and I wondered if this was what dying was like: bright lights and life flashing before your eyes.

Apparently it wasn't – the lights flickered one last time and held. The tremor itself became a consistent motion and I realized that the reactor had emerged from its hibernation and was now powering the boat and the electrical system. What had caused it to reanimate, I had no idea, but I unlatched the perspex canopy and lifted it an inch. I put my face to the gap and breathed in – I wasn't leaving the canopy until I knew that the air in the sub was capable of sustaining me.

It smelled fresh and clear. Satisfied that the oxygen generators were working and the ventilation system was circulating clean air, I pushed the canopy open, scrambled out and ran for Baxter's chamber.

He wasn't moving and, as I called out his name, I threw the perspex lid back. I think I knew, even before I saw his grey face, blue lips and staring eyes – Baxter was dead.

Even though I had witnessed a lot of death in my career, I felt a sting in the back of my eyes. His wallet was open and he was holding a photo of his wife next to his heart; while he was quite capable of forgetting his meds, I realized he would always remember the wallet that contained a photo of Sophie.

I bowed my head in sorrow: he was a fine man, a good partner I was sure, and a person who should have been a father; he had a lot of love to give. I reached out, closed his eyes and headed towards the door.

I had only taken a few steps when I felt a subtle change in the operation of the boat. I stopped, listening, concentrating; a low hum – barely audible, meaningless to anyone who had not served on a submarine – indicated that the massive high-pressure pumps used to discharge the ballast from the sub had started to work. Thousands of tons of seawater were being pumped out.

I could barely breathe. Somehow – either a person or the on-board computers – had initiated the emergency blow. If the pumps held, if the reactor continued to operate, if the hull wasn't compromised, if the sub could stay on course, if there were no faults in a thousand pieces of equipment, relays and connections – we were going to the surface.

19

I RAN OUT OF THE ENTRANCE OF THE MULTI-PURPOSE PLATFORM and down wrecked companionways. All the time I was calling, for somebody – anybody – to answer, my voice echoing through the wreckage of hanging pipes, crushed electrical conduits and a chaos of spilled and broken equipment.

I was heading to the primary command post, hoping that by some miracle Martinez and his officers – and not the computers – had activated the emergency blow. When we left Diego Garcia, there had been one hundred and sixty-eight people on board, and now they were silent.

My worst fears were confirmed a few minutes later. I had scrambled past a submersible pump that was pounding hard, draining water out of a storage room and sending it down long hoses into the bilge and out of the boat. Sprawled across each other on the side of the companionway were two women I recognized – the pair of fire-fighters who had extinguished the tiny flames in the electrical box. They were both dead, and it was clear from the red and purple splotches in their eyes and the foam that had dried around their mouths that they had suffocated before they got to the wardroom.

I glanced into an area behind them – the junior officers' quarters – and saw more bodies on the floor and near the bunks, all with the telltale red and purple discolouring in their eyes or faces that showed they too had died from lack of oxygen.

There was no point in yelling again – I was the only survivor – and in the oppressive silence, I kept moving forward, through the wreckage.

Despite the scale of it, the lights grew brighter, the hum of machinery louder and the pulse of the bilge pumps stronger. By the time I reached the central command post, the *Leviathan* felt, once again, like a vibrant, living thing. In stark contrast to the situation inside.

I glanced across and saw that while the reactor had awoken and the computers were running and attempting to save the boat, not everything was working correctly. The screens above the navigator's workstation had come to glitching life and they showed we were in the Hudson River, New York, lying four hundred yards off lower Manhattan. It had to be a malfunction, until I remembered Martinez saying when we first set sail that the navigation system had been given a notional destination in order to activate it. Obviously nobody had amended that – or the computers had not updated yet – and were still showing it as the end-point.

The clocks too had not recovered. The time and day might have been right for all I knew, but the year was clearly as improbable as our location.

Hoping the computers and clocks would self-correct, I turned to the communications area. The equipment had powered up and, though I knew little about it, I started by trial and error to scan different frequencies and try different messaging methods. I had no doubt there were a hundred different assets looking for us, and they would be trying to make contact. Surely I could connect—

I heard a faint voice. I grabbed a headset mic, ready to reply, and cranked up the volume: a man with a British accent was transmitting a message that defied my understanding. 'This is London Station,' he said. 'This is London Station, signing off permanently now. To anyone still out there – good luck and Godspeed. This is London Station, this is—' He sounded exhausted, defeated.

I put the microphone down. Who was London Station? I had no time to think about it. A speaker built into the ship control panel announced: 'Emergency blow status: Prepare to surface – ten seconds.'

I turned to the panel and saw that the boat, far lighter, and at an angle, was spearing up through the water. 'Eight seconds.'

I grabbed the photonics mast control – periscopes had gone the way of dial-up and been replaced by sophisticated 360-degree cameras mounted on a telescopic shaft – and tried to raise it to see my surroundings. It seemed to hit an obstruction—

'Four seconds.'

A graphic on the panel showed me we were at an even steeper angle of ascent; we were almost there. I grabbed the back of a swivel chair to steady myself for when the sub blasted out of the underworld and into the atmosphere. 'Two seconds.'

She was going to surface. I was going home. 'One second.'

Then we hit. And a moment later we got the Bounce.

20

THE BOUNCE WASN'T GOOD, NOT GOOD AT ALL. IT OCCURS WHEN A submarine trying to surface doesn't have enough speed or power to break through sheet ice covering the ocean. In that event, the ice bulges like a huge blister, but it resists the punch from below and sends the sub 'bouncing' back down into the freezing water.

The only explanation I could think of was that we had travelled further south than I had imagined and encountered an area of Antarctic sea ice. It was late enough in the year for it, I figured, but it was still strange.

And yet, according to the information scrolling across the ship control panel, the sub's computers had calculated from the Bounce that we were under four feet of ice. That was manageable; an ice-strengthened submarine – which the Leviathan surely was – could surface through at least ten feet of hard-packed ice. Apparently, the computers didn't think there was a problem either—

They had guided the sub lower, changed the angle of attack and, as we headed to the surface again, started to increase the speed. The sub's sail – the square tower on top of the hull, a structure that used to be known as the conning tower – would take the full impact on sections of hardened steel.

'Four seconds,' the voice said.

I grabbed hold of the swivel chair hard and braced myself again. This was going to be a heavy punch. 'Two seconds.'

I breathed deep and waited. 'One second.'

We hit. I managed to keep my grip on the chair but felt my right arm almost wrenched out of its socket. Another second and I would have found myself hitting the ceiling.

The Bounce didn't arrive. The ice surrendered and we were through.

I turned to the photonics mast and cursed my stupidity; I had not retracted it. There would be no images, just a mangled mass of cameras and steel extending above the sail.

Instead, I ran for a ladder that led from the command centre up the middle of the tower.

Heart pounding, I reached the sealed hatch that accessed the navigation bridge, an open-air space at the top of the sail that was used to command the sub when it was on the surface. The hatch was bolted and usually required a code to unseal it, but the emergency release would have to do.

I smashed the glass, triggered an alarm and ducked-and-covered as the six small charges exploded and broke the bolts. I pushed the hatch open and felt the freezing air engulf me. I breathed deeply and closed my eyes for a moment in an attempt to master a tumult of emotions. Miraculously, I had survived, I was alive, I was free.

I swung through the hatch on to the floor of the navigation bridge and stood up. I looked out at the world and didn't move—

I was frozen – and it wasn't the temperature.

21

SO, TELL ME – WHAT WAS IT LIKE TO WALK ON THE MOON, MR Armstrong? It was the only thought I could muster in the face of something so overwhelming.

I was in New York, staring at the iced-up Hudson and the remains of the Statue of Liberty; the torch gone, the head missing and her body cleaved apart. Beyond it lay Manhattan and the ruins of a

513

once-great city. I had come to the end of the world, and I had come at the waning of the day.

As far as the eye could see, New York's legendary skyscrapers – or what remained of them – lit by a setting sun, had collapsed or been burnt out. Magic hour indeed; dark magic. Pillars of smoke in the north, up past Central Park, rose into the sky, scattered fires were burning along the East River, the stunning multimillion-dollar apartments with views to die for were in ruins, some sort of attack drones darted among the towering skeletons, machine-gun fire loaded with red tracers blasting at them from dozens of wrecked penthouses. Down near Battery Park camouflaged howitzers were firing across the river at hollowed-out high-rises on the Jersey side.

Reeling from the sight of it, surrounded by the thunder of war and the acrid smell of rocket and artillery propellant, I thought of the message I had heard: London Station had signed off permanently, but New York – or so it seemed – was still fighting. Against whom, and what it meant, I had no idea.

I took hold of the railing and rocked on my feet, needing to feel something real to steady myself. It was like I was a child of the universe, standing on the edge of the infinite, everything in front of me ultimately unknowable and mysterious. Even so, the artillery sounded real, and a quadrocopter drone near the Empire State building spiralled out of control as it was apparently hit by a hail of gunfire.

I attempted to recalibrate my breathing, trying to force it back close to normal. I recalled the clocks that had gone wildly awry as the cloaking technology was activated and had never corrected themselves, I remembered the feeling of a railroad car jumping tracks when one of the tremors had passed through the boat as our voyage was going to hell and I heard a Nobel Prize-winner say that perhaps if you twist light, you twist time. 'Nobody knows what happens – nobody has ever tried it,' Baxter had also told me. Well, maybe the scene that lay in front of me now was some sort of answer.

I continued to look at a world I barely recognized: I had no doubt I was in New York but, almost overwhelmed by a sense of existential terror, I had to confront the next question – when?

I could not recall the date I had seen on the clocks and was about to go below to look at them when the howitzers on the battery fired another volley. Flashes of orange flames shot forty feet out of their barrels and illuminated acres of frozen water—

In the glow, speeding towards me, plumes of ice and snow thrown up in their wake, were an open-top SnowCat, three heavy-duty snow-mobiles and four modified jet-skis. All of the battered vehicles had machine guns mounted on their bodywork.

The lead vehicle – the SnowCat – had six figures on board, all wearing jeans, bandoliers and body armour. Equipped with hi-tech helmets and night-vision goggles, they looked like front-line guer-rillas or battle-hardened partisans. One of them activated a spotlight and trained it on me. The guns on the front fender, remote-controlled, tracked with the light and held me in their crosshairs.

There was no point in going below: I'd be dead the moment I moved. I raised my hands and interlaced my fingers above my head. I guessed I would find out the date soon enough.

'US Navy?' the man skippering the SnowCat yelled at me as soon as they were within hailing distance.

Squinting against the spotlight, the craft still bearing down fast on me, I managed to make him out. I was taken aback by how young he was; early twenties was my guess. Fair-haired, tall and lean, with a few days' stubble, he was – beneath the dirt and battle grime – a handsome guy. He had unyielding eyes and a strong line to his jaw. Sometimes you can just tell; whoever he was fighting for, he was a good soldier.

'Yes, Navy,' I called back, keeping my hands raised and watching the vehicles split apart and surround the sub. The young commander wasn't taking any chances, and with good reason, I thought: we were in the middle of a war zone.

He brought his vehicle to a sliding stop and, like the rest of his pla-toon, ran his eye along the glittering white sail and the small amount of the hull that had just emerged unheralded through the ice. I could only imagine what they must have thought when they first saw it.

He continued to stare at the boat then indicated the tangled mess of the photonics mast. 'That's not gonna polish out,' he said. 'What's her name?'

'She hasn't got a name,' I replied. 'Experimental, a research sub.'

'I believe it,' he said, obviously thinking it went a long way to explaining her extraordinary appearance. 'How many of you?'

'One,' I replied. Seeing a look of incredulity cross his face, I hurried on. 'We had a complement of one hundred and sixty-eight, then the oxygen generators failed.'

Behind me I heard men and women clambering on board the hull and I realized the snowmobiles and jet-skis were transferring a heavily armed boarding crew. I lowered my hands but kept them on the railing, in sight. 'Two of us managed to reach the decompression chambers,' I continued. 'The other guy didn't make it.'

'Decompression chamber? You a Navy SEAL, a diver? Hurry.' He was looking around now, worried – I was sure – that whoever was on the Jersey side was going to open up at any moment.

'No, scientist,' I replied. 'Like I said, she's experimental.' I wasn't going to disclose my real job or anything about myself. My mind was whirling, I had no idea what was going on, and I decided, if ever there was a time to follow one of the cardinal rules of espionage, it was now: live your legend. Always.

I heard a bracket of small explosions from the for'ard section of the hull. The boarding party must have just blown the door off the escape hatch to get access to the interior of the boat.

'Where did you come from?' he was asking now.

'Diego Garcia,' I said.

He couldn't hide his surprise. 'The Indian Ocean – the naval base? A good spot for the end of the world, I suppose. You were holding out there?'

I didn't know what he meant. Like everything else, it was a mystery. 'Pretty much,' I said.

'And then that fell?'

'Yes,' I responded, and decided to take a gamble. 'Like London.'

'You know about London?'

'I heard,' I said with what I hoped was authority. Keen to change subjects in case he questioned me more – and desperate to know one thing – I indicated the ruined cityscape. 'Can you tell me . . .' I paused. 'What do I call you? Commander?'

'Tokyo. We use call signs. It's easier than remembering names. It started early on – so many were dying, there didn't seem any point in knowing who they were.'

'So, can you tell me, Tokyo – what is the date?' I asked.

Puzzled, he looked at me for a moment – clearly he thought it was a strange question. Then he told me the answer and it took all of my self-possession not to react—

Twenty-four years had passed since the sub had activated the cloaking and subjected itself to forces far beyond any control or current understanding. Twenty-four years. Like the railroad car of my imagination, we had jumped a track, I guessed – a track in time. Two decades or so was nothing compared to the 5 billion years since the Earth was formed – barely discernible in the grand sweep of a universe 10 billion years even older than that – but a shattering event to someone living on a human scale.

So this is what the future looks like, I thought, staring at the plumes of explosions and miles of ruins. Tokyo was watching me, and I had the creeping suspicion that my attempt at normality wasn't convincing him.

I was so preoccupied that I didn't realize one of the boarding crew had emerged from below and was on the bridge behind me. It was only when his hand fell on my shoulder and – startled – I turned to throw it off that I realized he was there.

'Whoa! Easy, tiger,' he said. He was a big guy, a total warrior – six five, broad shoulders, narrow waist, arms and fists like a heavyweight – in his mid-forties and armed with a modified battle rifle fitted with a scope and a two-foot steel spear mounted under its barrel; I stared at it, I had never seen anything like it. As I tried to settle down, I saw that – according to the call sign stencilled on his flak jacket – he was MartinLuther.

He had found a tablet computer below and he yelled to Tokyo: 'I've got a crew list. He's right – one hundred and sixty-eight. Bodies everywhere, suffocated, by the look of 'em.'

Tokyo nodded and watched as MartinLuther took hold of the security necklace hanging around my neck, looked at the name printed on it and checked it against the crew list. 'Daniel Raymond Greenberg,' he called out. 'Photo matches. There's a lot of other data on the list, but it's him.'

'Okay, give Mr Greenberg a flak jacket and helmet,' Tokyo replied. 'Get him on board. We're gonna have to floor it.'

'Where are we going?' I asked.

'To see Kris,' Tokyo said gnomically, revving the SnowCat.

'That's his call sign?' I replied.

'No, his real name,' he said. 'Kristofferson. He's the leader of the Resistance.'

MartinLuther handed me a helmet and a flak jacket. As I put them

517

on I realized that Tokyo was still looking at me. Our eyes met, and his didn't waver.

'Kris is a hard man,' he said. 'A Marine colonel before The Fall. I'm looking forward to him talking to you.'

'Why's that?' I asked.

'He'll ask you all the right questions. There's something about you that I don't believe.'

22

LEAVING THE *LEVIATHAN* BEHIND WITH HALF THE BOARDING CREW still on board to guard her, the SnowCat crossed the ice at full throttle as two female members of the party used field glasses to scan the Jersey shore.

Shocked by miles of devastation, I pulled the collar of my jacket up and hunched my shoulders against the freezing wind; snow had started to fall and I thought of a phrase Falcon had used at Langley in what seemed like a lifetime ago. 'The bleak midwinter,' he had said, and I knew that at last I had found my way into the jaws of it.

The vehicle changed direction slightly and, earlier, I had seen the Brooklyn Bridge in ruins. I wondered if it had been deliberate; perhaps the Resistance – whoever they were – had made the island of Manhattan as inaccessible as possible. On the other hand, the endless craters and skeletal buildings in front of me indicated that little of the city had escaped the carnage.

'Maybe you think this is the Hudson,' Tokyo shouted to me above the wind, indicating the expanse of ice we were flying across. 'It's not. It's the fucking Volga.'

'We're in Russia?' I asked.

'Sure. Winter of '42, a huge city in ruins—'

'Stalingrad?' I said.

'You know your history, Mr Greenberg,' he replied. 'According to Kris, until now it was the worst battle ever fought. You know the average lifespan of a Russian soldier who was ordered into battle? Twenty-four hours.'

'He's probably right, two million casualties,' I said. 'Who are we – the Germans or the Russians?'

'The Germans, unfortunately – totally surrounded,' he replied. 'The water is all that separates us from the Orcs – like the German 6th Army, we have no hope of resupply, reinforcements or escape. Just holding them off is the best we can do.'

The Orcs? Who – or what – was that slang for? I wondered. But I said nothing; supposedly I had been one of the hold-outs on Diego Garcia so I should know the answer. 'What about other cities?' I asked.

'London was the final stronghold we knew about,' he responded. 'Sydney and Rio had been fighting hard, but we haven't heard from them in months. We figure everywhere has fallen.' He smiled ironically. 'This is probably our last stand.'

I turned away: he was saying Europe, Australasia, South America – the whole world had gone to war?

We were almost at the Manhattan shore, and I saw, ahead of us, a pier and boat storage sheds topped by a faded and shrapnel-riddled sign identifying it as the home of the Circle Line, a company that I knew had once offered boat tours around the island. Tokyo slowed the SnowCat as we headed towards it, forced to pick our way through a graveyard of wrecked and half-sunken pleasure boats.

I looked past them and saw, just to the north, the huge bulk of the USS *Intrepid*, a Second World War aircraft carrier that had survived five Japanese kamikaze attacks before being preserved as a floating museum. It had now fallen victim to whatever the current conflict was; she was barely above water, listing hard to port, her superstructure covered in rust and peppered with artillery damage.

Moored beyond her, protected by the huge piers used by cruise liners in years past, the tops of another seven vessels were visible. Astonished, I turned back to Tokyo. 'Subs?' I said. 'I can see the tops of their sails. Five fast attack boats, at least two boomers—'

'Sure,' he said. 'Their crews were probably the safest people on earth – how could they inhale the spore if they were six hundred feet below the surface? One morning alone, five subs arrived in convoy. There are ten others anchored over in the East River—'

He turned away and started shouting orders to people onshore to open the gates into one of the Circle Line's boat storage sheds.

I was riding an avalanche of information, fighting not to be buried alive: there was a spore, a worldwide conflict and the Orcs were at the gates of Stalingrad, the single outpost left standing—

And then it hit me like a shattering blow – what had happened to Maryland? How could those suburban houses and leafy streets have survived? Where was Rebecca? Did she give birth to the twins? Were any of my family still alive?

In panic, I looked around – desperate to know something, anything, but unable to ask. Somehow I had to get to Maryland, but, as I realized later: I was hardly thinking rationally – twenty-four years had passed. Whatever had once existed there would have been scattered by the winds of war, and the chances of survival were negligible.

23

THE SNOWCAT HAD ENTERED THE BOATSHED. MOMENTS LATER, AS A set of vast doors slid shut behind it – closing us off from the river – a row of overhead lights flickered to life.

By their glow I saw a pack of dogs was waiting – a dozen of them or more crowding around, tails wagging, excited, as the snowmobiles and jet-skis drew up at a concrete wharf.

I scrambled ashore and looked around at my surroundings. The large and shadow-filled space was covered – forty feet above – by a roof of reinforced concrete and steel.

Working in teams, about eighty people were servicing snowmobiles, snow scooters and even a military hovercraft. The mechanics, surrounded by the glare of arc welders, were dressed in dirty coveralls, and all of them – men and women – had their hair buzzed short, making them look like prisoners. In a way – trapped on Manhattan – I suppose they were. Everybody was staring at me.

'You've got their attention – we haven't had a visitor in years,' MartinLuther explained, coming to my side, carrying a bulging sack. The dogs – mostly German shepherds, beagles and black-and-white pointers – crowded even closer.

'You must be a dog guy,' I said, making a fuss of the animals. It may sound ridiculous, but it affected me deeply – this scrap of normality in the midst of the madness.

'We're all dog people here,' MartinLuther replied. 'We wouldn't survive without 'em.' He opened the sack, took out a stack of bowls and started to portion out food. 'The dogs warn us,' he explained. 'During the day the Orcs hit us with artillery, rockets and drones – so we use the subway and sewage tunnels. But during the night their raiding parties arrive. That's what the snowmobiles and skis are for – from sunset we try to patrol the island. The bad news is, the Orcs often get into the tunnels, too.'

I took several bowls from him, started filling them and putting them down.

'They'd surprise us if it wasn't for the dogs,' he continued. 'Most dogs use scent on the ground when they track, but German shepherds catch the scent in the air. It's a big advantage – they can smell an Orc hundreds of yards away. We couldn't survive in the tunnels without them.'

He put the last bowl down and closed the sack. The dogs headed off to piles of blankets, but MartinLuther kept one of the shepherds back – a young female called Ella, small for her age, and with bright eyes and a way of cocking her head that made her look like she was questioning everything she saw.

'What now?' I asked.

'Head uptown to see Kristofferson. We have to get to the first tunnel, and the only way to do that is along Sniper Alley. We can't risk that until it's dark, so – another few minutes.'

I looked once again at the chaos all around. My worry for Rebecca had not abated, but reality was intruding: Maryland was two hundred and fifty miles away, and travelling through this war zone already appeared far different to anything I had ever undertaken in my earlier life. If I was going to find a way to do it, I needed information. 'You from the East Coast, Martin?'

He gently pushed Ella's nose out of his pack – among the ammo and spears, she was trying to purloin a box of field rations: 'Philly, but I went to Atlantic City when I was twenty – a connected man I knew offered me a business opportunity.' He smiled.

'Yeah? Sounds suspicious,' I replied.

'That was what the FBI thought.' He laughed. 'They tapped his phone for over a year, raided his house and took him into custody. Early that evening they picked me up at a counting house I ran for him and locked me in the basement while they catalogued and bagged the money. That was Devil's Night, and I never saw any spore.' He laughed again. 'I owe my life to law enforcement – how many Black dudes can say that?'

'You ever been back – to Philly or Atlantic City?' I asked.

He looked at me askance. 'What – how could I go back? How could anyone? There are easier ways to commit suicide.'

'It was the same all along the coast?' I said, pressing.

'It was the same everywhere,' he replied.

'I had family in Maryland,' I explained.

He shrugged. 'We all had family somewhere.'

I heard someone behind me load a clip and then slide the action to cock a rifle. I turned and saw that it was Tokyo, about to address his assembled platoon. 'Okay – load and lock,' he said. 'Thirty seconds. Eyes to the sky for drones, everyone.'

MartinLuther put a leash on Ella and tossed me a battle rifle. I caught it, wincing at the pain. At least I was getting some movement back into my injured left shoulder. 'You know how to use it?' he asked.

'I'll figure it out,' I said.

24

IN ANOTHER TIME, ANOTHER WORLD, SNIPER ALLEY WAS CALLED 42nd Street. Taking cover, crouched next to a pile of debris from a collapsed skyscraper, the twenty of us looked across 12th Avenue: there were huge craters in the asphalt and piles of rusted vehicles half covered by the falling snow.

'Counting down from five,' Tokyo said. 'Then we go.'

MartinLuther reeled out the leash, giving Ella more room to run. 'Follow me,' he told me. 'I know where the doorways and hollows are. They use drones with fifty-cal remote guns. The rotors sound like egg-beaters – when you hear one you have two seconds. When I dive, you dive.'

'Four,' Tokyo announced.

'Twelve hundred yards to the Port Authority Terminal,' MartinLuther continued. 'It's a five-minute run – inside the terminal, there are half a dozen subway tunnels still viable; the rest are collapsed. We start running left, but the terminal's on the right—'

'Three seconds.'

'When you go, anybody gets hit, you don't stop to help. They won't do it for you – we all know the rules.'

'Two.'

'There's debris all along the route, it's easy to fall over in the dark. There's a flashlight strapped to your helmet. Turn it on—'

I swung to face him, objecting. 'The drone operator will see it.'

'Doesn't matter – he's got thermal imaging anyway. It's more important to stay upright and keep running. Maybe they won't be flying tonight, or perhaps the snow will help.'

'One.'

I turned on the flashlight along with everybody else, checked my rifle was cocked and, unseen, slipped the safety off; running fast was fine, but I wasn't taking any chances.

'Go!' Tokyo yelled.

25

CONTRARY TO MARTINLUTHER'S HOPES, THE DRONES WERE FLYING that night. The platoon had scattered when Tokyo gave the order, everybody taking a different route across the wreckage of 42nd Street, trying to make the wild run as target-poor as possible.

As twenty flashlights danced in the darkness, I followed MartinLuther close. My heart pounding, we passed Lucky Strike – a ruined bowling alley – scrambled over the rubble and raced down canyons of wreckage, while Ella was determined to take a different route and forced MartinLuther to snap her free of the harness.

As the dog veered away – tiny LED lights on her collar flashing – he suddenly hurled himself into a darkened doorway. I figured he had heard the egg-beaters and, even though I was only a few yards behind, there was no time to follow him. I had two seconds – so he had said – before I got red-misted; I threw myself face first on to the debris-strewn ground.

The drone was a false alarm, but the sharp rocks that split my forehead weren't. With blood streaming down my face from a long gash, I saw MartinLuther emerge from the darkness. He registered the free-flowing blood and ignored it—

'On your feet – move!'

I grabbed my rifle, scrambled up and followed him. Thanks to having to wipe blood from my eyes, I was falling behind as we passed what was once a large public square. Situated between the ruins of a series of high-rise office towers, the plaza was cratered with piles of earth interrupted by acres of splintered trees. It looked like Passchendaele in 1917.

Ella emerged over the top of a mountain of dirt in the middle of it and half ran, half slid, down the side of it. She hit the street sprinting, partway between MartinLuther and myself. Then I heard it for real—

The egg-beater. MartinLuther and myself dived to the ground, and Ella – highly trained – instantly dropped to her stomach and flattened herself.

I looked between my arms – wrapped around my head, trying to shield it – and saw the drone coming towards us, dive-bombing like a Stuka. It was a black and ugly thing with a rotor on either end of its curved wing, a forest of antennas on its head and a machine gun attached to its belly.

Fifty feet above the street, it levelled out and opened up. The sound was deafening, echoing off the ruined buildings, and the fifty-cal rounds and their red tracers blasted towards three flashlights diving for cover outside an old church.

The hurricane of lead and metal shredded concrete and brick and must have hit at least one of the targets – a woman's piercing scream rent the night.

The drone lost altitude and hovered, the remote gun moving on its axis as, I figured, the operator – miles away in New Jersey – scanned his night-vision screens for the exact position of the three fighters.

Abruptly, the drone soared higher and unleashed another burst of fire. I saw a red tracer ricochet off the church wall and fly forty yards across the street towards us—

I realized if a tracer was taking that trajectory, so could other rounds. 'Down!' I yelled as a warning, even though MartinLuther and I were prone on the ground.

I watched the tracer fly over Ella's head, thought she was safe for a moment, and then heard her yelp. She fell to the ground, writhing, blood pumping from a rear leg; another of the ricocheting bullets had struck her.

Whimpering, she tried to crawl towards MartinLuther, dragging her leg, but she was in too much pain and shock to make any progress.

I saw the drone climb into the night sky and turn away, but I was sure it wasn't finished with us yet. Tokyo, crouching further down the street, watching from the entrance to the Port Authority Terminal, started to yell: 'Leave her, Martin. Run! Move now.'

MartinLuther rose to his feet and appeared to be about to sprint for the terminal. Ella, whimpering louder, tried to get to her feet and follow him but fell back down, bleeding hard. MartinLuther hesitated. Then he turned, heading back for Ella. So much for leaving the wounded on the battlefield. Maybe that only applied to humans.

I started to get to my feet, about to shout that I would grab her on the way through, but the words never left my mouth. I looked up and saw the drone: it had wheeled around in the dark and was diving into the street behind MartinLuther, straight at his back. It would have him dead to rights – a fifty cal at that range would cut him in half.

A warning was a wasted breath. Instead, I crouched on one knee, unslung the battle rifle fast and thanked divine providence I had checked its action and unlocked the safety.

As I have said, I am not a great shot, but with a decent weapon and a scope I can usually do the business. More important than that, I had been taught to stay calm in extreme situations. It's not the weapon that saves you, it's the training.

I saw the barrel of the drone's gun track as it acquired its target. MartinLuther was sprinting now, his back to me. No flak jacket or body armour in the world would stand a chance against a gun of that calibre.

I slipped the rifle on to full auto, took a breath, clamped the stock tighter into my shoulder, steadied myself and opened fire—

The rifle kicked, but I was ready for it and compensated – the spent cartridges cascading out the side as I kept my eye on the scope and the trigger depressed.

Orange sparks flew as a dozen of my shots hit the barrel of the machine gun. The weapon was just opening up, but the velocity of the hits at such short range knocked its barrel off centre. As a result, the burst of fifty cal went awry, ripping up the asphalt within inches of MartinLuther as he dived to cover Ella with his body.

The hail of fire from the machine gun kept coming, blasting a trail across the ground straight towards me, sending up plumes of debris. My only hope was to keep shooting. I saw the drone's antenna turn to shreds and then hurled myself aside as its gunshots peppered the ground two feet to my left.

Without its sensors, the operator turned the drone, trying to adjust his aim, exposing it. I rose to my feet fast and, standing amid the dust and ruins, opened up again. My fire – at less than fifty yards – zipped its belly and then hit one of the rotors.

Shards of metal flew as the blade suddenly spun itself into oblivion. The drone pitched to one side, the remaining rotor fought to keep it aloft and the bullets from the machine gun flew in wild arcs as it spun out of control—

The fighters at the church, seeing their opportunity, had grabbed their wounded colleague and were racing for the terminal. They hit the dirt as the uncontrolled gunfire slammed into the walls all around them. One of them screamed—

Tokyo hurled himself aside as a stream of tracer approached him. Bullets ripped through what was left of the terminal's glass signage above his head.

The drone – out of control – spiralled faster, lost altitude and slammed into the facade of a branch of the Chase bank, exploding in a shower of metal and unspent cartridges.

I got to my feet, slung the red-hot rifle over my shoulder and sprinted to MartinLuther. He had already tied a tourniquet around Ella's leg and was trying to lift her but, in pain and distress, she was trying her best to bite him. I clamped my hand around her muzzle and together we lifted her on to his shoulder.

'She's gonna lose the leg,' I said as we started to run. 'At best.'

'I figured,' he replied. 'As long as she lives. I'll just rename her.'

'Rename her?' I asked.

'Tripod,' he said.

Despite the circumstances, I laughed.

'You shouldn't have done it,' he said seriously. 'Open fire, I mean.'

'You shouldn't have gone back for her,' I replied.

'I wouldn't have for you or anyone else. A dog's different.' Then he looked at me. 'Thanks,' he said.

I had no time to reply – we were at the door of the terminal and Tokyo was waiting. 'What the fuck were you two thinking?' he yelled. 'You could have both been killed.'

'I know,' MartinLuther said. 'It was a mistake, should have left her. It won't happen again.'

Tokyo turned to me. 'That was pretty fancy shooting,' he said. 'Where'd you learn that?'

I shrugged. 'I lived in Florida as a kid. I've been around guns all my life.'

'No,' he said. 'It takes more than growing up in Florida to face a fifty-cal chain gun and stay that cool. Do you want to tell me?'

I said nothing. The scepticism and questions could wait for Kristofferson.

Tokyo was about to press further, but one of the members of the platoon – a guy in his forties who served as the medic – interrupted. He was tending to the woman who had been hit outside the church – applying dressings to shrapnel wounds in her legs. Another member of the trio – a man in his fifties – was trying to pack bandages into a ricochet wound that had ripped open his shoulder. 'Marta's lost a lot of blood, Tokyo,' he said. 'We've got to get 'em both to Bergdorf's.'

Bergdorf's? I thought. What the hell was that? Before I could ask, Tokyo was calling out: 'Okay – we stop on the way to Kristofferson. Load and lock.'

The platoon shouldered their backpacks and weapons and started jumping on the spot; simulating running, to see whether any of their kit would make a noise. Satisfied, they knelt and began binding their shoes with cloth and rags to muffle the sound.

The exception was MartinLuther; he was hurriedly emptying his backpack and distributing the food, ammo and spare spears among the rest of us. I realized why and knelt to help.

As soon as his pack was empty we lifted Ella, put her in tail first and swung it over MartinLuther's shoulders. She didn't like it, yelping due to the pain in her leg, but we had no choice; it was the only way to transport her when we were running.

'Wait,' the medic said. 'I'll give her a shot to sedate her.'

'No,' MartinLuther replied sharply. 'She's gotta be alert to smell the air.'

26

ELLA WAS QUIET, MORE COMFORTABLE NOW, AS SHE LOOKED OUT from the backpack – just her head and ears showing – bouncing as MartinLuther ran along the old subway tunnel.

I was right behind her – rifle at the ready and burdened with a pack full of ammo and over a dozen of the mysterious spears – scanning the hostile environment for an enemy I knew nothing about. It was a terrible place: water running down blackened walls, sludge and rotting trash lying where the rails used to be, cables hanging from ruined conduits and the constant skitter of rats scurrying away at our approach.

Somebody – the Resistance, I guessed – had strung naked bulbs every few hundred yards to help them negotiate the subterranean thoroughfare, and the scattered pools of sickly yellow light, instead of alleviating the sense of claustrophobia and despair, only added to it.

I was breathing hard from exertion, and the air was rank and undisturbed. We were running in groups of two or three, spread out in case of attack, everybody silent, weapons raised and cocked, eyes darting into alcoves and peering into the darkness of numerous side tunnels. As far as I could tell, Orcs could be waiting anywhere, so I kept my attention on Ella, trusting her senses more than any of ours. I just hoped she could still function despite the shattered leg. She was slumped with her head laid on one side, panting heavily. It wasn't reassuring.

'Shit.' The word was whispered, but it was loud enough to carry to MartinLuther and myself, and we both knew it was Tokyo, leading from the front. He had stopped in the middle of the tunnel and, moments later, when we arrived, we could see why: the tracks went down a slope before rising up a steep incline. The long dip was filled with at least ten feet of filthy water – a large pond being filled by a broken storm-water pipe.

The obvious solution was to swim across, but with the water containing God only knew what toxins, the heavy packs, our weapons and the two wounded, it was impossible. 'A shell must have hit the drainage pipes,' Tokyo said.

'Or they flooded the tunnel,' I said. 'Force us to take a different route and we walk into an ambush.'

Tokyo looked at me, considering. 'It's possible, but we have to get to Bergdorf's if they're gonna have a chance,' he said, indicating the wounded.

'Can we go back and take a surface route?' I asked.

'No,' he replied. 'At night every route is like 42nd Street.' He turned and called to a member of the platoon. 'Quaalude.'

A tall, gangling guy in his late twenties – bearded and laid-back with a crooked smile and missing one eye – pushed forward. 'Maps,' Tokyo ordered.

Quaalude pulled old paper maps – detailed diagrams from City Hall of the subway, sewage and maintenance tunnels – out of his backpack. 'Find us the shortest way round it,' Tokyo said. 'Cupcake.'

A totally ripped woman – khaki T-shirt, flak jacket, high-tops – called from the back. 'Yo, boss.'

'As soon as we get a route, sprint back to the Port Authority, go topside and contact my sister. I don't know where she is, but she's in midtown somewhere. Tell her what tunnel we're taking and ask her to access it. If there's an ambush, we'll need help.'

Cupcake nodded and pulled a battered walkie-talkie out of her pack to check the battery.

'You can't call from down here?' I asked.

'Too deep. There's no reception from tunnel to tunnel,' Tokyo replied.

'Got it,' Quaalude announced, spreading the map out on the floor, showing a route down a narrow side tunnel to Tokyo.

I looked down and saw a code number on the tunnel. 'What does XR-236 mean?'

'Sanitation,' Quaalude replied.

27

THE TUNNEL WAS DARK, HALF IN RUINS AND DIFFICULT TO NEGOTIATE, but none of that was as bad as the smell. We were only forty or fifty yards in, splashing through a shallow sludge that it was better not to think about, turning a bend, when it really hit us – a stench so rank and fetid that we were forced to stop and tie bandanas over our mouths and noses.

MartinLuther tried to laugh: 'You think it's bad. We have four hundred scent receptors in our nose. A German shepherd has two hundred *million*.'

'Will she still be able to pick up the Orcs?'

'Doubt it,' he said. 'She'll probably be overwhelmed. Who wouldn't be?'

'You think that's why they forced us down here?'

He shrugged. 'Maybe – they know how good the dogs are.'

'What do we do?'

'What can we? Like Tokyo said, there's no going back. We make it to Bergdorf's, or I guess we go over the handlebars.' He smiled. 'Welcome to the Suck, Mr Greenberg.'

Bandanas in place, we headed deeper into the underworld until the forward scout turned on a battery lantern and held it high so that the rest of us could see the path was partially blocked. In its pale light we saw a rusting train that had been abandoned on the tracks.

A faded marking on the front of the locomotive identified it as Work Diesel 52, and I realized it had been part of the subway's sanitation system; behind it were dozens of skips on flatbeds filled with hundreds of rotting black garbage bags, torn apart by the rats. Their contents were partly liquefied, unrecognizable thanks to the passage of the years, but the overwhelming stench remained.

Beyond the last flatbed I saw the tunnel widen out and several side routes branch off it, and I recalled from the map that we had to take one of them next. To get there we would have no choice but to split into two columns and, single file, make our way either side of the train, squeezed between it and the brick walls.

A chill crept up my spine; if I was going to ambush somebody, I thought, I would do it once we were trapped alongside the flatbeds. Under fire, we wouldn't be able to advance, and retreating in the narrow confines would be almost impossible. But if that was true, where was the enemy? I scanned the entirety of the tunnel and saw nothing.

The silence grew as our muffled feet crept through the sludge. A slight breeze entered the darkness, ruffling the torn plastic in the skips. Slowly, the platoon split into two as we reached Engine 52. The only sound was the drip of water—

I lifted my rifle and trained it on a deep alcove. I had a chill – a premonition – that something bad was about to come down and I stared deep into the darkness; there was nothing. I took another step—

My eye ran across MartinLuther's back. Ella was panting, obviously in pain. She lifted her head and looked at me pleadingly, and then her eyes sparked to life, she raised her nose and sniffed, curled her lip to growl—

'Down!' I shouted, suddenly realizing in a panicked epiphany where they were hiding. One heartbeat later, I fired at the shredded plastic garbage bags piled in the skips.

As the rest of the platoon threw themselves into the sludge or took cover next to the locomotive, I continued to fire short bursts across the first three flatbeds. All along the train, the black garbage bags were moving, being hurled aside—

Scores of hostiles emerged, firing automatics from the shoulder. I stared at them, my shock almost stopping me from continuing to pull the trigger. Somehow, I kept firing, barely comprehending what I was seeing: the warriors were pale, hairless, and the few who were shirtless revealed they had a ridge of thickened and hardened skin running down their spine. Their eyes, green, streaked with gold, were devoid of fear or emotion; they seemed human without humanity. 'Orcs,' I muttered, swallowing, my breath coming in short gasps—

'Yeah,' MartinLuther said. 'Is that what you called 'em? Some places it was Ridgebacks or other names. The same thing, though – fuckers.'

I kept firing. I hit the four closest to me – I knew I did – and while the impact sent them staggering backwards, wounding them, it didn't put them down. They didn't seem to feel pain or suffer damage in the way I expected – their pale skin appeared to act like a form of armour – and their unbridled aggression forced them to recover and keep advancing. On every level, I was terrified.

I barely heard the weapons beside me open up, hurling a cyclone of shells at the enemy and driving them back. Just as well they did – I had kept the trigger pulled, but in my confusion, without realizing it, I had run out of ammo. Crouching next to Martin – partly protected by the loco's massive steel body – I was slamming in a new clip when I saw him take careful aim through his scope.

A huge Orc with a ragged scar creasing one side of his skull was advancing fast, peppered with shot but still able to raise a grenade launcher. At that range, even though we were huddled down, we didn't have a chance—

I raised my head and opened fire – to little effect – confused about why Martin didn't shoot and help drive him back. 'Fire, goddamnit!' I yelled in frustration.

He ignored me and kept sighting, adjusting his aim, crouching lower, appearing to be trying to get the angle just right.

The Orc was only yards away, and I registered his eyes focus on mine. I was lowering my weapon when I saw Martin press a button on the side of his rifle.

The spear, triggered by an electronic pulse and propelled by an explosive charge in its shaft, blasted free of its bracket under the rifle. It flew like a harpoon, lightning fast, straight at the Orc.

The range was so short the hostile didn't have time to move. The wide-flanged arrowhead struck him just below his left earlobe in a sharp upward trajectory, driving through flesh and bone, severing a blood-vessel, sending a spray of arterial fluid in a fountain—

It must finally have hit a major nerve centre, because his arms flew to his throat, spinning him in a pirouette. He seemed to shrink as his legs collapsed beneath him and fell into the trash-pile.

'Hit!' yelled MartinLuther in angry triumph. A ragged cheer went up from other members of the platoon as he turned to me: 'Spear,' he ordered.

Continuing to fire my own weapon – short bursts at the garbage skips, barely aiming – I reached into my pack, grabbed a spear and tossed it to him.

'You're doing good – keep driving 'em back.' He assumed I knew what I was doing. 'We would have been dead if you hadn't yelled the warning. Cunning bastards, aren't they? Worse than drug dealers.' He laughed.

I swept the barrel of my rifle in short arcs and saw another sharply angled spear flash out of a rifle on the other side of the locomotive. An Orc charging out of a tall pile of garbage bags went down. 'Hit,' a voice I recognized as Tokyo's yelled out.

Another cheer erupted but, as I reloaded, I couldn't take my eyes off the skips; more and more Orcs were emerging. We didn't have a chance. There were too many—

MartinLuther had fitted another spear and was sighting through his scope, sinking lower on his haunches, adjusting the angle of the barrel.

Crouching to avoid the blasts of incoming fire, I glanced at my own weapon and saw a bracket under the barrel and the small button near the trigger just as MartinLuther fired. 'Hit,' he yelled a moment later.

Instantly I grabbed two spears out of the pack, threw one to him and slotted the other under my barrel. I lifted my head, saw red tracers fly past, sighted through the scope and locked on to a hugely muscled Orc. He was missing the fingers of one hand, firing a pump-action twelve-gauge with the other.

I held the crosshairs square on a point just below his left earlobe, took a guess at the angle, altered my crouch and pressed the button.

The spear exploded out of the bracket. A silver streak, it flew out of the cover of the loco, skimmed the top of several flatbeds and hit the Orc under his earlobe next to the jawbone. He dropped the shotgun, wheeled but – face half shattered, grotesque – didn't go down. Panting, he reached for his weapon and staggered on, coming closer, about to fire again when another spear hit him just under the other ear. His head jerked violently and he dropped the pump action. He was dead before he hit the ground.

'Hit!' MartinLuther yelled, ducking back under cover, reaching for a spear to reload. 'Sharper angle,' he said. 'You gotta hit at close to sixty-two degrees. The magic sixty-two! It's the only way through the armour, it's their vulnerability – the skin is thinner to allow movement of the head and the bone isn't strong enough to protect them. One thing fucking evolution really screwed up there, thank God—'

He reloaded, let a blast of gunfire pass, raised his head and lined up a female Orc. 'A bullet can do it, but we've learned – the size and spread of the spearhead is way more effective,' he said, settling on his knees, sighting carefully. 'The lower velocity helps – modern ammo is so powerful the bullet can go straight through. A big exit wound looks great, but you need something that smashes the motherboard. Only works at short range, unfortunately—'

He fired as several Orc bullets ricocheted off the locomotive. I ignored them, watching, focused and intent. The spear buried itself in the Orc's neck, her eyes immediately filled with blood, and I didn't need the red-speckled foam at her mouth to tell me she was a dead woman standing. In the moment before she crumpled, I tried to slow everything down: concentrating on the exact angle of entry of the spearhead, trying to commit it to memory.

The woman fell in a heap on the trash, and I grabbed another spear, loaded it and looked up. The Orcs were coming in a more organized wave now, clambering over their own dead in a dozen places. It reminded me of the accounts I had read of Russian convicts being hurled into the murderous line-of-contact during the First Ukraine War and using their dead comrades as stepping stones.

I fired again and watched the spear bury itself in the neck of a young warrior, naked from the waist up, his pale skin glistening with sweat. He staggered, went to his knees, and I thought I must have got the angle right. But no—

He managed to rise and reach for his rifle. He was like a virus – he wasn't alive, but he certainly wasn't dead either. As he levelled his weapon at me, I loaded another spear. With the first one still protruding from his neck, he looked through his sight as I took aim at the other side of his face. His finger reached for the trigger while I adjusted my stance and altered the angle of the spear, trying to judge the magic sixty-two. I pressed the button just as he fired—

I threw myself aside, landing beside the loco's steel wheels, avoiding his raking fire, and looked up. My second spear was flying straight and true. The Orc saw it and raised his hand to protect the vulnerable entry point. The spear hit, flying straight through his palm, pinning his hand to his jaw and continuing uninterrupted.

His eyes filled with blood, and I knew. 'Hit!' I yelled. The magic sixty-two – and I reached for another two spears. As I did so, I saw Tokyo, curious at my success, staring at me from the other side of the loco; it was no easy task to get the angle right – especially not for a scientist, even if he had grown up in Florida.

I had no time to think about it; as I tossed one of the spears to MartinLuther, I saw how many Orcs were still attacking and how few spears we had left. We were going to be overwhelmed. 'We have to withdraw,' I yelled at MartinLuther, slotting in another spear.

'We're dead if we do.'

'We're dead if we don't.'

'We stand or fall here.' He raised his head from cover and fired again—

'It's not the Suck,' I said grimly, starting to aim. 'It's Rorke's fucking Drift.'

'Hit!' he yelled, reaching for another spear. 'Who the fuck was Rorke?'

I aimed, pressed the button and waited a moment. 'Hit,' I called.

'A hundred and fifty British Redcoats faced four thousand Zulu warriors at a mission station on the Buffalo River.'

We both reloaded as the smoke in front of us was pierced by more flying arrows. 'What happened?' he asked.

'The battle went all night. By dawn the Redcoats had fired twenty thousand bullets and had only nine hundred left. The acts of bravery were legendary.'

Martin and I both shouted 'hit' together and reloaded. I saw that we only had four spears left. 'Eleven Victoria Crosses were awarded,' I said. 'It was the most ever won by a single regiment in one action. At 7 a.m. the Zulus gave up and withdrew—'

'So, what the fuck are you bitching about?' MartinLuther said. 'Shows it can be done.'

We both lifted our heads from the cover of the loco, more bullets ricocheted near me, and I fired. 'Hit!' I yelled, and waited for MartinLuther to do the same. He was silent and I turned—

He was slumped against the loco, thrown backwards, bleeding from a wound in his chest: a slug had penetrated his flak jacket and it was only by virtue of that partial protection he was still alive. Nevertheless, he still seemed to be badly wounded.

'Maybe you were right,' he said, trying to smile, breathing in gasps. 'We should have pulled back.'

I shook my head, wanting to dress the wound but unable to ignore the advancing Orcs.

'You've got . . . no chance alone,' he said. 'Go under the loco, get to the other column.'

'No way,' I said. 'I'll drag you.' I loaded another spear, took aim at the closest Orc, adjusted the angle, fired and watched his eyes fill with blood as he went down. I didn't bother yelling 'Hit!', there was no time. I turned back—

'You can't drag me,' Martin said. 'And I can't get there alone.' He was stricken with pain, trying to remove the flak jacket. 'They're gonna overrun us. Get out.'

I shook my head and reloaded. 'Just go!' he repeated, insistent. 'Do one thing . . . take Ella . . .? Make sure you love her, okay?'

The dog looked at me; I swear to God, she shook her head.

I started to raise myself to aim and fire, but a blast of incoming forced me back. The Orcs were getting closer. 'This isn't Rorke's-whatever,' Martin said. 'The Redcoats aren't gonna win. Not today.'

I ignored him, waiting for a pause in the wall of fire. 'Please – just take her. Go,' he said.

I was lifting my head again to shoot when Tokyo shouted from the other side of the train: 'Pull back. Withdraw—'

'You heard him!' Martin said. 'Get the fuck outta here.' He began to unshoulder the backpack holding Ella, ready to give it to me.

I pushed his hands aside and grabbed his arms to try and drag him when there was a deafening explosion, amplified in the confined space, rattling the walls and sending a wave of garbage flying through the air.

I poked my head out of cover and saw the two nearest Orcs, one missing a leg now, cartwheel out of the nearest skip, hit the wall with a deadly crunch and fall to the ground.

'Grenade?' I said to MartinLuther. 'Who's firing grenades?'

He didn't have time to reply – another explosion, and then another, and into a syncopation of sonic booms which took out the skips and their occupants.

'It's coming from behind the Orcs!' I yelled, looking out at the smoke and debris-filled cavern, the rapid explosions reducing visibility to a fraction.

Despite the pain, Martin laughed, triumphant. 'Grenades? It's her,' he said. 'Gotta be.'

'Who?' I said, turning to him.

'Tokyo's sister,' he replied. 'They're the only platoon with a grenade machine gun.'

The number of explosions diminished, and I looked again at the shattered flatbeds. Orcs were lying dead all over them, and then, illuminated by burning bags of garbage, emerging through drifting clouds of smoke, a woman in perhaps her early twenties walked towards us.

Dressed in camouflage pants, combat boots, a ripped T-shirt and with a bandolier of heavy ammunition strung across her chest, she was fair-haired and clear-eyed, the grime and sweat of combat almost obscuring her high cheekbones and a forehead bisected by a long scar that had creased her skull.

As she walked towards Tokyo, the rest of her platoon appeared, two of them carrying a battered MK47 Striker grenade machine gun and its ammo; it was little wonder the Orcs had been decimated: the Striker was deadly, capable of firing close on two hundred and fifty grenades a minute.

I turned away and crouched next to MartinLuther, about to expose the wound and start battlefield triage. I glanced up and saw the woman and Tokyo embrace.

'Thanks,' Tokyo said, holding her tightly. 'Another few minutes . . .' His voice trailed off. I realized how frightened he had been, and how young he was.

I turned back to Martin, grabbed his black T-shirt, ripped it from navel to neck and exposed a gaping hole in his chest. Several shattered ribs were clearly visible. If it had not have been for the flak jacket—

'We came as soon as Cupcake called,' I heard the woman say. 'How many of you down?'

'Four,' Tokyo said. 'None serious—'

'It's damn serious here!' I shouted. 'Medic, now!'

The medic grabbed his backpack and ran towards us. The woman turned her eyes on me. As we looked at one another, I had the strangest feeling, as if we knew each other.

28

THE MOMENT PASSED ALMOST IMMEDIATELY. AWARE THAT MartinLuther was wounded, Tokyo and the woman scrambled over the coupling between the loco and the first flatbed and crouched at my side—

'QuikClot!' I was yelling to the medic. He opened his backpack, pulled out a package and, to save time, threw it the length of the loco. It wasn't the greatest throw, but the woman managed to stretch and half jump to take the catch.

She ripped it open and – our hands working together – we started to clean and pack the wound. A foot away, Tokyo was bending over MartinLuther's legs, using a spearhead to cut open the big guy's jeans; I hadn't even noticed – he had also taken a bullet in the calf.

Tokyo tore a strip off the black T-shirt to use as a tourniquet and began expertly tightening it with the spear. His sister opened another pack of bandage and brushed my hands away. 'I think I'm more experienced at this than you,' she said, her tone allowing for no opposition.

It was delicate work, manoeuvring around shattered bone, and I was sure she was right; I wondered if she had trained as a doctor. 'It's not as bad as it looks,' she said to MartinLuther, ignoring his gasps for breath.

Deftly, she continued to stem the bleeding and dress the wound while – unnoticed – I watched her work: she was fearless, obviously accustomed to command and highly accomplished, a leader to her core.

Impressed, I dismissed her brusque manner and, when the medic arrived and took over, I smiled and handed her a flask of water. She looked directly at me. 'I heard we had a visitor,' she said.

I nodded and met her gaze.

'Cupcake said you came from an island in the Indian Ocean,' she continued. 'Palm trees, golden sand, mangoes?' She gestured to the garbage-filled flatbeds and the dead bodies. 'What do you think – good decision?'

She smiled and – once again – I had that sense of something like déjà vu; I realized what it was – she reminded me of somebody.

She passed the flask to her brother and held out her hand. 'My call sign's Dior.'

'Like the clothes?' I asked.

'Yeah,' she said, indicating her ripped T-shirt and bandolier. 'We call it combat chic. I'm working on a new AK-47 for the fall collection.'

'Danny Greenberg,' I said, shaking hands.

'Danny's a scientist,' Tokyo added. 'But I think there's more to him than that.'

'Really?' Dior asked.

'No,' I said, anxious to move on. 'Martin said you were siblings.'

'That's right,' she replied.

I looked from one to the other. 'Who's the oldest?'

'Me,' Dior answered.

'By ten minutes,' Tokyo countered.

'Twins?' I said, surprised. 'Not identical, of course.'

'Thank God!' they exclaimed together.

As I smiled, I saw – over their shoulder – the medic rise from MartinLuther's side and pull off his plastic gloves. Dior and Tokyo turned to look. 'The bullet's still in there,' the medic said. 'His ribs and the flak jacket stopped it. Another inch and it would have hit his heart. I'll organize a team to stretcher him to Bergdorf's—'

He started barking out orders, and MartinLuther – pale from loss of blood, his chest and leg heavily bandaged – raised his hand in quiet salute to me. 'Thanks, man,' he said.

I shrugged, but Dior and Tokyo stared at us. 'For what?' Dior said.

'I took the round,' MartinLuther explained, indicating his chest. 'I told him to leave, but he wouldn't.'

Dior and Tokyo were silent, reappraising me. MartinLuther tried to give me a smile. 'You should ask them,' he said, pointing at Tokyo and Dior.

'Ask 'em what?' I replied.

'About Maryland,' he said. 'They were born there.'

'We weren't,' Dior said, correcting him. 'We were born here in the city. It was our family that was from Maryland.'

'Whereabouts?' I asked.

They shrugged. 'Some suburb,' Dior replied. 'Mom fled on Devil's Night. A terrible journey, of course – she was pregnant and alone except for a teenage friend, but somehow she fought her way through. We weren't born yet, but she saved us.'

'Remarkable,' I said. 'Alone? Your father was killed—' I indicated several of the dead Orcs.

'Oh, no,' Tokyo said. 'Dad had died a short time earlier.'

'Lost at sea,' Dior added.

Suddenly I was barely able to breathe, like I had a hole in my chest. A woman from Maryland . . . pregnant with twins . . . a dead father taken by the ocean – the world was shifting on its axis. I tried to find solid ground, but my mind was a maelstrom of emotions and possibilities so I stood motionless, rooted in the future but lost in the past.

Time seemed to pass so slowly that the seconds felt like minutes. Thankfully, Dior and Tokyo had stepped away and were organizing both platoons to move out. I looked at their backs and was no less lost: even if it was true and the twins were the children I had only ever seen on an ultrasound, how could I explain when we were at the end of the world, on the run in a ruined subway in New York City, that I had come from the past? That a stranger, barely ten years older than themselves and fighting beside them, was the father they had never known?

I was trying to find a way forward, to ask a question that would not characterize me as unhinged, when I realized that the twins had finished their work and were staring at me.

'You look pale,' Dior said. 'You okay?'

'Just exhausted,' I replied. 'And thinking about people dying too young.' Then it hit me, the way forward, I mean. 'You said "lost at sea" – your father was a sailor?'

'Probably,' Tokyo said.

'You don't know for sure?' I asked.

'No,' Dior replied, laughing. 'You see, Mom always glamorized him. According to her, he was a spy; he was on a submarine that sank.'

Tokyo laughed with her, and I smiled wanly, doing my best to join in, but as I looked at my son and daughter and thought of what an incredible job Rebecca had done to save their lives and raise them, I was forced to turn away. The emotion was too much.

Unwilling to even try to speak, I bent down to Ella, made sure she was comfortable and got ready to hoist the pack on to my shoulders. It gave me enough time to find my voice and pose the next question, the one I barely had the courage to ask.

'And what about your mother? Is she dead too?'

29

'MOM?' TOKYO GRINNED. 'IF YOU KNEW HER, YOU WOULDN'T ASK. "Tough" is the word most people use. She's a few klicks away, at Bergdorf's, probably driving her team crazy, as usual.'

Alive? I took a breath. I'd got my answer, but I didn't say anything, I couldn't – I just busied myself with putting the pack holding Ella on my back, managing to buy some time to control the turmoil running through me.

I stared into the tunnel as if I was checking the way forward, but in reality registered nothing of my surroundings. After a long moment, and a little more composed, I turned back to the twins. 'Who or what is Bergdorf's?' I asked.

'An old department store on Fifth,' Dior explained. 'The basements are huge, safe too – they doubled as a nuclear fallout shelter a long time ago. Eventually they became our hospital, and Mom has run it for years.'

With Rebecca's experience in ER, of course she had. I remembered her coming home from MedStar – her whole body sagging from exhaustion – and dragging herself up to bed.

And who, I wondered, would be waiting for her there now? 'Did your mom remarry?' I asked the twins quietly.

'Skipper!' a voice shouted, his voice echoing across the tunnel walls, and neither Tokyo nor Dior heard me. It was the medic, pointing at four teams of stretcher bearers with the wounded already loaded. 'Let's get 'em to Bergdorf's. I'm ready.'

I was glad he was. I wasn't so sure whether myself – or the children and Rebecca, for that matter – were prepared for what was coming.

30

THE FIRST SHOCK HIT ME WITHIN MOMENTS OF ARRIVING IN Bergdorf Goodman's huge subterranean space.

Surprisingly, it had nothing to do with seeing Rebecca, although – as we jogged through the tunnels towards the basement hospital – I had spent the previous thirty minutes preparing myself for just that event.

In skirmish formation, we had left the stench of the sanitation train behind and – guided by Quaalude and his maps – made our way through a labyrinth of passageways and narrow access tunnels without encountering any more Orcs.

Ella, God bless her, didn't complain, even though the motion of my feet pounding on the uneven surface must have caused her frequent pain. The combination of carrying her, keeping my rifle at the ready and a heavy pack on my chest containing ammo, food and a dozen leftover spears meant that I was fighting for breath by the time we emerged into a broad, well-lit train tunnel.

With Dior, Tokyo and myself – purely because of Ella's nose – in the vanguard, we rounded a corner and came face to barrel with two Browning heavy machine guns, weapons so fearsome they were called 'Ma Deuce' by generations of soldiers. Heavily protected by concrete gun emplacements, I saw that they were remote controlled, overseen by a forest of cameras and sensors.

Tokyo stopped to give a facial recognition camera time to do its job. 'Only four tunnels access the basement,' he told me as we waited. 'They're all protected like this – the Orcs haven't been able to penetrate the place in twenty years.'

'And you can do it with just two Brownings?' I queried. 'I would have thought—'

'Wait,' he said, smiling.

With the facial recognition complete, a massive blast-proof iron door behind the machine guns slid open. Ahead, I saw that the tunnel had been deliberately narrowed with massive steel and concrete walls, forcing us – and any invaders – into single file. Gun slits were cut into the walls on either side and I figured, like a medieval fortress, there were ladders and walkways behind the walls to allow the defenders access to dozens of firing positions.

'It's a kill box,' Tokyo explained as we kept moving forward.

'Has it been used much?' I asked, looking at the rust-coloured walls, noticing flashes of movement behind the apertures as we passed; we might have been identified, but the basement occupants weren't taking any chances.

'In the early days, all the time,' Dior replied. 'If you look carefully, you'll see that's not rust on the walls.' I glanced at her – she was serious.

We stopped at yet another steel door, waited while it opened and then – finally – we entered the emergency room. It was little different to dozens of other such facilities that I had seen over the years – except for the giant photos of muscular young men in their underpants, the woman in Louboutin heels walking a Great Dane and three society ladies sharing Ladurée macarons. They were among dozens of out-size advertising posters that had been salvaged from the store, probably years before, and used to line the walls. Their purpose was presumably to make the area seem less grim; they certainly added a surreal quality to it.

Milling in front of the posters was a crowd of warriors and staff: the wounded from half a dozen different patrols had arrived by the other tunnels and were being hastily assessed by nurses and delivered to triage teams. Despite the artefacts of a different era lining the walls, it was still an ER and it was the same as it ever was: a scene of barely controlled chaos, fear and noise.

Tokyo halted the platoon just inside the sprawling area, called for assistance for our wounded, and I immediately scanned the faces of anyone who appeared to be in command, searching for Rebecca. I saw no sign of her, and moments later we were swamped by nurses and orderlies – all dressed in combat fatigues painted with a red cross.

As I unhooked my backpack, I glimpsed a female doctor guide MartinLuther on to a gurney and immediately begin removing his bandages. Two orderlies came to my side and lifted Ella on to a table. The moment they saw her leg they shouted: 'Surgery!'

I turned and continued to search for Rebecca. I glanced across to check on Martin and – literally – almost dropped my rifle; the doctor leaning over and examining him was Laleh.

She was in her early forties, a far cry from the girl who had saved my life in the Persian Gulf, a strong and purposeful woman with ripped arms, hair greying at the temples and worry lines etched deep into her forehead. Even so, she had retained the thing that had first caught my attention so many years before: she still had the gentlest eyes I had ever seen.

I gaped. I knew Rebecca – of course, she would never have willingly abandoned Laleh. Masked by the chaos, I continued to watch her – it was not where you start that counts, I told myself, or even where you finish. It's the length of the journey that matters.

I couldn't think of anyone who had travelled a longer road than Laleh. And now it looked as though she had fulfilled at least one of her dreams; she had become a doctor. Maybe not Board Certified, thanks to the extraordinary circumstances, but with Rebecca's guidance and her practical experience, a doctor nonetheless.

'*Insha'Allah*,' I was saying to myself ruefully – if God wills it – when a woman's hand touched the back of my head. I froze, thinking for a moment it might be Rebecca, but it was a nurse, parting my blood-matted hair. I had forgotten about my own wound, but I remembered soon enough once she started probing. 'That needs to be stitched,' she said finally. 'It's not serious. And we'll have a look at that shoulder of yours as well. You're gonna have to wait, okay?'

I nodded. She turned to treat another of the walking wounded and I took a hand-mirror off her equipment trolley and looked at myself. My hair was lank and clumped together, my forehead and the area under my eyes were caked with blood and the rest of my stubbled face was covered in dirt, sweat and grime.

'Not a pretty sight,' somebody said, and I looked across to see it was Dior, taking off her flak jacket and smiling in my direction.

'Don't worry,' I replied. 'I look much better when I've washed up.'

'That's what all the guys say,' Dior said to a round of laughter.

She walked towards me. 'This could take a while,' she continued, pointing at my forehead, 'you should take a seat,' and indicated a row of chairs against a wall.

'I'll ask Mom to come and see you when she gets a chance. You can ask her about Maryland.'

31

I WAS SITTING NEXT TO A MAN WHO WAS EVERYTHING I WASN'T – immaculately dressed, with a confident smile, a wealthy sophisticate, without doubt – when I saw her.

She had walked out of an operating theatre and was making her way through a knot of medical staff and wounded, barely visible at first, but heading straight towards me and the ad on the wall behind – the one that showed the sophisticated guy standing next to his Rimowa luggage and directing us to their boutique on the fourth floor.

As Rebecca finally broke free of the surrounding group, I had a long moment to look at her, plenty of time for my heart to threaten to stop and for my mind to spin into uncharted territory. They tell you that forewarned is forearmed, but not that day and not at that moment.

She was on the downslope of middle age and clearly the years and the stress of trying to stay alive had taken their toll. Her hair, streaked with grey, was cropped short, and her eyes had a sadness to them that I had never seen before, as if life itself was no longer to be celebrated but simply endured. It was the biggest change, that loss of spark and joy, and it alone made me indescribably sad. Her face – lined and pale with fatigue, its youthful glow long since gone – had filled out a little, and so had her body – and she walked with a slight twist in her hip, and I knew from experience that at some time in the past she had been badly wounded in her leg or thigh.

It was clear, watching her, that so much had been lost in the fire, but at the end of the day – and surely the world was at that stage now – it didn't matter; once, years ago, I had seen a woman across another crowded room, in New York too, and had fallen in love with her. In a world that had become almost unrecognizable, one thing hadn't changed: my heart may have been breaking, but I knew exactly who owned it.

She came closer, stopped in front of me and nodded in a professional way. 'My daughter suggested I talk to you. Sorry you had to wait, we're kinda busy.'

The voice hadn't changed. I was far from certain if I could trust my own, so I looked at the floor.

She turned to a medical trolley nearby, pulled on a pair of plastic gloves and started to part and separate my matted hair. She glanced down at the name-tag hanging around my neck. 'Mr Greenberg, is it?'

I nodded.

'This is going to need quite a bit of work,' she continued, tracing the long line of the wound with her fingers. 'You need some pain relief?'

I shook my head.

'It's gonna hurt, but I can stitch it under a local anaesthetic. Any allergies, Mr Greenberg? Problem with injections?' She laughed. 'Not pregnant, are you?'

She waited for an answer. 'I take it that's a no,' she said at last.

I nodded in agreement.

'Talkative soul, aren't you?'

I nodded at her, but then I realized and shook my head – no.

She considered me for a beat, then put her fingers under my chin and made me look up, staring at me in the eyes. 'Are you okay, Mr Greenberg?'

Again, I just nodded.

She sighed in surrender and pulled the trolley closer, picked up cotton swabs and a kidney dish and started to wash the grime and blood from my face to check for other wounds.

'My kids told me what you did in the tunnel,' she said. 'Not abandoning MartinLuther – that was a courageous thing. Thank you.' She had cleaned my forehead and most of my cheeks and was starting on the jaw when she stopped—

We held each other's gaze. 'I'm sorry,' she said after a pause, shaking her head. 'You remind me of someone.' She tried to laugh. 'You know you have a doppelgänger? You look exactly like my husband did when he was your age.'

I didn't reply, I just kept my gaze on her. 'I mean – my *late* husband,' she said, trying again to shake herself out of it. 'I know it's silly, it's been a long time, but I miss him very much. I probably see things that don't really exist.'

I saw that her lip was trembling. 'I have our two children – the ones you met – that's all I have left of him. My greatest regret is he never got to meet them.'

I smiled at her. 'Don't speak too soon. How are you, Becca?'

32

I HAD MY HANDS READY IN CASE SHE FELL. SHE DIDN'T, BUT SHE staggered and I caught hold of her wrists to steady her. Just the touch of her was electric.

She stared at me, uncomprehending, and it was her turn now not to speak. Who was I? How did I know her name? 'Ridley?' she said weakly.

I nodded and kept hold of her hands. And so we remained, statues on the edge of the known world, while all around us the chaos of the emergency room seemed to fade into silence.

For several heartbeats it was just the two of us, touching each other across a mysterious span of time, and then I saw her start to return to reality, I heard the sound in the room surge and she looked at me and shook her head in mute disbelief.

'The submarine didn't sink, Rebecca,' I said. 'It was lost, but it didn't sink. They were running an experiment – a highly secret test – of a stealth technology called cloaking.'

She nodded, but I don't think it had much to do with understanding. She just wanted me to keep talking while she recovered.

'Think of the Manhattan Project. This time, scientists were bending light to try to hide the boat, to make it invisible,' I continued. 'Instead, the boat jumped a track; that's the only way I can describe it – not in the ocean, a track in time. It surfaced here – twenty-four years later, a blink really, a flash in a Milky Way of two hundred billion stars, a particle of time in a universe that is – ultimately – completely mysterious.'

I looked at her. She barely moved, overwhelmed. 'When did you realize . . .' she said at last, '. . . it was me . . .' She was struggling. 'That I was here?'

'An hour ago, when the children started telling me about their background.'

She nodded but said nothing. Then it hit me; what I had just said. 'The children, Becca,' I told her. 'Our children. What a job you've done . . .'

'Thank you.' She was about to cry. 'Alone,' she said, barely audible. 'That was the worst part of it – bringing them up . . . so alone.'

I pulled her wrists gently, bringing her closer and putting my arms around her, trying to still the tears. 'Alone? Not married, Rebecca? A relationship?' I asked quietly.

'There were . . .' she said, '. . . never marriage . . . in this . . .' She swept her hand around, meaning the circumstances of the world. 'There had to be . . . there were men.' She tried to smile. 'A woman, too.'

I smiled back. For her, I was dead, the world was coming to an end, and I was certain that anybody would have grabbed whatever comfort they could find.

'But it was you. In my heart, always you,' she continued. She looked up at me and I leaned down and kissed her on the lips. She kissed me back and I was not sure if she was about to laugh or cry. I took a small step backwards, looked into her eyes again – to make sure it was real, I suppose – and then glanced over her shoulder.

Tokyo and Dior were standing on the perimeter of the knot of people, staring at us in astonishment. It was clear from their expressions that they had seen us kissing.

Rebecca must have felt my body tense because she untangled herself from my arms and turned to look.

She and the kids considered each other for a beat. 'Chloe and Ridley,' she said at last. 'I want you to meet your father.'

33

THE STUNNED SILENCE WAS ONLY BROKEN WHEN THE TWINS, REELING in disbelief, launched an avalanche of barely articulate questions. Rebecca shook her head – she wouldn't answer any of them.

'Not without Laleh,' she told them. 'As much as anyone, she needs to hear this.'

Chloe immediately turned and half ran into the chaos of the emergency room. Moments later – while Rebecca, Ridley and I waited in strained silence – she emerged from an area used to treat the most seriously wounded with Laleh hurrying at her side.

They were accompanied by a tall, handsome guy in his late thirties: olive skin, dark hair and a smile that, despite the grim circumstances, seemed to constantly play in the corner of his eyes. He was a doctor, too, and I was taken aback to realize, from their body language, that he was Laleh's romantic partner. I don't know why I should have been surprised; I suppose it was because the last time I had seen her she was in her teens, totally naive about men and the ways of the Western world.

'Chloe said it was urgent,' Laleh said, out of breath, addressing Rebecca but nodding a greeting to Ridley. It was clear from their easy familiarity that she and the twins had grown up together. 'What's happened?'

Before Rebecca could answer, she saw me, my face still only half cleaned of blood. She put out her hand. 'You must be the new arriv—'

Suddenly recognition dawned. She wheeled to look at Rebecca, who already had her hand out to take her by the arm. 'Yes, it was urgent,' Rebecca said. 'He's back.'

Laleh could only stare in bewilderment, and Laleh's partner – Jonathan Gee, according to the name-tag on his jacket – being new to the party, had no idea what was going on.

Thankfully, the chaos of the ER hadn't abated and nobody noticed that something extraordinary was happening. 'Now that we're all here,' Rebecca said quietly, everybody's face turned towards her, but she was addressing the twins. 'Twenty-four years ago, your father left on a mission that was so secret he refused to tell me anything about it. You remember, Laleh?'

Laleh nodded. 'It was a very bad time.'

'Yes,' Rebecca replied. 'We didn't part on good terms. Far from it – and I've thought about it for all these years.' She shrugged with resignation. 'Act in haste, regret at leisure, I suppose. Plenty of time; not a lot of leisure, though.'

I took her hand and squeezed it.

'The fact is,' she continued, 'it was your father's job and I never accepted it – not until it was years too late.' She smiled at our daughter. 'Yes, Chloe – he really was a spy.'

Chloe smiled back, but her eyes were filled with tears. 'The mission was on a submarine,' I said, partly in explanation, partly to fill in the silence. 'And that meant there was one unintended consequence – I was never exposed to the spore.'

'Praise be to Allah,' Laleh whispered.

'A few minutes ago,' Rebecca continued, 'he told me the sub was conducting an experiment that turned into a disaster – as a result, and stranger than anything, it made a jump in time. And then it surfaced – twenty-four years later. With just one survivor.' She shook her head in disbelief. 'And here we are.'

Nobody said anything – mentally reeling – until Laleh broke the silence. 'I prayed for you every night,' she said, her voice almost breaking. '"Call upon Me and I will respond to you,"' she went on, quoting the word of God in Sura 40 of the Noble Qur'an.

'"Hope for a miracle, but don't rely on it,"' Jon Gee countered, smiling. I realized it was a quote from the Talmud, the Torah or a Yiddish proverb – I couldn't remember which – and I suddenly understood that he was Jewish. He nodded at me in quiet confirmation and pointed at Laleh. 'They always said the Muslims and the Jews wouldn't reconcile until the end of the world.'

'I guess they got that part right,' I replied, grinning back.

'It's overwhelming, crazy, incredible, everything about it,' Rebecca said. She looked around at the crowded ER – people were already starting to look at us. 'Especially for me and the kids. We need to talk in private.'

She took my hand and led us to the door. As we stepped into the corridor, I looked at Jon – I was happy for Laleh, he seemed like a good man, but in the weeks that followed he turned out to be far more than that: he was one of the smartest people I had ever met.

I think even then, heading for what passed for Rebecca's home, he realized – unlike the rest of us – the huge opportunity that my arrival had presented.

34

I STEPPED THROUGH THE DOOR INTO THE FAMILY HOME AND stopped. It was a long way from a suburban street in Maryland, that was for sure—

A suite of rooms that had formerly been the staff cafeteria had now been refashioned and decorated with furniture and fittings pillaged from some of Fifth Avenue's finest stores. The central, industrial-style kitchen with stainless-steel bench tops and a huge cooking island was surrounded by B&B leather sofas, a pair of Lalique cabinets and several magnificent oriental carpets, all of which were lit by a chandelier. The only discordant note – apart from being deep underground and having no windows – was a Bradley Fighting Vehicle, twenty feet long and weighing thirty tons, standing near the cafeteria's old espresso bar, ready to defend the two corridors that provided the only access to the area. 'Bizarre' didn't start to do the place justice.

'What happened?' I asked as soon as Rebecca had closed the door. 'I heard about a spore.'

'It was wind-borne and fell to earth everywhere,' Rebecca replied, ushering us towards the sofas. 'It was one of the most amazing things people had ever seen – as if the sky was full of sparklers, tiny pinpoints of falling blue light. How could something so beautiful be dangerous? Who would have imagined disaster would come cloaked in magic?'

'That was Devil's Night?' I asked.

'That's what people called it later. They left their houses, stood in the street or on the prairie and breathed the damned thing in. Within an hour, often less, the spore hijacked its host's body – it co-opted their DNA and a new life-form, nursed by the old, emerged. Now they didn't need us any more, they could procreate themselves, but they had to compete, didn't they? For resources, for dominance, for life itself.' She shrugged.

'It's no different to what we did. For five thousand years Neanderthals and Homo sapiens co-existed on earth. Seen any Neanderthals lately? They didn't just disappear – they were wiped out, and the winners inherited the Earth. That was us – until now.'

She headed across the huge space towards a large steel door set in the wall next to a row of gas burners. 'The only survivors – the left-behinders, if you like – were the ones who didn't join the crowds. I had no choice – I had the house closed up, mourning you.'

'Rebecca saved my life,' Laleh said. 'I wanted to go outside, but she wouldn't let me.'

'MartinLuther was in police custody—' Rebecca continued.

'He told me,' I replied.

'Jon was working in the family's deli on Houston Street—'

Jon smiled. 'Best pastrami triple-decker in New York,' he said. 'I know it's true because Grandad put it on the awning the day he opened the doors.'

He turned to the espresso bar and started to make coffee. 'I was fourteen,' he said. 'Working next to the deep fryer when a new guy dropped a glass of water in it. The fat flew everywhere, including into my eyes. Dad didn't wait for an ambulance – he drove me straight to Presbyterian Hospital.

'That's where I was, eyes bandaged, when the spore fell. There was no point in going outside to look at it, of course, but Mom and Dad called. They told me they were in the street filming on their phones and they'd show it to me later.' He tried to smile. 'I never saw them again.'

He handed me an espresso and I took a sip. I looked at him. 'I never expected such good coffee during the Apocalypse.'

'Starbucks had a huge warehouse full of crates of beans up on 129th Street,' Chloe said. 'At the beginning somebody had the good sense to secure it before the rats got in.'

'But it's almost finished now,' Jon said. 'Like us.'

'How long?' I asked.

'Six months,' he replied. 'Maybe less.'

'And then?'

'We've all agreed – everybody makes their own decision.' He took Laleh's hand. 'We either end it ourselves or we convert.' It was clear what path they had chosen, and I turned and looked at the twins. Neither of them said a word and I felt my heart fall off a cliff.

'Ridley,' Rebecca called – then realized the confusion it might cause. She was speaking to me: 'I mean Kane – come and look at this.'

35

STANDING NEXT TO THE GAS BURNERS, SHE OPENED THE STEEL DOOR. As I walked towards it – accompanied by Laleh, Jon and the twins – I saw it was a huge cool room that had been decommissioned years ago.

Rebecca turned the lights on, illuminating walls lined with tall shelves holding hundreds of file boxes, a pair of armchairs standing in a corner, rugs on the floor and a group of desks arranged along a wall. Despite its antecedents, it felt welcoming. Maybe it was the maps on the walls and several wonderful paintings that must have come from the Metropolitan Museum of Art just up the road.

'God, I haven't been in here for years,' Chloe said. 'It used to be our schoolroom, and then, of a night, we'd lie on the floor and he'd show us movies. Remember, Mama?'

'Who did?' I asked, looking at a Monet hanging just above a single bed on one side.

'Radar was his call sign,' Rebecca said, rifling through several boxes and booting up a desktop computer. 'Older guy, probably in his fifties back then – he was an archivist at the Library of Congress who got trapped in an elevator on Devil's Night. Go figure, huh? Just after he arrived he said he thought it was important we kept some kind of record for future generations – the History of the Great Unravelling, he called it. That was in the days when we thought we had a chance of winning.'

'What happened to him?' I said as Rebecca activated a projector fixed to the ceiling.

'At the end of the fourteenth winter things were turning very bad and we needed everyone at the front. There was no talk of winning by then. He got pinned down in a building on the line of contact – twenty of them died when the Orcs shelled it and brought the whole thing down. His real name was Don Steele – I'll never forget him. This was his work—'

The lights dimmed, the projector came alive and video footage started to play on one of the walls. It was spectacular, shot on a clear night in DC, and it captured all the great landmarks: the Capitol, the White House and the reflecting pool where I had met with Falcon and my part in the epic journey had begun. The entire panorama was filled with what looked like falling stars; the tiny, glowing spore was falling to earth and I stared at it in wonder. 'How could anyone have resisted going into the street to look at that?' I said.

'Don always said it was an important part of the spore's design,' Rebecca replied. 'Who would have stepped outside if it looked frightening? No, our species has always been tempted by beauty. Well – men at least.' She laughed.

Footage of other cities across the globe started to play, followed by shots from a space telescope that showed the whole of our planet – floating in a universe of darkness – wreathed in the tiny wind-blown lights. 'Where did it come from?' I asked.

Rebecca indicated the maps hanging around the room. 'Nobody knows,' she said. 'There was talk at the beginning – and still is today – of Asian wet markets, a virus that jumped species, a mutation that emerged from eating bush-meat in Africa, a massive leak from a Russian bioweapons lab—'

'Or a random event from space,' Jon added from the darkness to my left. 'A spore carried in on a meteorite or a fragment of debris that fell to earth.'

'That was Don's theory,' Rebecca replied. 'He always said it came from off-earth. He thought the spore was deliberately engineered, a package of DNA – basically a code – that was safe inside its hard shell. He believed that somewhere, sometime, someone or something had broadcast it across the universe.

'He thought the distances were too great, the time too long for an individual to really journey through the universe. Nothing would survive. He said if you wanted to populate the endless darkness, you wouldn't send yourself, you'd send the genetic code.'

'Scatter it on the cosmic wind and let it land wherever it could,' Jon added. 'Don and I spoke about it often. It'd lie dormant inside its shell waiting until it encountered something or some place that would sustain life.'

But I was barely listening. I was staring at one of the dozens of maps and a group of images projected on the wall. 'Where's that?' I asked, pointing at a bleak and windswept landscape. 'On the left. Is that the Steppes?'

She adjusted the projector, pulled it into sharper focus and consulted some data on the computer screen. 'Kazakhstan,' she replied.

'What else have you got on it? Where in Kazakhstan?'

I saw Jon and the others react to the tension in my voice. Rebecca searched for more information and brought up more images on the wall. One stood out for me: it showed the rusting hulks of a group of ships marooned in the Aral Sea. 'Baikonur,' I said softly.

'That's right,' Rebecca responded, surprised.

'Why was Don interested in Baikonur Cosmodrome?' I asked.

'He was interested in hundreds of places. He was always looking for what he called Patient Zero,' she said. 'Trying to discover the root of it, the first person to be infected.'

'And what did he find?'

'Countless possibilities,' she said with a smile. 'Hundreds of 'em even in Baikonur.'

'Show them to me. The ones in Baikonur,' I said, my tone so serious it cast a pall across the room.

Rebecca looked at me – worried – and started searching through the boxes lining the walls. She found one marked 'Baikonur', opened it and – surrounded by files filled with paper notes – retrieved an external hard drive. She plugged it into the computer and the ceiling projector immediately displayed its contents. Thumbnail images of men and women began to appear on the wall.

I walked forward, staring at the faces of people that the long-dead archivist had identified as being infected at Baikonur. I went from one to the next, row by row. There was a myriad of them, vastly different, but nobody else in the room was paying any attention to them; they were looking at me.

I stopped and stared at the profile of one man in particular: it was decades old and badly lit, not completely in focus, and a trimmed beard obscured the jaw line. I looked at the text underneath it: 'Name unknown,' it said, but I kept staring at him.

Was I mistaken? Was it just a trick of the light or nothing more than a passing resemblance? I couldn't be sure. 'Him,' I said to Rebecca. 'Number 129. What else have you got on him?'

She looked through the paper files and glanced at a couple of them. 'Not much here, really,' she said. 'But I can show him to you.'

I stared at her. 'In life, you mean?'

'Sort of,' she replied, smiling, her manner making it clear that she wasn't going to be any more forthcoming. Instead, she headed for the door—

36

IT WAS ONE OF THOSE NIGHTS, THE SORT YOU KNOW YOU WILL NEVER forget: the flurries of snow had passed, and there was a sparkling clarity to Manhattan, a yellow moon was on the rise and the orange glow of a myriad fires was scattered across the city.

The skeletons of the ruined skyscrapers surrounded us and, far below, Central Park had long ago returned to the wild. I saw feral dogs and white-tailed deer heading towards the model boat pond for water.

We were on the roof of the half-destroyed Bergdorf Goodman building, looking across the top of the shattered facade of the Van Cleef & Arpels store next door, with the entirety of the city laid out below. Dozens of surveillance and attack drones were weaving above the streets, trying to avoid the shafts of light thrown by dozens of Resistance searchlights, and every few seconds red tracer and the bright glow of rockets ripped across the sky.

The six of us were crouched deep in shadow, my arm around Rebecca, waiting – apparently – to see the man I had identified. Now, she kept checking her watch. 'Four seconds. I'll say one thing – they're punctual. Look to the east, down 57th Street, past old Billionaire's Row.'

I did as I was told, and then it appeared, floating slowly, rounding the corner of a high-rise: the Goodyear Blimp. As it came closer, I saw that it had been refashioned; the iconic colour scheme and name had been removed and replaced by the black-and-red flag of the Orcs, but it was still the same huge, bulbous airship. Giant video screens on either side were playing images but, as it was flying straight at us, I could not see what they were.

'Another few seconds and you'll see him,' she said. 'It's going to swing to the south.' She had barely finished when the giant craft started its turn. 'It flies over the island every night, relaying news of our latest defeats,' she said bitterly. 'That's how we knew about Sydney and London. The man you asked about seems to be a sort of military leader – he tells us to surrender then shows us pictures of our dead and wounded.' Rebecca's face conveyed her distress better than any words.

'Why not shoot it down?' I asked, looking closer at the blimp.

'Why waste a rocket?' Ridley replied, and he was right.

The blimp completed its turn and now, broadside to us, I saw the man clearly. Large-framed, heavily muscled and dressed in combat fatigues, his face was pale – almost translucent – and he was completely bald. If he had ever had a beard, it was long gone, and the skin of his bare forearms – undoubtedly like the rest of his body – had been transformed into the armoured shield. In huge close-up, he looked more brutal than anything I had ever encountered. The decades had passed, every year may have exacted its own host of changes, and clearly he was unrecognizable to Laleh. Of course, she had been very young in Iran and, unlike me, she had not spent countless months studying photographs and footage of him. Nevertheless, I am not sure I would have leapt to the conclusion had it not been for his eyes. Even though they had changed colour, they were as cruel and intelligent and arresting as they had ever been. The tattoo wasn't visible, but I still would have known those eyes anywhere.

'That's him,' Rebecca said. 'Like I told you, he seems—' She stopped, and I guessed she had felt my body go rigid. She unhooked herself from my arm and looked at me. 'What?'

'I'm certain – that's him, that's Patient Zero.'

They all looked at me as the giant image on the side of the blimp loomed above us. 'How can you be so sure?' Jon asked.

'I know him,' I said. 'I know him inside out. On Don's list it said "name unknown", but that's not true now. He was raised in Siberia, joined the military and rose to the rank of colonel in the Spetsnaz. He is called Roman Kazinsky.' I turned and looked at Laleh—

She had turned pale at the sound of the name and started to tremble. She reached out to hold on to Jon.

'Shoot it down,' I said. 'Shoot it the fuck down.'

Do what? the faces of everyone except Laleh said. Nobody made a move—

'Shoot it down!' I ordered, like the officer I had once been. I didn't want that man, or even an image of him, anywhere near us.

'Listen to your father,' Rebecca said as Chloe and Ridley hesitated. They started to fit rocket-propelled grenades to their rifles while Rebecca stared at me for an explanation.

'I met him, I spent days as his prisoner,' I said – and that rocked them even more.

'Met him – where?' Rebecca asked on all their behalf.

'In Iran.'

'You went to meet someone. Isn't that right?' Rebecca said, remembering. 'A courier, but he'd been crucified. You killed some men, you said, you saved the life of his two girls—'

Chloe and Ridley had stopped loading their weapons and were staring at one another – a prisoner? A crucifixion in Iran? Men were killed? And this was their father?

'It was Kazinsky who ordered the crucifixion,' I said. 'He was military commander of a terrorist group called the Army of the Pure. After that I tracked him from the border with Afghanistan, up to a port near Tehran, across the Caspian Sea, into Azerbaijan and then on to Russia. He ended up at Baikonur Cosmodrome—'

'Tracked him – why?' Jon said. 'To kill him?'

'That was the idea – mine, at least.'

'What happened?' he asked.

'Baikonur was a ZATO – a sealed city. The agency decided to step back, to watch and wait.'

'You think he was working at a bio lab there?' Rebecca queried. 'Something like that, and he got infected? Don said the place had a dozen of them.'

'No – there was one area of Baikonur pioneering a different technology,' I replied. 'Years ago, the Cosmodrome had led the way into space and now they had started to mine minerals from asteroids. Huge amounts of ore were being brought back, and I'm sure Don got it right: the spore came from off-earth.'

'Surely the Russians had safeguards, protocols against accidents—' Jon said.

'Maybe they did – but for years Kazinsky had been driven by religion,' I responded. 'My guess is he figured he was chosen; it was God's will. Knowing him, he probably released it.'

The idea seemed to rob them of oxygen. They turned and looked at the huge, pale face of the Colonel looking down on us.

'Fire in the hole,' Ridley said quietly, and he and Chloe shot almost simultaneously. The two rocket-propelled grenades flew across the moonlit sky, trailing a thin line of flame.

They hit the image of Kazinsky square and exploded, ripping the blimp open in a dozen places and, while helium is not flammable, the grenades caused so much damage the huge airship collapsed in on itself, plunging down, heading towards what was left of the Museum of Modern Art. For a moment it looked like it would crash into the street, but instead – spinning as its engine caught fire and exploded – it veered towards the wrecked museum and impaled itself on a tall shard of steel and glass.

The six of us crouched in silence for a long moment, staring down at the smoking debris, each lost in our own thoughts. It was a reverie finally broken by Jon: 'You know, when Rebecca first told us how you got here, I thought of something,' he said, and paused. 'Why don't you go back?'

I turned to look at him – what?

'Use the submarine, try and jump the track again – go back,' he said.

Rebecca was nodding her head. 'I had the same thought. Go to Baikonur. Complete the mission.'

'I thought you never approved of my work,' I said.

'I do now,' she replied. 'Return and zero him.'

I stared at them all – were they out of their minds?

37

'DON'T YOU REALIZE?' I SAID, TRYING TO CONTAIN MYSELF. 'NOBODY could survive the journey.' We had returned to the living quarters and I was leaning on the back of a sofa, confronting the five of them. Surely they understood what the *Leviathan* had endured on the voyage out? One hundred and sixty-seven dead and a boat almost ripped from bow to stern was a pretty good indication, I thought.

Moments after hearing their suggestion on the roof I gave Rebecca and Jon a curt 'No', got to my feet and led the way to the wrecked fire stairs.

Now, Rebecca was meeting my gaze across the couch. 'You say nobody could survive the journey back,' Rebecca said. 'But nobody can survive this.' She pointed at the Bradley Fighting Vehicle but meant the wider world. 'There's little food, no gas and we're almost out of heating fuel. People are dying all the time – we're sinking fast. You heard Jon – six months at the most.'

'It's six months longer than I'd get on the boat. The whole crew died on the way here.'

'You didn't,' she said.

'I was lucky. I might not be, going back.'

'We don't know that.'

'I say we do, and I'm the only one who can judge, the one person here qualified in submarines. No, I won't risk it – I can't,' I said. I saw the conflict on Rebecca's face; no sooner had we been reunited than she was making the case that I should leave. Whatever her feelings, it didn't stop her—

'You're wrong,' she said. 'You don't get it, do you? You're our only chance.'

'I'm not,' I retorted. 'More than anything, war is dynamic. The Resistance isn't finished – fortunes change, the whole situation can pivot overnight.'

'Not this war, not this time,' Ridley muttered.

'Are you gonna listen?' I said to all of them, snapping. 'Hope is not a strategy. I'm not leaving. This is where I belong. With my family.'

'We're not your family,' Chloe replied calmly.

I looked at her, shocked, and learned something most parents discover sooner or later: nobody can hurt you quite as ferociously as your children.

'Of course, you're hurt,' Rebecca said. 'But Chloe's right.'

'Mom might be your family,' Chloe continued. 'To us you were a sperm donor. Ridley and I don't know you. We never have.'

'Think about it,' Rebecca said. 'Please. Apart from anything, you can be a father. To raise them, for us to be a family. Go back, kill him and give the world a chance—'

'And what – change the future?' I said sceptically. 'Is that what you're telling me? You honestly think that's possible?'

'You think you can jump a track in time?' Jon said. I looked at him, but I had no answer—

'Of course you can change it,' Rebecca replied, coming around the sofa and taking my hands in hers. 'There isn't one future – there are infinite futures. It's like the universe, forever unfolding – that's the wonder, the majesty of it. The future we get is decided by what we do now – moment by moment, step by step, life by life. Kill Kazinsky, prevent the spore from being released and give us a new future – a different one. It can't be any worse than this.'

I said nothing. In my mind, I was travelling through time again. I was in Paris watching Saloth Sar about to cross the road. Had he taken a longer stride for two steps he would have covered an extra inch, the car would have hit him at high speed and the future of two million Cambodians would have been far different. Maybe, Becca . . . just maybe . . .

'What are you thinking?' she asked.

'About a man from years ago,' I replied. 'It's nothing.'

She spoke softly, forcing the others to lean closer. 'I don't know where your role in it started, and perhaps you don't even know yourself.'

I thought back to a Friday in my office, about to go to lunch on a winter's day, when I opened a file and a strange silence fell across the world.

'But you told me once about heading into a canyon and hearing gunfire from the future.'

The others looked at me in confusion. Again, I was standing in the tree-line, the brutal summer sun of Iran dipping towards the horizon, Sakab at my side, the canyon ahead turning from pink to orange and listening to a sound I could identify but not explain—

'I know about the Persian Gulf,' Rebecca continued. 'And how the waves and the night and the Shamal should have killed you.'

I glanced at Laleh, the young girl who had saved my life, and my gaze was returned by the woman and the doctor she had become.

'You went on a mission on the world's most advanced warship, a secret submarine, and only you know how bad it really was – yet you were the sole survivor. Why? What is that about?' Rebecca asked.

I said nothing; I couldn't. There was no rhyme or reason to what had happened on board; better men and women than me had died terrible deaths. But for a handful of pills, Baxter would have lived. I didn't know why I had survived.

'Do you still hear the wolves?' she asked. 'Are they still calling to you?'

For some reason, I felt an overwhelming emotion rising up in me, felt the wheels of fate grinding—

'There are people who say that omens are the language of God,' Rebecca said. 'What do you think?'

'The wolves?' Chloe asked. 'What wolves?' Rebecca and I didn't explain. How could we?

'I still hear them,' I said softly.

'I think you were kept alive for a purpose,' Rebecca continued. 'You've always been a lonely man, a solo voyager, someone willing to go where – as they say – the angels fear to tread. Why do you think you speak Russian?' She didn't wait for a reply. 'Because you were born for this.' She pressed my hands tighter. 'Some day people might say the story of the spore was written a long time ago. But so was yours, Ridley. This is your mission. It always was. Go back.'

I sat for a long time, nobody saying a word. I understood everything that Rebecca had said, but I also knew that even if fate was knocking, it didn't mean you had to answer. My mind roamed across a landscape of memory and I thought of Baxter lying in the pod with the photo of his wife, I recalled my mother in the cancer ward and the last words of my dad as he lay on the burning asphalt, but – more than any of it – I thought of being trapped in a submarine that I believed was doomed and thinking only of Becca and our unborn children. I suppose I was thinking about love – how difficult it was to find, how hard to live without.

I don't know how long I would have sat there had it not been for Jon. 'The sub's computers will have been programmed and logged the outward journey,' he said quietly. 'You can retrace the voyage.' He sighed. 'It might not be much but it will give you a chance. There are people here who know about this stuff.'

'I'd thought of that,' I said. 'But it's not the computers, it's the boat. What good will I be to anybody if I'm dead?' I looked at Rebecca. 'You're everything in my life, you have been for years. I may not be family to the kids, but they certainly are to me. It's like you told me once – there's a reason why DNA is built like a chain. This is where I belong, with the people I love, this is where I stay.'

I must have said it with a tone of finality, because nobody argued. Rebecca turned to Laleh and Jon. 'I think it's done,' she said quietly, indicating the door and the emergency room beyond it. 'We need to get back to work.'

Ridley and Chloe didn't bother trying to hide their anger. 'Sis and I will take the midnight patrols,' Ridley said to his mom. 'We'll see you in the morning.'

38

THE OTHERS HAD LEFT SO, ALONE, I GOT TO MY FEET, SLUNG A BATTLE rifle and half a dozen spears over my shoulder, returned to the fire stairs and climbed four storeys up to the deserted ground floor.

I scrambled over shattered display cases and dust-covered computer terminals and saw what I was looking for: what had once been one of the most valuable shop windows in the world. I squeezed past the heavy steel plates, anti-assault 'hedgehogs' and coils of razor wire that were defending it and stepped through broken glass straight on to Fifth Avenue.

The Orcs may have been a threat, but I needed to think. I needed to be certain of the decision. Alert for danger, I scanned the street. The sight made me pause: the grand avenue was a vision with the moon shining down, the snow hiding piles of debris and a pair of owls perched on a streetlight. It looked like some alien Christmas card. Silent night, holy night.

After a long moment, I turned and – recalling everything that had been said in the apartment – hunched my shoulders against the bitter wind and started to make my way uptown. Keeping tight to the shadows, I walked quickly through the crumbling foyers of once magnificent buildings, hoping that any surveillance drone would mistake a single moving body for one of the numerous foxes and dogs roaming the streets.

As I traversed the shattered glass cube of the Apple store and crossed the grand lobby of the Sherry-Netherland Hotel I told myself that I was a Denied Access Area spy and I knew more about assessing the likely success or failure of a mission – no matter how extraordinary it might be – than probably anybody still alive.

I stepped back on to the avenue, and started to think about my past and the one thread that ran through the tapestry of my professional life; I had experienced a lot of fear. First, on a freighter crossing the Andaman Sea, then in Syria and Turkey. Russia three times. Iraq and Afghanistan, Iran, Egypt and Pakistan – the list went on and on. On at least five occasions I had been almost paralysed when the fear threatened to overtake me, but my courage had never failed. Yes, I had decided against trying to go home, but nobody could say it was because I was afraid. I wasn't a coward.

Walking a little easier, starting to find some peace of mind, I looked across the rubble-strewn road to what was now the jungle of Central Park and I couldn't help wondering if the leopards, grizzly bears, apes and other animals in its zoo had escaped and turned the eight hundred acres into an unorthodox hunting ground. I didn't want to find out so, instead of taking one of the thoroughfares through the park, I unslung my rifle and stuck to my side of the road. What a world, I thought – worried about being attacked by wild animals in the middle of New York City. Then again, maybe things hadn't changed that much.

I picked up the pace and – as difficult as it was – had to admit that Chloe was right: I had no relationship with my children. I had not been in their lives and they had grown to adulthood without me. Now, for whatever time we had left, I somehow had to find a way to bridge the gulf between us. What was the alternative? To fight, and probably die together as strangers.

The towering facade of the Metropolitan Museum of Art looming ahead in the moonlight was half obscured by trees, its two 'tabletop' fountains at the entrance filled to overflowing with debris and fetid water. Perhaps more than any other building in the world, thanks to both its architecture and its contents – ranging from ancient Egyptian artefacts to three thousand European Old Masters – it had stood as a testament to the civilization humankind had built. Now in ruins, the building was a statement – both symbolic and literal – of what had become of us. It was worth a last look, I thought.

Crossing the road and out of the shelter of the buildings, the wind hit me. I glanced down the avenue, back the way I had come. And stopped dead in my tracks.

39

THERE WAS SOMETHING ABOUT THE WAY THE LIGHT WAS FALLING . . .
the arrangement of several ruined skyscrapers . . . the wind whipping
up dust in the street: I had seen it all before.

Heart starting to race, I recalled the early hours of a morning in
Maryland when a wedge of wild geese came in to land and I described
to Rebecca the ruins I had foreseen, the vision of her imminent death
and a large sign on a wrecked building with half its letters missing.
Be . . . Good . . . it said.

Standing on Fifth Avenue, looking downtown, I saw the half-
destroyed Bergdorf Goodman building and the wrecked name on its
side. All that remained of it were the letters—

I forgot about wild animals and attack drones and started to run.
Death was in the house—

40

SPRINTING DOWN THE AVENUE, I EXPECTED RANKS OF ORCS TO
have overwhelmed the Resistance's boats and patrols and to now
be swarming on the surrounding streets approaching Bergdorf's.
There was nobody, though, and only then did I realize: they had to be
underground.

A coincidence of circumstance confirmed my assumption: the wind
had dropped, the moon reappeared from behind a shattered skyscraper and I was scrambling over a mound of rubble. The increase
in height, the flood of light and the unexpected stillness of the wind
allowed me to see a thin column of dust rising vertically from a ventilation shaft next door to Bergdorf's. They were tunnelling deep
inside the Van Cleef & Arpels building.

Scrambling through the hedgehogs and razor wire protecting the
window on to Fifth Avenue, I reached the fire stairs and immediately

started yelling down to the emergency room. 'Out! Get out!' By the time I burst into the area, nobody had moved; Rebecca, Jon, Laleh and the kids, about to set out on the midnight patrols, were staring at me, along with everybody else, confused.

'They're coming,' I said, just managing to speak between breaths. 'They're tunnelling . . . in the adjoining basement . . . they're gonna come through the fucking wall,' I gasped.

Everyone looked around in fear. 'What wall – where?' Chloe called. 'How?'

I had no time to explain or argue. I made my way through them, pushing aside medical trolleys, scrambling past gurneys with the injured still on board. 'Which way is the jewellery store – Van Cleef and whatever?' I yelled.

For a beat nobody answered. 'The wall in front of you,' Rebecca said, pointing at the longest wall – a hundred feet of masonry decorated with the old posters. At least she wasn't dismissing the idea.

I ran to one end of the wall, trying to work methodically, and threw aside a tall cabinet and stuck my ear against the concrete, hoping I could hear the sound of movement or tunnelling.

I had barely taken a step when a thought occurred to me: they might not be digging at all. If they had managed to tunnel into the adjoining basement, why not rig a common wall with explosives and blast their way in?

Trying to concentrate, I moved along the masonry and put my cheek against an ad for 'Men's Underwear, Fourth Floor'. I moved past a model's immaculate thighs, straining to hear.

I saw Chloe – along with everyone else – staring. 'Move 'em out,' I ordered. 'Everybody. They'll slaughter us in here. Save 'em!'

Rebecca paused for a second, considering it, then turned to Laleh and the rest of her staff. 'You heard him – out now! Take everyone through the dispensary, the badly wounded up to the second floor. Jon – call in the patrols, tell 'em we're under attack. Go!'

Her reputation and authority were such that the huge space exploded into activity: nurses and orderlies dropped what they were doing and wheeled gurneys with patients towards a narrow doorway, the walking wounded limped as fast as they could on their crutches, staff piled medicine and equipment on to trolleys and the men and women capable of fighting threw open cabinets, grabbing rifles and spears.

I barely noticed it; I was moving along the wall, still listening for anything that might indicate a point of attack. I saw Ridley moving towards the other end of the long wall. 'I'll start from this end,' he called. 'We'll meet in the middle.'

It was a form of reconciliation, at least. 'Thanks, but no,' I yelled. 'The Bradley – get the Bradley. If they come through—'

'Yeah – I've got it,' he said, and turned, sprinting for the apartment, swerving past MartinLuther; he was hobbling, his chest strapped with bandages and a bag of IV solution over his shoulder feeding a tube in his arm. He was lifting Ella – her hind end heavily dressed and with only three legs now – off a post-surgery bed and putting her in a wheelchair; there was no way he was leaving her behind.

Seeing Ridley leave, he yelled to me across the room. 'I'll take the other end.' I nodded my thanks and watched as he wheeled Ella towards the wall, moved tight against it to listen and started working his way towards me.

I passed another four of the large glossy posters, heard nothing, and was starting to question whether I was wrong about the Orcs when MartinLuther whistled loudly to attract my attention above the din of the evacuation. 'What do you make of this?' he called.

I ran to his side, put my ear close and listened. I heard nothing. 'Quiet,' MartinLuther yelled to the room at large.

Something close to silence fell, I concentrated hard and thought I picked up something. 'You hear drilling?' I asked tentatively.

'Maybe,' he replied. 'It's what I thought.' We moved along the wall, trying to see if we could hear it more clearly. Martin was still using the wheelchair for support, pushing it along with us when Ella – lying completely still and panting after the operation – suddenly tried to stand. Martin and I stared at her. Unable to get up, she looked at the wall and started to snarl. 'There's no way she can smell through the concrete,' I said.

'No, but she can hear,' Martin replied, fear suddenly constricting his voice. He put his face to the masonry. 'They're there,' he said. 'I can just hear 'em. Four feet away.'

'Detonators?' I said.

'Yeah, punching 'em into the wall.'

I spun to face the room. 'Run – now!' I yelled. Instantly, the scores of people who hadn't yet evacuated surged towards the narrow doorway.

Chloe realized the door was going to be a deadly choke point:

'Gurneys first!' she yelled, wading in, moving people aside, clearing a path—

I looked across and saw Rebecca hauling a badly wounded warrior off a surgical bed and into a wheelchair; she was ignoring his cries, desperate to get him to safety. 'Get out!' I yelled to her. 'Leave him! They're gonna blow the—'

She heard me – she looked up – and disappeared instantly, lost in a deafening blast of dust and debris as a whole section of masonry exploded inwards.

A middle-aged orderly with a warrior tattoo on his forearm died from one breath to the next as a chunk of concrete hit his chest and blew it apart. I saw Quaalude – the one-eyed guy with the maps – fly across the room, hit a portable X-ray machine head-first and fall in a heap. I watched Rebecca's patient and the wheelchair somersault through the air—

Then the blast hit me and I was hurled backwards into a steel drug cabinet – the impact making it topple and fall on top of me, inadvertently protecting me from the secondary – and more deadly – wave of heavier debris.

The onslaught of concrete, bricks and copper water-pipes swept the room like a scythe. I heard the initial screams and then the sound common to every battle: people crying in pain or pleading for help. I threw the drug cabinet off me, but I couldn't see anything, let alone Rebecca.

The room was clouded with cement dust and the choking fumes from the explosives. Visibility was down to less than a foot. I scrambled to my feet and stumbled into the gloom to make my way to where I had last seen Rebecca. Somewhere nearby, Ella was whimpering, and then I heard MartinLuther try to calm her. At least they were alive. Now, dear God, one more miracle—

The rubble and the mangled wreckage of gurneys and trolleys made it difficult to stay on my feet, but I managed to grope and fall and half crawl my way forward. I had only gone a few feet when the dust started to clear. It was a bad development—

The Orcs had started running massive exhaust fans to expose the combat area to undertake their grisly work. I had a choice to make, one that was really no choice at all: to plunge onward and try to find Rebecca or arm myself and help repel the imminent onslaught.

I would be of no use to Rebecca if we were all dead. I scanned the wreck and ruins around me. There was a rack of weapons that had escaped the blast and I hurled myself towards them. I saw MartinLuther through the settling dust and grabbed a rifle and a quiver of spears.

I yelled and he turned. I threw the clutch of weapons to him. He had barely caught them before more men and women – rising from the rubble, white with masonry dust, looking like ghosts – started hollering for rifles and spears.

As I tossed them across the space, Chloe sprinted back into the room from the doorway and scooped up a rifle. 'Here they come—' MartinLuther called.

I turned and saw ranks of Orcs – huge, spectral figures in the gloom, wreathed in firelight and dust – emerge from where they had been sheltering from the blast. They started to advance across the Van Cleef & Arpels basement. 'Pair up!' I heard Chloe call. 'Number One take the spear, Number Two hold 'em back with auto fire. Wait for my order—'

I glimpsed more defenders – orderlies, the walking wounded, doctors – scrambling into the space from the dispensary, grabbing weapons and taking cover. The wounded, crying out, were all around us, but nobody had a chance to help them.

And then, there he was; older, incredibly powerful, heavily scarred and all the more terrifying for it. He was coming up the flank, about to lead from the front.

Kazinsky.

41

HE KEPT ADVANCING AND I REALIZED: HE WAS WITHIN RANGE AND there was nowhere for him to go. I lined him up through the rifle's scope, taking it steady, aiming just below his left ear, regulating my breathing and making sure that the spear would hit at the magic sixty-two. Whatever emotion I felt about him now that I was in his presence again, I put it aside and concentrated only on making the shot.

He scrambled over several wrecked crates and was partly obscured by the ruins of two concrete support columns torn apart in the blast. It was clear from the way he was yelling orders that the assault wasn't going to plan – he must have been counting on the element of surprise and for the explosion to have caused greater casualties, and now, without either, he was having to develop a new strategy.

Taking cover behind an upended gurney, I waited for him to step clear of the columns. My fatigues, thick with plaster dust, provided accidental camouflage, as good as any sniper could hope for. As I kept my eye fixed on the scope, I thought of the long road we had both travelled to a ruined basement on Fifth Avenue; one more minute, probably less, and his journey was over—

As he moved out from behind the pillars, he stopped to bark an order and his troops on either flank broke cover and stormed forward in a pincer movement. I loosened my shoulders, touched the button with my index finger and made one last check on the angle. He was done.

'Fire!' Chloe yelled – and all hell broke loose. A blizzard of spears and automatic gunfire from several dozen angles, let loose by the warriors and medical staff dug in behind the wreckage, hit the Orcs. God bless my daughter, but—

The enemy threw themselves to the ground. I was too far gone, I couldn't abort; the spear exploded out of the bracket, and I saw it flash through the dust at a perfect angle. There was only one problem: Kazinsky – diving for cover, too – was in mid-air.

The spear ripped open his cheek, but it passed him by without further injury and hit a female hostile behind him square in the forehead, knocking her off her feet.

Kazinsky, blood running down his face, scrambled to his feet and looked around in shock. At that range, under those conditions – what? They had a marksman? I grabbed another spear and started to reload. My hand was shaking, I knew what was coming—

I had barely slotted the spear into the bracket and was unable to get a clear line on Kazinsky when it started. I heard him yell the order in Russian and English and his troops rose up and stormed forward, firing from the hip or shoulder, using the crates and piles of debris as cover, their laser sights splitting the gloom and smoke, being hit time and time again, but relying on sheer weight of numbers to keep advancing. I saw several of them load rocket-propelled grenades and then men and women with large canisters on their backs and nozzles in their hands rush into the front rank.

What was it about flame-throwers that made them far more

terrifying than gunfire or grenades, even to battle-hardened troops? I
felt it as much as anyone and I heard cries of alarm ring through our
ranks. They were going to burn us out.

I fired, took a big man down, and had time to think as I reloaded
about what the next two minutes would bring. We were done – their
numbers were too great, the RPGs too deadly and the flame-throwers
too terrifying.

I looked up from my weapon and – through the smoke and the hail
of incoming – caught Chloe's eye. I motioned with my head towards
the door. She knew exactly what I meant: we had to retreat. Dropping
one empty ammo clip and slotting in a fresh one, she yelled: 'You,
Martin and the others first. We'll cover you—'

'No,' I called back above the half-deafening rattle of gunfire. 'You
go first. We'll keep 'em at bay.'

I didn't tell her, but I wouldn't be withdrawing with MartinLuther
or anybody else – not until I found Rebecca. I turned across to him to
explain about the covering fire, but he and the twenty men and
women on their bellies near him had all heard and were passing the
word along, reloading and changing position to initiate our own hail
of gunfire.

I had to pick my moment. A second later I saw my opportunity:
Chloe was about to move and Martin was making sure his makeshift
company was keeping Kazinsky and his men locked down.

I was on my feet, doubled over at the crouch, weaving through no-
man's land and then throwing myself forward into some rubble, losing
my rifle in the process and ending up flat on my stomach. The wreckage of the wheelchair had ended up on top of a shattered cabinet. At
least it gave me somewhere to aim for. Rebecca had to be near it.

From face down in the dirt, bullets were kicking up plumes of dust
and the smell of gasoline vapour was thick in the air as the flame-
throwers were primed.

I drew up my legs and waited for the covering fire from Martin to
reach a relentless roar. But Chloe and her troops had barely moved –
unable to retreat without being cut to pieces.

Light was filtering into the battlefield. I spun and saw two spotlights approaching from deep inside the corridor that led to Rebecca's
apartment: the thirty tons of heavily armoured Bradley Fighting
Vehicle with its 25mm Bushmaster chain gun – able to fire three
hundred rounds a minute, accurate at up to two miles, let alone a

hundred feet – and two four-barrelled grenade launchers was finally on its way.

I turned to Chloe, about to yell at her to halt the retreat when, in the light cast by the Bradley, I saw Rebecca. Half covered in dust, blood running from a deep gash in her cheek, she was emerging from a jumble of wrecked gurneys and trolleys, bending low to avoid the incoming, one leg clearly injured, but trying to drag the guy from the wheelchair to safety.

'Down, down!' I yelled, elated that she was alive. She looked up, saw me but didn't understand why I was telling her to drop – from her angle, she couldn't see the Bradley. But Kazinsky could. I spun round to see him staring down the corridor at the approaching lights. More than anyone – having seen the vehicle on battlefields from Iraq to Syria – he would have known what damage a chain gun could do. He yelled at his bugler, a kid of about fourteen, to sound the retreat.

As the piercing notes rang out, Kazinsky raised his assault rifle and, in an act of fury and defiance, unloaded the entire clip at MartinLuther and his comrades. Still not satisfied, firing from behind one of the pillars, he pulled out the empty clip – and saw Rebecca rise from her crouch, attempting to get more purchase to keep dragging the wounded guy.

Kazinsky slammed in a new clip and took a moment to take aim. I screamed at Rebecca, but she couldn't hear above the cacophony of noise. She struggled on—

I knew Kazinsky couldn't miss, not with his experience and at that range. I reached for my rifle to pin him down but, of course, I didn't have it. Instead, in desperation, I rose to my feet, about to try and sprint to her. Kazinsky pulled the trigger—

Nothing happened. The gun had either jammed, overheated or the ammo was stovepiping. I didn't care, it was my chance—

I launched myself forward. If I ran hard, I figured I could reach her and throw her to the ground before Kazinsky had cleared the jam.

Hurling myself forward, I looked to the side and saw the Bradley smashing into the ER, Ridley in the turret, scanning the battlefield from behind a transparent bulletproof plastic shield, as its tracks crushed the debris and rode over wrecked gurneys.

I could have cheered. The Bradley would open up on the enemy before Kazinsky could get a chance to clear the weapon—

Except Kazinsky didn't bother trying. He cast the rifle aside and – lacking a side-arm – pulled an MPL-50 out of a loop on his flak jacket.

Invented over a hundred and fifty years ago, it looked like nothing of consequence – unless you had seen one used in battle. It was an entrenching tool, a small spade with a wooden handle primarily used to dig foxholes, but, like the Swiss Army knife, it had a multitude of other purposes: a frying pan, a hammer, an oar for paddling a boat, a saw and – with its knife-like edges of hardened steel – it had replaced the bayonet as a deadly weapon for hand-to-hand combat.

Spetsnaz troops underwent advanced training with it, and it also had one other lesser known but darker purpose – it was perfectly balanced and could be used as a throwing axe.

Rebecca couldn't hear anything over the roar of the Bradley's massive engine. The Orcs saw it, though, and started to pull back. MartinLuther and the other defenders cheered the vehicle's arrival, laying down another screen of bullets at the retreating enemy. It was a symphony of movement and noise—

In the middle of the orchestra Kazinsky raised his arm, drawing the MPL-50 back above his shoulder—

I scrambled over rubble and wreckage, running faster.

Rebecca saw the Bradley and – relieved at its arrival and determined to get her comrade to safety – stood a little higher.

Abandoning any thought of retreat, Chloe caught sight of her mother through the clouds of dust. Her smile of recognition turned to horror as she saw Kazinsky with the MPL-50—

Ridley – concentrating on the enemy – opened fire at them with the chain gun; deafening and brutal, it cut through concrete, rubble and flesh.

Kazinsky's arm reached the top of its arc. A fire had erupted behind him and for a moment the MPL was backlit by the flame—

He let it fly.

I watched helplessly as it cartwheeled through the air, flying end over end, travelling unerringly through the dust and smoke. I tried to keep running, but my feet were like lead.

Ridley glimpsed Rebecca out of the corner of his eye, saw the axe and stopped firing momentarily to shout a warning.

Rebecca heard him, looked up and turned—

I watched the weapon fly closer, cutting through the air.

And finally Rebecca saw it too. She tried to throw herself aside, but it was too late. She just had time to scream as the axe caught her above the collarbone and buried itself deep in her neck.

There must have been a huge arc of arterial blood, but I don't recall seeing it. Rebecca fell, dislodging the axe, and lay crumpled in the rubble. I kept running, but I already knew what I would find – I had felt the light go out in my heart.

42

REACHING HER FIRST, I LIFTED HER INTO MY ARMS, FELT HER BLOOD run down my neck. I saw a flicker of recognition in her eyes. We looked at each other for one terrible, brief moment, she squeezed my hand—

Then her eyes glazed and she was gone.

People will tell you that looking at each other one last time in the face of death is some sort of consolation. Let me disabuse them of that notion – it isn't.

Somewhere behind me the bugler stopped, the chain gun – which had started firing again under somebody else's command – fell silent and the rattle of the automatics died. The hostiles had withdrawn; the Resistance had won a victory that felt like no victory at all.

Chloe was at my side, hugging her mother and me. I held her tight, and a pair of hands fell on my shoulder – I looked up, saw it was Ridley and he lowered his cheek on to my head. I felt his tears run down my face. At last, the four of us were a family united – united in grief.

Chloe raised her tear-streaked face to mine. 'You loved her with all your heart, she always told us that,' she managed to get out through the sobs.

'If love had been enough to keep her alive, she would have lived for ever,' I said.

A few feet away, Laleh and Jon had joined the circle of anguish. Laleh had her head bowed, praying, I am certain. Behind her, scores of Resistance warriors were standing in silent sorrow and respect for the woman who had saved so many lives.

I looked at Jon; he was ashen-faced. 'How many?' I asked.

'How many what?' he replied, confused.

'Submariners. How many here in New York?'

'I don't know,' he replied. 'Seventeen subs arrived in the first few years. What's that – two and a half thousand crew members? A lot of 'em have been killed, of course. Maybe five or six hundred left. Enough for a crew.'

'I don't need a crew,' I replied. 'I want people who have served on Virginia-class boats – men and women who know every last detail. I want engineers, nuclear power graduates, master welders and computer experts. I need the *Leviathan* seaworthy.'

The kids, Laleh and Jon all looked at me. Chloe squeezed my hand so tight it hurt. 'Dad . . .' she said. 'Really? . . . Are you?'

In her anguish, she couldn't continue, but I knew she wanted confirmation. I looked down at Rebecca's lifeless body.

'I'm going back,' I said.

43

I CAN'T SAY THAT HAVING A MISSION SAVED MY LIFE, BUT IT CERTAINLY saved my mind.

We sat for what felt like hours with our arms around each other, keeping a silent vigil over Rebecca's body, while all around us the fires were being extinguished, the dust was settling and the dead and the wounded were carried out.

Vaguely I saw work crews gather up the bodies of the Orcs and drag them upstairs to be dumped on Fifth and heard two forward scouts report that Kazinsky had been seen leading the survivors towards the river.

Then, a short time later, a crew on board the Bradley opened up with the chain gun, firing at the remaining concrete pillars in the Van Cleef & Arpels basement, cutting through them like a saw. The idea was to collapse the floors above and make sure that nobody could ever pass through the tunnel and enter the basement again. It also served as a sort of punctuation – it was time for myself and the kids to leave.

Good man that he was, Jon had anticipated the grisly task that lay ahead. Four orderlies were already waiting in the shadows. Gently, he allowed us one last look at Rebecca's shattered body and then shepherded us away. No sooner had we turned our backs than I glimpsed the orderlies move forward to load Rebecca into a body bag.

The three of us made our way out of the ER and down the corridor. As we approached the fire stairs, my operational brain kicked into gear and I started thinking about the road ahead: there was a mission to plan. I saw the door into the apartment was open and let go of Chloe's hand. 'Where are you going?' she said, surprised at my sudden burst of energy.

'Right now I'm the mission planner, the threat assessor and the case officer,' I replied. 'I'm going to work.'

44

NIGHT WAS FALLING AS THICK FOG ROLLED ACROSS A THOUSAND miles of empty prairie and towards the lights of Baikonur. I was sitting alone in the converted cold store that had once been Don Steele's lair – the repository of all his records and now my makeshift mission control – watching footage of Devil's Night playing on the walls.

In the forty seconds between speaking to Chloe in the corridor and entering the apartment, I knew my first and most critical step: somehow, I had to find the exact date and time of an event that had occurred twenty-four years earlier. Don's research was my only hope.

I had opened the steel door and entered the darkened room. Ignoring the Monet and other priceless paintings, working by the light of a single desk lamp, I rearranged the kids' old school desks into a workbench and started pulling down boxes from the tall shelves, projecting footage on the walls, opening files that had not seen the light of day for decades and trawling through stacks of ageing computer discs and hard drives.

My concentration was broken when the entire room was flooded with light. Startled, I turned and saw that Chloe – outlined in the doorway with her brother – had hit the overheads.

'We can help if you need it,' Chloe said. She sounded shattered.

'I sure do,' I replied.

'Do you have a name at the agency for untrained employees?' Ridley asked.

'Executives,' I replied.

Smiling, they sat down at their old desks. 'What's the plan?' Ridley inquired.

'I'm trying to find information from a host of sources,' I replied. 'Trying to triangulate the data. The aim is to track the precise journey of the spore. If we're lucky, we can trace the path back and pinpoint the exact date and time when Kazinsky released it.'

'Got it,' Ridley replied. 'I guess at least we have one advantage: we know Baikonur was Ground Zero.' He started opening boxes and examining files. 'Without it, we wouldn't have a chance.'

Instead of computing power, we had a whiteboard, maps projected on a wall and – very soon – endless pages of scribbled notes littering the floor. With Chloe in charge of plotting co-ordinates on the whiteboard, box after box and file after file were opened, scanned for information and discarded. Thanks to Don's painstaking research and supplemented by wind-flow charts, detailed atmospheric readings, eyewitness accounts from across the world and dozens of other metrics, Chloe added one more entry on the board, checked a range of information and – exhausted – leaned back on her heels. 'We're there,' she said.

I looked at her hesitantly; there was no room for error.

'It's okay, I'm certain,' she said. 'At some time between 1.16 a.m. and 1.57 a.m. on a Sunday – July the eighth – twenty-four years ago, Roman Kazinsky was in the off-earth processing plant at Baikonur and somehow unleashed the spore.'

I walked forward and stopped in front of the whiteboard, checking the complex plot lines and footnotes that were laid over a map of Kazakhstan – all leading to the day and time Chloe had identified.

'So it's straightforward, isn't it?' I said. 'The mission, I mean – I just have to get to Baikonur Cosmodrome before 1 a.m. on that Sunday and stop him.'

They nodded, but I stood unmoving, looking at the whiteboard but not seeing it, thinking about everything we needed to do for the journey back, to repair the *Leviathan*, somehow reprogramming the computers to take me back along the exact course and settings that had brought me to New York in the first place.

'Are you okay?' Chloe asked.

'Yeah, just thinking.' I turned to my desk, picked up a sheet of paper I'd been working on and fixed it to the whiteboard.

'What is it?' she inquired.

'A schedule for after I surface,' I replied, and smiled. 'You can't say I'm not optimistic.'

'A schedule – what do you mean?' Chloe asked.

'If we fix this right, the boat will surface in the Southern Ocean – but I still have to get to Baikonur,' I said, pointing at the sheet of paper. 'I've worked it out the best I can. It's going to take three and a half days to get from the sub to the Cosmodrome.'

'That means the sub has to surface almost four days before Kazinsky releases the spore,' Ridley said. 'That will give you enough time to make the journey and stop him.'

'That's right,' I replied. 'Sunday at 1 a.m. is the deadline at Baikonur. Three and a half days before it is a Wednesday. That happens to be the Fourth of July – Independence Day.'

'You have to surface about one hour after noon on the fourth,' Chloe said.

I nodded. 'Any later and I won't have time to reach Baikonur.'

'Eighty-four hours,' Ridley said, looking at the schedule and my notes. 'Eighty-four hours to get from the Southern Ocean to Baikonur. Can it be done?'

'Can any of it?' I replied. 'Will the boat even survive the trip and, if it does, was your mom right that there isn't one future but – like the universe itself – there are infinite possibilities? I guess we'll find out soon enough.'

I turned off the desk lamp and Chloe closed down the overheads. As tired as we all were, I knew none of us had any intention of going to bed: we would never sleep—

45

'STARSTUFF,' I SAID QUIETLY TO THE TWINS AS WE SAT, HUNCHED together on the roof. It was still bitterly cold, but the wind had dropped, the clouds had vanished and the stars looked close enough to touch. 'That's what she told me just after we met. Every atom in our body – the oxygen we breathe, the minerals in our bones and the iron in our blood was formed inside stars and scattered across space long before Earth even existed. We are made from the stars, it's where we came from. She always used to say that's the extraordinary thing about life – we really are children of the universe.'

I looked down and saw that the twins were smiling. 'What?' I asked.

'She told us that too,' Chloe explained.

'A hundred times,' Ridley added ruefully. 'When we were little and saw people dying every day and were terrified, she'd put her arm around us and tell us we were starstuff. She'd say that dying didn't matter, it happened to everyone – it's what we did before we died that counted.'

'And she did a lot in her life, didn't she?' Chloe said, her voice quavering.

'She did everything,' I said, hugging her. 'She had a dozen lives in one. More than anything, she had children she loved and who loved her. What more could anyone want? I was going to ask her about the names – where did they come from? I understand Ridley, but . . .'

'She was so excited about being pregnant, she started making a list the day you left on the sub,' Ridley said. 'One column for boys, the other for girls. She noted down her favourites on the back of her first ultrasound, the one that told her she was having twins.' The ultrasound I'd seen on the morning I left for Diego Garcia.

'In the five days after you left, the list grew longer and longer – you know Mom, she was nothing if not thorough.' He tried to smile.

'Then she heard that an experimental sub was missing, and by that time she already had a dozen names for a boy and the same for a girl,' Ridley continued. 'She didn't add any more – she was too choked. She was done – she ranked them, and the top two boys' names were Xander and Panama—'

'What?' I said.

'I know,' he replied. 'You being presumed dead saved me from that. She decided that I had to be named after my dead father.'

'Well, yeah,' I said. 'Every cloud has a silver lining. But Panama? Are you sure she wasn't joking?'

'We've seen the list,' Ridley explained. 'It was the first picture taken of us and she always kept it in her wallet.'

'On the girls' list,' Chloe said, 'the top two names were Megan and

Olivia. Chloe was the last choice, but then she realized they were her preferences, not yours. So she tried to guess the one you would like best. How'd she do?'

'Really great,' I said. 'Chloe is terrific.'

She paused and turned serious. 'Ridley and I have discussed it; we know the situation. You're going back, but you don't really believe you'll survive the journey, do you?'

I said nothing; she was right. 'We just want you to know – we'll never forget what you've done.'

'Here's the strange thing,' I replied. 'If I succeed, you'll never even know. There will be no spore being released, no Devil's Night, none of this reality. You will be born at MedStar in DC, you'll go to school, your dad will lie to you about the work he does. This won't have ever happened.'

Ridley looked at me anew. 'I never thought of that,' he said. 'You'll be an unknown hero, anonymous to the whole world – even to your wife and family.'

'Welcome to the spy world,' I replied, smiling. 'And if I fail, it won't matter – we'll all be dead. Nobody will know we even tried – as someone said, history is written by the victors.'

46

EVEN WITH THE ADVANTAGE OF A HUGE AND HIGHLY EXPERIENCED crew assembled from the surviving submariners, splitting them into two shifts and working around the clock, it took almost three weeks to repair and prepare the *Leviathan*.

Nobody knew for sure whether the sub was capable of making the journey back, but the consensus was that due to its experimental nature, the mysterious cloaking device had been constructed to a remarkable standard and had escaped serious damage. Without a dry dock, the same couldn't be said for the hull.

The best we could do was deploy a team of salvage divers loaded with a host of equipment taken from the abandoned subs to check for metal fatigue or other signs of weakness.

Finding none, the work topside continued unabated. Once the decision for me to return had been made, Jon and I had immediately organized for an abandoned Coast Guard ice-breaker to head out to the *Leviathan*. With a pair of battered New York fire boats, they towed her out of the Hudson and moored her between two deep-water piers in a bend of the East River.

A wall of ruined skyscrapers along the shore cast a deep shadow over the worksite and provided an effective defence against an airborne attack. With chain guns and artillery mounted on their roofs, Zodiacs and jet-skis patrolling the water and Resistance drones flying all day and all night, the Orcs had little opportunity to disrupt the work.

Towards the end of the third week – one of those clear and achingly beautiful days that you sometimes encounter in early spring – the fire boats pulled in close to the piers and launched heavy-duty hawsers on to the deck of the *Leviathan*.

With the tide running at the flood, men and women attached a dozen of them to quick-release bolts and prepared the sub to be towed from its mooring. I stood in silence on the pier with Chloe and Ridley, a kitbag at my feet and sporting the same clothes and identity necklace I had been wearing when I had arrived; I was back to being Daniel Raymond Greenberg again, a scientist from Oak Ridge Tennessee, and it was almost time for him to say goodbye.

We watched the last of the final shift emerge from the sub and crowd on to the pier. Most of them stopped to shake hands or exchange a few words with Jon. Without anyone asking, he had assumed responsibility for organizing the crews. Very little would have been achieved without him.

He had his arm around Laleh, both of them standing with their backs to us, when a large flock of brilliantly coloured orioles – yellow and orange with black wings – swooped low along the river. New York City was on what was called the Atlantic Flyway, one of the world's major migration corridors, and with spring's arrival the birds were heading north.

They made a spectacular sight, their vivid plumage highlighted against the blue sky and the sparkling water, enough to lift anyone's spirits – except, apparently, those of Jon and Laleh. As they swung round to follow the flight of the birds I saw a look of deep distress on Jon's face. It was clear Laleh was also close to tears.

'What's wrong with Jon and Laleh?' I asked.

'They asked us not to say anything,' Ridley said. 'But if you kill Kazinsky, they won't meet here in New York and none of the rest will happen.'

'Of course they want you to succeed,' Chloe added. 'But it's bittersweet – they know these might be their last days together.'

I nodded my head in understanding then called out: 'Laleh.' She turned, looking surprised – we had already said our goodbyes. I motioned them towards us.

'Do you remember when I was in the metal cage?' I asked her.

'Of course,' she replied. 'Why?'

'You were scared, you thought the US military would come and rescue their spy—'

'Yes. And I'd be abandoned, left alone with the men,' she said.

'Do you recall what I told you?'

'You said if you could escape, you wouldn't leave me, you'd take me with you.'

'Yes,' I said. 'I made a promise, didn't I?'

'And you kept it.'

'That's the point – here's another one. If I make it back, I'll make sure the two of you meet. The rest is up to you, but for that much – I give you my word.'

She looked at me and reached out to hug me. I glanced over her shoulder; the last of the workers had left the *Leviathan* and, along with everybody else, were packed on to the pier. The most senior chief of the boat was approaching.

He was elderly, his boilersuit stained with grime and oil from the weeks of hard work, but he straightened his shoulders and saluted. I knew word had spread that – despite my name-tag and the crew list – I was an officer qualified in submarines. Out of Diego Garcia, US Navy, once seconded to a spy outfit, so the story went.

I saluted back, and the irony of the situation wasn't lost on me. At last I had fulfilled the ambition I had held so close growing up in Florida: I was now in command of a nuclear-powered submarine. What a strange hand fate had played.

I turned and looked at the boat that my life – all of our lives – depended on. Somebody had arranged for her to have a US Navy identification number painted on the hull. She was now *SSN-212* – like all submarines, the SSN stood for Sub-Surface Nuclear, and 212 had once been the phone area code for Manhattan. In addition, hanging over the side of the sail was a removable wooden plaque emblazoned with the name USS *Leviathan*. Now she had the name and identity of a warship, ready for whatever battle lay ahead.

'Boat ready to cast off, sir,' the chief said. I nodded my thanks. It was time to go – just one last thing to do.

I took a moment to gather myself and turned to my children. I put my arms around Chloe and kissed the top of her head. 'I'll see you on the other side,' I said.

'Of life?' she replied, trying to fight back the tears.

'Of time,' I said.

I disentangled my arms from her and embraced Ridley. 'Take care of each other,' I said.

He nodded, seemingly unwilling to trust his voice, and as I leaned down to pick up my kitbag, he produced a small package wrapped in faded blue silk and bound with twine. He handed it to me and glanced at his sister, making it clear it was a joint gesture. 'This was from years . . .' He took a steadying breath and started again. 'It comes from years back. One of the first people to arrive was in Washington when it fell and he found it in what was left of the White House.'

'That was his story, anyway,' Chloe said. 'I'd say he probably bought it on the internet – if we still had an internet.' She tried to smile. 'He gave it to Mom before he died.'

'We thought you might want to use it,' Ridley continued. 'You know, like you, it's a survivor.'

'Thank you,' I said, no idea what it was, and picked up the kitbag. There was no point in delaying, so I turned away from them and, accompanied by the chief, walked towards the boat.

As we approached the gangplank a line of men and women in coveralls formed up on either side of it. The realization hit me. Somebody had found bosun's whistles on the other subs and once I stepped on to the gangplank the crowd on the wharf fell silent and – for the first and only time in my life – I was piped aboard.

As the high-pitched whistles rolled across the river and bounced off the ruins, I walked along the metal gangplank and stepped back on board the *Leviathan*.

It was time to go.

47

THE HEAVY ROPES ATTACHED TO THE TWO FIRE BOATS HAD SPRUNG taut and the massive sub was free of the pier and heading into the middle of the East River by the time I had made my way up the series of ladders and on to the *Leviathan*'s navigation bridge at the top of the sail.

Along the way I had left my kitbag in the command centre and opened the small package Chloe and Ridley had given me. Staring at what was inside for a long moment, I couldn't help wondering if it really had come from the White House. It certainly looked the part – thick with masonry dust, torn in a couple of places and badly tattered down one edge.

I tucked it under my arm, climbed the remaining ladder, clambered through the hatch and was hit by the cool spring breeze. Barely glancing at the shore, I found the lanyard I was looking for, attached the old piece of fabric and hauled it to the top of the repaired photonics mast.

The breeze unfurled it and blew away most of the dust. The Stars were all intact; the Stripes were torn and ragged at the end. On the pier, I could just make out Ridley and Chloe standing apart from the crowd. It must have been quite a sight: the glittering white vessel, the brilliant blue water, the two fire boats with wakes boiling at their stern and the ragged old flag flying overhead.

The ruins of the Statue of Liberty appeared in front of me, the howitzers on the Battery opened up with a deafening salvo – whether to suppress the Orcs or as a farewell, I don't know – and the fireboats released the ropes and blasted their horns, signalling that we were at the exact spot where I had surfaced.

I checked my watch. In three minutes, the computers would send a series of complex commands to the nuclear generator, the rudder and a host of other components and we would be underway.

Ahead, looking east, I saw the collapsed piers and twisted sections of metal that were all that remained of the once-towering Verrazano-Narrows Bridge, the gateway to the Atlantic. I turned away from it and ran my eye across the skeletal ruins of the buildings on the Jersey

Shore and Lower Manhattan, saw pillars of fire in the distance and the rusting hulks of freighters near Ellis Island.

And with that last look at the future, I swung through the hatch and went below.

48

THE TECHNICIANS AND PROGRAMMERS WHO HAD WORKED SO HARD to get the boat ready had given the computers a voice. They must have figured calm and reassuring was the way to go.

'Good day, this is Commander Alexandra Roberts,' she said quietly as I stepped off the final ladder. 'Boat preparing to dive. Three minutes.' Brilliantly, they had made Alexandra the first woman to ever skipper a nuclear-powered sub in the notoriously male-dominated United States Navy. Then again, it *was* the future.

In two minutes, according to the schedule, I had to be in the pod with all its systems activated and – sixty seconds later – the *Leviathan*'s pumps would kick in and start to fill her ballast tanks with seawater.

I headed into the well-ordered and spotlessly clean vessel; all the bodies had been removed and it was now a far cry from the floating wreck with waterlogged compartments, burnt-out electrical circuits and smashed companionways that I had surfaced in.

With a minute to spare, I entered the multi-purpose platform, hit the lights and moved to the electrical panel on the wall.

There were clear instructions on exactly how to set up one of the yellow decompression pods and, with those fresh in my mind, I entered the commands on the attached computer screen, adjusted the levels, heard the oxygen hiss as it entered the pod and saw the thermometer inside reach the correct operating temperature.

Right on time, I climbed inside, lay down on the bed and sealed the perspex canopy. I looked out and checked that the air-quality monitor fixed to the far wall of the room had been repaired. If we jumped the track and I made it to the other side, it would tell me if there was enough oxygen for me to leave the pod. Right now, it was the only light in the room, showing seven green bars; everything else dimmed to blackness, and I felt the *Leviathan*'s massive pumps start to fill the ballast tanks.

In the darkness, I stared up at the airtight canopy enclosing me, thought about the vast expanse of the ocean that lay ahead, and asked myself a question that I couldn't answer.

Was it right to pray to a God you didn't believe in?

49

I WAS IN A STATE OF SUSPENDED ANIMATION, A FLY TRAPPED IN amber – or so it felt to me. Trying to breathe slow and deep, drifting between dreams and imagination, I had no idea how long I had been in the pod. In an unexpected irony, time meant nothing.

Until, violently, I was hurled awake and upwards. With my face pressed against the perspex, my heart hammering, I realized that a tremor far stronger than anything I had experienced on the earlier journey was sweeping through the sub. I planted my feet against the pod's metal frame and tried to ride it out, wondering how the fabric of the hull could withstand it.

I twisted my head and looked across to check the air-quality monitor in time to see it black out; power to the rest of the boat had failed completely. Then the tremor passed and we started to fall—

Down into the abyss. I held my breath, God knows why – I was beyond thinking. Then it hit again, another tremor, another jump, bigger, stronger, more terrifying. Even in the sealed environment of the pod I heard – or felt – equipment smashing, metal groaning and the sub's superstructure screaming as the *Leviathan* twisted and fought.

Then, as the tremor passed, there was something even more terrifying: deathly silence. No light, no sound, just the sensation – real or imagined, I couldn't tell – of dropping more slowly. On and on – dropping, drifting – until, finally, I slumped back and lay there for what seemed like hours. It might have been minutes, it might have been days; I had no idea.

The light woke me. It was nothing really, only the red glow of the air-quality monitor, but to my unconscious eyes accustomed to complete darkness it seemed like a searchlight. It could mean only one thing – emergency power was being restored. Slowly, one of the seven bars turned from red to green; the oxygen generators were starting to work. Then Commander Roberts confirmed that the boat was coming alive. 'Stand by,' she said.

Stand by for what? I wanted to throw open the canopy and get out to discover what was happening, but with only two green bars on the monitor I knew I would suffocate.

I leaned back to wait; there was nothing else to do. If the sub had in fact made the jump, we were back in present time and it was clear from the monitor that the air on board was too toxic to breathe. As I had anticipated in New York, it would mean that the crew were once again dead and I was the only survivor—

Except, maybe, for Baxter. I had no idea at what point his heart had stopped. Perhaps he was in his pod right now, fighting for breath.

I checked the bars on the air monitor. Five of the seven were green, and that was good enough for me. I unfastened the canopy, leapt out and scrambled to Baxter's pod.

I grabbed the latches, looked through the perspex and didn't bother opening the canopy. His face was the colour of ash, the lips a faded blue and his eyes were glazed in death. He must have died just after he got inside – before we took the leap into the future.

I felt a surge of emotion well up, an enormous sense of loss. I guess I had always been hoping—

But I had no time to indulge my sadness. 'Stand by – four seconds and counting,' Commander Roberts announced.

Four seconds to what?

'Initiating emergency blow,' she said.

I didn't move, I could barely breathe; we had made the jump and I had survived.

As the realization landed, I started to run, scrambling over the wreckage in the multi-purpose platform, heading for the command centre. There, the computer screens would tell me what I had to know—

Where were we? What was the exact date and time?

50

THROUGH A SEEMINGLY ENDLESS DEBRIS FIELD OF SMASHED metalwork, twisted ladders and broken equipment and aided only by scattered emergency lights, I plunged forward and yelled: 'If you can hear me, answer. Anybody! Are you alive? If you hear this . . .'

My voice echoed through the sub's long companionways, but the only response was the barely audible pumps discharging the ballast or voiding water from several flooded compartments. I continued to call, still hoping, but in my heart I knew there would be no reply.

The crew had all died from lack of oxygen before the *Leviathan* made the jump and they were still dead when we came back.

Breathing hard, I finally reached the command centre. Martinez and the other officers must have abandoned it for the wardroom – more than likely in a desperate mission to try and restart the oxygen generators – because none of their bodies were present. A communications officer and a sonar tech were still in their chairs, both with a blue tinge to their skin and pinpoint haemorrhages on their faces; they had died at their posts.

Their computers were black, as were the screens in the other workstations, giving no clues to our depth and location, the time and the date. I could tell from the motion and angle of the boat that we were still heading for the surface, but without a working depth finder or echo sounder, I had no way of even knowing how long it would take. The only solution was to raise the photonics mast. Given the damage to the rest of the boat, I had no confidence it would still work, so I was taken aback when I tried to activate it and the control panel illuminated.

A graphic on the panel showed me the mast telescoping upwards. When it was fully extended, I put my face against the eyepiece in time for it to break the surface and the high-definition cameras on top of it to focus.

I looked out at a world I thought I would never see again. An expanse of ocean was rolling with a long swell, a breeze was combing spray off its crests and blue sky with scattered white clouds seemed to stretch for ever. The world had never looked more beautiful.

Pivoting the camera through three hundred and sixty degrees, I stopped abruptly: a warship was about a mile away, pushing hard through the swell: a United States Navy aircraft carrier, her rigging uncharacteristically adorned with bunting and scores of multicoloured flags. Even stranger, there were crew members everywhere, many of them in casual clothes. There were even barbecues on the flight deck. I realized—

It was lunchtime on the Fourth of July.

I stepped backwards, catching my breath. I had made it back. On schedule. I thought of holding Rebecca as she died, I thought of seeing her again, young and full of life. I thought of Chloe and Ridley, not even born yet—

I had eighty-four hours to kill a man.

51

ON THE BRIDGE OF THE US AIRCRAFT CARRIER, MESS-ROOM ORDERLIES were delivering platters of barbecue to the vice-admiral commanding the fleet, the skipper of the carrier and the other officers and technicians responsible for the largest warship in the world, all eleven hundred feet of her.

The sonar tech – turning to reach for a plate – suddenly clamped a hand to his earphone, listened for a moment and wheeled back to his screen. He entered a rapid series of commands, accessed a flood of information and watched as a few disparate lines started to appear on the screen. He kept listening and tweaking his controls—

The carrier's skipper – so the CCTV footage showed later – had seen him turn to his screen in alarm and was approaching. 'What you got?'

The sonar tech didn't take his eyes off the image in front of him. 'Not sure, sir. The visuals are only just starting to resolve themselves.'

Then he paused, gathering more information. 'It's a boat, sir.'

The vice-admiral and the other officers gathered around. The sonar tech was holding one of the earphones tight to his head. 'I recognize the signature of the reactor,' he said, and turned to his commander. 'She's back.'

It brought the bridge to a standstill. 'What? Where is she?' the skipper asked.

'A mile to port, sir,' the sonar tech replied. 'Surfacing, I would say. She's at periscope depth already.'

The vice-admiral looked at the screen; the image was establishing itself and they saw the unmistakable and ghostly shape of the *Leviathan* appear.

'Where in hell did she come from?' the skipper asked. 'How did she get so close?'

The sonar tech had no answer, but he wasn't waiting for one. He turned to his executive officer: 'Sound General Quarters.'

52

AN ALARM BLASTED OUT FROM THE CARRIER'S PUBLIC ADDRESS system, echoing down its companionways, through the storage hangars and across the flight deck. 'General Quarters. All hands man battle stations. Set material condition Zebra. Submarine contact one mile to port. General Quarters, all hands . . .'

The massive warship exploded into activity. One of the lookouts on the bridge raised his binoculars and scanned the area to port. 'Photonics mast visible, sir,' he reported, and gave a series of co-ordinates.

The skipper and the vice-admiral raised their own glasses, but they didn't get them to their eyes; the *Leviathan*'s massive hull – bow first – broke the surface of the ocean in a blast of white, boiling water.

As they watched, the six-hundred-foot vessel, under the force of the emergency blow, continued to emerge from the depths like a whale breaching, a battered wreck of a thing with stretches of its white tiles missing, kelp clinging to its hull, and its sail seemingly damaged beyond repair. For all the world, a boat back from the dead.

As she settled on the surface, the officers and crew on the bridge stared at the vessel. She was unlike any submarine they had ever seen. The vice-admiral – prematurely white-haired, a decorated war veteran in his early fifties – was shorter than the commonly held image of a very senior Navy officer and he made up for it with an imperious manner. He turned to the communications technician—

'Message the Pentagon under my name,' he ordered. 'Tell the Chairman of the Joint Chiefs and the Secretary of Defense that we have found the *Leviathan*.'

53

WITH THE RETURN OF THE SUBMARINE, EVENTS WERE ALREADY changing. Rebecca, who had been working in emergency at MedStar when she learned from the TV that a boat was missing, had returned home with Laleh and – distraught and unable to sleep – waited for news.

A host of alerts on her phone told her to watch the news, but this time the Pentagon spokesperson did not announce that the search for the sub had become a recovery mission. Instead—

'The experimental submarine known as the USS *Leviathan* has been found,' he said. Rebecca had to find a seat lest she fall. 'Surfacing fifteen minutes ago, a team of Navy SEALs are preparing to board the vessel. At present, there is no information about the welfare of the one hundred and sixty-eight personnel on board.'

He ignored an onslaught of questions from the scores of reporters in the room. 'We will provide more information as soon as we have it.' With that, he left the room.

Rebecca and Laleh continued to stare at the screen, but their sense of relief was short-lived. The news channel had just returned to the studio when the anchor looked at the autocue—

'This just in,' he said. 'A senior White House source, not authorized to speak publicly, has told us that the carrier strike group has been trying to contact the submarine since it surfaced. There has been no response. The source said that due to the condition of the sub and the time that has elapsed, there is little chance of finding any survivors.'

Rebecca shook her head. 'There's no way they can know,' she said to Laleh. 'They haven't even been on board.' She knew she was clutching at straws.

She walked out of the room and sat on the porch, looking down the road, dreading the approach of every vehicle.

54

TRYING NOT TO LOSE A MOMENT, I HAD ABANDONED THE PHOTONICS mast and headed for the ladders that led up to the open-air navigation bridge on top of the sail.

My plan was to signal to the carrier when – almost at the hatch that opened on to the bridge – I encountered an impassable tangle of shattered ladders and sparking electric cables.

Cursing, I turned back, climbed down and headed aft to the closest of the three escape hatches. As I ran – sloshing through water from a series of burst pipes – I finally reached a less damaged companionway. I heard a sound above and stopped to listen – boots were moving along the hull. A rescue team had landed.

I sprinted faster, climbed a ladder and was stopped by a series of small explosions echoing through the boat; the rescue team were blowing open the escape hatches.

I plunged forward until I saw a glow of light ahead, coming from the area that housed the oxygen generators – a form of emergency lighting, I figured, until I realized: they were headlights on helmets.

One of the SEAL teams had arrived and had been searching among the oxygen generators. I was about to call out when I heard the SEAL leader reporting to the carrier through his headset mic: 'We've just located the commander and most of the officers – all deceased. Signs of suffocation due to lack of oxygen. Moving towards midships. Anticipate all deceased—'

He took a step forward as I emerged from the shadow of a crushed bulkhead and his headlamp illuminated me. We looked at one another—

'Wait . . .' the commander said into the mic. 'Wait. We have at least one survivor.'

55

WHILE THE OTHER SEALS CONTINUED TO SEARCH THE *LEVIATHAN*, THE leader and three of his men shepherded me on to one of their Zodiacs.

With men and women watching from the flight deck and any other vantage point they could find – all staring at the haggard-looking civilian, I was winched up the side of the carrier and taken directly to the bridge, where the vice-admiral, the skipper, half a dozen other officers and the chief medical officer and her team were waiting—

'Mr Greenberg?' the vice-admiral asked, looking at the identity bracelet around my neck and consulting a crew list recovered from the sub.

I nodded.

'We're still looking, but you're probably the only survivor,' he said. 'You want to tell me what happened?'

'I'm sorry, Vice-Admiral,' I replied. 'I'm not at liberty to talk to you.'

He stared at me, so shocked he sort of smiled and glanced at the other officers: *did you hear this guy?* he seemed to say. There was no hope I could even begin to explain what had happened – nor did I have the time – so I waited.

'You're a civilian, Mr Greenberg, so I'll cut you some slack. You must have been under an enormous amount of stress, but let me explain – I command this battle group, and this is my flagship. That's my ensign flying from the tower. Now I have to give an account of the situation to the Chairman of the Joint Chiefs and the Secretary of Defense. What happened?'

'I am not at liberty to give you any information, Vice-Admiral. Call this number, please.' I turned, picked up a pen and notepad, wrote down an area code and phone number and handed it to him.

He made no attempt to take the notepad. 'You don't tell me what to do – not anywhere, and especially not on my ship – *Dr* Greenberg,' he said, making sure I understood that I held no military rank at all.

'You will call the number. Do you understand, *Admiral*? Now.'

As everyone stared in silence, he turned to the chief medical officer. 'Take him below. Check him out. There's obviously a problem.'

She nodded and was about to tell me to accompany her to the infirmary when the skipper picked up the notepad. 'There's no such area code,' he said, shaking his head.

'Just because you've never had to use it, Captain, doesn't mean it's not real. Call it,' I said.

He looked at me hard and handed the notepad to the communications tech. 'Call it,' he said. 'Maybe the doctor will realize he needs to be examined.'

The vice-admiral, still barely containing his anger, watched as the technician opened a phone line and dialled. Without a valid area code, they all knew that the line wouldn't connect so they couldn't hide their surprise when the technician started to speak to somebody at the other end.

'This is the United States Navy,' he said, then paused while he listened. 'Where did I get the number? It was given to me by a man called Daniel Greenberg. Who am I speaking to?'

He seemed to recoil as he heard the reply. He turned to the vice-admiral. 'I think you should take this call, sir.'

'Who is it?' the vice-admiral asked, as perplexed as everyone else.

'I think you should take it, Vice-Admiral,' the tech replied.

The vice-admiral grabbed the handset. 'Yes?' he said peremptorily and then listened. 'I understand . . .' he continued in a sudden change of tone. 'Well, yes . . . of course . . . yes, we will . . . thank you.'

He hung up and turned to me. 'So tell me – how does a scientist from Tennessee get the private cell number of the director of the CIA?'

'I'm sorry, Vice-Admiral,' I repeated. 'I am not at liberty to discuss that with you. I need a secure office, an encrypted satellite phone, some notepaper and a burn box for when I finish.'

He said nothing to indicate his agreement, either from reluctance or shock. I had no time to waste. 'I can call the president if you want,' I said, bluffing.

56

REBECCA DIDN'T HEAR HER PHONE RING – IT WAS STILL LYING IN THE kitchen – but Laleh did. She answered it, listened to the caller's identity and ran for the front porch. 'It's your phone,' she said as soon as she was through the door.

'You should have let it go to answering,' Rebecca said, fraught with worry, still watching the road.

'It's Falcon Rourke,' Laleh said.

Rebecca grabbed the phone.

'He's alive,' Falcon said. 'The only survivor.'

Rebecca sat back down, trying to breathe.

'Pack a bag,' Falcon continued. 'A car is on its way.'

'Where are we going?' she asked.

'Andrews,' he replied, deliberately obtuse; he never trusted a phone. 'Ten minutes.' The line disconnected and he was gone.

57

'REMEMBER GROZNY?' I SAID INTO THE SAT PHONE, SITTING ALONE IN a supervisor's glass-walled office, looking out at the dozens of planes stored just below the carrier's flight deck.

I had commandeered the space because it was soundproof. It had to be – surrounded by forklifts moving supplies, rows of maintenance bays and the constant thrum of power tools – which made it the most secure place on the ship in my view.

'Do I remember the airfield and the recruiting centre – sure,' Madeleine O'Neill answered from her office at Langley. 'Why?'

'I'm going there.'

'To Grozny – when?' she asked, shocked.

'Tonight, tomorrow – as soon as I can.'

'You're trying to get to Baikonur?' she asked, realizing.

'I'm going to sign up,' I said.

'Baikonur's a ZATO, Kane. The background checks will be unbeatable. Even with months of preparation and a good legend, it can't be—'

'It can be done. I'll have a legend that works.'

'And you're going to find that legend in a day?'

'Yes. I never realized it, but everything's been leading here. Every detail, every event, it all had a purpose. It's the mission of my life, of all our lives. I need your help.'

'Does Falcon know?'

'Not yet. I heard he was on his way to see me.'

'Are you on an aircraft carrier?'

'Yes.'

'Then you're right. He has your wife and Lucas Corrigan with him.'

'Rebecca? Thank God,' I replied. 'Lucas too? I guess Falcon wants a psychological assessment as well as a debrief. I'll tell him about Baikonur when I see him.'

'Will he agree to it?'

'I'll have to convince him. But you and I have to start now – we don't have much time.'

'What do you need?'

'Details, photographs; fingerprints are a priority. I'm going in as a Russian – he was a member of the Army of the Pure so he should be in the files you already compiled. He served with Spetsnaz in Aleppo then followed Kazinsky down to the badlands. We're lucky, I know a fair bit about him—'

'Where is he now?'

'Dead. But because he was killed and buried in Iran, the Russians won't know it.' I looked at my watch. 'Right now, we've got eighty-one hours to bring him back to life.'

58

WHILE MADELEINE AND I WERE IN CONSTANT CONTACT, WORKING AT speed to develop my legend, a GreenEnergy G800 jet, able to cruise at six hundred miles an hour, had left Andrews and was flying all through the afternoon and night to the far south of the Indian Ocean.

I was still in the supervisor's office, trying to marshal facts about my new identity, fighting to stay awake, when a naval rating knocked at the door and told me the jet I had been waiting for had appeared on the carrier's radar. I stood, shook myself alert and headed up to the flight deck.

I looked down three hundred feet of runway. The night sky was clear, the wind had dropped and the sea had resolved itself into a series of long and regular swells. Landing on a carrier has always been a dangerous exercise – the hardest thing a pilot will ever do – but at least the weather was running with us. The air boss and his team were already deploying the four arresting wires across the deck and the fire-control personnel and their fire truck were moving into position when I looked to the stern and saw the Gulfstream approaching, passing almost above the *Leviathan* – manned by an emergency crew and supported by inflatable buoyancy bolsters.

The Gulfstream was one of the agency's specially adapted jets and I saw the tailhook drop down from its belly.

The plane levelled up as the pilot adjusted his angle of approach, aiming for the third wire, watching a series of green lights projected from the carrier to guide him in—

Every time I have seen a plane land on a carrier, they appeared to be flying too fast. This time, it was no different. 'Slow down,' I said, then held my breath. I was sure the three passengers on the plane were doing the same.

The Gulfstream roared in over the carrier's stern, the wheels hit the rise and fall of the deck in a cloud of smoke, the tailhook snared the third wire, hydraulic cylinders below deck controlled the tension on it, and the plane, under full power, screeched to a gut-wrenching halt.

I ran towards it as the air boss and his team dragged the plane to the side of the flight deck and chained it down. The pilot was already lowering the jet's air-stairs and I sprinted up them to see Falcon, Corrigan and Rebecca, still shaken by the violent wrench of the arresting wire, gathering up their belongings.

Rebecca turned and saw me as I moved towards her; one look and she was close to tears, her face crumpling with relief. I took her in my arms and kissed her hair, her eyes. 'You're back,' she whispered. 'Thank God you're safe.'

'You too,' I said, looking at her half in wonder. 'I held you when you were . . .' I stopped myself before continuing. 'And here we are – alive.' I hugged her again and glimpsed Falcon and Lucas exchange a glance but ignored it.

'You held me when I was what?' Rebecca asked, puzzled.

'It was a long journey, I saw things – they were dark days, the end of our time, Becca.'

'Where? Where did you see them?' she asked.

'It doesn't matter.' Falcon and Lucas were looking at me, worried now. 'We can talk about it on the way,' I said.

'And just where the fuck do you think we are going?' Falcon asked.

'Morocco,' I replied. 'The agency has a black prison with an air-strip and I can be fitted with my legend there.'

'A legend for what?' he asked.

'Baikonur,' I said.

'You think you're going to Baikonur? A fucking ZATO? Have you lost your mind?'

'We don't have much time, Falcon – we have to refuel and leave.'

'No,' he replied. 'We get off the plane and, whatever happened, we talk about it calmly.'

'Falcon's right,' Lucas added in his best psychologist's manner. 'We start when you got on the boat—'

I shook my head. 'Time's too short.' I moved to a small conference table at the front of the cabin and sat down. If they wanted to talk, I would talk, but I wasn't getting off the plane.

59

THE FOUR OF US SAT AT THE SMALL TABLE AND I TOLD THEM – AS FAST and clearly as I could – everything that I thought was important. I described the submarine and the jump in time, New York in ruins and about the new world that had been created.

I recounted Don Steele's research, tracking the spore to Baikonur, and I spoke about the beauty of Devil's Night. I argued that evolution hadn't stopped with us and that our kind was out of step, out of place and desperately out of time. I reported Rebecca's death in detail and in the pervasive silence which followed I explained about love, our two children I had met and why I had to risk everything to try and return to the present.

Becca was clearly distressed by it, and the reason soon became apparent. 'It must have been terrifying – the suffocation, the fires, being lost underwater,' she said.

'God only knows how that plays with a person's mind,' Falcon said.

'But there are things that can be done,' Becca continued. 'Lucas would agree—'

I stared at the three of them. 'It's not fucking PTSD,' I said. 'If that's what you think.'

'Listen,' Falcon said gently. 'You locked yourself in a pod and saved your life. Maybe only a Denied Access Area spy, accustomed to surviving on the frontier, would think of it. It was brilliant.'

'Thank you,' I replied.

'So, let's be grateful,' he continued. 'You said yourself you were so exhausted you passed out. While you were asleep or unconscious, you dreamt terrible things. Some time later, the computers kicked in, the oxygen generators restarted and the software initiated an emergency blow. Just like they're meant to – that's what happened. The reality is, you never left the pod.'

I stared at him, turned to Rebecca for support and got none.

'Imagination is an incredibly powerful emotion,' Lucas said. 'It's the only explanation. You were in a sealed pod, which is little different to a flotation tank. There have been scores of experiments with those, depriving someone of external stimulation and inducing an altered state. Of course it seemed real to you. That's the point of experiments – they're meant to be.'

'And you were primed for it,' Rebecca said, taking my hand. 'The prospect of imminent death, the submarine plunging down into the deepest and darkest depths. Can you imagine a better cue for entering the subconscious? It's textbook.'

'The subconscious has nothing to do with it,' I said. 'You have to underst—'

'No, you have to,' Lucas replied. 'We're your friends. You were lost underwater and you thought you were going to die, your world was collapsing, you were terrified of never seeing Rebecca and your unborn children. So your mind reacted, it created a story about a terrifying man you have hunted for years. You imagined Kazinsky came back to destroy you. Don't underestimate it – all of our fears talk to us through our dreams.'

'It was a fever dream? Or you think I lost my mind?' I said, trying to tamp down my fury. 'Okay . . . you may be right. Maybe none of it happened. Maybe I never left the pod, there was no gunfire in a canyon or a silence that fell as if the universe was holding its breath, I never saw Rebecca dying in my arms or heard the wolves. Yeah, perhaps none of it was real, Lucas – but all of it was true. It saved my life in the canyon, Rebecca will pass in a basement in New York and the End Times are about to come out of Kazakhstan, I'm telling you.'

Lucas smiled and pointed out the window. 'The mind is like the ocean: no matter what you see on the surface, the real life is underwater. We have to get you home—'

'I'm not going home,' I said. 'I'm going to Baikonur.'

Falcon sighed, exasperated.

'I won't die in New York, but you'll die there,' Rebecca intervened, caught between anger and tears.

'She's right,' Lucas said. 'Rebecca told us she was pregnant. You can't do this to your children.'

'I can't? What about Saigon?' I retorted. 'Tell us about the last day of the war. What did your father do for his kid there?'

Falcon looked at me, confused. 'Saigon? Why the hell are we talking about Saigon?'

I ignored him. 'When the chopper turned around, Lucas – what was your father thinking? I'll tell you. Exactly what I am – he was thinking about his family and saving the life of his son. So don't tell me I can't do this for my children.'

That silenced Lucas, it had touched a nerve, but it meant nothing to Falcon. 'Saigon was a real event,' the director said. 'That's the difference.'

'Totally real,' Rebecca added. 'Yours was a dream—'

'A nightmare,' Falcon continued. 'I won't authorize anyone going to Baikonur. Ever. I can't, I'd be derelict in my duty if I did. Least of all you.'

I said nothing. The heavy stillness of unresolved conflict fell over us. They weren't going to change their minds, and I couldn't surrender. But they had one advantage – I could not enter the Cosmodrome without the agency's support and resources. I glanced at a digital clock on the wall; I needed a way forward and – hunting – I looked around the cabin, glanced at the open door into the cockpit and ran my eye across the table. I saw Rebecca's purse lying on the seat beside her—

Fortune smiles on the creative mind, I guess. Or maybe necessity is the mother of inspiration. 'Open it,' I said.

She looked at me in confusion. 'The purse,' I said. 'Take out the photo of the ultrasound.'

'How do you know I have it with me?'

'Because you always carry it with you,' I replied. 'You have since the day after I left for Diego Garcia.'

She stared at me, baffled.

'I saw the photo in the drawer of your desk that morning. Have I seen it since then?'

'How could you?' she answered. 'You were on a submarine.'

'Exactly. There are two lists of names on the back, aren't there? Both written by you after I left. Show them to Falcon and Lucas. Now, please.'

She looked even more perplexed at how I knew but did as I asked.

'The names are in order of preference, aren't they?' She nodded, even more nervous. 'And what did you do to rank them – underline your first choice, circle it, number them?'

'Numbered,' she said.

'How many names on each list?' I asked. 'Twelve, is that correct?'

'Twelve,' Falcon confirmed, looking at the lists, starting to look pale.

'You're starting to scare me, Ridley,' Rebecca said.

'Good,' I replied. 'I mean to. Look at the top two choices for boys, please. Those are Xander and Panama – yes?'

'Correct,' Falcon and Lucas confirmed almost together, very quietly.

'On the girls' list, it's Megan and then Olivia,' I said. 'Chloe is the last at number twelve.'

Nobody said anything, they didn't have to – their faces conveyed it all. 'How do you know what I wrote when you've never seen it?' Rebecca asked.

'That's the point,' I said. 'The twins told me. Just after Kazinsky killed you, we sat on the roof of Bergdorf Goodman's – remember "Be . . . Good . . ."? – and I asked them how their mother had chosen their names. They told me about the ultrasound you had kept with you and the list you had written on the back.'

Rebecca's lip started to tremble, but whether it was from fear or wonder, I would never know.

'On a rooftop? Twenty-four years from now?' Lucas said as evenly as he could.

'That's right,' I replied. 'How else would I know? What other explanation is there?'

'No idea,' he said humbly. 'Maybe . . . maybe there isn't one.' He looked at Falcon – the director was expressionless, trying to process something that was far beyond his experience or understanding. It was like faith, I thought – you either made the leap or you didn't.

'At worst, if I'm wrong and it was the work of an overwrought mind,' I said to Falcon, 'I will – *insha'Allah* – kill the most wanted terrorist in the world. At best, I save us all. What is there to lose?'

'No, at worst you're wrong and you die trying,' he replied.

Rebecca was trying to master her breathing. 'I've gone through more hard times with Ridley's work than most partners ever have to,' she said. 'I think it gives me some skin in this game.'

Falcon and Lucas nodded.

'I believe it. I don't know why, but I believe it,' she said. 'The gun-fire, the wolves.' She indicated the ultrasound. 'All of it. I think Ridley should go.'

I didn't know what to say; for somebody you love to believe in you, to have so much faith – well, maybe words weren't made for that. I lifted her hand and put it to my lips.

Falcon gave a small smile. 'You say he should go, Becca – weren't you the woman who gave me all that shit at MedStar? You said then I was happy to send young men and women into some dark place that many never came back from? And even if they did, they were torn apart. That cut me very deep. Now you're saying I should send Ridley to the darkest place of all – a ZATO, alone and probably with no way home?'

'Maybe I never understood how high the stakes really were. Till now.'

'That's the tragedy of the secret world – the public never does. But we've all been on a journey, and every one of them brings an insight. I went to Egypt and came back a different man. I'm sure none of us will ever forget the far south of the Indian Ocean.' He turned to the cockpit: 'Skipper,' he called.

Falcon looked at me. 'I have no idea how a man with no time to develop a legend thinks he can enter a ZATO, but I'm sure you've got a plan.'

The pilot appeared at the cockpit door. 'Boss?'

'Set a course for the agency's place in Ourika,' Falcon replied. 'We're going to Morocco.'

60

THE VIEW FROM THE JET WAS SPECTACULAR – THE SNOW-CAPPED peaks of the High Atlas Mountains fell through towering cliffs into lush and verdant valleys thick with almond and cherry trees, fast-flowing streams tumbled over waterfalls and small Berber villages clung to the banks in hidden canyons.

I was exhausted, and so were Rebecca, Falcon and Lucas – they had flown through a day and night to meet me – so any further discussion was put aside and we were all asleep shortly after the jet had been catapulted off the carrier's deck and made the turn to the north.

It was only when we hit turbulence surrounding Mount Toubkal, the highest peak in the Arab-speaking world, that we woke. I raised the window blind to see that we were descending, through air so clear I saw the village of Ourika – discovered by the hippies decades ago – surrounded by wild-flowers. In the middle of it, rope bridges crossed a wild river and brightly coloured barbecue tents were scattered among the stalls of a small souk.

Losing altitude, we flew deeper into the mountains and then, approaching a precipitous cliff, turned hard into a valley that was inaccessible even by the mule tracks that criss-crossed the landscape. The walled compound that lay at the far end was identified on most maps as a 'royal hunting lodge' – and maybe it was once – and it certainly went some way to explaining the long, sealed runway, the no-fly zone above it and the small cluster of barrack-style buildings. Our place was a black prison built into caverns inside one of the mountains and was invisible. A safe house set in its own gardens – as befitted its cover as a royal hunting lodge – was beautiful: a collection of pavilions with pink rendered walls and Moorish arches faced a large swimming pool.

The jet's wheels touched down and I saw there was a Jeep on the side of the runway. Its driver, Madeleine O'Neill, was standing beside it, waiting—

61

THE FOUR OF US PILED INTO THE VEHICLE, AND IN THOSE LAST, desperate hours – as I hurtled towards the final leg of the longest journey of my life – Madeleine did more to help me than I could have ever expected; or probably deserved. As it turned out, in at least one way, I owe my life to her.

As we headed towards a magnificent palm-lined avenue that led to the pink house, she pointed to the runway's concrete apron, where a C-17 Globemaster freighter – the size of a wide-bodied passenger jet – was parked under camouflage netting. 'Falcon told me to organize the transport of everything we'd need and I brought it in on that.'

The plane had small winglets to land on short runways and was usually solely a military jet, but, painted white, boasting an impressive but unidentifiable crest on its fuselage and with no serial number or letters, it could pass, at least to a satellite, as some sort of private jet. It was, in fact, part of the agency's version of ConAir, used to transport high-value prisoners, CIA staff and supplies to a network of black prisons scattered across the world.

'It's funny, isn't it,' Falcon said to me, pointing at the prison entrance. 'According to your legend when you first missioned into Iran, you were searching for your brother. We knew you'd never find him, because he was in a black prison in Morocco. There he is, a few hundred yards away. The circularity of life, I suppose.'

'And Buster?' I asked Madeleine. 'Is he here, too?'

'He'd better be,' Falcon said, smiling. 'He's not taking early retirement, I told him that a few days ago.'

'Margaret's with us, too,' Madeleine added. 'Vaping up a storm and organizing the intelligence on Grozny. I grabbed the armourer and two of his technicians – I figured you'd need a weapon that could be concealed – and I also hijacked four members of TripAdvisor, our two best forgers, the production designer and her team so you would at least look like your legend, and six researchers, including Clay Powell from the Tomb and Darren, our resident Russian speaker.'

'Good,' Falcon said drily. 'The crazy gang's all here. What could possibly go wrong?'

62

'OKAY, WHAT HAVE WE GOT?' FALCON SAID TO MADELEINE AS WE trooped into the house's entertainment pavilion and he dropped his backpack on to a marble table. The area had been chosen by Madeleine because of its size and seclusion, and she had already turned it into command central for the imminent mission.

Rebecca and I paused on the threshold and looked around: a huge sweep of limestone flooring was anchored at either end by a monumental fireplace – ideal for the cool mountain nights – the walls were decorated with beautiful Moorish tiles known as *zellige*, a backgammon table stood near the large open-plan kitchen and a host of comfortable white loungers which looked out through an open wall of glass to a barbecue, the black-bottomed pool and the snow-capped peaks beyond. 'Looks kinda like Tahoe,' Rebecca said, referring to that town's spectacular beauty and extravagant mansions.

Already at her makeshift desk, Madeleine picked up a cardboard file-folder with an old, grainy photo of a young soldier in a Russian uniform on the cover and containing twenty or thirty loose pages. 'This is from my archives, one of the terrorists we tracked into Iran. Most of it was hacked by the NSA from the Russian Defence Department.'

She handed it to Falcon, who looked at the photo of the man on the cover. 'This is him?' he asked me. 'The legend – the man you told Madeleine you'll be masquerading as?'

'Yes.'

'Why choose him? What's the advantage?'

'He's dead, for one.'

'You're certain?'

'Absolutely, buried down in the badlands with military honours – but the Russians don't know that. To them he is a former member of Spetsnaz, a corporal who fought in Aleppo, joined ISIS, threw in his lot with the Army of the—'

'And now he's returned to Mother Russia, looking for high-paying work in Baikonur. Being former military, he knows he'll pass the security checks. They like Spetsnaz, don't they?'

'Exactly. And apart from the file, I know a lot about him – we don't have to spend time inventing a legend and then have me try to master it. We've got a flying start—'

Falcon looked questioningly at me. 'How do you know about him?'

'It's in the file. Open it and you'll see – it's got his name, birth-place, family. Service record. Physical characteristics. Injuries and impediments—'

Falcon opened the file, leafed through the pages and stopped. I fig-ured he had come to the section with the details of the legend's identity. He read it and then, shocked, looked at me. 'You're going in as him?'

'I'm gonna try.'

He shook his head. 'No . . . no. You're crazy.' Then he thought about it more. 'You sure about this?'

I nodded. Rebecca was looking from one to the other of us: 'What's the problem?' she demanded.

Falcon handed her the file, still open at the identity page. 'The English translation is at the bottom.'

Rebecca looked at the page for a long moment then raised her eyes to me. 'Jesus,' she said. 'Are you out of your goddamned mind?'

63

MARGARET HAD THE FLOOR, STANDING NEXT TO ONE OF THE monumental fireplaces in the darkened room, facing another half-dozen people who had joined us, using a digital pointer to highlight footage on a large-screen TV normally used for movies or sporting events but now featuring satellite images of the hangar on the desolate airfield outside Grozny.

'We tried everything, but we couldn't get inside the hangar, so exactly how recruitment for Baikonur works is uncertain,' Margaret said. 'Maybe with more time ... but that's a luxury we don't have.' She glanced at a clock on the screen. 'Fifty hours to get to Baikonur, and that means we've pulled together whatever we can.

'You can see – two car parks. One for prospective recruits and the one we're interested in: for the staff. Satellite observation, the number of vehicles present and time-lapse photography indicate that something like one hundred and forty people work at the facility.'

'That many?' Falcon asked, as surprised as I was.

'Yes, I know, we would never have guessed,' Margaret replied. 'We ran an analysis of the Grozny power grid – the hangar has a dedicated power supply with full battery back-up and that indicates they are running their own independent computer network. We figure they have total access to the files of Russian law enforcement, intelligence, military, state archives, gossip – the whole nine yards.

'Then we used facial recognition on the employees where we could and got a dozen hits, enough to tell us the personnel are mostly intelligence agents or researchers from the Moscow and Saint Petersburg academies.' She paused. 'This isn't Russia's usual Rube Goldberg organization, Falcon – this concerns a ZATO. This is deadly serious.'

'I can see,' he replied grimly. I glanced at Rebecca – with each new fact, anxiety was being written larger on her face and I realized what a unique situation she found herself in; for probably the first time ever, the significant other of an American spy – a civilian – was witnessing the planning, the dangers and the fear that accompanied a secret mission. Some people might say it was a privilege. Instead, her eyes met mine and she shook her head despairingly.

'Next, the satellite captured audio from six rejected applicants talking to family after they had left the building,' Margaret continued as the faces of those who had been overheard appeared on the screen: violent-looking men and women, and not the people you'd want to spend time with.

'From what they said, with the interrogators having access to every file created on the man you have chosen to impersonate, it will be intense and extremely dangerous,' she said. 'Frankly, I don't think we have ever dealt with a situation so potentially disastrous.' She paused, looked around the room, and her eyes came to rest on me—

I always knew it was going to be tough but, even so, her assessment was sobering.

'During the process, they will strip-search you, full cavity version,' she said. 'Then they'll examine every item you want to take in with you and X-ray as much as possible. Primarily, they'll be looking for phones, recording devices, cameras – the usual stuff – but drugs, too. The trade in ZATOS for heroin, coke and ice is hugely lucrative. Life is so restrictive; people look for ways to escape. Weed, they don't care much about, and vodka, of course, is nearly everyone's poison of choice, but other drugs are a different proposition. Take your clothes off, please.' She was still speaking to me. 'Everything except your underpants.'

Rebecca looked at me. 'I hope you changed them this morning,' she said, deadpan, and at least it made everyone smile – we needed it.

A woman in her late thirties – chewed fingernails and ink-stains on her shirt and jeans – stepped out of the gloom near the kitchen. I recognized her as one of the agency's top forgers and, nervous as hell in front of Falcon and Buster, she took hold of the TV remote.

Immediately, images of a dozen tattoos appeared on the screen. With me standing in my underpants, she explained: 'Given the man's history, these are the inks we believe make sense for the agent – the Grim Reaper with an assault rifle for Spetsnaz, of course, the man's rank and regiment, battlefields where he fought, a map showing where he was born, and the date. Some of the front-line warriors did that for identification in case their faces were burned or their hands were taken as trophies.'

I avoided looking at Rebecca and was relieved that the forger started fiddling with the remote control and the tatts suddenly appeared – superimposed – on my mostly naked body. 'This is where we suggest placing them, but I need agreement before we start,' she said.

Rebecca shook her head at the forger. 'If I'd wanted a guy with tattoos, I would have gone for a rock star. Are they permanent?'

'It's a special dye that survives water, soap and almost any examination. They'll start to fade after about a month.'

'A month?' Rebecca replied. 'Okay – I'll get the spare room ready for him.'

The screen went to black, and Margaret took the remotes. 'We're all in agreement with the tattoos?' Nobody objected. 'Now we need to deal with the stuttering.'

I stopped, halfway through getting dressed. 'The stuttering?' I asked. 'In Russian?'

'Childhood trauma, apparently,' Margaret replied. 'He was very smart, a good soldier – the stuttering is the reason he never achieved higher rank. It's mentioned in all the files – we have no choice.'

Successfully negotiating the recruitment process under relentless stress, terrified of making one small mistake, my life depending on every answer, recalling instantly every aspect of the legend's history and contending with highly qualified interrogators in a foreign language would be hard enough. Having to do it without forgetting to stutter and carry it off convincingly added a degree of difficulty I hadn't bargained for. It must have shown on my face—

'It's not too hard,' Darren said in his monotone, speaking from out of the darkness. 'There's a total of six key elements.'

'How do you know that?' Falcon asked.

'When I read the file on the man, I studied it on Google.'

'I should have known,' said Falcon. 'How's your father?'

'Well, thank you. He says he's moving to North Korea – less government surveillance.'

Rebecca had turned to look at Darren; whatever doubts she had about the mental state of the people at Langley were clearly being dispelled. 'I can help you, Mr Kane,' Darren continued.

'Thanks,' I said. 'That would be invaluable.' I meant it, too.

'Time's short. We should move to the plane,' Madeleine said, turning off the screen.

64

A BACKPACK – OLD, FILTHY AND BATTERED – WAS SITTING ON A BENCH in a pop-up workshop just behind the plane's cockpit.

In a small convoy, we had left the entertainment pavilion and, as the sun was dipping behind the mountains, swung under the camouflage netting and climbed the steps into the cabin of the Globemaster freighter.

We followed Madeleine down the length of the aircraft. It had been transformed: virtually all the seats and fittings had been removed and the interior turned into workspace for the TripAdvisors and their charts, the Oscar-nominated production designer and her racks of aged Russian clothes, a barber with a chair and blades, the fingerprint experts surrounded by racks of moulds and plastics and – lastly – the armourer and his assistants with their precision tools and a 3-D printer.

'I didn't know the agency had anything like this,' I said to Madeleine.

'Nor did I,' Falcon added.

'We only had three hours to pull it together,' she explained. 'A crew at Andrews stripped out the interior while another team was constructing the workshops. It took twenty-five trucks to transport everything from Langley, and the last of it was loaded and in place with five minutes to spare.'

We stopped at the armourer's corner, and the bear of a man – the technical virtuoso who I had last seen just before I missioned into Iran – smiled and put out one of his giant paws to shake. 'I heard the navigation system on the old AK-47 worked out pretty well.'

I stared at him. 'You're kidding? I got lost more times than I could count.'

His laugh was as big as him, and he turned to an assistant, a slightly built guy in his late twenties who looked like he hadn't seen daylight in years: 'Show him our latest failure, Matty.'

Matty stepped up to the bench with the backpack on it and hit a stopwatch lying beside it. Deftly, he pulled apart six Velcro attachments, released two clips and stripped the filthy nylon webbing free of the backpack's metal-and-plastic frame. Laying the nylon aside methodically, he unscrewed and broke the frame down into its constituent parts before expertly reassembling them into something entirely different and far more deadly: a short-barrelled rifle.

I stared at it in astonishment. Matty hit the stopwatch. 'Forty-three seconds,' he said. 'And you're loaded for bear.'

I picked up the weapon and turned it over in my hand. 'Incredibly light,' I said.

'Titanium and 3-D-printed plastic where we could,' the armourer answered. 'The Russians will probably empty the backpack and weigh it. Too heavy and they will really start to look at it, so we had to get it right. Did you see – the firing mechanism is hidden in the grab handle on the top?'

I nodded. 'Really, really smart. Bullets?'

'Around your neck,' he replied, picking up a silver necklace from a bench. Hanging from it were a set of grimy dog tags and three cartridges. 'Each bullet is engraved with a date and place – they memorialize the US soldiers you killed in combat.'

'Did they really do that – the bullets?' Rebecca asked.

The armourer shrugged. 'Why not? Shrivelled ears were the most popular souvenir.' He turned to me: 'Three shots enough? It's all the magazine can hold. The weapon's accurate up to ten metres.'

'Three should be okay,' I replied. 'Can we make it even lighter? I need two spears mounted on it, gas powered, fired one at a time by the rifle.'

Everybody looked at me; they had no idea. 'Spears?' Falcon asked. 'Why?'

'In case I get delayed, a fail-safe if everything goes to hell,' I replied.

'Yes, but why spears?'

'Trust me, Falcon. I need spears.'

He nodded, and I turned to the armourer. 'Give me a pen and paper. I'll sketch the shape of the arrowhead – beyond everything, that might be crucial.'

65

I FELT LIKE A CUSTOMER IN A NAIL SALON IN THE WORLD'S MOST fucked-up strip mall. Surrounded by the plane's pop-up shops, wearing a dust-resistant smock, I had both hands inside electric dryers as three fingerprint experts – two men and a woman, all in their forties, their faces covered by surgical masks – waited at my shoulder.

A timer rang and they motioned for me to remove my hands. Immediately, the team leader – the woman – took off her mask, grabbed a magnifying glass and started to examine my index finger. Her two assistants took my other hand, placed it under a microscope and studied every whorl, ridge and furrow of my thumb and middle finger. Together, they were assessing the thin prosthetic sheaths they had created and fitted over my three fingers to duplicate the prints of the dead man I was impersonating.

'The fit's fine,' one of the men at the microscope said, lifting his face from the eyepiece. He picked up a copy of the fingerprints contained in the Russian military file and compared them to their own work. 'No problem with the match – the patterns are identical.'

He and his two colleagues sat back, tension easing. 'Okay – that's three fingers,' I said. 'Won't they take prints of four fingers, thumb and the palm of each hand? Twelve prints in total, and we've just got three. What happens if the recruiters look at the other ones?'

The team leader handed me the military file. 'We're lucky – the man joined the Army years ago, and back then they did a total of five fingers and the palm print of the left hand.'

'Okay,' I replied. 'That's six prints, and we've still only got three – we're missing two fingers and a palm.'

She nodded. 'We can't do a prosthetic of a palm print; it's not possible. And we have to conceal the place on the finger where our fakes meet your skin. We think three's the limit.'

I stared at her in dismay. 'I can't just go in there and hope they choose the fingers with the prosthetics. I'm a dead man walking if they don't. What do we do?'

I glanced at Falcon – clearly, he had no idea about any of this – then I saw the team leader looking at Buster for help. Uncomfortable, he made a poor attempt to tuck his shirt in, bracing himself. 'We're going to have to burn the other two fingers and the palm of your left hand.'

'Burn them for real?' I said.

'Yes. They'll be blistered and raw, as if you've had an accident a few days previously,' he replied. 'The Russians won't be able to lift a print off them so they'll have to rely on the three that they can. That will be our fake ones.'

'Apart from that,' the team leader added, 'we'll use the bandages to cover the joins where the prosthetics start.'

I thought for a moment and shook my head. 'Even if it works, why would they accept me, Buster? Nobody is gonna be able to work at Baikonur with burnt hands.'

'You'll have a letter from the hospital in Grozny saying the injuries are minor, you'll be fit for work in three days,' he replied. 'The forgers are working on it now.'

'How badly burnt?' Rebecca asked.

'Badly enough to be convincing,' Buster told her.

'The fingertips are loaded with sensory neurons,' Rebecca explained. 'Even minor burns, if they have to blister enough, are going to hurt—'

'We've thought of it; we'll do it under anaesthetic,' he responded.

'You can't,' Rebecca replied. 'If the Russians blood test him, they'll find traces of IV anaesthetic and they'll know something is wrong. It has to be done conscious.'

Nobody said a word. Falcon looked at me quizzically. 'Okay,' I said with a shrug. 'Conscious it is.' But I kept my eyes on the director; he was clenching and unclenching his fist. 'What's wrong?' I asked.

'The gun. It worries me,' he replied. 'I've got cash money that says the Russians will look hard at the backpack and then strip the frame down.'

66

FOR PRIVACY, OUR SMALL GROUP HAD MOVED TO A SECTION OF THE plane that had been converted into a dining area: banquette couches and a wall lined with vending machines that dispensed bad coffee and even worse snacks.

The backpack was lying on the table in front of us and Falcon was stripping off the canvas covering and breaking down the frame. I had once heard that – back in the day – he could field-strip an assault rifle in nothing flat, and it was obvious he had retained most of the skill. He twisted the concealed firing mechanism free of the grab handle, slotted it into the rifle and cocked it, ready to fire.

For a moment, he was an agent back in the field. 'Forty-three seconds – that's an incredible piece of tech,' he said. 'The problem is – once somebody realizes the frame can be unscrewed and reattached, it's like Rubik's Cube – just a matter of time before they get the right sequence. From what Margaret said, there are plenty of men and women at the recruitment centre capable of it.' His eyes turned to me for a reaction—

'If they find the gun, I'm dead as well – so is the mission,' I said, picking up the weapon and making a decision. I turned to the armourer. 'I'm sorry – after all your work – but Falcon may be right, the risk is too great. I won't take the backpack.'

The silence as they all absorbed it was broken by Margaret. 'What are you going to do?'

'Go in without a weapon,' I said.

'You can't – that's suicide. You can't go in unarmed. Period,' Falcon said harshly.

'I don't have a choice,' I said, just as uncompromising. 'What's the alternative? I have to get into Baikonur. Once I'm there, I'll extemporize.' The thought of confronting Kazinsky armed only with what I had found on the run was terrifying, but what else could I do?

'Extemporize?! It's a fuckin' ZATO,' Falcon said as we glared at one another. 'You can't go – we're stuck here in Morocco; flying out and abandoning the mission is the only option. I won't authorize it unarmed.'

I knew Falcon so well I was sure from the set of his jaw he wasn't going to back down.

'Burn his leg.' It was Madeleine talking.

'What?' I said.

'Burn it,' she repeated.

'Why?' Falcon asked, as lost as anyone. But realization was dawning for me—

'That's brilliant,' I said. 'It means I'll have to use crutches—'

'Yes,' Madeleine said. 'It will give them something else to concentrate on. We'll use the crutches as a diversion—'

'They'll draw attention away from the backpack?' Falcon asked.

'That's the theory,' Madeleine replied.

'And we can burn the leg very deep,' Margaret said. 'That'll sell the hand injuries.'

'Thanks, Margaret,' I said. 'Very helpful.' But my eyes didn't leave Falcon. After a long moment's thought, he turned to the armourer. 'Can you do something with crutches? Enough to arouse suspicion?'

'Sure thing, boss. It's not like we're short of time, is it?' the armourer said, smiling.

Forty-two hours.

67

I WAS USING BOTH HANDS TO HOLD A METAL BAKING DISH – RETRIEVED from a cupboard in the entertainment pavilion's kitchen – as a half dozen of us stood around the island bench listening to Margaret explain the scenario.

'You were staying at a friend's apartment en route to Grozny when you decided to cook *pirozhki*,' she said. 'You know it?'

'Traditional Russian dish. Pastry stuffed with cabbage, cheese or meat that it's better not to ask about. You bake or fry 'em,' I said.

'Yours are baked,' Margaret said. 'Using mitts, you took the baking dish out of the oven, put it on a countertop, dispensed with the mitts and – not thinking – decided to move it. Okay, drop it.'

Buster immediately noted where the dish hit the calf of my left leg. He rolled up my jeans and, using a mark-up pen, circled a few square inches. 'Hands now,' he said.

I held out both hands and he marked the spots on my fingers and left palm where I had been holding the handles of the baking dish. 'Okay?' he asked Rebecca.

She nodded and took bandages, swabs for a local anaesthetic, antibacterial wipes and gauze dressing out of a first-aid kit. She turned up one of the gas burners and put the long-handled soup ladle which she had decided was the best instrument for the job ahead into the flame.

'You need help with that?' Lucas Corrigan asked; he was a doctor too, after all.

Rebecca shook her head. 'Thanks, Lucas – it's probably better if we're alone.'

He nodded, and Falcon led everyone to the door and closed it behind him as Rebecca turned the cold-water tap on. 'We'll start with the fingers of the right hand,' she instructed. 'As soon as I'm finished, put the hand under the water – it'll reduce the swelling and pain.' She tossed me a tea towel.

'What's this for – to dry it?' I asked.

'Your mouth – roll it up and bite down on it. This is really going to fucking hurt. Ready?'

I nodded, put the tea towel in my mouth and watched as she took the red-hot ladle out of the flame and moved it towards my out-stretched fingers. 'Try not to breathe in,' she said matter-of-factly. 'The smell of burning flesh makes some people gag.'

The glowing metal approached the skin of my index finger, I braced myself and felt a knife-like pain rocket up my arm as Rebecca grabbed my wrist to stop me pulling my finger away. I bit down hard on the tea towel as she kept the metal pressed to the flesh. I felt my closed eyes water, opened them and saw the smoke rising from my skin, the pain getting exponentially worse. Gasping, biting down even harder, I realized she was taking the metal away and releasing her grip. The skin on my finger was red raw and bubbling already with blisters—

'Superficial hurts the worst,' she said. 'I have to be careful, I don't want to destroy the nerves—'

'No, don't do that,' I said, gasping, trying to recover. 'When I come back, I won't be able to feel anything when I touch you.'

'That's right,' she said softly. 'When you come back.' There were tears in her eyes and she turned away, ostensibly to reheat the ladle. 'I'll do the other two fingers and then the palm and the leg. An hour and you'll be on your way.'

68

IN THE CLEAR MOUNTAIN AIR, WITH A SPECTACULAR STARFIELD ABOVE and a full moon illuminating the highest peaks, four of us waited on the edge of the runway.

The backpack with its concealed gun and spears was over my shoulder, I had a pair of specially designed battered crutches at my side, my hands were partly wrapped in dirty bandages, my cheap Russian jeans had been ripped at one knee to reveal the bad burn on my calf, the seaman's reefer jacket I was wearing had tags inside from a Goodwill shop down south near the Caspian, my hair was cut short and badly, as was the style among former warriors returning from the badlands, and the waterproof pouch strapped around my waist held my birth certificate, internal passport, military discharge papers and a host of other forged documents that were indistinguishable from the genuine.

The small jet taxied to a halt just in front of us and the stairs were already being lowered as I turned to Lucas and put out my hand. 'In Saigon,' I said.

He smiled. 'Yeah, the city of my childhood – if only it still existed.'

'Sure it does – in your memories.'

'So – in Saigon then,' he replied.

I turned. 'In Cairo, Falcon.'

He nodded. 'In Egypt – where all my changes were.' He reached out and embraced me.

Rebecca tried to smile. 'In Soho,' I said quietly to her. 'In a bar full of sharp-elbowed people where everybody talks and nobody listens.'

She had realized how it worked. 'In Soho,' she replied. 'Where everything started so long ago.'

We hugged each other tight, then I disentangled myself, tucked the crutches under my arm and walked for the plane. I didn't look back; I couldn't, I might have lost my courage.

Instead, I climbed the stairs, ready to journey into a place where – *insha'Allah* – the past, the present and the future would all collide.

69

THE PILOT GREETED ME AT THE TOP OF THE STAIRS AND LOOKED OUT at the surroundings. 'It's a dry heat,' he said. '*Definitely* a dry heat this time.' I laughed – it was the same guy who had flown me into Riyadh and, as I battled the overwhelming anxiety of what lay ahead, I was pleased to find a familiar face.

'Baku?' he asked as he walked me to my seat and helped stow my backpack and jacket. I nodded.

'Ever been there?' he asked. 'Ever seen the fire surf?'

'Just once,' I replied.

'That's enough – you never forget it, do you?'

'No, it's like it's from a different time – when the Earth was young,' I replied.

'Exactly. You want me to run the GreenEnergy promo video again?'

'Once is enough for that, too,' I said.

'Good choice,' he replied.

Instead of the video – as we hurtled down the runway, climbed steeply to escape the valley and grazed the moonlit peaks – he played a map of the plane's route and progress.

Skirting Marrakesh, the map showed, we would turn east at Casablanca, fly down the Mediterranean, travel below the boot of Italy, cross the Greek islands, pass a scattered chain of islets with barely a name but home to a fragrant pine forest and a beautiful villa hidden by red bougainvillea, head into Turkey, traverse the length of the country, enter Azerbaijan and be guided into Baku by the glow of the LED screens on the Flame Towers. The journey would take eleven hours, according to the TripAdvisors.

From the airport, I would take a taxi belching diesel to the glass-roofed Ganjlik shopping mall and, following a map that I had memorized, go down to the supermarket, head out the back door and into the city's bustling bus terminus. From there, shuffling through the crowds and stopping at a dozen store windows to see in their reflection if I was being followed, I would make my way on foot to the Street of Gold.

On my crutches, moving slowly to make sure the CCTV captured me in all my threadbare glory, I would stop and haggle with three currency dealers to guarantee I got the best rate for my *tolahs*. By the time I had a fistful of rubles in my hand, any intelligence agent in a hangar in Grozny who decided to check the route I had travelled would be inclined to believe I was yet another disillusioned believer making his way home from Afghanistan or Iraq, Iran or Syria. By the grace of good planning, the truth would be blown away. You never leave a footprint in the sand.

I was following the exact route taken by Kazinsky not so long before, and though he had no way of knowing it, by the time I limped out of the Street of Gold I would be little more than twenty-four hours behind him—

And closing fast.

70

FOR ONCE, ON A DENIED ACCESS AREA MISSION, EVERYTHING WENT to plan. With my newly acquired rubles, I left the Street of Gold, stopped at one of dozens of stalls selling some of the best street food in the world, bought a *tantuni* wrapped in bread and headed to an underground car park well beyond the reach of any camera surveillance.

On the basement level, in a distant corner, I saw a nondescript Toyota with its trunk open and two grocery bags and a baby stroller waiting to be stowed.

Cautiously gliding between pillars and parked cars, I approached the Toyota by a circuitous route from behind, making myself as difficult a target as possible. Two agents-in-place, a man and a woman in their thirties – a 'tandem couple', in the parlance of the agency – were supposed to be sitting in the car. I saw two people who fitted the description but, in my heightened state, that meant nothing at all. They had not seen me, and I unslung the backpack, ready to drop to the ground if all hell broke loose, silently reminding myself that I would have forty-three seconds and three bullets to make an escape. What I would do after that, I had no idea.

'Where's Dasha?' I called, my voice echoing across the dimly lit space. The plan was for me to speak when I was almost at their side, but I had long ago dispensed with that idea; it would have left me far too exposed.

My voice startled them – neither of them seemed well experienced in working at such a dangerous level – and they both scrambled out of the vehicle. They would have been shot there and then if the circumstances were different.

The woman was the first to recover. 'With the nanny,' she replied, looking around, trying to see me.

The code phrase had been given and answered and I scrambled out from behind a pillar, tucked the crutches under my arm, sprinted towards them, immediately got into the back seat and simply said in Russian: 'Drive.'

In the long-established way of these things, we rode in silence until we reached a blaze of light in the darkness on the edge of town – a truck stop on the E119, the same coastal route that Kazinsky had taken to Grozny.

We drew up next to an eighteen-wheeler that was parked in the darkest corner of the lot and, well shielded from any cameras, I slipped out of the back seat of the car, threw the backpack and crutches into the cabin and within moments was riding shotgun beside another agent-in-place.

A lean and wiry guy in his early thirties with unruly hair and a ready smile, he pulled out of the parking lot on to the highway and hit the accelerator. In less than nine hours, looking out at every mile and the ten gas stations whose images I had once pored over in the Tomb, I would be at the airfield in Grozny.

For the first time, I really thought we had a chance—

71

TIME WAS ONE OF OUR GREATEST ENEMIES, AND IN MOROCCO WE decided we had to take a risk. As a result, the big-rig bypassed Grozny train station. I dispensed with getting a taxi and covering my tracks even further, and we drove straight on to the abandoned roadhouse, saving several hours.

On the long trip from Baku, the driver had proved to be a highly skilled agent – a former rider on the European MotoGP circuit who had translated his love of danger to the secret world – and it was his brilliant idea to give me a pistol.

'It's none of my business,' he had said when we were passing Truck Stop Seven. 'But you told me earlier you were unarmed. Do you think somebody who has travelled from Afghanistan, into Iran and across the Caspian would do that? I mean, we're in Chechnya – even the imams carry guns here.'

I turned to face him, recognizing his forethought and silently cursing the lack of my own.

'Arrive naked and they're gonna be suspicious,' he said, reaching under his seat and pulling out a 9mm Glock 17 with a thirty-three-round mag, probably the most common pistol in the world. 'It's a ghost – untraceable, of course,' he said. 'Hand it in when you arrive – if nothing else, it'll show you're military; you know you can't have an undeclared weapon on base.'

I nodded my thanks and took it. 'It's the details, isn't it?' he said.

'Yeah, it's the details that sell the story,' I replied. 'We tell a million small truths to make them believe the one big lie.'

We probably both had that in mind as we pulled into the roadhouse parking lot. Almost certain that we were under surveillance – either by satellite or from cameras on the high-voltage electricity towers that ran along the road – I clambered out of the cabin and made a show of handing over three of my remaining *tolahs* in supposed payment for the ride.

I waited for the semi to turn out of the overgrown lot before I swung the backpack over my shoulder, fitted the crutches under my arm, limped past piles of old shell casings and walked along the side of the road, putting my thumb out to the few cars that passed. Nobody stopped; given my appearance it was hardly surprising.

I didn't have to walk far, but with the uneven terrain and the unaccustomed crutches biting into my armpits, my face was drawn with fatigue and running with sweat by the time I arrived. It was a blessing; I looked exactly like a down-at-heel warrior as I approached the steel security gates and concrete blockhouse guarding entry to the airfield.

Speaking through a glass window, stuttering, I told the young Army lieutenant in command the reason for my visit and was met with a look somewhere between incredulity and disdain. 'You?' he said in clipped Russian, indicating my ragged appearance and bandaged hands. 'You want a job in Baikonur?'

I nodded, unbuckled the waterproof pouch from around my waist and handed him my military discharge papers. He glanced down at them and underwent a total change in demeanour: 'Spetsnaz?' he asked.

'From Syria,' I stammered. 'By way of Iraq and the badlands near Afghanistan.'

'Spetsnaz in Syria,' he murmured, with even more respect.

'Presenting a weapon now,' I said, and a flash of alarm crossed his face. I withdrew the Glock from my jacket pocket, its barrel pointed at me for safety, and handed it over.

Relieved, he took it. 'Good to meet a professional,' he said, smiling. 'Internal passport?'

I indicated the waterproof pouch and felt my tension rise as he ran his eye over its pages and checked on a computer to see if it had been stolen. Satisfied, he handed it back. Thank God for the agency's forgers, I thought.

'I'll organize a car to take you to the recruitment centre,' he said. 'While you're waiting, there's a washroom in the back. Clean yourself up – they're hard people over there, even to veterans. Try to avoid a man called Strelnikov – you'll recognize him; he's cold enough to send your temperature to zero.'

72

A BEATEN-UP UAZ-469 – THE RUSSIAN EQUIVALENT OF A JEEP – dropped me outside the isolated hangar and, with my face freshly washed, hair slicked back and a clean bandage wrapped around my calf, I joined the queue of would-be recruits.

The line was much shorter than the satellite footage I had seen when Kazinsky was making his way towards the door, but the type of people – civilians, many of them downtrodden and sullen – was unchanged and the same document detailing the special regulations at Baikonur was circulating among the new arrivals.

It was handed to me, I read it through for appearance's sake, and by the time I had finished I was at the door. One of the three military guards gave me a numbered disc, noted down my name from my internal passport, and stood aside to allow me to enter—

The decrepit and rust-streaked exterior of the hangar completely belied what lay inside. Painted a brilliant white and lit by hanging fluorescent tubes, the vast space was grim, antiseptic and totally intimidating. With a floor of pale grey linoleum, rows of interview desks also in white, armed soldiers at every door and banks of black computer terminals and X-ray machines, it looked like it had been designed by someone with a wrought-iron soul. Maybe that was the intention.

I sat on a straight-backed chair next to several dozen other interviewees and looked at a screen on the wall that was announcing numbers, telling the holder of the relevant metal disc what desk to attend. Anxious to see where I would confront the greatest danger, I looked to my left and saw that a queue of men and women had stripped to their underwear and were loading all of their clothes, luggage and possessions on to X-ray conveyor belts. Half naked, they waited at stainless-steel tables while uniformed security officers followed up with a fingertip examination of all of their clothes and goods.

I glanced down the tables and – with alarm – saw that every backpack was having its outer shell removed and the exposed metal frame taken apart and inspected.

The savage twist in my gut made me want to leave, but I couldn't back out. There were a host of cameras on overhead gantries monitoring the entire space, their operators undoubtedly alert for anything suspicious, while above them – on a glass-walled mezzanine floor – I could see men in suits observing the floor below. Margaret had said it wasn't the usual Rube Goldberg outfit, and she had got that right; I was trapped and alone with zero options.

Mind racing, I watched another group of recruits, still in their underwear, pass through body scanners and then wait at flimsy booths to undergo full cavity searches. This was no place for modesty.

A loud voice – surprising in the silence – suddenly called out. I turned and saw that it was a hard-ass orderly yelling angrily at those of us on the chairs and pointing at the screen on the wall.

I glanced down at my metal disc and saw that I had been concentrating so hard on what lay ahead that I had ignored the present – my number had come up.

73

I GRABBED MY CRUTCHES, LOCATED THE NUMBER EIGHTEEN ON A pole above a desk near the front and, negotiating my way past several other recruits being interviewed, saw a lean man – clean-shaven with a cruel mouth, a sharply pressed uniform and wire-rimmed glasses – sitting behind the desk and watching me from grey eyes.

With a jolt, I guessed his name even before I saw the patch above his breast pocket: Strelnikov. The rest of his insignia told me he was a major in military intelligence. In his early thirties, he was young for the rank – and his sharp-eyed dedication reminded me of the photos I had seen of the men who had kept the new arrivals running down the chutes at Auschwitz.

I stopped in front of him, propped the crutches against the desk, and – like any good corporal, even a former one – saluted. He didn't stand, didn't acknowledge me, he just stared, assessing. Like measuring me for a coffin.

I had expected him to tell me to sit in the chair facing him, but he didn't. He adjusted his glasses and opened a file of papers in front of him. 'Aleppo,' he said as he looked closely at one of the papers.

'Yes, sir,' I replied, stuttering. The impediment made him look up and, again, he just observed me. I reached out and took the crutches to support myself; if he was going to keep me standing, at least I was going to play up the injury.

'You were there for the worst of it?'

'I was, yes, sir,' I said, continuing to stutter.

'At the end, the Americans went out and buried the Spetsnaz dead,' he said. 'What did they do, Corporal, as they put them in the grave – do you recall?'

'You mean, how they took off the dog tags, the watches, the photos – everything personal?' I replied.

'Go on.'

'They put them in a box and returned it to us. A mark of respect, the Americans said, warrior to warriors.'

He gave no acknowledgement that I was right. 'Take your shirt off,' he said.

I did as ordered, and he motioned me closer so that he could look carefully at the tattoos. I had no idea how good the inks were or how much Strelnikov would know about them. One thing was certain; my life was now in the hands of the woman in Ourika with the stained jeans and the chewed fingernails.

The major focused on the battlefields and the dates listed on my chest, comparing them with those in my military records, and then, seemingly satisfied, turned to the date and map of my birth. 'Your mother left when you were very young,' he said, consulting different pages in the file. 'Ten years after that your father died violently and you were orphaned. Correct?'

I nodded; I think he was relieved he didn't have to wait for me to get any words out.

'You were an eyewitness to your father's death and that trauma led to the stutter.'

'Yes,' I replied. 'It prevented me taking any command position in the military.'

'So it says,' he replied, indicating the file. 'It also claims you were a good soldier.' With a wave of his hand, he indicated I could put my shirt back on. I was through that part, thank God, but my relief was short-lived. 'Fingerprints,' he said, and switched on an ultrasonic scanner – the most accurate of the four types available to law enforcement – sitting on the desk.

I held out the index finger of my right hand and the thumb and middle finger of my left hand – the three fingers that had been fitted with the prosthetics – and waited for the machine to finish booting up.

He kept his eyes fixed on me. 'Take the bandages off,' he ordered.

If he saw the join between the prosthetics and my skin I was finished, and so was the mission, but I had no alternative. He watched as I unwrapped the bandages from both hands. 'You're sweating,' he said.

'It hurts, Major,' I replied. 'Release the pressure, the blood flows in, the pain increases.' I was thankful for the stutter; it helped mask the fear in my voice.

I removed the last bandage but kept my hands half balled into fists, making out I was trying to reduce the pain but trying to hide the joins. He took my wrists – his hands were surprisingly soft and feminine – and I was certain he was going to straighten out my palms and would see what I was trying so hard to hide. Breathing hard, with no way out and no fallback, I waited—

He didn't unball my hands. He merely pulled them closer, wanting to see if my fingers really were injured. I made a conscious effort not to sigh with relief. He looked at the blisters – most of them had already burst and were raw and weeping, appearing even worse than they felt – nodded in acceptance of it and let go of my wrists.

'What happened?' he asked.

'Cooking *pirozhki*, sir,' I said, trying to force my heart rate back to normal. 'I had the baking dish out of the oven, gloves off, when I decided to move it. I burnt my hands.' I shrugged. 'Then I dropped it.' I pointed at my bandaged calf. It's the details, I thought, always the details.

'What meat did you use?' he asked. 'For the *pirozhki*?'

'Beef, Major,' I replied.

'Not dog?'

'No, sir. They were for friends; I wasn't selling them.'

He pointed at my hands as I was rebandaging them. 'You won't be able to work,' he said.

'Beg to differ, sir. I have a letter from Grozny Hospital Number Four – they say three days and I will be fit.' I pointed at the waterproof pouch and, as he retrieved the forged letter, he nodded at the scanner—

'Use your three good fingers,' he said. 'That'll have to do.'

The subterfuge had worked. With my fingers under the scanner, I waited while sound waves mapped the exact contours of my prints. The green light stopped and I knew they were now being compared to the dead man's prints on file in some massive military database in Moscow.

Strelnikov's eyes alternated between watching me and looking at a computer screen on the side of his desk, while, all the time, I kept my gaze fixed on the middle distance, seemingly paying attention to the men and women in the glass room above us.

'Sixty seconds and we get the result,' he said. 'I've had my doubts about you, Corporal – the bandages, the limp, the accent from the frozen north that doesn't sound quite right. Maybe it's the stutter. It's my job, though – to doubt everyone and everything. Certain people would love to get somebody into Baikonur. The Americans have a group of elite spies, skilled men and women called Denied Access Area agents – that's the sort of person they would send.'

'Really, sir?'

'Yes, really. I'm certain of it. Ever heard of them?'

'What was their name again?' I asked.

He was about to repeat it when the computer pinged. He looked at the screen and frowned; whatever suspicions he might have harboured had been allayed. 'It's a match.'

I bit my lip with relief, but there was still one hurdle left.

'Pick up your things,' Strelnikov said. 'Bring them over to the X-ray machine.'

74

I STRIPPED DOWN TO MY BOXERS, EMPTIED MY BACKPACK AND LAID the pack, its contents, the clothes I had been wearing and the crutches on the conveyor belt.

I was still sweating hard but – for once – I didn't try to mask it. I knew what I had to do and, in a minute, maybe less, every sign of anxiety and stress was going to help me. It might even save my life.

I watched my possessions disappear into the X-ray machine and then turned my attention to the operators – a man and woman, sitting at separate screens – as they slowly examined the image of every item. If nothing else, they were thorough.

The clothes emerged, then the crutches, followed by the empty backpack. With Strelnikov at my shoulder, I moved to the stainless-steel table, fussed over some of my clothes and meagre possessions, kept glancing at the crutches and waited for the four officers on the other side of the table to start their fingertip search.

One of them picked up the empty backpack and carried it down the table to where three of his colleagues were waiting to take off its outer shell and examine the frame. Despite the ice-cold fear rising out of my stomach, I didn't even glance at it; I just kept my eyes darting back and forth between my clothes and the crutches. Acting casually, I reached out, picked them up, and was about to put them under my arms as if my injured leg needed the support—

'Wait,' Strelnikov ordered.

Everybody, including the three officers at the end of the table who had just taken possession of the backpack, stopped. I looked at the major.

'You seem nervous, Corporal,' he said. 'You're sweating again – it can't be the wounds this time. Why did you keep glancing at the crutches?'

'Did I, Major?' I replied. 'I just want them back. I need them to walk.'

'No,' he said, stepping forward, his face close to mine, looking at me intently. I could feel his breath on my cheek. 'No,' he repeated, shaking his head for emphasis.

I shrugged – making out that I had nothing to hide. The man and woman operating the X-ray machine stopped the belt and watched. The fingertip searchers, the other recruits waiting in line and the officers with the backpack were just as silent.

Strelnikov's thin lips separated into a smile. 'Give me the crutches.'

I looked at him for a moment and handed them over, apparently unwillingly, managing to make my hand shake a little. He signalled to the three officers with the backpack to join him: 'Look at these,' he ordered as I watched them abandon the backpack. 'Take your time.'

I stepped aside to give the three officers room and they took possession of the crutches, ready to lay them out on the steel table and examine every joint and length of tubing.

'They're heavier than you would think,' a middle-aged guy, his belly straining against his jacket, said as he balanced one of them in his hand.

'Maybe somebody lined the tubes with lead or aluminium to block the X-ray?' Strelnikov said, looking at me.

'Possible, sir,' the pudgy guy replied. 'There's plenty of people who think they're geniuses. Is everyone in the world corrupt?'

'I don't know everyone,' Strelnikov replied icily.

I said nothing, just kept my eyes on my clothes, studiously ignoring the backpack as it sat, untouched, further down the table.

The three officers continued to look at the crutches, turning them over in their hands, trying – unsuccessfully – to unscrew the lengths of tubing from each other or find some other way to take them apart. 'We should be able to disassemble them,' one of them – a sharp-faced woman – said. 'They can't have been moulded in one piece.'

'Is there a locking device, some sort of mechanism?' the pudgy guy suggested. Everyone, including the other officers and the recruits in line, had moved closer to watch the drama.

'What do you think, Corporal?' Strelnikov asked. 'Some sort of lock?'

'I wouldn't know, Major,' I replied. 'I bought them at a second-hand store in Baku.'

'Ah,' he said. 'Of course – a second-hand store.' He turned to the sharp-faced woman. 'Strip off the cushioning.' He pointed at the faux-leather padding where the top of the crutch fitted under the armpit.

She took a multi-purpose tool off her belt and with a knife cut it away, exposing the metal. 'There's a large screw,' she reported, opening a screwdriver and trying to loosen it. 'At least that's what it looks like. It turns, but it won't come out.'

'Broken, maybe? A stripped thread?' the pudgy guy asked.

'Not sure,' the woman replied.

'Cut open the padding on the hand grip,' Strelnikov ordered, pointing to the area halfway down the crutch.

The woman did as she was told. 'Another large screw, identical,' she said, and used the screwdriver on it. 'Same problem.'

Everybody looked at the stripped-down crutch, trying to work out what, if anything, it meant. 'Strange, isn't it?' Strelnikov said to me. 'Two large screws, identical, but neither of them seems to work.'

I opened my hands in confusion – apparently as lost as anyone. Still thinking, the major looked at the man and woman on the other side of the table. 'Turn both screws together,' he said.

The officers each fitted a screwdriver into a screw. 'Clockwise,' the woman said. 'Now.' They both turned—

The crutch – its various components spring-loaded – suddenly sprang apart. Strelnikov smiled, triumphant.

The other recruits stared at me in surprise while the officers looked at the crutches, nodding their heads in grudging admiration.

'Quite a bargain you got at the second-hand store,' Strelnikov said. 'You do it yourself?'

I sort of slumped, acting as if there was no point in denying it, and nodded. 'I'm good with machines, technical stuff, building things,' I said.

'It's very clever,' Strelnikov replied. 'But not quite clever enough. You should learn a lesson from it – sometimes you can meet people who are a lot smarter than you.'

'Yes, Major,' I said, barely looking at him. 'Learn a lesson – you're right.'

'What's inside?'

'Weed,' I replied. 'I like a smoke – it helps with the stuttering if I'm relaxed.'

'Where did you get it?'

'Afghanistan,' I replied.

'You carried it all the way here?' he asked, taken aback. 'Where in Afghanistan?'

It was a question I hadn't anticipated – adrift, panicky, I tried to think of a town or a village. A region, even. Then it came to me:

Connor Bryant, I thought, recalling the young drone pilot from Huntington Beach.

'I bought it in Balkh,' I said. 'They say it grows the best weed in the world, but I went there for another reason – the town is home to the Mosque of the Nine Cupolas, the oldest in the country. It's sacred—'

'The Mosque of the Nine Cupolas?' Strelnikov said; clearly he'd never heard of it, but it had the ring of truth to it.

'Major?' The pudgy officer was calling Strelnikov's attention to the large pile of marijuana they had now removed from both crutches.

'If it was any other drug, you'd be under arrest, I can promise you,' the major said to me. 'You burnt your hands and leg yourself – so you'd have an excuse to use the crutches?'

'Yes, sir,' I replied, downcast. Other officers had gathered at the table, examining the armourer's handiwork while Strelnikov signalled to the X-ray operators to restart the belt. For that moment, everyone was distracted. *Carpe diem*, I thought—

As unhurried as I could manage, trying to suppress the crushing anxiety, fighting to ignore the terrible consequences of failure, I started to pick up my clothes and other possessions from the steel table. Casually, with my arms full, I walked a few steps down the table—

I wasn't breathing, I knew it, but my body was working to its own reality. I pulled the backpack towards me and began to repack it, expecting at any moment that Strelnikov or one of the officers would yell an objection and order me to stand aside. Nobody said a word.

Instead, the recruits were unloading their gear on to the conveyor, the officers at the table were starting the fingertip search, backpacks were being pulled out for further inspection and Strelnikov was watching the pudgy man and the sharp-faced woman reassemble my crutches.

The two officers saw me approach and handed me the reassembled crutches. Neither they, nor the major, said anything about the backpack. They didn't even appear to notice it. Thank you, Madeleine, I thought, thank you – you've brought us this far.

'You went to a lot of trouble,' Strelnikov said, indicating the crutches. 'And you've obviously got a lot of technical skill, but don't ever try anything like that again.'

'Yes, sir,' I said, barely willing to hope. 'Does it mean I'm going, sir?'

'You're Spetsnaz, Corporal – we know we can rely on your loyalty. That has tipped the scales for you.'

'Thank you, Major,' I replied, and for once I wasn't faking the sincerity.

He laid my file and a batch of movement orders on the table, signed and stamped them in triplicate and handed a copy to me. 'There's a canteen and bunks at the back of the hangar. Your plane leaves at noon tomorrow.' He turned and walked away.

I stared after him in shock. Back in Morocco, we had monitored all the flights between the air base and Baikonur and I knew there was a flight leaving in two hours. That was what we had relied on; if I wasn't on board, there was no reason to go – I couldn't get there in time. 'Permission to speak, sir,' I called after him.

Officers and the people queuing at the X-ray machine looked. Strelnikov turned. 'What?' he said in a tone of exasperation.

'I believe there's a plane leaving soon,' I said. 'Can I catch a ride on that, Major?'

'It's full,' he replied, turning away.

'It's a family matter,' I said, reclaiming his attention. He turned back. 'A birthday,' I continued.

'What?' he said, hearing what I said but irritated.

I walked closer to explain, more people turned to listen and I was almost at his side when a siren blasted through the hangar. It was a signal to the officers and guards to gather up their files and possessions – the shift was changing.

It drowned out my voice and I had to lean in close to the major, speaking almost into his ear and preventing anyone else from hearing.

The siren lasted for barely twenty seconds, but by that time I was finished and, in the silence, Strelnikov looked at me and sighed. He consulted a list in his files and called loudly towards the canteen at the far end. 'Abramovich!' he ordered.

A guy in his early twenties in a tight T-shirt walked forward. 'Yo,' he called.

Strelnikov glared at him. 'You're flying out tomorrow,' the major told him. 'Give your boarding documents to your replacement here.'

He handed them over. In two hours I would be flying to Baikonur. Once I arrived, I had two hours and seven minutes to kill Kazinsky.

75

THE ILYUSHIN IL-76 TRANSPORT CAME IN LOW OVER THE ARAL SEA, its bleak expanse of spinifex and sand transformed to silver in the bright moonlight. Through the window I saw a herd of camels roaming among the flotilla of marooned ships.

Dozens of other recruits were crowding the windows and as the plane turned to prepare for landing several of them called out: 'Wolves.' I scanned the landscape and saw a pack of four, powerful and wild, standing on a ridge-line; they were perfectly still, the alpha male in front, all of them looking in the direction of the plane.

They were silent and, it seemed to me, I would never again hear their howls: behind them were the orange bursts of flame from the blast furnaces at the off-earth processing plant. They would no longer be able to call to me: I had arrived.

76

IT WAS A SPECTACULAR SIGHT — BAIKONUR'S PILLARS OF LIGHT RISING high into the sky and the long runway ablaze with light — as the Ilyushin came into land.

Captured from a satellite, the image was playing on the large screen in the entertainment pavilion at the black prison in Morocco. Rebecca, Falcon, Buster, Madeleine and several of the experts were standing in front of it, watching silently as the plane's wheels touched down and a convoy of buses drove across the apron to meet it.

'We have to assume he got on board and he's arrived,' Buster said and turned to Falcon. 'You gonna make the call?'

'I'd prefer to be certain,' Falcon said. 'What about when the passengers disembark? Will we be able to see him?'

'No,' Buster replied. 'The air-stairs are covered because of the elements. The passengers will walk down and straight into the buses.'

'Okay,' Falcon said. 'We have to believe he made it then. I'll trigger it now.'

He walked outside for privacy and, standing near the pool, pulled his phone out and waited for the encrypted call to be connected by satellite.

'Trigger what?' Rebecca asked.

'He's calling Langley,' Buster said. 'To tell them to use one of our most highly classified systems to contact an asset we have in place.'

'In Baikonur?'

'Yes. The message will alert her – she'll know the agent has arrived and the mission is live.'

'Then what does she do?' Rebecca asked.

'Nothing. She waits,' Buster said. 'Kane knows that as soon as he's killed Kazinsky he has to hit an emergency button in the plant that's used to summon urgent medical help. We've made sure the asset is on duty tonight. She goes to the plant immediately, just as she would in any situation—'

'To help him if he's injured?' Rebecca asked.

'Yeah, that too,' Buster replied. 'But mostly to get him the fuck out of there.'

77

THE ONE HUNDRED AND FORTY OF US ON BOARD THE ILYUSHIN watched as three officials made their way down the aisles, consulting clipboards and allocating the men – and half a dozen women – to different sites scattered across the sprawling complex.

A man in his late forties with the physique of a bar-room bouncer and an attitude to match stopped in front of my row. 'Abramovich,' he demanded.

'Abramovich was pulled off the flight,' I stuttered, handing him a folder with my documents. 'I got sent instead.'

He didn't bother opening the folder; he just looked me up and down dismissively. 'Not much of a bargain,' he said, examining his clipboard. 'Take the ground transport to stop three. You're a labourer Class 2 – north-east oil storage depot.'

'No,' I said. At the recruitment hangar I had been too concerned about getting on the plane to worry about what facility I would be sent to. Once on board, however, I'd had plenty of time to think about it.

'No?' the Bouncer asked, taking a step towards me. 'What you mean, no?'

'Abramovich was the labourer,' I replied evenly. 'I've got an engineering background – that's why we were swapped. I've been assigned to the off-earth processing plant.'

'Says who?'

'Strelnikov.'

'Strelnikov – the asshole?' he muttered.

'Yeah, that's him,' I replied.

He looked at me and almost smiled. 'You get on the *motovoz* – the plant is in Siberia, the last stop on the line. Okay?'

I nodded, relieved, as he handed back the unopened folder and called out the next name.

I looked at my watch: 12.47 a.m. In New York, Chloe had calculated that the spore was released some time between 1.16 a.m. and 1.57. I had twenty-nine minutes to get to the processing plant.

After that, I would either encounter Kazinsky, or I would meet something that was more than a man, but less than human.

I grabbed the backpack out from under my knees and got ready to disembark. Twenty-eight minutes—

78

THE *MOTOVOZ* TORE THROUGH THE DARKNESS, ITS OLD LOCOMOTIVE belching black diesel and shattering the silence.

The four carriages were almost empty; most of the other recruits had already got off at previous stops. With escalating anxiety, I had watched as we pulled into five of them – two more than we had anticipated in Morocco – and there was no doubt I was really running against the clock now.

We slowed down and pulled into yet another rickety wooden platform. This one served a vast waste-water complex. Tumbleweeds were blowing through its decrepit buildings, a handful of rusting pumping stations and a series of huge sludge ponds.

The smell – carried towards us by a wind howling out of the Great Steppes – was almost overwhelming as a dozen recruits tied handkerchiefs across their mouths, gathered up their belongings and stepped on to the platform.

The Bouncer and I were alone on board now. The locomotive blasted its horn and the train gathered speed, heading deeper into Siberia, fast approaching the last stop on the line.

'You're in luck,' the Bouncer said, pointing ahead. Through the window, a long glow of lights and flashes of orange flame were visible on a small rise in the ocean of darkness.

It was my first sight, in reality, of the off-earth processing plant, and I stared at it for a long moment.

'It's been offline for a couple of days,' the Bouncer continued. 'Some fuck-up took the whole electrical system down. You can see, though – they've got it back online.'

He was about to turn away from the window when he stopped. 'Look at that, will you,' he said.

I followed the direction in which he was pointing and saw a huge spiral of ash, smoke and glowing embers suddenly whirling out of the roof of the plant.

'What the hell is that?' he said.

But I knew – I knew that despite what the Bouncer had said, we weren't in luck at all. Kazinsky had just opened the large cooling vents in the roof.

One more step and there was nothing that could be done—

THE TRAIN TOOK A LONG SWEEPING CURVE AND STARTED TO SLOW. I looked at my watch again: 1.21 a.m. – five minutes past the deadline – but I was still within the window. Maybe things would work out, but the truth was, I had no idea what I would find inside the plant.

We came out of the curve far sooner than I had expected, and there it was, right in front of us – the plant's towering brick walls rising up into the night, its huge doors standing open, out of which poured noise and heat and a sickening, acrid smell.

The train continued to slow. I had come to the ends of the Earth, where night had fallen and the darkness was truly upon us.

The Bouncer came to my side. 'The guy in charge is called Kazinsky,' he said, his voice raised above the roar of the machines. 'He was in the Spetsnaz – a colonel – and you either call him that or the Emir, okay? He whipped two men to death the day he arrived, so that probably tells you all you need to know.'

He laughed and took out my file of documents and opened it.

I looked through the doors, saw the interior of the plant for the first time. In the glow of the furnaces and scattered overhead lamps I saw a crane passing in front of the faded murals of Lenin and the heroic Soviet workers. I couldn't see what was suspended from its large hook until it passed close to one of the furnaces and a shadow of a vast bucket appeared on the far wall.

'We should hurry,' I said to the Bouncer.

He looked at me quizzically. 'Keen, aren't you?' He had the documents open. 'I am going to need him to sign the transport form, showing you've arrived—'

He stopped. 'That's a coincidence,' he said.

'What's that?' I asked.

'The name,' he replied, seeing it on my documents and then lifting his eyes to look at me.

'Not really,' I said.

'How come?' he replied.

I started to speak but the *motovoz*'s brakes were screeching us to a halt and I had to lean in close to his ear for him to even hear—

I GRABBED MY BACKPACK AND LED THE BOUNCER OFF THE TRAIN.

Together we walked into the glowing, pounding interior. I saw the glass-enclosed pod, a massive bucket hanging from the crane and, steadily approaching it, the river of lava-like metal. Off to one side was the empty cafeteria with the emergency button that would summon urgent medical help if and when I needed it.

'Colonel Kazinsky,' the Bouncer called loudly, respectfully.

'What is it?' a voice answered.

I tried to compare it to how he had spoken to me in Iran to see if it had changed in any way, but he was yelling and the sound of the machinery was too great.

'A new recruit, Colonel.'

'Leave his papers there. I'll sign them and return them to you tomorrow. Tell him to wait – I'll be there in a minute.'

The Bouncer grinned at me and called back, 'It's your brother, Colonel.'

There was a momentary pause. 'My brother died in Iran, shot by the Americans.'

'Well, he's back,' the Bouncer called. 'And he's here.'

'Not possible!' Kazinsky yelled in answer.

'Does he speak with a stutter?' the Bouncer asked.

'Yes.'

'Then it's definitely him,' the Bouncer said, and looked at me. I smiled back, as if we were both in on the surprise, then looked up at the overhead crane, which had stopped momentarily. But my relief was immediately swamped by apprehension: Kazinsky was on his way.

A horn blasted from outside – the train driver signalling it was time to go. The Bouncer handed me the documents he wanted signed. 'Make sure he gets 'em back to me tomorrow. Good luck with the family reunion.'

He turned, headed out the door, and I immediately dropped to my knees and started pulling the backpack apart. Forty-three seconds.

Partway through, with the canvas shell stripped from the frame, I looked up and saw a shadow appear on the wall. My hands flew across the frame, trying to release the parts more quickly.

A moment later he walked in. I was twenty-two seconds short.

81

TWENTY-TWO SECONDS SHY OF ASSEMBLING THE WEAPON – AND probably four minutes too late in arriving – I saw that Kazinsky had already been transformed.

Across ten feet of toxic air – and unarmed – I looked at the enormously powerful frame, the prominent musculature, hairless body and the skin so pale it was almost translucent, that I had seen in New York. If I survived long enough to catch sight of his back, he would have a ridge of hardened skin running down his spine.

He stared back at me, momentarily astonished. 'You,' he said.

'You told me in Iran you couldn't wait to see the next surprise.' I was looking past him, playing for every second, gathering the half-broken-down frame of the backpack, trying to plan for when he attacked. 'They just keep coming, don't they?'

I tightened my grip on the different parts of the frame. Lose one of them, and I would have to fight without a weapon. I was a dead man.

His dark eyes, with their luminous streaks of gold, flashed as astonishment was supplanted by a wave of sheer fury. He hurled himself at me. 'For my brother,' he snarled.

His hands reached for my neck. He was much younger than he had been in New York, stronger and more agile. One twist of my neck and he would snap the vertebrae, killing me instantly.

But I was at least ready for him and launched myself to the side. I felt his shoulder brush my elbow as his hands missed my throat by an inch or less. I hit the ground and combat-rolled over and over, sliding under a heavy-duty trolley on large steel wheels—

Any well-trained soldier would have kept rolling, emerged from the other side and started to run. But I wouldn't have had a chance against Kazinsky in a flat-out foot race.

Instead, I grabbed the underside of the trolley, wrenching my shoulder, to bring myself to a halt. I rolled back the way I had come and saw his feet leave the ground as he leapt over the trolley.

He landed, and I was behind him now. I drove the trolley hard into his back as he looked ahead, trying to locate me in the gloom. It sent him sprawling to his knees. I hit him again, harder, forcing him even lower and running one of the steel wheels over his outstretched arm, crushing part of his elbow.

Now I ran – stuffing the parts of the rifle into my jacket and zipping it to keep them safe and my hands free. Ten paces and I was in the heart of the deserted plant, the blast furnaces spewing out sparks, the molten river aglow, the ash whirling through the overhead vents, and the steel door into the supervisor's office gaping open. High above me the huge bucket was dangling from the crane.

I barely paid it any attention. In my head, I had a sort of plan. I ran for the far wall, past the furnaces and the slag heaps, skirting the molten river and grabbing a shovel from a large barrow as I passed.

On the concrete behind me, I heard Kazinsky's feet pounding, ever closer, then I saw him reflected in a stainless-steel water hopper. Only a few feet back and gaining fast. Three steps and he would be able to—

Just as he lunged, I suddenly swerved, grabbed a ladder and swung myself on to one of the lower overhead gantries. He couldn't make the turn and cannoned past, cursing.

Charging along the rickety walkway, I saw him just below, keeping pace.

'Tired yet?' he shouted, laughing maniacally.

I ignored him and reached the wall, where I took a breath and swung the hardened steel blade of the shovel with all my strength at the heavy chain.

Breaking apart, the chain flew upwards, spinning free with an almighty rattle, and with a clang, the huge glass vents in the roof slid shut.

Kazinsky stared at them; it might not prevent the release of the spore, but it would certainly slow it. Roaring with anger, he leapt, grabbed an overhead pipe and swung on to the walkway, coming straight at me—

I wheeled, scaled another ladder, scrambled on to a higher and even more unstable path and jagged to the right, running for the supervisor's office.

Behind its thick glass walls designed to muffle the sound of the machines, and with the steel door bolted behind me, I might be able to buy just enough time to finish assembling the rifle. Armed, I could do it, I could take him—

Sprinting hard, Kazinsky followed me on to the upper walkway, and I felt the structure shudder and swing under our combined weight. I had to grab the handrails to steady myself, slowing me down. I wasn't going to make the office.

Instead, I threw my weight to the right, swung over the side, dropped to the walkway below, landed on it for a moment and then leapt again, on to the ground. A shower of embers from one of the furnaces sprayed me, but I kept going through it. I looked behind—

Kazinsky had taken the drop in one leap and made up several crucial yards. I darted left and reached an old metal bridge across the broadest section of the molten river.

I was halfway across, expecting to feel his feet hit the decking behind me, but there was nothing. Still running, I looked back—

He was bent over, about to use his brute strength to try and rip the end of the bridge from its rusted moorings. If he did, I had no chance: the whole structure – with me on it – would plunge into the river of metal.

I heard the sound of splintering metal and ran harder as the bridge suddenly lurched downwards, unmoored. I was only inches above the white-hot metal now, and I launched myself forward, into the air.

There was another sound of tearing metal, and I reached my hands out as far as I could to grab an upright post at the far end of the bridge.

Hauling myself forward, I pulled my legs up tight behind me, just as the bridge collapsed into the molten metal. It started to melt and disappear into the lava.

I dragged myself to my feet, checked that all the parts of the rifle were still inside my jacket, and ran for the supervisor's office once more. Looking back, I expected to see Kazinsky shadowing me from the other side of the river, but he wasn't there.

I sped up and was ten yards from the office – increasingly confident I would make it inside and assemble the gun – when I saw him. Remarkably, he wasn't running in hot pursuit. He was standing in front of a rack on the wall, calmly unclipping a remote that operated the overhead crane. With rocketing alarm, I looked up and saw that the huge bucket, filled to the brim with scrap metal, was almost directly overhead.

There was no cover. I glanced back and saw Kazinsky press a button on the remote.

From directly above there was a mechanical *snap*, and I made a wild, desperate dive—

The bucket plunged down, smashing through the gantries surrounding the supervisor's office, tearing its glass walls apart and sending the steel door flying. Hitting the ground, it exploded in a hailstorm of deadly, flying metal—

82

IT WAS A MASSIVE ROCK-CRUSHING MACHINE THAT SAVED ME, probably the only thing in the entire building that was strong enough to withstand the onslaught of flying shrapnel at such short range.

I had dived to its side and had just enough time to roll between two of its short pneumatic legs when the bucket detonated on the floor.

But it was a pyrrhic victory: a steel flange underneath the machine tore a long gash down my shoulder and a jagged corner of its oil sump opened up the left side of my face – before doing the same to the back of my head – as I rolled and crawled beneath it.

Lying flat under the machine, miraculously the wave of shrapnel swept past me. I felt the blood soaking my hair and shirt but it didn't matter – somehow, I was still alive.

I listened: the exploding bucket must have killed the power to different sections of the plant, halting most of the machines and probably plunging large areas of the plant into darkness. Rolling on to my stomach, I looked out at the piles of wreckage and metal covering the floor. Out of the gloom, a pair of boots suddenly appeared and started to move through it. Kazinsky had emerged from his own cover and was now searching for me – or my body.

Not finding either, I knew he would soon realize that the crawl space under the rock crusher offered the only chance of survival. Seconds after that, he would find me.

I silently elbow-crawled my way backwards, moving away from him and out from the far side of the machine. It was only when I tried to stand up that I realized how badly injured I was.

My head and face were pounding, the gash down my shoulder made my left arm difficult to move and I only realized now that I had cut my right calf very deeply and was losing blood fast.

I forced myself to ignore it and moved as quickly as I could towards the massive entrance doors, keeping to the shadows and trying not to make a sound. Halfway there I swung left and sprinted for the canteen.

The whole area was in complete darkness – perfect for my purposes – and I ran to the cooking area. The pilot flames on the gas burners were alight and, by their glow, I scrambled to the sinks, grabbed a dishcloth and knelt in a corner of the kitchen.

Concealed by the darkness and an island bench, I unzipped my torn and filthy jacket, pulled the parts of the frame out and laid them on the floor. With my hands trembling a little from pain, exhaustion and God knows what else, I started to break them down exactly as I'd been shown.

Less worried about time now, I cleaned everything as best I could with the dishcloth and reassembled the major parts of the short-barrelled rifle. Lastly, I grabbed what had been the handle of the backpack, converted it into the firing mechanism and fitted it in place. The weapon, truly a marvel of engineering, was now complete.

I removed the two spears from inside one of the frame's tubes and pulled the three bullets free from the necklace around my neck.

I put the first slug into the magazine when I heard a footstep and froze.

The kitchen bench was on small legs, and I peered underneath it. Kazinsky was silhouetted in the doorway, looking carefully around the room. He reached out and flicked a light switch – there was nothing.

He stood very still, listening, and I could hardly breathe, willing him to leave, but he stepped quietly inside and started to search.

Silently, he moved further into the room, passing through pools of greater darkness, looking at everything, coming closer to me.

I moved slightly so that I could watch him around the side of the bench. The darkness was my greatest ally.

'Are you in here?' he said softly. 'I wonder.'

I wanted to load a spear and shoot, but I couldn't risk it – he'd hear me long before I had it slotted into the special brackets under the barrel and had a chance to aim and fire.

Keeping the long bulk of the bench between us, I shifted my position, making sure he couldn't see me. To keep track of him, I had to look under the bench, so I lowered myself carefully and saw his feet moving closer.

Barely five feet away, separated only by the bench, he stopped. He was listening, I figured. Then his hand dropped into view and I saw it touch the knob that controlled one of the gas burners.

He continued to stand, unmoving. Satisfied that his hand meant nothing, just a casual gesture, I kept watching, waiting for his feet to start to walk away—

Then his hand moved lightning fast, sweeping along the row of knobs, igniting all the gas burners, turning them up to full, throwing a warm glow across the entire room.

Its light revealed the dishcloth spread out on the floor and a small length of discarded frame. He immediately leapt on to the kitchen bench to scan the room.

He was right above me. He looked down, saw me, and our eyes met for a moment. I lifted the rifle with its single bullet as he started to leap—

I aimed the best I could and pulled the trigger. In mid-air, the bullet hit him in the jaw, destroying part of it and knocking him aside. I rolled to my right and, in spite of his momentum, he missed me.

I scrambled to my feet and started to run for the door, dropping the two spears but managing to keep hold of the last pair of bullets.

I felt him right behind me, but maybe less than two steps later his hand grabbed my shoulder and pulled me to the ground. If I hadn't crushed his elbow earlier, I wouldn't have had a chance – both his hands would have grasped my throat and killed me.

I squirmed, throwing my weight forward, ripping my jacket and loosening his grip. I pulled free but in the melee dropped the rifle.

Completely unarmed, I jagged to the right, circled away from the door, glanced back and saw he was closing fast. In a few moments he would be on me. There would be no escape, not this—

Just ahead I saw the row of fire extinguishers standing under the first-aid kit. I recalled a hidden villa on a tiny island, body-swerved to avoid Kazinsky again, and plunged headlong towards them.

I grabbed one in each hand, dived to the ground and rolled out of the way just as he hurled himself at me.

Missing me, he lay sprawled in the dirt. I rose to my feet and ran for the rows of blazing gas burners. I looked back, saw that he was up and sprinting towards me, but I reached the bench top and threw the first of the extinguishers.

It landed in the flames, and I threw the second one. It hit a different set of burners and, as it started to ignite, I threw myself to the ground and took cover behind the bench.

I saw Kazinsky slow – confused – staring at the fire extinguishers. He must have realized, he started to drop—

Too late. The first extinguisher exploded, shrapnel flew kinetically across the room and a large chunk of metal hit him in the chest. It sent him reeling, but he was still on his feet.

The second extinguisher blew up. Another wave of shrapnel hit him across the legs and thighs and sent him to his knees once more.

I stood up, ran a few yards, scooped the two spears off the ground, along with the rifle, heading for the door.

I was still alive, thanks to the Magus, and now I had to load a spear and red-mist him. I looked back.

He may have been injured and breathing hard, but he was on his feet and heading in my direction—

83

MOVING AS QUICKLY AS I COULD, I SKIRTED ONE OF THE NOW-silenced rock crushers and found an area of deep darkness near the Number Four blast furnace. Enclosed on three sides by a sheer brick wall, the blast furnace and the steel side of a rock crusher, it meant I couldn't be taken by surprise.

Working by the light of the furnace, I knelt and cleaned the two spears with my shirt. I fitted the first of them into the brackets, checked the rifle's firing mechanism was still in order and put the second spear through my belt at the small of my back, ready to grab if I needed it.

I reached into my pocket for the two remaining bullets – and cursed. There was only one – its companion must have fallen out during the chase. I shrugged it off – one bullet and two spears would be enough. It had to be.

I inserted the remaining bullet in the magazine and then checked the entrance to the cafeteria. There was no sign of Kazinsky but I saw – partway towards it – a ruined gantry was dangling down. A work-light, still operating, was hanging from it and providing some visibility for me to hit a target.

Above it, the crane was still moving according to its own broken system – but it wouldn't affect the shot. I crouched, trying to assess the magic sixty-two, when Kazinsky emerged.

Wounded, but still a menacing, super-strong force, he stopped and looked at the ground. I glanced down at my wounded calf and realized: in the glow of the blast furnace and the hanging light, he would see a trail of blood spots.

It was good, very good, I told myself – he would follow it, walk directly under the light, and it would be finished.

Barely moving, shutting everything else out, I watched him approach, estimating the steps he would take until he was directly under the light. Nine, I figured.

I shifted my stance, crouched a little lower and locked the sight on to the point just below his left earlobe where the carapace could be penetrated. He was still following the blood trail, searching to see where I was, steadily coming closer. Six steps.

I measured the distance with my eyes, made a tiny adjustment for a crosswind through the front doors and started to regulate my breathing. Three steps.

I squinted through the sight and pulled the stock tight into my shoulder. One more step; I wasn't going to miss—

There was the sharp retort of splintering wood from high above at exactly the same moment I pulled the trigger.

The crane had hit the wreckage of a gantry and sent it plunging down. It hit the ruined section supporting the light and everything tumbled towards the ground—

The spear, triggered by its electronic pulse, blasted free of its bracket and flew like a harpoon straight at Kazinsky. The aim and angle were perfect.

Except that the falling light and wrecked gantry intercepted the spear and its target, striking it a glancing blow, but deflecting it off course, where it hit Kazinsky's ear, tearing it clean off.

I stared in shock.

Bleeding hard from the wound, he barely paused, assessing the flight of the spear and looking directly at my hiding place. It wasn't safe, not now – I was trapped between the three walls.

I had to move fast – there was no time to reload. I scrambled out, sprinted around the back of the blast furnace and threw myself into a hollow of darkness. I grabbed the last spear from the small of my back. Just that and one bullet left. I slotted the spear into its bracket, checked the firing mechanism.

Kazinsky emerged out of the gloom, still searching for me. The fallen light was still working, casting a huge shadow of him on the wall which I watched as it came ever closer.

I raised the rifle and aimed, but I couldn't get a clear shot.

I forced myself to wait, watching him approach – I had to be certain: it was this time or never. He stopped at the row of oil-stained gauges next to the blast furnace, peering into the darkness.

He was still partly obscured, and I kept waiting – sooner or later, surely he would walk into clear air.

He continued to scan his surroundings and then – to give himself a better view – he leapt on to the flat steel tray that fed slag into the blast furnace. Looking across the nearby area, he was suddenly clear of any obstruction. Thank God—

I levelled the rifle, lined him up through the gunsight, checked for the magic sixty-two, aimed for the nerve junction just below his missing ear, took a breath and fired.

The spear exploded out of the brackets, flew through the gloom and into his neck.

I knew instantly I'd missed. Maybe it was the shimmering waves of heat or a blast of air out of the furnace that had affected my aim – more likely I had got the angle wrong – but while he went down to his knees and one eye filled with blood, he was a long way from dead.

Instead, he staggered to his feet and looked in my direction. I had to finish it now – hand-to-hand combat would be suicide. One chance left.

I stood up and rushed out of the darkness – he couldn't get off the stainless-steel tray. He saw me, we looked at one another and he started to scramble in my direction.

Any moment and he would be on the ground, coming for me. I raised the rifle to my shoulder—

He laughed – what good would that do? But I wasn't aiming for him. He swung first one leg off the tray, and was about to do the same with the other when my last bullet exploded out of the barrel, a moment later hitting the button that controlled the tray, triggering the system—

The tray tilted up fast, tipping at a steep angle towards the opening into the blast furnace. Kazinsky, losing his footing, fell backwards and started to slide down towards the flames.

He tried to grab the sides of the tray with both hands, but his smashed elbow meant only one obeyed.

Even so, his great strength meant he could pull himself up the sloping steel tray, but I was there, ready for him. His one good eye fixed on me, his lip curling into a snarl. I stood barely two feet away from him, met his gaze and raised the rifle butt before smashing it down on his fingers.

For a second, he held on, but I smashed the butt down again and his fingers betrayed him. He started sliding, not taking his eyes off me.

His boots hit the flames first and he screamed as they enveloped him. For a moment, as the skin was burnt from his face, I saw his death's head skull disappear into the furnace. A sight I shall never forget.

Then he was gone, consumed by the fire. I kicked the door of the blast furnace closed. It was almost finished.

84

A LARGE PART OF THE PLANT WAS IN RUINS – THE FALLING BUCKET had made sure of that – but the sealed chamber was still intact.

I dragged myself across the river of molten metal, found my way through a tangle of collapsed walkways and cut one hand to pieces on a shard of glass – hidden in the gloom – from the ruins of the supervisor's office.

I tore a strip off my T-shirt to stem the bleeding and, cursing the pain and my carelessness, reached the control panel outside the sealed chamber. I powered up the control panel and, much to my relief, saw it come alight.

I scrolled through the Russian menu and found what I was looking for: a series of commands accompanied by large red triangles. They were, the notes alongside them explained, to be used in the event of the sealed chamber being breached or seriously damaged in any way.

I entered the commands, did not know the final access code, but put the cursor over the words *Critical Override* and saw a steel lid next to the control panel slide open. Inside it were two levers and I pushed the first of them into the 'on' position.

The rows of industrial nozzles ranged along the steel ceiling dropped lower, swivelled and started to spray the chamber with disinfectant, sterilizing it. I activated the second lever—

The lights inside the chamber dimmed and a port on the back of the nozzles opened. A grey gas shot out, swirled in the air for a moment and startled to settle.

In the gloom, I saw the tiny glow of myriad spores. As they were hit by the deluge of disinfectant or were touched by the gas, I watched the glimmers of light – the legacy of some distant and terrifying place – fade and die.

Now it was finished.

85

REBECCA, FALCON AND THE TEAM IN MOROCCO HADN'T LEFT THE entertainment pavilion since they had seen the Ilyushin land in Baikonur. They continued to sit in front of the large-screen TV even though it was now blank—

Until a direct feed from the satellite monitoring the Cosmodrome kicked in and the screen flickered back to life. Clearly the engineers at the NSA thought they had something.

Rebecca stood up, took a step forward and stared closely at the sweeping, seemingly empty landscape, lit only by ladders of moonlight. 'Can you see anything? What is that? An ambulance?'

'Even if there is a vehicle, don't let's get ahead of ourselves,' Margaret, ever the realist, said. 'Kazinsky or somebody else might have called the security services. It might be them.'

For a moment longer nothing was visible, then Falcon pointed to the top-left-hand corner of the screen. 'There,' he said. 'Dust – a vehicle or vehicles.'

Everybody stared at it as it grew more distinct. 'It's one vehicle,' Falcon said. 'It's not the security services – they'd come in force. I think it's an ambulance.'

He was right. Moments later – according to Rebecca's account – the screen showed a much closer shot of the solitary vehicle: a half-track painted a military khaki with large red crosses on its roof and hood.

Rebecca slumped, almost in tears from relief. 'He's alive?' She turned to Falcon, spirits soaring, and repeated it, but not as a question now. 'He's alive.'

Falcon nodded, but with greater restraint – I guess he'd seen too many missions fail at the final hurdle. 'We don't know what state he's in physically – and we still have to get him out.'

86

MY PHYSICAL STATE WAS NOT GOOD.

After I'd slammed the door on the blast furnace, I made my way towards the cafeteria, but the pain pounding in my head, the loss of blood from the wound in my calf and the sheer exhaustion of it all were taking their toll.

The machinery and wreckage around me began to twist and distort, and I started to reel. Worried that I might pass out, I stopped three times before finally reaching the door to the cafeteria.

The gas hobs and the remnants of the extinguishers – a melted, toxic mess – were still alight, several areas near the bench top had caught fire from flying debris and were smouldering. The atmosphere was thick with choking chemical fumes from the foam contents of the extinguishers.

Between the fumes and the smoke, I knew I couldn't reach the emergency button unaided. Wearily, I pulled my shirt off, soaked it under a drainage tap, wrapped it around my face, marshalled the little strength I had left, and plunged in.

Holding my breath, eyes stinging and half closed, I staggered through the chaos to the emergency button. I hit it as hard as I could and saw it flash red. Medical help was on its way. Lungs screaming, I took a breath – and immediately wished I hadn't.

Coughing, my throat burning from the acrid air, I reeled out of the cafeteria, and – gasping for breath – slumped to the ground near the plant's large entrance doors.

I don't know how long I laid there. At one stage I thought I heard a siren approaching and dismissed it as a product of my imagination; why would anyone need a siren in a trafficless wilderness?

The hands that took hold of my shoulders and rolled me on to my back were real enough, though. Turning my head, I saw a fair-haired woman in her late twenties wearing a doctor's jacket kneeling over me. The name on the identity tag stitched to her breast pocket said Tatyana Zhukov.

Emotion almost overwhelmed me; maybe it was then that I realized it was almost over.

She turned to the two orderlies that had accompanied her and told them to get a gurney, an oxygen tank and a range of other medical supplies from the ambulance and wait there for her instructions. She had to buy herself some time alone.

'How's your mother?' I asked as soon as they were out of earshot.

She stared at me for a moment. 'No change,' she replied. 'But thank you for asking. And Falcon?'

'No change either,' I said.

'He's still the best-dressed man in America?'

I tried to smile, and she took a pair of shears out of her medical bag and cut open my jeans to expose the wound in my calf.

'Give me your papers,' she said as she started to dress it with QuikClot bandages.

I pointed at the breast pocket of my shirt. Reaching inside my jacket, she took them out and put them inside her medical bag. Looking around to make sure she wasn't observed, she swiftly replaced them with another set.

'You are Fyodor Petrov. Understand?'

I nodded.

'Repeat it.'

I did as she demanded, and she turned to the wounds on the back of my head and my face, gluing several long cuts as a temporary measure and then bandaging them.

'Petrov is due to take the 5 a.m. medical evacuation flight to Grozny,' she said. 'You are going in his place. There are thirty men and women on board, the staff will be overwhelmed and won't have time to talk. Petrov is seriously ill, so you won't even have to try.'

I nodded – the bandages made my condition look even more serious and they had the added advantage of obscuring a large part of my face, making any comparison with a photograph almost impossible.

'What will happen to him?' I asked.

'He will stay here.'

'And?'

'He will die.'

She must have seen a look on my face. 'Don't worry about it. He's a piece of shit, a wife-beater,' she said. 'In Grozny, a fleet of ambulances will meet the flight and all the patients will be taken to Grozny Hospital Number Four. In the confusion of emergency and admissions, you will be transferred to another ambulance to be taken to a different hospital.'

'Who'll be driving it?' I asked.

'Two people with the right uniforms, clipboards and the correct documents. You will know them.'

I looked at her questioningly.

'The couple you met in a car park in Baku on the way out here.'

'Okay – yes, I know. They won't be transferring me to any hospital, will they?'

'No, Fyodor. They will take you to a disused shipping terminal popular with ambulance drivers stopping for a smoke. Inside a building, unseen, you will be transferred to a semi-trailer—'

'Driven by another agent-in-place who may have used to compete in MotoGP,' I said.

'Correct,' she replied. 'He will take you down the E119 to Baku. Someone will meet you at a truck stop just outside the city.'

'And take me to the plane.'

'Yes,' she replied, smiling. 'Maybe one day – God willing – I will go the same route.'

87

THE GREENENERGY JET, ITS ENGINES ALREADY TURNING OVER, DIDN'T wait around. As soon as I was on board, it swung off the apron and headed for the end of the strip.

I felt it pause and then, the engines rising to a crescendo, it began to accelerate. Even in my anaesthetized state, I felt us lift off. I looked out the window as we climbed and saw the Flame Towers below and then, as we banked hard, the whole of the Caspian Sea open up before us.

I continued to look out the window as we turned for Turkey. When the seatbelt sign was turned off, the on-board doctor and the nurse approached down the aisle.

They wanted to give me something to help me sleep, but I waved them away; there would be time enough for that later.

They returned to their seats and I heard them speaking quietly.

'Who is he?' the nurse, a guy in his thirties, asked.

'I don't know,' said the doctor. 'Some Russian, apparently.'

'Yeah,' the nurse replied. 'Name of Fyodor Petrov.'

'Never heard of him,' the doctor said.

They both fell silent as the door into the cockpit opened. The pilot, the same one who had flown me into Saudi and, more recently, to Baku, came and knelt next to me.

He smiled. 'Four seconds,' he said, looking at his watch.

'Four seconds?' I queried, but he ignored it.

'Two seconds,' he continued, with no explanation. 'One second. We are now in international airspace. You're going home.'

EPILOGUE

THE LETTER ARRIVED AT THE HOUSE BY COURIER, ADDRESSED TO Rebecca, the first hint I had about what lay ahead.

Six weeks had passed since the GreenEnergy jet had landed at Andrews, and Becca – waiting on the apron with Falcon – had accompanied me in an ambulance to Walter Reed. I spent several days there, more for evaluation than anything, and was then released to recuperate at home.

She read it and turned to me. 'I've been invited to a private function at Langley,' she said, perplexed, handing the sheet of paper to me.

I skimmed the three paragraphs below the impressive seal and saw that it simply said that Falcon Rourke, the Director of the CIA, would be pleased if she could attend the Original Headquarters Building at 7 p.m. the following Friday. 'Please note,' it said in conclusion, 'this event is private and classified.'

'What does it mean?' she asked.

'I'm not sure,' I replied. 'Normally partners are only invited to Langley when an agent has been killed and a star is unveiled on the wall of honour. And that's not until years after the mission has lost any intelligence value.'

'Well, you're not dead yet – although sometimes . . .' She smiled. 'It's the same day and time when you're supposed to meet Falcon, isn't it?'

'Yes,' I replied, my turn to be perplexed now. 'I guess they want us both there.'

We drove out to Langley together, passed through the security checkpoint, parked in the lot adjoining the Original Headquarters Building and walked through the front doors into the impressive foyer.

We crossed the marble floor, passed the wall bearing the quote from the Gospel of Saint John – 'And ye shall know the truth and the truth shall make you free' – and took the elevator to the seventh floor.

The guard at the security desk directed us to Falcon's private conference room, I opened the door – and we stopped on the threshold.

A small group of men and women turned to face us: most of the brains trust were there, Falcon and Lucas Corrigan standing at the front.

Falcon smiled as we entered, walked forward and shook hands with Rebecca. 'Thank you for coming,' he said. 'How's it going?' He indicated her stomach.

'No problems so far,' she replied.

'And it's still Chloe and Ridley?'

She smiled. 'Of course. How could we ever change that?'

He turned and shook my hand. 'Thank you,' he said. He stepped away, took a small velvet box from a side table and, facing the small group of onlookers, opened it.

I stared at the contents. I had never seen one in reality, few people ever had, but I knew what it was: the Distinguished Intelligence Cross, the agency's highest honour. Of the twenty-two crosses that have been awarded since the agency was formed just after the Second World War, only four have been presented to a living recipient. The other eighteen were given posthumously.

Falcon hung the ribbon around my neck. 'For conspicuous gallantry,' he said. 'For service above and beyond the call of duty.'

I took Rebecca's hand and placed it over the medal. It was ours to share – I might have built the boat, but she was the wind that brought me home.

I turned and acknowledged the applause from everyone who had been part of the epic journey and I was filled with an overwhelming sadness. I knew what the small ceremony really signified—

Once the applause had passed, Falcon ushered Rebecca and me through a door and into his adjoining office.

'It's over, isn't it? My time at the agency?' I asked as soon as the door was closed.

Falcon nodded. 'I can never send you over the border again,' he said gently. 'You've seen too much, you know too many secrets.'

Rebecca looked from one to the other of us – she'd had no idea what was coming. 'Leave the agency?' she asked, confused. 'I thought there'd be a desk job, running other agents—'

'Me too,' I said. 'I always thought – in a year or so, Buster would take early retirement and I might move into his role.' I looked at Falcon. 'Why?'

'You know the answer. I think we all do,' he replied. 'Years ago, the psychologists said you would never command a boomer – you've always been your own man and you always will be. You broke all the rules at the crucifixion and followed your own compass. God, how I admired you for that. But take a desk job and you work as part of a team. That was never your karma – you were made to work alone, to be a Denied Access Area spy. Now the race is run and it's time to go. Settle down, raise a family, that's my advice. Try to be happy.'

He turned, picked up a dozen paper files and spread them out on his desk.

Rebecca took my hand and looked at me. 'You've earned it. Falcon's right, we need to be happy – all of us.' She touched her stomach.

I turned to the window and looked out at the campus laid out in the moonlight. All of my secret life was there, so many memories. I looked back at Rebecca and tried to smile. 'Maybe there's a time in everybody's life when they have to accept . . .' My voice trailed away and I started again. 'We both have,' I said. 'Earned it, I mean.'

She embraced me, her eyes shimmering with tears of relief, and then she turned and looked at the files Falcon had laid out. 'What are those?'

'Safe houses,' Falcon replied, and spoke to me. 'In light of your service, the government has agreed to grant you one at a peppercorn price.'

'The government knows about the LOCUST mission?' I asked.

'Of course,' he said with a shrug. 'They know that an unnamed Denied Access Area agent went into a ZATO and killed the world's most wanted terrorist. Why – did something else happen?'

I shook my head. 'No, that pretty much sums it up,' I said, smiling. I turned to look at Becca. She was leafing through the files, pulling out photos and information pages.

'This one.' She pointed at a file.

Falcon looked over her shoulder. 'It's a beautiful property,' he said.

'Why?' I asked Becca. 'Why that one?'

'It's a horse farm,' she replied. 'What was the name of the pony, the one that saved you?'

'Sakab,' I said. 'It means a horse so graceful it moves like running water.'

The house we chose is a rambling old colonial with mellow brick walls, white shutters and wide verandahs. It stands in a hundred and twenty acres, hidden at the end of a valley in the most scenic corner of Virginia.

Falcon had said it was a safe house, and there is little to disturb the peace out here; the nearest neighbour is ten miles away and the only approach road – little more than packed earth and overgrown with knotweed – runs into a small river that is never easy to ford.

Beyond the entry gates and a winding drive, night-vision cameras monitor the miles of chain-link fence, and concealed pressure pads dot the woodland trails. They were installed at my insistence, and I check them every night. Even though it is seven years since I left Langley, old habits die hard.

Much of that time I have spent in a book-lined study – looking across the white-railed paddocks and watching the horses run free – writing this account of the LOCUST mission so that there will be some kind of record. They say that every bad thing that happens in the world starts with forgetting.

Oftentimes – even tonight – I hear Becca and the kids laughing or arguing deeper in the house. There are three children now; several years after the twins were born, we had another boy. There was no list of names this time; Rebecca and I agreed very early that we would call him Baxter, and I sit with him sometimes as he falls asleep and tell him about a fine man I knew once who had won a Nobel Prize.

There is one other member of our family. Shortly after we moved in, Rebecca went to the local dog shelter and brought home a rescue dog – a cross-breed a little over a year old – who had lost a leg in a road accident.

'What do you think of Tripod as a name?' she asked.

I shook my head and, while there was little evidence of German shepherd – more beagle, I thought – I knew what it had to be. 'Ella,' I said.

Becca stared. 'You realize – it's a male dog,' she said.

'Sure, I know that.'

'So?' she said.

'So – he's a modern dog. His name is Ella.'

Madeleine O'Neill has continued her rise through the agency and two years ago was appointed head of research and analysis. Six months later her father died unexpectedly and, with her wedding already planned, she called me. I flew to Boston, met her wife, and had the privilege of escorting Madeleine down the aisle.

Every year, on my birthday, a postcard from an exotic location and addressed to me arrives at Langley. Jeddah, St Tropez, Cairo, Sofia. The message is always the same: 'Best wishes to you – from one magician to another.' The agency has never caught the Magus, and I suspect it never will.

Margaret never stopped vaping, not even after she was diagnosed with stage-three lung cancer. Nor did she dispense with her cynicism. 'I've always cared deeply about humanity,' she said at the small gathering to mark her departure for medical leave. 'It's just people I can't stand.' She died four months later.

Three years after leaving Langley for the last time, I returned on a warm spring morning and made my way to a secluded area near the campus's memorial garden. Gathered on the lawn, surrounded by flowers in full bloom, were several hundred relatives of the crew of the USS *Leviathan*. They had been invited to witness the unveiling of a memorial to their loved ones, which, due to the highly secret nature of the boat, could only be erected in a secure location.

Surrounding a bronze rendering of the sub's extraordinary profile was a list of its officers, crew and observers. 'Lost at Sea,' it read simply. There was no mention of a sole survivor.

Underneath it was the dedication, and I recognized it. During the Second World War, British forces confronted the Japanese 15th Army at the top of a strategic pass at a place called Kohima and prevented them from sweeping out of Burma and invading the greatest prize of all: India. In the cemetery, the last resting place of several thousand Allied soldiers, is a fifteen-foot-high stone column topped by a cross, with just one sentence chiselled into it. Known as the Kohima Epitaph, it says:

WHEN YOU GO HOME, TELL THEM OF US AND SAY, FOR YOUR TOMORROW, WE GAVE OUR TODAY.

Whoever had designed the *Leviathan* memorial had borrowed it, and I could think of no better words to pay tribute to those who had died on a boat that had journeyed into the future; a craft that had travelled into all of our tomorrows.

Buster finally took his retirement and moved to the Gulf Coast in Florida, where, according to his posts on social media, he has never been happier: he spends nearly every day of the year in a T-shirt, shorts and flip-flops.

Immediately after we had decided on the house in Falcon's office, I asked him if he could organize a modest government pension for Laleh. He did it the following day, and it allowed her to stay in Washington, keep studying and – even though Rebecca had left – to continue doing informal work experience at MedStar.

The following year, with her Christmas break approaching, I organized to take Rebecca and the kids to New York and meet her there. Rugged up against the chill – winter had come early – we spent a morning at the Metropolitan Museum, walked down Fifth Avenue, saw the Van Cleef & Arpels building, and I stopped for a moment and looked at Bergdorf Goodman's.

'Are you okay?' Becca asked.

'Sure,' I said, and put my arm around her.

'Do you miss all of this?' she asked, sweeping her arm around. 'The bright lights, the crowds, the energy?'

'No,' I said. 'I'm a full-on country hick now – when I come to the city, I'm surprised to see people walking on their hind legs.'

She laughed, and I guided the five of them towards the subway and rode it downtown. We walked around Soho, looking in the windows of galleries and boutiques until we found ourselves on Houston Street.

'Let's get something to eat,' I said. 'What about a deli?'

Rebecca looked at me. 'I'm hungry – but really?' She had gone almost completely vegetarian over the previous year.

'Why not?' I said. 'What's New York without a deli lunch?'

She raised her eyebrows in a long-suffering expression and allowed me to lead them across the street to a large deli on a corner. Inside, I glanced around at the different seating areas and found the one I was looking for.

I spoke to the hostess, convinced her to let us have a booth at the back, took a cursory glance at the menu and waited for the waiter to approach.

He was a good-looking young guy, mid to late teens, with olive skin, dark hair and a smile that seemed to be constantly playing in the corner of his eyes. I checked his name-tag. 'What do you say, Jon Gee – is it the best pastrami triple-decker in New York?'

'It must be, sir,' he replied, smiling. 'That's what it says on the awning out front.'

'I bet that was written by your grandfather,' I said.

He laughed. 'How did you know?'

I saw him stealing a look at Laleh as he took the orders and then – again – as he cleared the plates. 'You work here full-time, Jon?' I asked.

'No,' he replied. 'I just help out over the holidays. I'm planning to go to med school.'

'Me, too,' Laleh said, overcoming her shyness. They looked at each other for a moment, then he brought the bill, ran the credit card and, while Laleh didn't see it, I did. He slipped a paper napkin under her purse.

It wasn't until we were getting ready to leave that she found it. She opened it up, saw what it was and looked at Becca. 'It's a phone number,' she whispered. 'What do I do?'

'Call it,' I said, unasked.

'Do you think so?' Laleh said, nervously.

'Yes, I do,' I said.

Becca looked straight at me. 'What do you know?' she asked.

'I don't know anything.' I shrugged. 'Sometimes, though, I just get a premonition. I think she should call.'

Laleh and Jon plan to marry next fall.

Lucas Corrigan left the agency two years after me and, without any family or entanglements, took passage on an old TransPac freighter out of San Francisco, crossed the Northern Pacific, entered the South China Sea and made his way slowly up the Saigon River to what is now Ho Chi Minh City.

The following day he bought a ticket from a street vendor and visited the large compound that had once been the US embassy, now a museum. With few other visitors, he walked undisturbed through the courtyard, saw the car park where the embassy staff had cut down a tamarind tree to allow the Sea Stallion heavy-lift choppers to land, imagined the rain pouring down and the constant rattle of small-arms fire.

In a far corner he found the spot, marked by a small plaque, where his father had burnt the five million dollars in US currency. He entered the old chancery building and saw a host of large, vivid photographs of the night that the embassy fell.

A very elderly Vietnamese man in a museum uniform saw Lucas and approached him, smiling. He explained that he was a guide and would be happy to answer any questions. 'American?' he asked.

Lucas nodded, and the old man pointed at a Pulitzer Prize-winning photo dominating one wall: red tracers flying through the air, the compound walls collapsing and thousands of frightened people crowded into the courtyard.

'I was here that night, you know,' the elderly gentleman said, pointing to the roof of the chancery building crowded with young NVA and Vietcong troops.

Lucas nodded. 'So was I,' he said.

The old man stared, laughed and shook his head. 'You couldn't have been – you'd have been far too young.'

Lucas pointed at another, equally large photograph that showed a young boy – wrapped in an American flag, being held by his father – being hoisted up to a hovering Air America helicopter.

The elderly man looked from the image to the reality and back again, scarcely able to believe it. Then, satisfied, the parchment-like skin of his face crinkled into a grin. 'The CIA station chief,' he said. 'The man who came back for his son. You were the boy?'

Lucas nodded. 'Me.'

The old gentleman reached out and took Lucas's hand in his. 'We probably should have shot your father—'

'I'm glad you didn't,' Lucas said.

'Me too.' The old man indicated the other photos showing a city in its death throes. 'We couldn't do it.' He paused. 'The most memorable damned day of my life.'

Lucas smiled again. 'Same here.'

Now, he goes back twice a year, stays with the old gentleman and his family, and together they conduct walking tours for tourists, taking in the city's landmarks while recounting the vivid history of Old Saigon. The highlight of every tour is when they stop at the shattered embassy gates – preserved as a memorial – and tell the story of the night they were both eyewitnesses to history.

Following the death of Clifford Montgomery and the rise of an administration he had little respect for, Falcon retired. Despite approaches from several wealthy industrialists and a group of powerful politicians, he declined to seek either party's nomination for the presidency. Maybe it was because he knew, first-hand, just how high that wall in the Oval Office could be.

Instead, he bought a beautiful home in Marrakesh. Nearly three centuries old – shaded by ancient date palms and full of fountains and hidden courtyards – it is located just inside the Kasbah, the walled district containing the royal palace. More importantly, it is less than a day's drive away from the Sahara – for the greatest spymaster of his generation to find the peace he has always craved.

He spends several months a year there now, but whether he is in Morocco or at his home in Georgetown, most of his time is devoted to writing. Only several people know, but he is the author of an anonymous column in *Vogue Homme* called 'Dress for Success'. Published every month, it is by far the most widely read column in Washington. Despite its title, nobody reads it for its fashion advice – woven through its thirty paragraphs is the best and most reliable gossip available in the capital.

And as for me? Sometimes, late in the year, if the wind is out of the north and the snow starts to fall, a profound silence falls across the land. If I stand and listen, I can find myself back in my office at Langley, opening a secret file and starting on a journey that would take me across oceans far stranger than I could have ever imagined.

On those nights, I climb the stairs, look at the children in their beds and then, quietly, walk the acreage until I remember – sometimes, in order to be found, you need to get lost.

For a long time, I thought that the wolves were threatening me. They weren't, they were calling to me, trying to show me the path ahead. I don't hear them any more – their job, and mine, is done.

I don't believe that anything in the universe can ever surprise me now. If I have learned one thing, it is this. We're riders on the storm, that's all we are and can ever hope to be—

Riders on the storm.

TERRY HAYES is a former journalist and multi-award-winning screenwriter. He wrote screenplays for *Mad Max 2 – Road Warrior*, *Dead Calm*, *Mad Max Beyond Thunderdome*, *Payback*, *From Hell* and *Vertical Limit*, amongst others, as well as writing for a host of other movies, including *Reign of Fire*, *Cliffhanger* and *Flightplan*. *The Year of the Locust* is Terry Hayes' second novel. His first, *I Am Pilgrim*, was published in many languages and was an international bestseller. He lives with his wife and family in Lisbon.

Also by Terry Hayes

I Am Pilgrim

THE GLOBAL NUMBER ONE THRILLER

THE YEAR OF THE LOCUST

I AM PILGRIM

TERRY HAYES

THE INTERNATIONAL PHENOMENON

A YOUNG WOMAN MURDERED.
All of her identifying characteristics dissolved by acid.

A FATHER PUBLICLY BEHEADED.
Killed in the blistering heat of a Saudi Arabian public square.

A SYRIAN BIOTECH EXPERT FOUND EYELESS.
Dumped in a Damascus junkyard.

SMOULDERING HUMAN REMAINS.
Abandoned on a remote mountainside in Afghanistan.

PILGRIM.
The codename for a man who doesn't exist. A man who must
return from obscurity. The only man who can uncover a flawless
plot to commit an appalling crime against humanity.